Because Beards.

BENEFITING THE MOVEMBER FOUNDATION

Alexis Alvarez – Faith Andrews – M Andrews
Jeannine Colette – Hayley Faiman – Angelita Gill – Ace Gray
Ruthie Henrick – Scott Hildreth – Evie Lauren
Jerica MacMillan – RC Martin – Emmanuelle de Maupassant
Leslie McAdam – Maria Monroe – Adrienne Perry – J Quist
Renee Rose – Kacey Shea – Martha Sweeney – Tom Sweeney

Copyright © 2016

ISBN-13: 978-1539141044
ISBN-10: 1539141047

This book is a work of fiction.

Names, characters, places and incidents are the product of the authors' imaginations and are used fictitiously.

Any resemblance to actual events, locales or persons, living or dead, is coincidental.
Copyright © 2016 by Alexis Alvarez, Faith Andrews, M. Andrews, Jeannine Colette, Hayley Faiman, Angelita Gill, Ace Gray, Ruthie Henrick, Scott Hildreth, Evie Lauren, Jerica MacMillan, R.C. Martin, Emmanuelle de Maupassant, Leslie McAdam, Maria Monroe, Adrienne Perry, J. Quist, Renee Rose, Kacey Shea, Martha Sweeney, and Tom Sweeney.

Cover Photography: Wander Aguiar from Wander Aguiar Photography
Cover Model: Jacob Rodney
Cover Design: Jessica Hildreth
Formatting: Champagne Formats

All rights reserved, including the right to reproduce, distribute or transmit in any form or by any means.

All proceeds from this anthology will benefit The Movember Foundation.

Published in the United States

Dear Readers

Twenty-one authors have come together to give you the ultimate in bearded pleasure. The heroes of our stories are ready to win your hearts and steam up the pages.

All proceeds from this anthology will go to *The Movember Foundation*, a charity that raises money for prostate and testicular cancer and research, men's mental health and suicide prevention. You can find them here: us.movember.com

There are many men who are important in our lives: Fathers, sons, brothers, husbands, teachers, and friends. Many of us enjoy reading about amazing fictional men as written by our favorite authors. With your purchase of this anthology, you are helping to fund the life-saving research that will benefit all of the real-life men we love. Thank you.
We hope you enjoy this book!

Sincerely, your authors...

Alexis Alvarez, Faith Andrews, M. Andrews, Jeannine Colette, Hayley Faiman, Angelita Gill, Ace Gray, Ruthie Henrick, Scott Hildreth, Evie Lauren, Jerica MacMillan, R.C. Martin, Emmanuelle de Maupassant, Leslie McAdam, Maria Monroe, Adrienne Perry, J. Quist, Renee Rose, Kacey Shea, Martha Sweeney, and Tom Sweeney.

Note: This anthology is meant for readers who are 18+ years old. The stories contain sexual content, explicit language, and adult situations. Don't read this where people can see you blush!

SPECIAL THANKS

Thanks to everyone who graciously donated their time and talents to make this anthology a success. We'd like to give a special thanks to:

Jessica Hildreth
Wander Aguiar Photography
Jacob Rodney
Martha Sweeney
Stacey Blake, Champagne Formats
Heather Roberts & Social Butterfly/PR
Southern Belle

JESSICA HILDRETH

Jessica studied graphic design in college and just recently made it her full time career. She is well known for her adult coloring books and cover designs and has had her work on the covers of "big 5" publisher's books. When she isn't busy designing, she can be found on a beach in Florida spending time with her husband and kids.

Website: www.jessicahildrethdesigns.com
Facebook: Facebook.com/creativebookconcepts

WANDER AGUIAR

Brazilian born and San Diego based photographer Wander Aguiar has variously been a civil engineer, model and painter. His photographic work reflects similar eclecticism and spontaneity. "I like challenges and the freedom to create," he says. "I try to use my experience as a former model to bring out the best in each model I work with. Being a model is beyond just having a beautiful face; you have to perform and show a different personality and attitude no matter what you have on." Wander shoots beauty, fashion, editorial and fine art. His creative vision and coaching abilities have helped develop new faces and placed him with the best agencies. His work has appeared with magazines worldwide.

Website: wanderaguiar.com/
Facebook: www.facebook.com/WANDER.AGUIAR.PHOTOGRAPHY
Fan page : www.facebook.com/Wander-Book-Club-461833027360302/

JACOB RODNEY

My name is Jacob Rodney Hogue. I was born July 10, 1987 in Owatonna, MN but I grew up most my life in Great Falls, MT and Yuba City, Ca. When I was 19 I joined the United States Army Reserve. I spent 8 years enlisted and deployed to Afghanistan in 2014. Once I had fulfilled my commitment I decided I wanted to do something different and made the decision to move down to Southern California to pursue acting and modeling. I soon after landed on a cover for 'Obvious' magazine and shortly after began shooting for book covers. It's been a hell of experience and I look forward to the future.

Instagram: www.instagram.com/jacobrodneyhogueshow/
Facebook: www.facebook.com/Jacob-Rodney-Model-526442767542569

Heather Roberts at Social Butterfly

Heather Roberts provides authors personalized attention to their stories so that their voices can shine. She may be a trained attorney but she's a lover of all things romance at heart. Heather is a voracious reader who adores falling in love with a new book, and is a fierce collector of book boyfriends. She is passionate about helping authors - both brand new and established - build their brands and connect with readers. Being a publicist is her dream job and she wouldn't trade it for the world. Heather is originally from Pennsylvania but currently lives in West Virginia with her husband, their dog and a cat.

Email: heather@socialbutterflypr.net
Facebook: www.facebook.com/socialbutterflybookpromos
Website: www.socialbutterflypr.net
Instagram: www.instagram.com/owmyshelf/
Twitter: https://twitter.com/OWMyshelf

Stacey Blake, Champagne Formats

Website: www.champagneformats.com

Southern Belle

Two best friends with a mutual love for romance novels, Erin and Katie formed Southern Belle in December 2013.

We strive to promote our favorite books and authors from a variety of subgenres. Concentrating mainly on Contemporary/New Adult/Young Adult romance, we endeavor to give authors honest reviews with a side of love and to share our excitement, enjoyment, and anticipation with other readers.

Our blog provides reviews, spotlights, takeovers and giveaways.

www.southernbellebookblog.com

CONTENTS

Special Thanks	iv
No Joke by Kacey Shea	1
Wild Proposal by Angelita Gill	23
How to Kill a Lady Boner by Ace Gray	65
Fortune Favors the Beard by Alexis Alvarez	103
The Beard Made Me Do It by Scott Hildreth	137
To Beard or Not to Beard? by J. Quist	153
Scruff You! by Faith Andrews	183
Theirs To Protect by Renee Rose	207
One Kiss by Martha Sweeney	251
Asshole Calling by Maria Monroe	279
Talking to the Moon by Jeannine Colette	315
Thou Shalt Not Beard by Leslie McAdam	337
Background Noise by R.C. Martin	353
Rough and Reckless by Hayley Faiman	391
First Class Distraction by Ruthie Henrick	425
Opening Hearts by Jerica MacMillan	455
Hometown Prince by Evie Lauren	479
All or Nothing by M. Andrews	511
Confessions of a Beard Lover by Adrienne Perry	531
Eternal Embrace by Thomas Sweeney	561
Highland Pursuits by Emmanuelle de Maupassant	575

No Joke

BY KACEY SHEA

A COVER MODEL, A PHOTOGRAPHER, AND A ROMANCE WRITER all walk into a bar.

What's the punch line?

There isn't one. This is my reality on a Thursday night.

Four years ago when I hit publish with the aid of free Wi-Fi at my favorite hipster coffee shop, I never in a million years dreamed this would be possible. Though had I dreamt this scenario as my life, it would've looked a little different. For one, it would've included more sex. Hell, any sex would be nice.

Don't get me wrong; I'm thankful for the success I've achieved. The career I've been able to grow. Back then I worked retail between late nights of writing just to make rent, living in a dingy, cheap apartment and chasing my dream of becoming a published author. My last two releases hit the USA Today's Best-Selling Books list. Again, more than I ever hoped.

Still, I'm sitting in this dive bar just outside of Nashville after a day of shooting for my next book cover and I'm left unsettled, restless, and on edge. My career's success is due in part to my ability to write mind-blowing sex. Sex which my readers assume I enjoy on a regular occurrence. Except I can't remember the last time I orgasmed while getting some. Actually, that's not true . . . I can. But it's been over five years and I don't allow my mind to wander that far down memory lane. My own sexual frustration has me feeling very much a fraud as I pick at the label on my beer bottle. Not wanting to wallow in my own self-doubt a second longer, I twist my seat away from the bar.

Bryan, my fucking fabulous cover model, cuddles up in the back booth with the hottie ranch hand we met before the shoot. Gary, with his southern drawl, tight jeans, and scruffy beard could pass for a model himself, though I doubt he has six pack abs underneath all that flannel. The way things are headed, though, Bryan will find out for sure before the clock strikes midnight.

My photographer and bestie, Lauren, sits perched on stage next to a karaoke machine as she belts out lyrics to the latest Taylor Swift single. I cross my legs, kicking one calf length boot to the rhythm of the music and cringe as Lauren hits a high note. She sobers enough to glare my way and I right my face into a smile.

Tipping my beer, I take a long pull and throw my right hand in the air, thumb holding the two center fingers down so my index and pinky rock on. *You go, girl.* This seems to encourage her, and if possible her voice screeches an octave higher. I fucking hate karaoke, but she's up there having a grand ol' time so I force a smile and pray the ringing in my ears dissipates before the night is over.

"What's a pretty thing like you doing sitting alone in a bar?" A mammoth of a man slides onto the stool at my right and breathes his whisky sour into my ear. "I'm Johnny. What's your name, suga'?"

I straighten my spine and uncross my legs, and scoot as far away as possible without falling off my own seat. Closing my eyes, I inhale a cleansing breath. *Be nice; don't be a total dick to the dickhead.*

"Can we please not do this?" I try for sweet but my inner bitch always rules. My lips pull into a smile but it's too forced and I'm sure looks more threatening than approachable. "Please don't fucking hit on me." *I said please.*

Johnny Bad Breath's smile drops and his face twists up as though

I've kicked him in the nuts. He scoffs. "Your loss," he says, and moves on to another poor undeserving soul.

See. This is why I don't get laid, good, bad, or otherwise. I have no patience for the song and dance of the bar pick up scene. And online dating? *Fuck that shit.* Never in a million years. I'd rather my vagina elect a permanent sabbatical.

I glance up to find Bryan and Gary acquainting their tongues with the other's and I almost smile except Lauren chooses this moment to tackle an Elton John number. I twist my body away from the spectacle and shudder. "Not Rocket Man," I mumble and shake my chin. A few strands of hair escape the knot atop my head and brush my bare shoulders. I glance up to find the bartender watching me; his ocean deep eyes almost dance and lips pull up at the edges.

"Not a fan of watching gay men hook up?" He raises one eyebrow.

My eyes widen and I shake my head. "Not that. I love *that*. I just can't take it when someone murders one of the greats! Especially when said someone is my best friend."

He nods, a lazy grin pulls at his face, and that's when I notice the shape of his lips and how his thick trim beard frames them just right. I bite my lower lip. *Damn.* I'm such a sucker for good lips. His lower one more plump than the top, it's a mouth perfect for kissing. I imagine, anyway.

"Well, I hear alcohol has been known to dull one's senses, so here." He pulls a glass bottle from where it chills in a bucket of ice. "On the house. In the name of great music and all things holy. I feel as though you've earned it."

I can't fight the smile that pulls at my lips. "I don't know how you do it." I take the offered glass container and ignore the shiver of lust that works its way down my spine and between my legs when our fingers barely brush.

He steps back, leans against the counter, and shrugs. "It's a job. Getting me by until my ship comes in."

I take the moment to appreciate his body. He's not overly tall. I'd guess maybe a few inches over my height of five foot seven. His caramel brown hair is a little long and has a slight wave at the ends of his mostly straight locks. Lashes, thick and long enough to make any woman jealous, frame his irises blue as the sea. The glint in them is teasing and all knowing.

I take a pull from my bottle and clear my throat. "I know how that goes. Just don't give up on that dream. It always gets shittier before it gets better. But stick with it and you're sure to achieve great things."

"You sound like you speak from experience."

"Yeah—Well—I—" I take another drink. *Damn it, Amanda, fucking act like you're literate.* "I know what it's like to chase something that once seemed impossible and come up on the better end."

"Something tells me you're not talking about a man?" He smirks.

I chuckle. "No, not a dick. I never chase dicks."

"You've got quite a mouth on you." He runs his hand over the whiskers of his beard and raises his brows. "I like it. So, what is it you do chase?"

"I'm a writer." I state proudly.

"Oh . . . that explains it." He nods as though he already knows my life story, and I bristle.

"What is that supposed to mean?"

He leans forward, resting his elbows and forearms on the counter so our faces are inches apart. I'm trying to be pissed here, but with him this close I get distracted studying the way the blue in his eyes catches the dim light.

"People watching," he murmurs, his tone a seductive allure.

"Huh?" I'm still lost in those eyes and don't remember exactly what we're discussing.

"The way you watch people. It's something a writer does. Finds entertainment and joy in the mundane of life. It's beautiful, really."

"I never thought of it that way."

"So, what is it that you write?" His voice is back to a casual pitch and I relax.

"Romance."

"Ah . . . I knew with that mouth you'd have to have a naughty side. What kind of romance? Fifty Shades or the Fabio-grandma type stuff?"

I roll my eyes. "You do realize there's so much more to it than that?" A little laugh escapes my lips and his gaze drops to my mouth. I feel the need to lick the parched skin. *Fuck. I'm so screwed.*

"Only if you want to be," he says and his eyes blaze with the same heat I feel all over my skin.

"Huh?"

"You said, 'Fuck, I'm so screwed,' and not gonna lie. I'd like to help you with that."

Shit. Double shit. I said that out loud. His perfect beard and kissable lips must have magic powers because I'm flustered.

"That's a really lame pick up line. I'd expect so much more from you. In this line of work I'm sure you witness all the bad ones." I gesture around the bar with my hand.

He pushes off the counter and laughs a deep, straight from the belly sound, and it fills me with pleasure.

"You're fun. I like you." He reaches out a hand. "I'm Brax."

I place my hand inside his larger one and shake. "I'm Amanda. But you can call me Manda."

"Nice to meet you, Manda." He releases his grip and looks around. "I've got to check on my other customers, but I'd love to spend more time getting to know you."

My joy fades and I study the label on my bottle. Discontent sours my mood. We've only just met, and yet I can't help but wish for more time to explore this city and my attraction to this handsome man. "I won't be here long. I've got an early flight to catch tomorrow. Back home to Phoenix."

He nods and I wonder if he's not disappointed, too. "Well, Manda. I'm sure you write about all sorts of mind blowing orgasms and unbelievable one night stands."

I nod, and my lips pull into a wide grin. *Why, yes. Yes, I do.*

"If you want the real life version, I get off in an hour. No pressure. Just know that I'll do everything in my power to deliver." He winks, those lush lips pull up with his smirk, and he saunters to the other side of the bar.

Holy *fucking* hell.

"Come on, Lo. That's enough." I grip Lauren's arm and pull her from the stage, and more importantly, the microphone. She squirms out of my reach and stops, hands on hips.

"You don't like my singing?" One tear escapes the corner of her face, and her chin trembles. Oh, jeeze. How much has she had to drink? She's such a lightweight. It doesn't take much and she's an emotional drunk. I don't have it in me to babysit tonight.

"I love your voice. You know I do!" I skirt the singing topic and thankfully she doesn't notice. "But I need girl advice. Like now. Impromptu meeting in the ladies' room."

"Ooh . . . does this have anything to do with sexy bartender?" She raises her brows and nods his way. "He's totally staring at you, by the way."

"Hey, bitches!" Bryan interrupts and loops one arm around my shoulder, then pulls Lauren beneath his other.

"Having fun?" Lauren giggles.

"Yeah. I'd say today was one for the books." He pulls back and drops his hands to shove them in his back pockets. "Thanks for picking me for your book, Manda. It's a huge honor and I can't tell you how thankful I am."

This is one of the main reasons I selected him over the thousand others. He's humble and a class act to work with. Hasn't let the social media hype and fame change him or inflate his ego. Oh, and he looks really good naked. That's a plus.

"You're the best, Bryan. I'm so glad this worked out." I nod over at Gary the ranch hand standing near the door. "Looks like that's working out, too."

Bryan's lips pull into his signature megawatt smile, his natural sexiness on display. Even though I know he's gay my heart can't help but give a little stutter. "Yeah. Gary and I are gonna head out."

"Yeah, you are." Lauren winks and then captures Bryan in a big hug. I wave a goodbye to Gary before Bryan wraps me in a squeeze next.

"Have fun tonight," I say.

Bryan nods, backing away. "You, too. Safe flight tomorrow, ladies."

I wave and with my free hand lace my fingers in Lauren's to drag her toward the restroom. We push through the door and into the tiny space. The bar isn't packed tonight, but with only one working stall there's a steady line of women. They crowd the room and simultaneously retouch lipstick, poof hair, and adjust bras so their cleavage pops just right.

"You needa pee?" Lauren asks and squeezes herself into the tiny fraction of open real estate in front of the only mirror.

"No. I need advice." I stand behind her and lower my voice. "The bartender. He's cute, right?"

"You have contacts in." She runs her fingertips under her rolling eyes to wipe away the smearing liner.

I study my reflection over her shoulder. I'm attractive. I know this. Not in line with pop culture standards, but pretty to look at nonetheless. I've always loved my hazel eyes but they're a little too big for my face and non-existent eyelashes. And although my frame is full of curves, I've always felt a little jilted in the curvy department. It should be a requirement to be blessed with nice big tits since I've got the ass to go with them. Instead, I'm lucky to fill a B cup.

"You're doing that weird thing again." Lauren narrows her stare in the mirror and snaps her compact shut. She turns to scrutinize my face and then pokes at my cheek with her index finger.

"Stop." I swat her hand away but her frown remains. "What?"

"It's like you're throwing daggers at yourself. What's got that beautiful mind in overdrive?"

I lower my voice to just above a whisper. "Sexy bartender just offered me a night of no strings lust and I'm actually considering it."

Lauren's eyes widen and she nods aggressively. "Yes, yes, yes."

"I don't know. He's a stranger. He could be a creep. He could abduct and kill me."

"With orgasms!" She shouts and draws the attention of every other woman in the restroom. "You must fuck the sexy bartender! If not for yourself, then do it for single women everywhere!"

"Lauren!" I chide. She's not even single.

"She's right, honey, and Brax ain't no manwhore. He's a good southern boy. He'll treat ya' right," Red Lips to the left offers helpfully.

Great, now everyone is in on our conversation. I groan.

A hand rests on my shoulder and a brunette I recognize from the dance floor nods solemnly. "Your friend's right. Do it for the single ladies. Chelly and I have been trying to get that man in our bed for months now to no avail."

My eyes snap back to Lauren and she bites her lip, having the grace to look slightly embarrassed. She smirks and shrugs her shoulders.

I blow out a frustrated breath. I'm not sure if I'm more irritated at myself for having second thoughts when presented an opportunity for no strings bearded bartender sexy time, or at Lauren for announcing it to the entire ladies' room. I want to go with my gut but it's giving me conflicting advice. My body recommends one thing, and I'm not surprised—the man is walking, living, breathing sex on a stick. My mind though, she's wary—and for good reason. Life has shown me time and again that if something looks too good to be true, it most likely is. But that's not what has me uncomfortable or indecisive.

No, it's the fact my heart is attempting to weigh in on the decision. She's the real hangup, because I don't have confidence in her, not one bit. My heart has led me astray before. She's a liar. She gives too much. Hopes too easily. Yeah, I don't trust that unreliable bitch.

Lauren takes my hands in hers, gives them a squeeze, and her lashes blink over her pleading gaze as her lips pull wide into a drunken grin. She waits patiently. Knowingly. She won't pressure me to do something I don't want. Though it's clear her vote is for orgasms. She bounces up on the balls of her toes and it jolts me out of my indecision.

I reach up and pull the band from my hair, smooth the strands and twist it all back atop my head while I worry my bottom lip between my teeth. "He says he gets off in an hour." *Oh, hell, I only live once. I'm doing sexy stranger.*

"Fuck yeah, he will." Lauren holds up her hand, waiting, and I hold her gaze but narrow mine. "What? You're gonna leave me hanging? That's five worthy!"

I roll my eyes but don't slap her hand because I'm freaking the fuck out. Now that I've decided to do this, or rather him, I have no clue how to follow through. My stomach rolls and Lauren's eyes widen as she drags me away from the inquisitive eyes inside the restroom.

In the open hallway I already feel less anxious. "Sorry." I stop before we reach the dance floor to blow out a deep breath. "I just . . . what am I supposed to do now?"

"Like it's been so long you forgot?" She tilts her head as her lips pull to a pout then points one finger and sticks it in and out of the circle she forms with her other hand.

A giggle escapes my lips and her smile tells me that was her intent.

"Why are you freaking out? You've got this, babe. Sexy bartender is a sure thing and you've earned this. Enjoy it."

"I know. I agree, even. That's not what I'm asking. What should *I do now*? Like do I give him a thumbs up? I can't slide him my room key . . . though that's a shame because I've always wanted to do that."

"God! Please don't do that. I need my sleep."

I laugh because I'd never kick Lauren out of our room. Even for a one night stand. I'm not that hard up. Well, I kind of am . . . but I'm not a bad friend. "I assume he has his own place, or at least a room. I just don't want it to be awkward. Like do I sit at the bar? You know I flirt for shit."

"Manda. Breathe. Go. Sit. Be you. If it feels right, go home with him. If not, get an Uber and bail. But you best not miss your flight home tomorrow."

"Right. Good. Yes." My head bobs as though it's attached to a loose spring and the nerves from my belly tingle with excitement and anticipation. "I can do this. I'm doing this." I've got this.

Lauren glances toward the bar. "Chalk it up to research for your next book."

"Mmm hmm." I resist the urge to roll my eyes. As yummy as Brax is, there's no way he'll live up to my book boyfriends. Boys are *always* better in books.

"Do you want me to stick around? I'm kind of tired, but I can get back on the mic if you need the support." We make our way out to the dance floor.

"God, no!" I clear my throat and let loose a giggle. "I'll be fine. I swear. You are the best girlfriend a woman could ask for but please don't sing—er—stay."

She lifts a brow and her lips twitch as if she wants to laugh. I'm trying to spare her hurt feelings but even she's gotta know her singing sucks.

"Whatever!" I laugh. "If you really want to sing, stay. I'll find earplugs, or liquor."

Lauren's lips pull into a smile even after she stops walking to place her hands on her hips. "Fine. I'll leave. But you need to appreciate my boss karaoke skills. Not everyone knows all the lyrics to 'Father and Son.'"

"True. I'm sorry." *Though Cat Stevens doesn't sound like a cat being murdered.* I keep that last part to myself. See. I'm a good friend. I can censor my thoughts when it's important. "Thanks for everything today. Including the pep talk."

"Love you, Manda." She wraps her arms around me and squeezes tight.

"Love you, Lo." I hug her back. "Do you want me to walk out with you?"

"Nah! That's what cabs are for." She waves a hand but stumbles in the process and reaches out to steady herself with my arm.

I narrow my gaze, not sure she should be leaving alone in her state. "Text me when you get inside the room. You sure you don't want me to go with you?"

"Fuck, Manda, I'm fine! The bouncer'll get me a cab. I'll text you. Now, go get 'em, tiger!" She releases her hold and I give her a little nod before turning to face the bar. She gives me a little slap on the butt and I squeal.

Brax glances up and when our eyes meet through the crowd his lips pull into a smile that's made for melting panties. At least mine. I keep my gaze trained on his tempting stare all the way back to my perch at the bar.

"Your friend left." His lips pull up at one side.

"She had to practice for her *American Idol* audition."

He grins. "So does that mean I'm the lucky one who gets to take you home?"

"That depends."

"On?"

I consider his question while I lick my lips. His gaze follows and I feel sexy, wanted, in control. Empowered. "Whether you act like an ass between now and when you get off."

"Oh, I'll get off, but not before you. Because although I'm many things, a selfish asshole isn't one of them." His brow rises with challenge.

"Witty." My lips pull in a smirk.

"So are you."

"Hmm." I'm smart and funny, but I'm not sure he really knows that or is just being complimentary at the promise of getting laid. "Can I get another beer?"

"What's your pleasure?" He draws out the words.

I squeeze my legs together with the rush of need that pulses at the timbre in his voice. "I'll take a Lagunitas for now." I admire his body with the concentration of a naughty voyeur as he twists to bend over and pull one from the cooler.

"IPA. Nice choice." He pops the top with the cloth tucked into his belt and sets it on the counter. His lips soften to a sweet smile. "But that's the last one for you."

"What? Why?" I lean away, more than a little taken aback at the fact he's cutting me off. I'm not drunk and it's nowhere near last call. Who in the hell does he think he is?

Brax grips the bar top and leans forward. No trace of his smile remains. "Because when I fuck you, I want you to feel every inch of my cock slamming in and out of your sweet pussy. Good?"

My mouth drops open and before I say something stupid, or more likely respond with an embarrassing sound that's not really a word, I grip my bottle in both hands and let the liquid ease my sudden thirst. Only it doesn't, because what I want most is the bearded bartender across the counter. I set the beer down, and the glass hits with a thud louder than I intended. "So, how soon can we get out of here?" I manage, and as my lips pull into a smile, his mirror the movement.

"Not soon enough. Let me check with my boss. Maybe I can scoot early." He backs away and glances over his shoulder.

I'm anxious to leave with him, but I don't want him to get in trouble with his job. I can wait. "Oh, you don't have to—"

"Oh, but I want to, Manda. I want to." He cuts me off and his gaze is so full of promise, heat, and dominance that I have to pick up my drink again. He chuckles. The sound washes over me and fills me with excitement while he walks to the opposite end of the bar to talk with one of the waitresses.

Knock, knock. Who's there? *Horny romance writer about to get some.* Who? *Me, motherfuckers.*

"It's not much, but it's where I call home for now." Brax hops out of his truck and I follow out the passenger side as he slips his key into the door to his trailer. Yes. That's right. My sexy bartender lives in a trailer park. And maybe that's reason to be wary for some, but my childhood best friend spent many years of his life in a double wide, and as I look around this park of trailers I'm more fearful we're about to disturb the peace. That is, if Brax follows through on his promised orgasms.

Friendly Pines, as the sign read on the drive in, contains mobile homes in well placed rows, but it's the yard décor that gives it away for me. Paved squares of decorative white rock grace more than one lot, while another holds every lawn sculpture my grandmother ever collected. That and the fact it's completely silent at nine o'clock on a weeknight.

"Brax, do you live in a retirement community?" I try to keep the laughter out of my voice, but I've never been good at faking.

"Er—don't judge me, okay, but—well, I do actually." He twists the lock, grins over his shoulder, and pushes open the door, holding it for me to walk in first.

I step inside but stop short when my gaze falls on the old man asleep on the recliner. The blues and greens of the muted television screen cast his face in an eerie glow while his snores rattle the otherwise quiet space. "Brax . . ." I whisper. "You have an old guy in your house."

Brax's soft chuckle sends goosebumps across my flesh and his hands brush softly over my hips. His body is close behind mine, not quite touching, and my own begs him to just take me now. Well, not *now* now. Not with the snoring spectator.

"That's Dick."

"Pardon?"

"Richard. He's my roomie. Don't worry; he's cool. Come on." Brax grabs one of my hands and pulls us to one end of the small home until we're in front of a bedroom door where he inserts his key again.

"We won't wake him?" I'm still a little concerned about Dick down the hall. Also, who the fuck has a lock on their bedroom? Maybe I should be more cautious, though my gut tells me I'm safe with Brax. My eyes narrow at the handle, my mind and heart battling out for a legit purpose to the lock.

"Nah, he can't hear shit without his aids in." Brax twists the handle and glances over his shoulder to find my stare. "Oh, I lock it when I'm gone. Bartender life. I try to get to the bank regularly, but I have a lot of cash on hand and I don't really trust Dick's caretakers with the temptation."

That makes sense. I release the breath I didn't realize I was holding and step inside his room. The small window at one side allows the light of the moon to illuminate the space. It's clean, thank God. Even the bed is made. Fuck, I don't even make mine on a daily basis. If it weren't for the boots in the corner, a half empty water bottle on a wooden crate next to the mattress along with the clock radio, I'd think no one lived here. The soft click of the door locking pulls my perusal back to the man of the hour.

"This okay?" Brax says. His hands skim down my arms, a feather of a touch, but settle at my waist with a strong hold. He steps forward, just as I do.

"Perfect," I murmur into his lips as they meet mine for the first time. They're as lush and kissable as I imagined. My tongue comes out to play with his and I hush his groan by sucking his lower lip into my mouth.

"I'd ask you if you want a drink, but we already covered that at the bar," he says between breaths.

"I didn't come here for a drink," I sass.

His fingers hook the waistband of my jeans and he pops open the button. "No. You didn't. What did you come here for, Manda?" He yanks the zipper down and his lips meet mine with all the force of our attraction. He owns my mouth. His tongue and lips lead every bit this time. I arch my body into his, needing, wanting to be closer. His fingers dance along the top of my panties, not quite touching where I ache for him.

His other hand holds the back of my head so he can control our kiss even more. When his fingers dig into my scalp and tug, a rush of need storms through my body.

Oh, fuck. That's hot. I like dominant Brax. I wonder just how in charge he likes to be. I pull back enough to meet his hooded gaze. "Why, whatever do you mean, Brax?"

He growls. Like a fucking animal. Growling from the lips of anyone else and I might've laughed, but with Brax I want to melt in a puddle. Or get on my knees. Beg. Suck him off. God, I want to do everything.

His hand at my nape tightens almost painfully, but instead of hurt I only experience more desire. His other hand dips inside the waistband of my panties and he strokes two fingers over my clit and inside my slit. "You came here so I could fuck this pretty pussy. Didn't you? Is that what you want, Manda?"

"Fuck, yes."

He holds me to him while his fingers languidly slide in and out, his breath at my ear. "That's right. You're so wet for me already. I'm going to eat you out but first I want a taste. You want that?"

I groan as his fingers pump inside me faster, harder. We're both fully clothed and yet it's the most erotic thing, his naughty words at my ear and his fingers inside me. His lips kiss along my shoulder and move up to my ear. He sucks on my earlobe, his tongue dancing around the shell of my ear, and more lust shoots down my spine and to my core. He pulls his fingers from between my legs and sucks them into his mouth, releasing them with a pop and a smirk.

"Tell me what you want, Manda. I need to hear you say the words." His rough voice is a gentle command as his hand goes back to my pussy.

"Fuck me. Taste me. Eat me. Now. Please."

His deep, throaty chuckle tightens my belly with even more pleasure than his ministrations bring forth. "I thought being a writer you'd have a more elaborate vocabulary."

"I like to get to the point."

"I appreciate that. Let's do that." His hand vacates my panties and I almost whimper until they go directly to my shirt, pulling it up and over my head in a swift moment. I unhook my bra. He peels off his shirt. Which I'd love to replay in slow motion but I'm too occupied with kicking off my boots and shimmying out of my skin tight jeans. When the flurry of clothing settles we're left naked and very much aroused.

And thank fuck he's big and long and hard for me. I drop to my knees and relax my jaw, my lips falling open inches before him. My breath comes heavy and I glance up into his baby blues. The storm rages within their depths and hold me in place.

He palms his erection. "Damn, you're gorgeous, Manda. You know that? You're fucking beautiful on your knees for me. You want this cock in your mouth?"

My answer is a lick of my lips and a wide open mouth.

"Fuck, yeah, you do." He holds his cock at the base and feeds it in along my tongue. I tighten my lips around it and moan. With our eyes still locked, his pleasure and control etch in the draw of his brow and the tightening of his own mouth.

I try to take him deeper but gag instead, and come off for a deep inhale before I do it again.

"Fuck, that's sexy." He thrusts his hips, slow and methodically, while both hands hold my head steady. "You like choking on this cock?"

I'd answer him, but my mouth is currently full. This time I'm determined to take him deeper, maybe not to the base, but close to it. I inhale and exhale through my nose, hold his stare and lean forward, relaxing until I do almost choke on the size of him.

"Fuck!" He shouts and steps away.

Shit. Maybe he's not into that.

"Bed. Now." He holds out his hand to help me stand, only to pull me into another of his battling kisses and backs me until my legs hit the mattress.

"You lose your words, too?" I whisper against his lips. He shoves my shoulders and I fall back onto the bed. The pale moonlight sneaks through the window and his beard pulls up at the sides of his face before I'm rewarded with his dazzling smile.

"Just eager to return the favor." He drops to his knees and the pads of his fingers travel from the skin just under my knees to the tops of my thighs.

"You gonna suck my dick, too?" I retort before I even think.

His throaty chuckle causes my center to tighten with need and I attempt to squeeze my legs together as moisture, my own arousal, rushes between my legs. But Brax's hands on my thighs keep me in place. He pushes my legs open and dips his head so his mouth is just out of reach.

"Oh, Manda. Manda, Manda, Manda . . . I love your dirty mouth, but I think I'm gonna like this better."

Before I can come back with a smart remark his lips lock down on my clit and steal all words and thoughts. My senses overwhelm. The musky aroma of sex fills his room. The wetness of my pussy with the smack, lick, suck of his mouth. The stroke of his strong and steady touch all over my skin, rubbing, learning, enticing.

I'm so close to my orgasm, the taunt and teasing of the night building quickly at my core. I want to come, but I want to feel him break apart, too.

"Fuck me. Please, Brax." I grab at his scalp and tug him to my mouth. He finally works his kisses over my body, from my belly to my breast, my shoulder to my neck, until they meet my eager lips. We kiss; all the while our hands grasp, caress, and scrape across skin. He's close but not enough. I rock my hips but the weight of his body holds me down.

"Condom." He croaks and scrambles off the bed in a flash.

I attempt to still my quickened pulse but he's back over me, fully protected and ready, before I can catch my breath.

Our bodies come together in a rush. *Heat. Need.* I spread my legs wider. *Lust. Pleasure.* He shoves his cock into me harder with each thrust. *Want.* We're both selfishly chasing our orgasm, but neither seems to care. He bites my shoulder with a groan. I dig my nails into his back. It's a battle but no one loses.

"Fucking come on my cock, Manda," he demands but his words are lost. I already am.

My body spasms in that most unattractive way it does when I come really hard, but Brax doesn't seem to notice. His head is buried in the sheets while he braces his shuddering body over mine.

He lifts his head. "Fucking hell. Are all writers like this?" He pulls out and rolls to his side.

My heart hammers in my chest and my breath is ragged. I feel as though I've just run a sprint, when in reality he did most of the work. I turn to my side so I can better admire his naked body, and tuck one arm to rest beneath my cheek. "I don't know. I've never fucked a writer before."

"Fuck!" His breath heaves with the staccato rise and fall of his chest. "Well, you really should. That was phenomenal. You were a goddess."

"Were?" I sass though I can hear the smile in my own voice.

"Are. Still are. Fuck." He blows out a breath and twists his head to meet my gaze. "But good for you, too?"

Brax's hair falls every which way, a delicious mess. His skin glistens with a sheen of sweat, and his lips, oh God, those lips are now even more plump in appearance than earlier tonight. But it's the blue irises of his eyes that catch the only light in the room and appear so sincere, capturing my gaze. It's endearing that he's genuinely concerned about my enjoyment despite the fact we're practically strangers.

"Good. More than good," I manage as my heart rate picks up speed at his return smile. God, he's handsome as fuck.

"Good." He leans closer and his lips find mine in a taste so gentle it could be considered chaste, if only I didn't smell my arousal on him. I lick my tongue along the seam of his lips and he opens for me. It doesn't take long before our innocent kiss becomes hurried, passionate, and sexual. I nip his lower lip and am rewarded with another one of his growls—my new favorite sound. He flips me completely onto my back and when I lift my hips to grind into him I'm surprised to find him already hard.

"Again?" He asks the stupid question, rubbing his erection over my swollen nerves.

"Why not? I'm already on my back."

"Not for long." His body comes off mine in one fluid motion and before I can ask, the rip of another condom wrapper breaks the silence. I'm captivated and eager as he rolls the ribbed latex over his hard on. "Hands and knees, Miss Naughty Author."

"Oh, what are we playing now?" I'm almost giddy as I crawl to all fours. The bed dips with his weight and I don't know what exactly I expect, but a sharp smack to the ass is not it. I gasp at the sting of pain. His hands brace my hips and I gasp again as he fills me in one hard thrust.

His chest covers my back while one arm snakes over my breast and to my throat. He doesn't squeeze, but instead pulls against my ribs so my body arches back against him. His breath is at my ear. "All the positions."

"What?" I pant out as he holds me and thrusts in and out at a tortuous, steady rhythm.

"The game we're playing. I'm going to fuck you in all the positions. Good?"

"Yes. Good. More."

He really has reduced me to a woman unable to form proper sentences.

After our second round, a bathroom break, and picnic of cheese sticks, pretzels, and yogurt atop his moonlit bedspread, I'm totally spent in the best possible way, lying next to Brax and fighting the urge to give in to sleep.

While I did not fully expect him to deliver on the sex tonight, at least not to the extent he had, I'm also more than gratified from our exchange of banter, his humor and positive outlook on life, and the timbre of his voice and how some words twang in a manner particular to the south. God, I'm almost smitten. Must be sleep deprivation.

"Manda, darlin' you are lookin' rather sleepy. Did someone wear you out? Need a nap?" Brax props his head on his hand, his elbow against the pillow. His fingers skim across my shoulder, down the center of my chest and then brush over one nipple, causing goosebumps to scatter across my skin despite the warmth I feel down to my bones.

I glance over to the digital clock on his makeshift bedside table and cringe at the time. I'm not sleeping tonight. Not that I'm complaining. I just can't believe how the past few hours have flown by with him. Conversation and making love—no, fucking—with my sexy bartender shouldn't have lasted longer than an hour or two.

"I should probably leave soon. My flight's in three hours and I need to grab my stuff from the hotel room before Lauren thinks I overslept."

"Can your friend meet you? I'll take you to the airport." He braces his body over mine and scrapes his beard between my naked breasts. His lips sneak kisses, a soft, whispered tenderness that spikes need and lust at my core.

"You don't have to do that." My words lack conviction, though, and my fingers brush into his hair as he peppers kisses down my body and low to my belly.

He lifts his head, our eyes lock in the moonlight, and his honesty catches my breath. "But I want to."

"Why?" I bite my lower lip because his own are dangerously close to where I already ache for him again.

As if he understands my need, his lips pull into a wide smile while his hooded gaze holds me in place. "Because I'm not close to being done with you. One night and I'm not close to having my fill. I'm not sure I could ever get enough of this pretty pussy." He dips his chin lower and swipes his tongue over my clit. My hips lift, wanting and needing more, but his hands grip my body and hold me down.

His fingers dig into my flesh when he licks me again and damn if that doesn't turn me on even more.

"Maybe I need to schedule another event in Nashville. Sometime soon . . ." *Fuck!* He's so good at this. I'd take notes for my next book, but it's impossible to concentrate on anything other than the wet heat from his mouth and his tongue working in, over, and around my bundle of nerves.

"Oh, yes, Brax, do that." I can at least be encouraging.

He sucks hard and then releases it moments before I'm about to break apart. I almost protest but he replaces his mouth with his fingers, leisurely working one and then two fingers inside me. I lean forward and rest my weight against my elbows so I can watch him better.

"If you come back to Tennessee I won't be here. At least, I hope I won't be. I've got big plans to get out of this town," he says. His fingers pick up the pace, and the sounds of my heavy pants and the wetness between my legs fills the small room. It's entirely erotic. Bold. Delicious.

"Well, if you ever find yourself in Phoenix, look me up. You can eat my pussy any day," I sass and Brax uses the opportunity to flick my clit with his tongue again. "*Fuck!*"

"Maybe I will." He lifts his lips for one brief moment before locking them down.

"Yes, yes, yes, yes!" The shouts leave my lips of their own accord, matching the desire that surges and pulses from my center. I'd be gushing wet if it weren't for Brax's lips lapping up my release as if it's his favorite meal. And he's made me a fucking liar. Because there's no way any book boyfriend has ever compared to the way Brax just played my body. Working my clit with an expertise that should be illegal, it's so sinful.

"Why are you so good at this?" I practically growl.

He smiles up at me with those ocean hued irises, wanting, needing, greedy. "It's the beard."

I tug his body over me and my lips find his. Our tongues battle and stroke, fueling my yearning until my legs fall open, willing and wanting all of him inside me again. He rolls on another condom and his rock hard length sheaths in my pussy in one hard slam.

My heart beats a little too quickly and it's not only from his kiss. I'm afraid it's more than a beard thing. It's a Brax thing. God damn it. Of course. Only I would go and fall for a one-night stand. A man who lives nowhere close to the place I call home. Someone who makes me feel things while he rocks my world so hard I can't see straight.

I spend the remaining hours relishing in his touch, his kiss, the rub of the bristly hairs on his cheek as they skim over my most sensitive skin. I get lost in his ocean blues, my heart a ship without anchor as we ride the waves of pleasure and desire into the early dawn.

When my alarm signals it's time to leave, I dress in last night's clothes, my body sore and completely satisfied, but my heart squeezes with an unfamiliar pain. It's not shame. It's not doubt. Not even regret. It's dangerously close to a feeling of love. Which is crazy because I've only known this man for one night.

Love doesn't happen that way. Not in an instant. I must be mistaken.

But my heart begs to differ.

Damn. Joke's on me.

About Kacey Shea

Kacey Shea is a mom of three, wife, and indie author who resides in sunny Arizona. She enjoys reading and writing romance novels as much as her son loves unicorns, which is a lot. She has an unhealthy obsession with firefighters. It could be the pants. It could be the fire. It's just hot and on occasion she has been known to include them, without their knowledge, in her selfies outside the grocery store. Kacey's contemporary romance novels are a mix of humor and heat, all the while weaving a story that brings readers joy and keeps them guessing every turn of the page!

Website: www.kaceysheabooks.com

Newsletter: eepurl.com/b5FI4f

Instagram: www.instagram.com/kaceysheabooks

Twitter: www.twitter.com/kaceysheabooks

Facebook: www.facebook.com/kaceysheabooks

Goodreads: www.goodreads.com/author/show/13919697.Kacey_Shea

Reader Group: www.facebook.com/groups/booksbykaceyshea

Wild Proposal

BY ANGELITA GILL

Chapter One

OH, NO HE DIDN'T.

Antonia climbed out of the rental car, pulled the sunglasses from her face and dropped them on the seat. She couldn't believe her eyes.

During the six-hour drive from Seattle, she imagined her boss brooding in a rustic cabin on a hilltop where no one could reach him without four-wheel drive. Or hiding out in his fancy Airstream by a river. Maybe staying low in a cozy bungalow near a famous bike trail or something.

But not this.

Justin Faber had swiped her dream. That hipster-genius-CEO-millionaire took her vision and made it *his* reality.

It probably didn't occur to him she'd find out, or that she'd ever track him down. No one else had a clue where he'd taken off to, and his hiatus was supposed to end the Sunday before last. However, Monday morning came and she was told he'd sent a message to Chloe, his assistant, that the date of his return was currently "indeterminable."

Most of the employees at It's Handled were unfazed by his prolonged absence.

But then there was Antonia. Furious, agitated, and done with his bullshit.

She'd asked Chloe to have him call her, but although her message had been relayed by the assistant, it had been ignored by the CEO. So were her emails.

After fuming for a week, she decided to go to *him*, and there she was, standing in front of a beautiful glass house on a raised platform with a glittering, private lake behind it.

She stared at the magnificent but modest-sized structure in awe, shut the car door, and walked up the broken seashell path.

She had the right place; his Range Rover was parked near a shed with a gleaming, brand-new Airstream hitched to it.

With no doorbell in sight, she knocked. The sound seemed foreign in such a serene environment.

No answer. She knocked again. Because of the curtains, she was unable to see inside.

With a frustrated sound, she marched down the steps and went around the deck to the rear of the house. Checking her cell phone, she cursed when she realized she had no service that far away from civilization. Apparently, her network carrier didn't bother putting any towers out this far in Washington state.

She rounded the deck, mouth agog. There were no curtains blocking her view of the interior now.

It was an open floor plan, with gleaming wood floors, chrome paneling, and a primarily neutral palette of crème, tan, white, and gray. A California king-sized bed was positioned on one end, and a social area with a couch and coffee table in the middle. There was a fireplace and dining table on the other end, stacked with books. A modern glass desk was littered with gadgets and monitors. The kitchen had beautiful cherry wood cabinetry, stainless steel appliances, and a glass-door fridge.

She sighed with envy, then went down the back steps and roamed around the massive backyard, when she heard the buzzing of an engine in the distance. Raising a hand to shield her eyes from the sunlight, she saw a boat heading to shore.

Her heart skipped a beat.

Justin.

At the helm of a cruiser boat, wearing a blue flannel shirt unbuttoned with its tails flapping behind him, the sleeves rolled to his elbows, was the ruggedly handsome owner and CEO of It's Handled.

Not only was he smart as a whip and insanely successful, he was also hotter than a ghost pepper, and probably just as dangerous to touch…and taste.

Dios mío. He'd grown a beard.

He didn't appear to see her while he switched off the engine, jumped onto the dock, and pulled the boat over to secure it.

She swallowed, heart beginning to pound, neck heating up, breath shortening. Justin's two-month absence somehow made her forget that being in his general vicinity evoked physical reactions she could never control.

What the hell was she going to say to him? Why was she there, exactly? Justin had a low tolerance for people who came to him unprepared, or for those who spoke impulsively. That wasn't him. Every word out of his mouth seemed to come out as though he thought of them five minutes before you finished speaking.

He hopped down, swiped his hands on his cargo shorts, and headed in her direction with that notable swagger. Then he looked up, and halted.

Those soulful, hazel eyes locked with hers. There was no surprise. No shock.

She raked her gaze over him, raising a brow at his…casual appearance.

At the office, he never appeared unkempt. Every day he wore his signature vests, ties, and custom-made shirts. The poster child for the hipster entrepreneur. Yet, he was just as devastating in a flannel shirt and shorts that looked like they'd been plucked from a crate at a fisherman's market.

The outfit made him look boyish, but his expression was hard as volcanic glass. "Antonia. How the *hell* did you find me?"

Chapter Two

Antonia preferred that hard tone. She'd heard it a hundred times, and could match it. "*What* the hell are you doing for two months while the rest of us are trying to keep It's Handled afloat?" God, he should really button that shirt.

His gorgeous eyes narrowed. "The company is more than afloat. In fact, last time I checked, it's practically floating in the clouds, we're doing so well this quarter. Have you forgotten we raised our estimated IPO to $10 billion?"

You patronizing... "Just because it's doing phenomenal doesn't mean you can jump ship."

"Newsflash: I can do whatever I want. I own the ship."

Oh, it felt too good to hear his deep, sexy voice. The unprofessional in her wanted to run to him, hug him, tell him she missed him, missed his voice. That was how out-of-whack his absence had made her.

She crossed her arms and steeled her nerves. "As your VP of PR, it's my job to make sure your reputation doesn't get caught in the net of rumors and conjecture, putting the company in a shadow when it's really starting to shine. Being gone for a couple weeks is fine. A month? Manageable. *Two* months with no immediate date of return? There are rumors you're out here brainstorming something epic. People are starting to talk."

"When you say people, to whom are you referring?"

"Clients," she emphasized, her Spanish accent coming out. "Employees. Business associates. It's a matter of time before the media gets wind of what's going on, and starts printing theories about your absence."

He shrugged, hands on hips. "Do your job and handle it. That's not something I need to concern myself with."

"I *have* been doing my job! Part of it is anticipating fires, and putting out the flickers before they turn into infernos."

"You're being a little dramatic, don't you think?"

"Dramatic? Dramatic would've been here weeks ago. Panicking after a month. Taking ulcer medication after two. By the way, I took a week of vacation just so I could find you. I'm doing what you pay me for. If you want a passive PR executive, then fire me and hire someone else." She inwardly gasped, disbelieving her blurt. Justin could easily retort, *Okay, you're fired*, and walk away, leaving her unemployed and ashamed. Her mouth could get her in so many places, including in trouble.

Everyone and their cousin wanted to work at It's Handled. Slack dress code. Health benefits. Free gym, free food, sleeping pods for afternoon naps…the benefit list went on. If she was smart—and she was—she'd do everything to keep her job. To keep working beside Justin.

Eyes forward, chica. Don't look at the defined chest and rippled abs. No, no. You might be away from the office, but that doesn't mean you can openly ache at the sight of your boss's fantastic body.

He said nothing, continuing to hold her gaze, his expression blank. Usually she was good at reading people, but like a spotted leopard, Justin Faber was a rare breed. Growing up with four brothers, she thought she knew everything there was to know about reading men's body language, tone, mannerisms.… But he was unlike any man she'd ever encountered.

That made him fascinating, to the point of *obsessively* fascinating. Which was probably why she was standing there in front of him, instead of forcing Chloe to put him on the phone.

Done with the drawn-out silence, she said, "You haven't returned any of my calls or emails in weeks. Why are you being like this?"

"I don't know. I've been busy."

"Doing what?"

He made a gesture to the structure behind her. "Enjoying myself. What do you think?"

She turned around to stare at the house in all its glory. "I think you stole my idea."

"I guess I did," he said in an amused tone.

Must be nice to be wealthy beyond reason, able to purchase a unique glass house built on a lake. Her salary was generous, and the company perks were unheard of, but it would take her years of hardcore saving to afford something like this, let alone the land it sat on.

"How could you?" she whispered.

"Have I upset you?"

She jerked at his nearness. When had he snuck up behind her? She could feel his heat, smell his musk. Little awareness bumps raised on her skin.

"Upset? Pfft. I'm happy for you. I just…didn't know you were listening. Or paying attention to my wistful little dream." She'd often spoke of buying a glass house by some body of water whenever they went out for company socials.

"I'm always listening. I'm always paying attention. When it comes to you."

When had his voice taken on a sensual quality? She'd never heard it before, in the office or otherwise. Was he *flirting*? Justin didn't do that. Not with her. In fact, he was the opposite when they were alone. Short, terse, succinct. Though there were moments in meetings when they tended to finish each other's sentences. She'd look at him, he'd look at her, and time kind of time stopped. She secretly lived for those moments.

Antonia slowly faced him. However, there was no teasing light in his eyes, twist in his lips, or any obvious sign he was flirting. It was all in her head. She kept her tone sharp. "When are you coming back?"

He took his time answering, searching her gaze. "Eventually."

"That's a vague answer."

"That's the only one you're going to get." He walked past her.

What the hell was going on with him?

She followed him up the steps. "Are you having an early mid-life crisis or something? You're only thirty-five. Maybe it's different for you because you've accomplished so much at a young age, but if you're going through some existential crisis, I need to know." Actually, she didn't. She was his employee, not his therapist. But she'd do anything to get him out of his funk and back to where he belonged.

He stopped so abruptly, her face was almost introduced to his ass. "What if I was going through something? What would you do?"

"*Are* you going through something?" She looked up, trying to read him, but as usual, got Nowheres-ville.

Instead of answering, he resumed his climb.

She uttered a series of low curses in Spanish and forced her legs up the stairs. When she reached the top, her unlady-like swearing came to a stop.

"I don't blame you for wanting to stay, but you can't. You should be in Seattle." What would he do if she just fell on his bed of white sheets and snuggled in for an hour?

He sauntered to the kitchen and pulled a pitcher of water from the fridge. "I don't have to be physically present at the office to work. Besides, the place isn't falling apart without me."

"It shouldn't have to fall apart in order for you to be there. Don't you miss it?" *Or, maybe even me?*

He met her eyes briefly before pouring a glass of water. "Miss what?"

"Your company."

"I've lived and breathed it for six years. I'm never that far from it. But I had to get away for a while."

"Why?"

He raised the glass to his mouth, looking past her shoulder. "I don't know."

That was the second time he said that. Justin didn't utter the phrase *I don't know*. It was disconcerting because he always had an answer. He always *knew*. Maybe he was under some kind of pressure she wasn't aware of. Maybe he was bored. Maybe this rumored new idea was sucking up all his energy.

A dog barked from somewhere in the house, and came jaunting from around the corner. She grinned at the adorable golden retriever. "Who's this?"

"Fletch."

She smiled. "Hi, Fletch." She bent down, petted his head, and scratched under his chin.

Now that she couldn't talk Justin out of staying, she didn't know what to do. If he wouldn't come to work, then she might as well bring work to him.

"Can I go over a few things with you before I leave? I did drive six hours, almost hitting four different species of animal, and narrowly missing a rogue boulder on the way."

"Damn, you're incorrigible. If it's absolutely necessary."

She gritted her teeth. "It is." She went to the car to grab her tablet, laptop, and purse. Even though he'd been short with her, she couldn't help but smile.

Just like old times.

Justin watched the woman of his fantasies from the window.

His heart hammered, his hand tightened to a fist. How dare she come out here and disrupt his peace?

Somewhere in the back of his mind, he *knew* she would. He couldn't explain it, but he had an inkling if he stayed away, Antonia Ruiz would eventually hunt him down, especially since he'd been ignoring her for too long.

That was intentional. He'd been attempting to purge the lustful ache, clear his mind, and become whole again with self-discipline and isolation. He knew if he heard her voice or even responded to her emails, he'd be back at ground zero.

So he'd been cruel and dismissive, cutting off communication with her until he felt ready.

Well. The past two months had been an effort in goddamn futility. His reaction to her arrival proved he'd been in denial the entire time. The second he laid eyes on her, the suppressed feelings revived like a violent volcano, gushing, fiery, and melting any inner strength he'd had carefully built.

Damn her.

He strode to the wireless router and disabled it. She had to leave. He didn't trust himself not to blurt out how he felt. He didn't want her to know how much he missed her, how dependent he'd become on seeing her smile to remind himself life was good. He couldn't let her know how much he fed off her enchanting, unspoiled energy to get through a hard day, even when they argued.

Before she came along, he didn't need anything in his life except his company, his friends, his coffee bar, favorite bike trails, and the occasional one-night-stand.

Then Drew, his IT guru, told him he needed to hire a public relations pro, and brought Antonia in for an interview. Quite frankly, he'd pictured…someone else.

She was vivacious, intelligent, articulate, and witty. Something told him to hire her, and it'd been one of the best decisions he'd ever made. The office became a lot more colorful with her in it, swearing in Spanish and donning her colorful blouses. She had to be the best-kept secret in the city, and he'd been shocked no one had scooped her up with her credentials, a Gonzaga grad who'd interned at one of the most respected PR firms. Not to mention, she was a stunner. All that long, dark hair, caramel-tinted skin, and those healthy curves, particularly an ass that had him—at many frustrating times—inwardly groaning, his cock twitching to brush between those plump cheeks.

He rubbed the back of his neck. "Fuck." Five minutes ago he wanted her to leave, and yet…since she was there, and they were alone, he couldn't help but think this was what he'd needed all along.

Her with him. No more of this solo crap.

No one else hovering around them. No office etiquette between them. If there was ever going to be a perfect time to explore their chemistry, and discover if what he felt was real, or if it was plain physical attraction, then he'd never get a better opportunity.

He leaned his forearm on the glass. Telling her could derail everything. If she didn't want him…if he exposed his desire and feelings only to have them rejected, then he'd be humiliated, and he'd lose her.

Everyone at the company would lose. She'd go work for someone else and make another man's day brighter, someone else's company better.

Part of him would be grateful, because then the suffering would end.

Was it worth the risk? The attraction was mutual. He could see it. Passionate woman that she was, she couldn't help but show it at times. Everything was in the eyes, and her sexy browns told him the yearning wasn't one-sided.

With a frustrated growl, he turned from the window, shoving his hands in his pockets. A few years ago, he would've mocked a man with a similar problem. How cliché: the boss panting after the sassy, bewitching VP. Willing to fuck up a successful professional relationship for the slim chance at a successful personal one.

But he'd tried to fight it. Honestly, he did. No matter how clever or logical he was, he was just a man, and every man had his weaknesses. Antonia happened to be a notable one of his.

Like so many other times in his life, he was going to set logic aside, and go for it. Give in for once, instead of resisting forever.

Running a hand through his hair, he frowned. He couldn't seduce her like this, covered in dirt, sweat, with greasy hair. He needed a shower before he spoke one more word to her.

A half-smile tugged his mouth, the first in a long time since he'd been out there.

It felt good, and just a little bad.

Justin wasn't anywhere in sight when she returned and placed her belongings on the dining table. Then she heard water running and saw the bathroom door ajar.

She gasped, eyes wide. Her boss was showering just steps away, soap and water sluicing along his plank-hard stomach and butt, down those muscled legs.

She plopped down in a chair and squeezed her eyes shut, blindly typing in her username and password for the laptop. Was her lack of a sex life the cause for this constant fantasizing about one man?

Sex was awesome, but it wasn't vital to her like it was for some of her single friends. Ever since she'd started working with Justin however, the very thought of it had become oxygen. She'd been experiencing unprecedented sexual cravings.

Six months prior, her friends had talked her into participating in a bar crawl, and she'd met a charming, sexy Chris Hemsworth lookalike. Many empty bottled beers between them later, one thing led to another and they ended up at his place, where he rocked her world. Or, at least she'd moaned like he had, because the only man she thought about was Justin.

His mouth searing along her skin. *His* tongue leisurely licking her pussy. *His* cock stroking in and out of her body. She'd been having sex with a good-looking guy with stellar skills in bed, and yet all she could think about was doing her boss, wishing it was his hands squeezing her ass, his voice choking out her name as she rode him vigorously.

"Antonia."

She shot her gaze to Justin's. Her cheeks flamed with guilty heat. "What?"

"I asked if you wanted anything to drink."

An ice cold bucket of water would do. She cleared her throat. "Juice if you have it."

He opened the fridge door. His hair was damp and run-through, and instead of the rags he'd donned earlier, he wore jeans and a light blue V-neck. Hmm. She sort of preferred the rags in a weird way, but damn, he looked good. Especially with the beard. It made him even more masculine, and with his new tan, he looked like a rugged, nature god—

"How about lemonade? Bought it fresh from a neighbor kid down the road," he said.

She cleared her thoughts and focused on her laptop screen. "You have neighbors? How far are they?"

"A mile down. And on the north side of the lake."

God. They were so isolated it wasn't even funny. Normally she'd love it, but being secluded with Justin seemed to make her world smaller and harder to breathe. "What's your Wi-Fi password?"

"It's on a sticky-note underneath the mouse pad."

"Not exactly a prime hiding place, Mr. Faber."

He shrugged. "I'm hiding enough as it is."

When she typed it in, a message popped up that there was no signal. She tried again. Still didn't work. She restarted her Mac and got the same results. "I can't get online. It says there's no internet access."

"That's weird. Let me check the router."

He squatted behind the desk in the corner and assessed the equipment. "Something's wrong. It's not showing a signal. I'll restart it." Five minutes later, and it seemed technology had failed them. "Sorry. Looks like we won't be doing any work."

She held back a frustrated groan. "Justin! You're a man who made millions on the latest workstations for the nomadic professional. How can you not have the best reliable network here?"

"We're in the middle of nowhere. What do you want me to do? Move satellites with my mind?"

Ugh. She was so fed up. "So I came out here for nothing? I can't convince you to come back to Seattle, and I can't get any work done while I'm here. Just great." She yanked the power cord from the outlet, wrapped it up, and turned off the laptop and tablet.

Justin took a sip of water, his eyes narrowing. "I didn't ask you to come out here."

"Well, you can rejoice now, because I'm leaving."

"Fine." He set down the glass on the desk with force. "Take your attitude with you. I don't need it and I definitely don't need you."

That stung more than a slap to the face. She wanted to get out without looking back. She slipped on her jacket, gathered her belongings, and charged to the front door. "By the way," she said, turning the knob. "I quit."

Chapter Three

Years back, when she was an impulsive teenager, every time she did something stupid, her grandmother's words of outrage would sound off in her head. *Idiota! You never think before you speak! You spit on the Lord's blessings.*

Her grandmother would be right this time, but she had too much pride to turn around.

"Antonia!" Justin angrily shouted behind her, but she kept going.

Too emotional to confront him, she yanked the rear passenger door and threw her stuff in the backseat.

"Antonia."

He jogged down the steps and marched toward her. Just when she opened the driver side, he slammed it shut before she could get in. "You can't quit, damn it."

"I can and I did." Part of her celebrated the fact he'd come out here, furious with her decision.

"Did you mean it?" he asked.

"Yes." No. But she couldn't admit it, and she sort of wanted to see the man grovel.

"Why? Because my router isn't working? Because I refuse to obey at the snap of my VP's fingers? These are *illogical* reasons."

Whoa. He looked really pissed. "I don't have to give you a logical reason."

For a lengthy period, they stood facing each other without speaking. His hand remained splayed on the door, blocking her from opening it. The air became cooler with a light mist accompanying the breeze. His skin took on a wet sheen, and small drops of rain clung to his beard.

"Antonia. I didn't mean it. I do…need you. You can't quit."

She blinked. It wasn't the words he said; it was how he said them.

"I'm sorry," he said, shocking her. "For being a jerk. I guess I've been by myself for too long. You've made me realize I can't stay out here forever."

"Does that mean you'll come back?"

He dropped his hand from the door. "Yes. Under one condition."

"Name it."

"I didn't ask you to come…but I *am* asking you to stay."

"Stay? You mean for dinner or something?"

His gaze dropped and he appeared to be fighting a smile. "No. Stay the week. Help me get my groove back, so to speak. I'll work. I'll tell you what's been going on in my head. I'll even help you write media kits. At the end of the week, I promise I'll drive home. Just don't quit."

Her mouth opened and closed, opened, and shut again. *That was his condition?* "Are you loco? I can't do that."

"Why not?"

"Because for one thing, I…I have to get back to Seattle."

"I thought you took the week off."

"Er, I did. But that was to give me enough time to find you."

"And it only took you one day. You figured out what no one else could. I think you deserve a week off. Consider it mandatory."

Didn't he get it? "Staying with you is inappropriate. How about I grab a hotel room in the nearest town? We can meet up at a local diner or a library and work there for the next few days."

His gaze turned hard again. "No. It's here or nowhere."

You entitled ass. "I can't share the CEO's vacation house with him! Period. You don't have a spare bedroom."

"No one will know you're here." He glanced behind him. "I'll sleep in the Airstream. You can have the house. Think about it. You'll have my full, undivided attention for five days."

Tempting. Very tempting. Most tempting offers were classified as such because they fulfilled desire. Desire usually meant one wanted something enough they were willing to be stupid. Stupid decisions led to regret or consequences. Consequences sometimes weren't worth satisfying a selfish act.

Then again, it was her dream house, and she'd love a few days off. And, of course, there was *him*.

"If I stay, you'll leave this weekend? For good?"

He gave a single nod.

"And you won't tell anyone I was here?"

He shook his head.

As a friend of hers would say, this was a PNR situation. Point of no return. Having Justin to herself was a dream come true and a total professional nightmare at the same time. Too much proximity. Too much one-on-one. But she couldn't say no. "All right. Deal."

Without a word, he grabbed her items from the car and headed back to the house.

Justin blew out a relived breath. That was close. During her tantrum about not getting work done, he didn't take her that seriously, but when she announced she'd quit and stormed out, the panic hit him like a freight train.

Two thoughts popped in his head: *Get her back. Say anything.*

If she hadn't agreed to stay, he was scary close to blurting, *Yeah? Well I think I'm in love with you, so maybe it's better if you quit!*

Good thing he didn't have to go that far.

Eventually he'd switch the router on—they *should* get some work accomplished—but for tonight, that wouldn't be part of their evening.

"Make yourself at home," he said, putting her bags on the sofa. "There's wine. Beer. Snacks. Cheesecake. The pantry and the fridge are full. Take whatever you want."

"I'd really like to clean myself up, if that's okay."

A vision sprung to mind. The two of them in the shower, him mapping her entire body with his tongue. *Yeah, scratch that from your mind before you get hard.* He pointed to the left. "Through there, as you've already guessed. There's a tub too, but it's not in the bathroom."

Her eyes lit up. "Where is it?"

He gestured for her to follow him. Around the kitchen, on the other side of the house, was an acrylic freestanding tub with a handheld sprayer. He'd had it placed in the corner for an exclusive view of the lake and backyard.

By the way her mouth parted in awe, she loved it. She traced her fingertips along the edge. "It's perfect."

God, he wanted to kiss her. Was the time ever going to be right? He cleared his throat. "I'll show you how to control the lights and curtains."

He gave her a quick demonstration on how to operate everything with the remote, including the fireplace. He turned on the TV, even though he'd killed her ability to watch movies without the internet, except by his DVD collection.

She perused his bookcase. "Hm. Goonies. Spaceballs. Lethal Weapon...someone likes male-driven shenanigans movies."

He hid a smile, and gave a fake cough. "Want to know a secret?"

Her brows lifted.

"*Legally Blonde* is in the *Rocky* case, hidden beneath the special features DVD."

She laughed. "I'll take it to my grave."

A few moments of silence passed between them before he realized there wasn't anything else he needed to show her. "Right, so… you should have everything you need." He scooped up his books and laptop and tucked them under an arm. "I'll be in the Airstream if you need me."

She opened her mouth to say something, then smiled. "Gracias. I'll see you in the morning."

His smile faded as he opened the door to the trailer. What was he doing, walking away from her? He should've offered more. He should've found a way for her to need him so he wouldn't be stuck in his trailer all night. He had Antonia Ruiz all to himself and he'd just… left her there.

For now.

He killed time writing in his brainstorm journal, and listened to a podcast he'd saved on his laptop. When the sun slid behind the horizon, he was beyond restless.

He put on a jacket and grabbed his flashlight, thinking he should check on the boat, make sure it was anchored and secured. Deliberately keeping his eyes *off* the house, he strode to the beach.

The boat was fine.

He walked along the shore, threw rocks in the water, then cut through the forest to make sure birds hadn't made nests on the septic tank.

The lights coming on from the house illuminated through the trees.

He looked up.

Antonia stood in front of the window, wearing a silk robe, loosely tied at her waist, showing a wealth of womanly breasts and lacey panties. She stared out at the trees, tracing her fingertip along the edge of the robe's collar.

His stomach dropped, and he let out a disbelieving breath. He swung around, wiping the sweat from his upper lip, knees weak.

He shouldn't look. Squeezing his eyes shut, he cursed, took two steps forward...and stopped. No matter how much he *burned* for one quick glance, to take advantage of this moment, it was wrong.

"Shit." The flashlight. She might've seen him out here. He switched it off.

Wait. Did she know he was in her direct line of sight? Had she done that on purpose? He hesitated, debating whether he should march forward to the beach, or let his eyes drink up the ultimate view.

I'm so goddamn weak.

He turned around, squatted behind the tank, and looked.

She untied her robe, slowly, and let it drop to the floor.

He couldn't breathe, couldn't move, but damn if his cock didn't twitch. Every line of her captivated him. Full breasts with dark, little nipples, a soft waist, thick hips and thighs. A lacy thong covering that part of her where he'd imagined his mouth to be over and over.

He slowly lifted his gaze to her face. Was that a smile? He couldn't really tell from the distance.

She turned around and reached into the water.

He made a fist and bit it with a groan. He relished this showcase of her deliciously plump ass while she gathered her hair in a loose bun, removed her panties, and climbed in.

With his cock hard as steel, he trudged back to the trailer and slammed the door. He needed a drink. The only thing he had in the trailer was warm tequila.

Good enough.

He splashed a good portion over ice and sipped on it for a while, listening to a favorite Seattle band, when there was a knock on the door.

Half buzzed, he dropped his head back before forcing himself up and opening the door.

Antonia smiled up at him, wearing a white, ankle-length dress with a modest slit on her left leg.

God have mercy. "Hey." His voice was rough.

"I'm starving. I found salmon in your fridge and thought you might be hungry? I made enough for the both of us."

He didn't respond, tongue-tied, remembering her luscious body naked.

She started to back up, a gleam in her eyes. "Come on. I like my food hot."

As soon as he walked in, his mouth watered. Two plates with salmon, a side salad, and the rest of his quinoa. A bottle of wine stood near her plate, a third of it empty. He raised a brow, glad to see he wasn't the only one drinking.

She'd cooked the salmon to perfection. It practically melted in his mouth, and when he finished, she seemed pleased that he'd cleaned his plate.

She set her chin in her hand and smiled. "I'm good, no?"

Ah man, she's so lovely like that. "You're good."

"Found your cheesecake. Thought I could smother it with some chocolate syrup, but only if you share it with me."

She created their dessert, swirling a generous amount of chocolate over the slice. His buzz started to wane now that he'd eaten, but his lust hummed consistently, especially when his gaze kept traveling to the center of her breasts every time she leaned over to cut a bite of cheesecake.

"It's so quiet out here," she said, bringing the fork to her mouth. "And dark. Are you ever scared being alone in a glass house in the woods?"

He shook his head.

She laughed softly. "I suppose a man like you isn't afraid of much, no?"

Her accent came out a lot more when she drank, with her putting "no" almost after every question, something he'd picked up on at the summer BBQ and Christmas party. Each time, he found it more adorable. He swallowed his bite. "What is there to be afraid of? The forest monster coming to eat me?"

She leaned in. "*Anything* coming to eat you. Come on, admit it. You've heard a noise or saw a movement in the trees and got a little scared."

"A bird flew into the window once. I think I jumped."

"Oh, the poor thing! Your house treeked it."

"Treeked? You mean tricked?"

She rolled her eyes and shrugged. "That's what I said."

He grinned, then pointed to the last bite on the plate. "Are you going to claim that?"

She pushed away from the table, shaking her head with a grin. "I never take the last bite. It's rude."

He chuckled. Maybe it was the fact he'd rarely interacted with anyone in person for a long time, or maybe he was just sick of his own company, but he hadn't felt this—content? in ages.

It was her. She made the difference.

Shit. He was in trouble.

Antonia got up and picked up the dirty plates. He caught a whiff of the soap she used, and he had the urge to moan, haul her across the table and into his arms. It was getting ridiculous how much he had to fight his impulses.

He shot up from his seat. "Thanks for dinner."

Her brows rose. "You're leaving?"

"Yeah."

"All right. If that's what you want." She held his gaze, almost challenging him.

He *wanted* to split her dress down the front, spread her legs, and fuck her hard and deep until she cried happy tears. The invitation in her eyes was unmistakable, and yet he couldn't make a move. He opened the back door. "See 'ya."

"You saw me, didn't you?"

He paused and met her gaze. "What?"

"I know you did, because I saw you first. In the trees." She took a step toward him. "I wanted you to see me."

"Antonia—"

She groaned, shoulders sagging. "I don't want to fight anymore. Let's stop pretending. You want me. You think I'm blind? I see it. You want to be close to me. And I want you. There. I said something I thought I'd *never* say." She searched his face. "Am I wrong?"

He swallowed. "You're wrong."

"You're lying."

"You know what you look like. You're beautiful and sexy, and… I've been out here alone for a while. Of course I'm going to look at you when you're standing naked in front of a window, but I'm not going to…touch you."

A fucking lie if he ever told one. His stomach plummeted at the hurt look on her face. He'd humiliated her to save his pride. He shot her down because he didn't like being told he was so transparent, or that he was weak, and that it was okay. With a soft curse, he left the house and walked toward the trailer.

To his annoyance, she followed him. "Justin."

He kept marching, ignoring her, feeling the weakness closing in.

"Why are you pushing me away?"

"I'm not. I've always been like this."

"You don't have to be. I think I know why you came out here. You're unhappy. You imagined getting away from it all would fill that…that void. We all experience it. Sometimes our dreams let us down, even when they're fulfilled—"

He whipped around so quick she bumped into him and gasped. Locking an arm around her waist, he swooped down and claimed her mouth. Her lips were hot, and she tasted like chocolate, sugar, and pure woman. A helpless sound escaped his throat.

Her hand slid inside up his chest and raked his hair while she swirled her tongue with his with greedy passion.

He moaned and ran his free hand down, inside the open slit of her dress, caressing her thigh, finding her skin warm and silky. He boldly went around her hip and grabbed her ass, pressing her body closer to his so she could feel how hard he was.

He wanted her so badly he could barely stop his body from shaking with need. The more and more they kissed, the closer he got to falling to his knees and confessing she had him, owned him, that he could lose himself in her if she let him. That was real power she had.

He broke away and took a step back.

Their deep breaths made white clouds in the dark, cold air. Her lips were swollen and her breasts rose and fell.

Eventually, he was going to succumb to her. It was inevitable. A matter of time. But not tonight, with her tipsy enough to regret it and blame it on the alcohol.

He drew in a deep breath, jaw clenching as his exhaled. He should get a fucking award for rejecting his ultimate temptation. "Go to bed." He turned for the trailer.

"You're walking away again?" she asked.

"As I said, I've always been like this."

Chapter Four

THE FIRST THOUGHT THAT CAME TO HER WHEN SHE WOKE UP the next morning?

It was the vino. Wine made her confident. *Overly* confident it seemed, because even though she'd gotten the kiss that destroyed all memories of kisses before it, she'd essentially been rejected.

She didn't know why. Unlike most men, Justin seemed to get angry about his attraction to her, he kissed like a man starved for sex, and yet wanted to punish her for it.

She'd been so wet and turned on, she'd been seconds away from begging him to take her to bed, which appalled the hell out of her. Antonia Ruiz didn't beg any man for anything. *They* did the begging.

She grabbed a pillow and screamed her frustration into it. The dog barked and she took the pillow away from her face with a smile. He wagged his tail eagerly. It was as though he smiled at her. She sat up. "Yes, I know, Fletch. I threw myself at him, but I don't regret it."

She got up, dressed, and let him out to do his business. She glanced at the Airstream. Justin had better keep his promise. Mad-hot mutual attraction aside, they had things to do. When she checked the wireless router, she found the cable connection wasn't in all the way, and realized he'd sabotaged it on purpose.

She smiled and shook her head. "Men."

The internet worked perfectly after that, and even though she was supposed to be on vacation, she checked her email and spent an hour catching up on social media. It was after nine o'clock and Justin had yet to make an appearance, so she turned on her favorite playlist on her laptop and started making breakfast. He had enough food to feed a small country.

She was singing along, flipping pancakes, and occasionally tossing the dog fatty pieces of ham when Justin appeared. She didn't notice him until he cleared his throat and shut the door.

How long had he been standing there? "Morning," she greeted.

"Smells good in here."

"I'm making strawberry pancakes with a side of ham. Need coffee?"

"Desperately."

She made him a plate of food and poured him a mug, then went to turn down the music. "You'll be impressed to know I fixed the router."

Head down, he cut into his pancakes, a hint of a smile on his lips. "Did you?"

"Now nothing can stop us from getting work done."

"Hooray," he said dryly before sipping coffee. There were dark circles under his eyes.

"Did you get much sleep?" she asked.

"Define much."

"More than four hours?"

"Then no, but that's usually the case for me."

Feeling guilty, she refilled his coffee. He probably missed his insanely comfortable California King. "I can sleep in the Airstream. You shouldn't be kicked out of your own bed."

"Thanks, but it doesn't matter where I sleep, the result is the same." He looked up and saw the concern on her face. "Excuse my crankiness. It takes me about thirty minutes until I'm myself in the morning. I forgot you're always so—chipper."

She smiled. "It's been a long time since I've been able to sleep in and take my time. I'm always late, running out the door, posting on It's Handled social media before my eyes even open."

After breakfast, he switched on his computer with dual twenty-inch monitors and started on his emails.

She created her own work area at the dining table and began reading off current headlines out loud, as she usually did before the morning meeting to get everyone talking and productive.

"Hot topics of the day. A UK microchip manufacturer is on the verge of being bought out by a Japanese company. Some reality star is having a Twitter war with some pop star. Wildfires continue to eat up southern California. And a panda is pregnant at the zoo."

"Read the articles to me."

"About the panda too?"

He chuckled. "Why not?"

For the next hour, she read to him, though at first he didn't appear to be listening. Whenever she paused, however, he'd turn around and ask why she stopped. Apparently, he enjoyed hearing her read to him.

Later on, his cell phone rang. "It's Chloe," he said.

She jerked her gaze to him, as if they'd been caught, her pulse racing as he answered the call and put it on speaker. Justin, however, was nonplussed.

"Hey, Chloe. What's new?"

"The natives are getting restless," she said without preamble. "Especially now that Antonia is gone."

Justin swiveled in his chair and raised a brow. "What do you mean 'restless'?"

Chloe went on. "With you out, nothing really changed around here, but without Antonia, some of the employees seem lost. Out of the blue, she said she had to take a week off for a personal matter. Didn't she message you about it?"

"Of course she did. I saw her email this morning," he fibbed.

"Well, not for nothing, but with you *and* her gone, the office seems a little out of sorts. Every day before our meetings she makes us play a game of Guess-Which-Celebrity-I-Am to wake everyone up out of their morning stupor. Even people who thought it was silly are hooked on the tradition. When I told them we wouldn't be playing any games without Antonia here, they looked at me like I'd stolen Christmas."

While Chloe continued to give details about the office staff, he placed her on mute. "I didn't approve this game."

She shrugged. "When the cat's away…"

He gave her a chastising look before unmuting his assistant. Once she finished, he asked, "Anything else to report?"

"Shawn is demanding a conference call."

"Set it up for tomorrow."

"Really? He'll be ecstatic."

"And let everyone know I'll be back in the office on Monday."

"Monday? Oh, thank God. You and Antonia will both be back at the same time. She'll be so happy. She misses having you here."

A hot blush fired up Antonia's cheeks. Why did Chloe have to say it like *that*?

"She does? How do you know?" he asked, stroking his beard with a smug smile.

"I can just tell. We miss listening to you two hash it out in your office like David and Maggie from *Moonlighting*. Without the door slamming. You don't let anyone else talk to you the way she does. Have you ever noticed that?"

Antonia shook her head and avoided Justin's amused gaze. She had no idea people paid attention to their dynamic, but she guessed with sharing space in a huge, loft-like area, it was hard not to notice when the CEO and VP of Public Relations raised their voices.

Mostly, she was embarrassed because Chloe was right; she'd missed Justin more than she'd ever admit out loud. Every day, she woke up excited to go to work. Not just because she loved her job, but because of him. He challenged her and vexed her, when most men at her previous jobs had degraded her. She'd finally found a position she loved, where she could be herself all day. She finally worked for someone she truly respected…and wanted more than she could bear.

Yes, she thought wearily, she might be just a little in love with him.

Justin answered a few questions from Chloe regarding his schedule, then ended the call. There was a long stretch of silence between them, and she felt more exposed than ever.

"Antonia…" he started, then frowned, as though debating. Raising his gaze to hers, he finally said, "Pack us a quick lunch. We're going outside. I need to talk to you."

Oh, God. Could he see how she felt all over her face?

She didn't ask questions, even when he said she needed to change into something more suitable for going out on the boat. After switching from pants to shorts, she went to the kitchen to make sandwiches and cut up some fruit. She loaded their lunch in a backpack with two bottled waters.

When she made her way to the beach, she found Justin pushing the boat farther into the water, and she reveled in how cut his calves looked as they strained from the effort.

"Need help?"

He glanced over his shoulder and shook his head. He flattened his hands on the edge and hoisted himself up, then untied the rope.

She waited on the dock. He held out his arms, grasped her by the waist and set her down with ease.

God, he is so strong. She tried not to think about how *easily* he could hoist her up against a wall and—

The engine roared to life and they eased out to the lake. Antonia closed her eyes and let the wind blow her hair. He took them around a bend to the right, and anchored the boat near a shaded spot under an overgrown tree.

"I thought we could use some fresh air," he said. "I like to come out here and be on the water. Helps me think."

She leaned back on her elbows, heart thumping. "What did you want to talk to me about?"

He remained standing and crossed his arms, looking like a bearded god with his defined biceps and chest. "There's something I've been thinking about since I came out here. Something…I haven't told anyone."

And yet she was going to be the first person he shared it with? She took off her sunglasses, and set them aside. "Sounds important."

"Could be nothing. Could be something. Something new."

Excited, she grinned. "Tell me."

He smiled too, as though happy to see her enthusiasm. "At the core, we rent out co-working space for the wandering professional so they can work from virtually any major city. That's it. We're a leasing middle man, which by-and-large is a success in its own right. What if we went bigger? What if…what if we *also* offered co-living space to rent out to those same customers? Apartment living beyond the basics. Offer a community vibe that the average, on-the-go, isolated joe can call home for a day, a week, or even longer. What do you think so far?"

It was kind of brilliant. "Tell me more."

"Picture this: we offer it all. Beds, couches, kitchen. Month-to-month flexibility with benefits. Wi-Fi, cable, and basic utilities. All the beer, tea, and coffee they want—"

She sprung up, inspired. "And then add communal spaces like meditation and yoga rooms. And...a community chef's kitchen. Laundry rooms with karaoke."

"Ha! I like it! They'll have access to It's Handled Community events."

"Full-time housekeeping," she suggested.

"A concierge on-site."

"And encourage social engagement with an It's Living app."

He cocked his head. "It's Living?"

She flinched. "Sorry. What did you call it?"

"It didn't have a name yet." He shook his head and grinned. "It has a name now."

She laughed. "Just like that? This was *your* idea! You should christen it."

"No way can I top that. It's Handled for work. It's Living for non-work." He paused. "I've been thinking about this for months. You know how risky it is? Flipping the script on traditional apartment living could be huge. It could also be a huge disaster for us."

"As far as ideas go, it's just an embryo right now. We'll beta test the hell out of it first and go from there."

"You're right. It can start out as an experiment."

"Exactly. We'll use our own city. If an idea like this is going to thrive or dive anywhere, it'd be Seattle. Or San Francisco. That'd be a good place to test with the traveling techies coming and going."

He cupped her cheek. "I'm glad you get it. I knew you would, Antonia."

His smile made her smile, and for a second, time stopped...a new connection formed. How come at the office they acted like brats, but out here, they were practically in sync? Maybe their attraction was the problem. They had to fight it, hide it, and tension could never be released. Not at work.

He took a step closer, jaw clenched.

The nearness of him had her heart creating a tattoo against her ribcage, and she parted her lips, finding it hard to breathe.

Just kiss me, Justin. Please just do it.

It was as if he heard her. "If I kiss you, I won't stop. I'll go on and on and then I'll want more than kissing. I'll want you naked, open for me, in every way I can have you. But I don't want to do that on this boat. Not for our first time."

Her throat was drier than the Sahara. She had to swallow to make her tongue work and form a coherent word. "Okay." That was all she could mutter.

He turned then, grabbed the backpack, unzipped it, and began taking the items out. The moment was broken, and her legs were weak as she groped behind her to sit down again.

They resumed their conversation about It's Living, shooting pros and cons back and forth for an hour. How easily they could flip from blistering sexual tension to a productive conversation. She was frankly amazed it was possible, and how easy it could be with him. If she hadn't fallen for him yet, she had now.

Later that afternoon, they cruised around the lake for a bit, and headed back to the house. Clouds were coming in, and it looked like it might storm, winds disturbing the peaceful trees.

Once he docked the boat, he helped her out and they walked toward the house.

He stayed behind as she climbed the steps. "I have to go into town. I'll be gone maybe a good hour or so," he said. "Need anything?"

What could he have to go into town for that he didn't already have stocked twice? She shook her head. "Nothing I can think of. What do you want for dinner?"

"You don't have to make every meal for me."

"A word of advice. If a woman asks you what you want for dinner, it's because she wants to cook for you."

A corner of his mouth lifted. "I'll be happy with whatever you whip up."

"I know." She smiled and resumed her climb.

"Antonia?"

She stopped and met his gaze.

"Thank you," he said.

"For what?"

"For the perfect day."

Chapter Five

Over an hour later, she was setting down the plates on the dining table when the first rumble of thunder shook through the house.

She'd showered, let her hair air dry in untamed waves and put on a comfortable, form-hugging cotton dress. Tonight was the night she was going to give herself to him. They both knew it.

It started to rain, then pour, and soon after, the thunder and lightning interrupted the night. Fletch whined and hid under the table. She soothed him as best she could, and kept an eye out for Justin.

She switched off all the lights and the TV. It was amazing to listen and watch the rain in a glass house with the fire going. She tried not to look at the clock, but it'd been over two hours.

What if something had happened? Who would she call? Where would she go to look for him? She paced, fiddled with her hands, tormented with each passing second.

The dog barked once, and she saw headlights coming up the driveway. At first she was beyond relieved, then she was pissed.

Worrying about him was something a girlfriend or wife would do. She had no right. She didn't like how it made her feel.

When he came in the door, completely soaked, she gaped at the mud all over his clothes. "What happened?"

He began peeling off his jacket. "There was a flash flood on the main road, so I had to go around the entire county to come in from the other direction. Then I saw a couple stuck in a ditch, so I tried to help them, and ended up like this."

Well, she couldn't really be mad, since he'd basically been a hero while she was in there, warm and dry. "I'll get you a towel."

"Don't bother. I'll need more than that." He untied his muddy shoes and set them on a mat. "I didn't realize how late it was. I missed dinner."

"Yep." She shuffled to the kitchen. "It's no big deal. Just spaghetti and garlic bread. I kept a plate in the oven for you."

While he went to shower, she sat in front of the fire on the sofa, finally able to relax.

Minutes later he came out, and touched her shoulder from behind. "Something wrong?"

She decided to be honest. "I was worried about you. I'm just glad you're home."

"No one has been worried about me in a long time."

He came around the couch, and she softly gasped. No shirt. Just pajama pants and a bare chest. He sat down in the corner of the sofa with a languid grace, stretching his arms out. "Come here."

Eager to do just that, she scooted between his legs and laid back, the heat and strength of his body warming every inch of her.

It was comfortable too. Oh so comfortable. She gathered the giant blanket over her and watched the flames jump in the fireplace. He felt good. It felt like home. "Did you get what you needed in town?" She didn't notice any bags or items in his hands when he walked in.

"I did," he said. "Everything I need."

They didn't talk for a while, until he broke the silence with a question she knew he was eventually going to ask.

"How did you find me? I want to know."

"Why? So the next time you disappear I won't be able to locate you with the same method?"

"Come on, tell me. I thought I'd covered my tracks. How did you manage to make me look like a fool who thought he could hide from everyone?"

"That wasn't my intention." She sighed, wondering how loca she'd sound divulging her research skills. "All right. I was borrowing Chloe's computer because mine had crashed, and spotted a message from your Gmail account to her. I remembered a trick IT showed me, about how to display the email header. It shows your IP address. I copied-and-pasted it onto an IP-finder website, and it gave me your approximate location. Karakoh, Washington." She paused, waiting for his reaction.

"Go on. I know there's more. You didn't just drive around and happen upon my well-hidden home."

She sighed. "Right. Well, from there I did research. I looked for any property or homes that'd been purchased within a year, since there were no hotels in town, and I knew you took your Airstream with you. It took me a whole Sunday of research, but I finally found a very expensive piece of land on a lake that had been purchased recently. Your name came up in the public records. I got in the car, drove all day, and boom. That's how I found you. Mystery revealed."

A moment passed. "Impressive."

"Not really. Without all of that available information on the internet, I would've never stood a chance."

"Even so, I'm in awe. I guess you really wanted to find me."

"You think I'm crazy, don't you? I would."

He pressed a kiss on that place between her neck and shoulder. "I think you're incredibly clever and resourceful. I've never met a woman like you."

She closed her eyes, heart pounding. "I know."

Slowly, he slid his hand down her arm, and linked their fingers together. "If you hadn't found me, this would've never happened. Ever. I would've come back to Seattle and things between us would've stayed the same. I would still want you…" he traced his mouth along the curve of her neck, "and I'd still fight it. Every day. We'd still be apart. Every day. Instead of this. No, Antonia, this is where we should be."

With a helpless sound, she shoved the blanket to the floor, sat up and turned around, hiking her dress to straddle him. There was heat and desire in his gaze, and she knew there was no going back.

She kissed him, and instantly he came alive from his languid state, sitting up and grasping her face. His beard scraped her chin, his mustache tickled her nose. His lips, however, were soft, and he tasted like mint and warm male.

He moved down her throat, and she dropped her head back, enjoying the rough sensation of his beard scratching along her sensitive neck. His hands settled on her thighs, pushing her dress to her waist.

"I want you so much it hurts," he uttered. "What do you want? Be honest."

She made a noise of surrender. "I want to touch you, and taste you, and make you want no one but me," she whispered.

She lifted her arms. He pulled the dress up and sent it to the floor. Her bra was undone quickly, and before she could take her next breath, Justin's mouth was on her nipple, his hand gripping her butt.

Closer. She needed him closer, strong and alive, and holding her. His cock was hard and big through his pants, pressing against her sex. She started moving on him while he sucked and bit on each nipple and groaned with every pump of her hips.

She held his face and brought his lips back to hers, hungrily opening her mouth over his. His hands roamed along her back and cupped her backside, his breathing becoming ragged. Pulling back, she kissed either side of his mouth and eyes before sliding to her knees on the floor. "Don't move," she whispered.

She kissed each of his nipples, planting her hands on his chest, and making her way down. Once she found the end of the drawstring, she used her teeth to undo it.

"Oh, God," he groaned, head falling back.

She smiled wickedly, then pulled the waistband with her fingers. He lifted his hips so she could slide the pants off, freeing his cock.

Her eyes widened at how much of him she would have to take in her mouth, and eventually in her body. It thrilled her to the point she arched her back like a cat and licked her lips. She smoothed her palm along the silken, hot shaft before grasping it, and licked from the balls to the head, eliciting a loud moan from him.

He linked his hands behind his head with an expression of a man lost in bliss.

She worked his member in her mouth, swirling her tongue while alternating between a hard grip and a soft one. A fast suck, and a slow lap. He hissed and cursed, lifting his hips. She continued pleasuring him until he gripped her hair and pulled her off him.

She laughed huskily. "What's the matter?"

Breathing hard, he closed his eyes. "Witch. I already worship you as it is. But you have to stop."

She gave a little pout. "Fine. Then worship *me*."

She lay down on the blanket, brought her knees up, and removed her panties, before slowly spreading her legs. He made a feral sound and went down to crawl toward her, capturing her mouth for so long she had to drop back to breathe.

"Condom?" She didn't know *what* she'd do if he didn't have any.

"That's what I went into town for," he said with a crooked smile. He sat back on his haunches and grabbed his pants. Marveling at the beauty of his body, she rested her foot on his shoulder, watching him roll the protection on.

Once done, he held her leg and kissed her ankle, making his way along her inner leg from calve to thigh. When he rubbed the pad of his thumb on her pussy, she cried out at the electric, torrid sensations shooting to every nerve.

"So wet for me already," he murmured before taking a long lick of her. "And you taste good."

"Justin...I can't wait," she pleaded. "Come here."

He chuckled. "All right. I'll save that for later when you're trying to sleep." Moving up, he planted his hands on each side of her, meeting her gaze. "You're so beautiful."

He ran her hand down the side of his face. "So are you." She bent her knees and drew him down to her, kissing him.

He locked his arm at her back and plunged his iron-hard cock inside her.

She softly cursed, gripping his butt, wanting him as deep as he could go. They soon found a rhythm, and with each push of his hips, the ecstasy increased and expanded in her body and soul.

He kissed her temple, nose, mouth, and switched to his back. She rode him for a while, increasing her speed, moaning louder and louder.

"No, wait," he uttered, sitting up, and slowing her down. He smoothed the wild tresses from her eyes. "Not yet."

With their eyes locked, she complied, and eased her pace.

He buried his face in her chest, and she held them there, moving her hips at a languid measure. "I'm going to come," she whispered, lying back, letting him guide her hips for a little bit. The look on his face was what she'd been waiting for. Undiluted lust. Need. Surrender. And...something else.

Love?

Or maybe that was just what she wanted to see. She sat up and wrapped her arms around him, frightened he might not feel the way she did. That she was just wishing so hard, it was making her see things that weren't really there.

Justin shifted her to her back and brought the blanket over them. He held her close, penetrating hard and deep.

She was lost. It was time to let go.

When she cried out for the last time and scratched her nails down his back, she felt him shudder, heard him call her name.

Time stopped again. All she could hear was their mutually unsteady breathing, and feel his tightly muscled body on hers, keeping her warm, keeping her close.

Too bad she was eventually going to have to push him away.

Chapter Six

MEN IN LOVE ACTED LIKE IDIOTS. THEY DID FOOLISH THINGS to make women happy because doing so seemed to make *them* happy.

Justin never understood.

And he still didn't, even though he was well aware he was in love with Antonia, and finding himself channeling his inner fool to please her playful side, make her smile, or just surprise the hell out of her. Her opinion of him seemed to be that, because he had a high IQ and had started a multi-million-dollar company before the age of forty—and grown a beard—he was more serious than the average man.

Not true. Not with her.

The morning after the storm, they made love again, then cooked breakfast. He caught up on his emails, started a file for the notes on It's Living, and she read him the headlines.

His conference call with Shawn went well, until Antonia walked by him wearing nothing but his shirt. His brain temporarily froze. He caught her by the hand, muted the call, and proceeded to punish her with illicit kisses and groping until she was panting in his arms. Then he set her off his lap and told her he had to get to work.

She smacked him hard for teasing her like that.

In the afternoons, they took Fletch for a walk or a boat ride. One day, he got a perfect picture of Antonia leaning over the side to feed the ducks. He'd called her name, she looked over, smiled, and he caught the moment on his smart phone.

They had rowdy sex in the trailer, with him spanking her ass while he bent her over the tiny table. And they got naughty in the lake, with her forcing him to swim out far to catch her before he could touch her.

She insisted on making dinner, and he insisted she be the dessert. He laid her on the table and licked her until she screamed in Spanglish. He got a kick out of that.

Every night after dinner, they'd pour wine—or tequila—and discuss details about It's Living. For months he'd been chewing on this venture, but it wasn't until he told Antonia did he finally feel *excited*. They discussed it for hours, building on one another's ideas and at times arguing until one of them gave up.

But no matter what, the night ended with them making love slowly, intensely, because the end of another day meant they were closer to bringing their week to its end.

She gave him all of her; his woman didn't hold back. There was nothing lovelier than her clinging to him, seeing her eyes glitter with passion, her hair spread over the floor. Sometimes she'd bow her back and cry out, and sometimes she'd bite her bottom lip and barely make a sound when she came.

No other woman fascinated him like she did.

In five days, she became his best friend, lover, and confidant, though she'd been two of the three for the past year. When she asked him if they could stay until Sunday morning, pushing back his return to Seattle, he readily agreed. He didn't want to leave either. He slept better next to her, and a lot longer than four mere hours. Amazing what one woman could do.

There was the one thing they hadn't discussed: what would happen to them once they were home. He knew what he *wanted* to happen, but didn't know if it was what she had in mind.

He had to know if she was his. But then again, why the need to define it after only six days? Since when was he the sensitive one in the relationship?

Sunday morning after a swim, he yanked open the back door to find the music on, Antonia singing, making waffles, and tossing Fletch bits of bacon in between.

Since when? Since right that moment. He wanted to come home to this, every day.

She beamed a smile at him. "Hey! I taught Fletch a new trick. Watch." She took a piece of bacon and shouted. "Speak!"

To which the dog responded with a single "woof!"

"Speak, speak!"

"Woof! Woof!"

She laughed and gave him the bacon. "See?"

He grinned and lifted her on the counter. "Is there no male who won't bend to your command?"

She licked her finger, shook her head, and set her arms on his shoulders. "Not that I know of. How was your swim?"

"Enlightening."

"Oh? You came up with another dazzling idea?"

"I think so." He moved a lock of hair away from her face. "You and me. Making this official."

The smile faded from her mouth. "You mean…?"

"I want you to be mine. And I'll be yours. Only yours."

She pushed off the counter and away from him. "We can't. I just…am not sure we should do that while working together."

"It's 2016. I don't believe in regimented office rules. It's my company. I can be with whomever I want. That includes my gorgeous and intelligent VP of PR. Of course we'll be discreet and keep our personal relationship separate from our work. But everyone is going to know we're together. I'm not keeping it secret."

"Even so, you know some employees will take issue with it."

"I don't care. It's not as if you'll get any special perks no one else gets." He tried to lighten the discussion. "Except my body. You're the only one allowed to use it."

He had only annoyed her with that remark. She groaned, and ran her hands through her hair. "I don't know if I can sleep with my boss and go into work every day like it's no big deal."

"I'm not just your boss anymore. Just tell yourself it isn't a big deal, and it won't be."

"But it is, Justin!"

His heart hammered at the thought that he might not get what he so badly needed. "Then what do you want? Because I want *you*. You and I can't end here. We just started." No way was he going to lose her over an ethical technicality. Looked like he had to put it all on the line to convince her. "I love you."

She gasped, her gaze shooting into his. Her chest rose and fell with every unsteady breath.

"I love you," he repeated.

Still, she said nothing in return.

Surprised her again. And she was about to get another one. He dug in his pocket and gently set the simple silver ring with the chip diamond on the counter, and his heart and future on the line. "What if we got engaged?"

Chapter Seven

She stared at the ring, shocked beyond reaction, except the stunned-into-a-stupor kind. "When did you get that?" she exclaimed.

"The other day at a boutique shop, right after I got the condoms. I knew that day you were the one. Actually, I've known for a while…" He crossed his arms and leaned against the counter. "It's just a little thing, but it'll do until—"

"Marry you? I haven't even told you I love you yet!"

"Well, don't you?"

She gave a shaky laugh, overwhelmed. Of course she did. She'd been in love with him for months, but planned to keep it to herself. However, it appeared Justin didn't want to wait. Thank God. "Yes. You smug jerk. I love you."

His gaze softened with relief. "Then let's make it easy. Marry me."

"Typical man! Marriage is *not* easy!"

"It can't be any harder than staying apart was."

"Oh, it can be *a lot* harder. You know that."

"Okay, we won't get married right away. Think about it. If we get engaged, people will forget the scandal part and focus on the engagement. They'll know we're in love and not just having sex for fun. Come on baby, you're in PR. Put a spin on it."

She put up her hands. "You are *crazy*, mi amor."

"So are you. Let's be crazy together."

But he had the right idea. She could spin the hell out of it, especially when she started leaking tidbits about the new side project. The coverage on that would override any personal news. Would anyone at the office really be that upset?

She still had one more argument. "People will think I'm marrying you for your money."

"Unfortunately, we can't stop people from thinking all kinds of things about us. But if I'm not mistaken, you just said yes."

"What!"

"You said 'People will think I'm marrying...' So you *are* marrying me. Good."

Before she could move, he came in and kissed her, stopping time, and temporarily making her forget how fast they were moving. There was just one more thing... Hands on his cheeks, she shook her head. "How long have you loved me?"

"Since day one, I think."

"Oh, really? Well, I lied to your face on day one so you might want to rethink your wild proposal."

"Lied? About what?"

"I...don't actually have a degree in public relations." She made a face. "I'm sorry. I really wanted the job."

He straightened. "What! Did Drew know?"

She groaned. "Yes. It was true I learned everything at the PR firm, but it wasn't exactly an internship. My aunt was a director there, and she made me work for her for free, as punishment for spending my first semester exploring Italy instead of taking classes. I fell in love with public relations. I found my calling! I planned to go back to college, but then Drew said there was a new, small company in need of a PR expert. When he told me about It's Handled, I jumped at the chance. I was going to tell you at the interview, but then you were so impressed, I bit my tongue." She searched his face. "Now, do you still want to marry a fraud and a liar?"

He stepped back, brows drawing together.

Her heart squeezed and she swallowed the lump forming in her throat. If she lost him—and possibly her job—she'd be devastated. But he had to know. She'd wanted to tell him for a long time.

"Justin, I'm sorry. It was wrong to lie about my qualifications. Everything else is the truth."

"I can't believe it." He gripped her shoulders. "I can't believe you thought I wouldn't want to marry you because of *that*. You've more than proven your worth at your position, and thank God your path brought you straight to me. With or without higher education. I only went to college because I thought I'd take over Microsoft one day." He started to tickle her. "So you do accept? What do you say now?"

Out of breath with laughter, she pushed him. "All right! I say yes. I'm yours for life, Justin Faber." She paused, folding her hands behind her. "Mm. Antonia Faber. I like that."

He kissed her tenderly, and she melted back on the sofa, starting to unbutton her shirt. He retrieved the ring and slid it on her finger before coming down to nuzzle her neck.

"I love you," he said, kissing between her breasts and moving down.

"And I love you." She ran her fingers through his hair while his mouth charted a path down her stomach. Her world was about to change in so many ways, but she didn't have to think about that now. "When can we come back here?"

"Next weekend. We'll fly. As many weekends as you want to. You were meant to find this place. Meant to find me, and bring me home."

She smiled, cupping his face and guiding him to her lips. "And I always will."

About Angelita Gill

Angelita is the author of fun, sexy contemporary romance, where the heroes tend to drop sexual innuendo, and the heroines have all the real power.

When she's not torturing them to their happily-ever-after, Angelita loves volunteering for the arts, spending time with her own alpha hero and dancing with her friends while she tries not to spill her wine. Sign up for her newsletter here.

Website: www.angelitagill.com
Fan Page: www.facebook.com/authorangelita

How to Kill a Lady Boner

By Ace Gray

There was a frantic energy around us, bouncing like ping-pong balls off every surface, and pummeling into me. With each announcement, the electricity seemed to ratchet up. So did the volume. I couldn't tell if it was excitement building inside me or something else completely.

I was out of place in my cut off jean shorts that put my long legs on display and my vintage AC/DC t-shirt that showed off my cleavage. I wasn't dolled up in green and yellow and shaking pompoms. Instead, I was still wearing my dark Ray-bans and was touching up my deep purple lipstick.

It was at that moment where sunset switched to dusk and, with a big thunk, all the lights of the stadium flooded on. Mandy went to say something but the combination of a disorienting amount of energy and the roar of the crowd cut her off.

"Wait, what?" I turned and shouted at her.

She had no prayer of hearing, let alone answering. Apparently, the stadium had been operating at a dull roar until now. The new wave of sound crashed down and split my ears as it rang and reverberated off every surface, making my teeth chatter. Mandy was caught up in whatever I had missed, and she was screeching down at the field.

When I looked down, nothing much had changed. The Timbers were still walking out one by one with their backs to us, each had a miniature soccer player at their side. The announcer was more excited than he'd been a minute ago but even his words were drowned out.

Why is everyone losing their shit?

I knew people in Portland took their soccer seriously but this was unreal. I rolled my eyes, and when Mandy jabbed me in my side, I did it again, this time so big it almost hurt my eyeballs.

The players lined up with the kids squarely in front of them as an American flag unfurled overhead. The crowd only silenced when our anthem started playing. Automatically, Mandy and I placed our hands over our hearts. My question was still burning my throat, but I bit my lip until the cheering started back up at the end of the song.

"What was that eruption earlier?" I asked as I started to sit but she grabbed my arm and hauled me back up. I stood, narrowed my gaze at her, and put my hands on my hips.

Mandy just laughed. "Livy, that was The Beard."

"Oh Lord." I rolled my eyes again. "*The Beard*?" I said it as thick with disgust as I possibly could.

"Yeah." Mandy wasn't deterred in the least. "Check out number four." My eyes scanned the field only to find the dark wavy haired Hulk sprinting up the field.

Number four barely fit in his jersey, the seams had to be close to splitting. I was surprised there weren't cracks in the lettering of his last name. *Foster* read like a neon billboard, drawing me to the dips and grooves in his shoulders and back, then my eyes dropped lower. His ass was so high and tight that his shiny jersey couldn't naturally slide down over it. It just rested on top of his mountain of muscle instead, like a shelf. I happily pictured biting it. Every inch of him could do with a nibble or a lick.

But then he turned around.

"Ugh" I couldn't help it or that I faked gagging.

"Ugh? Did I just hear ugh? What on earth are you ugh-ing about?" Mandy threw her hands up.

"He has a beard," I whined.

And it wasn't just close shaved scruff, it was full-on, inches long, dark and bushy. It was a beard's beard.

"Well duh." She drug the word out and made it sing-songy. "How did you think he got the nickname?" She was probably rolling her eyes now. "Ya know he's one of the best players in the MLS."

"I just don't get it. You know I don't get it. We're in a stadium of wanna be lumberjacks, watching perfectly toned lumberjacks, and all I can think is why in the hell do you want to be a lumberjack?" I sighed dramatically and flopped into my seat behind me.

Soccer was fine, tight pants were good—specially on the right man—and I'd never complain about artisanal roasted coffee, but the sheer amount of flowing hipster facial hair in Portland was starting to kill my soul. Well, actually, my snatch, but some days that felt like the same thing.

"Stand back up, stop pouting, and watch a real *man* play soccer." Mandy knocked me on the shoulder. "A real *gorgeous* man."

I stood, making sure to keep my arms crossed tightly, and grumped, "Call me old fashioned, but I think it's the dick that makes him a real man."

"I bet his D is fabulous." Mandy actually clapped as she went starry-eyed at the thought.

"I bet his D is buried beneath so much fur, we couldn't tell up from down in bed."

The game was good. Bearded or no, watching grown, sweaty, sculpted men play the game was a good evening. The beer and cheesy pretzels made it even better. By the end, I roared just as loud as Mandy when the Timbers won.

"Worst night of your life?" she asked smiling and short of breath.

"Absolutely." I couldn't keep a straight face while I said it. "You know once you start watching the feet rather than the faces, it ain't too bad."

"What is wrong with you?" she screeched.

"My mother dropped me on my head. Repeatedly. I ended up with good taste," I snarked.

"Hey sis." Out of nowhere, Mandy's older brother, JJ, threw his arm around both of us. "Hey Livy." He pulled us both in to a sandwich hug, like he had done since we were in high school. "You guys enjoy the game?"

"Totes. Thanks for the tickets bro." Mandy stepped back and punched him lightly on the shoulder the same way she had hit me earlier.

"Livy?" He arched his eyebrows.

"I'm looking into getting the team sponsored by Gillette."

JJ laughed loudly and affectionately yanked me into his shoulder.

"Beards aren't all that bad," he said as he bent down and rubbed his short scruff against my temple.

"Good God, get that sandpaper off me." I shoved against his chest.

He stumbled backward but laughed even louder.

"You guys wanna go get drinks with me in a bit?" he asked as he caught himself and casually leaned against the railing.

"You owe me at least one shot for the filth of the earth your beard probably just spread across my face." I made a show of rubbing the skin he'd just scraped against as hard as I possibly could.

Dr. Jason Jones, or as I'd known him for thirteen years, Nurse JJ, sent us to a low key modern bar that I'd never heard of. The lighting was low and the music seductive but it had pool tables. Sleek, black felt ones. A wicked smile spread across my face.

While we waited for the good ole doc to finish up evaluating the team or whatever it was he actually did lounging around big ole virile men, I'd schooled any and every one willing to go head to head at the table.

I was bent over the pool table, about ready to sink the eight ball, when a pair of skinny jeans came into view. The legs those pants wrapped around were muscular, and the man was obviously tall. What was even better was that they barely contained what made a man a real man. I couldn't help but smirk and shoot the ball right at, well, his balls.

"Nice one." A smooth, rich voice traveled down my spine and made my skin goose bump. I was incredibly glad I'd worn a V-neck that put my cleavage on display. I tried to shimmy the well-worn fabric down as I stood up.

My face fell. Of course, a beard waited for me. One of the big ones you could easily confuse with a grizzly bear vagina.

On second look, *The* Beard waited for me. I scrunched my face up and bent back down to fish for pool balls so I could re-rack and move on. I kept my head down and my hands busy despite the full weight of his stare.

"Can I play?" he purred at me, literally purred like a jungle cat or something. I arched my eyebrows and looked up at him from underneath my lashes at the ridiculous sound.

"I'm playing with my friend. You can have winner if she doesn't care." My eyes dropped back to the table as I spoke.

"Deal." There was a hint of laughter in his voice and it had me pursing my lips as I stood.

It only took a quick scan of the room to see Mandy had disappeared from my side. She was halfway across the bar, standing next to her brother and some bearded dude. Her hand rested on his pec as she threw her head back and laughed a little too loud. I'd been abandoned in favor of facial hair. Rough, haggard, stringy, wiry pubic hair. I couldn't help but roll my eyes.

"Looks like you're up," I said begrudgingly.

"Don't sound so disappointed. I'm decent enough." His voice was laced with humor again.

"I'm sure you are."

I shook my head and turned to pick up my pool cue. The Beard kept watching me, his eyes had a way of boring into the back of my skull that I felt resonate through me. When I turned around, he was chalking the end of a cue stick with long fingers and self-assured ease, while his eyes stayed fixed on me. He obviously hunted women like prey and, considering his face looked like something straight out of the year 1880, I wasn't surprised. I had to stop myself from rolling my eyes again.

When he quirked his eyebrow up and stepped confidently

toward me, I settled for shaking my head instead.

"My name's Graham by the way. Graham Foster."

He held out his hand and I eyed it like he'd extended a rabid weasel.

"I know who you are." The very idea that he had probably run his hand through his beard kept mine in place. He probably grabbed his balls then stroked his chin and that made my stomach turn.

I bent back down and his crotch was in view again. His big, bulging, about to break free of his denim crotch. Apparently, my snatch was more alive than I'd originally thought. Even the hint of a giant salami made my knees falter. I shook my head and blew out a deep breath before I took a shot. The balls hit against each other with a crisp clack and then shot across the table.

"Are you a Seattle Sounders fan or something?" His laugh was still peeking out through his voice.

"Nah. I prefer Euro Leagues, actually, but the Timbers do just fine for an evening of entertainment." I pocketed another stripe then shrugged.

"An evening of entertainment? Wow." He laughed and it was husky, warm, almost like a blanket you could cuddle into during a Pacific Northwest winter. I wanted to lose myself in that laugh. "That's all you see when you watch me? I'm like an old episode of Friends or something?"

"I was always partial to Sex and the City or Gossip Girl, but yeah, essentially."

I nailed two balls in before missing. Only then did I stand and meet his gaze.

"You always this hard on a guy trying to buy you a drink?" He watched me plop onto a stool before bending over to work the solids.

I was treated to the perfect ass-shelf again and everything below my belly button clenched. He hit in two balls, each shot making his muscles ripple beneath his perfectly fitting clothes before missing a third. He'd made his way over toward my perch for the botched shot and, when he stood, we were almost pressed against each other. He turned, putting his chiseled chest smack in front of me. I sucked in a deep breath in spite of myself.

"I have a drink," I stammered.

He wordlessly pulled it from my hand and slugged it back.

"Whiskey, neat?" He was close enough that his beard grazed my cheek when he asked. My lady boner laid right back down.

"Bourbon," I corrected him in monotone. "And I'll buy my own drinks, thanks."

"You're sure fighting this hard." There was still an undeniable warmth to his voice that spoke to something deep inside me, despite the beard. "What is it? Because I'm an athlete?"

I sputtered a weird laugh thing as I bent back to the table. Two balls went in with a single shot, and I smirked at my good fortune. If it were some clean-shaven hunk of man meat watching, I would have died and gone to heaven.

"Ah, sexually inexperienced. A real man terrifies you." His voice was lower, husky, the definition of sex itself as he poked fun.

"Honey, I got moves you've never seen." I stood and gestured up and down on the pool cue, making sure I took long leisurely strokes as I poked my tongue into the side of my cheek.

"Show me," he challenged.

"In your dreams."

When I bent over to line up my next shot, Graham shifted behind me. Even through my jeans, I could feel the warmth of his body radiating against mine. Like this, I could forget about the pube forest running wild on his face and surrender to the sexual tension bubbling up between us. I was lucky to sink an easy shot.

My body vibrated and I fought the urge to back up into him. The tiny space between us was as electrically charged as the stadium had been this evening. My breathing picked up pace, and I'm sure he could see how my body trembled against the thin fabric of my shirt.

He put his hands on my hips just as I let loose a shot. Realistically, I was too jittery to sink it but the shock of him touching me sent my cue shooting upwards and the ball ricocheting all wonky across the table.

"What are you doing?" I shrieked loud enough that half the bar turned.

He held up his hands in surrender and started in on an apology.

Out of the corner of my eye, I noticed both Mandy and JJ making their way toward us.

"I'm really sorry. I thought we were flirting. I thought it would be okay." All trace of lightness had left his voice. I hated that I liked his desperate, tormented one even more.

"First, it is *never* okay to put your hands on a woman without her permission." I made the number one with my finger to emphasize my point. All too quickly, my number one turned into a sharp pointed finger that I pushed into his chest. "Second, I could never flirt with you."

"Why?" His face seemed to fall but it was too hard to tell, buried as it was.

"Hey, is everything okay over here?" JJ and Mandy asked at the same time.

"It's your God damned beard. I'd never flirt with a guy that had a disgusting yeti blanketing their face, and I'd certainly never go home with someone who thought they were God's gift to women because of overactive testosterone."

With that, I chucked the pool cue onto the table, scattering the remaining balls then turned on my heel to storm out.

"Well last night was…interesting." Mandy started in when I answered the phone without any preface.

"Sorry. Probably not the best way to make an impression on your potential soccer studs." My voice was crackly, fresh from sleeping off the bourbon. "I know you had your heart set on a sleepover where you guys could braid each other's hair."

"Eh, you come first. Always do." She ignored my jab.

"Awe, that's sweet," I groaned, as I stretched out in bed.

"Besides, I landed one anyway. Number twenty-two." She laughed loudly.

"Does he have a name?" I chuckled along with her.

"Not yet. Twenty-two is fine for now."

"And is Twenty-Two good in bed?"

"His beard is amazing between my thighs." She moaned the words like she was mid-orgasm.

"Mandy that is gross on so many levels. I can't even." I made sure she knew how disgusted I was with the tone of my voice.

"Don't knock it till you try it."

"I'm hanging up now." I waited just a beat but when her full, bright, busting up laughter rang across the line; I did exactly what I said.

I tossed my phone onto the bed and the down of my comforter poofed around it. With another morning groan, I turned over and burrowed back into my pillow. I was on the verge of drifting off when my phone rang again.

Without looking at the screen, I answered, "I'm not putting a beard between my fucking thighs, Mandy."

A big, brash, and definitely male laugh boomed across the line. I shot up from my mattress and pulled my phone back to look at the caller ID. *Unknown* flashed across the screen and I yelped, "Oh my God."

"Livy, I got the point last night. No need to kick a man while he's down." The man was still chuckling as he spoke.

I was disoriented to say the least. That voice struck a honeyed chord inside of me just like The Beard had last night. But The Beard didn't have my number. The Beard didn't even have my name.

"Who is this?"

"Graham Foster." He laughed through his name, which mercifully helped him miss the sigh of relief I breathed into the phone. "I got your number from Jason, hope you don't mind. I wanted to apologize."

"Oh. Ummm, yeah," I managed, still slightly off-kilter from his call in the first place.

"Look, I just felt really bad about the whole thing. I misread the situation big time, and I was a real fucking prick to put my hands on you. I didn't sleep thinking about what a jackass move that was." Just like last night his voice hit me hard, that powerful rich tone was every bit as manly as the crotch shot I'd first gotten of him.

"Wow." I breathed in deeply to steady myself. "Thank you for that." I whistled lowly. "I guess I'm sorry if I lead you on."

"You didn't. You've been pretty clear about where me and my beard stand with you. Twice now, actually." His husky chuckle was back.

So was the inexplicable want centered right between my thighs.

"Sorry about that too."

"No worries." He was good on the phone, every bit as sexy as he had been in person—when I wasn't looking at his face that is. My lady boner was back and would be seriously tenting my covers if physically possible. I was going to have to show her a picture of the beard to remind her to tuck herself away. "Can I ask you what's so terrible about the beard anyway? Out of sheer curiosity?"

"Oh. Sure." I shrugged even though he couldn't see. I'd explained myself plenty of times before. "It's just a turn off. A massive one. Like the way some girls just can't do short guys or some guys can't do red heads. I can't stop thinking about where they've been and what's crawling around inside them. They're rough and brittle on my face. I mean, they're a great way to keep Chapstick in business, but me, my lips, both up top and down low, can't get down like that."

"Huh," he answered thoughtfully. "Never heard that one before. I mean, the way you put it, it makes sense, but damn if I'm not disappointed."

"What do you mean disappointed?" I leaned back in bed, settling into the conversation.

"Well I'd be lying if I said that it didn't bother me that you find me the opposite of sexy. Particularly because I find you to be the definition of sexy."

"You don't even know me." I laughed loudly.

"I know you like soccer. I know you like bourbon neat. I know you could probably run the table playing pool. All of which are things I like."

"Oh yeah?" I couldn't help the big dopey smile spreading across my face.

"Yeah. I also know that the curves of your body are absolute perfection. I thought about kissing every inch last night."

I bit my lip. The idea of his lips dancing against my skin had my blood boiling.

But the beard...

"You'd scratch my skin all to hell," I whined but it was a little breathy.

"Oh Livy." He said my name in a way that sent shivers down my spine. "Have you ever been kissed by a man with a beard?"

"No," I admitted.

"God, I'd make it so good for you." Desire was thick in his voice, and my body responded to it.

"You would?" I couldn't help myself—the voice, without the visual, spoke to me on a primal level.

"Hell yes I would." There was a hint of determination, maybe even force behind his statement.

Splooge.

"What would you do to me?"

My question hung in the air between us. Graham's breathing was still coming across the line but he didn't answer for what seemed like hours.

"Are we really doing this? I mean, you started this conversation by shouting that I essentially had no shot with you." He sucked in a breath and I swore he held it.

"I believe I said your beard had no shot with me. Phone sex doesn't involve beards," I purred hoping to tempt him.

"So you're using me for an orgasm?"

"Holy fuck..." I trailed off. I'd been too caught up in the moment and the lust churning wildly inside me to see it for what it was: a real bitch move. "Looks like it's my turn to apologize. I'm an asshole. And I'm sorry. So sorry. Thanks for the call. Thanks for the apology. Bye." The last few words all mushed together just before I pulled the phone from my ear and hung up.

"God Livy, you're a dumbass," I mumbled to myself as I tossed the phone aside and slid further under the covers.

My ring tone blared again but this time I didn't make a move to grab it. When I let it ring to voicemail twice, the text messages started popping up. I grabbed it, thinking I would just silence it but then I saw the first few messages.

Hey don't disappear

I didn't mean it like that

I definitely want to take it further but it kills me I won't get it in person

I sighed. It was true. He wouldn't. The idea of finding the dark curlies of his beard in my teeth was enough to cool my jets permanently. It wasn't fair to ask him to use his sex on a stick voice to get me off.

Sorry. I shouldn't have just hung up but it really was a dick move on my part.

Your parts make my dick move

HA! Good one Graham.

I like it when you call me Graham. No one does.

What do they call you? Beast?

The Beard.

Ohhhhhhh, riiiiiighhtttttttt... I can't believe your nickname is even The Beard.

It was so easy to forget when he wasn't in front of me. I started to type again but I saw the telltale three little dots pop up from his incoming text.

Would The Beast be a better fit?

My brow crinkled for a second, I wasn't quite sure where he was going with this. But then a picture popped up.

A picture of a big, beautiful, and incredibly hard dick popped up. "Holy shit," I exclaimed to my empty apartment.

I couldn't stop staring. This was the kind of dick you found on Tumblr and sent to all your girlfriends just to get their reactions. The emojis alone would be worth it. There would be the shocked faces, purple devils, and at least a million eggplant emojis, all peppered with hallelujah hands. He was thick and long, a combination almost no one had in real life. His tip was perfectly shaped, so perfectly, in fact, that I salivated over the idea of it pushing into me.

And it was manscaped. Perfectly so. Not a single one of his dark hairs was anywhere in the picture, making him seem all the bigger, all the more delicious.

Livy...???

Oh shit.

Right.

Hi.

I got a little distracted looking at this fucking phenomenal dick pic I just got.

You like? ;)

Like? I might be all sorts of wet right now... Beast is good. Beast is way better.

I flipped back to the full screen photo and cursed the heavens. Why on earth would they give a man with that voice, this dick, and an insanely magnetic pull over me, a mother fucking beard? I wanted to scream. And rub one out. Then scream again but this time the good kind.

With you, Beast it is.

Remember how we established there really can't be a "with me"?

He started typing a few times just to abandon it then start again.

How about a game of pool?

I thought about it for a while. Part of me liked the idea—the snappy banter was delicious in person and over the phone—but then I'd be face to face with be the beard and the reality of the two of us. I couldn't go. I couldn't hang out with him. But I didn't want to end our conversation on such a sour note.

Without thinking too hard about the ramifications of my actions, I whipped my shirt up, made a kissy face, and took a perfectly framed pic of my tits and lips.

We can't. How about I leave you with this instead?

I sent the photo immediately afterward and then shut my phone off all together.

I'd left the phone off while I was at work, leaving me disconnected for a good part of the day but now that I was home with sunset coming I figured I couldn't avoid reality any longer. Honestly, I wanted to peek at the giant beast luring on my camera roll too.

The second the small little apple faded from the screen and the picture of Mandy and I in t-rex costumes boxing each other took over, a few more messages popped up and blurred the screen.

Leave me?

What?

Livy, where are you?

I got harder when you sent that pic.

There was another picture of his dick and it did look harder. His balls looked tighter and there was the smallest bead of liquid pooled at the head of his cock. I wanted to lick it from top to bottom and back again. I'd suck his balls too just for the opportunity to be between those thighs.

I flipped to the next message.

Until I got off using that pic.

There was another picture of his slightly soft dick resting against the washboard of his stomach framed by an abstract halo of cum splattered this way and that. I wanted to lick his stomach clean.

God, all the times Mandy calls me a dirty whore are pretty accurate.

I started texting Graham back but stopped short. What did I say after that?

Thanks? Glad I could help? I'd suck your semen off your stomach if you shaved? Nothing seemed quite right.

While I was deciding, his three dots started back up on the text screen.

I've been waiting.

Looks like you've been rather busy if you ask me.

You like?

I'd lick.

That can be arranged.

Graham...

My phone started ringing a second later, *unknown* flashing across the screen.

"Hello?" I answered.

"I was hoping you'd scream something about my dick now that we've put that on the table." Graham's warm carnal voice was enough to knock my knees out from under me and flatten me to the bed.

"If your dick was on the table, I think I'd be well fed for the next few weeks or so." I laid back against my mattress.

"Oh come on, a few months at least. I mean, did you see it or do I need to send you a few more pictures."

"I could handle pictures of your perfect dick all day." I tried to match his lust-laced voice.

"Imagine how I feel about your tits."

"You like 'em?" I bit my lips.

"Good Christ yes. They're perfect plump little peaches with rosy little nipples. I can picture fucking them." Whatever sexiness dripped off his words, mirrored the drips between my thighs.

"Yeah?" I settled into the comforter and my hand automatically drifted up to my chest.

"Shove them together," he commanded, "right now."

"I have to put you on speaker." My voice was getting breathy.

"Good. I want your hands free."

I clicked speaker on the phone and plopped it next to my chin. As soon as my hands were available, I shoved my tits together until they were flush against each other.

"I don't know that you'd fit."

"Oh, I'd fit," he growled. "I'd lick every inch of you, get you all nice and wet. Then I'd straddle you and palm them both up together and shove in."

"Yum." I smiled widely. "The picture of your abs over top of my tits is downright drool worthy."

"I'll drool all over you."

"Would you play with my nipples?" I asked, my voice rough and coy.

"So much." The pleasure was obvious in his voice. "Will you touch yourself?"

"If my arm could reach around your tree trunk legs." I smiled at the image.

"No. Now."

I swallowed hard, but before I could stop my little bastard fingers, they travelled down my body and pressed beneath the waistband of my shorts. I sucked in a deep breath when my finger hit my clit.

"Jesus, Livy," he groaned. "Tell me about it." His voice got low and needy.

"My pussy?" I gasped as my fingers kept working.

"Yes."

"It's wet. Really wet. I think it gets like that just at the sound of your voice."

He groaned across the line.

"Graham, are you jerking off?" I asked with a breathy whisper.

"Fuck…yes…I am." His words were a little more choppy. "Back to business."

"Ummm, okay, yeah." I could barely refocus. I was picturing his big hands wrapped around that horse-like cock and, mixed with my own teasing touches, my mind was as close to vacant as possible.

"Your pussy, Livy," he encouraged.

"Likes it when it's flicked but likes it more when it gets tiny circles." My hips bucked against the rhythm of my hands.

"I'll remember that." He laughed. "Is that what you're doing now?"

"That and teasing little pokes. There's this spot on the front entrance of me that's so sensitive as I slide in and out."

"That's your G-spot, Livy. I know how to work a G-spot," he snarled.

"No, my G-spot is higher." My fingers slid in deeper looking for the exact spot.

"I wanna feel your G-spot. I wanna feel you come when I stroke it. I wanna feel you splash on me." I could tell Graham was speaking through gritted teeth.

"I got news for you, I don't squirt."

"I could make you." His voice snapped and it was this yummy lusty thing.

I could picture the body that went with that voice. The flexing muscles, the writhing body. I wanted to be the one fisting up and down on his beastly cock. I wanted that beastly cock inside me. More than that, I wanted to squirt all over him like some porn star. With that voice commanding me, that body working me over, I would do anything on the planet he asked. Trashy porn star sluts of the world would go slack jawed with shame at the things I was imagining.

The film reel I'd conjured up had me coming. Hard. My skin was slick with my wetness as I ground on my own hand. I couldn't stop moaning in time with the orgasmic waves wracking my body. It barely took a split-second for Graham to start moaning too. That sound on speakerphone was toe-curling and renewed the orgasm that consumed my body.

"Oh my God," I groaned a few times.

"Send me a pic." He barely got the words out through the sounds of his trembling voice. "It's the closest I'll ever get to being inside you." This time it was more of a desperate plea.

I clicked off the phone and shoved off my shorts. I propped myself up on my elbows and angled the camera down at my pussy. It glistened and was a little red and swollen. For a second I thought about cleaning up but then I thought better of it. He'd want to know what he did to me every bit as much as I liked knowing what I'd done to him. I snapped the pic and sent it.

Goodnight Graham.

"What have you done to Graham?" JJ asked when I walked into Mandy's apartment for dinner a few days later.

"I haven't done anything to Graham." I rolled my eyes.

"Oh yeah you have. He's going insane. I'm debating whether to commit him."

Something inside me twinged and not in the usual spot, this something was about a foot higher, right underneath my left breast.

"We've just been texting." I couldn't help but crease my brow.

"They're not texting, they're sexting," Mandy added as she brought over wine.

"What? No…That's not…Mandy." I scowled at her even though I turned a furious shade of red.

I mean, she was right. The phone sex we'd had was just the start of some really filthy moments. Calling, texting, pictures, all were becoming an addiction. I found myself running to the bathroom at work to snap something or rub something out. We'd talked about whether Graham's hand would fit inside me, whether I'd let him in my back door, sex on a pool table, and I'd given him a virtual blow job he was still talking about.

"I saw your phone. You should delete that shit after you send it."

I almost choked on the rosé.

"Besides, I thought you were decidedly anti-beard. He's kind of the definition of a beard guy." She put her hand on her hip and arched an eyebrow at me.

"It's just over the phone. It's not in person." I let my eyes fall to my glass, hoping they wouldn't see all the times I'd gotten myself off to the sound of Grahams voice or his return videos reflected there.

"Livy, first and foremost, you're like a sister to me. I don't want your tits or…or…or…" JJ stammered, flustered, until he gave up. "…out there. With the team no less. What if they pass those around? What if I see your…your…your…"

"They pass me around?" I screeched.

"They're passing your pussy around the locker room all imagining their beards latched onto it," Mandy added with a wicked laugh, finding herself hilarious, while JJ turned a darker shade of red.

"And second…" He raised his voice trying to wrangle us back to the matter at hand. "…Graham doesn't play well when he's frustrated. He gets in his head and starts screwing things up."

"You think I'm frustrating for him?" I asked and I cocked my head to the side.

"Not getting the thing you want desperately? Having said thing dangled in front of you every day? Isn't that the definition of frustration?"

"He wants me desperately?" I couldn't help but smile.

"This isn't a game, it's his livelihood, Livy. If he loses focus, his stats drop. If his stats drop, the team doesn't do well. If the team loses and it's on his shoulders, he doesn't get resigned."

Each offense he listed was dropping like a boulder in my stomach.

"I didn't know that. He never said anything…"

"Well why would he? He's gotta be hoping to, ya know…" JJ made a circle with one hand and then stuck his finger in it from the other.

"Get it in?" Mandy spoke for him. "Jeez JJ, you're a doctor. It's okay to say sex."

"I'm in denial either of you have sex thank you very much." He was a brilliant shade of red.

"We both have lots of dirty, filthy, animal sex. Sometimes with the players you treat." Mandy stuck her finger in her mouth and then angled to give her brother a wet willy, tormenting him so thoroughly they started roughhousing. When Mandy spilled her wine, they pulled apart, breathlessly laughing and the whole room was light again.

"Look, Livy, all I'm saying is that a man's not going to admit his short comings to someone that he likes. Keep in mind the power you have over him and use it wisely, okay? Graham's a good guy, and I don't want to see him get hurt any more than I want to see you to get hurt when this is done."

I gulped and nodded before slugging back the rest of my wine.

The energy of the stadium didn't fight me this time, it ebbed and flowed through me, as Mandy and I both stood and clapped in front of our seats.

"So is it different this time around?" Mandy asked when the roared response to Graham died down.

"Not really." I shrugged.

"Oh come on." She was a little too excited. "You've seen his dick!"

I almost choked on the beer I was drinking as every head in the neighboring two rows turned toward me. A few of the guys smiled, one even reached out his hand and introduced himself. Mandy shoved him away.

"And this is the day I murder you. Hope JJ has triage equipment,"

I said under my breath as I flashed a giant, forced smile.

"Well it's true." She slapped me on my back. "It's gotta change something. At the very least, are you watching his shorts rather than his feet?"

"I fucking hate you," I mumbled.

"Jesus Christ Livy, get a sense of humor!" She screamed so loud that JJ and a few of the players turned around from the sidelines.

Of course, Graham was one of them. He put his hands on his hips and his eyes danced when he looked up at me. He jerked his chin and nodded an unmistakable hello in my direction.

"That's whose dick you've seen?" a random girl asked from beside us.

Four cookie cutter girls, with perfectly ringed curls all leaned out to look at me. They all wore team scarves covering barely there midriff baring shirts. They all shot me daggers too.

I collapsed into the seat behind me and my white summer dress puffed out around my knees. I leaned back and pinched the bridge of my nose.

"Oh God, he must be desperate," one said.

"Or really small," added another.

"There's no reason he'd be with a girl who wore Doc Martins."

I thought about taking one off and chucking it at one of them. Or all of them.

"Livy, stand up and watch that man play soccer. These jealous *HAGS*," she shouted, "couldn't land a soccer player if they were the last pussy on earth."

I dramatically dropped my hand but I stayed draped across the stadium seat. Graham was watching me, his eyes still twinkly. I lifted my pointer finger and signaled for him to turn around. He arched his eyebrows then did as I asked only to start stretching in the most inappropriate ways. I vividly pictured smacking his ass when he bent over to stretch his hamstrings.

But then he stood up and stroked his face. His salty, scraggly, yak face. I almost choked on my own tongue.

This was going to be a long afternoon.

Graham played like shit and the Timbers lost. It made the girls behind us all the more relentless. By the end of it, I had a nickname, beard gag. The unoriginal take on a ball gag really made my temper flare. The heat of the Portland summer hadn't helped my mood either.

We went to the same bar after the game and I was playing pool while Mandy and JJ talked about some family reunion. I was slamming balls into pockets far more forcefully than necessary. Once or twice, they even jumped out of their pockets and onto the floor.

"You look like you could use someone to play with." Graham's voice still sent shivers up my spine.

"If you want." I handed him a cue.

"Why are you so upset? I'm the one that needs his wounds licked." He slipped closer to me.

"Don't ask," I grumbled as I picked up one of the balls that had gone rogue across the floor.

"I liked having you at the game."

"I shouldn't have gone."

"There's a small chance I could see your little pussy when you were sitting at the stadium earlier. Thanks for wearing a dress." His fingers danced along the edges of the fabric but he didn't touch me.

I looked over, studying the sculpt of his arms, the slope of his back and chest. But then I looked up. The snagglepuss that was clinging to his face ruined everything.

"Let's just play pool." I sighed and stalked around the table and took the liberty of breaking.

He let me roll for a little while before he grazed against my inner calf with a pool cue. My skin tingled and I twisted to playfully scold him but I got beard-slapped and the reality check made my face fall.

"Please don't."

"What?" He read the complete shift in my body language.

"I can't. I honestly keep trying and I can't. I'm sorry." I placed my cue on the table and turned to walk toward Mandy.

When I found her wrapped around Twenty-Two, and JJ in deep

conversation, I slid onto a bar stool in the corner and ordered bourbon. It only took two minutes for the sheer hunk of muscle that was Graham to slide onto the stool next to me. He ordered a beer then sat silently next to me, just screwing around on his phone.

Mine buzzed against the bar where I'd left it.

How about this? We're really good at this.

That we are.

I smiled as I looked down at my phone then over at him. He seemed to be smiling too but it was so hard to tell with shag carpeting covering his face.

Can I tell you that when I saw your pussy today before the game, framed by white cotton and combat boots, I got hard. I wanted to bury myself in you. I wanted to pull up the video you sent me a few days ago.

Only if I can tell you that I stared at your dick almost all game.

That's gonna get me hard all over again

Don't tease a girl

I'd only tease you with the tip

No way I'd accept just the tip. I'd swallow you whole.

He groaned next to me beneath his breath. The sound was so full of want and need I couldn't help that my hand went to his thigh. He sucked in another deep breath and laced his hand into mine.

I should tell you to get your hands off me

I should get my hands off you

We were both slower texting one handed but we managed.

Please don't

He pulled on my hand and placed it on his dick. The thick column was coming to life beneath me and I couldn't help but flex my hand into it and rub.

"Holy fuck," he whispered under his breath. I kept stroking.

The palm of my hand was getting hot and it wasn't just friction. It was the chemistry between us that threatened to singe my skin. I looked around to make sure no one had crept into our dark corner of the bar. Everyone had gravitated to the pool tables and high-top tables that peppered the space. It was safe to flip his button and unzip his fly.

"You're a minx." He laughed breathily.

"I can't help myself with you." I wormed my hand under the waistband of his boxer briefs.

"Perfect."

I rubbed on him harder, adding flicks and twists of my wrist. I leaned over and sipped on my bourbon at the same time, trying to be nonchalant.

"God, I've been dying to feel you against me," he said it so quietly, so haggard I didn't think I'd ever made a man that excited before.

"Are you going to come?" I angled toward him, less concerned with my bourbon.

"In your hand if you give it one second."

Everything inside me clenched. Here in the dark it was the man with a beastly cock and the silver tongue. That man I wanted to get off. I wanted to feel his hot cum in my hand the way I had felt my own when I masturbated to videos he'd sent or things he said.

"I have to kiss you," he said in a breathy, choppy voice and he started leaning in.

For a split second, I stayed still. I wanted to kiss the man I'd been phone fucking too. I wanted to feel what his lips would be like against mine. How his hands actually would explore my body. My eyes fluttered shut and I surrendered.

Until he rubbed a Brillo pad against my cheek.

"Stop." I shot back from him and yanked my hand from his pants.

"Wait. What?" He was breathing heavy, slumped against the bar with the tip of his dick still poking out over top of the Calvin Klein elastic.

The unmistakable heebie-jeebies crawled up and down my neck. I felt like there was a ghost trying to grate the skin of my cheek off.

"I'm sorry, Graham. I really am." I bit my lip and turned, all but running out the door.

My phone pinged while I sat on the fire escape outside my window. I knew it was Graham without getting up. Part of me wanted to read it, part of me was sure there was nothing he could say to get us out of this pickle.

Did I just suck it up? Find a way to choke the bile down and kiss him despite the fact that I was likely kissing everything he'd eaten in the last few hours and his sweat from practice and any pussy he'd had in the last few weeks? I shuddered at the thought.

The clatter of my phone buzzing wildly against the dresser was becoming obnoxious so I pushed up from the warm steel of the fire escape and snatched it.

I know it's because I kissed you

I should have just let you keep touching me

As soon as you stopped I was...

His next photo was an exaggerated pouty face. Despite the beard, I could see the hint of big, full lips. The small pelted critter trying to eat his face made me shudder.

And The Beast was...

His second photo was a picture of his dick only he'd drawn on it with a black marker like that dude that made memes for Tumblr. It had tiny eyes and a giant frown. It was big, bold, noticeable lines that were obviously actually drawn on. To top it off, Graham had obviously jerked off because cum coated his frownie dick, making it look like it was bawling.

It was ridiculous. Well, more like riDICKulous, but still…

I busted up laughing, even doubling over, and slapping my knee. I couldn't catch my breath as I studied the giant crying dick over and over. It was this big, beautiful monster with an adorable child's drawing of a face. It was like the worlds most twisted children's book, and I loved it.

How would he explain Sharpie on his cock to his teammates? How did he plan to actually explain the dopey face to me? Why couldn't I make out with the sports god that had a sense of humor?

> I'm gonna go out on a limb and say there's a crying pussy out there too. I know I made you wet…

I bit my lip, knowing it was a picture request and immediately had an idea.

How would I explain marker on my cooter? Since no one but Graham was seeing it, it didn't much matter. He'd find this shit funny. Lucky I was shaved clean for the perfect canvas. What on earth possessed me to draw on myself was beyond me. I stepped over to my desk and dug around for a Sharpie.

I only found a pink one. The idea of a pink pussy made me snicker even harder as I hiked up my dress. I threw my leg up on the radiator so I could see myself in the mirror. I slipped for a minute and a stray line gashed down my thigh.

"Fuck."

My cinematography skills had to get good and quick. Otherwise, I'd look like a kid had at my thigh before I went full filth. It was another one of those moments when I thought about what a dirty little hooker I actually was then shrugged it off with a mischievous smirk. Mandy would find it funny, except that I was thinking about her while touching myself.

I was a little slick at just the sight of The Beast. After all, he was enough to make a river run wild. And the humor just made everything below my belly button clench. So I stuck my tongue out as I scribbled tiny little ears across the hairless plane above my snatch. I laughed at the tiny triangles enough to tumble again and scribble all over my other thigh, making my legs look even more absurd. When I stopped giggling, I added two tiny little crinkled eyes, then whiskers shooting out from my clit.

It was probably the stupidest, weirdest, and least sexy thing I could have thought up but I'd managed a pretty cute doodle. I snapped a picture and sent it with the caption "meWOW" then busted up laughing all over again. A second later my phone rang, Graham's name popping up on the screen.

I meowed into the receiver instead of saying hello.

He snarled a little bit before he answered, "I think someone needs to feed that pussy."

The knock on my door surprised me, I wasn't expecting anyone. The sharpie kitty I'd drawn over a week ago was still fading from between my legs and since I'd been sitting around in nothing but a t-shirt I had to scramble to cover it up. I checked my appearance in the mirror and I looked exactly like the hot mess constant late night phone sex was making me out to be.

As soon as I covered up, I yanked open the door to find JJ casually leaning against the doorframe.

"Nurse J, what are you doing here?"

"He's single-handedly lost two games in a row Livy." Dr. Jason Jones had swiftly replaced Nurse JJ and he pushed into my tiny apartment. "I told you to be careful because this wasn't some random Tinder hook-up but you didn't listen."

He strode right into the kitchen and helped himself to a glass of water. He gulped it back way too fast then leaned against the counter, rolling the empty glass between his hands in an anxious movement as he did.

"We're just having fun." It was a weak defense and I knew it.

"*You're* having fun. He's risking everything Livy. And I see the way he looks at you. He's happy to do it, thinking you'll change."

"Maybe I will." There was absolutely no conviction in my voice.

"Yeah and maybe monkeys will fly out of my butt."

I couldn't help but laugh at the Wayne's World reference.

"You're stubborn as hell Livy, and I have years of ridiculous stories to use as evidence."

I sighed with absolutely no defense.

"Look, Livy, we're leaving for New York on a red eye tonight. Go out. Get laid by someone who shaves and stop answering his calls." It was a brotherly warning, serious but warm all at once. "Please, Livy. Do it for me?"

My phone ring was blaring from somewhere. I rubbed at my eyes as I searched for it mixed in with the blankets. I had gone out, like JJ had suggested, but there wasn't a clean shaven face in the house. Or maybe I just wasn't looking. I tried to remember the finer details as I patted around.

"Hello," I finally answered and it sounded like I smoked six packs a day.

"Hi minx." Graham had started calling me the nickname after the bar. My smile split my face each and every time he used it.

"Did you get to New York okay?"

"Yeah, the red eye always sucks. Then trying to get some privacy to call you took forever. It's nice to hear your voice now, though."

I couldn't help but hum into the phone.

"Jason was telling this story about you and his sister camping tonight on the plane. I turned off my headphones to eavesdrop. You guys were trouble."

My stomach bottomed out and my eyes shot open. It didn't matter that it was 5 a.m.

"And for the record, you topless, yelling at the cops…"

Graham went on telling the story but I couldn't make myself listen. Usually this was one of my favorite tales, full of humor, shenanigans, and nudity. Mandy and I telling it together was a sight, full of hand motions, sound effects, and visual aids courtesy of her camera roll. But tonight it was a frigid cold reminder of what JJ had begged for yesterday.

"Graham," I interrupted, my voice a little shaky.

"Livy?" He must have sensed something was off right away.

"Are you okay Graham?" My voice was far too timid and shaky.

"Of course, why wouldn't I be?" His voice wasn't as convinced as his words.

"JJ, I mean Jason and I were talking. He's worried…" I gulped.

Why is this so hard to get out?

"About me?"

"Yeah." My bottom lip quivered. "Since this isn't ever going to be…more…"

"You still think that? I mean, I thought things were changing. That you'd give me a chance." The voice on the other end of the line wasn't Graham's anymore. It wasn't smirktastic *or* strong and assertive.

"I'd be lying if I said I didn't like you Graham. And The Beast is delicious, but…" Tears were starting to knot in my throat but I had to follow through. Dragging out the flirtation was selfish, relishing the orgasms was even worse.

"You're going to throw this away because of the beard?" he snarled. "Really?"

"Graham…" My voice broke as I whined into the phone.

"Don't Graham me." His voice was an echo of mine. "I know it's new and I know it's mostly tit pics and dirty videos and phone sex but it's more too. I want to take you to dinner. I want you to come to a game with *me*. A night at the movies would be awesome."

"I can't date you." My voice was small, mousey almost.

"Because you don't want my beard between your legs?" He was almost shouting at me now.

"Because I can't kiss you." The words were barely more than a whisper. "The idea still turns my stomach."

The line went dead and the three tones of a hang-up blared in my ear. I couldn't blame Graham for disconnecting. We'd danced around the subject until I up and smacked him in the face with it. Hard.

A tear or two dripped down my cheek. He'd never really been mine—I wouldn't let him be—but I missed him all the same.

Just for shits I Googled him. There he was with his big, dark bush covered face and, for the first time, I missed it. I couldn't kiss it, I couldn't cuddle it, but something deep inside me yearned to have that pube face back.

I couldn't force my body out of bed all day. I only managed to turn on the TV around 4 p.m. ESPN all but obliterated Graham during their telecast of the game. And rightfully so. He was a disaster, almost scoring in his own goal. My guilt was as large as the goal deficit the Timbers were dealing with.

Twice I went to text him. I wanted to say I was sorry, beg forgiveness, tell him that we might never kiss but the way his voice decimated me was worth it. But then a full face shot of an angry, rabid beaver would still my hand.

I opened my phone just once and scrolled down to his name in my favorites. With a few clicks, I deleted the number. I needed to stay 500 yards from The Beard at all times, and forget about The Beast all together.

"Please?" Mandy begged. "Please, please, please, please, please!" She was even tugging on my shirttail.

"Mandy, stop." I shoved at her hands. "You know damn well why I don't want to go. I need to get over him."

"You were never under him." She smirked then broke into a full-blown giggle at herself.

"You're hilarious." I rolled my eyes. "And trying really hard to get me to go." The sarcasm was thick as frozen peanut butter in my voice.

"Is it really so bad to see him? Doesn't seeing him help? Seeing him means you're gonna look at that big ole Sasquatch face and remember all the reasons you stopped talking to him."

"JJ told me to stop talking to him. The beard was the only reason I followed through." I blew out a heavy sigh.

Mandy was partially right. Every time they flashed his face on the jumbotron or he turned toward the crowd, I'd feel that familiar lurch and or sucker punch to my insides. But if he was playing poorly, I'd blame myself for letting it go where it had in the first place. If they interviewed him and I heard that voice, there was a chance I'd pass right out. But then there was the beard…

"Why can't he just shave it!" I snarled in frustration at no one in particular.

"Because the Timbers gift store is filled with jerseys that say *Beard*…t-shirts, lumberjack costumes…Hell, there are foam beards you can buy. They're all based on Graham."

My insides twisted. Mandy was right. She usually was. But hearing that Graham was there and there was still next to no hope was obliterating me. And, honestly, I needed to piece myself back together.

"You're right." This time when I sighed, I blew the layer of hair hanging in my face skyward. "About all of it. He'll never shave and I'll never change. I need to get over it. Game time it is."

The roar of the crowd was deafening in my ears but I couldn't manage much more than a slow clap. My insides balled and writhed and tangled up on themselves. In a few seconds number four was going to jog onto the field. Long, sculpted arms were going to wave at the crowd, and that shelf of an ass was going to make my mouth water. He'd smile but it would be buried deep beneath that creature suctioned to his face.

I'd feel all the things that I couldn't quite explain. And likely all at once. I'd have to tie them up in a long stringing pube hair bow to get through this.

His silken jersey slinked up and down on his perfectly sculpted frame. The number four crinkled and flattened just above God's gift to women conveniently wrapped in white shiny shorts.

I waited to go deaf. For the crowd eruption to chatter my teeth and threaten to dislodge my head, but it didn't come. Across the stadium from us the crowd deflated, one by one people became slow clappers just like me. Soon an eerie hush rolled over the stadium that was only punctuated by gasps and the cricket like noise of whispers.

"What's going on?" I asked Mandy out of the side of my mouth, unable to take my eyes off Graham.

She shrugged as we both watched him turn in time with his name being belted over the sound system.

"Holy Fuck!" I shouted loud enough that my voice became a ping-pong ball bouncing around the stadium. Graham smirked where I could see him and rubbed the back of his neck, then let his hand trail down his jaw.

His sharp, defined, and clean-shaven jaw.

Mine was about ready to hit the floor. Graham, The Beard, Foster had shaved. The whole stadium was shocked. The silence slowly shifted toward angry boos and hisses. My heart would have broke for Graham if it wasn't busy going ape-shit in my chest.

Clean shaven Graham was gorgeous. His striking face put his perfect ass to shame. Beneath that monstrosity he'd been sporting, he had plump, full lips, and a dimple that hollowed his left cheek. I wanted to drag my teeth across both.

"He shaved." I was still shouting at Mandy.

"Yes, it would seem he did. You wanna lower your voice about it?" She shot me a look. A few other people pursed their lips and grimaced in my direction. I squinched my face up in return then stuck my tongue out when they turned away.

"Do you think he…" I trailed off when I realized how vane it sounded.

"Shaved for you?" Mandy had no problem finishing the sentence. "Probably. It sure as shit wasn't a career move."

That earned me far less friendly looks from the girls around us. I didn't care. Those bitches could be all kinds of angry. I had Graham. Glorious, gorgeous, and completely clean Graham. I couldn't take my eyes off him.

He played like a god. He played like David Beckham in his prime or Cristiano Ronaldo. It had me knocking my knees together far too frequently. The Timbers were up by three goals, two of which were scored by Graham himself. The more on fire he was, the more the crowd bought into the beardless wonder too.

Sweat dripped down his forehead and shone on his arms and legs. His jersey was plastered to his back as we were all treated to sight of him running everywhere. Because he was *everywhere,* I almost got whiplash stuck to him as I was.

When the final whistle blew, the crowd erupted. The lumberjack disappearance from earlier seemed to be completely forgiven thanks to the massive win. The sound chattered through my bones and up into my teeth but it paired perfectly with the pure need coursing through my veins. Grown men, screaming, celebrating, muscles flexed, and then jumping on each other was downright primal and surprisingly hot.

Mandy and I were still chanting with the crowd, smiling ear to ear when Graham broke away. A few cameras tried to stop him but he simply darted out around them, as nimble as he'd been on the field.

My heartbeat ratcheted up and my breathing went shallow. Watching him run could do that to a girl. In that moment I think it became my new favorite hobby.

Then I realized he was cutting a path in my direction. He had to slow when he got to the random people milling about on the sidelines but he jostled them aside easily enough. I stopped breathing all together when only the metal railing separated us. It took him a moment or two to find his footing in his cleats but then he hurdled over it in one hell of a smooth move, bringing him and I face to face.

His rugged, abtastic torso was in front of me. His drenched shirt clung to every single inch of his perfect chest. He shifted his weight side to side, no doubt an anxious movement, but it highlighted the definition of his thighs. I wanted to touch every inch, lick every inch.

And then I looked up.

Graham Foster truly was a god. He'd kept his hipster haircut, long on top and short on the sides, and it fell haphazardly where it wasn't slicked back from sweat. His eyes seemed more green without the dark reflection of his beard, and his jaw was most definitely chiseled from stone.

"Hi." His smooth voice came from the most luscious shaped lips just before he smiled the most panty-shredding smile I'd ever seen. That he'd been in hiding seemed a really cruel and heinous joke.

"Hi." I barely managed the word.

"I'm gonna kiss you now."

I started to nod but it only took a moment for him to crash into me and stop me from doing anything but melting into him all together. Cheers erupted from the stadium and shrill cat calls too. I smiled wide while I breathed him in.

Kissing him was better than Christmas, the smell of rain on warm pavement and fresh baked cookies combined. His lips knew how to work it, tumbling against mine but also owning them. His tongue crept between my lips, gently exploring. Graham grunted into my open mouth as his big hands wrapped around me and yanked me to his sticky chest. The dampness spoke to my animal instincts right along with the salty taste of him. I couldn't help myself when I curled my claws into his chest.

"Still turn your stomach?" he asked, his lips brushing against mine.

"For a very different fucking reason," I murmured before leaning back in to explore his mouth a little more.

"Good." His word was more a breath in between our fevered kisses.

When I thought I might melt into a puddle or off the face of the earth completely, he picked me up and cradled me to his chest as if he knew. He kissed me hard one more time then took off, dodging people filtering out of the stadium. When we got to the stairs, another cheer erupted for us and the crowd parted. Graham ran the stairs as easily with me in his arms as he probably did without.

"It's like they know how desperate I am to be inside you," he said low and husky in my ear just before he bit it. There was a chance I was going to come right there in his arms.

Once we got up to the top of the stairs he bolted against the flow of traffic to a players only entrance, security stepped swiftly aside to let him pass. We made two quick turns down successive hallways to find ourselves in a dark tunnel lit only by distant sunlight.

He set me down then slammed me up against the wall, his lips coming back to mine like they'd never left. His hands were everywhere, peeling up my t-shirt and gripping at my ass. Mine were desperate to do the same. When the wet fabric of his jersey kept getting in the way, I yanked it clean off. Graham snarled then returned the favor.

"Is anyone gonna see?" I asked panting.

"Don't think so," he answered as he dove down to kiss the swell of my breasts. "Not that I'd mind. They can watch me fuck you in the center circle for all I care."

"Are they mad about the beard?" I couldn't help myself.

"Are you?" He roughly yanked my tits up out of the soft bra cups, and I arched against the cool cinderblock wall up into his hands.

"No." I drug out the last letter like it was a howl to the moon.

"Then I don't fucking care."

He latched onto one nipple while he pinched on the other.

"I needed you, Livy. Couldn't sleep, couldn't breathe, couldn't play without you. Tell me you needed me too?" He kissed down my body and fell to his knees.

"I missed everything about you." I was gasping for air against the cool blocks.

He hooked his fingers into the waistband of my shorts and yanked them and my underwear off in one quick movement.

"Liar," he shot back just before he latched onto my clit. I moaned wildly, and the echo bounced down the empty hallway. "You don't miss the beard one bit."

The puffs of his laughter against my pussy were enough to drive me wild. I bucked my hips up and he leisurely lapped me before pulling back. With his finger, he traced the skin that had worn the sharpie drawing of a cat far too long.

"Minx?" He was talking directly to my clit. "You ready to meet Beast?"

He didn't hesitate and in one swift move, Graham stood and shoved his shorts down, notching between my thighs precisely. He pushed into me hard and fast, and I screamed again clawing my hands into his chest. He cried out too, pushing hard and fast up into me and almost knocking me off my tip-toes.

"You're big," I whined.

"And you're tight," he shot back as his hands wrapped around my thighs and lifted me. "I like tight almost as much as I like you, Livy."

The full weight of our bodies rested against my shoulders on the scratchy concrete. As soon as he started thrusting, I knew it was going to mark me, and the idea made me drag my fingernails down his back. He groaned again, adding to the wild cacophony of sound.

Over and over, we moved with each other. I closed my eyes, relishing the feel of blissfully good sex and the gratification of finally being together. I started repeating his name in time with his thrusts. They started as low, hushed whispers but quickly escalated to ragged shouts and screeches as my orgasm neared.

It seemed like the tunnel was getting brighter but that had to just be my orgasm detonating my insides. Graham had been able to do that before I had his mouth and cock claiming every inch of me. I was about to shatter, and my senses were slipping away one by one as I went.

Then he shoved up in me and I actually felt him coming. His dick twitched inside me as heat flooded into me. It triggered me and I howled as my body went a little rigid and my joints unhinged. My body shuddered against him in uncontrollable twitches.

"Fucking shit, my little Minx." He was breathing hard and his voice was a fragile thing.

My eyes were still closed when I finally found words. "Worth shaving for?"

"I'd shave anything in the whole wide world if it meant I could stick it inside you," Graham purred back.

"That sounds like a challenge." I rolled my hips against him and felt cum drip down me.

"It's more of a proposition. Call it a…"

"Answer, Graham." Some unknown female voice yelled, finishing the sentence unexpectedly. My eyes split open. "Come on, answer whether this was a publicity stunt or something different."

The bright lights of a portable camera showered down on us. My arms immediately shot to cover my rucked up tits. Graham moved a second later to cover me with his body and smash me up against the wall.

"What the fuck are you doing down here?" he roared.

"Looking for answers," the journalist replied. "To the million dollar question." She smiled as she raked her eyes over the two of us. I'd turned the darkest shade of red imaginable and curled into Graham's shoulder. "Well, I guess it's actually the six million dollar question, but still… Why throw it all away?" She shoved her hand on her hip. "Please tell me it wasn't for a girl," she remarked, her voice thick with disdain.

"And if it was?" Graham tried to find a way to hide me further from prying eyes.

The reporter smiled her wicked smile and my world washed cleaned out. I was only grounded by the firm muscles beneath my fingertips and the bright white light of the news camera that blinded me. She still wore her smirk while she answered, "Then this is getting bumped from Sports straight to front page news."

About Ace Gray

Ace Gray is a self-proclaimed troublemaker and connoisseur of both the good life and fairy tales. After a life-long love affair with books, she undertook writing the novel she wanted to read, which culminated in her first release STRICTLY BUSINESS then the remainder of the MIXING BUSINESS WITH PLEASURE SERIES and now the TWISTED FAIRY TALE series. Often she is referred to as the creator of adult Highlights and the Oprah of D. Insert winky face emoji here…

When she's not writing, she owns her own business teaching Pilates and slings brews at Deschutes Brewery. She loves rainy days, shellac manicures, coffee shops and bourbon—all of which are bountiful in her adopted home of Portland, OR where she runs amok with her chef husband and two huskies.

Sign up for the wild and crazy newsletter here:
www.ace-gray.com/extra-extra-read-all-about-it/

Please follow Ace on social media at:

Instagram: www.instagram.com/acekgray
Facebook: www.facebook.com/acekgray
Twitter: /www.twitter.com/acekgray

Fortune Favors the Beard

BY ALEXIS ALVAREZ

Arie

He's built, he's hot, and he's totally in my way. "Move," I urge mentally, even though I've never been successful with telekinesis. Part of me wants to stay stuck behind him so I can keep looking at his ass. It's perfect – taut, sexy, and it moves in such an enticing way when he shifts his weight to do something to the bicycle chain.

But the other part of me – the part that needs to just get into the supermarket and buy an emergency stash of flour – really needs him to stand aside. After all, one does not simply work on one's bike *in the automatic entrance doors* of the grocery store.

Myler speaks into my ear via Bluetooth. "Arie, hurry. You need to get back here so we can finish the last batches."

"I'm trying." My voice rises as I sigh in frustration. "I'm stuck behind Lance Armchair Biker who's, like, blocking my egress."

Shit. Did he hear me? Well, maybe I said it louder than necessary.

Oops! He glares at me, but when our eyes lock, a spark of attraction so fierce and powerful surges through me that I almost gasp. If his butt was amazing, his face is even more gorgeous. All planes and lines and dark eyes. Holy fuck, he's sexy. He has perfect proportions, chiseled cheekbones, luscious lips. Strong jaw. Green eyes and a smooth forehead. And that beard! It's short and trimmed, barely more than scruff, but on him, it looks so incredibly sexy that I almost die.

The thing is, I don't feel this just because he's hot. There's something about him that calls to me. It's like I know him, or something – even though I don't. I know how corny and stupid that sounds, but I can't help staring.

He holds my gaze. "Ingress," he says. "When you want in, it's called ingress." His voice is low, and as his eyes move up and down my body, assessing, bold, I blush hard. He makes it sound so dirty… in a wicked, delicious way.

"Thanks for the grammar lesson," I say. I don't want to let him know how he's affected me, because he probably doesn't feel the same, so I act cool. "But, you know, and someone needed to say it, you're sort of creating a fire hazard. If nobody can get past you, what happens in an emergency?" I wouldn't talk this way to a client or to my mom, but this guy – I want to push his buttons. I want him to push mine.

I raise my eyebrow and cross my arms over my chest, tossing my red-gold curls over my shoulders.

"Vocabulary." His voice is smooth, and he twists the pedal on the bike while grabbing the chain.

"What?" His hands are so strong, his fingers long and quick.

He doesn't answer, but bends back down to do something again with the bike chain. I don't know what someone as sexy as he is – in a suit that expensive – would even be doing with such a ratty-ass shit-trap of a bicycle. I'm not the only irritated party. I can see a few people waiting to leave the store, three carts backed up like a train, the lady in front starting to blow out her breath and tap her slip-on sandal on the ground.

He stands up and says, "There. All fixed." He gives an apologetic wave to the carts, wheels the bike out of the walking path, and looks directly at me. "You wanna put on your helmet, Sugar, and I'll take you for a ride?" This sounds even dirtier than his last comment. It's so inappropriate, so utterly forward, and so…hot. My heart hammers in my chest.

"Where you gonna take me?" My voice comes out lower than I mean, sultry. His eyes are locked onto mine again.

"The library. A person who doesn't even know the difference between grammar and vocabulary needs a lesson indeed." He smirks and props the bike up on the kickstand.

"But. I." This is all I can manage. First of all, he has some nerve insulting me. And second of all – or maybe this is really the first reason, he was supposed to say something flirty. Then I say, "I know the difference. I was only not able to think of the right word because I was thinking of something else." My face gets hot.

He laughs. "I'd like to know what." He grins, then gestures to someone hovering near a display of discount patio chairs and charcoal briquettes, and a teenager wearing a "Golden Wok Delivery" apron takes the handlebars. "I got the chain working," he tells the kid, "but you're going to need to take this bike to a repair shop. The teeth are worn down and it's loose."

"Dude, you saved my life. Thanks." The kid gives off a waft of sesame oil and egg rolls. He hangs a sagging plastic bag over the handlebars, gets onto the bike, waves, and pedals off.

My man examines his fingers – black grease marks. He frowns, looks around.

I dig into my purse and pull out a clean batch of brown napkins from Starbucks. "Here." I offer them to him and as he takes them, our fingertips brush, sending a shock of sparks directly into my belly. "That was, um, sweet of you. I didn't know you were helping someone. Otherwise I would have been more…" I give him a shy smile.

"So, I'm playing bike repair man for the afternoon. What's your story?" He smiles back.

I look into his eyes and I'm gone. His eyes are green and hazel, bright and gorgeous. I want to touch his beard. I want to kiss his lips.

He puts his hand on my arm, and the feel of his fingers makes it hard to breathe properly. "You look like you need something important."

"I need flour," I say. "Three bags." His cologne drifts over to me on the breeze and I lean in slightly, as if to smell him. I can barely resist the urge to put my finger onto his cheekbones, my mouth onto his.

He's still holding my arm, and I look down at it, and he does too, and then he lets go, as if he just noticed. I feel an immediate loss. I liked his firm grip. I want those fingers on my body again.

"Three bags." A smile tugs at those sexy lips. "And exactly what –"

A horn honks and startles me and I jump. A voice calls out, "Dude, we gotta get moving." There's a BMW at the curb, and another suited guy driving. This one is cute, too, but blond where my guy is dark.

My guy looks up. "In a minute, Nate." He turns to me again, opens his mouth to speak, but as he does, Myler's voice explodes into my ear. "Arie! For the love of everything holy, you have to get back. All the lights went off and I don't know how to find the fuse box and – did you get the flour? Arie?"

The job! My stomach lurches. I cannot mess this up.

All I can think of is getting back to my bakery. "I have to go!" I exclaim. "You can keep the napkins. Here are some more, even." I grapple with my purse, shove a few more into his hands. "Good luck with everything and bikes and it was, you know, nice meeting you."

I want to ask his name. I want his number. I want to take him home and make mad love to him. I want to forget my stress in his arms, lose myself in his glorious eyes. But I hesitate. I'm afraid to ask, because what if he says no? It would be embarrassing, horrible. I turn to the door.

"Wait –" he says, but I don't. Better to leave it this way, a fantasy. Besides, I'm on a mission. I race into the store, breathless, and soon I'm back at my shop, ready to make more fortune cookies.

"We did it!" I grab Myler into a hug, do a short victory jig, and lean theatrically onto the counter. "Our biggest order yet and it's done. One thousand, three hundred and twenty five custom fortune cookies are now on their way to the Carter Hudson Analysts annual gala, full of the most inspirational and uplifting phrases about success and leadership ever uttered."

Myler claps and points. "Lao Tzu, Steve Jobs, and you."

I blow out my breath in a long exhale of pure relief. "I wasn't sure we'd pull it off until I loaded the last box into Jitter's ride. The back of his VW van has never been a more beautiful sight." I bite my lip as anxiety bubbles up. "What if he broke down on the way? Or lost his GPS signal? I better text him to make sure he got there okay."

I send a quick message to my delivery guy, Maxwell "Jitters" Jones, who works part time at the coffee shop next door, spends a lot of hours playing guitar out front for dollar bills in his bucket, and also drives my orders around. You might think he's irresponsible, especially with a nickname like Jitters, but he's the most reliable driver I've ever hired.

"Arie, Jitters is a traffic guru and he has magic in his pants." Myler smiles. "When he's on the prowl, legs and cars part in front of him, like the Red Sea."

It's true. He can work his way through any traffic jam, and drop any panties he wants – mine and Myler's excluded, of course. She's with someone, and I'm, well, it would be unprofessional, for one. He's hot, but I'm waiting for someone who can commit to more than a night of quick passion. His vehicular prowess, however? That I will sign up for any day, no question.

I get a reply.

No worries. Just dropped off the boxes at the service entrance and got sig on paperwk. Hding back now.

"He did it." I rub my eyes. "Now I can have some wine. Want some wine? You and Bree can come to my place to celebrate."

"Sorry, wish I could, but we're going to her mom's for a family dinner. I have to jet and get ready." Myler puts away the last shiny baking tray and swipes her hands together. "Look, perfectly clean and ready. It's like the kitchen is just waiting for our genius hands to arrive again tomorrow and bake up another batch of pure fortune perfection."

"Yeah." I smile as I look around my silver and marble domain. "Ever since I opened last fall, business has just kept increasing."

Myler picks up her purse and jacket. "I'm too hot to even put this on. The cold air outside will feel so good. And yeah, you make the most delicious baked goods in all of Chicago. This, I'm certain about. Plus, custom fortune cookies are hot these days. You get more orders for those than all the cakes and cupcakes combined."

"Mmm." I take another deep breath. The kitchen smells fresh, like lemony cleaner, but under it is the ever-present lure of vanilla and baked crumbs, caramelized sugar spun from my dreams. It's a good mix.

Myler hesitates, touches my arm. "I really think you need to consider hiring more helpers than just me, Arie. Today we barely squeaked by. And that final flurry when you were racing to the van to get the last boxes in with Jitters? My heart almost exploded."

I bite my lip. "Yeah, I know. But I only tripped a little. Didn't spill the box of cookies. And we got it all baked in time."

"It was close." Myler narrows her eyes. "I know you want to do it all alone, but you have to reach out and trust more people. Honestly, and I hate to say it, but we got lucky today. It could easily have blown up in our faces. I know you have a hard time delegating, but – be bold. You even have it here."

She picks up a long strip of white paper from the box of extra fortunes on the counter. "*You can do anything, but not everything. David Allen.* Or this one. *Don't be afraid to give up the good to go for the great. John D. Rockefeller.* Or, *The world cracks open for those willing to take a risk. Frances Mayes.*"

"I need to get more of a financial cushion before I do that." But when I see her face, I worry that maybe she'll quit or something. I am lucky to have someone so talented and hard-working as my number one assistant. I don't want to lose her, so I amend it with, "But I'll think about it. Thanks."

"Coolness." Myler gives me a quick one-armed hug. "Great job, A. See you next week!"

When she leaves for her Prius down the street, it's just me and the aromatic silence, pressing thick on me like humid air in the summer. The lights are bright and pure in the kitchen and the freezer hums, a low soothing purr. Outside are faint honks and engine revs that create the constant flow of Chicago traffic, punctuated by calls of pedestrians on their way to parties and bars.

I run my fingers over a smooth counter: Mine. It's cool to the touch but warms up as I lay my hand there, absorbing my heat. I think this whole endeavor has been like that: I started with something cold, empty, and warmed it up with the beat of my own heart and the power of my imagination. All my life I've dreamt of owning my own bakery, creating custom pastries to tempt tongues and entice interest from people all over the city.

Before I started, I thought it would be easy. Now I know better. It's back-aching, soul-searing work, and less than I'd like is actual baking. Marketing is just as critical; it's more than critical; it's the lifeblood of the place. Half of the time, my veins flow not with sugar and vanilla but with ad-space content and vendor outreach plans, thousands of words and papers and emails bursting out of my computer with vehemence and ardor.

It's a little scary, knowing that my baking talent alone is nowhere near enough, not even a fraction enough to succeed long term in this city. It would be nice to have a partner.

I think about Myler's comments. She's probably right, it's just – this is my baby, my prize. It's hard for me to trust Myler with things, and she's been my assistant from the beginning. I know the saying, You have to spend money to make money. But taking chances on the unknown isn't easy yet; no matter how many times I do it, even calculated risks make me cold in the stomach. Unknown things are like having to do a tumbling routine in the middle of a marathon.

A knock on the door flips me out of my reverie, and I turn the lock. "Jitters! You did it."

He gives me his cocky grin that melts hearts all over town. "Smooth ride, A. They've got a fancy set-up there. I helped the, uh, girl, bring all the boxes into the prep room."

"Of course you did." I make a face at him and smile.

He laughs. "It would have been ungentlemanly to let her carry those boxes by herself." He raises one eyebrow. "Plus, I needed a little more airtime to get her number."

"Did you?"

"Did I what?"

"Get the number."

"Oh, I got more than the number." He smirks. "I got pure unadulterated passion in the form of an eye-fucking. We're getting together later when she's done catering."

"You're such a whore." But my voice is affectionate. I like Jitters; he's funny and kind, even though he sleeps around. He never leads his women on, that much I can say. He's clear up front that he's not going to stick, and he doesn't leave a path of shattered hearts. His exes seem to still love him. Now that takes skill.

Speaking of eye fucking, I can't help but think about the handsome man at the store today, and a rush of regret hits me.

Jitters is eager to tell me more about his latest exploit-in-progress. "When she signed the acceptance form, she wrote her number on my hand. But then I just told her to program it into my phone anyway. She's into Cross Fit like I am, did you know that?" There's a note of something extra in his voice, a tone I don't usually hear when he talks about his dates.

He shows me both palms, one of them with smudged marks, and I shake my head. "Well, thanks for delivering, as always." I hand him the wad of cash waiting on the counter. "Here's your tip, Romeo."

"Want me to give you some tip?" He gives me such a dirty look that I have to roll my eyes. "Or more than the tip, if you think you can handle it, that is." He wiggles his eyebrows. But he doesn't mean it.

"Ugh. Go away and have fun with your catering kitty."

A hint of red stains his jawbone, and I look twice. Interesting. Must be something about this one that makes her stand out.

"See you later, A." He hesitates. "You're not staying here too late, right? Want me to hang out and walk you to your car?"

"I think I can manage." My voice is dry, but I appreciate his concern. There was an armed robbery a few blocks down last week, and everyone is being extra cautious.

"All right." He peers down the street. "You got your pepper spray, right?"

"Yes, I'm fine! Go. And check the schedule on line, okay? I have a ton of jobs next week that still need drivers."

"Will do. Not available Wednesday because that's my calculus final, but I can do the rest." He gives me a jaunty wave, blows a kiss, and takes off.

The silence is thicker this time, more oppressive. Being alone before was a respite from the craziness of the day, but now it's lonely. I don't want Jitters, but I want – someone. Myler has Bree, someone with whom to share joys and triumphs. Wine's no fun when you drink it alone.

My mind flits back to the sexy man at the grocery store. I never got his name. I don't even know if he was single! What if I had asked him for his number?

It's probably better that I didn't, though. Rich, powerful sexy men like him order directly from the Bond Girl catalogue and get some supermodel who also cures cancer in her spare time, because she's a doctor, and who runs marathons on her way to volunteer at the homeless shelter.

I run my hand down my flour-spattered jeans. I'm pretty and fit, but I'm not ever going to be strutting on a stage in a weird lampshade gown and hurling cell phones at people who irritate me. My medical knowledge comes directly from Web MD and makes me so anxious that I need to stress-eat cupcakes whenever I google some symptom, and the closest I got to a marathon was delivering fortune cookies to a post-runners party for a client.

But as I lock up the bakery and head to my car, I still see that enigmatic smile on his lips. I wish I'd taken the chance to give him my name and to ask for his.

Carter

The chandeliers in the vast hall send shimmering sparkles of light across the marble floor and the multitude of impeccably set tables, and the string quartet – all in evening wear, are tuning up. It reminds me of a night at the opera, hearing them talk in low voices as they twist wooden knobs and run bows across string. I can already see how in-sync they are with each other, relying on more than visual cues to match tempo, tone and timber. The lead violin sways her body in a certain way and the other violin follows even though her eyes are shut. The viola player jumps in at the exact right time to run a scale over the flittering high notes. It's amazing how a group of people can communicate without words and work like one seamless organism.

Too bad Nate and I don't have that with our company yet. Ever since Dad died five years ago, we've run the investment business together. Although we're doing well, it's rocky – and I don't feel like we're in our groove yet.

Nate comes up with a smirk. "Bro times." He slaps my back and grabs for my hand, and I twist into him, easy, the motions a routine. Feeling his strong grip and seeing his broad smile make my confidence soar. "We're going to fucking kill it tonight."

"As long as you don't say fuck in front of Caroline Baker. Dad never got her to sign with him, but we can do it if we're on point tonight. She's my main target. Her company is huge. It would be a million dollar deal over the next five years. Can you imagine?" I can taste the money.

Nate grins. "Maybe dad was too nice to her. People say she's stone cold mean. She's got a backbone of steel and a pussy of–"

"Stop." I hold up my hand. "One wrong word hits the wrong ears and we're in trouble. You know how important image and perception are." I give him my stern, older-brother glare.

He shrugs. "Carter, I love you, man, but you're obsessed with image and numbers. There's more to life than pure money. You need to have fun, too." He swings at an imaginary golf ball.

"You spend too much time fucking around and not enough time actually working."

"Ah, Kohai, but it is work. Merely a different kind. And the struggle is real for me, too. I have to match shoes to pants on a daily basis."

"Thank you for your suffering. Dad would be so proud." I give him the finger, even though I'm grateful he has the magic touch – he signs as many clients on the golf course as I do in the office.

He laughs. "Seriously, though. Maybe if you lightened up, you could reel her in. People respect other people with balance in their lives. *Carpe Diem*. Seize the day, and enjoy the pleasures of the moment without regard for the future. Someone smart said that."

"Oh, right. Because forgetting about the future is the very best way to run a company."

"Dude, you don't forget about the future forever. Jesus. Just for a while, while you're having the fun. The point is to take time for enjoyment, and when you do, throw yourself into it utterly. Then, later on, you're refreshed and sharp and you work better than ever."

He's about to say something else, but morphs into the epitome of sophistication as a client approaches us. "Jonathon Harcourt!" He gives a firm shake. "I'm glad you could make it." They walk off together.

When I spot Melissa heading my way, I take a deep breath. She works at a different accounting firm, and I can never tell how much of her interest in me is personal and how much is financial. Her golden gown is painted onto her body and her sinuous curves pull the eyes of all the men, like cats watching a toy. She uses sex as her hook, but she's fucking brilliant when it comes to investing, I'll give her that.

I chuckle before I realize that I'm watching her, too, as caught up as anyone else, nearly batting at her with my useless paws, and that pisses me off. She treats it like a game, bedding high-powered men.

She'd be good in bed. But I don't want good in bed. I don't want leverage in bed, or manipulation, or insider gossip traded for sex. I want magnificent. When I fuck, it's no game. I like it rough and passionate and primal. Fierce. A connection that drowns out any power either of us have or don't have in regular life, because it's not about business, it's an inevitable explosion of passion that bursts out and consumes us.

If that's what Nate is talking about? I'm already in. I just need to find the right woman.

My mind flickers back to the girl from the grocery store, the one who gave me attitude about the bike. I got the feeling she could give what I wanted – not just in bed, but out of it, too. How I could possibly know this from a one-minute interaction is impossible to say, but I'm convinced that I fucked up.

Why didn't I follow her into the store and ask for her number? Because I was too focused on this event, that's why. I sigh. Well, I blew that chance…there's no way I'd find her again in this huge city. For a split second, I imagine going to that grocery every day just in case she comes back. Or maybe hacking into their computer system in case she paid with a card that can be traced back to her. I could hire a hacker. With the right connections, it's possible to hire anyone to do anything.

"Carter!" Melissa drops an air kiss near my face, avoiding any makeup mishaps. Her eyes tell me she'd be willing to mess up her makeup later, but I keep my expression neutral as she winds her slim, toned arm around mine. "I am so glad to see you."

"You too." I nod, squeezing her shoulder. "Thank you for supporting us tonight."

She reads the banner atop the main podium. "*Charity Ball for the Fortune Family Foundation. Mentoring for underprivileged kids.* Getting high school kids to college is the best way to improve our financial status in the world – by growing our youth."

Whatever I do or don't think of Melissa, she's right about this.

"I love the theme," she continues, pointing at banners around the room. "Fortune Favors the Bold. And you even put fortune cookies by each plate!"

"Yes." Out of the corner of my eyes, I see more people meandering into the room, greeting each other with calls, handclasps, or hugs, depending on their level of person and fiscal intimacy. Some wind their way around the room, others find their seats. The chatter starts to rise, and it reminds me of the orchestral tune-up from earlier.

Melissa spots someone more important to her than I am, or perhaps – to be more accurate: someone more apt to treat her with importance. She gives an air kiss, and evaporates from my arm.

Nate is back. "Where'd you get the cookies, anyway?"

"I told my PA to hire a bakery in town to make personalized fortune cookies," I explain. "He said that the owner created a list of quotes by famous philosophers and innovators throughout history. I hope it will impress potential clients."

"Nice going, bro. They'll be eating out of your hand by the end of the night. You ass-licking bastard."

"That's the plan." We grin at each other. At a table nearby, small cracks, like the shattering of tiny brittle bones, let me know that people are opening the fortune cookies.

A young woman and her date compare fortunes, and their reaction is not what you'd expect. Her eyes goes wide and she claps a hand to her mouth to stifle a screech of laughter, glances around, then leans in to whisper into her boyfriend's ear. He looks at his and laughs so loudly that his friends notice. They crack open their cookies: More guffaws. Now one of them lopes to the baskets of cookies on the center table. He takes about ten.

Huh.

What about "*Your life does not get better by chance, it gets better by change,*" is so hilarious?

Nate pokes me. "Carter?"

"Yeah." I feel a distinct sense of unease as my eyes dart around the room. A colleague of my father, a stiff-lipped gentleman with white hair and an impeccable suit, a man who's been hesitant to entrust his financial planning to me and Nate after dad died, scowls and tosses his fortune to his plate. When his wife reaches out, he puts his hand over hers and shakes his head.

"Dude, I think the cookies are poisoned or something." Nate takes one from a nearby empty table and starts laughing. "Jesus, Carter." He reads aloud. "*For rectal use only?*"

"What the fuck? Let me see that." I grab it, sure he's messing with me, but that's exactly what it says, in bold, easy-to-read font.

I open another. "*Fuck me if I'm wrong, but a steak is a vegetable, right?*"

Oh, God. This is a nightmare. Are they all like this?

Nate's in on the action. "*Sit on my face and I'll eat my way to your heart.*"

"*Never give up, unless defeat arouses the hot girl with the big tits in the red dress.*"

"*I'll bet you 10$ my dick can't fit into your mouth.*"

I grab my phone and speed-dial Marconi. "I need you to get in here with all of the staff you can find. Remove every single fortune cookie from the room. Now."

Trying not to look frantic, I take the basket and start tossing in unopened fortunes. "Nate, give me a hand," I snap.

He's laughing so hard that he can't focus. "Dude, these are hilarious!"

"Yeah. Hilarious career killers. We need to get these disappeared."

He recognizes my urgency, starts collecting cookies, and my unease lifts when Marconi and the staff pick the rest from the tables like vultures on a fancy carcass. Thank God. Okay, so some got opened. Maybe more than some. But we've got the majority of them covered.

But, oh shit, here comes Caroline Baker, and she does not look amused. She holds up a strip of paper and glares at me. "Carter Hudson. Your father would be ashamed." She holds it out. "Read it aloud, young man." She narrows her eyes and puts her hand on her hips, a challenge.

"Caroline," I begin, "I apologize. There was apparently a mix-up at the bakery and they sent the wrong cookies."

"Here's a fortune for you," she snaps. "Confucius says that wise men admit mistakes and don't blame them on others. Read it."

"I really don't think that's necessary –"

"Read it. I knew you when you were a pimply-faced teenager with an attitude problem, young man. Show me the respect I deserve." Titters break out in her stafftourage.

I scan the paper and read. "*Wanna do a 68? You go down on me, and then I'll owe you one. I am so sorry. I apologize. Yes, it was my mistake. We're removing them, and I'd love to talk to you about how our new algorithm for analyzing options –*"

She breaks in. "And do you know what my colleague's fortune said?"

It's a lost cause. "What did it say?" I cross my arms and try to look apologetically confident.

She points her chin at him, and he hands me the paper. I read it. "*There were nine planets in the Universe, but they agreed to take it down to eight because I'm going to destroy, ah, Uranus.*"

She snorts. "And that one doesn't even make sense. Pluto is not a planet anymore, but a planetoid, so there would only be eight to start, Carter. At least next time hire a perverted bakery that knows their astronomy."

I'm not sure, but I think I hear one of her entourage mutter, "ASS-tronomy." Muffled giggles and "shush" sounds happen.

I can't believe this. I've planned for this night for so long, not just for the charity, but because I want to get Mrs. Baker into financial bed with my company. And now it's all fucked to hell because of some idiot baker who gave me God knows whose shitty-ass fortunes.

Nate steps in, all unctuous placation, and takes her hand, acting like some patronizing elder statesman instead of a thirty-year-old. "Caroline. My brother may be no genius when it comes to fake fortunes, but he has a real gift for reading the futures of the stock market."

She pulls her hand from his. "Mistakes like this don't happen to people who execute flawlessly. I'll stay and donate to the charity, but I'm going to give some hard thought as to whether I want to do business with you." She sniffs and walks away, although I think I see her stifle a smile.

The same intern whispers, "She said HARD," and giggles with his counterpart before they scamper after her.

FUCK.

I'm seething.

Nate and I make the rounds, and it's not as bad as all that: Although a few people walked out, other guests who read the dirty fortunes loved them. Thank God that many of our clients are pervs with a good sense of humor. In fact, and this is an unexpected relief – I get so many requests for business cards that I have to text Marconi to bring me another batch from my backup stash.

Someone tells me that I really know how to appeal to the younger investors. Another person tells me that I have an edgy, bold flair that sets me apart from the competition. One guy asks if he can get the basket of unopened ones for his weekly poker night, and when I say no, he says, "At least tell me where you got them."

And that raises an excellent question. Who, indeed, is responsible for this fortune almost-fiasco?

While the guests are eating and a guest speaker is extolling the virtues of donating to childhood foundations, I text Marconi. *Look up the name of the baker who fucked me tonight.*

It's not even twenty seconds before his reply comes across the screen, practically making my phone vibrate in sympathy. *Mr. Hudson I am so incredibly sorry I was not on top of this please give me a chance to make this right. It's Caked With Love, and the owner is Arie Blair.*

He shoots me the website, and I ignore the cute frolicking lacey logo and go right to the "Arie's Bio" to see the idiot herself. It's like when a person cuts me off in traffic, weaving and driving like a drunken douche squirrel, I have to pass – but it's imperative that I look over to get a good look at the asshole in person. Just passing? That's not nearly as satisfying.

But when I pull up the page and see her picture, it's like a punch to the gut. Arie Blair is the girl from this morning, the one who sassed me about the bike and gave me napkins to clean my fingers. I can't believe this. How in the fucking world?

She's gorgeous in the picture, almost as pretty as in real life. Her long red-blond curls are loose on her shoulders, and her blue eyes look like the sky, even on my phone screen. I stare at her luscious kissable lips that I immediately imagine wrapped around my dick.

Marconi texts again. *Do you want me to call her right now or tomorrow to complain? Or I'll go in person tomorrow when they open.*

Nate thinks I need to have fun? To liven things up? I can do that. And there's no way in hell I'm passing up a chance to meet Arie Blair again. If fortune is offering this to me, I'm taking.

A smile spreads across my face. I bite my lip and put one foot up on my opposite knee while I type back. *I'll take care of this one myself.*

Arie

The bistro tables and metal chairs with curled floral edgings are filled with my breakfast crew. Since I started serving coffee and croissants, morning business has boomed.

"I feel good," I tell Myler. "I think we've turned the corner into supreme profits. I can feel it. A good recommendation from the Carter Hudson team on Yelp could totally level us up." I wave to a few customers who leave, and add, "I need to call them this morning and see how it went."

"I love that you do a personal follow up." Myler pulls a tray out of the glassy display, and deftly arranges a four by six display of Cherry Surprise cupcakes from her rolling cart.

"I think it sets us apart. We're in the business of building good customer relationships." I crouch down to help, loading a fresh batch of Birthday Cake Sprinkle Joys from her cart onto another tray. "Personalized service makes a difference."

"Oh, is that what you call it?" A deep voice startles me and I bump my head on Myler's tray as I stand.

"Ouch! Ow. No, I'm fine." I rub my temple. "Hello, can I help…you." My voice trails off because it's him. The guy from the supermarket.

He's even sexier today, if possible, in blue jeans and a black sweater that clings to his muscular arms and chest. I know I'm staring, but I honestly can't stop. He's drool worthy. He runs a hand over his stubbly beard as he regards me.

I'm entranced by his eyes. "It's you. Bike Guy. From the store. I gave you napkins." I hesitate. "You remember me from the store?" I blush.

"Yes, that's right." His mouth twitches into a grin. "I definitely remember you." His eyes study mine. "I even offered to tutor you. And I guess," he glances at the samples of fortune cookies, "you must be Fortune Cookie Girl."

"Otherwise known as Arie Blair." I whip off my plastic glove, wipe my hand on my jeans, and stick it over the counter. "And you are?"

"Someone who'd like to talk to you about a large, important order of fortune cookies." He takes my hand and I feel the sparks, just like the other day. I try not to gasp. His hand is warm and firm and he holds it just a second longer than necessary before he lets go.

"Oh! Yes. Okay." I swallow. Part of me hoped he tracked me

down because he liked me, not because he wanted to order baked goods. But it's fine. "I'd love to talk to you right now, and get an idea of what you're looking for. And then, I'll get my laptop and show you samples and prices. Unless – you'd prefer to talk later?"

"Let's talk right now." He crosses his arms over his chest. "Unless you're busy preparing for a bachelor party or something."

"Now is fine. Myler will watch the counter, right?" I grab my client notebook from the lower back cabinet.

She nods, so I come out from the half-door and gesture to a table. "Can I get you some coffee?"

"No." He sits down, leans back, and crosses his arms again. "Tell me about your quality control." A little smiles plays on his lips. If he'd said anything else, I'd swear he was undressing me with his eyes. His thighs look powerful in the denim, and between them there's a good-sized – I flush, not wanting to be obvious about checking out his body.

"My quality control?" I daydreamed about him, and now he's here, but he's not asking me for a date, he's grilling me about – I don't know. Is he going to hire me?

"Sure." He raises an eyebrow. "Let's say I ordered, oh, one thousand three hundred twenty five custom fortune cookies for an important financial event, and asked for phrases and saying about success and hard work. How would you assure me that I wouldn't somehow get something, let's see, like this."

He pulls a wad of little strips from his pocket and dumps them onto the table between us, where they start to curl outward slowly, drowsy snakes unfurling.

He clears his throat and reads. "If I'm a pain in your ass…we can add more lube."

A horrible feeling lurches through my gut. Oh my fucking god. Oh, no way. No, no way.

My eyes must widen because he puts up a hand. "No, no, just let me read you a few more. Oh, this one's really special. Imagine if a very conservative client found this little delight. I'm no weatherman, but you can expect a few inches tonight. Or my personal favorite, I must say, Every exit is an entrance for new experiences. For example, the anus." He smiles. "I'm Carter Hudson. You sent some really filthy fortune cookies to my important donation banquet last night."

I clap a hand to my mouth and gaze around the restaurant in dismay, but no help is forthcoming. I look back at him. "Those are for next week! We saved them in the back, in a box. It was labeled, *Matt's Bachelor Party*. There's no way."

"Apparently, miracles do happen, because these were they very fortunes that ended up at my fundraiser gala last night. And lost me a very important client, I might add."

"But we sent you all of the good ones! The regular ones." I half stand up, craning my neck to look at the entrance to the kitchen. I'm positive that box of inappropriate fortunes is right where I left it.

"Oh, you did. After the event, my friends and I opened a lot of them, and found that most of them were the ones I'd ordered. It was obvious, though, that special ones had been mixed in with the good ones." He does air quotes on "special" and raises one eyebrow.

"I'm so sorry." I don't even know what to say. "I can," and this makes me die a little inside, but it's unavoidable, "refund your money. Give you a discount. I'm so sorry."

Giving his money back will be a blow to my finances, but how can I not offer? My voice is frantic. "I don't even understand how it happened. I had that box separate, with a huge label. I was so careful."

Then I remember helping Jitters load boxes, how I was stressed and still thinking about the fuse and the flour, the guy with the bike. I distinctly remember taking that box anyway. I was going to put it aside. Then I must have handed it to Jitters, like a stupid weird robot on drugs. Gah! I'm an idiot. Myler is right. It's clearly well past the time to hire another assistant. If I'd done that earlier, I could have avoided this mess.

He looks around the bakery, and I wonder what he sees. Standing up, I put my hands flat on the table. "I'll do a PayPal refund today. Please accept my apologies. This is the first time this has ever happened, and I take full responsibility. I'll make sure it won't happen again." I swallow hard, imagining ways to recover.

One time, I saw this meme on Facebook. It was a picture of a chalkboard menu sign outside a café: Try the sub sandwich that one

Yelp reviewer called the worst thing he's ever eaten! The guy's humor actually gained him new fans and business. Could that work here?

"Sit back down," he orders, then, at my expression, tempers it with a "please" and a half-smile, his hands up, so I do. This time I cross my arm and tap my foot. How is it possible that even now, I'm entranced with his lips?

"It's not the end of the world," he says thoughtfully. "I lost the big client I wanted, but the dirty fortunes actually appealed to some people and I gained some clients."

"So do you want the refund, or don't you?" I almost don't care anymore about the refund, as long as I get to look at his face, listen to his voice.

"Well, I don't feel it would be fair to penalize you for the full amount." He grins. "I'd accept a forty percent refund, because the clients I lost didn't quite make up for the ones I gained."

I open my mouth to agree, but he adds, "And you'll meet me for dinner." He leans in across the table and his cologne wafts over to me, a tantalizing aroma, sexy and spicy. "Okay?" His eyes are clear. Those lashes.

"I'll do what?" I feel a slow burn start in my stomach and spread lower. Oh, God. I look at his lips and imagine them on mine, his hands stroking my bare skin. Maybe he likes me after all.

"As my baker. I'm trying one last effort to win back my biggest lost client. I'll need the real fortunes." He raises an eyebrow. "I'd like you to hand-deliver them yourself. A batch of ten. No mistakes."

"Oh. I see! I can do that." I flush hard. He wasn't asking me to dinner, dinner. Duh. I take a deep breath to steady myself. Easy.

"And if I get her back, I'll refund you the refund."

"Uh…okay." Now I'm a little confused. "So when is this event?"

"She's available tomorrow night. We're meeting at Chez Joel. Be there at eight pm with the cookies. And wear something nice." He looks me up and down, at my jeans and T, and smirks.

I stick up my chin. "And you assume I'm available just because you say so?"

"Well, are you?" His voice is lower, intimate.

I flush. I don't know what he's asking. From the look on his face,

I'm not sure he does, either. My hands are on the table in front of me, and his are on the table too. I stare at his fingers, willing them closer. I want to touch him.

And like magic, he leans in and puts both of his hands on mine. The impact is instantaneous. I gasp, and he doesn't smile. His face is serious as he watches me. "Are you available?" he asks, and I feel like he wants to know more than about a dinner date.

"Maybe," I say softly. My heartbeat is staccato, a hummingbird. I can't think. His skin is soft, warm. He brushes my thumb with his. "Are you?" I ask.

"Maybe," he repeats my words, and smiles. "I'd really like to see you. For you to come. Tomorrow. Will you?" His eyes are intense.

"Okay." I breathe out, soft. "I'll bring the cookies to your dinner tomorrow."

Carter

While I wait for Caroline, I sip a glass of whiskey and scan my phone for urgent texts from clients. Then I check the door, but it's not Caroline I hope to see. I want Arie. Since I talked to her in the bakery, she's all I can think about. Maybe it's insane, but I'm already into this girl, even though I don't know her. I shouldn't have teased her that way, maybe, but hell, it was fun seeing her blush. I want to give her attitude, and then I want her to give me attitude, like with the bike. Then I want to fuck it out of her. Then I want to do it all over again.

God, I hope she comes tonight.

"Carter." Caroline takes my hand in her wrinkled one. Her face is lined but her eyes are shrewd and bright, light.

"Caroline. Thank you for meeting me." I gesture at the table. "I appreciate the second chance."

"Yes." Her voice is dry. She raises a hand, nearly imperceptible, but the nod of her head has the waiter at her side. "We'll take a bottle of the Mount Eden Vineyards Chardonnay." She looks at me. "When your father and I used to have lunch, this is the wine we'd order."

"I didn't realize you knew each other that well." My brow creases as I try to understand this revelation. My dad sparred with her for years. She was his nemesis, always evading his attempts to reel her in as a client.

"There are many things people don't know about each other," she replies, and her voice is a little distant.

"I'm sure." I glance around the room.

"Are you looking for someone?" She tastes the wine; nods at the waiter. He pours and disappears. "I hope you didn't invite your brother. One Hudson at a time. My personal limit."

"That's fair. I asked the baker to deliver the real fortune cookies here. I'm just," and I clear my throat, "seeing if she arrived yet."

"Young man, I've been on this earth longer than a while, and I don't take offense at many things. The cookies were nothing."

"You certainly seemed offended." Arie's not here. Maybe she won't come at all. The truth is that I don't really give a fuck about the cookies, not anymore. If I never hear the word "cookie" again, I can die a happy man. It's just that, well, I want to see her again. Just to find out if that spark I felt is still there. Because –

"I was disappointed that you thought cookies with fortunes were the best way to impress me, and irritated you then assumed accidental vulgar words would color my entire perception of your abilities and personality. Surely you can do better."

I nod. "I'd like a chance to try."

"Send me your proposal. If I like what I see, I'll call for more details. We'll have lunch and discuss it."

"That's what you always said to Dad. But you never hired him." I raise an eyebrow.

She laughs. "It was more fun that way. Then we could get together for wine and gossip about obnoxious people we know. Share advice."

"Dad did that?" My voice rises despite my best efforts.

She nods. "I believe he enjoyed my company more than he wanted my business. And he was far too erratic with his options trades, in my opinion."

I blink. That my father had friends – that this woman was his friend – never crossed my mind. New ideas burst forth. "So you were partners, after all. Just not in a financial way."

"You could say that," she says. "I recommend the sole meunière. It's never overdone and the sauce is miraculous." She takes off her spectacles. "Carter, there are many relationships in the business world, and not all of them involve monetary exchange. It's possible to help each other out without trading a dime."

"No, I know that." But do I? Maybe this is what Dad meant when he told us we'd grow into the business. He lectured to us often, from his hospital bed. There was a grace to him, and below the surface he carried an entire universe of knowledge. When he died, and that went with him, it felt like losing something as critical as an arm. We didn't just lose a father, we lost our foundation.

It's his business still, but entirely not his, because now it's mine and Nate's, run by our thoughts, our personalities, our relationships. A sudden burst of clarity makes me realize that we need to work harder at building the bonds between people, just as hard as pushing the financial transactions. That was the glue my dad had, the magic that kept it all together. Nate has that. I need more of it.

"But I'm definitely more conservative than he is in my trade choices, so I think you'll be pleased," I can't help but add.

I feel a presence at my shoulder and turn, and there she is. Arie. Dressed in a tight black dress and silver heels, her hair loose and flowing on her shoulder, she's like some goddess. I stare. I don't want conservative now.

"Arie." My voice comes out hoarse, and I clear my throat. I stand to greet her, lean in, and kiss her cheek. She smells of perfume, something sweet and musky, and I can barely resist the urge to bite her neck, lick her skin, take her lips with mine.

Yeah, the attraction is real. I feel it, she feels it. Fuck, probably everyone in the room feels it. I see the pulse beating in her throat. I want to touch the hollow there, but I step back. Thank God she showed up, even though I was a dick. She surely can see from my eyes that it's not the cookies I care about.

I pull myself together to do introductions. "Caroline, this is Arie. Arie, Caroline."

Arie has a fancy box in her hands tied with a ribbon. "It's so nice to meet you. I'd like to apologize for the fortunes. Here are the ones I was supposed to deliver." She hands over the package.

Caroline snorts. "You two are completely fixated on these, aren't you? Join us." She gestures at the table.

Arie bites her lip, looks at me. It's like she needs to hear it.

"Please." My voice is firm. "I want you to." Our eyes lock and something sparks between us, and I know she knows. And for some reason, although we've not spoken more than a handful of words together in our lives, I feel that I've known her longer, or that fate means for us to have something together. Because against all reason, against all normal human interactions, something about Arie makes me feel comfortable and right.

I can't say that trite phrase, "I feel like I've known her forever," because that's simply not so. But there's a feeling there I can't describe. I don't believe in love at first sight, but sometimes you just fucking click with another person, and the sound of you and them falling into place reverberates through your entire brain and body and soul, making echoes that come out through your eyes.

"Well, then, all right. Thank you." She smooths her dress down her thighs and although it's not an obviously provocative gesture, I can't help but feel my arousal grow. Her belly has just the slightest curve and her arms are toned. The swerve of her calf transfixes me. I can't stop looking.

Caroline smiles. "Tell me about your bakery."

Arie looks up fast. "My bakery?" She flushes. "Can I just tell you how entirely sorry I am that–"

"No, you can't." Caroline lifts her fork and puts it down, firmly. "Both of you. You're like sweet fluffy baby chicks walking on an expressway. Listen. Mistakes happen. Own them. Learn from them. Use them. You're here, with me," and she gestures grandly. "Use this opportunity, Arie, to sell me your products. And you, Carter. Take advantage of the people who thought those cookies were hilarious. Offer discounts to those who didn't. Use the mistake to your advantage. No publicity is bad publicity. Work it like it's an opportunity, not a setback. Next time someone bitch-slaps you in public, handle it like a boss and get charge of the situation. I'll tell you how."

I nod. Okay, so she wants to be a mentor. I can use a mentor. Maybe this is the kind of thing Dad meant when he told us, "Find the people who matter, all of them, and keep them close."

"Uh, okay." Arie swallows. "Great! So, okay." She takes a breath and starts talking.

By the end of the meal, Arie has obtained a promise from Caroline to use her bakery for the next event she needs desserts catered in exchange for a five percent discount.

Caro (we're on a nickname basis now) smiles at me when she leaves, and I get the feeling that she's never going to hire me as her financial advisor, but that we're going to have a long and mutually satisfying relationship, regardless.

It's just me and Arie, looking at each other across the dimly lit room. And now that we're alone, I don't know what to say. So I blurt out the first thing that comes to mind. "Want to come back to my place?"

Arie

"To your place?" I put a hand to my cheek, feeling it redden. Sure, I want to, but that's a bold move on his part, especially since our only big conversation so far revolved around a refund of a refund. And since he originally invited me here as his baker.

"Yeah." He eyes me and smiles. "Just for a drink. You and me. Let's talk, get to know each other. I just – I feel like there's something here, you know?"

He's confident, but under it there's something else, a need I recognize, a desire that matches the one inside of me. And that makes it easy to say, "Yes."

He puts his hand on top of mine and leans in, his dark eyes flashing. "I'll drive you and we can come back for your car, later."

My stomach leaps into a flurry of excitement, wondering what might happen before the "later" and whether it will be along the lines of my fantasies, late at night, in bed. But I simply nod.

My car is safe in the lot here, and when he looks at me sideways from the driver's seat of his Panamara 4S and grins, I melt inside. Yeah, there's something about him that I crave on a fundamental level.

Sometimes two people just fit so well that they seem meant to be together. Except that it's random, life is, and probably nobody is "meant" to be anything. Fate doesn't exist, and who knows if karma is real. Life is chaotic and strange, and we're all just hanging onto this spinning globe by our fingernails. And despite all that, sometimes two halves of the same whole find each other. And that is more magical than fate; it's nothing short of miraculous that those two souls — in all these billions of humans crowding the globe – find a matching heartbeat. If you find that person who fits you, you need to try your goddamned best to make it work because that it is it– your one snowflake from a blizzard, your one perfect moment to fly. Your one chance. You don't let that pass.

I'm not going to let this pass.

He has an apartment downtown near the lake, and the lights of the city are breathtaking, sparking in the black like fireflies of desire, buoying my desire for him higher, ratcheting the tension between us taut. A wire, ready to snap.

"Wine?" He pours something red into glasses and I taste it without taste, because all I can focus on are his lips on the wine, and my brain is consumed with wondering how he would taste. I want him so badly I'm ready to cry out.

We talk, and it's both inconsequential and weighty, because each word we trade lingers in the air between us, bridging the gap between our bodies, creating a twisted cable of ideas that pull us closer and closer, inch by inch, until his lips hover over mine. Our glasses are gone and his hands are holding mine, and he whispers, "Arie?" and all I need to do is smile into his mouth and nod, and now there's no distance between us at all.

His mouth is warm and skilled, his tongue playing mine, teasing me, and he tastes like the wine, grapes exploding on my tongue into their full flavor, all of the undertones of cherry and leather and sunshine they talk about in catalogues, but it's mine now. He's mine.

He wraps one hand in my hair and tugs me closer to him, even closer, and we're kissing so tightly that there's no air, we're sharing one breath, and when we break apart, panting, the feral look in his eyes sends a spire of desire right to that place between my thighs, an arrow of urgent need.

His hand glides up my thigh, his fingers lingering at the apex, before he gently pushes aside my panties and finds my wetness, touching softly at first, then more boldly, and I spread for him, a moan on my lips.

"You like that?" He murmurs and I nod, tossing my head back, eyes closed, leaning back onto the couch. He bends over me to take my lips again, running his fingers up my belly to touch my breasts under the dress, drawing my moisture along my body with his fingers, his magic touch. His other hand is in my hair again, tangling, playing, and he strokes my cheek before he devours my mouth. This kiss is more passionate than the last, and when he breaks it to bite my neck, I cry out in pleasure, arching my body up to him.

I run both of my hands over his strong shoulders, his powerful arms. I can feel the muscles under his suit, and I squeeze hard, wanting to be skin to skin with him; run my hands over his ass through his pants, then grab him in for a fierce hug. He laughs but returns it, then splays his hand across my stomach. "Arie? Can I take you to my bedroom?" His eyes are liquid lust and I nod. Yes, please. Please.

I scream out in a startled laugh as he scoops me up, but I'm light in his arms, and he kisses me as we walk, our mouths merging, and he drops me onto the bed with the rough order, "Stand up and strip for me." His eyes are so full of passion and light that it's an order I willingly obey, shimmying my dress up and over so I stand there in just my lacey panties. He growls and grabs me to him, cupping both of my ass cheeks in his hands as he takes my mouth, pulling me up and into his body so I can feel his hard arousal between my thighs.

"Take off your clothes," I demand, when we break for air, and he nods and does it: Cufflinks, shirt. Pants. When he's just in his boxer briefs, I catch my breath. He's ripped with a 6-pack of a top athlete, his muscles are perfection.

"You like what you see?" he teases.

I nod. "So far, so good. Keep going." My voice is low and full of desire.

When his shorts come off, my eyes widen in surprise and pleasure: He's big and thick, gorgeous. And I've never wanted a man more. He stalks toward me and gestures – lie down. I do, putting my arms above my head on the pillow and spreading my hair out, hoping he'll find it sexy. I know he does, because the growl he makes as he straddles my hips tells me more than any words could.

He pushes his cock into the warmth of my body, resting against the crotch of my panties, and teases me slowly, drawing his body up and down, pushing against me, then away, until I'm moaning, little breathy sounds of passion. When he bends his dark head down and flicks my nipple with his tongue, I cry out his name, so he does it again, and again, and again, until I'm squirming under him. He bites down and I gasp with the small pop of pain, delighted at how it sends a burst of pleasure through my entire body.

"Like that?" he asks, and when I nod he licks and bites the other one until I'm almost crying with need. But then he slides down my body, pulling my panties down to mid-thigh, and spreads them as far as the fabric allows, and puts his face into my body. "Let's see how well I can lick you with these on," he suggests, and his tongue barely flicks my most sensitive skin, making me wail out in pleasure. I need more, I want more, and I try to open my legs further, but I'm trapped, bound in my own lingerie.

He laughs and uses a finger to stroke the place I need a touch, but continues to tease me with the tiniest flicks of his tongue, and soon I'm delirious with desire. I'm going to die if I don't get more than I'm getting. The feeling is building so slowly that it's painfully powerful and I can't take it, I need more, I need release.

"Please, take off my panties, please," I pant.

"Where do you want my tongue?" he whispers. "Tell me."

"Where it is, but more," I urge him.

"Say it," he demands, pushing up on his forearms to look into my eyes.

"My pussy," I whisper back, feeling my face redden, but I don't care because I need him so badly. "Carter, please. I'll do anything."

He moves back down my body and tugs the fabric lower until it's around my ankles, but then he winds the fabric over itself until my ankles are tightly bound and I can't spread them at all. I make a sound of surprise and he orders, "Onto your hands and knees. Your turn." Then he smiles at me, a sly smile, and he deliberately lies back and puts his hands behind his head on the pillow, his cock jutting up, strong and thick. "Do a good job and I'll untie you and finish my job," he says, raising one eyebrow.

I could take my legs out of the panties in a heartbeat, but I want this, so I nod and crawl forward until my hair brushes his body. "Your wish is my command," I murmur, and smile to see his eyes darken with desire and his cock harden even further. I suck his nipple like he did mine, then trace my tongue across his belly, the dips and flats of his abs. He sucks in a breath as I move my mouth down his hip, dropping kisses and bites, until I reach his groin. When I take him into my mouth, he groans and flexes his thighs, and I know he's mine.

I suck and use my tongue on him, doing my best to drive him insane, repeating the things that make him grunt and clench his muscles, until I can feel the tension in him, wound so hard he's ready to explode. I pop him out of my mouth for a second and turn myself around, so my ass is presented to his face, my knees beside his body, and lean back down to continue licking.

"God, Arie," he moans and puts both hands on me immediately, running them over my ass, touching, squeezing. He slides a finger into my pussy and I groan around my mouthful and push my hips back towards him, so he does it again, finding a rhythm that matches mine; when my head goes down on his cock, his fingers go out; when I come back up, he goes in. He moves his hand forward so his fingers brush my clit and I cry out; I'm close, so close. With his other hand, he slaps my ass, a hard crack that echoes around the room, and the mix of pain and pleasure makes me even more insane with want.

I come up for air. "Carter, please, I'm going to come," I wail, and I don't know if it's a warning or a plea.

"Not yet," he orders. "Suck me again. Don't come." I put my head back down and continue, and this time he doesn't touch my pussy, but spanks me again. The need to come fades just a bit, but in a different way, my arousal is further whetted. The sting on my ass is making me crazy for him, and the whole scene – wet panties around my ankles, the smell of his sex, the feeling of his fingers, the illicit dirtiness of this – is overwhelming me. "Tell me when you're ready," he says, and I murmur something incoherent as he strokes my skin, touching me, teasing me.

Finally, he pulls me up. "I'm going to fuck you now, Arie. Lie back." I didn't say I was ready, but I am; he can tell.

I'm delirious with relief and passion and when he pulls the fabric from my ankles and spreads my thighs, I'm dying for his cock. When I feel his tongue instead, I scream with the soft touch on my clit. "I just need a taste," he says, his voice hoarse and fierce. "Your smell has me wild." He thrusts into me with his tongue, firm and strong, and swipes across my clit again.

I scream and twist in his arms; it's too much, but I love it. I want less and more at the same time. I can't take any more of this, but then he's back up, his mouth taking mine in rough possession, tasting of me and still the wine from earlier. He rolls on a condom and his cock slides into me, hot and tight, and we both exhale a breath at the same time, and when he starts moving, it's the best bliss I can imagine.

I usually close my eyes at orgasm, but this time I want to see, I want to see him come. I want to see him burst with passion for me, and we lock eyes. It's too intimate but I can't look away. He reaches down to finger my clit and says, "Come," and I let go, tossing back my head and closing my eyes finally as the feeling surges and bursts in an unreal explosion. He comes too, and gives a rough cry, his body so hard and tense on mine, and then we fall together side by side, spent, letting the bliss flow over us.

It's fast, but it's right. And when he reaches over and grabs my hand and kisses it, still out of breath, my heart melts and I'm confident that this night is a beginning, not an end.

Arie

"I'm so glad we met at that grocery store exactly one year ago today," he says, kissing me on the mouth.

I blush and touch his face. "Happy one year dating anniversary to you, too. I got you a present." I smile at him and bounce on my toes.

"Oh, you did?" His voice goes low and husky. "Can I unwrap it right now?" He undoes the top button of my blouse and flicks the material aside. "Can I guess what it is?" He drops a kiss onto my neck, letting his lips linger.

I close my eyes and sigh, enjoying the feel of his mouth and his hands on my body. "Of course. You get three tries."

"Oh, I do? Just three?" He opens another button and cups my breast through the bra. "Here's one." He reaches back to squeeze my ass. "Two." Then he strokes the front of my skirt right at the apex of my thighs, a touch that melts me even through the fabric. "And three. How about these three?"

"Good choices," I murmur, grabbing both of his ass cheeks through his jeans. I'll never get tired of his ass – so hard and sexy. "But there's something else, too."

"Something else? Really?" He bites my earlobe and I squeak out.

"A real thing! A present."

"Oh, this is as real as it gets," he argues, and smacks my ass once. I yelp. "Something in a box."

"I want the box," he agrees, and laughs, rubbing more insistently.

I push his hand back. "First you can open this, though. Then you can have my...box. You're gross."

"You love it." He's arrogant and confident and he's right. I do love it. But I really want to give him his present.

I grab a gift bag from the counter and thrust it at him. "Here. You can open it now."

"For me?" His face lights up, eager, like a kid at Christmas, and he grabs out the fluffed up tissue paper and tosses it to the floor. "I still have no idea why you women put this crap in here." But he's pawing through it to get to the prize. "What it is?" He pulls out the small black velvet box and shakes it. "I hope it's a jeweled butt plug that I get to put into your ass."

"Stop! It's not that. If I get you that, you're not going to find it in a box. I'll surprise you by wearing it to bed one night."

His hands freeze on the bag. "Really?" I've never heard a more interested voice.

"Yes, but right now focus on the present. Come on!" I can't wait to see how he likes it.

"Fine." He flips the lip open. "Aw, Arie, that's sweet." He takes it out.

"It's for your desk," I say, suddenly nervous that he won't like it. That it's dumb. "Like a paperweight thingie. Decoration, I guess. To be cute. Although, I mean, if you don't like it, you can just leave it… on the counter." I wave around the room.

"Babe, it's awesome." He smiles and kisses me. His beard tickles but I love it.

I've given him a silver-plated fortune cookie with our names inscribed on it, and a fortune on paper wound through it: "I love you."

Fortunes have become our joke, now, along with refunds. Sometimes when we're in bed, I'll tease him: "You still owe me a forty percent refund, you know." And he'll say something really awesome and dirty like, "Sorry, babe, I only give one hundred percent all the time. Here's your refund right now. Enjoy." Bam. Or maybe, "You can get as much refund as you can suck out of my nice hard dick, Arie." And then he'll stick his cock in my mouth, or my pussy. You get the idea. It's fun. We have fun. Oh, we spend a lot of time talking – our conversations range from politics to literature to TV shows. We argue and laugh. Ever since that first night when we drank wine and made love, those first few words together were the start of a waterfall of sentences, torrents of thoughts that we share on a daily basis.

But the sex is fantastic, and I'm not sorry to say it.

"I'll put it at work tomorrow," he promises. "And I don't care how many jokes Nate and the guys make about it."

"They won't!"

"Uh, probably. I can see it now. They're all going to take turns putting horrible fortunes in there. But it's all good." He smiles and puts the box on the counter. Then he looks at me. "I got you something, too."

"You did?" I'm excited. We discussed dinner for our one-year anniversary, but said we wouldn't do gifts. I cheated by getting him this one. I have no idea what he's giving me.

He pulls a small box out of his pocket, smaller than the one I gave him. My heart starts to hammer in my chest.

"Is it earrings?" I babble. "I love earrings. Everyone knows that they're a perfect gift. Or a keychain." I give a weak giggle. I can't breathe. I don't want to assume anything.

There's a stain of red on his face and I think I see his fingers tremble. Oh, God.

"It's not earrings," he says, his voice low. "Or a keychain. It's a promise."

"A promise?"

He nods, and takes my hand. "A promise to be yours forever, and to take care of you as long as I can. A promise to stick by you, even if the wrong fortunes get delivered to our doorstep. What do you say?"

He lets go of my hand and gives me the box. When I open it, I can't see anything, because tears blur my eyes, but when I blink, there's a diamond on a platinum band, a simple beautiful diamond. And there's all the love in the world, everything I've ever wanted.

"Yes," I say. "Yes."

"Yes?" He stands up and takes me into his arms.

I was right when I met him; I felt that we belonged together, and it was true. We fit, we work, we complete each other in ways I could never have imagined. I don't believe in fate, but I do believe in grabbing opportunities while they're there. And I can't deny that some part of me feels that fortune has been smiling on us.

"Yes." I reach up to kiss him, and nothing has ever felt more right. Together, we will make our own fortunes.

About Alexis Alvarez

Alexis Alvarez is an author, photographer, and digital designer who loves writing steamy romances. Her female heroines are always strong, intelligent women who fall for the sexiest guy around…and get the happy-ever-after ending of their dreams.

You can usually find Alexis hanging out with her family or her sisters, who are also romance writers, at their website, Graffiti Fiction. The three of them love to drink wine together and laugh like hyenas while making dirty jokes and inappropriate comments. Their mom is very proud.

Alexis loves meeting new people on Facebook, so please come on by and say hello. Thanks and happy reading!

Website: graffitifiction.com

Facebook Author Page: www.facebook.com/AlexisAlvarezAuthor

Goodreads: www.goodreads.com/author/show/14127116.Alexis_Alvarez

Twitter: twitter.com/AlexisAlvarezWr

Instagram: www.instagram.com/alexis_alvarez_writer

The Beard Made Me Do It

BY SCOTT HILDRETH

Chapter One

7:21 p.m. Saturday

"WE'RE GOING TO NEED A COMPLETE STATEMENT," THE detective stated flatly. "Something that makes sense. So far, all we've got from you is a bunch of jibberish. We can't go to the District Attorney's office with what you've given us. We need more. A lot more. You're in a world of shit, missy. Now, help us help you."

There were at least two problems. One, I didn't want them to go to the attorney's office. And, two, if I told them the complete truth, I'd be stuck in prison.

Visions of being prison bitch to some woman named Bad Betty filled my mind. Within a matter of seconds, I began to blurt out lies infused with bits and pieces of the truth.

Only because I knew I'd never make it in prison.

Well, that, and the fact I really, really liked Bradley.

And his beard.

"What do you mean, help you help me?"

Cop number two sat down across from me. He smelled like fast food and unwashed polyester, which made sense considering the fact his suit was grease-stained and made of the age-old fabric. I glanced at cop number one.

He shrugged.

I lowered my head for a moment, feigned deep thought, and looked up. The interrogation room was just like what I had seen on T.V. – small with windows on one side and a stainless steel table in the center.

A table I was handcuffed to.

Cop number two cleared his throat. "We don't want to see you take the fall for the crime. We know you weren't involved. But, if you don't help us get the man who is involved, you're all we've got. So, you'll go down for the crime. We want to help you walk out of here, but we need your help to make that happen. Does that make sense?"

I lifted my head. "I suppose."

"Now," he said. "Tell us exactly what happened, and don't leave any details out. Try to remember *everything*."

I nodded. "Okay. The truth, right?"

He shook his head. "We can't help you if you lie to us."

I looked at cop number one. He tossed his hands in the air. "Let's lock her up."

"Hold on," I blurted. "I'll tell you everything."

"Start talking," cop number one said.

I nodded, and then relaxed into the chair as much as the handcuffs would allow. "Okay." I sighed lightly. "I was walking, and this guy came running up behind me. He was in a big hurry."

Cop number two cocked an eyebrow. "At the bank on Tenth and Cormack?"

"Yes. Well, around the corner from the bank."

"Continue."

"I was just out walking. I do it all the time. So, I was walking by, and he came up and handed me this bag. He pointed the gun at me, and said *here, hold this or I'll drop you where you stand.*"

"And what did you take that to mean? What did you think that he meant by that?"

"He was going to shoot me if I didn't accept the bag."

"What happened next?"

"I took the bag, followed him—"

Cop number two interrupted. "Did he say you *had* to follow him?"

"He had a gun, remember?"

He nodded. "Continue."

"So, I followed him to the car, and I tossed the money in the back. In the trunk. And then he said *get in or die.* Those exact words."

"And you got in?"

"Uh huh. I didn't think I had a choice. Basically, he took me hostage."

Cop number one came to the edge of the table, leaned over, and looked right at me.

"The silent alarm sounded at 6:01. At 6:08, there were officers on the scene. He – and you – were gone. You were apprehended at 6:28. What happened for those twenty minutes? What did he talk about? Did you hear anything about what his name was or where he was going? Did anyone call him?"

"Oh, yeah," I lied. "He got a phone call."

"Did you overhear anything?"

"Well," I feigned deep thought. "He said *this is Steve* when he answered, so his name must be Steve. And, he said *meet me at the warehouse on 143rd and Racine.*"

Cop number two's eyes shot wide. "143rd and Racine?"

143rd and Racine was actually ten miles from where we were at the time, but it was pretty obvious they knew nothing regarding who Bradley was or where he was going. I nodded nonetheless. "That's what he said."

"And then what happened?"

"Well, we were at the corner of 13th and, I don't know, about

Belfast, I think. He turned the wheel, smashed the gas, and spun the car really fast in a circle. While it was spinning, he reached over and opened my door. That's when I spilled out in the street."

"Where was the gun?'

I returned a confused look. "When?"

"If he was steering with one hand, and opening the door with another, where was the gun?"

I shrugged. "I have no idea."

They looked at each other, shared a silent moment, and then cop number two looked at me. "So, you weren't with him earlier in the night?"

"Oh, no. Not at all," I lied.

"And, you weren't an accomplice?"

I shook my head. "A hostage. I was a hostage."

He pursed his lips, eventually nodded his head, and then unlocked the handcuffs. "Alright. You're free to go. See the desk sergeant to get your cell phone and purse."

I stood up and looked around the room. "Just like that, I can go?"

"Yeah," he said. "But don't leave town. We may have some other questions."

"Okay," I said with a shrug. "I'll be at home or at work."

And, just like that it was over.

The interrogation, anyway.

But, it was at that moment that my life, for the most part, began.

Chapter Two

4:02 p.m. Saturday

I grinned a grin until it hurt, and thanked God that Josh was no longer a part of my life. Shari and I decided if there was one sure-fire way to rid myself of the memories of him, a celebration at the neighborhood tavern was it.

We'd been planning it for over a week.

"Here, drink it." She handed me a shot of something milky. "The douchebag is finally gone."

"What is it?"

"Rumchata. Just drink it."

"Okay."

"Here's to no more Josh." She raised her glass.

"Hear, hear," I said. I downed the cinnamon-flavored drink and slammed the glass down on the table.

It felt good to be rid of the asshole who had done his best to intimidate me, control me, and limit my activities away from home.

The bar was mere blocks from my home, but I had never been in it. A hang-out for the local men of the single variety, Josh obviously felt uncomfortable with the level of competition the establishment offered him.

With Shari and I planning an all-day drunk-fest, I raised my bottle of beer to my lips and scanned the bar. Although it was filled with attractive men, one clearly stood out as being exceptionally nice-looking.

"Oh my God. Three o'clock," I whispered.

Shari shook her head. "No, it's already after four."

"No." I tilted my head to the side. "The guy. Three o'clock."

She turned to her side and glanced over her right shoulder. "Holy crap," she gasped. "He's—"

I nodded. "Yeah, I know."

Dressed in black slacks, a powder-blue dress shirt, and a vest, he looked like he just finished a business meeting and came to celebrate his having secured a new client. He was tall, had a broad chest, and short, well-groomed hair. His hazel eyes glistened unlike any I had ever seen, and were drawing me in like a magnet.

But. One thing that made him stand out more than anything was his awesome beard.

Groomed close to his face where it met his hairline, but rather long and bushy along his jaw and chin, it was nothing short of beard perfection. I stared in awe of its – and his – magnificence for several long seconds.

With his eyes fixed on the back door, he lifted his glass to his lips and took a long drink. The fitted shirt he wore clung to his bicep like a coat of paint, leaving nothing of his muscularity to the imagination.

"Holy crap," I whispered. "Look at his arms."

"Stop it," Shari said through her teeth. "He'll see you."

"Another shot?" the waitress asked.

I tore my eyes away from my bearded friend and glanced at the waitress. Shari did the same.

"Sure two more." Shari's eyes met mine. "Rounds, not shots."

I grinned. "This is going to be an awesome night."

"Early starts make for the best nights," she said. "We're going to make up for three years of lost time."

I nodded in agreement and raised my bottle of beer. Our overly efficient waitress delivered the four shots to the table with a grin a moment later, and we downed them without a moment's thought.

Beers and shots followed one after the other, and within an hour or so, I was feeling little – if any – pain.

"I've got to pee," I said.

"I'll go when you get back," Shari said. "I don't want to lose our table."

"Okay."

I grabbed my purse, turned toward the bathroom, and began to walk away. Carefully placing each foot in front of the other, and at least attempting to look sophisticated, I intentionally walked past the bearded wonder positioned between me and the restroom.

As I walked by, I glanced over my shoulder.

I would have sworn our eyes met.

Maybe it was because I wanted them to.

Either way, he was the most handsome man I had ever seen.

His beard?

Perfection defined.

After relieving myself of the afternoon's alcohol, I stood at the sink and stared blankly into the mirror. Mentally preparing to talk to the magnificent stranger, I was convinced I had what it took – short of a little courage – to impress him.

I turned toward the door, inhaled a breath of bravery, and pulled it open.

Oh shit!

Standing on the other side of the door stood the bearded wonder. Wearing a shitty little smirk, it appeared he knew I was coming. Although I had many things planned to say, and many more I wanted to say, I executed none of my plans.

Instead, I stepped to the side, gazed at him with wide eyes, and muttered a half-hearted apology as I passed. "Sorry," I squeaked.

His hand gripped my shoulder lightly. "Wait."

Oh God.

My legs began to shake. I turned around.

"Yeah?"

"You're single, adventurous, and have no problem keeping a secret," he said flatly. I couldn't help but notice that his teeth seemed as white as the winter snow, but it was his beard that commanded my attention.

I stared back at it – and him – in disbelief.

His eyes narrowed slightly. "Am I right?"

My eyes were still fixed on his beard. I nodded. "Uh huh."

He reached for my hand, turned toward the back door, and paused. "You're going to come with me."

I would have followed him to the fiery depths of hell, but I wasn't sure I heard him correctly. "Huh?"

He met my gaze. "Can I trust you?"

"I uhhm…I'm…You," I stammered. I swallowed hard and

nodded. "Yes."

"One hundred percent?"

I nodded again. "Yes."

He tugged against my hand. "Come with me, then."

I stumbled toward him, half-drunk and slightly confused. For the last three years, I'd lived a life filled with the rules, regulations, and restrictive requirements of a manipulative boyfriend, and following a man I didn't know toward the back door of the bar was in complete contrast to what I was accustomed to.

"Okay," I said with a smile.

He reached the door, which was clearly marked "FIRE EXIT ONLY". He glanced over each shoulder, and then studied the sensor at the top of the door. After searching in his pocket, he reached for the sensor, messed with it for a second, and shoved the door open.

I waited for the alarm to sound, but nothing came.

"What did you do?" I asked as I followed him up the steps. "To the alarm?"

"Disabled it."

When we reached the top of the stairs, I had a moment, albeit brief, of clarity. "What are we doing?"

"You said I could trust you, right?"

I shrugged. "Yeah, but—"

He stopped, then turned to face me. "But what? Can I trust you?"

"Sure. It's just—"

"Just what?"

"I have a friend back at the bar."

"Shari?"

I nodded. "Yeah, how'd—"

He shook his head. "I told her you'd be leaving with me."

"Seriously?"

He sighed. "Seriously."

He turned around and began briskly walking down the sidewalk. Needless to say, I followed. After a few hundred feet, he stopped and turned toward me. We were standing beside a black sedan. Behind it sat another car, one I immediately recognized.

A 1967 Shelby GT 500KR.

"Can you drive a stick shift?" he asked.

My Volkswagen was a stick shift, and I was quite versed on driving one, even with a worn-out clutch.

"Yes," I responded proudly.

"I'll drive this one." He pointed toward the sedan. "Follow me in *that* one."

I glanced at the Shelby. I couldn't believe I was even considering getting in a car I didn't own and following a man I didn't know to an unknown place. I shifted my eyes toward him.

His beard stared back at me.

No one in their right mind would have agreed to what he was asking, considering the circumstances. Saying no to him was quite possible, saying no to his awesome beard, however, would be difficult.

Forfeiting a chance to drive the car of my dreams wasn't an option.

"Okay," I said. "But how'd you get them here? Both of them?"

"I drove the red one. And, I stole this one." He handed me a set of keys. "You sure you're alright driving a stick shift?"

I didn't bat an eye at the stolen car remark. At least, I guessed, I wasn't driving it. "Positive."

"It'll just be a few miles."

"Okay."

When I wasn't gazing into his amazing green and brown speckled eyes, my focus was his beard. Standing only a few feet in front of him, I became lost in his handsome qualities. He cleared his throat.

I blinked.

"You're going to follow me," he said. "I'll park along the street. After I park, drive past me, turn right, and park around the corner, out of sight of where I park my car. Make sure wherever you park has ample room for me to pull in behind you and park without having to take time to parallel park. Lastly, leave the car running in neutral with the brake set, and get into the passenger seat. Okay?"

It seemed mysterious and sketchy.

I loved it.

"Okay."

"Now," he said. "Tell me what we're going to do."

"I'm going to follow you for a few miles. You'll park along the street. I'll drive past, turn right, and park around the corner at the curb out of sight of your car. Leave room for you to pull in behind me. Car running, in neutral, me in passenger seat."

He smiled.

I smiled in return.

"Follow me," he said.

"Wait," I said. "What's your name?"

"It's best you don't know."

"Listen. You caught me at the right time, on the right day, and in the right mood. This deal is sketchy as fuck. Tell me your name, or no deal."

He sighed. "Bradley."

"Nice to meet you, Bradley. I'm Jessie."

He nodded and turned away.

Chapter Three

5:58 p.m. Saturday

Bradley had parked in front of the First National Bank, further feeding my suspicions of the entire event being illicit. Thoughts of him robbing the bank and us escaping Bonny and Clyde style ran through my mind.

As I sat in the passenger seat, the sound of the exhaust rumbled from behind the car. I appreciated cars since my childhood, primarily a result of my father – who I idolized. He was a collector of fine autos, and taught me everything he knew about cars. One of his favorites was the Shelby GT 500KR, but finding one that suited him proved all but impossible.

He passed away in prison when I was in high school. Serving time on an auto theft charge that I wasn't sure he even committed, he died after a long bout with pneumonia. Later in life, I blamed my penchant for bad boys to his love of fast cars and his untimely death in prison.

It hadn't been long, but it seemed the alcohol I had consumed was beginning to wear off. Second guessing my decision to assist Bradley altogether, I pulled my phone from my purse and sent Shari a text. While I waited for her to respond, I checked my makeup in the rearview mirror.

Just as I finished adjusting my lipstick, Bradley came around the corner at a rather aggressive pace. His car came to a stop immediately behind the Shelby.

The door swung open.

He tossed an oversized duffel bag into the back seat, jumped in the driver's seat, and pushed in the clutch.

"You buckled?" he asked.

I glanced at the bag, turned toward him, and calmly nodded.

He shifted the car into gear, pressed the throttle, and released the clutch. While sirens wailed in the distance, we pulled away from the curb as if we were driving to dinner.

"What's in the bag?"

"Three million bucks, give or take, why?"

"Just wondering."

"We didn't meet by chance," he said.

I shot him a look. "What do you mean?"

"I'm Rocky Larucci's son. Your father's cellmate from prison."

My heart skipped a beat. "Really?"

He chuckled. "I'd have found you earlier, but I just got out of the joint three days ago. Did a four-year bit for auto theft."

"You robbed that bank, didn't you?"

I knew the answer, but I wanted to hear it from his mouth.

"I did. But. Half of that is yours. Your father insisted on it."

Other than my irregularly beating heart, I felt remarkably calm. "So, you just got out of prison?"

He turned another corner and shifted gears. "Few days ago, yeah."

"Grow that awesome beard in there?"

He laughed. "Yeah, didn't shave the entire time I was in. Thought it'd be a good disguise."

"I like it," I said. "A lot."

He rolled to a stop at a traffic light. "Maybe I'll keep it."

While we sat at the light, my mind tried to digest all of what he had said. While processing who he was, and his odd ties to my father, the sound of a police siren grew closer.

"Shit," he said. "Cop coming up behind us."

I turned around. The officer was coming straight for us, with lights blinking and sirens wailing.

Before the signal turned green, he revved the engine, released the clutch, and shot through the light.

In seconds, we were flying down the sparsely filled street at 130 miles an hour. Excited, scared, and fearing capture, I clutched my purse and prayed. Within a matter of thirty more seconds, we were a block ahead of the cops and quickly gaining distance.

I'm going to take this corner pretty fast," he said. "And about half-way up the next block, I'm going to stop. As soon as I come to a complete stop, get out and lay in the street."

I glanced over my shoulder. The closest car was a block and a half away. "You're outrunning them, you can't *stop*."

"They'll stop pick you up. Tell 'em you were walking by and I grabbed you. It'll buy me some time."

"How will you find me?"

"Don't worry," he said. "I found you once, didn't I?"

He had a good point. I nodded. "Okay."

He took the next corner at 80 miles an hour, and then hammered the gas. Half-way up the block, he came to an abrupt stop.

"Get out," he shouted.

He revved the engine and waited.

Reluctantly, I opened the door, got out, and did as he asked.

Sprawled out in the street with my purse spilled at my side, I waited. A few seconds later, the sound of the approaching cop car screeching around the corner caused me to divert my eyes toward the intersection.

The car came to a stop twenty feet from me. Two officers jumped out and pulled their guns.

"Don't fucking move," one officer shouted. "Or I'll shoot."

I remained motionless and glanced up the street in the other direction.

And Bradley was nowhere to be found.

Chapter Four

7:03 p.m. Wednesday.

I walked down the stoop and stepped onto the sidewalk. I really didn't know where I was going, but I felt the need to go for a walk. And, I was hungry.

I hoped the late evening stroll would clear my mind.

The last four days had been filled with thought of my father, Bradley, and coming to terms with the fact my father was more than likely the criminal the courts portrayed him to be.

Two blocks away from my home, and across the street from my favorite pizzeria, I stood and waited for the signal to cross the street.

The unmistakable sound of a muscle car shifting gears rang out through the otherwise silent night. I glanced in the direction of the sound.

Round headlights, round fog lights…

My heart raced.

The car came to a stop in front of me.

"Need a ride?"

I bent down and peered inside. "Oh wow. I was beginning to wonder."

"Get in," he said.

"Do you like pizza?" I asked.

"Do I like pizza?" he chuckled. "My name's Larucci. What do you think?"

"Want to get a slice?"

He nodded, and then pulled the car to the curb.

That night, we shared a slice of pizza, had a few glasses of wine, and talked of our fathers. When we finally reached a point that we were comfortable, we simply drove off into the night.

I never returned to the city. Not. Even. Once.

Some claimed I was kidnapped.

I knew better. I wasn't kidnapped.
But I was forced.
Well, kind of.
In short, the beard made me do it.

About Scott Hildreth

Born in San Diego, California, Scott now calls Naples, Florida home. Residing along the gulf of Mexico with his wife and children, he somehow finds twelve hours a day to work on his writing. A hybrid author who has published more than two-dozen romance and erotica novels, his three book Mafia Made series through Harlequin is due to start release with the first book in summer 2016.

Scott has spent his entire life pushing boundaries, and his writing is no exception. His books are steamy, however, they always include an HEA, and have no cheating, no sex outside the relationship, and no OW OM drama.

Addicted to riding his Harley-Davidson, tattoos, and drinking coffee, he can generally be found in a tattoo shop, on his Harley, or in a local coffee house when not writing.

Loyal to the fans and faithful followers who allowed him to make writing a full-time career, Scott communicates with his followers on Facebook almost daily. He encourages his readers to follow him on Facebook and Twitter.

Twitter: @ScottDHildreth

Facebook "OFFICIAL": www.facebook.com/ScottDHildreth

Facebook: www.facebook.com/sdhildreth

Goodreads: www.Goodreads.com/ScottHildreth

Website: www.scotthildreth.com

To Beard or Not to Beard?

BY J. QUIST

Chapter One

There are people in the world you don't notice...until one moment you do. And then they are *everywhere*. At your favorite coffee shop. At your CrossFit gym. At your soccer league. Getting his haircuts and beard trims in your barbershop.

Only not with me.

"Hey, Roxy," says the object of my attention in his usual black tank top as he strolls in the shop and towards Jerome's chair. The gun show—all biceps and triceps and delts—is on full display.

"Bowie." I give him a nod of my head and flex my own guns.

Though he comes here every Saturday, I never shave him.

Not that it bothers me.

"Did you see that crazy motherfucker with the shark fin beard walking out of here?" Jerome asks him as he preps him for a shave.

"What?" Bowie says, sitting up at attention, halting the prep process. "I missed it!"

"Man, it was amazing. Weird, but amazing," Jerome replies.

"Just like Roxy," Bowie says. He tries to catch my gaze in the mirror, but can't cause I'm too busy rolling them. The clippers vibrate in my hand as I trim the neck of my client.

"Bow, my man, I hear you took a cheap shot at the Rox the other night." I still my hands over Marvin as his drill sergeant voice booms over the noise of the shop: jazz trumpets, buzzing clippers, chattering men.

A snort of laughter escapes from under the hot towel covering Bowie's face. "It was clean, man. She's such a diver."

"Shut your shit talk," I say, almost making a dip in Marvin's flattop. "You totally missed the ball."

"Your revisionist history is lacking," he says and his broad, cocky smile crinkles his eyes. "It was all ball, baby."

I respond with a rub of a middle finger across the side of my nose and cough "bullshit" into my shoulder while brushing stray hairs from Marvin's shoulders.

Marvin chuckles and says, "When you gonna let her take care of that beard, Bow. I mean, Jerome's getting up there, a li'l shaky and this gal here is a master." He rubs a hand over his freshly shaven chin. "You'd be fancy with a Batman goatee."

Bowie's ability to answer is negated by my boss' razor scraping along his jugular region, demonstrating that his precision is not affected in any way. Jerome's laugh comes from deep within, voice low and slow like James Earl Jones. "Probably not the best idea if he keeps trashing her on the pitch. Can't have an accidental slip in the shop."

"Plus, I'm more of a Wonder Woman kind of guy," Bowie says as Jerome adjusts his head position.

This time he does catch my reflection in the mirror. He's smiling that fucking smile—a full three dimple level with *all* the teeth. His charm is wasted on me. I'm still pissed about that game. And he *knows* how I feel about the Wonder Woman. I shaved the symbol on the side of my head at the last soccer tournament.

But sweet baby Jane—that smile—if he didn't have a serious girlfriend and wasn't such a pain in my ass, I'd be drinking what he's servin'.

He does *not* need to know that information.

I pick up my razor and hold it up to the light as I shoot him a glare. One should always fear the girl with a straight blade. But his smile holds and is accompanied by a playful challenge in his eyes.

I'm busy cleaning my station. Bowie's leaning back in Jerome's chair, smiling and laughing and filling up the room with his charm. And that's fine. I mean, normally its fine, it's just that recently his presence takes up more space in my head. I don't need him there. I need the space.

"Oh don't mind her," Jerome says. "She's still moody from the break-up."

Fuck me. This is why I need the space. So I can pay better attention to other's conversations, especially when they are about me. "I am not moody." The growl in my voice causes every dude in the room to look at me with the same *you're full of shit* expression.

"Fine." I say with a dry laugh. "But I'm not moody about the break-up. Christ, y'all are worse than my grandma's book club." Bunch of mother hens. I duck around to the back room to change my shirt for the gym.

"The break-up?" Bowie says while he pays Tommy at the front desk. "So that's why the pretty princess doesn't come around anymore."

"That girl wouldn't dare show her face here," Tommy replies. "She is banned from all things Rox."

I step out from the back room, pulling my tank top down over my abs. "Are you insinuating *I'm* not the pretty princess?" I level him with a direct gaze, raised eyebrows and all.

At first Bowie looks caught, eyes wide, no smile, just a parting of lips as he looks at my stomach then my eyes. I think I've got him. Finally shut him up.

But then he smirks, never breaking eye contact and says, "You're not the princess, Roxy. You're the queen." And with a deep bow, he disappears in the flash of a blinding smile.

The place erupts in laughter, Jerome's roaring over all the others.
Damnit.
The Bowie invasion continues.

Chapter Two

The girl is late. At least by my standards. Late for me is a minimum of ten minutes early. Being a six-foot, one-inch tall female with swimmer's shoulders, a generous C-cup and a jawline of a dude, I already attract enough of human nature's curious attention. Some humans are better at observational subtlety, but most are not. It's best not to draw further attention by being tardy.

The girl, Penny is a friend of one my CrossFit buddies and new to the city. He thought it would be "nice" of me to chat with her and maybe show her around so she doesn't end up eating bad Chinese at the buffet on Smith Street or dancing at shady clubs.

I told him I didn't need to be set up. Can get my own date. Fine being single.

"Oh, it's not like that," he assured me.

"She's straight then?" I said, cranking the fire under his hot seat.

"Well, no."

"Dude."

"But it's not a set up. I swear. It would be nice for her to have another friend in town."

And me being a sucker for helping people, said yes. Now here I sit, waiting for this person who is not a date and maybe a future friend, but is probably expecting something else.

Ten more minutes and then I'm getting my coffee. My caffeine headache decreases my tolerance for decreased punctuality. The new Jack Reacher novel only distracts me for so long.

The door opens and my heart kicks me. My strategic viewing position from the corner table reveals not the red headed girl I am expecting, but four guys in snazzy suits talking and fucking around on their phones.

In my experience, Bowie usually comes in the shop dressed in gym clothes or a ratty T-shirt and jeans. I never envisioned him in suit. But today he wears an expertly tailored maroon one that's fitted to his lanky, athletic form in exquisite perfection. The skinny pants display the right amount of tight and stop an inch above his bare ankles and brilliant black patent leather loafers. My grandma always said it pays to advertise. And well, he's a fucking masterpiece of a billboard.

While the suit catches me off guard, his hair is really the shock. Usually it manifests itself in a gorgeous 'fro, shooting rays of his crazy energy everywhere. It's pulled back into a small knot at the base of his skull, but it does not extinguish his charm. Only enhances the open depth of his eyes, the height of his cheekbones and fullness of his mouth framed by his full beard. I itch to get my hands on that beard. For no other reason than to shape it into a modern work of art, of course. His presence fills the room, even though he's only standing in line, long fingers flying over the screen of his phone.

My paperback provides inadequate cover, so I'm forced to keep my head down and hope to avoid any attention garnering eye contact. With Bowie bearing witness, the tale of my humiliation of being stood up would be embellished beyond recognition at Jerome's. Those busybodies don't need any more fuel for their gossip fire, especially at the expense of my social life.

My phone vibrates. Not Penny. Just Bowie.

I see u

His profile is visible from my vantage point and his cheek curves up to a one-dimple level, which I know exists under today's overgrown beard. I flip a couple of unread pages before typing my answer.

Nice suit

Wait.

My finger hovers over the send icon.

Does that sound like flirting? I shouldn't flirt with Bow. He's not my type—too shiny and charismatic. And that beard. I may shave them for a living, but they're not an attractive attribute to me. But the suit is nice, so the statement is merely a compliment. Nothing more.

Send.

Nothing. Not another smile. Not a glance at his phone. Not even a glance at me. He just shoves his hands in his pant's pocket, which is in extreme defiance of the laws of physics. Shit. I'm looking directly at his pocket region. I mean, I'm clearly not the only one checking out that area. The barista just dropped a giant iced coffee because her eyes have melded with his crotch.

The other dudes trickle out with their afternoon beverages and Bowie waves to them in parting as he veers over to my table in the corner. I gesture for him to sit down because I'm nice like that. And because I want to let him know I'm controlling his presence at my table.

He takes a careful sip from his cup. Double dirty chai latte. Tea and coffee together is completely bizarre. Pick one.

I wait for him to speak. He waits. I wait. The sparkle in his eyes says, *mischief, mischief.*

"So. . ."

"So. . ."

"So. . .you like my suit," he says. His white teeth match his crisp white shirt.

"Nice to see you not looking like a slob." His tie is slim and black with little white dots. I kind of want to wrap it around my fist. I kind of want to wear it. "Who knew?"

"Got a date?" His smile is more of a smirk. Eyes making a quick pass over one of my nicer black shirts, which dips to reveal a bare shoulder.

"No," I say too quickly.

"You've got on your 'going out' shirt and do I detect a little lip gloss?" He strokes a lazy finger over the patch of hair just below his lower lip. My tongue tastes my berry bombshell lips.

"Tell me, Mr. Fashion Man, should I have gone with the heels instead of the Chucks?" I ask and take a sip from my water bottle. I probably should make more of an effort at work.

"Heels are always sexy."

I cough up that sip of water.

"So you got ghosted?" he asks and mops up the water that splatters the table.

"Of course not," I cough-say, a little defensively.

A red headed girl enters the coffee shop; the bright pink flush of "I'm late" panic stains her cheeks. I wave to her as a rush of relief passes over me.

"Sorry I'm late. I got lost," she says in a rush. "I'm Penny. So glad to meet you, Roxy." She sticks out a freckled hand with perfect French tips. Her immaculate eyebrows pull together as her gaze skims over the large hunk of male at the table.

"No worries," I say, shaking her hand with what I hope is a relaxed smile. "This town is crazy. Glad you found the place."

Bowie is in full manspread position, legs apart, heel tapping, casually leaning back in his chair as he sips his coffee/tea concoction, waiting for I don't know what. An introduction? A fucking parade? A live sacrifice?

He smiles the fucking smile—perfect teeth and crinkly eyes and all the dimples. Of course he does. "Bowie Carlson," he says and extends a hand to Penny, who is clearly captured in his net of charms even though she's here for me.

"Oh. . .hello. Nice to meet you." Her eyes dart between the man and me, trying to determine if she's intruding.

I kick the leg of Bowie's chair to end this awkward standoff of his presence on my date that is not a date, but probably is. "Don't you have to go, wherever it is that you go?"

"Yes, yes, back to work for me." And he struts from the shop like a supermodel in his fancy suit. "See ya later."

"Friend?" Penny asks a question loaded with unspoken curiosity because I'm clearly engaged in the Bowie Runway Show with more than a passing interest.

"Kind of," I say and her confused expression matches my thoughts.

I don't even know what that means. He was initially just a dude who came to Jerome's. Then my CrossFit classes. Then the bar after soccer games. But recently, he's more than just taking up friendly space. There's a level of attraction to which I am not accustomed since I haven't dated a guy for several years.

"Come on. I know the best place for sushi," I say. She gives a brilliant smile, where I notice the cute freckles across her nose.

In a shocking turn of events, my not-date turned into a date with Penny, hoping to clear Bowie out of my head.

Chapter Three

"REFEREE, ARE YOU GOING TO BLOW THAT WHISTLE BEFORE this jackbag kills my ability to breastfeed my future children?" I say to the dumbest fucking center ref to ever center ref the game of soccer as my team sets up for a free kick. He ignores me as he walks the players off the ball.

"REFEREE!" I yell again while bodies jostle in the box for position. I wave my hands above my head in an *I'mnotdoinganything* gesture while the offender pushes both forearms into my girls. "DO YOU NOT SEE THIS!"

Having boobs is usually not a hassle in the co-ed league. But all it takes is one dirtbag getting offended after you make him look like an uncoordinated toddler to start off an avalanche of cheap fouls and crude remarks. Grabbing jerseys, elbowing the gut behind you, shoving in the back is all part of the game. I'm as physical as the rest of them. I just don't use other people's breasts to do so.

My teammate signals his kick and I shove the prick off of me. I cut to my spot and jump above another dude and head the ball laser sharp into the back of the net, giving us the lead with only five minutes left in the game.

I'm surrounded in a team hug. A few of the opposing guys bitch out the molester for his poor defensive skills while a couple others grumble in passing, "That's the only way she can score."

"No one likes a fucking fish taco," the dirtbag says.

"That's not what your girlfriend said," I say, jogging past. I'm followed by echo of "Oh, shit, man. You burnt."

A few minutes later, the asshat tackles me causing me to slide along my hip. The pain hints at one hellava turf rash. The ref blows his useless whistle to signal the end of the game.

During the good sportsmen's handshake line after the game, the jackbag slaps my ass in a supposed "good game" gesture.

I. AM. DONE.

He's the same height as me, which provides me a perfect angle to grab him by the shoulders and kick my knee into his boy parts. Hard. He drops like a sack of shit, screaming and coughing up obscenities of the unoriginal fucking dyke bitch variety.

"Oh, pardon me for the accidental dick graze, you perverted fucktrumpet." I step over his crumpled body and pat myself on the back for not crushing his hand with my cleats.

The rest of his teammates as well as mine clear the hell out as I make my way to the sideline. I snatch my bag and don't even bother to change my shoes. When I exit the park gate, Bowie steps in front of me. His game was before mine and apparently he stayed to watch.

"Holy shit, Roxy." There's concern, but also crinkles of humor around his eyes. "You okay?"

"I am not in the mood to talk to anyone with a penis right now," I say and step around him.

"Wait, Roxy. You're limping." He falls in step beside me.

My hip throbs and stings as I lift my slider shorts higher to reveal a four-inch turf burn.

"I hope that motherfucker can't get it up for a year!"

"Christ, Roxy. You gotta take care of that." Bowie leans over, basically looking at my ass. It's awkward and sort of intriguing at the same time—if I wasn't standing here in public with a gaping wound and smelling like an old gym bag. Oh, yeah and his girlfriend. Must always remember the girlfriend.

"I can just do it at the shop," I pull down my shorts and adjust my bag over my shoulder. "I gotta stop by there anyway."

"My place is closer. Come over and clean up."

I know this is only Bowie being nice. That it's logical not to wait to take care of the burn. But being in his space. Using his stuff. Seeing where he lives. Feels like stepping beyond this imaginary boundary I set around us.

The wound rubs on my sliders and the friction will only increase the pain the longer I leave it open. And well, maybe I'm a little bit curious about his place.

"Fine." I try not to notice the little smile on his face.

Bowie's studio is filled with well, not much—a bed, couch, coffee table, big ass TV, a couple of bar stools at the extended counter that separates the small kitchen space from the rest of the room. His walls are bare, except for a giant black and white photograph of a beach. His bed is half-assed made, gray comforter pulled up over the pile of sheets. There are breakfast dishes in the sink and a covered plate of muffins sitting on the counter. The scent of this morning's coffee lingers in the air.

Nothing overtly feminine grabs my attention. *Interesting.* This should not be interesting to me.

"This way," he says and directs me to the back corner. The bathroom is tiny and modern with gray and white subway tiles patterning the small shower stall. He rifles in the cupboard under the square sink and sets antibiotic cream, bandages and towels on the counter.

"Here ya go," he says. The walls feel too close. The oxygen content minimal. The scent of his sweat fogs my mind. I only nod.

He doesn't step away toward the door. "You can shower if you want."

"Oh, I. . ." *Want.* "Thanks." I step toward the counter and unzip my bag for clean clothes.

"No problem." And after a moment, he exits the room, leaving a little breathing room.

He's being nice. Bowie's a nice guy.

It's logical. Putting clean clothes over a sweaty body is gross.

He has a girlfriend. Though there is no physical evidence of her here.

I'm standing in the same place he showers. Sans clothing.

The two of us could fit in here. Only a slice of space between our bodies. Only room enough for the water to slide between. Only room enough for soap to glide along each other's skin. Barely room for the citrus scented steam to join us.

"Ouch! Motherfucker, that stings," I say as the hot water hits my turf burn. The pain overrides the sliding bodies daydream.

I check out his shaving products as I dress and notice the beard oil I use at the shop. Not Jerome's preferred scent. *Interesting.* No, Roxy, not interesting.

Bowie stuffs an entire muffin in his mouth when I emerge from the bathroom. "*Hmphf*" is his attempt at greeting with his mouth full.

I laugh and shake my head. "Pig."

He shrugs, still able to grin with a mouth full of food. He swallows and takes a long drink from the glass of juice in his hand. "Sorry. You hungry? Muffin?" He extends the plate to me.

"Thanks," I say and take a normal sized bite. My mouth fills with blueberry and sugar and a hint of lemon. Whoa. "That's incredible. You bake?"

"Ha! No. The older couple of ladies down the hall make them for me."

I stuff the last piece into my mouth. "Of course they do. I bet you walk the hallways shirtless and the next day you have pumpkin bread."

His finger rubs along his chin the way he always does when contemplating an answer. "I just dazzle them with my smile. I think they'd be more interested in you shirtless."

I burst out in full laughter. "I'm not opposed to flashing the goods. Those muffins are awesome."

He laughs, but turns to the sink with his glass. "Not sure they could handle that entertainment." The tips of his ears are pink.

I snatch another muffin from the plate. "I'm taking one for the road."

"You coming to The Pit?" he asks in sudden change of topic. The soccer crowd congregates there after Saturday games.

"I don't know. I gotta hit Jerome's and I'm kind of beat from today." I'm not really sure if I'm up for The Pit today. Too many dicks—literally and not literally—for my mood.

"Okay." He fiddles around with covering the remaining muffins.

"Okay, then," I say and shuffle from one foot to the other. He's not making eye contact. It's weird. "Thanks for. . .uh, the use of your facilities."

"Anytime," he replies and gives me a half smile that just dimples up his cheek. "See you later?"

He watches me walk down the hallway in a full lean pose against the doorjamb. Even in sweaty, dirty, nasty soccer attire, he's still in fine billboard form.

"Maybe," I say and give him a little wave as I step into the elevator.

The fresh air of the open street should make me feel free. But my head is crowded with citrus body wash and steamy small spaces and blueberry muffins. I crossed the imaginary boundary and entered his personal space, where he cooks and sleeps and shaves. He's checked right into Libido's Campground. I shouldn't have let him in the tent.

Chapter Four

"Hide your jewels, gentlemen!" the bartender roars at my entrance to The Pit. "The Ball Buster has arrived!"

The male patrons cheer and cover their precious manhood, while chanting, "Rox, Rox, kicked his box!"

I high-five my adoring fans on my way back to where a few of my teammates and Bowie camp out. The table is littered with sauce-smeared plates of wings and bowls holding a few left over chips. By the rosy glow on many cheeks, much alcohol has already been consumed.

Bowie's arm is draped, almost protectively over an empty chair next to him and he nods toward it. "Our hero," he says, bumping knuckles with me. "That guy has been a dick all season."

Jerry from my team says, "What did you call him?"

Another teammate chimes in "a perverted fucktrumpet! It was so awesome!"

"I'm sure everyone will be on the lookout for your accidental dick graze," pipes in Jerry.

"As they should," I reply. "Now where's my beer?"

The story of my glorious game grows more hyperbolic as the booze continues to flow. I'm happy to observe and occasionally chime in a comment or two. This is normal. Just Bowie and the guys and beer and wings. Simple.

A couple of girls at the table next to us are fascinated with all the tales from the pitch and join our little group. One short blonde sits next to me and while she keeps asking Bowie questions, her knee presses into mine. He responds, but he isn't his usual boisterous self. He scans the room and returns to the conversation, constantly engaging and disengaging.

"I'm gonna get another drink," I say once the little blonde wanders away with her friends. "Our waitress has disappeared."

Waiting off to the side for my turn, I scan my phone for updates and messages. Which is why the voice behind me takes me by surprise.

"Hey, Rox," my ex-girlfriend says.

Oh, this day is just all kinds of fucked up.

The last time I saw Riley was a couple of months ago and though our break-up was definitely for the best, seeing her irritates me. She's not supposed to be *here*. She got the apartment. I got the gym and The Pit. It was a fair trade knowing I wouldn't run into her in the neighborhood.

"Hey," I attempt my best lean against the bar impersonation of Bowie, hoping the causal stance masks my shock.

"You cut your hair." Her eyes map the curve of my head, my neck and travel back to my face. That look used to give me goose bumps and made me want to kiss her until we were breathless.

Now nothing.

"Oh, yeah," I say, rubbing my hand over the fine layer of black fuzz. Cutting is an understatement. I'd already shaved the side of it for my Wonder Woman logo, so I figured what the hell and buzzed off the rest a few weeks ago.

"Very Mad Max," she says with a little smile.

That's a personal compliment that almost makes me return her smile. We both lusted after Charlize with the butch haircut in the movie. It's weird to feel this indifference instead of the usual comfort of familiarity. We were together over two years. I was totally in love with her. I figured I'd feel hollow when I saw her again. Maybe I'm not as empty without her as I thought.

A drunken chorus of "Rox, Rox, kick his box" rings in from behind us, interrupting my response. The chant was endearing at first, but is now more irksome than cute.

"Jesus fuck," I murmur under my breath with an eye roll. "I'm gonna kick yours if you don't shut it!"

"What's up with that?" she asks and motions to the bartender for two drinks.

"Soccer revenge." Bowie answers as he throws an arm over my shoulders.

"Bowie," Riley says with an irritated sigh and a quick glance at the display of affection. "Playing body guard now?"

Riley is the one person who isn't overtaken by Bowie's gargantuan personality. In fact, she was snippy and highly annoyed whenever he appeared at my gym classes or Jerome's. It was as if there wasn't enough space for all their charm in the room.

"Oh, the queen doesn't need protection."

I'm trapped between the bar and Bowie and a whole lotta awkward. "What brings you to The Pit, Ri?"

"Oh, Caroline was dropping off something for her brother." She points toward the entrance where her new girlfriend and the brother are talking.

Seriously. This day can just eff off.

"Cool," I say because I'm nice like that. "Good to see you."

"Take care, Rox." She grabs her bottles of Stella from the bartender and makes her way through the crowd.

I'm leaning on Bowie more than I realize. He's warm and cozy like a boy-scented blanket. *Just so fucking tired.*

"You okay?" he asks, steering us back toward the table with his hand at my back. "With the princess here?"

"Oh, yeah." I shrug. "It's just weird, I guess."

He picks up his glass, sets it down, making a ring pattern with the condensation puddle on the table. "What's she up to?"

"I didn't ask. You have excellent timing for rescuing people from awkward ex encounters." I take a long swallow from my bottle. "That's a useful superpower."

"At your service, your grace." His smile is slow, almost lazy, showing only his top teeth. I imagine he would smile like that the morning after great sex.

"Do you have other powers?" I ask. *Fucking hell.* That is a regretful question. No flirting with unavailable people!

"Oh, I have many—" His eyes are full of *mischief, mischief.*

The only sound in my head is my heart's erratic rhythm. My ability to move, to look away from his dark eyes is lost somewhere with my good judgment.

Until his phone vibrates on the table, signaling the girlfriend's call.

Our connection is broken. Which is a good thing. His superpower was only moments away from storming the sex castle.

Chapter Five

Bowie strides into Jerome's wearing his usual Saturday uniform—loose tank top that dips to the bottom of his ribs, ripped jeans, and gold and black high tops. He's shocked to find that Jerome is out sick with food poisoning.

"Damn, man," he says pulling at the whiskers under his chin. "I've got plans tonight and I need to look pretty. Kordell, you got time?"

Kordell shakes his head, "I'm booked up, but Rox can take you."

Every eye in the place flashes between him and me, waiting to see who will win this rally. I lift my straight blade and polish it with gentle strokes. My smirk reflects in its shiny face.

"Don't be such a baby, Bow," Marvin says and pulls on his jacket. "She hasn't killed anybody today…yet." The room fills with teasing laughter.

"Fine." An expression of defeat falls across his face and he trudges to my chair as if he's facing lethal injection.

I brandish my cape with the flourish of a matador, luring a bull for the kill. "Are you ready?"

"For what exactly?" he asks, trying to maintain his cocky demeanor.

"My mad skills," I say, standing behind him, trailing my fingers over his beard. A whisper of touch. He hasn't been in for a trim with Jerome in a few weeks. An ideal overgrown canvas. "I have an idea. You game?"

His shoulders rise as he takes a breath. "No Batman?"

"Definitely not."

After another deep breath, he nods his surrender.

Routine. Routine is my savior. The automation of my movements masks my nervous energy. I wanted to get my hands on his beard long before I wanted to get my hands on him. My equipment and supplies line the workstation in the usual sequence.

Mint.

Fresh breath is absolute priority at all times. My favorite peppermint is nestled in my cheek.

Bowie watches my face from his reclined position as I tuck a towel into his collar and place another across his chest.

Hot towel.

I drape it over him and follow with a deep pressure over his face. He's quiet under the lemon-scented wrap. The guys' latest gossip conversation hums in the background.

Electric clippers.

I even out his chin, cheeks and jaw into short symmetry. His mustache is trimmed shorter than the rest of his face and I design a square over his chin. His fingers tap, tap, tap the rhythm of the overhead song.

Beard oil.

His skin is soft and my fingers tingle as I massage the oil throughout his beard and along its edges. I pass along his neck and his throat muscles spasm as he swallows hard.

Shave cream.

The soft foam is warm from the dispenser and I apply it with my fingers along all the borders and his chin. He's a statue and I whisper for him to breathe.

"Don't worry," I place my hand on his forehead in preparation for turning his head to the side. "I'll be gentle your first time."

He gives me a smile laced with trepidation and rolls his eyes as Kordell chuckles behind me.

I pull his skin tight and my razor glides in small strokes, making the initial straight line from the top of his ear to the corner of his mouth. I stand at the top of his head as I shave his neckline. The curves of his chin are tricky and I remind myself to breathe. His breath quickens and brushes over my fingers.

Knowing he'd be lost without it, I leave a soul patch below his bottom lip. His lips. Seriously. The fullness. The symmetry. They're insane. When he smiles the top one curls under.

I perfect my lines with a dry run of the razor, shaping to the highest level of crispy before I apply a cold towel. After a gentle pat down, I warm the spicy citrus oil in my palms. My fingers glide along his jaw, circle the muscles there and then follow my routine pattern up to his temple and forehead. I pause at the facial pressure points and then sink my hands into his glorious hair to complete the scalp massage. My pulse accelerates and the hair on the back of my neck stands at attention. Thank fuck for my padded bra or the nipple situation would be beyond embarrassing.

"He's alive!" I exclaim in my best Dr. Frankenstein voice as I fan his face with a towel. I stand above him as he opens his eyes, pupils wide and warm. Hip lips tip up just at the corners as I raise him to an upright position.

"Damn, Roxy," he says, eyes popping at his reflection. An index finger strokes his beautiful soul patch.

"Still not pretty," Kordell says. The shop bursts into laughter and applause.

"I'm always pretty," he says and flashes everyone a full wattage grin in the mirror as he admires my handiwork. Or himself.

"Got a hot date?" Tommy asks him while he pays.

"No, man. Just mixing at Cubes with Jomo," he says, looking first at me, then Tommy. "Y'all should come."

Tommy's eyes practically pop out of his head with this invitation. "Yeah, cool…"

"Your, grace," he says to me with an exaggerated bow. "Thank you."

I'm so not going to Cubes. It's not a good idea, despite what my lower body tells me. I must remain in a Bowie-free space while entranced in this fog of lust.

Chapter Six

After not much begging and bribing, I agree to meet Tommy and his friends at Cubes. Begging and bribing isn't required to convince my roommates to tag along. Melly has been crushing on Tommy for months and Jolene and Jessica AKA the JJs are always up for a night on the town.

Bowie is a tour de force up on the stage—the hair a glorious sunburst shape, the crispy beard, the black Golden State tank top clinging to his long chest, guns on full display. Images of my hands in his hair flash before me. I need a drink. Or a girl. Or a guy. Something to take the edge off.

He gives us the cool nod and smile while his body is one with the beat.

The dance floor is packed with a wide variety of beautiful people. Our group drinks and dances and misdirects the unwanted attention while it directs the wanted attention. Melly is living her up close and personal dream with Tommy. The JJs find suitable conquests for the night. I'm dancing with both guys and girls. I've been keyed up since Bowie left the shop earlier. His unavailability makes my hands ache with emptiness. So I fill them with another.

Jack is a fucking fine dancer. Bonus: Buys drinks. Not Mr. Grabby Hands. Very, very male. One way to get a certain man out of my head is to have another in my hands.

Jolene and Jessica vacate the place and head for another club with their new friends. I give my blessing to Tommy and Melly as long as they promise to inhabit somewhere that is not our place.

The bass bumps my blood and the lyrics breathe with innuendo as I kiss Jack. Our arms tangle around shoulders and waists as our bodies press together. His just shaved skin is smooth and smells of sandalwood after-shave. Not my preferred citrus scent.

We are still entwined when we break from the kiss and I find Bowie standing completely still, eyes unfocused in my direction. The scowl on his face confuses me. I'm not known for public displays of affection, but honestly, he shouldn't be so surprised that I make-out with people.

I wave my fingers at him. He shakes out of his stupor and acknowledges me with a belated half-smile before returning to his duties.

"You know him?" Jack asks, his lips brushing my ear.

My eyes are locked on Bowie. "Yeah, he comes to my shop." *And my gym. And my coffee shop. And my head.* "We're just friends." A friend I wanted to lick a few hours ago.

"That's it?"

"Yeah."

"Cool." He moves to kiss me again, but his friends interrupt us. "Jack-Jack, let's gooooooooo," one of them says leaning on him.

The other leans on me. "Pauly is waiting for us at the diner and he's pissed we're not there yet." The dude realizes I'm an actual person and shows me a drunken smarmy smile. "Hey, lady."

Jack pushes his face away from me and says, "You want to join us?" But something in his face tells me he's expecting the no.

"No worries." I pat his cheek and smile. "You have fun."

I send a text to the girls and Bowie informing them that I'm closing up for the night. All by myself. Catching Bowie's eye, I motion to my phone and wave good-bye to him. He mouths "wait" and I send him a message that I'm tired and will see him at the game on Tuesday.

Chapter Seven

THE DOORBELL SCREAMS AND SHOCKS ME AWAKE. TWO-THIRTY a.m. The idea of leaving a dumbass roommate to sleep on the front steps seriously crosses my mind. My neck is kinked from sleeping on the sofa without a pillow. The reading light, still clamped to my book illuminates the underside of the coffee table. I'm still dressed in my halter dress.

A surprising form fills the peephole. "Bowie?" My heart stutters as I open the door a crack.

"Roxy," he says. His shoulders collapse as if he'd been holding his breath waiting for an answer. "Sorry, I know it's late. Or early. It's just . . .Can I come in?"

"Bow, what—" But he doesn't let me finish.

"Just for a few minutes. I need—" He's pulling on his soul patch, eyes shifting down and up like a lost boy.

"Sure," I say and open the door wider. Because I'm nice like that.

He blows in like a hot wind that is non-existent on this muggy summer night. Kinetic energy pops off him—his magnificent hair shoots every which way as though he's grabbed a live wire. His fingers twitch as he shifts his weight from one foot to the other. His eyes search the room as if looking for monsters in the dark.

I flip on the table lamp and he asks, "The girls home?"

"Ah, no. Found some love at the club," I say with a wink.

He nods—not even a crack of a smile to my joke—and catches my gaze for a nanosecond before he shifts away and flashes to the TV, his feet, out the window.

"Have a seat. Want somethin' to drink?" I walk toward the kitchen. My tongue sticks to the roof of my mouth. "Water? Gatorade? Apple juice?"

"Apple juice? Who's the preschooler in the house?" he asks and for the moment he sounds like the Bowie I know.

"That would be Melly."

He laughs at that. Almost normal Bowie.

I hand him a bottle of red Gatorade and seat myself on the opposite end of the couch, reclining back into the corner and propping my feet up on the coffee table.

His perfectly symmetrical lips press to the rim of the bottle and he drains half the liquid in a few gulps. Must stop ogling the lips.

"You okay?" I crack open the lid of my water bottle with a twist.

He turns toward me and holds my eyes for a moment. I take a sip, breaking his gaze, but I feel it on my lips, my throat and lower like a waterfall. He's focused on my mouth as I tip the bottle down.

He jumps up with a jolt and paces back and forth on the far side of the coffee table. Four steps. Turn. Four steps back. Repeat. He finally says, "You have fun tonight?"

"Sure?" I say. It's more of a question than an answer. There is no way he came here in the middle of the night to find out the evening's fun level.

"Well, y'all left early, so I thought, you know. . .maybe you didn't."

If he wasn't lit up like a Christmas tree, I'd kick his ass to the curb. Instead, I smile with raised eyebrows. "Fishing for compliments?"

"Not fishing." A familiar little smile tinged with his typical swagger breaks the panic look. "But I'm happy to accept all commendations."

I tap my finger to my lips, considering. "Well, you didn't suck."

My reward is a flash of a smile—a burst of electricity shot straight at me. "Seriously, it's almost three a.m. What gives?"

His smile disappears, but the residual current hangs smoke-heavy between us. Bowie rubs his fingers—long and lean like the rest of him—over his cheeks, once again pulling the spot of hair under his lip before he says, "I need you to shave this off."

Water shoots through my nose. I wipe my face and coffee table with the throw blanket. "What the fuck, Bowie. . .It's the middle of the fucking night. I'm not shaving you."

"But. . ." he says. He dodges out of my way to the kitchen for a paper towel. "I need you to. I'll wimp out if you don't do it now."

I'm debating whether to open the door and toss him out or just go to bed, leaving him and his ludicrous beard to fend for themselves. "No."

"Roxy." My name pleads from his lips.

"I don't have my stuff." Not true. "Just my clippers and a worn down Venus disposable I shave my pits with."

"Bullshit," he says, cocky, yet not his playful cocky. "You've got to have one of your shiny demon barber friends here."

True. I shaved my head with it a few weeks ago. *But still.* "I could have a thousand blades here, but I'm not gonna do it."

"Why?" He's fired up, pacing again with his hands knotted behind his neck.

"Because I'm tired and that beard is a fucking masterpiece and you're being a jackass." *Did the masterpiece part slip out?*

He scrubs his face with both hands and stops still.

"You kissed a dude," he says. My heart skips a beat or two as though he's tripped the breaker.

"So?" I wave my fingers for him to continue as my pulse kicks up.

"You had a girlfriend!" He gestures wildly as if attempting to conjure a woman before me.

"You *have* a girlfriend!" I counter with my own arm flailing.

"Not anymore."

"What?" The air is sucked out of the room. "Since when?"

"Since the night we were at The Pit a few weeks ago." He shrugs and pulls at his hair. "Jerome didn't tell you?"

I shake my head. I can't believe those fucking busybody bastards didn't mention any of this. What are they even good for?

"Do you make out with guys often?" he asks, steering the conversation back to me. So serious. Not a hint of humor, just wide-eyed intent.

I'm still reeling from the no girlfriend revelation. The lack of sleep and dehydration from the night's alcohol consumption along with the *weirdness* of this entire conversation combine together into a hysterical cocktail. Which apparently I'm the only one drinking because Bowie is just standing there...perplexed and pulling at his patch.

Maybe...just maybe he's as clueless as he looks.

"Bow...man," I take a few deep breaths to help swallow my laughter. "Did you not know?"

"What?" The word is a breath of disbelief.

"I like guys and girls."

"Pardon?" He appears quite stupefied. "But—"

"I've had girlfriends and boyfriends, but more recently more on the female side of things." The edge of the dining table is sharp against the back of my legs as I lean back, the need for external support falling on me.

"For real. . .you're attracted to guys?"

"Yes, Bow."

His index finger strokes along the cleft of his three a.m. shadowed chin. "The dude tonight didn't have a beard?"

"Christ." Good thing for the table, otherwise I'd be flat on my ass. "You're not making fuck's sense right now…"

"You prefer no beard?" His thumb rubs across that exquisite lower lip.

He stands a couple of feet away. I only have to tip my chin to look straight at him. His eyes are not sparked with his typical Bowie mischief, but a wild, unchecked power.

"Uh. . ." My brain short circuits, zapping the words from my mouth. "I've never kissed anyone with one."

"No one?"

"No," I attempt to take a breath. "Technically, my Uncle Rubin had a moustache and kissed me on the cheek—"

"I want to kiss you," he starts, but stops as my fingers stretch to touch his cheek. His beard. There are only inches between us. "Do you—"

A wet blanket falls on our fire when the JJ's burst through the front door, a little tipsy and giggly, meaning they're more likely sex drunk versus vodka drunk.

Jolene stops. "Whoa." Jess, who's on her phone, crashes into her.

"Hey, it's the DJ man," Jess says and looks around the room. "Was the party here?"

"Rox, you know hot DJ?" Jolene asks, incredulous.

"It's Bowie, you dumbass," I step away from the table. And the hot DJ that I was about to kiss the hell out of a few seconds ago.

"Shut the friggin' door," Jolene says, slapping a hand to her forehead. "The Bowie? Like the always hanging around Bowie?"

"Like the hot tight pants Bowie?" Jess chimes in. Maybe they are more booze drunk.

Fuck me. This is why you should never gossip about boys to your roommates. They blurt out privileged information at the most inopportune time. I can't look directly at him. He fills himself with this information and promptly assumes the famous Bowie lean against the breakfast counter, complete with a self-confident smirk.

"No, no, no," I say and start corralling them toward the stairs. "Just annoyingly arrogant Bowie."

"Nice to meet you," he says with all the teeth grinning.

"Your night is over, my darlings," I say.

"Good night, ladies." He spreads the charm like buttercream frosting on a cake.

The JJs eyes glaze over until I nudge them, ever not so gently toward their destination. The whispers crescendo up the stairs, peaking at the top with a "She's gonna fuck the hot DJ!"

With my back to this humiliation, I lock the forgotten front door and note the green paint is chipping away by the dead bolt. My chest expands in an attempt to fill myself with some type of gallantry in the face of this man who snuck his way into my space—*my life* over these last few months.

This man who always makes me laugh and smile.

This man who treats me as an equal.

This man who looks at me as though I'm the queen. His queen.

This man whose face I want to kiss instead of shave.

He stands behind me, not touching, but close enough to blanket me from head to toe with his scent, his breath, his heat.

"Roxy." My name brushes the back of my neck and crackles down my spine, lighting up every nerve ending.

He's so *close*.

Or I am.

We lean forward and backwards. The space between disappears as his fingers slide down my bare arms and entwine with mine—thumbs pressing another hot switch in my palm.

His lips. *His beard* skims along my bare shoulder, the side of my neck to the shell of my ear before he says, "You're killing me. You've been killing me forever. I never thought I could have this." He presses a kiss behind my ear, causing our chests to rise and fall in staccato rhythm.

"And tonight, Jesus, I didn't think I'd survive. This dress." He bites the knot of my halter top and whispers kisses along my spine. "Your skin. . ."

With the electric shock of his touch—lips, tongue, stubble against my neck—my heart races, pounding through my veins in a frantic beat that makes me want to dance until we shatter.

I turn and face him

"I. . ." My voice is heavy and thick. My hands on his chest provide a pocket of space filled with unanswered questions and unreleased tension. The distance gives me room to gaze at him. He's dark blue. His fingers blaze. His eyes sear. His tongue is a flickering flame against his bottom lip, framed by a masterpiece, *my* masterpiece of a beard.

"What?" he asks, his hands resting—branding the tops of my hips.

"This," I say, slipping my hands over the coiled muscles of his shoulders. Over the racing pulse in his neck.

With trembling fingers, I trace along the immaculate cheek line, the skin there still smooth from my blade. I continue across the hair above his top lip, shorter than the rest of his beard and down the square outline of his stubbled chin before settling my fingers on the soft thickness of his cheek. My thumb rests in the cleft just perfectly.

His body is still, coiled in anticipation, waiting to spring into action at the right moment. I'm not sure he's breathing. I'm not sure I am.

"I've wanted to kiss you forever." I confess. To him. To myself.

His lips curl up just enough to change the curve of his cheek and signal a hint of the first dimple under my hand. His body uncoils, arms cinching around my waist. His breath brushes my lips before we touch.

So close.

No space. He's the blood in my veins, the oxygen in my lungs, the electric current down my nerves. He's no longer only in my headspace. He's in every space.

The kiss is soft and stubble. Slick and sweet. An infinite dimple smile.

It's fingers in his thick hair. Palms on my bare back. Teeth nipping earlobes.

It's his throat. Smooth shaven. Bowie scented. Thunder rumbling under the drag of my tongue.

It's the sum of all these months—every smile, every teasing joke, every hour spent sweating at the gym.

It's the door at my back. Wall of Bowie at my front. And nothing between us.

It's fucking *finally*.

The kiss ends with foreheads pressed together, bare chests rising to each other in breathless wonder, while his long fingers refuse to leave my spine. By some miracle, we're still standing.

"So. . ."

"So. . ." he says and leans back just enough for me to catch the mischief in his eyes. "To beard or not to beard?"

I kiss him, nipping at his bottom lip. His stubble tingles against my chin.

"Beard." I'm blinded by a full three-dimple smile. "Most definitely to beard."

About J. Quist

Whether growing up with five sisters in a small midwestern town (population 700), cleaning campground restrooms in high school (yes, totally gross), teaching patients to walk again (awesome career), J. Quist is always surrounded by interesting people. Where there are people, there are stories. So many stories to tell.

Some of her favorite things include Duran Duran, iced tea, all sports, books, musicals, soccer boys and neuroanatomy. Oh, and tacos. Don't forget the tacos.

J. Quist lives in the concrete desert metropolis of Phoenix with her husband and three daughters. You can find her on the sidelines of her kids' soccer games, working with special needs children as physical therapist, reading all the books and cheering for her beloved Nebraska Cornhuskers and Liverpool Football Club.

Facebook: www.facebook.com/J-Quist-1120589968009818
Twitter: twitter.com/JQuist_Writer

Scruff You!

BY FAITH ANDREWS

Chapter One

"VENTI, ICED CARAMEL LATTE, SOY, NO FOAM, TWO PUMPS of—"

"Hazelnut," I spoke over my shoulder. Without a nudge of help the new dude would no doubt mess this up. And from the little I knew about our mysterious daily visitor, she wasn't the type of chick who tolerated people fucking things up. Part of me wanted to see him botch the order just to get a reaction out of her, but I was once in his position and I sympathized with the poor guy. Tony was yet to learn the secret motto most baristas mumbled at least ten times a day: *If your coffee takes more than three words to order, you're part of the problem.*

Complicated shit aside, I glanced her way, hoping to catch a glimmer of appreciation flash across her face from underneath her dark-rimmed glasses, but nope—nothing. Just like always. I was beginning to think she needed better glasses *or* I was invisible. Not likely, though, since the sexy-bearded-barista-thing was irresistible to most of the women populating the hipster-lined streets of Williamsburg. And I fit that description to the T.

Tony finished ringing her up and then scribbled her name—I use the term *her* loosely here—across the plastic cup. I busied myself behind the counter doing barista-ish things while checking her out. *A daily pastime.* She fumbled through her wallet—a fuchsia vinyl piece of junk held together with a strip of zebra washi tape—while biting on her burgundy painted and silver-ringed lip. *Shit! That again?* Did she not know what that did to me?

I ignored the current of neediness that pumped through my body from tongue to cock, like the double shot of hazelnut I'd infused into *Greta's* coffee.

"Greta?" I mumbled, rolling my eyes as I turned to face her. I thought about calling her out on it because I'd finally caught on. Yesterday it was Ava, the day before Marilyn, and last week she had the cashier squiggle *Rita* on her cup. *Hollywood starlets.* Quite clever for a chick her age. She couldn't be more than twenty or twenty-one, if that. I only hoped I wasn't drooling over jail bait, for Christ's sake.

"Yup. That's me. Thank you," she whispered grabbing her order with her eyes toward the ground.

I extended the cold, perfectly brewed beverage into her hands and held on a second longer than usual, hoping her eyes would meet mine.

Nothing. Not a smile, not a flush of embarrassment, not so much as a glance at our fingers that were mere centimeters apart, wrapped around the cup.

She was indifferent. I hated that. There was nothing worse than wanting the attention of someone who couldn't care less that you existed. *But it was a challenge.* The cocky part of me didn't have to question that the opposite sex liked what I had to offer. Hell, I lived in the most diverse slice of Brooklyn. Forget about the opposite sex; *dudes* liked what I had to offer, too. But regardless of my carefully groomed, bearded armor there was a dormant insecurity from many moons ago that was awoken by this mystifying woman who was hell bent on ignoring me.

When I noticed that the morning rush had simmered to only one last customer in line, I took it upon myself to end this charade for once and for all. *Fuck it! What did I have to lose?*

"I'm on to you, you know," I blurted with a crooked grin while I rubbed my fingers scraping over scruff.

"Excuse me?" she muttered with a scowl, her brows angling inward to the bridge of her cute little nose. I guessed she was offended that I finally spoke more than the four typical words to her.

Too bad. There's more where that came from, Miss Garbo.

"I know your name isn't Greta, or Rita, or Marilyn for that matter. So, now that I figured out your clever name game—which was pretty slick, might I add—why don't you tell me what your real name is so I can ask you out the way I've been wanting to since you strolled in here ordering your obnoxious concoction and made me mad, wondering whether you'll lose your glasses and the pencil in your bun when you finally let me kiss you?"

Starlett-Wanna-Be's brilliant green eyes went wide behind those sexy-as-hell specs. Her alabaster skin flushed pink along her faultlessly sculpted cheekbones. Stunned speechless, she took a half step backwards and gulped back the sip of coffee she'd taken before I'd started making the moves on her.

I leaned forward, rested my elbows on the "pick up your order here" counter and waited for her to say something. Anything. I might've gotten a hard on, even if she told me to fuck off. But what I hadn't expected was for her to run to her regular table in the corner, grab her notebook, and dash out the front door at the speed of a freight train on a one-way track to get-me-the-fuck-outta-here.

"Real slick, Ezra. I've never seen that girl jet out of here like that. What did you say to her?" Tony was behind me snickering as he wiped his hands on his apron.

I shook my head and made my way back to the coffee machine to brew a fresh roast for the mid-morning crowd. "Eh, nothing. Guess she had somewhere to be today." I waved him off as if I hadn't a care in the world, when in reality I wouldn't be able to stop thinking of how she'd blown me off all day.

Lucky for me, she'd be back. Not because of me or for another coffee fix. No. I was certain she'd return, because on the table in the far right corner–*her* table—sat the white electrical cord to her MacBook Air. That was my in. When she came back I'd make it a point to get her name—and her story—once and for all.

Chapter Two

I'D STARED AT THE CLOCK FOR SO LONG, MY EYES WERE STARTING to cross.

Mid-morning had turned into lunch, and lunch had turned into evening quicker than I expected. It didn't help that Tony's shift ended hours ago and Shelby had some kind of crisis with her cat or her iguana, or was it her chinchilla, and had to jet out of here to tend to her ailing pet.

I was holding down the fort—solo—and aside from the hum of the music which had become an annoying blend of whiney indie rock, the rain pelting against the front window of the store was all that was left to keep my mind off the clock.

A bright burst of lightning animated the darkened sky, a loud crack of thunder booming shortly after.

"Shit! It's getting bad out there," I mused aloud as I dried one of the pots I'd just cleaned. Not only was it pouring buckets, but now the lightning and thunder had become impossible to ignore. Not like I was scared or anything, but the streets were deserted and I'd rather be home binging on *Game of Thrones* than here in this lonely coffee house waiting out a storm. *And keeping an eye out for a girl who wasn't showing up.*

Stupid me had jumped at the chance to tack on an extra shift just so I could be here when *Greta*-or whatever her real name was—came back. Stupid me never did shit like this—wait around for a chick. Stupid me . . . Who was I kidding? If the weather wasn't apocalyptic out there I'd still be holding out hope that she'd walk through those doors.

I took one more glance at my wristwatch, another meandering gaze around the empty shop, and decided to call it quits. Didn't matter that closing time wasn't for another half hour. Who was braving this storm for overpriced caffeine or stale scones? Definitely not my mystery woman. "I guess I scared her away." I laughed to myself, scratching my beard as I thought about what I said to her. I allowed the memory of her shocked expression to penetrate a moment too long and warm my weary body. I jangled the set of keys I was given once I'd made management and walked to the door to lock it shut.

With one hand twirling the key ring and the other undoing the string around my apron, I blinked twice as I approached the foggy, rain soaked glass. "No. Fucking. Way."

I had to be imagining things. But who in their right mind would ever conjure up the vision of an enormous red umbrella and hideous yellow and white polka dot rain boots?

"Greta?" I shook my head and unscrambled my eyes to make sure they weren't playing some kind of pathetic trick on me. But sure enough, as I hurried closer to the door and swung it open, the rain and wind rushed in as if they were welcome guests and the umbrella lifted ever so slightly to reveal the girl behind the dark-rimmed glasses that had me counting the seconds, minutes, and hours all day.

Even protected by the parachute-sized umbrella, her dark hair was matted to her face with tiny drops of rain dripping down the bridge of her upturned nose. "You're soaked. Come in!" I shouted above the sound of the torrential downpour and another deafening crash of thunder.

The snap and crack of the boom sent Greta jumping straight into my arms, the red umbrella an afterthought as it flew out of her hands and floated behind her. I was momentarily stunned by the feeling of her body against mine—wet, cold, trembling—but then looked over her shoulder to catch the path her umbrella was headed on.

Call me a hero—or a dumbass, your choice—but I felt as if that umbrella was some kind of lifeline. She'd need it to get back home in this storm and although it had failed her from the look and feel of her saturated clothing, the need to retrieve it before it was lost for good overtook me.

"Hang on." I peeled myself away and darted toward the door. As soon as I stepped outside, the rain assaulted me, clouding my vision. I managed to catch sight of the flyaway umbrella to my right and took a few bounding steps through puddles that soaked the hems of my jeans. With a leap and a stretch that was action-movie-hero worthy, I clutched the red fabric and held on for dear life before it had a chance to drift further down the stream of water that had formed in the gutter. "Got ya, you son of a bitch!"

I didn't bother closing it, or thinking about anything but getting back inside, for that matter. Once I did, however, and after I shook off the rain like a shaggy dog just in from a jaunt in the mud, I realized the umbrella might have been safe, but the keys to the shop were not.

Chapter Three

I watched from the dry warmth of the shop as the keys drifted downstream. They did not share the same fate as the red umbrella. *They* were goners.

"Mother fu—" I started to yell, but thought better of it when I remembered I had company. Unexpected, albeit welcome, beautiful, but wet *company*. I scared her off once, I didn't want to risk her running out into this stormy night. "Welp." I shrugged. "Guess this is something we can tell our grandkids one day, right, babe?" I ran a hand over my drenched hair, slicking it back while arching an equally drenched brow as I sized up my lady friend from head to toe.

Greta's eyes narrowed behind misty lenses. Her nostrils flared and her hands balled into merciless little fists at her sides. She couldn't have known that the rain boots threw off the whole *I'm mad as hell and I'm not gonna take it anymore* vibe. But she was angry, nonetheless, and if her ears could have produced smoke, their cue would've been now.

"Oh . . . oh . . . just . . . scruff you, alright! Scruff you *and* your lumbersexual, I'm God's gift to Williamsburg attitude. For your information, I did not risk my life—nor my dignity—in this shitty weather to hear more of your cheesy pick-up lines or to be harassed. I'm on a deadline and I left my charger and I'd like it back so I can get out of here and be on my merry way!"

I didn't want to laugh. I really didn't, but *scruff you*? Did this girl have any idea how adorable she was? I tried as hard as I might to hide the humor staining my *lumbersexual* features, but there was no use. Laughter erupted, escaping my nose and pissing off Greta even more.

"You're a real piece of work, Ezra!"

Now *that* got me to stop laughing. "Hey, that's not fair. How do you know my name? I'm stuck labeling you with made-up monikers because you're too cool for school and here you are bitching me out on a first name basis."

"I can read," she smarts.

"Huh?"

"Your name tag, genius. You wear one every day on that ugly green apron."

Oh, duh. Here I was thinking she took the time to learn my name when in actuality an occupational hazard was to blame. "Well, in that case . . ." *What?* I froze, void of a clever comeback. What could I say to get this girl to stay a little longer and to stop hating me. I was out of pick-up lines or anything worthy of what this feisty girl was looking for.

But I was also saved by the bell, or in this case the crash of thunder that forced Greta back into my arms. The world—or the tiny bubble of a coffee shop the two of us inhabited at the moment—turned pitch black.

"Ezra? What the hell was that?" The sprightly, smartass demeanor I was so fond of dissipated with every second she pressed herself into the protection of my body.

Underneath a wet shirt, my heartbeat picked up. I prayed it wouldn't give me away, but when I finally mustered enough courage to reciprocate her embrace, I felt her shivering.

I cleared my throat of gravelly nerves and explained as if it weren't obvious, "Lights must've gone out." *No shit, Sherlock.*

But she didn't retreat or retort the way I imagined she would. I relished the momentary peace and quiet between us. I closed my eyes, although there was no need in the darkness provided by the storm, and sucked in the deliciousness of her rain dampened scent. Strawberries and cream mixed with a tinge of earthy steel.

I could've stayed like this all night, just to get closer to this mystifying woman. Funny how in my arms she no longer felt like a stranger; she let down her guard. That had to count for something because nothing about Greta screamed *damsel in distress*. From the little I'd observed, she was meek but confident. Independent, yet delicate. *Damn, did I want to know more.*

Against my better judgment, I cleared the silence before I took the liberty of indulging in what had become my most current craving. "You okay, sweetheart?" I hated how the endearment slipped off my tongue so cheaply. She deserved better, but was I really supposed to call her Greta when I knew damn well that wasn't her name?

She backed away, her hands against my chest for support, and I could make out the silhouette of her face looking around the blackened room. "Yeah. Sorry about that. Not a big fan of thunderstorms."

"Yet, you braved this one just to get your charger? I'm not complaining, but couldn't it have waited till tomorrow?"

She scratched her head and then put her hands in front of her, feeling around the room. "I was on a roll. The idea of calling it a night just because my Mac had no more juice seemed kind of . . . amateur. Plus, I planned on pulling an all-nighter so I thought I'd grab another latte."

I followed her around like a lost puppy even though my eyes were adjusting to the darkness and the familiarity of my home away from home. "Aw, come on. You can admit it already, Grets. You wanted to see me again."

She stopped dead in her trek around the opaqueness of the shop, causing me to bump into her. "I should've known you couldn't control yourself for more than a minute." She huffed as she turned back around and then squealed a frustrated *ouch*. "Stupid chair! Don't you have any flashlights, or candles?"

"I might," I joked, taking advantage of her exasperation simply because I could.

"Seriously, dude? Why are you doing this to me?" Even in the dark I could tell her nose was crinkled and her hands were at her hips.

"Doing what to you?"

"Being so . . . so . . . aggressive and elusive and . . ."

"Oh, no. Don't stop. Please continue. You seem to have painted quite a colorful picture of me."

By this time, we'd reached the far end of the store where upholstered booths lined the wall. She plopped down on one and grumbled. "I know nothing about you."

I sat next to her, keeping a safe distance as not to piss her off further, although what I was about to say would surely do the trick. "I could totally change that, you know."

Her arms flew into the air and landed in her lap with a loud slapping sound. "See what I mean!"

I couldn't help but laugh. "You walk right into it, honey. I'm resourceful."

"You're relentless."

"I never said I wasn't." I raked my hand through my still damp hair and rested comfortably against the booth's cushioning. "Welp, since it looks like we're stuck here for a while, whadda ya say we kiss and make up?"

Greta remained silent, dejecting my come-on save for the heavy, irritated flow of her breathing.

I stifled another bout of laughter only to jump out of my skin at the sound of the crash and shattering of glass that came next. "What the fuck is going on here tonight?" I yelled, my attention darting to the source of the smash. One of the small windows on the side of the store had blown out. Out of nowhere.

Greta scooted closer, wrapping her legs over mine and anchoring me to my seat. The safety of the shop—and both of us—should have been my priority. What I *should have* done was find the reason for the broken window.

But that's not what I did.

Instead, I gripped Greta's tiny waist with ravenous hands and lifted her off the seat beside me. In one swift movement, she was straddling me, our mouths inches apart. She didn't speak and neither did I. The only sound filling the room was our staggered breathing and the rain hammering the pavement outside.

With one last inhalation of her sweet, intoxicating scent, I crashed my mouth over hers and nearly lost control of all sense and sensibility when she didn't object.

Chapter Four

Her fingers dug into my scalp and then traveled to my face with feather soft caresses over my scruff as *she* deepened the kiss. Her legs coiled around my waist as *she* ground her core against mine. Her moans filled the dim and otherwise quiet room, as *she* nipped and sucked and drove me mad with her lips.

She was also the one to stomp on the brakes just when things were getting good. "Stop. No. We can't." Her words came out in breathy spurts, her ribcage rising and falling underneath my grasp.

I didn't want to let go, or to stop, but she clearly had other plans. "No, no, no. Keep going. We get along so much better when we're not talking." I leaned forward and tried to connect with her succulent, seductive lips again, but she backed away and practically catapulted off my lap.

"I'm not this girl. I don't . . . this isn't . . . I should go."

Fortunately for me, another bang of ear-splitting thunder ripped through the silence, causing Greta to return to the safety of my greedy arms.

I nuzzled my nose into the crook of her neck. It was an intimate act, but I couldn't help myself. If she kept jumping into my arms, I'd be an idiot not to take advantage. Or maybe I was a creep because I was taking advantage. Either way, we were here together and I was nothing if not an opportunist. But rather than try my luck and risk a swift kick in my manhood, I opted for actually daring to learn a bit about her. "Can I ask you a silly question?"

"Mmm hmm." She nodded, staring at the tempered glass window that was no longer a solid sheet but a web of crushed glass. The broken pieces created a beautiful sea of iridescence as the moonlight glinted off the rain-dropped fragments.

I ran my hands up and down her arms, fingering the prickle of goose bumps that coated the bits of skin exposed by her rolled up sleeves. Deep down I hoped I was the cause for the gooseflesh, but

I knew the chilly dampness was probably the reason for her chills. "You're obviously petrified of thunderstorms, right?" I finally asked.

"Clearly," she grumbled in response.

I stifled a laugh and continued. "Then what in the world ever made you think you'd be okay in a storm like this? I know you're hell bent on getting your charger and finishing up whatever it is you're working on, but for someone so freaked out by thunder, you could've waited. I tucked it away in a safe place. I knew you'd eventually be back."

"Must I repeat myself?" She sighed. "I told you. I'm on a deadline. You wouldn't understand." This time her voice was low as it trailed off.

She was right. I didn't get it. "So why don't you *make me* understand? Let's start with: what exactly is this project that has you on such a strict time constraint that you'd confront a storm *and* one of your biggest fears?"

With her arms wrapped around herself she stood, leaving *my* arms with that empty, lonesome feeling again. "That's just the thing. I'm facing yet another huge fear by working on this project." It was a bold statement that made me want to unravel more of her mysterious charm. To say I was intrigued was an understatement.

"Well, brave lady, spill it. Or are you planning to keep me guessing, like with everything else about you"

Before she could respond with a snarky quip, a slash of bright light illuminated the sky, and her head snapped to the window to ready herself for the boom that was sure to follow. When it didn't, she glanced my way and arched a brow, a slight smile creeping at the corner of her lips. "Could it be over?"

This chick was a master of distraction, I had to give her that. She darted to the front door with a childlike excitement only to be slammed with disappointed when the door failed to reward her with the freedom she was obviously hoping for. "Uh, Ezra?"

I shot up from the booth when I realized she wasn't just making a show of pushing the door with all her might and getting no where.

"Well, ain't this grand." I couldn't help but laugh at the irony. We were locked inside thanks to a mammoth-sized tree branch that must have snapped off in the storm and landed, yep, you guessed it, right in the path of our escape.

Before I could even appreciate the humor in the situation or say a silent prayer to whoever was in charge of my and Greta's fate, she was shrieking. "This is some kind of trick, isn't it? You, you . . . trapped me in here on purpose!" Gone was the girl who was loosening beneath my touch. In her place was the guarded enigma from before who made nothing but inaccurate assumptions about the kind of guy I was.

I no longer had it in me to play nice. "Yeah, that's what I did, *Greta*. I snuck outside, chopped down the tree like good ol' George fucking Washington, and then super sleuthed my way back inside. In fact, this whole thunderstorm is a diversion, too. Smoke and mirrors. I did it all to get you alone and have my way with you."

Her eyes narrowed on me, her hands on her hips. Before she could come back with something to further sour my mood, I took it upon myself to deflate the ego I'd played a part in giving her.

"Listen, sweetheart. I want out of here just as much as you do. You think I want to spend my night holed up in here with *you*? Pssh! I've got shit to do, too. You're not the only one with deadlines and projects, ya know?"

"Is that so?"

"Yes, it is. And to think I stayed around here just to—" Oh, no. I wasn't about to confess that I stuck around for her. I'd already given too much and gotten nothing in return. It was time to forgive and forget and to put the fantasy of *winning over the coffee shop chick* to rest. I shook my head and scrubbed a weary hand over my drying facial fuzz. "Never mind. I'll see if I can get us out of here through that broken window. Or maybe there's an ax or something around here. I don't know. You think you can stay put or will you need to use me and my lap again for false protection when you're spooked by the thunder?"

"Don't, Ezra. Don't be a dick."

"Why, not?" I laughed, shaking my head. "If it walks like a duck . . . quack, quack, baby. You've already made your judgments about me. I might as well fit the bill." I had no idea what came over me. In the short amount of time I was trapped with this girl—this *stranger*—my emotions ranged all over the place. It wasn't normal to *feel* anything because of her. I hardly knew her. In fact, I didn't know anything about her! Not even her goddamn name.

With the dismissive flick of a wrist, I started off to the back room to find a way the hell out of here. Before I could take a step further into the awkward, silent shadows, Greta spoke. "I guess I was right about you, even if I hoped I wasn't. My observations—the research, if you will. You're perfect for the part because you *are* the part. Typical cardigan wearing, Kings of Leon lovin', not-trying-to-be-cool-but-totally-trying-too-hard hipster who thinks his trendy beard can melt the panties off any lady with a simple finger trail through his scruff."

I ignored the part about the research—for now—just to knock her down to size. "*Me?* Have you looked in the mirror, darlin'? You're the poster child for Hipster Magazine. With those thrift store glasses—that're probably fake, by the way—and your chunky bangs, and your cutesy wardrobe of shabby chic threads, sipping on your expensive artisanal java every day like a walking cliché. Not to mention the whole Hollywood starlet shit. You're what, barely legal? What the hell would you know about the classics and the silver screen? I'm no more of an act than you are, sweetheart. I've got your number. You, on the other hand, know nothing about me. I don't even drink this fuckin' coffee, for Christ's sake! America runs on Dunkin'!"

In the darkness, I could make out the moonlit silhouette of her face. She was stunned still. Not angry, definitely not indifferent, maybe a bit hurt. I'd worked myself up with my little tirade, my breathing erratic. I took a deep inhalation to calm myself and expected her to react before I was able to simmer. What I didn't expect were tears. *Fuck! I was a sucker for tears.*

Chapter Five

"Shit, Greta. I'm sorry. I didn't mean to make you cry." I rushed to her side, treading lightly as I reached out to graze her arm.

"Jane," she whispered, cupping her hands over her glasses to hide her eyes.

"What?" I sidled up to her once I was sure it was safe.

"My name. It's . . . Jane." It sounded like an apology and for the life of me, I couldn't understand why. Yes, we'd just gotten into it over nothing. Yeah, she'd been a bit presumptuous in judging me based on very little knowledge. *But* I made her cry and that wasn't cool. I should be the one apologizing to her.

"Jane," I let it slip off my tongue with ease. It was simple and delicate, timeless even. "It suits you."

"What's that supposed to mean?" Her tears wavered and she sniffled, but her stiff stance told me she thought I was being sarcastic.

I laughed then. To myself, of course. I didn't want to rouse the fierce tiger that lived inside this petite, adorable kitten. Jane was a mixed bag of personalities, and not in the schizophrenic way by any stretch of my wild imagination. In fact, it was that blend of sweet and spicy that found a way to creep under my skin—every day since she first walked into the coffee shop right until this very moment.

By some cosmic twist of fate, we'd spent more time together tonight than we had in the months I'd pined over her from afar. I couldn't exactly say it was time well spent, or that it was under the most luxurious of circumstances, but hey, I'd take what I could get. Only, I wanted a do over. I needed a chance to show her that there was more to me than good looks and a furry face. I wasn't just some wanna-be Brooklyn Flea, following the fads. I had depth, interests, a heart. If she got to know me, she'd learn to like me. *One could only hope.*

We stood in silence another moment, stagnant yet peaceful. We weren't getting out of here any time soon, and I thought it would be nice to make the best of it and walk through those doors—whenever that happened to be—as friends, if nothing else. Taking a step closer, I cleared my throat and swiped a few loose strands of hair from my forehead. "Why don't we start over?" I rubbed my hand across my jeans as if to brush away any cooties she thought I might have and then extended an open palm to her. "Hi, Jane. I'm Ezra. Nice to meet you."

Jane peered over the top of her glasses, some of her lashes sticking together from the tears she shed. She took a beat too long and for a second I thought she'd snub me—yet again—but to my contentment, she took my hand in hers and shook it with a gentle squeeze. "It's nice to meet you, too."

"Phew." My chest deflated with the breath I'd been holding.

Jane's did too.

Relief filled the air with a refreshing vibe, so I ran with it. "Your clothes are still damp; you've got to be cold. Want me to see if I have an old uniform shirt in the back?"

"That would be great, but can you not leave me out here alone? I'm still kind of spooked." She adopted a low tone as if she had to keep her fears secret, as if I didn't already know she was a wuss when it came to thunderstorms. I thought it was cute, like everything else about her. But I was getting ahead of myself. *Friends first, Ezra. Play it cool.*

"Sure. Come with me. Then we can munch on some not-so-fresh bagels until we figure out our escape plan. I don't know about you, but all this bickering made me hungry."

Jane laughed—a melodious chuckle—as we felt around in the dark and made it to the employees' lounge. I managed to feel out the utility closest where a flashlight would be waiting for us. "And God said . . . let there be light." I flicked it on and accidentally shined the bright beam into her eyes. She raised her hands to shield them from the light and I changed the direction of the stream so it hit the ceiling and gave the room a low glow.

"Better?" I asked.

"Much."

"Sorry about that."

"No worries."

This being nice thing without cracking inappropriate jokes was harder than it seemed. It was awkward not being able to hide behind the defense of sarcasm. I could tell she felt the same as her eyes perused the small room filled with lockers, chairs, and a water cooler.

After ogling a second too long over how timid she'd become, I made my way over to Shelby's locker—which she always left open—to look for something suitable for Jane to wear. Rummaging through a mess of unopened mail, crumpled napkins, a pair of ugly Crocs, and lots of female toiletries, I found something promising. "Do you mind green and yellow plaid? I actually think it'll go perfect with your eyes."

She smiled shyly when she retrieved the garment from my hands and then ordered me to turn around with the twirl of her index finger.

"There's a bathroom, you know?"

"Yeah, in the dark. I'll trust my luck out here instead, just don't get any ideas by sneaking a peek."

I arched a brow, a dirty comeback on the tip of my tongue, but I thought better of it in light of how nice it was to actually be getting along with Jane rather than at each other's throats. Although, being at each other's throats had sparked an aggressiveness in her that I hoped would resurface before the night was over. *What? You can't teach an old dog new tricks.*

Crossing my heart, I nodded and did as I was told. "Want me to check for a pair of pants too?" I asked as I stared ahead into blank space, fantasizing about what her pert breasts looked like underneath her clothing. Were they more than a handful, or less? Were her pink nipples at attention because of the circumstances? Was she soaked down to her bra, and needed to shed that too? Or did she even wear one at all? God, the possibilities were endless, and much like the anticipation of solving a mystery, what the mind invented in the crevices of its wonderings could drive a man mad.

"You all right over there, Ezra?"

"Um . . . yeah," I croaked, covertly adjusting my crotch. To my surprise, just the mere *thought* of her naked body right behind me, so close, had my dick straining against my jeans.

"You can turn around now," she finally said.

But I wasn't sure I should. It was dark but I was tenting big time and I didn't want to get her all worked up again. Wait. Let me rephrase that: I *totally* wanted to get her worked up again, just not in the way I knew she would if she saw that the head in my pants wanted to get to know her before the head on my shoulders did.

"Fits like a glove," I mumbled, walking past her and gesturing for her to follow me back out front. Our quarters were too close in the lounge and I couldn't trust myself not to go back to my old ways of flirting and teasing her onto my lap again.

"So . . ." I finally said, trailing off with a smirk she couldn't see. "You mentioned research earlier. How 'bout I set us up with something to snack on and then you fill me in. Looks like we have all night. Might as well make it a working evening since you're on deadline, and all. Whadda ya think?"

Her gulp was audible; her embarrassment almost was, too. I relished the idea of putting her on the spot and making her squirm the way I had while she was undressing behind me only moments ago. Something told me Jane's secret project was *very* interesting.

Chapter Six

WE SAT TOGETHER IN A BOOTH ADJACENT TO THE TABLE she usually parked herself in when she did whatever she did behind that computer of hers. I'd scrounged up a few still-decent croissants and muffins, and created her signature beverage like a boss. A green tea with lemon was my poison tonight, though a few finger widths of scotch or whiskey would have been much better.

The weather had subsided somewhat, although every now and then a rumble of thunder caused Greta . . . I mean, Jane . . . to look my way. My fingers itched to touch her skin, my lips tingled with the thought of hers on mine, but I kept my hands to myself and my dick in my pants because we were getting along in the peaceful silence by the glow of a single-bulbed flashlight. I ignored the elephant in the room—her mortified expression at the mention of her secret project—as long as possible, hoping she'd spill the beans on her own. She picked at the cranberry muffin like a cautious bird, hardly ever making eye contact.

I decided to break the ice because my curiosity was killing me. My fingers made a show of dramatically rubbing my beard. "I'm thinking of shaving it," I blurted out of nowhere.

Jane's eyes abandoned the muffin and popped open, honing in on mine. "The hell you are," she spoke matter of factly.

Taken aback, but loving every minute of her bluntness, I narrowed my eyes in question. "What's it to you?"

Jane took a deep breath and pushed her glasses up the bridge of her nose. I could tell she was nervous because her hands were busy with mindless tasks—making a pile out of muffin crumbs, smoothing her fingers through long strands of dark hair, wiping the corners of her pretty mouth. When she finally rested them on the table in front of her, I reached forward and clasped my much larger hands over hers. "Would you sit still? You're making me dizzy."

"*Dizzy*," she mumbled with a chuckle. Her green eyes met mine again and I couldn't help but bite my bottom lip to stop myself from saying something inappropriate.

What she said next, though—all bets were off after that.

"The beard stays. I like it. Even if it is a bit . . . *generic*." She was fucking with me but it was all in good fun because I could tell she didn't give a shit that it was generic. She dug it! I knew it! Before I could ruin the moment by babbling something along the lines of *I told you so*, she continued. "It's kind of what got me here in the first place. You. You're my research, Ezra."

I wasn't sure if I should be flattered or offended, but either way this got my attention. "Huh? What are you talking about?"

She removed her hands from underneath mine and started to fidget again. She lost her perfect posture and slouched into the upholstered booth. Closing her eyes and gnawing on her lip she divulged her best kept secret. "I'm writing a screenplay for class and you—well someone based on you—is the lead character." If not for the fact we were locked in here against our will, I expected her to jet out of here faster than I could say *manbun*.

But I wasn't letting her off easy. No fucking way. All this time I'd been practically obsessing over her and she was writing a goddamn story about me. "You totally want me, don't you?" I leaned over the table, resting my head in my hands and batting my eyelashes obnoxiously.

Her defenses were up but her eyes told a different tale. "Who said anything about wanting you? I'm intrigued by you, for my story, of course, but that doesn't mean I want to sleep with you."

"Whoa, whoa, whoa." I raised both hands in the air. "Look who's jumping to conclusions. I said nothing about sleeping together. I was only looking for a *date*. A good, honest night on the town with the quirky customer with the annoying coffee requests. But if you're game for skipping all the small talk and getting-to-know-each-other shit, I can up the ante on your *research* and give you something *really good* to write about."

"I knew I shouldn't have told you." She rose from her seat and shimmied out of the booth.

I followed her to the center of the store, came up behind her, hands on her shoulders, and spun her around to face me. "The jig is up, darlin'. Don't play shy now."

Our mouths only inches apart, her sweet breath tickled the tip of my nose. I wanted to kiss her. *Terribly*. But I also wanted her to initiate. To succumb and validate that she had it as badly for me as I did for her. "Jane," I whispered, teasing her.

"Ezra," she moaned, her eyes shielded by lowered lids and those adorable specs.

"I've done my own kind of research, too," I admitted, pressing my forehead to hers. "But it's not for any book, or screenplay. Just for *me*, Jane. I've watched you every day since you came in here. Talk about intriguing . . ." I trailed off and groaned, nuzzling my scruff covered cheek against her soft one. "You think you can finally stop snubbing me? Can you give me a shot—*Greta*?"

To think that only this morning she was a mystery. She still was, but I was slowly unfolding so many interesting details about this girl and I had this stupid job at this stupid coffeehouse to thank for it. *Of all the coffee joints, in all the world . . .*

"You don't think I'm a weirdo?" She inspected my face, from the dyed tips of my lumbersexual hair to the bushy depths of my whiskers.

"Oh, I totally think you're a weirdo, but you're an adorable weirdo. So whadda ya say?"

In the middle of a dark room, locked away from the world, with the rain still coming down in heavy sheets, we stood together in each other's arms—strangers with the possibility of becoming so much more.

Jane giggled, rested her head against my shoulder and then peered up at me with a devilish grin. "I think I can arrange that. For research, of course."

About Faith Andrews

Faith Andrews is living out her dream right outside the greatest city in the world, New York City. Happily married to her high school sweetheart, she is the mother of two beautiful and wild daughters, and a furry Yorkie son named Rocco Giovanni. When she's not tapping her toes to a Mumford & Sons tune or busy being a dance mom, her nose is stuck in a book or she's sitting behind the laptop, creating her next swoon worthy book boyfriend. Coffee addict, lover of wine and cheese, and sucker for concerts and Netflix, Faith believes in love at first sight and happily ever after.

Author website www.authorfaithandrews.com

Facebook www.facebook.com/authorfaithandrews

Twitter www.twitter.com/jessicafaith919

Instagram www.instagram.com/jessicafaith91

Theirs To Protect

BY RENEE ROSE

Chapter One

SLOANE DROPPED THE HEAVY STACK OF CASE FOLDERS INTO THE leather passenger seat of her white Prius. The back of her neck prickled and she paused, spinning around to scan the parking lot outside the Tucson city courthouse. For the third time that week she had that creepy feeling of being watched.

She shook it off and climbed behind the wheel. Probably she was just being paranoid. She sighed. At three in the afternoon, her day was only half over. She had to review the stack of files before Judge Tell's retirement party that night.

Starbucks, here I come.

She needed about ten Venti Red Eyes to make it through the files for tomorrow, most of them her least favorite—child protective services cases. Being a public defender wasn't glamorous—not even remotely—but she was still idealistic enough to believe she served the greater good.

She turned on her signal to pull into the Starbucks parking lot, only to have a cop cut her off as he pulled into the lot in front of her. What an ass. Seemed like most cops she dealt with had serious ego and control issues.

She followed him into the lot and managed to whip into the last parking place before he got it.

Ha.

The squad car zipped past and double-parked beside the row of vehicles. Must be nice to be a cop.

She grabbed her purse and headed into Starbucks, stealing a surreptitious glance at the policeman over her shoulder. Make that *men*. Two of them, and actually not unappealing specimens of Tucson's finest. Not that she was into that kind of guy.

She stood in line behind a trio of University of Arizona sorority girls in their matching T-shirts and short shorts. Damn, some of the girls wore them so short, their butt cheeks showed below the fabric. The police officers entered behind her.

Okay, they were beyond appealing. They were hot. Even for someone who didn't have the "man in a uniform" fetish. These guys could actually tempt her to into a game of *Good cop, bad cop*. Or would it be *Hot cop, hotter cop? Seasoned cop, youthful cop?* The taller one was older—maybe mid-forties—with salt-and-pepper hair and piercing blue eyes. He wore a neatly trimmed beard, also peppered with silver, and his uniform clung to broad shoulders. The other cop might be in his late twenties or early thirties, like her. His broad, muscular chest stood out in fine definition, and the corded muscles of his arms showed beneath his short sleeves. He had brown hair and green eyes and also sported facial hair—a goatee distinguishing his youthful face. The TPD allowed facial hair? They probably had a "neat and trimmed" policy, at the very least.

His eyes sparkled when he caught her ogling. "Sorry for cutting you off back there."

Unable to hold a grudge—he was too damn cute—she smiled back. "Sorry for taking the last parking place, but I figured it would be better for you to double-park than for me."

Youthful Cop's eyes traveled down the length of her body, taking in the fitted skirt, bare legs, and high heels. The corners of his lips curled in appreciation. Seasoned Cop smirked at both of them.

Damn, Starbucks needed to turn up the air conditioning. It was getting hot in there.

The sorority girls moved on, and she stepped forward, blood singing. She ordered an iced Red Eye and then told the cashier the policemen's drinks were on her. The young barista beamed.

She walked to the next station to pick up her drink. As she tapped a straw out of its wrapper, she heard the barista telling Hot Cops what she'd done. "It's in appreciation of your service," the barista said.

The sorority girls watched with curiosity, and the two women standing behind the policemen smiled, also listening.

"No, it's not, it's because you're so good-looking," she called over to them as she sailed to the counter with the half and half.

The coffee shop broke into twitters. Seasoned Cop threw back his head and laughed while Youthful Cop's watchful eyes crinkled.

Sloane winked at them and put the top back on her creamy iced coffee, swirling the cubes. The sound alone brought on a Pavlovian response of joy from her weary body.

She strutted out the side door, finding no reason to blow a great exit line. As she rounded the corner toward her car, Youthful Cop sauntered out the door, his neck craning sideways.

She smiled to herself and sashayed toward her car, the click of her heels on the pavement punctuating each step. The momentary thrill passed as she wondered whether he planned to ask her on a date. She hoped not. She didn't date—especially not cops.

Three failed relationships in her twenties had soured her on men in general. She'd been the type who went all-in, so when they ended, her life had been torn apart. *Controlling*, one ex hand called her. Needy, another had said. Okay, she wanted a lot from her man. So what?

So, yeah. She'd learned to live without a man. Problem solved. Life was easier now. Much easier. Love wasn't worth the heartbreak. Besides, she had a busy enough life with her career.

She opened her car door and slid into the seat, but Youthful Cop caught the door before she could swing it shut.

Oh boy.

He draped an arm over it and leaned in, standing between her and the door. She'd never understood the meaning of "twinkling" eyes before, but this guy's eyes definitely twinkled as he smiled down. "Thanks again for the coffee." His deep, sexy voice sent frissons of heat rippling through her body.

Seasoned Cop arrived behind him, holding two large cups of iced java. He handed one to his partner and perched his hip against the body of her car, filling the remaining space between her door and the car.

The words "Cop Sandwich" flitted into her mind, and she pushed them firmly away when they inspired an entirely different, far more explicit picture in her brain.

Damn. She must be ovulating. She didn't usually get this turned on by random guys she met at Starbucks.

She blinked up at them. Both smirked in a confident, hot-man kind of way. Jesus, they were cute. Almost blindingly so. "Okay, guys, I have to go—"

"I'm not sure those legs are legal, Johnboy, what do you think?" Seasoned Cop drawled, his eyes traveling the length of her bare legs.

Heat bloomed in her core.

Youthful Cop—Johnboy—took on a mock-serious expression and made a tsking noise. "I'm not sure they are."

She needed to shut them down. Because, really, this wasn't going to go anywhere. "Very funny boys. Okay, I need to get going."

"Uh oh, I think we're getting the brush-off now." Seasoned Cop's eyes slid sideways to his partner.

"Damn, and I thought she might enjoy a frisking." Youthful Cop flashed a wolfish smile.

Her breasts ached, nipples hardened into tight beads at the thought of the two men running their hands all over her body. How long had it been since she'd had sex? Two years? Three? Way too long.

No—just no. This was stupid. She didn't have time to even sit here and flirt right now, and the flirting wouldn't be going anywhere.

She stiffened her spine. "That's never going to happen, fellas." She made a shooing motion to get them out of her door.

When they didn't move, she upped the deep freeze. "Buying you coffee wasn't an offer for sex." Her tongue faltered on the word *sex*, as images flashed through her brain of all the possibilities available to three bodies, namely, the two of theirs and hers. She flushed.

End the conversation, Sloane.

"Sweetheart, women beg us for sex, not the other way around." John beamed at her as if she might start begging any minute. When she didn't, he accepted defeat and took a step back. "Well, you might consider it sometime. It could help with that monster icecap you have going there."

His partner's lips twisted into a rueful smile, and he hooked a large hand through Youthful Cop's arm and tugged him back, obviously realizing his partner had crossed a line and offended her.

"Right, like I'd need to resort to screwing *Super Troopers*," she spluttered. They didn't need to know she mentioned one of her favorite movies.

Great, Sloane. Was that the best you could do?

The guys had stepped back, out of the way of her door.

"Who wants a mustache ride?" John called out one of her favorite quotes from the movie as Seasoned Cop swung the door shut.

Seasoned Cop chuckled as he continued to tug his partner away from her car.

Seriously? Monster ice cap?

As if.

The whole drive home she thought of sassier comebacks she could've given to the two men, and not because her panties were still damp from thoughts of how the two of them might fuck her monster ice cap off.

Two men at once? Two *cops*?

Insane. She needed to get that thought out of her brain as quickly as possible.

Officer John Hathaway jotted down the hot blonde's license plate number before he met his partner's raised eyebrows.

"You going to check her record?" Keith asked with a snort.

"Maybe." He grinned and pocketed his notebook. As he drew a long sip of the coffee, he willed his thickened cock to relax. "Seriously, what happened back there? I know I came on too strong, but there was just something about her."

"Yeah. There was." Keith sounded as interested as he felt.

"For a half-second, I thought she might give us her number. She definitely thought about it."

"Aw, don't worry about it. I think you nailed it—she's a little uptight. We tempted her and then she got scared of her own desires and lashed out. Don't take it personally."

"Okay, Dr. Phil. Or is it Dr. Drew?"

"Yeah, just bring all your sex-related problems to me. Clearly, I have it all figured out." A shade of bitterness bled through in his voice. Apart from two threesomes they'd had with women who had a multiple cop fetish, Keith hadn't had sex in the four years since his wife died.

They headed to the squad car but before he had a chance to punch in her license plate, dispatch called. "A silent alarm has been tripped at the Circle J on Park Ave. All vehicles in the area please respond."

He flicked on the lights and siren and pulled out as Keith grabbed the handset. "Hathaway and Swenson responding. Estimated arrival, three minutes."

The tires screeched a little as he rounded the bend out of the parking lot. Swenson tensed beside him, readying for the scene. They were good partners—had been from day one. Somehow, they just synchronized immediately, "getting" each other, almost like brothers, despite the fifteen-year age difference.

He turned the siren off as they grew closer, to avoid tipping off the perps. When he whipped into the Circle J parking lot, both officers jumped out of their vehicle.

A tall, skinny figure emerged, yanking a mask off his head and stuffing it in the paper bag he carried.

John drew his gun and aimed it, creeping forward. "Freeze, hands in the air!"

Keith also drew his weapon and yelled at a young woman just getting out of her car, "*Get back in the vehicle. Stay down on the floor!*"

The perp took off running, clutching the bag under his arm. John cursed and took off after him, Keith right behind, shouting into the radio. "In pursuit on foot, following perp southbound, behind the building. Backup requested."

"I said, *freeze*, asshole," John yelled. The young perp's eyes were wild, which probably meant he was scared enough to be dangerous. Operating under the assumption he was armed, he would have skirted behind the cars for protection, but they all had occupants, and he wasn't willing to draw fire toward innocent bystanders.

Thankfully, two more squad cars pulled in, and one of them whipped around behind the building to cut the perp off from behind. The second closed in behind him and Keith. In seconds, Officers Franks and Sherman were out of their car, weapons drawn.

"Freeze, right where you are! Hands in the air!"

The perp drew up short, glanced over his shoulder at John and Keith bearing down on him, and pulled up to a defeated stop. He thrust his palms in the air.

"On the ground, face down," Keith yelled as the four officers circled the perp, each of them keeping their weapons trained on him.

The other two officers jumped out of the car behind them and worked on clearing the area of bystanders.

He darted forward and cuffed the perp then patted him down for weapons, removing the gun from his jacket pocket.

Keith came up beside him. "You went cowboy again." His way of saying John had been too reckless, but he heard the affection in his voice. He wasn't pissed—this time.

Chapter Two

By the time Keith finished booking the offender and interviewing witnesses, he and John had missed all possibility of going home to change into civilian clothes before they had to represent their precinct at some judge's retirement party. Not that he minded— much—his uniform was better than a suit any day. Still, he would have preferred to shower and freshen up first.

The pair had lost the department-wide rock, paper, scissors game or else he'd be at home with his feet up. Instead, they strolled the swanky outdoor patio of Starr Pass Resort, amidst the politicians and lawyers circling the area like sharks.

"Too many alpha males," Keith's wife Becky used to mutter when she had to attend these things with him. "Too many Type A personalities. It makes me want to run for the door."

The pang didn't hurt as much anymore when he thought of her. That bugged him. He'd never thought he'd forget her and move on. It had been only four years since she'd lost the fight to breast cancer.

John constantly tried to get him to date again. So far, it hadn't worked. He'd never even picked up a woman on his own, although twice they'd been picked up by women wanting to fulfill their *ménage a trois* fantasies. He thought it'd be weird the first time—he'd have to see his partner naked, and all that, but they made a good team. They were tight. Real tight—like brothers.

"Starbucks Ice Queen, two o'clock," John murmured.

Keith's head jerked up, and his gaze shot across the patio. *God in Heaven.*

There she stood, her body-hugging black cocktail dress accenting her perfect hourglass figure. The fabric of her dress swooped around her neck, leaving her shoulders bare, the slender line of her throat set off by a simple but elegant up-do with a few wisps of blonde hair framing her face.

Whoa. She looked amazing. Like, needle

screeching-across-the-record, show stoppingly gorgeous. Her figure, which had been sexy enough in her professional dress earlier in the day, now looked Hollywood-worthy.

"I'm going to get her this time," John said, filled with determination. "You in?"

He grinned. "It's on."

They headed straight for her, wolves hunting their prey. She stood talking to a couple of stuffed shirts, but her gaze slid over to them and she did a double take. He was half-afraid she'd ignore them completely, or, worse, make a beeline in the opposite direction, but, to his surprise, she broke away from her cronies and headed toward them. They met her near a concrete pillar and she skirted the side of it so it hid them from view.

"I didn't know they invited the Super Troopers." She folded her arms across her perky breasts.

"We just booted your car, Ice Princess," John said. "You really should've paid those parking tickets."

"What parking tickets?" she spluttered. "What in the hell are you—" Catching the amusement on Keith's face, she relaxed. "Very funny."

He tilted his head. "Well, I'm definitely writing a ticket for that dress. It should be illegal."

Her sensuous lips curved into a smile. "Oh, really?" She infused a heavy dose of skepticism into her words.

"On you, at least. It could incite a riot." He stuck out his hand. "Keith Swensen."

She gripped his palm, her slender handshake firm and professional. "Sloane Walters."

"John Hathaway." John offered his hand. "How do you know Judge Tell?"

She pointed to her lovely chest, giving them the excuse to ogle her cleavage. "Public defender."

John snorted. "That explains it."

Her jaw dropped in clear offense. "That explains what?"

"Type A personality. Never lets her hair down. Dying to get laid if only she didn't have to touch anyone to do it."

Her beautiful aqua eyes narrowed. "You don't know me."

His boyish grin appeared. "Oh yeah? What kind of woman buys two guys drinks, flirts, and then bites their heads off when they show interest?"

A flicker of regret—or defeat—flashed across her face. Keith didn't like it. They didn't seek to insult her or make her feel bad, but to incite her to action.

He spoke up before she could answer. "The kind who is secretly dying to know what it feels like to have two men make love to her at once."

Their gazes tangled. His eyes went to those full, glossy lips, close enough to kiss, as he imagined what it would be like to take her mouth. His heart gave a double pump, a sort of lurch that made the hair on his arms stand up with recognition.

He'd experienced the same lurch the day he'd met Becky.

"You know what I think," Youthful Cop—John—drawled. "I think you're the sort of woman who actually is dying to have control taken away from her." He looked even sexier than earlier, filling that uniform out with bulging muscles. She glanced at the handcuffs on his belt and wondered if he ever used them for sex.

Her eyebrows shot up to her hairline. "Oh please."

He held up a hand. "No, hear me out. Have you ever been tied up in bed? Taken roughly?"

Her cheeks heated, lips parted, but no words came out. Her body had a visceral reaction to his words, belly fluttering, heat flooding her core.

But that couldn't be. She didn't have any interest in giving up control, especially not to these guys.

Did she?

John backed her up against the pillar and rested a hand beside her head, invading her personal space. Keith leaned on his shoulder on the other side. Neither one actually touched her, but her skin prickled at their nearness. "It might be just the thing you've been missing," Keith said.

"I'm not interested," she managed to say, her voice shaky.

Keith's mouth twisted into a knowing grin. What he thought he knew, she wasn't sure. John's eyes dropped to her breasts. "You sure about that? Your nipples are so hard they're poking through the fabric of your dress."

She looked down, face growing warm. Oh God. He was right. Possibly about all of it.

"And I know you have a thing for my handcuffs because you've eyed them three times."

Shit. Really?

"I'll make you a deal. You leave here with us now, without any problems, and we'll forget all about the way you turned polar ice cap on us earlier."

She stared into John's moss-green eyes, sensing only good-natured teasing under the cocky posturing. "And if I don't?"

A slow, wicked smile spread across his face. "If you don't, then when we do finally get you in bed, I'll spank that perfect ass red and make you beg for every orgasm."

Her pussy contracted. If the pillar hadn't been holding her up, she'd have been swaying on her feet.

They knew just how to get to her, didn't they? Her competitive side couldn't back down from a challenge, and the sex talk? *Jesus.* She'd nearly orgasmed right there. And she knew she'd be safe—they were cops, after all. Despite the aggressive talk, she trusted them to respect her.

Keith, the older and the more serious one—the one with the haunted eyes—leaned over and nibbled on her ear. "We'll make it good for you," he murmured, and held out his hand. "Give me your keys."

She stared at him for a long moment. If she gave in, she'd not only be saying yes to a threesome, but she'd be letting them drive, both literally and metaphorically. Could she handle giving over control?

She reached into her purse, dug out her keys, and dropped them into his palm.

"Meet you at the elevators," Keith said.

It took her a minute to understand he intended to make it less obvious they were leaving together. She watched his back as he walked away—the wide shoulders that tapered to a narrow waist, the muscular ass...

"See you in the parking lot," John murmured, heading in the opposite direction.

Classy. These guys definitely knew their business.

She headed toward the elevator bank, her high heels clicking over the marble floors when she stepped inside.

Keith stood off to the side, casually thumbing the screen of his phone. He let her pass without making eye contact, but then followed her into the elevator before the doors swished closed. She hit the P3 button for the parking garage.

In a flash, Keith had her up against the wall, one wrist pinned beside her head, his other hand cupping her ass. The heat simmering since the moment she'd seen the cops in Starbucks burst into white-hot flames.

She lifted her face for his kiss, parted her lips for his plunder. His mouth twisted over hers, tongue swept into her mouth. She ground her hips against the thigh he'd wedged between her legs.

"We're going to make you feel so good, baby," he growled in her ear, just before he nipped it.

She panted, close to combusting right there in the elevator.

The elevator bell dinged and he pulled away, casual as if nothing had happened. She, on the other hand, probably had swollen lips and a dazed expression.

Chapter Three

Keith held the passenger door open for Sloane then climbed in behind her wheel, adjusting the seat to accommodate his long legs. John idled nearby. Keith gave him a mock salute and pulled out in front to lead the way.

Following Sloane's crisp directions, he pulled up in front of an Armory Park Victorian house.

They climbed out. A grey tabby came running down the sidewalk toward her.

"Molly!" She scooped up the cat. "What are you doing out?" Sloane frowned. "Hmm?" She rubbed her face in the fluffy fur as she led them up her porch stairs.

Dropping the cat, she unlocked the door, stepped in, and peered around as if something made her suspicious.

"What is it?" He watched her rub the back of her neck.

"Just trying to figure out how the cat got out. I know I left her in today."

"Want me to have a look through the house?"

She shook her head with a forced smile. "No, I'm sure she just slipped out when I wasn't paying attention."

Keith looked around Sloane's charming brick bungalow. They stood in the living room, which featured a large plush L-shaped red couch and a thick gold oval rug over the hardwood floor. The walls were brightly colored plaster in yellow, orange and brick and the ceilings sported the original metal ceiling tiles from the late 1800s. He only knew about that shit because he and Becky had renovated an old barrio house when they first married.

It had a warm, comfortable feel. Sloane, however, appeared uncomfortable. He'd have to take care of that.

"Okay to use your shower?" John asked, stepping past them.

"Oh! Yes, down on the hall on your left."

John disappeared and Keith stepped up close and unzipped her dress, letting it fall to a black puddle at her feet. As he'd suspected, she wasn't wearing a bra. She stood in nothing but a pair of black satin panties. He caught her wrists. "Hands behind your back."

She shivered, but obeyed. He slipped on the cuffs but kept them very loose. Bending close to her ear, he murmured, "Let me know if these bother you, okay, baby?"

Her shoulders visibly relaxed, and she smiled.

Keith kicked Sloane's feet apart and slid his large palms down her outer thighs, squatting in front of her.

The moment his thumb brushed her panty-clad pussy, she jerked and attempted to shift her feet, her hands twisting in the cuffs.

"Uh uh." He fixed her with a mock-stern gaze. "I told you not to move."

She swallowed and drew a deep breath.

This time he pressed his mouth right up to her mons and used his teeth, biting.

Her head dropped back, and she closed her eyes.

Jesus, she was beautiful. His thumb returned to stroke her pussy over her panties, and her legs trembled at the effort of remaining still.

Holy public defender and all things glorious. John emerged from the hallway with a towel around his waist to find the most erotic visage of Sloane he could have imagined. Hands cuffed behind her back, her eyes were closed, face and perfect, peach-tipped breasts facing the ceiling. Apparently, he'd been right. She'd been dying to surrender control.

His partner had the gusset of her silky panties shoved to the side as he palmed her ass and licked into her.

The little mewl escaping her lips nearly undid him.

"My turn," he muttered when he joined them.

Keith pulled away, appearing reluctant. Her juices glossed his beard. "She tastes like heaven."

He grabbed Sloane's hips and spun her around to face the arm of the couch. "Bend over, baby."

She obeyed, folding her torso over the furniture, hands still cuffed behind her back.

He brought his hand down, slapping the place where her ass emerged from the black lace panties and met her thigh.

She gasped but didn't move.

She liked it.

He slapped her on the other side, a little lower this time, watching his red hand print bloom on her bare skin. "You have the most beautiful ass I have ever seen, counselor."

She made an unintelligible sound.

Hooking his thumbs in the waistband of her sexy panties, he slid them slowly down her legs. She kicked off her shoe to step out, but he scolded her again. "The shoes stay on—don't you agree, Keith?" he called toward the bathroom where the shower had just turned on.

The water turned off. "What's that?"

"Her shoes stay on?"

"Oh definitely. They are the perfect accent to the most beautiful pair of legs I've ever seen." A blush stained Sloane's face, at least the side he could see with her head turned. She seemed far more innocent than the other women who had jumped into bed with him and his partner. He honestly hadn't been sure they'd coax her into it, especially since lawyers tended to be tightly wound. Gazing at her trusting surrendered pose now, he vowed to show her the time of her life—she definitely deserved it.

She twisted her wrists in the cuffs.

He checked the tightness. Keith had left them loose enough she could slip out of them if she wanted.

"Don't tug against these, baby. They can hurt."

"So did that spanking you gave me."

He chuckled. "That wasn't a spanking, sweetheart, just me warming up your ass." He rubbed the beautiful posterior in question. "It hurt?"

"Kinda." She sounded pouty, the cutest thing he'd ever heard.

He leaned over her back, still rubbing. "I'm sorry, baby. Do you want me to stop?"

"No." Her voice sounded small.

He slapped her again, rubbing immediately. "Mmm, I really do love this ass." One more slap, then he lowered to his knees and pulled her cheeks apart, running his tongue along her moistened slit.

She let out a little cry.

He stiffened his tongue and penetrated her then nibbled at her lips. "You're being a very good girl, Sloane." He stood up and stuck two fingers in her mouth. "Suck these."

Her eyes widened in surprise, but then she obeyed, swirling her tongue around his fingers, making his cock nearly explode with jealousy. He removed his fingers from her mouth and teased her entrance with them.

Her pussy dripped with moisture. He screwed one finger inside her, delighting with the way her back undulated and she squirmed and squeaked as he stretched her wide. His second finger fit beside it, and he pumped them in and out, her feet stamping beneath him.

The water in the bathroom stopped.

He called out, "What do you think, Keith? Has she earned an orgasm yet?"

"Make her scream, man."

Sloane whimpered.

He pumped his fingers in and out of her, aiming high against her front wall, his fingertips seeking her G-spot.

There. He found it. An area of tissue thickened and hardened beneath his stimulation, and her moans grew more frantic. He reached around her hips and found her clit with the middle finger, still pistoning in and out of her with the other hand.

"Oh God…please…oh my God. Oh please… *Oh!*" she screamed. Her muscles clamped around his fingers, squeezing and clenching as she orgasmed.

"Now, that's what I'm talking about," Keith rumbled from the doorway.

When she'd finished, he eased his fingers out of her and unlocked the cuffs from her wrists. She flopped on her back on the sofa with a satisfied sigh. Her eyes slipped closed, a smile curving her lips.

He climbed up beside her. "You need anything, baby? Are you hungry?"

Her smile widened, and her eyelids fluttered back open. "I'm okay."

Keith sat on the other side of her, stroking his palm up one leg and over her flat belly to cup her breast. "You're my dinner." He thumbed her nipple, teasing it back into a stiff bead.

Her hips twisted on the cushion. She moved to sit up, but they both held her down. "Where do you think you're going?" he teased.

"To reciprocate?"

His cock jerked at the offer, but he shook his head. "Not yet. Your only job right now is to receive." He pinched the nipple on his side while Keith drew circles around the other.

She moistened her lips with her tongue, and the sight of it had him groaning. Her hips swiveled again, legs rolling.

He reached down and cupped her mons. "Do you need me to touch you here again?" He undulated his fingers.

A wanton sound came from her lips. "Spread your legs, baby."

She shook her head. When she didn't move, Keith shifted to sit behind her, and pulled her up to lean her back against his chest. "Hand me those cuffs."

He tossed the cuffs to his partner, who attached them to her wrists in front, then lifted the loop of her arms up over his head, so her bound wrists rested behind his neck. Keith cupped both her breasts and pinched her nipples.

John crouched on the floor beside the sofa and shoved her knees up, spreading her wide. "The way I see it, if you don't have beard burn by the time we're done, we haven't done our job right."

He slid the tip of his tongue all along her slit, licking and sucking at her outer lips, nibbling.

Already, her hips lifted and pressed against his face. Keith continued to work her breasts, biting her neck and ear.

John circled her clit with his tongue, flicked it, sucked the swollen nubbin until she kicked and writhed beneath him. She panted, her chest heaving, belly fluttering. Her pussy juices dripped by the time he tested her entrance with his fingers. He worked one into her then two. He curled them, tickling her inner wall as he went to town on her clit with his mouth.

That quickly, she shattered again, screaming so loudly Keith laughed and covered her mouth with his hand. He held her bucking pelvis down and continued to lick and finger fuck her until she'd followed the spiral of release to its beautiful conclusion.

"Oh," she moaned when it had passed. Moisture leaked from the outer corner of one eye.

Keith licked it away. "Are you okay, beautiful?"

"Yeah," she panted. "I'm just…blown. Blown away. Blown out. I don't even know."

Keith ran a series of kisses along her jaw and down her neck. John had never seen his partner so affectionate with a woman. Well, not since his late wife, anyway. But, then, this one was different. John found himself wanting more than just a hot sex scene. He wanted to please her, wanted to earn not just her moans, but also her smiles, her esteem, and yeah…her affection.

He went to grab a bottle of water from her refrigerator and twisted off the cap. He held it up to Sloane's lips since Keith still had her hands cuffed behind his neck.

She drank, dribbling a little down her chest.

He licked the cool drops, dragging his tongue between her breasts and up the length of her neck to her jaw. "Admit it. I pegged you right."

"Great, are you going to do the I'm right dance?" She rolled her eyes. "Just because I got off doesn't mean you know what I like."

He gave her a "don't bullshit me" lift of the brows.

"What?"

He glanced at his partner. "Looks like we're going to have to play hardball."

Keith uncuffed her wrists and swung her around until she lay face down on his lap. His hand connected with her ass.

"Hey," she yelped.

"Admit it," John drawled. "You like giving up control."

"I do *not*!" She yelped again when Keith's hand connected a second time.

"For once in your life, you don't have to worry about being right or not screwing up or winning. You're just a helpless victim of our most depraved desires and you love it."

Keith smacked her ass again.

"Admit it."

Another smack.

"Ow, okay, okay, I admit I fucking love it, okay?"

Keith laughed and rubbed her ass. "Did you record that confession?"

He grinned. "Yep, I sure did."

Keith's cock throbbed beneath the beautiful lawyer. She rolled off and dropped to her knees in front of him, tugging off the towel around his waist. Fisting his manhood, she lowered her pouty mouth. He nearly came just watching those full lips part for him.

She took a long, slow swirl of her tongue around the head of his cock then took it into her hot, wet mouth.

He groaned. He wouldn't last long at this rate. He'd been hard for her since the first flirty smile she'd flashed at Starbucks that afternoon.

She licked a long line from his balls to the rim of his cock then took his length deep into her throat.

Jesus *fuck*! His eyes rolled back in his head.

Behind her, his partner produced a condom and rolled it on his dick. Sloane rested on her knees, bent at the waist, presenting in a perfect position to be fucked from behind.

He buried one hand in her hair, stroking her head. "John's going to fuck you now, baby," he warned her, wanting to be sure they had her consent.

"Mmmph," she moaned and waggled her hips as she hollowed out her cheeks and sucked his cock hard. Incredible to see how she'd given herself over to them, her trust in them clear, her surrender beautiful. He felt a strong desire to protect her—from them, from life, from anything that might ever threaten her. She brought out the most primitive male in him—the caveman who wanted to provide and protect.

John gripped her hips and held them still as he pushed into her.

She momentarily stopped sucking him, just held him engulfed in her deliciously hot mouth.

"Don't forget Keith, baby girl," John murmured, his voice deepened with lust as he glided in and out of her slowly.

She started and lifted her eyes apologetically. Keith stroked her cheek with his knuckles, watching, transfixed, as she started up again. Damn, the woman could suck the chrome off a bumper.

His balls swelled.

John picked up his speed, holding her hips steady as he shoved in deeper, harder.

She sucked faster, matching John's pace, her eyes wide with panic. She was close.

Damn, he was close, too.

"Fuck, Sloane," he muttered.

John's jaw tightened and his brow furrowed. He plowed into her with more force, their bodies slapping together.

Sloane lost all rhythm. She pulled off him and pumped her fist over his cock with the head bumping against her outstretched tongue. It was enough. His thighs gripped.

"I'm coming," he warned her, but she let it spill onto her tongue.

"Fuck, yeah," John grunted behind her, his strokes growing rough as he, too, lost control. "Yeah," he roared, shoving deep into Sloane.

Keith pinched her nipples, and she jerked with release, her mouth opening into a surprised sort of O.

Beautiful. Exquisite, really. He took a mental picture, not wanting to forget the way she looked in that moment.

Chapter Four

A MALE VOICE MURMURED SLOANE AWAKE. SUNLIGHT STREAMED in through a crack in her curtains. Holy shit. She stiffened. Had she actually *spent the night* with them? She blinked, rubbing her eyes as she sat up.

No. Freaking. Way.

Both cops lay in bed with her, one on each side.

"What time is it?" she croaked, panic seeping in. She had to be in court by eight.

"It's only five thirty, but I figured you might need to get going." Keith stroked a lock of hair from her face as he spoke. It had been his voice that woke her.

John leaned up on one elbow, his bare chest as perfectly defined as his partner's.

Holy shit. How had she ended up letting them spend the night?

What had she expected to happen? That they'd put their clothes on, say goodnight, and go their separate ways, she supposed. But when she'd collapsed on Keith in utter exhaustion, he'd picked her up and carried her to the bedroom. That was the last thing she remembered. She must have fallen into the deepest sleep she'd had in years.

"Yeah, I need to get moving."

Keith climbed out of bed, still naked—gloriously so—and stood back to let her pass. Wow. Had she really had a cop threesome last night?

She stood up and tried to pull the sheet with her to cover herself, but John snapped it back. "No way, baby girl. There's no being shy with us on the morning after."

She scrambled to pull on a robe. When had she taken her shoes off? One of them must have done it for her. "Oh really? What's your usual morning-after routine?"

The two men exchange a glance.

"We don't have one," Keith answered. "You're our first overnight."

Her cheeks flamed. She shouldn't have fallen asleep. Did they think it was weird?

"I had a great time last night, but you guys have to go." She shifted from one foot to the other.

"We know," Keith said, but those blue eyes appeared haunted again, the way they had before the sex antics had begun. "We want to see you again." He said it so plainly, so seriously, she stopped her fidgeting and stared. Had they discussed it? After she fell asleep? Or did they just read each other's minds?

"I'm sorry?"

John climbed out of the bed and pulled on his boxer shorts "Yeah. We do."

"What? Both of you again?"

John gave a sheepish shrug. "Either. Both. However you want us. We want to see you again."

She gaped at the two beautiful men who had rocked her entire world the night before.

No.

She couldn't. Once hadn't been rational. Twice would be stupid. "I had a great time, but, uh, I really can't do this again."

Keith's solemn gaze grew more sober. He tossed a card on the dresser. "You know where to find us." His voice sounded heavy, disappointed.

She shoved back her matching disappointment and bobbed her head. "Yep, I sure do. I'm going to hop in the shower. Just let yourselves out. Thanks, guys. Bye!"

In the bathroom, she turned on the water and stepped into the shower. Her throat grew dry as she washed away their scents, memories of her night with Keith and John flashing through her mind. It had been worth it. A positive experience in her rather limited logbook of sexual adventures.

But no. Seeing them again wasn't a door she wanted to open. How would it work? Three people couldn't be in a relationship. Would it just be booty call kind of action? She didn't have time for either option in her life.

So why did the thought leave her feeling so damn empty?

John watched his partner stomp toward the squad car. He hadn't seen Keith this surly in years. Not since his late wife, Becky, got the three-months-to-live diagnosis. Depressed, yes. Shut down, robotic, barely there. Those versions of Keith were more familiar, or had been in the years since Becky's death.

The fact his partner had been truly animated, truly engaged with Sloane last night, explained his foul mood today. Not that he could point any fingers. He had definitely been tempted to snap those cuffs on her for real and refuse to let her leave until she agreed to see them again.

Or just see Keith. Maybe he should step back and let his partner take this one.

But even as he had the thought, the pressure in his chest increased. He damn well didn't want to give up Sloane, not even to Keith. Not that he minded sharing.

"We'll change her mind," he said as he climbed into the passenger seat.

Keith didn't answer.

"We know where she works. We'll wait for her this afternoon. Convince her she needs more of us."

"Great, and how will you explain this to the chief when we're arrested for stalking?"

He rolled his eyes. "If she really doesn't want us, we'll leave her alone, but I think she had the morning-after jitters and there wasn't any time to talk her down."

Of course, they'd never spent the night with a woman before. Sex, yes. Cuddling up afterwards, waking beside her was all new territory. So he wasn't any expert on this situation. But he did know people.

Lawyers were cautious by nature. Cerebral. They weighed decisions thoroughly. Last night, she'd let go and given herself to them with pure abandon. They'd set the sheets on fire together. Without a shadow of a doubt, they'd rocked her world.

That probably scared her.

Hell, it almost scared him, and he feared nothing. She was so damn perfect—for both of them.

"I want her." Keith, the king of summing things up in as few words as possible.

"Yeah, me, too."

"I mean, for keeps."

Oh. Fuck. He wanted her. For himself.

John drew in a breath. The most selfish side of him said, *Fuck that. You've at least had a wife. I've never had the chance.* But he hadn't watched the guy suffer for the last four years without wishing he could cut out his own heart and give it to him so he'd be whole. He would die for his partner. He'd give a kidney, take a bullet. Keith had saved his ass more times than he could count.

"That's cool. I'll stand down. You deserve her, man."

Keith took his eyes from the road, brows low. "What? No, that's not what I meant." His partner shook his head and scrubbed a hand across his beard. "Wait…do you want her? Like, for a serious relationship?"

John hesitated. He, as a rule, didn't do serious relationships. Never had. He liked women too much. Multiple women. Different women. Yeah, he'd been a player. But, damn, a woman like Sloane?

For a moment, he pictured her as his wife. Imagined coming home to that sultry voice, those legs, that whip-smart brain of hers. But they hardly even knew each other. He opted for a shrug. "I don't know. Maybe."

Keith was silent for a long time. So long, John thought the conversation had been dropped, but just before they reached the station, Keith said, "Sometimes, you just know. I knew the moment I met Becky she was the one. Irrational—we had nothing in common. I liked sports, she liked the ballet. I loved the outdoors, she liked to stay in and read books. But none of that matters. There was just something there. Something indescribable. Not just chemistry, either, even though that was off the charts. It was like she knew me, the moment she saw me. And I knew her."

Inexplicably, his heart pounded hard in his chest, like they were about to go in and defuse a bomb or chase down an armed burglar.

"*I felt that way about Sloane.*" His voice cracked.

Keith parked and turned in his seat. "Me, too." He looked miserable.

His heart pounded harder. His mouth had gone dry. "You can have her, man. I don't want to stand between you and—"

"Fuck that. You can have her. You're young like her. You could start a family, make a life together. I'm not going to stand in the way of your future." He scrubbed his beard again and hesitated then turned away and opened the door, climbing out of the car.

Keith took down the information from the distraught college student whose car had been stolen. Fourth one that week—all from the university area. Someone was definitely running a ring, because none of them had turned up abandoned, as often happened with stolen cars.

He and John had a few leads—just rumors, barely enough to start digging. But, today, he couldn't concentrate on the case, couldn't shake his rotten mood. He ought to be happy. He'd had the hottest blonde in town last night. But Sloane was like an addiction—one taste hooked him. Apparently so was his partner.

He'd meant it when he said John could have her—if she could be convinced to see them—or him—again. A girl like her only came around once in a lifetime. Or maybe twice, in his case. He considered himself lucky to have met his soul mate early on, to have had ten glorious years with her.

Watching John settle down and have his own happiness would be enough for him.

They finished up with the report and climbed back in the car. "In-N-Out Burger?"

"Yep." He started the vehicle and drove to the fast food joint.

"Let's leave it up to her."

Although picking up a conversation they'd left off discussing three hours ago, Keith knew exactly what he was talking about. Or rather, *who*.

He nodded slowly. "I'm down with that. But I just want you to know there will never be any bad blood between us if she picks you."

"Same here," John promised. "Listen, man. I'm not going sappy on you, but I had that same thing with you. Minus the chemistry. Like we knew each other right from the start. I mean, I trust you more than my own brothers."

Already in the drive-through for In-N-Out Burger, he ordered their food, grateful for the momentary distraction.

"All I'm saying, is maybe all three of us would work as a long-term thing."

Keith snorted. "Come on."

"I'm serious. Why not?"

"So, what? We're all going to live together like we're on some some crazy hippie commune?"

John grinned his boyish smile. "Except with deodorant."

Keith gave a short bark of laughter, the first time he'd felt like laughing all day. "You're fucking nuts."

"Well, let's just see. First, we gotta win back the girl."

A reluctant smile stretched across his face, a primitive flare of hope sparking in his chest. John was the Golden Retriever of men. He liked everyone and generally figured things would always turn out well. He might not feel the same way, but he couldn't help but love his asshole partner.

Chapter Five

Sloane's feet were killing her. After trotting out in the spike heels last night, she should have opted for flats today. She limped up her sidewalk and unlocked the door, kicking her shoes off onto the hardwood floor the moment she stepped inside.

The cool air of the AC hit her in the face, and she drew a deep breath, happy to be home. She'd spent the entire day fighting off the memories of two pairs of manly hands on her body, of being bound, ordered into position, and pleasured.

She wanted to remember it all. She'd draw a bath and pour a glass of wine and just…go over the entire experience. She'd give herself this one night to remember it all and then put it behind her.

Brrrr. She checked the AC, ready to turn it up, and then froze. *Seventy-three?* She didn't set her thermostat that low. Not ever.

The now-familiar chill she'd been feeling lately swept through her with a rush. What in the holy hell was happening?

Someone had been in her house.

Goose bumps rose on her arms and neck. She crept from room to room, holding her breath. Were they still here? What did they want?

She stepped in her bedroom and looked around. Opened the closet door. Everything looked normal, except…

She clapped a hand over her mouth to stifle her scream, then stumbled back.

It's okay. It's not that scary. It's just shoes.

But, Jesus. Someone had arranged them— set all her shoes in a neat line, toes pointed outward. The laces of her sneakers had been untied and pulled straight out to the front.

Creepy. Super creepy.

Someone with a case of OCD couldn't stop themselves from moving her stuff.

She ran for the front door, leaving her shoes but grabbing her purse. She got in the car and locked the doors, her phone already out in her trembling hands. She wished she had Keith's card here, but it remained inside, on the dresser.

"911, what's your emergency?"

"Someone broke into my house—322 West Avenida Bonita."

"Are you in the house, ma'am?"

"No, I'm in my car in the driveway." She was pretty sure there wasn't anyone in there, but thought she'd better wait outside, just in case.

"Okay, stay out of the house until the police arrive."

"Can I request particular officers? Sergeants Swensen and Hathaway?"

A long pause. "I'll relay your request, ma'am. I don't know whether it can be accommodated."

"Thank you." Her voice shook.

What the fuck, what the fuck, what the fuck? Seriously? What the fuck was happening?

She closed her eyes and rubbed her temples. She needed a do-over on this day in a really bad way.

The minutes ticked by. It felt like hours. Her car grew warm, and she had to turn on the engine to run the AC.

Who had been in her house? Was it some kind of prank? Some kids playing a joke on her? Or something more serious? Nothing had been stolen. At least, not before today, nothing she'd noticed. A peeping Tom? Oh God, had someone been there while she'd been home?

The thought had her quaking.

The sound of screeching tires brought her head up and eyelids open. Her officers. She leaped out of the car and went running for them before their squad car had even pulled to a stop.

Keith jerked the car to a stop and flew out, not even bothering to shut the car door. He wrapped her up in his arms, seeming to know exactly what she needed. "It's okay, baby. It's going to be okay. Tell us what happened."

In the next moment, John was there, too, stroking the back of her head. "What happened? Someone broke in?"

She pulled away, still trembling. "Yeah." Her voice sounded shaky, but she was proud of herself for not crying. "Someone's been coming into my house. The cat was out last night, remember? Today, the AC setting had been lowered and"—she beckoned them to the door—"come and see my shoes."

They exchanged a glance, and she stopped.

Great. They thought her a nut job. She had to admit, her accusations sounded pretty benign and stupid out loud. "I'm not making this up."

"I believe you." Keith held out his arm to prevent her from coming in. "Let us search the place first, then you can show us the shoes."

She nodded and stayed on the porch as the two officers slipped inside the house, looking every bit as lethal as their weapons.

Several minutes later, they emerged. "It's empty. Show us what you saw."

She brought them in and pointed to her shoes, explaining how she'd left them in a big heap.

"I don't like this," John said.

"Nor do I." Keith took out a notebook and pencil and made notes on it.

"Can you think of anyone who might want to fuck with you? Some guy you pissed off in court? A former client?" John asked.

Her mind ran over her recent cases. She hadn't had any dissatisfied clients or anyone who seemed to blame her for the outcome of their cases as far as she could remember. She shook her head.

"Ex-boyfriend? Angry co-worker?" Keith prompted.

"No—no one like that."

"You're not staying here alone until this has been resolved," Keith said firmly.

"Right," John agreed. "We'll stay here with you. Either in shifts or together, whichever you prefer."

In seconds flat, she shifted from terror to turn-on. The single word *together* had her blushing at the memories of the previous night, heat swirling in her core, her skin prickling with a new awareness of their bodies and nearness. Her resolve not to repeat the night flew out the front door.

She swallowed. "Okay."

"Which do you prefer?"

"Huh? Oh…both of you," she spoke without hesitation then flushed again. Maybe she asked too much. They probably had other things to do. "I mean, unless you'd rather split up."

"No," they answered simultaneously.

"I'm glad you called us," John said. "We appreciate your trust."

"Yeah… *Of course* I trust you. I mean…" She had let them do anything and everything with her the night before, hadn't she? She realized she trusted them implicitly. Individually and separately. "Thanks for coming. I'm really glad…we met."

Met. What a funny way of putting it. She had a feeling they'd be meeting again soon, in many new configurations.

"We'll check the place for prints, but I'm not sure we'll be able to get any good ones," Keith said. John stalked through the house, checking behind doors and under beds while Keith dusted the door knob and closet door, trying to pick up any good prints. After about a half hour, he shook his head ruefully. "Nothing. The perp may have been wearing gloves. You see this smudge here? Doesn't look like it came from a bare finger."

Something about the gloves reminded her of something else, but the more her brain tried to retrieve the thought, the deeper it hid from her. She shook her head and sighed, feeling like she was going nuts.

"All right. I think our investigation is wrapped up here. I'll head home and get a change of clothes and some takeout. Does that sound good?" Keith asked. "John will stay with you while I'm gone."

She nodded. "Sounds great."

"What are you in the mood for?"

"How about pizza?"

"What's your favorite?"

"Rocco's Old Chicago—sausage and jalapeño."

He grinned and put the pencil and pad he'd been scribbling notes on away. "You got it." The wink made her knees weak. "I'll be back in an hour."

He headed out, and she turned to face John, who still stalked around her little house, inspecting everything with a dark look.

She loved how protective they seemed. Honestly, she couldn't remember when someone had taken care of her. She was a do-it-yourselfer by nature—prided herself on being able to handle her problems without calling in the cavalry. And she'd never dated guys who offered much more than what she could do on her own. But she had to admit, knowing two strapping policemen willing to rush over to her house and protect her with their lives made this situation a helluva lot easier.

But would they be able to solve the case? How long would it take? They didn't have much to go on. Worse still, her willpower to resist the two men sexually wouldn't last a half hour. And the more involved she got with them, the more complicated and painful it would be when things ended.

This was why she didn't do relationships.

John's protective instincts went wild. The idea of someone fucking with Sloane made him want to rip his or her face apart. Who would do this to her? And why? It seemed like a mind-fuck. A subtle form of intimidation. Who would be after their beautiful public defender? What grudge could they hold?

His investigative wheels turned as he circled the outside of her house, checking all windows and doors. One of the window locks appeared forcibly broken, and he found a large male footprint in the dust outside. White-hot fury surged through him.

Who the fuck had been here? He took photos of the print and tried to get a cast of it, but the dust was too fine and dry, the print not deep enough. He wanted to kill this guy, he really did. He circled the house again. The sound of a scream made his heart lodge in his throat. He threw the front door open.

A tall, thin man backed away from Sloane, who slowly advanced on him, clutching a butcher knife.

He drew his gun. "Freeze."

The man whirled, caught sight of John, and his already panicked face distorted. He lunged back toward Sloane.

"Touch her, and I'll shoot you in the back."

The man froze, a choked sound coming from his throat.

"Hands in the air, real high."

The guy slowly lifted his shaking fingers toward the ceiling. He stooped like an old man, but he couldn't be more than fifty, with thinning hair and broken front teeth. His clothes were wrinkled and unclean.

"Face down, on the floor." Without taking his eyes or his gun from the guy, he hit his radio. "Sergeant Swensen, return to premises *immediately.*"

"Copy that. En route."

The man sank to his knees, desperation streaking his face. "Ms. Walters is my friend. Aren't you, Ms. Walters?"

"You know this guy?" He didn't move his eyes from the perp.

"Yeah," Sloane gasped, her face white. "He was a client."

Outside, the screech of tires signaled his partner's return.

John ran forward and shoved the guy the rest of the way down then cuffed him roughly.

"Take it easy," Sloane said, her voice shaky. "He's mentally ill. I don't think he meant to hurt me."

He struggled to dial back his need to protect, but he agreed the guy didn't seem aggressive.

"What were you doing here?" he demanded. "Huh?"

"N-n-nothing. I just wanted to see her again. She's my friend. She's nice to me."

"Not like this. You scared her. Did you want to scare her?"

"No," the man sobbed. He attempted to lift his head and look at Sloane, but John didn't allow it.

Keith rushed in, stopping in the entry to take it in then easing past them toward Sloane. He closed his fingers over hers around the handle of the knife. "Let me have it," he murmured when she didn't let go. "You're safe now. We're not going to let anyone hurt you."

She let out her breath in a gush and released the knife.

Keith instantly pulled her into his arms.

John wrestled the guy's wallet from his pocket and tossed it to his partner. "Where did he come from?" he asked Sloane. It bugged the shit out of him he'd somehow missed the guy being in the house.

"He came in the back door."

The one he'd just exited through and left unlocked. Damn.

"Where were you hiding? Were you in the house when we got here?"

"Outside," the guy panted. "I went out the back door."

"You hid outside? What was your plan, asshole?"

"Nothing. I just wanted to see her," he pleaded. "I wouldn't hurt her. I would never touch her."

Jesus Christ.

"What was he accused of when you represented him?"

"Breaking and entering." Sloan sounded miserable, as if she bore the guilt of his continued law breaking.

"Did he steal things?"

"No."

Keith rifled through the wallet, the anger on his face matching John's.

Maybe the guy was mentally ill. Probably. It didn't make it any less creepy to find him in Sloane's house. John leaned his head low to the guy's face and snarled through gritted teeth, "You don't break into someone's house. You don't touch their things. You scared her."

"I'm sorry," the man wailed. "I didn't mean to scare her. I didn't mean to."

Sloane's eyes swam with unshed tears. "Please take it easy on him."

He pulled the guy up to his knees and turned him to see Sloane. "She's *crying*," he snarled. "Because of you."

"I'm sorry!" the guy cried. "I didn't mean to."

"Okay, let's get him down to the station. Sloane, you'll need to come, too, so we can get a statement. We'll make it as fast and painless as possible."

Chapter Six

After getting Sloane's stalker booked, John headed home to shower and change then returned to her place while Keith went to get the pizza. They hadn't even questioned whether they were still spending the night at Sloane's. Nor had she.

He tapped on the door and entered to find Sloane slicing vegetables for a salad. Something about the domestic scene made his cock thicken. Not that a professional woman wouldn't also be good in the kitchen. Sloane seemed ultra-capable. But the idea of domesticating with her was doing all kinds of things to his body and mind.

He wrapped his arms around her from behind.

She stiffened at first, but then her body went soft and she leaned back. Her head fell against his shoulder, her moon-pale hair smelling sweet.

"Keith was so pissed we let you get away this morning," he murmured.

She stiffened again, but then turned in his arms, her aqua eyes curious.

"I haven't seen him take a genuine interest in a woman—not since he lost his wife a few years back."

Her expression softened with sympathy. "Is that why you two—?"

He shrugged. "Yeah, partly. I had hoped to get him back in the dating scene. I never expected we'd fall for the same woman."

Her eyes widened, lips parted. Worry crept across her face.

He lowered his head and brushed his lips across hers.

Any doubt he had about her receptivity fled when her arms slipped around his neck and she slanted her lips over his, kissing him back with fervor.

Lust kicked through him. He wrapped an arm around her and kneaded her ass, yanking her slender hips up against his, pressing his swollen cock against her belly so she'd feel his interest.

She moaned into his mouth.

"Is this wrong, then?" she asked when they parted, her brows knit together in the sweetest show of concern.

"It's not wrong," he murmured. "Nothing between you and either one of us could be wrong. We both want you so much. We agreed we'd let you decide. If you want one or the other of us, fine. If you want both, even better."

Her lips parted in surprise. "On an…ongoing basis? A threesome…*relationship*? Or just sex?"

"Relationship." He flashed his most devastating bad-boy grin. "Think you could handle two men?"

She licked her lips. The sight of that little pink tongue made his cock throb painfully. "I can think of a few ways…"

Game on.

He felt no remorse in not waiting for his partner. His lips came crashing down on hers again, twisting over them, licking into her mouth. He grasped the back of her head to hold her still for his onslaught, determined to show her every bit of pent up frustration that had grown since they'd parted earlier.

He backed her against the counter and palmed her breast, slipping his hand inside her silky pink blouse. "Mmm," he rumbled. "You smell so good."

She bit his neck, worked the buttons open on his shirt. "So do you, Officer."

He dragged the hem of her pencil skirt up to her waist, groaning at the sight of her yellow polka dot panties. He picked her up and plunked her down on her counter, pulling her knees apart and settling his thumb over her clit. He brushed ever so lightly over the silky fabric. "You want me to touch you here, Counselor?"

Her breasts moved up and down with her rapid breath.

She grasped his hand and pushed it against her mons, urging him on.

He made a tsking sound. "Uh uh, Counselor. I'm calling the shots right now. I asked you a question. Do you want me to touch you here?"

"Yes," she whispered hoarsely.

He brushed again, ever so lightly. "Like this?"

She shook her head. "No-o," she moaned. "More, please. Harder."

He applied slightly more pressure and slid his thumb up and down over her sweet little button. "Do you think you deserve to come?"

"Ye-es."

"I'm not so sure."

Her thighs clamped shut around his wrist and she stiffened, eyes snapping to his face with a question.

"There is the matter of your dismissing us this morning. We were both highly disappointed." He rubbed his thumb in a painstakingly slow circle around her clit.

Her inner thighs trembled around his hips, her breath ragged. "I just—"

She didn't finish the explanation, a low whimper coming from her lips as he added a little more pressure.

Remembering how she'd responded to his domination last night, he said, "I think a little punishment might be in order."

Her gasp sounded wanton. Her nipples stood out under her blouse in stiff points and she squirmed against his thumb. "What kind of punishment?"

He heard the front door open and close and the clomp of his partner's footsteps coming down the hall.

"Well, there are many ways we might address displeasing behavior in our partner." He raised his voice to make sure Keith would hear. "Orgasm delay or denial, for one."

She shook her head from side to side with a low moan. "Nooo."

"Spanking." Keith's deep rumble came from the doorway to the kitchen.

Her hips jerked with excitement, eyes dilated.

"Punishment fuck."

The baby blues flew wide.

"Mmm, I think she liked that one," Keith murmured, leaning his hip casually against the counter to watch.

"Punishment fuck, it is."

"Do you have any lube?" Keith asked.

Sloane's expression took on a slightly panicked look.

He laughed. "How about coconut oil? Or olive oil?"

She pointed toward a cabinet. Keith opened it and pulled out the oil.

John caught her wrists and twisted them behind her head. "Bedroom," he ordered and nudged her in that direction.

Keith poured a little oil into a small bowl and followed them into the bedroom where John stood, arms folded across his chest. "Clothes off."

Sloane looked from one to the other, the uncertainty or discomfort returning. They didn't want that. He strolled over. "I'll help," Keith said easily and reached around from behind her to unbutton her silky blouse.

John started to strip off his uniform.

Keith slid the silky fabric from her shoulders and let it fall to the floor then unhooked her bra and dropped it. He cupped her firm breasts in his hands, squeezing. Her head fell back on his shoulder.

"This is crazy," she murmured. He cut off further verbalizations of her worry with his mouth, twisting his lips over hers as his hands slid down her belly and worked the button on her pencil skirt.

"You're so beautiful," he murmured.

She sighed.

"Punishment," John reminded him, but amusement rang in his voice. He moved to stand in front of her so they formed a sandwich, and took her mouth when Keith released her. Keith urged the skirt and her panties down over her hips and off. He gave her bare ass a slap that made her gasp into John's mouth.

"Fold her over the bed, here I think we need to work that tight little ass of hers open so it's ready for me."

He'd already decided he was the ass man. They actually hadn't tried double penetration with a woman before, but he knew John would be on the same page as him. John maneuvered her over the bed and pushed her torso down. He caught her wrists and pinioned them together, stretched over her head but resting on the bed.

Keith gave her beautiful ass a few more slaps, enjoying the bloom of pink from his handprints. He dipped his index finger in the coconut oil and lubed it completely. He brought it first to her slit, not that she needed lubrication there. He found it dewy wet, the folds plump, her entrance swollen and ripe. "Mmm, she's ready for you here, man," he murmured to John, who had slid his free hand under her chest to tease her nipples.

"Spread your legs wider," Keith commanded.

She obeyed. It was amazing how the stiff-spined lawyer transformed so quickly into this soft and willing partner. Her cheeks flushed with excitement, eyes already turning glassy. Just a little more work and they'd have her fully in a space of surrender to her erotic desires. His cock had gone rock hard at the sight of her, and he shifted it in his pants to ease the discomfort.

He teased her clit lightly, circling it with the lubed finger then flicking it until she whined with need.

He moved up to her back hole, massaging the tight ring of muscle with the coconut oil. She tightened, as if to keep him away.

He gave her ass a couple of slaps. "Naughty girl. This is a punishment fuck, remember? I'm going to take you back here while my partner fucks your pretty little pussy. You want that, don't you?"

She moaned.

He slapped her ass again. "Don't you? Speak up, baby. I need your consent."

"Yes," she moaned.

He chuckled. "That's what I thought." He rubbed away the sting of his spanks and began to massage her anus again, circling the rosebud then applying a little pressure. She moaned again. He kept the pressure steady until she opened for him, then worked the finger inside, massaging all around, stretching her opening to prepare her.

Her breath rasped, moans grew frantic. John took her mouth roughly, holding her face captive as he plundered with his tongue, sucking her lips, nipping, devouring.

"Oh my God," she gasped when he released her.

Keith pushed his finger in and out of her anus, and her breath came in sobs.

"Please," she begged.

"What do you need, baby?"

"You. Both of you. All of it."

He grinned at John and eased his finger out.

John climbed up on the bed and rolled a condom on his dick.

"Okay, baby," Keith said. "You're going to climb on John and ride his cock for a little while. But I don't want you to come. Understand?"

"Yes," she said breathlessly. She moved swiftly, obviously eager. She straddled John and lowered herself onto his cock, giving the sexiest little gasp as she did.

Keith's cock throbbed. He stripped out of his clothes, watching his partner and Sloane in their exquisite mating dance. She rocked her hips over him, obviously seeking her own pleasure.

"Don't come," he reminded her. "You don't get to come until we give you permission. Got it?"

She slowed and made an unintelligible sound.

John smirked. "She's pretty close. I think you'd better fuck her ass now."

He rubbed a generous amount of oil over his cock then climbed over them and held Sloane's hips to quiet her movements. He rubbed more oil on her little rosebud.

She whimpered with desire.

"Don't move, baby. I'm going to work that ass open."

Once more, he worked one finger inside her then two. Her flesh was more taut in this position, with her pussy full of John, and she moaned louder than ever.

He slid her knees lower, to straighten her legs and give more slack, then brought the head of his cock to her anus.

"Oh...oh...oh my God," she babbled as he eased the head in slowly. "Oh please. Oh wait...oh please...yes...no..."

He eased back out. "No?" He definitely didn't want her to feel violated.

"No, no, no. Please. More. Go on. I'm sorry." She sounded delirious with need and probably overwhelmed by the intensity of the sensation produced by having both holes filled simultaneously.

He rubbed more oil on and pushed again. This time, the bulb of his cockhead slid in.

"Oh yes," she screamed. "Holy hell, yes."

"Yeah?" He panted from the effort of holding back. Her tight heat had his cock ready to explode.

"We're going to fuck you at the same time, baby, and then you're going to scream both our names when you come. Got it?"

"Yes….yes, please…let's go. Please."

He grinned and he and John both began to rock into her at the same time, keeping it slow and gentle.

She buried her face in John's neck, whimpering. Keith felt her body trembling beneath his, the rasp of her gasps in her chest. They stroked in and eased back a dozen times until she started to come unglued.

"Oh my god, please, oh please, please, please. I need more, I need…"

"You need to come, baby?"

"Yes, *please.*"

He gripped her hips and picked up the rhythm. John, too, thrust harder.

Sloane began to sob. "Oh…oh…oh fuck…it's so good…it's too much…it's—" She let out a scream. "Johnkeithjohnkeithjohnkeith," she yelled, as he'd instructed.

He muttered a curse, holding back so he didn't hurt her, as his own orgasm exploded. Stars danced before his eyes.

John waited until they both finished. When Keith eased out and moved back, he flipped Sloane onto her back and pounded into her until he, too, came with a roar of satisfaction.

Sloane laughed, tears leaking out of the corners of her eyes.

He settled beside her, thumbing them away, thinking at how fucking beautiful she looked, limp and undone like this, her hair a golden haloed mess around her head, her eyes bright, cheeks flushed, lips swollen from kissing.

Ours, he thought.

Sloane sprawled on the bed, boneless, weak from the most incredible orgasm of her life.

Had that really just happened?

Keith stroked light circles around her breast, watching with those intense blue eyes. "You'd better not be thinking about how to kick us out this time."

She gave a short bark of laughter.

Nope, that hadn't been her thought, although she did still have a million What-*in-the-hell am-I-doing* thoughts.

"So what's your plan, Officers? How do you see this working?" Time for an honest discussion about how in the hell they thought there might be a future for this situation.

John settled on the other side of her, propped on one elbow. He stroked her hair.

She closed her eyes for a moment. All their attention, both physical and emotional, felt amazing. Too amazing. She should not get used to this, because it wouldn't work.

"We want to keep you. Clearly you need us," John said.

She scoffed and started to push up onto her elbows.

Keith put his hand on her sternum and pushed her back. "Ignore my cocky partner. *We* need *you*. You're special, Sloane. I know we don't know each other that well, yet, but we'd like to know you better. We'd like to keep this thing going, whatever it is."

"Like…all three of us?" She made a motion with her finger to all of them.

"Yeah," they answered in unison.

"Just for sex?"

"No," Keith replied, without even hesitating.

She glanced at John. "We want a relationship," he stated, completely serious, not teasing for once.

"Seriously?"

"Let's try it. Maybe it won't work, but it feels perfect to me," Keith said. "I haven't felt anything so right since the summer I met my late wife."

She touched his face when his eyes clouded. Then the corners of his mouth lifted and his eyes cleared again. "Give it a shot?"

"Just for argument's sake, assuming things work for us as a

threesome, what would we do? All move in together?"

"Sure." John grinned. "And you can have our babies. They'll have two dads. Or you can pick one of us, if you really can't do both, but we believe we can share."

She thought of her three failed relationships. She'd brought too much intensity to them. She'd wanted too much—more than the guys could give. Maybe what she'd needed all along was *two men*. She'd never be needy again, would she? She almost laughed out loud.

"Okay."

John's eyebrows shot up. "Okay?" Apparently, he'd expected more argument.

She grinned. "Yeah. Let's try it." It might not work, but not giving it a chance seemed like too much of a chicken move.

Keith rolled on top of her, smothering her with a kiss. His beard tickled. Both their facial hair added even more sensation to every kiss or lick.

She laughed, her heart feeling so full it might burst.

"My turn," John said, the moment Keith came up for air. His lips came down on hers just as eagerly, and she lost her breath with the intensity of their affection.

Two men, all for her. She'd hit the jackpot. Warmth filled her chest, and she reached for each of their hands, pulling them in toward her chest.

"Are you sure you can handle me? I hear I'm rather demanding as a girlfriend, which I guess is why I'm still single."

Both men grinned. "Oh, we have plenty of ways to handle you, baby girl," Keith said and rolled her to her belly, delivering a light slap to her ass. She pushed up to her hands and knees and crawled over Keith, ready for round two…

About Renee Rose

USA TODAY BESTSELLING AUTHOR RENEE ROSE is a naughty wordsmith who writes BDSM and spanking romance novels. Named Eroticon USA's Next Top Erotic Author in 2013, she has also won The Romance Reviews Best Historical Romance, and Spanking Romance Reviews' Best Historical, Best Erotic, Best Ageplay and favorite author. She's hit #1 on Amazon in the Erotic Paranormal, Western, and Sci-fi categories and is a contributor to Write Sex Right and Romance Beat. She also pens BDSM stories under the name Darling Adams.

To receive free copies of her books Theirs to Punish, Her Billionaire Boss, The Alpha's Punishment and Disobedience at the Dressmaker's, sign up for her newsletter here.

Website: www.reneeroseromance.com

Facebook: www.facebook.com/reneeroseromance

Instagram: www.instagram.com/reneeroseromance

Twitter: twitter.com/reneeroseauthor

Goodreads: www.goodreads.com/reneerose

One Kiss

by Martha Sweeney

Harper

"Stop sulking, Harper," Adele says for the sixth time tonight.

"I'm not sulking," I challenge with a dramatic pouty face.

"Yes, you are," supports Ayris with an unamused and unaffected expression.

"No, I'm not," I lie as I mock whine and drag out my words. I lose composure and a smile cracks slightly on my face.

"It's New Year's Eve," Brooke states the obvious. "It's going to be a new year, therefore, a new *you*."

"I don't want a new me," I say, continuing to fake fuss.

"You just need a new attitude," Adele corrects, throwing some sass my way with a smack to my hip.

"My attitude is just fine," I reply, sticking my tongue out at her.

"Not since you dumped Owen's ass two weeks before Christmas," Ayris reminds with a snicker followed by her own tongue's appearance.

My smile lowers slightly in a moment of defeat, but I swallow the pain quickly, causing the very pain the girls are talking about to surface a little as I try to brush it away. "Fuck off."

"Someone needs to get laid," Brooke quips.

"No," I counter. "I just need my heart removed."

"Owen is a loser," Adele announces. "He didn't deserve you."

"We told you he was a player," Ayris comments.

"No, you didn't," I deny.

"Well, in a round about way we did," Adele defends.

"On several occasions," Brooke adds. "You just didn't want to listen."

"It's not our fault that you were blinded by hot sex, hot abs, hot arms, and that smile," Ayris states followed by a sigh as she looks off into the distance as if picturing Owen's glorious body. She catches herself quickly, righting her expression and tone. "And, it's not our fault that you didn't want to see that he was sleeping around until you caught him," Ayris states.

The fucker was screwing some chick on my couch — my couch!

"At least he asked if you wanted to join them," Ayris reminds.

"After the fact," I say heatedly.

"Fucking models," Brooke huffs.

"Fucking men," Adele proclaims.

This gets a smile from me. My girlfriends always know how to cheer me up. We know how to raise each other's spirits when the time comes. There's the initial sad and depressed phase that includes a lot of tissues, takeout food, and junk food that is filled with understanding and compassion. Then, there's the anger phase where we hate all men and where I workout my frustration in the gym on a punching bag, which is then quickly followed by the love of men as soon as we spot a sexy one with a great ass and smile — which then eventually leads us right back to the beginning of the cycle.

"You know what you need, Harper?" Ayris asks.

"What?" I reply nervously.

"A one night stand," Ayris returns.

"No," I object. "I don't need any man in my pants right now, unless he's battery operated."

"How about your mouth?" Adele snickers.

"What?" I reply, choking on my sip of my sour apple martini.

"You do need someone to smooch with when the clock strikes twelve."

"I don't think that's a good idea," I counter.

"It's a *great* idea!" shouts Brooke.

"Making out with a stranger on New Year's is the best way to get over a guy," Adele confirms.

"Uh…no," I counter.

"Uh…yeah," Ayris interjects. "It helped me two years ago and Brooke the year before that.

"It definitely helped," encourages Brooke. "Especially if one of us takes a picture of it and then sends it to Owen."

"No," I reply as my eyes inflate a little. I pause for a second, considering the option. I wouldn't mind having a picture of me making out with a hot guy sent to Owen. It would show him that I've moved on and that he's missing out.

"I've got an idea," Ayris announces. "He's got to be *not* your usual type."

"What?" I laugh nervously.

"Yes!" Adele shouts supportively.

"No," I challenge, though I'm kind of excited by the idea.

"Shut up. It's happening," Ayris directs.

I smile to myself as the idea settles in.

"No pretty boys," Brooke begins plotting.

"And, no average ones," Ayris adds. "They don't have as much stamina or experience as the ones with a good body."

"We can't have our girl hooking up with a guy who hasn't had enough experience kissing, let alone look any less attractive than Owen," Adele adds.

"He's got to be hotter and sexier than Owen," Brooke comments.

My mouth opens to comment, but they keep shooting off ideas and at least one or two of them are talking at the same time, not giving me a second to be heard even if I did jump in. My eyes dart back and forth between them as I watch diarrhea of the mouth flow freely around me.

"Tall. He's got to be tall," Adele says.

"She always goes for guys who are eye level when she's wearing heels and she won't wear anything taller than three inches," Ayris claims.

"So, he'll have to be over six foot," Brooke says.

"His eyes," Ayris adds. "They have to be dreamy…and sparkle."

"Yes," agrees Adele.

"Dark and brooding with a hint of softness," Brooke includes.

"What color?" Adele asks.

"Doesn't matter," Ayris returns. "It'll depend on the gaze and feeling he gives off."

"What about his clothes?" Adele asks. "He can't be too nice or preppy looking."

"Or sloppy," Brooke mentions.

"I would say that depends on his face," Ayris returns. "Ooh….he needs to be scruffy or have a beard."

"No!" I interject, but they ignore me.

I hate, no, I loathe beards, especially the ones that just grow and aren't well taken care of. It's a pet peeve of mine.

"Yes!" the three of them shout at the same time.

"You hate beards," Ayris reminds. "So, a beard is a must!"

"Fuck me," I mumble, knowing that they're not going to stop until they pick a guy, and even worse until I actually kiss him tonight.

"Okay…so, I think we have our description of him," Adele states.

"A badass vibe, but with sweet, intense eyes, at least week old facial hair, or more, but it has to be well trimmed, 'cause you ladies know how if he's not willing to keep his face looking nice, then the rest of him is icky…tall, handsome and rugged at the same time… definitely *tats* if we can see them above the collar or on his arms with the sleeves rolled up." Ayris summarizes.

"No," I object.

"You don't have a say in this," Adele challenges.

"If my lips are connecting with his, I do," I argue.

"Nope," Brooke interjects. "You lost the ability to weigh in on this."

"Since when?" I huff.

"Since you had a bad judgment call on the last two guys you dated," Adele comments.

"Now, ladies," Ayris states excitedly. "Let's see who we can find."

They stand up at the same time from our booth and I watch the three of them scan the party and cringe at the very idea of all of this. A dreadfully nervous feeling stirs in my belly, causing me to stand in hopes of seeing who I'm going to be paired with just in case I'm going to have to drink more for it to happen.

"There!" Adele shouts, pointing in a direction.

I shift to see where they're looking as they whisper to each other, but they're blocking my view. The three of them quickly turn around and sit before I can see who they've chosen from the blob of bodies.

"Who?" I inquire, plopping down in my seat again.

"We'll tell you...." Brooke snickers.

My head tilts in request for her to expound, but she doesn't.

"We'll tell you...but, when it gets closer to midnight. That way you don't try to run and hide," Ayris replies with a devious grin.

"Here," Brooke says, handing me her drink. "You're going to need some liquid courage."

"No," I refuse. "I don't want to be hammered."

"You need to have a good enough buzz if you're going to do it," Ayris states.

"Fine," I huff, taking Brooke's martini and chugging the rest of it.

"Ten minutes," Adele announces after checking her phone. "Let's take our positions for who we're going to kiss."

"I'll keep an eye on this one," Ayris announces. Her head tilts in my direction.

"What?" I question with mock hurt feelings.

"You can't be trusted," Ayris says. "So, I'll pick one of his friends to kiss."

"You all suck," I announce.

"We know," Adele confirms happily.

"I've been told I *suck* really well," Ayris quips.

The four of us giggle and then chug the last of our drinks before getting up in search of our grand finale for the night.

Reese

The guys drag me out for New Year's, knowing that I'm not in the mood to party, let alone be with a bunch of rowdy strangers. Do I like to have a good time? Yes. It's just that I'm on-call for work and can't really relax. I'd much rather be at my place or one of theirs hanging out with a few friends, playing video games, pool, or anything other than being at this club with over four hundred people in it. We're crammed in and you can barely move two feet without bumping into several people at the same time, let alone the loud music and flashing lights that are making it hard to see.

Any other night, when I can actually relax and cut loose, I'm always up for getting out of the apartment. The guys keep me sane when it comes to being social and I don't mind chatting, having a few beers, and checking out the hot women in the bars and clubs we frequent each month. Tonight, however, I have to be a bit more reserved with my choices of drinks and who I'm willing to socialize with other than my friends.

I got used to working so much at the last hospital I was employed at that I had forgotten what it was like to have friends, let alone a social life, until I moved back here to New York eight months ago. My last job was too stressful. There should have been at least three more doctors on payroll, but the manager was cheap and an ass. He'd have us work twenty-hour shifts if he could, especially us younger, newer vets. I started working there while I was in college and stayed on once I graduated. When work consumed my life to the point where I wasn't even getting the chance to visit any family during holidays for an entire year, I quit and came back home. I had enough money saved up to afford to move in with the guys and look for a job for at least a year. With my excellent grades and the fact that I had worked at the same place for as long as I did, the first place I interviewed with hired me. Overall, the hours are better and the pay is much more.

"Come on, man," Gabe encourages. "Relax at least a little." He hands me a beer.

"I can't," I counter.

"It's almost midnight," Logan states. "Don't be a pussy and at least have *a* drink."

"I am what I eat," I reply with a grin, wanting to redirect our conversation off of me.

I've been with a few kind-of-serious girlfriends and none of them have complained about my *bikini burger* munching ability as Gabe calls it. I snort to myself at the phrase.

"Nice," Carter laughs, high-fiving me.

"Drink it slow," Gabe states. "You're not going to find a chick to kiss if you don't have a drink in your hand."

"A drink doesn't sway a woman to kiss a guy or not," I argue.

"At a place like this, it does," Gabe replies. "I've already got three potential chicks."

"How?" I investigate.

Gabe's always has fucked up logic when it comes to dating and the opposite sex.

"'Cause I got skills, man," Gabe boasts.

"You wish," Logan interjects. "Remember last weekend?"

Logan, Carter, and I laugh at the memory. A chick walked out of Gabe's bedroom, complaining about how he was unable to *eat her peach* properly after trying for about thirty minutes.

"That's bullshit," Gabe challenges. "And, like I said, she did *not* have a peach. It was more like a shag carpet. I mean…come on ladies. Wax that shit!"

"And…that's why you have a challenge with the ladies," Carter roasts.

"No, I don't," Gabe argues.

I take a sip of the beer Gabe gave me, chuckling at their banter as I scan the room. It's been three months since I've been in a relationship and I'm missing the benefits of one. The last chick I dated, Lily, was interesting. I'm not one to bash women, but she was a pain in the ass when she was trying to change me just two months into us seeing each other; this while she was apparently fucking two other guys and also blatantly tried hooking up with Gabe too. So, I dumped her that night and never looked back.

As the night ticks on, I nurse my beer and shoot the shit with my friends when they aren't talking with a chick. A number of drunk ones, really drunk ones, come up to us, but I don't pay them much attention. Yeah, they're cute, but I'm not into the slutty-drunkard chicks who are as obvious as the ones that I'm seeing tonight. I'm all about having a good time, but to get yourself that inebriated is not my thing.

At some point, I check my phone for the time and notice that it's almost midnight. For starters, I'm double checking to make sure I didn't miss a call alerting me that the hospital needs me as well as to find out how much longer until I can head home and get some sleep since I have the morning shift.

Suddenly, someone bumps into me.

"Sorry," a female voice says.

I look down and am met with sparkling, amber eyes that are surrounded by golden, long hair. My eyes immediately drop to her lips and I feel my caveman instincts kicking in. I lose my breath when she smiles. My dick hardens instantly and my throat dries, forcing me to chug the rest of my beer.

"Ayris, back up," she shouts, pushing her friend off of her.

The friend looks drunk, but I'm not sure about the goddess before me. Her mouth moves again when she looks back at me, but I can't make out her words.

"What?" I ask, leaning forward to hear her.

"Sorry," she repeats, leaning the rest of the way into me.

Her warm, plump breasts press into my chest and it feels like I'm about to come in my pants. Man, does she smell fucking amazing.

"My friend gets a little excited at New Year's," she states as her lips brush against my earlobe two times as she speaks.

Instinctually, my free hand darts to her hip, holding her steady when her friend and two others bump into her, pushing her further into my body.

We exchange a nervous smile when she pulls her face away from my chest. Our eyes stay locked and it's as if all the commotion around us dissolves. Time stands still at this very moment as I stare at her lips. Now I know who I'm going to kiss tonight.

Without warning, her mouth is on mine. When she pulls away for a breath, my hand moves quickly from her hip to her back, capturing her neck and pulling her closer. My tongue darts out, eager to taste more of the candy flavor of her lips. She returns the embrace, snaking one of her hands up my chest, behind my neck and into my hair. Her tongue tastes just as sweet as her lips and my dick gets even harder at the thought of her pussy having the same flavor.

"See," Logan's voice says in my ear. "We told you there'd be a chick to kiss."

My eyes dart around, wondering where she has suddenly gone.

"You okay, man?" Logan asks.

"Where did she go?" I search feeling dazed and confused.

"Who?"

"The chick I was just kissing," I state.

"Don't know," Logan replies. "I just saw the back of her head. The first time just before you two kissed and then again right before her friend kissed me after I just kissed some other chick."

"Fuck," I groan.

"Do you think they'd be up for a three-way?" Logan inquires.

Ignoring him, I look frantically for the goddess who blessed me with the taste of heaven. I dart through the crowd that seems still caught up in the rush of the new year arriving, desperate to find her, but my Cinderella is nowhere to be found.

Harper

It's been four weeks since New Year's Eve and I can honestly say that I feel great and that Owen has barely crossed my mind. The girls keep saying that it's all because of the kiss I had with Mr. tall, grey-eyed, sexy beard, at least one partially hidden forearm tattoo, dreamy hunk. I don't agree with them one hundred percent, but that was the best fucking kiss I've ever had in my whole life.

I'm no slut, but I've kissed a lot of boys since I was fourteen. I'd have to say I've made out with at least twelve, maybe more during my drunken bouts in college, but have only slept with five of them. I'm a firm believer in a girl getting to know her body as well as her own wants, desires, and fantasies before getting married.

That kiss replays in my mind several times a day and especially when I masturbate. He smelled divine, his lips were so soft yet firm enough to know how to kiss, his tongue was tasty and I actually enjoyed the scratch of his scruff against my skin. I found myself gliding my fingers along his chin twice as we made out for some strange reason. I hate the look of beards, but his was mesmerizing. He looked rugged and sexy and I loved the way it tickled my lips and cheeks. I walked away from that kiss reluctantly, but I'm glad I left when I did. My chest was pulsing. I was panting, and I felt like if we kept going that I was going to do more than just make out with the guy.

Part of me wonders if I'll ever see him again. I chide myself at night when masturbation only goes so far for not at least sticking around to see what would have happened with him. I've had a one-night stand before. It didn't go well, mind you, but for some reason, this guy seemed like he would have been more than just one night.

Today, I head out about a half hour before the sun is scheduled to rise. The girls can sleep through almost anything, so I don't have to walk around the apartment like a cat. The four of us live together in New York to keep our rent and other expenses low, live safely, and somehow save money when we're not spending it on clothes, shoes, books, food, and wine.

Brooke's a nurse, Adele is a bartender, Ayris works for a fashion magazine, and I'm a photographer slash graphic designer. I work mostly from home, running my own online business. I do a wide range of photography, trying to always keep myself open to new opportunities and to keep it interesting. Ayris' magazine has used me for a few spreads, mostly last minute photo shoots where something happened. I never asked what occurred exactly for them to need me in just a few hours notice, but I was grateful for the money, the exposure, and what it did for my portfolio. My shots have never been on the front cover, but I've at least have those as a part of my resume if I ever need it. I've started a collection of each magazine I'm in aside from a general portfolio online.

Mondays are my favorite day when everyone else in New York hates them. While people are late getting up to head to work for the day, I'm already finishing up either a workout class, a jog or a long walk (paired with the occasional ride on the subway) through the different streets of New York, taking photos of anything that inspires me.

Today's trip is with a hot chocolate through Central Park and my camera in hand, enjoying the hazy, cool morning as most avoid the outdoors during this time of year. On my way back to the apartment, I grab another cup of hot chocolate and relax in the cafe's window box that overlooks the street. I read a little when I'm not peering out the window people watching.

After hanging at the cafe for at least twenty minutes, I make my way home. The cool nip in the air doesn't bother me too much since my body is warm from the hot liquid I just had, so I lazily make my way down an extra few blocks to the next subway station. The platform is a bit crowded, but I'm able to get through pretty easily. With my camera already packed, I reach into my bag and grab my book to start reading.

Once the train arrives, my eyes stay on the page as I use my peripheral to maneuver through the people getting on and off of the train. I don't bother taking a seat, knowing most people need it more than I do. With my left arm wrapped around the pole to steady myself for when the train disembarks, I keep my nose in my book.

"Hey," a male voice shouts.

Normally, I don't bother reacting to people on the subway, but for some strange reason, my gaze lifts. My mouth gapes in astonishment as I see him; the hunk I kissed at New Year's. The doors begin to close as he tries to get close enough to get on. It's as if time stands still for everything except the doors. Our eyes stay locked as the train begins to move. Neither of us says anything as he tries to follow the train. His gorgeous eyes suddenly vanish from my view and my head jerks to the left, wishing they could see more of him.

Reese

I can't believe I fucking saw her. I was starting to wonder if I'd ever see my Cinderella again. I was instantly jealous of her teeth, having her sexy lips captured between them. Blood drained quickly to my groin, giving me an instant boner and temporarily slowing me down as I tried to get back onto the train. My legs couldn't move fast enough to get to her, and when the doors closed, I was devastated.

Everyday since our second encounter, which was three weeks ago, I've gone to that station at the exact same time, unless the trains are running late, hoping to see her. I don't know if she was leaving for work or just getting home from it. It doesn't really matter, I just need to find her.

She consumes my thoughts and dreams. I'm a guy, so yeah, my carnal urges crave her. I want nothing else but to be buried inside her. I masturbate before going to bed, dreaming that it's her and wake up with a raging hard on that needs my fantasy to become reality.

Once I satisfy my physical needs, my mind races to discovering her name, favorite color, favorite thing to eat, was the book she was reading for school or pleasure and so much more.

"Dr. Langford?"

"Hm?" I reply as my eyes flit across the iPad while I struggle to finish making notes.

"Dr. Langford," she repeats.

"Yes. Sorry, Mrs. Hildreth," I reply.

"Puppy love," she states.

"What?" I ask.

"It's in your eyes," Mrs. Hildreth informs. "What's her name?"

"I...I don't know," I answer truthfully.

"What do you mean you don't know?"

"It's complicated," I sigh.

"Love is complicated," she declares.

"We only met twice," I inform. "I'd hardly call it love."

"You're young, so I know you don't recognize it as such," she presents. "But, it is definitely love...regardless of whether you know her name or not. Soulmates from past lives who are working to find each other again."

"Sure," I comment, brushing it off.

"So...tell me about her as you examine Charlie," she encourages.

"There's nothing really to tell," I lie, shifting on my feet.

"Come on," Mrs. Hildreth coaxes.

"Besides, it's not professional for me to divulge personal information with patients," I remind.

"I'm not a patient," Mrs. Hildreth counters.

"You know what I mean," I state with a smile.

"Charlie doesn't mind…do you, Charlie?" she asks.

Charlie meows and then brushes his head up against my arm.

"Hello, Charlie," I greet, petting him. "How are you today?"

"He's good," Mrs. Hildreth informs. "I think he got one of the neighbor's cats pregnant."

"Pregnant?" I repeat. "He's fixed."

"That's what I thought," Mrs. Hildreth laughs. "Looks like the surgery didn't take."

"Did Dr. Manning do the procedure?" I inspect.

"No," she confirms. "When I adopted him they said on his paperwork that he was fixed."

"Well, we need to check…and if he's not, would you like us to schedule it?" I check.

"Yes," Mrs. Hildreth replies. "I don't need any more baby mamas getting mad at me and Charlie here."

I snicker at the phrase *baby mamas* coming out of Mrs. Hildreth's mouth since she's in her sixties or seventies.

"You'll find her," Mrs. Hildreth announces.

"Who?"

"Your lady friend," she clarifies. "Love never fails."

I smile and nod, hoping she's right.

Harper

It's been six weeks since I saw him at the train station. When I can, I veer from some of my daily routine and visit that stop, hoping to bump into him again. I still take a different route heading out for my morning workout class, jog, or photography journeys, but always make sure that when I go home that I take the same train at the exact same station as close to the same time as possible. I don't get to hang around the station because of what happened the fourth time I did. A few guys tried to mess with me, but when I threatened to use the mace I have on my keychain and lied about being a black belt, they backed off. I'm not so sure it was the mace, my threat, or as much as it was the homeless man that came to my so-called rescue. Though he smelled, he wasn't weird and didn't try to bother me after coming to my aid. So since then, I've gotten to know him a little more each time I'm there.

The first five times I saw the homeless man, he was just sitting on a bench in the back, minding his own business. He never begged for money and didn't have a cup out or anything like that. I know I'm not supposed to talk to strangers, but to me, he doesn't seem like one since he stood up for me.

"Hey, Allen," I greet, sitting down next to him.

"Hey, Harper," he returns with a smile.

"I brought you something," I say, extending my right hand.

"You shouldn't have," he replies, taking the lemonade and bag that has a sandwich and danish. "But, thank you."

I usually get him a black coffee, his favorite, but decided to change it up a little since today is a little warmer than usual for the middle of a New York March.

"Don't argue with me," I tease.

"You…never," he laughs. Allen gulps down half of the lemonade. "It tastes different this time."

"It's almost spring," I remind. "So, they add lavender to it. Don't you like it?"

"No, I love it," he praises.

"Good," I giggle. "I'll make sure to get it again next time."

"Yes, please," Allen encourages, munching on his sandwich. "So, have you found him yet?"

"No," I sigh.

"Part of me wants you to find him," Allen shares, taking a huge bite. He chews for about ten seconds and then swallows a little. "But, part of me doesn't."

"What? Why?" I ask with a laugh.

"If you find him, you'll forget all about me," Allen returns with a grinning mouthful of food.

"I could never forget you," I say with a smile.

"I know," Allen replies confidently. "So, what can you give me to identify him?"

"Why?"

"Well, I might have seen him and most likely will again. And, if I do, I can tell him something for you," Allen offers.

"Aww. You'd do that for me?" I ask, touched by his gesture.

"Of course," Allen confirms. "You take good care of me." He holds up the last bit of his sandwich.

"I don't know," I return nervously.

"What do you not know? You want to find him, right?" Allen checks.

"Yeah."

"Well, what's the problem then?" he searches.

"I kind of like the mystery behind it all," I confess.

"Clues are good for a mystery," Allen suggests.

"True," I agree.

"So?" Allen checks after about a minute.

"So, I don't know," I say.

"Worried that the reality isn't as grand as the fantasy?" Allen asks.

"Kind of," I sigh.

"You women make it more complicated than it needs to be," he states.

"Complicated can be fun," I return with a devious smile.

"Yes. But, it can also be a pain in the ass," Allen goads.

"True," I reply.

Reese

I'm starting to lose hope. It's been eight weeks since we saw each other at the train station. I've gone every day and haven't found her and I'm starting to think that it was just a coincidence that we ran into each other. The guys and I have even been back to the club a few times, but I haven't seen her there either.

I do my best to distract myself at work, at the gym or with the guys, because I know it's not completely healthy that she consumes as much of my thoughts and desires. I don't notice other women unless they possibly look like my Cinderella. When I've gone up to a few of them, thinking they were her, I was instantly disappointed. The women seemed excited that I stopped them, but not so happy when I walk away without a word or explanation.

"Why are we going back to this place again?" Gabe whines.

"Because..." Carter replies. "Reese is in love."

"I'm not in love," I challenge, scratching my beard.

"Yeah, you are," Logan states. "It's okay. We know how you get."

"How do I get?" I ask.

"You get one taste of a woman and you're hooked," Carter shares. "You don't see any other chick until things end with the one you want."

"That's not true," I counter.

"Yeah, it is," Gabe laughs. "The last two months, you haven't even made eye contact with another woman."

"Yes, I have," I argue. "I look directly at my patients and their owners."

"They don't count," Logan presents.

"Sure they do," I counter.

"I was referring to potential chicks to date or fuck," Logan reiterates.

"Whatever," I huff, despite my crumbling opposition.

"It's okay, man," Carter soothes. "We get it. It's just funny since you've only kissed her at New Year's and haven't seen her since."

"I have seen her," I mention.

"What? When?" Carter asks.

"It was about a month after the party. I had gotten off the train for work and saw her getting on," I explain. "We saw each other, but I haven't seen her since."

"Why didn't you tell us?" Logan asks.

"Because you'd make fun of me," I inform.

"No, we wouldn't," Carter replies.

"I would," Gabe states.

"We know you would," Logan replies. "But you weren't included in the *we*."

"Why don't you put out flyers around the station?" Gabe teases. "I'm sure she'd see them and would contact you."

"Ass," I hiss.

"It kind of makes sense," Logan defends.

"Maybe you could talk to one of the station workers," Carter suggests. "Is there anyone who's regularly there each time you get off for work."

"You said *get off*," Gabe laughs.

"Mature," I reply unimpressed.

Normally, I would laugh at Gabe's vulgarity, but not today. I'm too stressed out with not being able to find Cinderella.

"There are thousands of people that go through that station each morning," I remind. "There's no way in hell a worker would remember or recognize her," I comment.

"You never know," Logan returns. "She could be friendly with someone there."

"What are the odds of that?" I quip.

"Probably slim," Carter says. "But, anything is possible…even if the odds are slim in your favor."

"Thanks, Mr. Physics," I tease.

"Happy to help keep your hopes up," Carter replies with a grin.

"What's her name?" Logan asks.

"Don't know," I return.

"You didn't get it on New Year's?" Logan checks.

"Nope," I confirm. "We were too busy kissing…and then, she was suddenly gone."

"Man's on a mission,"Carter comments.

"I'm on a mission," Gabe interjects. "On a mission to get laid."

"Shocking," Carter replies.

"Don't hate the player," Gabe states. "Just hate the game."

"You aren't a player," Logan jabs. "You're on the sidelines most of the time by your own default."

"Am not," Gabe argues. "You boys are on the sidelines. You've put yourselves there…especially you, Reese."

I roll my eyes even though Gabe is right.

"What?" Gabe asks. "It's true. You could have been getting some all this time while you look for her. It's not like you two were or are dating."

"He does have a point," Carter supports.

"I bet she's already forgotten about you," Gabe adds.

"Don't be a dick," Carter says. "Just because you've been having trouble getting some."

"I haven't had trouble," Gabe shouts, walking away.

Logan, Carter, and I look back and forth at each other for a few beats, smiling at the jab.

"Well, I'm sure you'll find her again," Logan encourages.

"That's what Mrs. Hildreth says," I share.

"Who?" Logan checks.

"One of the patient's owners from the hospital," I reply.

"You saw her a second time," Carter reminds. "So, the odds are definitely more in your favor that you actually see her again."

Harper

"Harper," Ayris hollers from outside the room.

"What?" I reply as I get out of the shower.

"I have an emergency meeting at the office," she shares, barging into the bathroom.

This is typical behavior for all of the girls in the apartment, so her seeing me naked is nothing new.

"So?" I say, grabbing my towel and wrapping it around me.

"So, I will love you forever if you can do me a huge favor," Ayris states.

"What do you need?" I ask, getting a second towel for my hair.

"Mr. Darcy is supposed to have his checkup today and I really don't want to cancel," she informs.

"Why not?" I ask. "It's not like you haven't rescheduled before."

"I know," she sighs, grabbing the deodorant and handing it to me when I reach for it.

"Then?" I coax.

"I called," Ayris explains. "The problem is that they're booked solid for the next three months."

"So?"

"So, with the way that his insurance is, it can't wait three months," Ayris replies. "Besides, it's not like you have anything to do."

"Ouch," I reply with a pout.

"Oh, stop it," she directs. "You know what I mean."

"Do I?" I goad playfully.

"Come on," Ayris whines. "You know I love you. It's just that you've got more flexibility than the rest of us since you work from home."

"So, you do admit that I work?" I check with a grin.

"Yes," she huffs. "I acknowledge that you do work, making a good living from the comfort of our couch…which I'm jealous of… but I need your help for this."

"You're not jealous," I tease. "You love the drama that comes with your job."

"True," she confirms. "But, I really don't want to have to be paying out of pocket for the appointment if I don't have to."

"Got your eye on some new shoes?" I goad.

"No," she returns.

I study her for a second to see if she's telling the truth. "What time is the appointment?" I check.

"Ten-thirty," she replies.

"What time is it now?" I ask.

"It's only eight-thirty," she states, looking at her phone. "Shit, I'm already late."

"Sure," I agree. "I've got plenty of time to finish getting ready."

"Great!" she shouts. "I love you." Ayris wraps her arms around my shoulders.

"Love you too," I reply, patting her arm. "Now, get out of my way so I can finish getting ready."

"You're the best," she says, darting out of the bathroom.

"And, you're running late," I tease.

"Shit!" Ayris exclaims. There's commotion somewhere in the apartment. "See you later," Ayris says with her voice sounding more distant.

"See you later," I yell.

Mr. Darcy hangs out with me in my room as I get dressed. Ayris got him about a month after the four of us started living together in this apartment three years ago. We had just graduated college and we have been practically inseparable since, unless we're at work or naked with a man.

Mr. Darcy has a sweet temperament, acting more like a dog sometimes than an actual cat. He loves to snuggle, be petted, and plays most of the time he's awake. He's definitely spoiled by the four of us, but he doesn't seem to mind.

When it comes time to leave, Mr. Darcy happily climbs inside his crate. He's never really minded it and likes to hide in it some days. The two of us make our way down to the station just two blocks from our building, only having to wait for the train for about three minutes. A few children seem interested when they see the crate, peering in from a distance.

Ten minutes later, I exit the train and stop over to see Allen.

"Hey, cutie," Allen greets when I'm a few feet away.

"Hey, yourself," I reply with a smile.

"Who's your friend?" Allen asks.

I look around me. "There's no one with me silly," I tease.

"I meant the fur ball in the cage," Allen corrects, pointing to Mr. Darcy.

"Oh," I giggle. "This is Mr. Darcy. My roommate's cat."

"Hello, Mr. Darcy," Allen greets, placing his finger against the gate.

Mr. Darcy wraps his paw around Allen's finger.

"Looks like he likes me," Allen chuckles.

"Yeah," I encourage. "He's pretty friendly."

"Where you two headed?" Allen asks.

"Mr. Darcy has a checkup," I inform. "After that, we'll be having lunch."

"Wonderful," Allen praises.

"Do you want your usual?" I check.

"You're too good to me," Allen states.

"I'll take that as a yes," I return with a smile. "We should be back in about an hour or two. Can you wait that long?"

"I'll wait for you as long as I need to, cutie," Allen professes.

"Don't tease me," I challenge.

"Me? Never," Allen returns with a wicked smile.

"I'm still job hunting for you," I inform. "I wish I was more successful to be able to hire you."

"You buying me lunch most days is more than enough," Allen says.

"Behave," I tease.

"Never," he laughs as I walk away to get onto the train.

Mr. Darcy and I get to the vet's office about ten minutes early. As we wait, I see that there is a sign looking for someone who can help with the night shift watch for the animals and I instantly think of Allen. I inquire to the woman at the desk and she happily gives me some information and answers my questions about the position. Looks like today is going to be an even better day.

Reese

"Dr. Langford," one of the nurses calls as I inspect a chart outside of a room.

"Yes," I reply, keeping my eyes down on the iPad I'm using to call up patient files.

"Fifi is in room three," she informs me.

"Great," I return.

"Her owner has been here for about twenty minutes already," the nurse states. "Might want to get to her first since she's a little concerned with the pregnancy."

"Thank you," I reply.

I finish making notes, hit save, and then call up Fifi's information after clicking the schedule listed on the calendar. I review the files and the recent notes that were typed in from the call Mrs. Donahue made this morning for her appointment. The office, where I've been working for the past six months, has always been busy. There's never a dull moment. We do leave slots open for emergencies, but our time is usually limited with them since we're always so busy. The practice actually needs to hire at least another doctor to handle the constant flux of patients coming in and out on a daily basis aside from a few other staff members. They are interviewing, but from the looks of it, no one is promising yet.

After checking Fifi's vitals and noticing that her eyes lack moisture and her mouth, gums, and nose feel a bit dry, I give her water, a lot of water, and wait to run a quick urine test. From what Mrs. Donahue has told me, and from the looks of Fifi's symptoms, Fifi appears to be a little dehydrated. Waiting for the test results, I direct one of the nurses to let me know as soon as the test is complete. I use the restroom really quick before heading to the next patient.

"So, Ms. Reagan," I greet, keeping my eyes fixed on the iPad I'm holding as I open and close the door. "How's Mr. Darcy doing today?"

The only sound I hear is a cat meow followed by a faint purr after a few seconds of silence.

When I don't get a reply, I look up. "Ms. Reag…." I pause, awestruck by the sight in front of me.

I'm not sure what happens next, but the sound of the door opening paired with the nurse calling my name snaps me back to the present.

"I'm sorry, Dr. Langford," she apologizes. "I didn't mean to interrupt you…."

I turn to look at nurse Hannigan. "It's okay. What is it?"

"Fifi's results are negative," she informs me.

"That was quick," I reply. "Great. Thank you."

"You're welcome," nurse Hannigan says. After a short pause, she adds, "Would you like me to tell Fifi's owner that you'll be a minute?"

"Yes. Please let Mrs. Donahue know that I'll be right in."

"Sure thing, doctor," nurse Hannigan confirms and then leaves the room, closing the door behind her.

I turn sharply to find my Cinderella staring at me. Her eyes are wide and her mouth is still hanging open. "I'll be right back. Please, stay right here?" I instruct rather than request.

She nods slightly.

I rush out the door, quickly closing it behind me. Before I move away, I ask nurse Hannigan to make sure that no one leaves room five. She offers a small, but odd smile and nods her understanding. There's no way in hell I'm going to allow this woman to walk out of my life again.

Time seems to tick by exhaustingly slow as I inform Mrs. Donahue that Fifi is just a little dehydrated and needs to drink a little extra water. I recommend having her eat some celery or watermelon to help and which will have additional nutrients that will be beneficial to her and the puppies. It feels like it takes forever to get Mrs. Donahue to stop talking or asking me questions. She continues to speak as I escort her out of the room and down the hall to the waiting room. I appreciate the praise she's giving me in front of the other patients' owners who are waiting to be called, but this woman is tiresome and I need her to let me get back to the beauty in room five.

Standing in front of the door, I take a few deep breaths before opening it. A reassuring smile finds my face when I hear Cinderella chatting away on the other side, obviously talking to Mr. Darcy from some of the words I catch. I check my breath, run my fingers through my hair, and scratch my beard to make sure there's nothing on it from Fifi, then knock, which is quickly followed by me opening the door.

Cinderella bolts to a standing position and then adjusts her clothing and hair. The two of us stand still, not saying a single word as we hold each other's gaze.

I glance back down at the chart to catch her name so I don't sound stupid when I go to speak. I take three large steps toward her, surround her soft cheeks with my large hands and lower my lips to hers, imitating the beginning of our kiss from New Year's. She quickly returns the embrace, matching my tongue movements as her fingers return to the hair on my head once again. Her free hand cups my chin and her fingers gently rub back and forth over my beard, almost like she's petting it. I'm not sure how long we kiss, but it's long enough that both of us are panting and I'm not willing to let her go anytime soon.

"Ayris…."

"That's not my name," she interrupts.

"But, the chart says…."

"My roommate, the one who kissed your friend, is Ayris Reagan," she informs.

"Oh," I reply, clearing my throat. I suddenly feel nervous keeping her in my arms, but I'm afraid that if I let her go she'll disappear.

She offers a reassuring smile as if she just read my thoughts.

"I'm not letting you leave here until you tell me your name," I inform.

A sexy blush pops onto her cheeks, she bites her bottom lip momentarily before saying, "Harper."

"Reese," I reply. "Dr. Reese Langford."

"Nice to meet you," she replies.

"Again," I add.

Just a few seconds later and my lips are back on hers. I've got a raging hard on that she can probably feel on her belly. We kiss for what feels like only seconds, but I know it's longer than that thanks to all of the images of things I'd like to do to her that flash through my head.

"Are…are you going to check on Mr. Darcy?" she asks after I let her mouth go for a few seconds.

"Shit," I curse under my breath.

Harper giggles.

"Once you tell me your full name," I state.

"What? Why?" she laughs nervously.

"So after today, it's that much easier to find you," I confess.

Her brows lift, but she doesn't say anything.

"I haven't stopped thinking about you since New Year's," I admit. "And, I haven't stopped trying to find you since seeing you in the subway."

She looks down timidly for a second before her eyes return to mine. "Harper. Harper Collins."

"That's a cute name," I praise, kissing her again.

"Thanks," Harper replies in-between breaths.

"Why does that sound familiar?" I question.

A look of dread creeps onto her face.

My head tilts to the side. "As in...?"

Harper doesn't answer or ask to what I'm referring.

"As in the publishing company?" I check.

"Yes," she huffs. "My mom thought it was cute."

"I think it is," I comment, pulling her closer.

"You think that it's cute?" she asks with a shocked tone and expression.

"Yes," I confirm with a smile.

Harper shakes her head. "I don't."

"Well, I do," I return confidently, kissing her nose.

"Not," she denounces with a smirk. "It was worse when my mom actually worked for them."

"How long did she work for them?" I inquire.

Harper lets out a long sigh. "Ten years, when I was little."

"Where did she go after that?"

"Penguin gave her a better deal," she shares.

"Deal? As in she was...is an author?"

"No," Harper replies. "As in an executive editor."

"Oh," I say.

"Um...Mr. Darcy?" she reminds.

"Oh, right," I chuckle, forgetting for the second time where I am.

We gradually move apart, fixing our shirts as I grab some of the equipment needed to check the patient.

"So...how long have you been a vet?" Harper asks.

"Five years," I reply. "Who named him Mr. Darcy?"

"Ayris," she confirms.

"A fan of Pride and Prejudice, I see," I comment.

"How do you know about that?" she asks speculatively.

"I've got two older sisters," I return. "Them and my mom watch it every year in November."

Harper smiles and all I want to do is kiss her again. Strike that, I want to do more than just kiss her. Oddly, it's taking longer than usual for the blood in my dick to subside.

We're both quiet as I continue to inspect Mr. Darcy. We catch each other's gaze off and on, causing us to just smile and Harper to blush occasionally.

"Well," I say. "He's healthy."

"Good," Harper replies.

"However," I begin.

"However?" Harper asks nervously.

"However," I repeat with a smile. "I can't give him a clean bill of health until you agree to have lunch with me."

"Lunch?" she repeats.

"Yes. Lunch," I confirm. "Along with your phone number."

"Getting a little daring aren't you, doctor?" she returns with a grin.

"Yes," I confirm. "I'm known to be many things."

"Really," she giggles.

"Really," I affirm.

"On one condition," Harper states.

"Name it," I encourage.

"We go to my favorite place that's nearby," she informs.

"Done," I say quickly.

"And…" she begins, "…you seriously consider hiring my friend for the night position."

"Done," I agree. "Wait. Which friend?" I look down at the iPad. "Ayris?"

"No," Harper giggles.

"Then, who?"

"You'll meet him," she mentions.

"Him?" I ask.

"Yep."

"Him…as in a boyfriend?" I ask nervously.

"No," she replies with a giggle.

"Then, consider it done," I agree. "I've got one more patient before I'm clear to go."

"Okay."

"Will you wait for me, or am I going to have to hunt you down?" I check.

"Well…" she returns with a sexy smile. "Seeing that you know my name…even if you don't believe it is my name…you do have access to where Mr. Darcy lives, which is also where I live."

"You could be lying about living with him," I challenge playfully.

"True," she replies. "But, you do have access to my friend's home address and phone number." Her head nods slightly toward my iPad. "So, if I did run, it wouldn't be too hard to find me."

I take a few steps toward her and yank on the edge of her jacket after placing Mr. Darcy into his cage. "Just give me fifteen minutes."

"Done," she replies, sealing it with a kiss.

About Martha Sweeney

Martha Sweeney is an Amazon Best-Selling author and plans on writing in a variety of genres other than just romance, some of which will overlap into mystery, suspense, and science fiction. She has already released a book themed coloring book entitled "Bookish," for book lovers who are thirteen years of age and older.

Martha has been creative since she was little, always drawing, coloring or making crafts. When her adult life kicked in, her creative outlet disappeared until she discover Adobe Creative Suite products. Now, Martha is a self-taught graphic and website designer, works with her husband on their business, and writes into the wee hours of the night.

She lives in sunny California and has recently begun to enjoy reading in the past few years, unlike in high school or college which has sparked her new creative avenue of writing.

Website: www.marthasweeney.com

Facebook: www.facebook.com/AuthorMarthaSweeney

Twitter: www.twitter.com/MSweeneyAuthor

Instagram: www.instagram.com/MarthaSweeneyAuthor

Pinterest: www.pinterest.com/MSweeneyAuthor/

Goodreads: www.goodreads.com/MarthaSweeney

Google+: google.com/+MarthasweeneyAuthor

Asshole Calling

by Maria Monroe

A LOCAL FOLK BAND HAS TAKEN THE STAGE, PERFORMING A heart-stopping version of "Blowin' in the Wind." I take a sip of cheap but cold sauvignon blanc from my plastic wine cup, then lean back on my hands, legs outstretched on the grass.

Everyone in the park is quiet, even though we're outdoors, raptly listening to the perfectly harmonized voices of the performers on stage. I glance at my best friend Jessica, who's sitting on the picnic blanket next to me, and smile. Thanks, my grin says. I needed this. She smiles back before returning her attention to the band.

I close my eyes and take a deep breath, finally relaxing after a busy week at a brand new job.

"Asshole calling!"

Startled out of relaxation, I sit up, confused. Then I hear it again.

"Asshole calling! There's an asshole on the other end of the line! Asshole calling!" It's a recorded male voice, and I'm fairly sure it's a ring-tone, set to the highest volume possible. And it's right behind me.

I turn my head to see who the jerk is that forgot to turn his ring tone off during the concert, even though the band expressly asked everyone to before the music began.

Holy crap.

Directly behind me on a park bench is the hottest guy I've ever seen in person. Despite his beard—my ex had one, and I'm looking for somebody who is nothing like that jerk—I feel like time stands still while I take him in. He's sitting on top of the back-rest of the bench with his black leather boots resting on the seat. And although he's totally man-spreading, it's all right because nobody's next to him, and besides, *look at him*.

Curly dark brown hair, slightly too long. Chiseled nose and masculine jaw covered in a dark brown beard. Worn jeans that not only give him this totally cool casual look but also cling just enough so I can see the outline of his quads, which are totally yummy.

He's wearing an open leather jacket over a white T-shirt, and though I can't see his arms, I know (or imagine, at least) that they're a) lean and muscular and b) sporting at least one tattoo. There's something about him that screams *bad boy*. And even though I know better, I stare hard for a few seconds.

Until I realize what he's doing. He's holding his phone, which is blasting the ridiculous "asshole calling" ring over and over, and he's laughing instead of shutting it off.

"Jerk," I whisper to Jessica.

She nods. "Rude."

"You should say something," she whispers.

"No way," I respond, shaking my head.

"You have to. It's your next assignment. *Tessa's Time*, remember?"

The ringing is still going on. The glorious jerk behind me must have his phone set to ring like a thousand freaking times before it goes to voice mail. I need to say something, especially because Jessica's been helping me be more assertive. She calls it Tessa's Time, and says it's my time to stop letting people walk all over me and stand up for myself. Ex asshole boyfriend. New amazing job. She says I shouldn't settle, and she's absolutely right.

"Fine," I agree. "I'll say something."

"Yay!" Jessica gives me a quick round of silent applause as I get up.

My heart is pounding as I stand and turn around so I'm facing the guy on the bench. He doesn't notice me because he's just staring at his stupid phone like he's in a trance, a grin on his face.

I take the few steps separating us and sit down on the bench next to his right leg. And of course at that exact second his ringer shuts off.

He glances down at me, and his smile almost stops my heart. It's so genuine, with a hint of trouble-maker in it, like he's the kind of guy who'd go skinny dipping or dress up in a tux with the express purpose of crashing a wedding. Of course, it's hard to imagine him in a suit and tie when he's all leather and jeans and scruffy beard.

He slides off the back rest and sits next to me, so close I can feel his leg against mine. He raises an eyebrow at me in question, and I shift, suddenly unsure. The reason I came here is moot, and I feel stupid.

"Your, uh, phone was ringing. It was really loud and rude," I finally whisper, trying to be quiet so I don't annoy the people around us.

"It was," he agrees. "Sorry my phone was being rude. It can really be an evil little bastard." He tilts his head at me and grins again.

"It isn't your *phone* that's rude." For some reason his disarmingly good looks make me feel snarky. "Nice ringtone, by the way," I whisper.

His laugh surprises me, deep and rumbling and genuine. "You have no idea," he finally says. When he leans over so I can hear his whispering voice, a minty scent mingled with a clean, soapy smell makes me tingly.

Suddenly all I can hear is the band singing about "blowing in the wind," and all I can think about is whether or not he's thinking about *blowing* too right now. I blush so hard I can feel it in my ears.

His eyes brighten and he smirks, like he can read my freaking mind. *God.*

I manage to meet his eyes. "So yeah… just…" Words are suddenly hard, and I gesture at his phone with my head, unable to speak.

"Should have set it to vibrate, I guess." He looks directly into my eyes as he says it, and I will myself not to blush again. How immature am I that the word *vibrate* makes me squirm?

"Sorry," he adds, winking at me. His voice is so low, even more so because he's speaking quietly, and my stomach flutters. "Leaving anyway," he adds.

I nod once. I want to say *Good*. I also want to say *No!* and *What's your name?* and *About time* and a host of other things, all conflicting. I want him to ask me for my number. I want to ask for his. I want him to leave, because I'm positive he's trouble, that he's got more girls than he knows what to do with. And I don't want to be another notch in his sexy leather belt.

When he stands, he's all tall and lanky, and his jeans fit him so well he could be in a Stetson ad. I should have known he'd have a swagger. As he walks away, he looks over his shoulder once at me, as if he knew I'd be staring. He grins and lifts an eyebrow at me. Cocky bastard.

I return to the picnic blanket, where Jessica crinkles her brow. "Um, how did it go?" she asks. "And can I just say, he is delicious!"

"Yeah, but he's a jerk," I whisper back. Except he wasn't. Not really, at least. OK, letting the phone ring and ring and laughing about it was a jerky thing to do. But still…

"He could have a Britney Spears ringtone and he'd still be sexy as hell." She grins at me, then downs the rest of her wine.

"This round's on me," I whisper back, taking both our cups and standing up. "Be right back."

I wander over to the refreshments stand, where for $5 you can get a good pour of boxed wine. The sugary scent of freshly spun cotton candy from under the next tent fills the air, and a stand of watercolors on display catches my eyes, but I'm too distracted by him to take a better look. I need a drink.

The band's playing "Last Thing on My Mind," so at least I'm not thinking about blow jobs anymore. Or I suppose I am, if I'm thinking about not thinking about then.

The bartender hands me two cups of wine, so cold that condensation immediately coats the plastic, and I take a big sip.

I'm turning to head back to Jessica when a loud roar gets my attention. A motorcycle's revving, and there, being disruptive and sexy once more, is the guy with the phone.

As he speeds away I'm equally pissed that he's being loud again, and that my heart beats this fast because I got to see him again. That's junior high stuff. That's like seeing your crush in the hallway and being giddy for the rest of the day, and then all night too, because he's out of your league but still, somehow, noticed you.

No way. I'm an adult, not a teenage girl with a crush on the class trouble maker.

But as he rides past, he glances my way and waves. And my stupid heart, the betrayer, picks up its pace.

"Hey, Banjo!" I stoop to pet the black and white dog, who nuzzles into my hand and whines happily.

"You're here!" Jessica rushes around the counter at Happy Endings Animal Shelter and Veterinary Clinic to sweep me into a hug. "Thanks for coming by!"

"No problem. I love coming here." I do.

Jessica's both the head of the shelter and owner of the veterinary clinic her husband, Eric, helped fund when the old clinic got knocked down. I love the animals, and the fact that Jessica spends her life doing what she really loves inspires me to do the same.

I'm thrilled that I, too, have my dream-job, as an associate professor in the English Department at Maine University at Deerfield, commonly referred to as MUD.

"Sit down," says Jessica, scooping a giant orange cat off the chair across from her desk and placing it gently on the floor. The cats have a special huge room with cages and beds and toys in the back, but Marmalade is allowed to wander freely through the shelter during the day. He's fat and friendly and never tries to escape, and everyone who visits loves him instantly.

I sit, and Marmalade mewls, then jumps up onto my lap. Laughing, I pet him while he settles down and starts kneading my leg with his front paws.

"I have a huge favor to ask you," says Jessica, sitting down at her desk.

"What is it?" I scratch Marmalade behind the ears, and he starts to purr loudly.

Jessica takes a deep breath and sits up really straight, like she has to brace herself to say it. "OK. It's kind of weird."

I tilt my head and narrow my eyes. "What kind of weird?"

"Fun weird!"

"Okaaay....." I draw out the word.

"All right. Eric is involved in a charity that raises money for prostate cancer. There's a big fundraising event coming up next week, and one of the participants was injured and can't make it. We need someone to fill in, and I was hoping you'd do it."

"What do you mean by *participant*? I thought charity events involved glamming up and making small talk at a fancy dinner or something."

"Well. Uh, this is a little different." She scratches her cheek and looks away.

"Jessica?" I squint my eyes and crinkle my forehead.

She takes a deep breath, then a smile breaks out on her face. "It's going to be fun, Tessa! You'll have a great time."

"Tell me!"

"It's the annual Wife Carrying Competition." She says it really fast, but I'm pretty sure I heard her correctly.

For a second I just stare at her. "The *what*?" I finally ask.

"Wife Carrying Competition."

"I don't... what... isn't that something they do in Finland or somewhere?" I vaguely remember watching a YouTube video about it once, laughing as the women were carried over hay stacks and up hills, some over the guys' shoulders like sacks of potatoes, and some dangling upside down behind the guys in what looked like a really uncomfortable position.

"Yeah, but it's also a thing every year in Maine. Actually, it's in a town not far from here. Every year a different charitable organization benefits from the money raised, and this year it's the foundation my husband works with. A woman from one of the teams got hurt, so

Eric asked me if I knew someone small that might be willing to fill in."

"And I'm the lucky person." I narrow my eyes at her. "Anyway, isn't it called the Wife Carrying Competition? I'm not a wife."

"You don't have to be married. Lots of the participants aren't. Please? It's really important to Eric, and the event raises a lot of money, this year for prostate cancer."

"Why don't you do it?" I challenge her. "You're petite."

"I can't. I'll be out of town this weekend at a veterinary conference."

"This weekend? That's not short notice at all!" I sigh. "And honestly? It's way out of my comfort zone, and you're the one telling me to put my foot down about stuff. What if I say no?"

"I'd be really sad?" she asks, plastering a fake frown on her face.

"Jessica, stop! *Tessa's Time* is all about me being assertive, right? And I'm fairly certain this isn't something I want to do."

"You're right. You're right." She puts her hands up defensively. "But let me just tell you a little more about it, OK?"

"Fine," I mutter.

"So your partner is—I mean *would* be, if you decide to do this…" She turns to her computer and types something. "Dr. B. Maxwell."

"What's he like? Do you know him?" I ask.

She shakes her head. "Nope. But let's Google him! What if he's hot? And single? And you two fall in love while practicing various wife-carrying techniques? You know, like the one where the guy backs you up against a wall, and you straddle him with your legs?"

"This isn't some porno!" I laugh. "Though it would be a really great concept for one, now that I think of it."

"Are you sure you're not thinking of wife *swapping*?" asks Jessica with a giggle.

I move my chair over next to hers, laughing.

"Oh. Wait. No. Sorry for getting your hopes up." She clicks on a photo and a handsome man in his sixties pops up on the screen. "He's a little old for you. I mean, he's a silver fox and all, but you probably want someone at least thirty years younger."

"True," I respond, "but there's no way a man that old could pick up a woman anyway, let alone carry her!"

"Hold on," she says. "Here's an article. *Dr. Benson Maxwell and his wife Carla Maxwell are officially retiring from Maine's annual Wife Carrying Competition. After thirty years of participating, Maxwell, sixty five, says it's time for the couple to enjoy the competition from the sidelines instead of from the course.* The article's from about a year ago, right after the last competition."

"So if he's retired from the race, why does he need a partner?" I ask.

"Let's see. It mentions later that he's a prostate cancer specialist. So that's probably why he's back in, since the competition is benefiting research in his line of work. And maybe his wife, like, broke her hip or something? Oh look. Here's a video of last year's competition. Let's watch."

I stare at her screen while the video starts. The camera person is following a couple in the competition, and I absolutely cannot imagine doing this.

The guy is jogging along the course, the woman in an embarrassingly strange position on him. She's hanging upside down along his back, facing his body. Her face is pretty much lined up with his ass. *At least it's cushioned*, I think, because the girl's getting shaken up as the guy progresses through the course. The girl's butt faces up into the air, the back of the guy's neck against her crotch. Her thighs grip his neck, and her feet are crossed in front of him to help her stay in position. He's holding on to the backs of her knees as he rushes into a man-made water section of the course, and the woman has to raise her head up to keep from being drowned.

No. Freaking. Way.

There's no way I'm going to be in this competition, making a fool out of myself, and being carried about by a guy in his sixties, silver fox or not.

Jessica stops the video and looks at me, her face braced for the "no" she already knows is coming. "So?" she asks.

I shake my head. "Nope."

She leans her head back and closes her eyes. "OK. You don't have to. It's just that…"

"What?"

"I kind of already said you'd do it. You're supposed to meet him tomorrow morning at his office. I'm so sorry. Don't hate me!"

"Jessica!"

"I'm sorry," she repeats, and I can tell she feels bad. "It was a really shitty thing to do. Here, I'll call him right now and tell him you can't do it."

I watch as she dials the phone, mouthing sorry to me, and waits as it rings. "His office is closed for the day," she whispers. "Should I leave a message?"

"No," I say with a sigh. "Hang up. I'll stop by in the morning and tell him in person. I feel bad letting him down through a voice mail."

"I can go," says Jessica. "I'm the one who got you into this."

"It's fine, Jessica. Seriously. I've got time in the morning, and it will be interesting to meet the local wife carrying celebrity."

"Let me write down his info for you." She hands me a piece of paper on which she's scribbled *Dr. Benson Maxwell* and an address.

"In the office? Isn't he a little old to still be practicing?" I ask.

She shrugs. "I don't know. Yeah, maybe? Anyway, call me tomorrow and let me know how it goes. And don't hate me!"

"Never," I say with a grin as I get up to leave.

The office is in a converted Victorian house on a quiet tree-lined street in a town about a half hour away from Deerfield. Classes haven't started yet, and I don't have any meetings till the afternoon, so I head out first thing. I kind of wish I'd let Jessica leave a message, because I dread meeting this doctor and telling him no. It's too late to turn back now, though, so I park my silver Prius in front of the office and make my way to the house.

Lush dew-dropped ferns hang from the front porch, which is freshly painted a gorgeous shade of light blue and white, and a sign that reads "Maxwell Medical" confirms I'm in the right place.

Inside, there's a reception desk, and off to the side a large waiting room in what must have previously been the house's living room, octagonal and bright, sunlight streaming in through the many windows. Two comfortable couches and a handful of chairs are interspersed with side tables stacked with magazines. A coffee table in the middle of the room has coloring books and crayons on it, and I wonder how often kids come to a prostate specialist, but my thoughts are interrupted by an older woman hurrying to the desk.

"Sorry!" she says. "Just getting coffee." She lifts her steaming mug, then sets it on the table. "Do you, um, have an appointment?" She pushes her spectacles—they definitely look like spectacles and not glasses—up on her nose and pulls a pencil from behind her ear. Her grey hair is pulled back into a bun at the back of her head.

"No. Not really. I'm here to see Dr. Benson Maxwell? I'm supposed to meet him at nine?"

Her brow furrows. "Dr. Benjamin Maxwell?"

I pull the paper Jessica gave me and double check. "No. Benson. Am I in the wrong place? I'm here to talk to him about the, uh, Wife Carrying Competition?" I feel silly saying it.

She smiles broadly. "No, you're in the right place! He's with a patient now, but why don't you have a seat in the waiting room. He should be done soon."

"Thanks." I sit in a comfy arm chair and pick up a copy of *People* magazine.

A woman enters the office, smiles at the receptionist as if she knows her well, then sits across from me in the waiting room. Her brown hair is pulled back into a sloppy pony tail, and she's wearing jeans and a T-shirt, carrying a big slouchy purse, her face worn but friendly. She grins at me when she sees me looking at her.

"Hi," she says. "I'm just waiting for my son." She's one of those sweet talkative people who seems to need to get stuff off her chest.

I nod and smile, then turn back to the magazine.

"I'm sorry if you have to wait to see the doctor. We weren't on the schedule, but Dr. Maxwell always sees us, even if he's booked solid. When my son has a meltdown, sometimes there's no other way to calm him down."

"It's not a problem," I say.

"He's such a life saver. At first, I was a little put off by his appearance. But Trevor—that's my son—immediately responded to him in ways he hasn't responded to anyone before. Dr. Maxwell's helped bring out Trevor's sense of humor—I didn't even know he had a sense of humor! He's so serious all the time..."

Her words break off as the door between the waiting room and the exam rooms opens. A boy of about ten enters the room. He's slim and pale, with brown uncombed hair, and he shuffles in, head down, like he's trying not to be seen. He ignores me completely but he smiles at his mom.

"Bye," she says to me as she gets up to leave.

I smile and nod at her, and the boy tugs at her sleeve, apparently eager to leave. I pick up my magazine again, ready to settle in and wait, when the door opens again. I take a deep breath, ready to be friendly and make small talk before dropping the bomb that I won't be Dr. Maxwell's new Wife Carrying Competition partner.

And then the doctor comes in. Except it's not the friendly old man I was expecting. It's the guy from the concert in the park.

Light blue button down shirt rolled up to his elbows—a hint of scrolled black tattoos showing—and tucked into a pair of dark blue jeans. Black leather belt and boots. Rakish brown hair and bearded jaw and chin.

Jesus.

He freezes for a moment when he sees me, then one side of his mouth turns up in a grin as he realizes the coincidence he just walked into.

"Bye, Dr. Maxwell!" says the boy, who's waiting as his mom signs some papers at the front desk.

"See you next week," says the man in front of me, who I assume must, inexplicably, be Dr. Maxwell. "Oh, and I'll get you back for that prank you pulled!"

The boy laughs loudly, and his mom smiles fondly at the doctor as the two of them leave.

He turns to me, his brown eyes flecked with gold as he smiles. "Please tell me you're Tessa Jones and you're my new partner for the Wife Carrying Competition."

"I... I wasn't expecting you," I manage, despite the fact that my heart is pounding and my mind is an eddy of confusion.

"Likewise," he says, extending his hand. "I'm Ben Maxwell."

"Tessa Jones," I murmur, though he already said it. "I mean, you already know that. I'm here… I thought… I expected someone older. Benson Maxwell?"

"Ah," he nods, letting go of my hand. "That's my dad. He and my mom did the competition every year for a long time, but he officially retired from it last year. He roped me into doing it this year because the event benefits prostate cancer research, his field. And then my partner hurt her knee… Anyway, thanks for agreeing to fill in."

"Yeah. No problem," I answer. Somewhere in the recesses of my mind I remember that I came here to say I wouldn't participate. But what girl wouldn't jump at the chance to wrap her legs around this guy?

"Come into my office," he says, his smile charming me into speechlessness.

I follow him down a hallway into a big room with a desk, some bookshelves, and a sitting area with chairs and lots of books and toys, some scattered on the floor.

He gestures—with a strong and sexy forearm, I can't help noticing—toward one of the chairs, and I sit down.

"Coffee?" he asks.

"Oh. No. Thanks."

"You sure? I'm getting one for me." His voice is teasing and playful, and his eyes hold my gaze for a second.

"Yeah, sure," I finally respond. "I'm kind of an addict," I admit.

"Then why did you say no?" he asks, heading to the door.

"I didn't want to make you go through any trouble."

"Getting a cup of coffee from the other room is an *awful* lot of work," he responds.

"You know what I meant!" I laugh.

"Don't ever be afraid to say what you want," he says. His eyes narrow ever so slightly, and I swear he's talking about more than coffee.

He opens the door and there's the secretary, hand up about to knock. "Oh!" she exclaims. "You startled me!"

"Just on my way to get some coffee," says Ben.

"Oh, I'll just get it for you," she answers.

"You don't have to, Mrs. Spelling. I'm an adult, fully capable of pouring hot liquid into two mugs and carrying it down the hall."

"Benjamin Maxwell. I used to fix up your scraped knees when you were a boy. If I tell you I'll bring the coffee, then I'll bring it." She scowls at him, but it's evident there's a long history between them, and her eyes are filled with love.

"Yes, ma'am," drawls Ben.

And I swear she blushes! His gray haired grandmotherly secretary blushes! She recovers quickly, though. "Also, your mother called a little bit ago. She wanted to know... oh, I wrote it down, because she wanted me to use these exact words..." She reads from a paper. "She wanted to know if you *look like a legitimate and respectable doctor today or like a member of a disreputable biker gang*. Her words, not mine."

Ben throws back his head and laughs.

"And she wants to remind you to come over for dinner tonight. I'll be back with the coffee."

"She's known me since I was a kid." Ben sits across from me, his smile relaxed and handsome, his eyes filled with laughter. "She worked in my dad's office from the day he opened it till the day he retired. And now she works for me."

"What kind of doctor are you?" I ask.

He tilts his head. "Well, let's see. My patients say I'm fun. Their parents find me at the very least competent. I was written up in Down East Magazine for being one of the top new doctors in the area when I opened up my practice..."

I roll my eyes and laugh. "You *know* what I meant. *What kind of doctor* as in *what kind of medicine do you practice*?"

He smiles and rubs at his scruffy beard. "I'm a behavioral neurologist working primarily with children and adolescents. I do a fair bit of research in the area of neuropsychiatry as well."

"Oh." I'm a little bit astounded, and very impressed.

"And you?" he asks. "What do you do, Tessa?"

"Um, well, let's see. In the mornings I drink coffee. You know, since I'm an addict. Sometimes I go jogging. I like to watch funny movies and documentaries..."

He chuckles and nods approvingly, a dimple showing in his right cheek. "Touché. I think you know what I meant."

Grinning, I tell him I just got a new job as an associate professor of English at MUD.

We stare at each other for what feels like forever. I can't tell exactly what he's thinking, but his eyes are intense as they gaze into mine, and I feel my body fill up with heat. Something's happening, even though we just met. Even though he's some crazy, sexy, hot doctor who rides a motorcycle. Even though I'm going to be his partner in the Wife Carrying Competition, and we haven't even talked about that yet.

Even though he was being an asshole in the park, I remind myself.

He clears his throat and shakes his head slightly. "Anyway," he says, "about the competition. It's less than a week away, which doesn't give us much time. Have you watched any videos about it?"

"Um, yes. I have."

"So there are a few different carries that the men use, including the Estonian Carry and the Fireman's Carry, though some people do the old fashioned Piggyback..." He breaks off with an embarrassed-not-embarrassed smile. "Sorry. I should probably wait till tonight when we practice to give you a run-down on all the carries and moves. I get carried away..."

"No pun intended," I interrupt.

"Ha! Right. I get carried away with this stuff because I grew up watching my mom and dad participate in the contest."

"What was it like when you were a kid, watching your parents compete?"

Ben laughs. "Crazy. Cool. I went through a brief period of being embarrassed by it, but I'd probably have been embarrassed by anything they did at that age. Later, I realized how cool it is, though. My dad wrote the book on different carries and strategies."

"Yeah, I read he's sort of a local hero because of the competition."

"I mean he *literally* wrote a book on wife carrying."

I laugh. "Seriously? That's so random and cool! Your family

sounds amazing." My parents don't live far away, and I love them and visit regularly, but we were never the loud and boisterous families who laughed a lot that I always watched with envy.

The door opens, and I expect it to be Mrs. Spelling with the coffee, but instead a drop-dead gorgeous woman comes in. She has blonde hair cut into a chic pixie cut. Her silk blouse tucked into a slim pencil skirt shows off her slim yet curvy figure.

Perfect, in other words. Her shiny pink lips grin, revealing pearly white teeth, and she sashays into the room with her arms out.

"Benji!" she squeals.

Benji?

"Gemma!" Ben gets up and she rushes into his arms for a hug that, in my opinion, is a few seconds too long.

Not that I care. Of *course* I don't care! I seriously just met the guy, so how long he hugs random women isn't my concern. But my stomach clenches all the same. I like Ben. Not just the way his muscles flex or the way he idly scratches his strong jaw. But also the part that laughs easily and smiles often, and the part that chose to dedicate his life to helping children.

He gently pushes her away so he can hold her shoulders and look into her eyes. "How you doing?" he asks, tenderness in his voice. It's girlfriend-level tenderness, and I sigh in resignation. "How's your knee?"

She shrugs. "I'm getting x-rays today. It hurts." She makes a fake pouting face, which I think is stupid but apparently Ben likes because he laughs.

"Let me know when you hear something. Oh hey! You want to meet your replacement?" He turns to me with a smile, and I awkwardly stand and walk toward them. "This is Tessa. She's friends with the wife of a big organizer of this year's event, and she got roped into competing with me."

"Hi." I manage a weak upturn of my lips. "Nice to meet you."

"You too!" Instead of taking my hand, she gives me a quick hug, and I smell her floral perfume, delicate and unique and pretty, just like her.

"You didn't hurt yourself practicing for the competition, did you?" I ask her. "I need to know what I'm getting into!"

"Oh, no. Ben's really careful." She winks at him before turning back to me. "I was doing a trail run last weekend and I twisted my leg. My knee's been kind of swollen and really painful ever since."

"Yet you've waited this long to get x-rays," says Ben under his breath.

"Oh you! You know doctors make the worst patients," she says.

Great. So she's a doctor too. I suddenly feel so stupid, like my Master's degree in English holds absolutely no weight compared to these two.

"What kind of doctor are you?" I ask.

"I'm a neurologist," she says. "Ben and I met during our fellowships." She gives him a side hug that, I notice with jealousy, he reciprocates.

"It was great to meet you, but I need to get going," I say just as Mrs. Spelling returns with two mugs of coffee.

"You're leaving, dear?" she asks. "What about your coffee?"

"I'm sorry, I need to get…" I stammer.

"Oh, no worries. I'll have hers." Gemma takes the mug from Mrs. Spelling with a broad smile. "Pleasure meeting you," she says to me, then she grasps Ben's arm and leads him over to the chairs where we were just sitting.

"Meet me at the gym tonight? I'll email you the address," says Ben over his shoulder.

"Right. Tonight." I force a smile on my face and leave before I can embarrass myself any more. I haven't done anything overtly cringe-worthy, but I feel humiliated, as though I just ran down the hallway at school naked. Except all that happened was some sexy doctor came in to take over my time with Ben. Or maybe I was taking over her time with him.

Because I'm only the understudy. The replacement. And this is all just temporary.

He's an asshole anyway, I remind myself. He might be handsome, and an amazing doctor who changes children's lives, but he was still being a jerk in the park letting his stupid phone ring. So he's not perfect after all.

But my heart feels sick all the way back to work.

Oh my god.

Ben in jeans is hot. Ben in sweat shorts and a ragged T-shirt? Even hotter.

It's obvious he's no stranger to the gym. His thighs could be used to teach med students about leg muscles, because every single one is perfectly defined. He's got the calves of a soccer player and the grace of somebody completely comfortable with his body. And I can't keep my eyes off him.

We're meeting at his buddy's Brazilian Jiu Jitsu studio, which is closed right now so nobody else is here. The room we're in is large, one wall all mirrors like a ballet studio and the floor covered in mats.

"Floor's padded. In case I drop you," he says with a wink, running a hand through his slightly-too-long brown curly hair.

That dimple. It makes me wish I could kiss him until he was no longer smiling.

"I hope you've got a third partner lined up," I joke.

"I only dropped my last partner a few times. And if you want, you can wear a helmet in case you land on your head."

"Land on my head?"

He shrugs and grins. "Trust me," he says.

"I guess I should trust you when it comes to matters of brain damage. You know, since you're a neurologist and all," I mutter.

"The biggest issue is if you fall during the contest, we suffer a five second penalty. So don't fall."

"Don't drop me," I counter.

He chuckles. "So there are a bunch of different carries we can use, but the best, and the one I've been practicing with Gemma, is the Estonian Carry."

I nod, adjusting my running shorts and trying to block out the mention of her.

"Take off your shoes and socks."

"What? OK." I sit down on the mat and untie my shoes.

For some reason, taking my shoes and socks off in front of Ben makes me feel like I'm stripping naked. I try to fight down the blush that threatens because it's silly to feel this way.

Finally in bare feet, I stand. "Ready."

"Forgot something," he says, digging into his gym bag and pulling out a worn leather belt.

What the hell is he going to do with that?

He fastens it around his waist, on top of his work-out outfit.

"That's a good look you've got going on there," I say with a laugh.

"Right?" he responds. "I'm surprised more guys aren't walking around sporting the sweats and belt look. OK," he says, kneeing down on the mat. "Come here. This is going to seem weird at first, but you'll get used to it."

Right. My brain immediately imagines he's talking about something sexy. A new move he wants to try. Something we just watched together in a dirty movie. I need to stop that. I need to focus.

Except the way he's grinning lets me know he might be thinking the same thing.

I stand in front of him, and he puts his hands on the outsides of my thighs, pulling me closer to him so his face is right in front of my, well, shorts. This isn't awkward at all.

He holds my thighs instead of letting go while he tells me more about the move we're going to do. "So you're going to be hanging upside down behind me, facing my back, with your legs around my shoulders, holding onto my waist. The belt is there to give you something to grab on to at first till you get comfortable in this position."

"I'm not really athletic or anything," I say, suddenly really unsure about this. He's hot, and it was fun to imagine, well, *riding* him, but the actual carrying part makes me nervous.

"You don't have to be. All you're going to do is hold on tight with your legs so I don't have to support you much. The course itself is relatively short—253 meters, I think. And the challenge is mostly in the carrying. You just get to enjoy the ride." His voice is easy, comforting.

"Fine," I say. "Let's do this."

"I knew you'd come around," he says, his voice low, and all I hear is "I knew you'd come." His brown eyes flash with something—desire?—and he pulls me even closer, which is a little weird since he's kneeling and I'm standing right in front of him. I mean, right freaking there.

"Spread your legs," he says, tapping my right thigh with a finger.

"What? Right." I widen my stance, my stomach fluttery.

"Perfect," he says. "Now I'm going to put my head between your legs, and you're going to lean your body down my back. Got it?"

"Yup," I murmur.

And he does it. His head goes between my legs, the back of his neck right there. I bend my body down along his back.

"Good," he says. "Now as I stand, cross your ankles to grip on better with your legs, and grab the belt if you need stability. Ready?"

"Ready," I say, though I'm not at all sure I am.

He stands smoothly, lifting me up into the air. I squeal as I hang upside down, my face practically against his butt, which, I should add, is nice and firm, and grab his belt.

"You're a natural," he says, not even the hint of a grunt or struggle in his voice.

"There's nothing natural about this position," I laugh.

"Eh, you'll get used to it. Are you comfortable?"

I laugh again. "Really? I'm hanging upside down with my legs around your neck and you're asking if I'm comfortable?"

"You know. Relatively comfortable. I'm just trying to be a gentleman." I can hear the smile in his voice.

The blood has all run to my face, and I'm feeling lightheaded, but I take a deep breath and focus on not passing out as Ben starts to walk around the studio. After a few minutes, I feel more comfortable in the position, confident I'm not going to crash down to the ground at any second.

Instead, though, I become aware of the way his beard tickles the insides of my thighs, rough and prickly on my tender skin. The back of my legs face upward, and every once in a while, when he brings his hands around to grip the hollows of my knees, I can't help wondering what those hands would feel like touching my skin in a different scenario.

"Today we'll just work on getting you used to this," he says after a while. "Tomorrow I'll start going faster and we'll practice obstacles."

"Obstacles?"

"Yeah. The course has two logs to climb over."

"Anything else?"

"Just, uh, the *widow maker*," he mutters. Or at least that's what I think he says.

"Wait. The what? Put me down!" I slap at his ass.

"Geez!" he laughs, but kneels down until my feet touch the mat, and I stand, awkwardly untangling my legs from around his head and shaking the dizziness away.

He grins up at me. "That was fun, right?"

"Sure. If you define *fun* as having all the blood rush to your face that's hanging against some random dude's ass. And what's the widow maker?" I demand.

He laughs. "Is that what I am? Just some random guy?" His tone is light, but his eyes are searing as he gazes at me. Though it's pitch black outside now, the studio's lights are bright, and flecks of gold glint in his eyes.

My mind goes blank. What were we even talking about?

"What's the widow maker?" I repeat.

"You know." He shrugs. "I need to carry you through water."

"Water? How deep?" I imagine myself hanging off his back, my face dragging through liquid so I can't breathe. I watched those videos, saw the women lifting their heads up to avoid a mouthful of muddy muck.

"Almost up to my waist." He smiles. "I can see if snorkels are allowed." His strong hands reach down to unbuckle the belt he's still wearing, and my breath stops for a second.

Watching him, with his insane body and messy hair and scruffy jaw undo his belt buckle almost undoes something inside me. *God.* It's an innocent move, a necessary gesture, but I can't help my mind from wandering.

I sit down on the mat and pull my socks on, then my shoes, which I tie while he puts away his belt. When I'm finished, he reaches out his hand to help me up.

His grip is solid. His hand feels so big around mine. I let him pull me, allow myself to feel his strength as he swiftly but gently brings me to a standing position. Right in front of him.

"Look. Um, thanks. For doing this." His hand rakes through his hair as he looks down at me. "It means a lot to my dad. And with Gemma getting hurt…"

Ugh. Gemma. "No problem."

He nods, still looking at me. For a few seconds we stand there, neither of us moving. It passes the point at which it's normal to stay staring at someone, but I can't back away.

He reaches out a hand toward my face. Is he going to touch my cheek? Wrap his hand around my neck and bend down for a kiss? But then he lets his hand fall. "Come on," he says. "I'll walk you to your car."

The next evening we meet at the gym again, and I'm looking forward to spending some time alone with Ben. Instead of running shorts, I opted for long yoga pants. Because what's the point of getting turned on by some guy's beard on your thighs if he's already taken?

This time the gym is open, a class going on in the second studio. Ben's set up two obstacles, giant boxes covered in mat material, so I can get the feel of what it's like to be carried while he's climbing over things.

"Tessa," he says with a grin as I enter the gym. His outfit is similar to yesterday's, and again I am stunned into momentary silence by his lean and strong body. But it's his smile that really disarms me, genuine and reflected also in his eyes, glinting with mischief.

"Hey, Ben." I sit down immediately to take off my shoes and socks. I made a point to get a pedicure today on my lunch break, and even though I told myself it was because I needed it, I knew the real reason was because I wanted Ben to think I have pretty feet. Especially since they'll be in his face while we practice. Also? I bought a pack of baby wipes so I could clean my feet in the car right before practice, just to make sure they didn't gross him out.

A guy enters the studio, well built and grinning as he gives Ben a tough man hug. "Bro! Good to see you." He turns to me with interest.

"Joel, this is my new partner for the competition. Tessa. Tessa, this is my long time friend Joel. He owns this place."

"Hi!" I say, standing up and shaking his hand. "Thanks for letting us practice here."

"Yeah, no problem. Nice to meet you." He turns back to Ben. "How come you always get all the pretty ones? One after another with this guy," he says, pointing at Ben with his thumb.

"Oh, we're not… we're just doing the competition together," I say lamely, not even sure what Joel's getting at.

"Yeah yeah, I know. I didn't mean anything." He puts his hands up defensively. "I gotta get back to my class. Dude, if you finish up early in here, I need to work on my shoulders. Think I could borrow her for a little bit?" He winks at me.

Ben laughs, but it's not his usual genuine and generous laugh. It's forced, but I'm not sure why. It could be because Joel's being a pig. Or it could be because he's being possessive. Which makes no sense, since we barely know each other. But I can't help the fact that my heart skips a beat at the tone.

Joel leaves, smiling over his shoulder at me as he does, and Ben kneels down right away. "Let's get started," he says.

I approach him, standing directly in front of him like last time. He grins up at me, then urges me forward by giving me the "come here" signal with his finger.

I swear it's like he's a magnet and I'm a helpless little metal shaving, unable to resist his pull.

"Get on," he says with a drawl.

Holy crap.

I straddle his shoulders again, lying my body down his back, and he stands with no hesitation. It still feels weird to be hanging upside down, but not as bad as yesterday.

We practice for about half an hour, broken down into segments of about ten minutes of carrying and a few minutes of rest in between. I'm getting the feel of holding on to him, both with my legs around his neck and my arms, sometimes clinging to the belt and sometimes curled around his body, my hands clasped together over his rock-hard abs.

When we're done, he's sweaty, and I have a headache, though I'm more than mildly turned on by clinging to his gorgeous body for so long. We sit on the mat next to each other while I put my socks and shoes on.

"Do you think we're ready?" I ask. It's our last chance to practice before the event on Saturday morning.

"Yeah," he says. "And even if we don't win, which honestly we probably won't, we're still raising money for charity, and that's what it's all about."

"Who says we won't win?" I ask, tying my right sneaker and tightening the laces on my left.

"Eh, there are people who literally practice all year for this." He laughs. "Of course, I would love to win your weight in beer and five times your weight in dollars."

"That's the prize?"

He nods. "Yup." Sweat glistens on his neck, and I want to touch it, to run my hand through his damp curls.

"Who knows? Maybe we'll get lucky." I smile up at him.

"Oh yeah?" He turns to me so our eyes meet. One of his eyebrows is cocked, and there's the hint of a grin on his lips.

I roll my eyes, but my breath hitches when he reaches out and tucks a strand of hair back behind my ear. His finger makes a trail from my ear down to my chin, slowly, as he stares into my eyes. He puts gentle pressure under my chin, like he wants me to stay just like this, face tilted up toward his. It's not like I could look away; it's not like I'd ever choose to.

"Tessa?" It's a question. He's asking permission.

All I can do is nod. Yes. Of course yes!

Slowly he bends his head, his lips moving closer to mine. My mouth parts a bit, ready for his kiss.

"Bro! You ready for the big weekend?" Joel enters the studio, loud and boisterous and the worst interruption I've ever experienced.

"Yeah. We're ready," says Ben, looking at me for a second before breaking his gaze away and standing. "You coming out to watch?"

"Of course, man!" says Joel. "Hey, listen. If you're done here, could you take a look at my hand? It's been giving me some trouble."

"Find a girlfriend and you won't have to overuse it." Ben winks at him. "You know I practice in neurology and psychiatry, right? Not orthopedics?"

"Just take a look. Tell me who to see."

"Yeah. Sure." Ben looks at me with regret in his eyes, and I wonder what he's thinking. Was the almost-kiss a one-time deal, with us both caught up in the moment, or something I'll have a chance to experience another time? "I'll see you this weekend?" he asks.

"Right. OK." I wave awkwardly as I take a step backwards, then turn and leave the studio. At my car, I take a deep breath. He was going to kiss me! But what if he never tries again?

Frustrated, I unlock the door and start to slide into the driver's seat.

"Tessa! Wait!"

I spin around and see Ben jogging to my car, his quads so muscular I'm pretty sure they'd be hard as steel if I touched them. And even though I probably won't ever find out, I feel a little breathless anyway as he approaches me.

I tilt my head as he gets closer, about to ask what's going on. But I don't have a chance. He backs me up against the open door of my car and, with one hand behind my neck, pulls me toward him. Fast. No hesitation at all.

His lips are tender at first, kissing mine gently like he's asking a question without words. He pulls back to look into my eyes. His are hungry, and any trace of his usual jokey demeanor is gone, replaced by stark and unadulterated desire.

This time when we kiss it's hard and greedy, like we're both acknowledging the fact that we want each other. That someday we'll have each other. That eventually we won't be able to hold back until we've drowned ourselves in the passion we both feel. But for now it's just a kiss—a promise of what's to come.

I've never been kissed like this. Never felt this weak, like I'd float away if he wasn't here with one hand wound in my hair and the other on my waist to keep me down here on solid ground. My head is a kaleidoscope, tiny scraps of desire and sexy songs and love poems all spinning and spinning and arranging themselves in an array of unpredictable but beautiful designs.

I cling to the soft material of his worn T-shirt as we end the kiss.

"You all right?" he asks, tilting my face up with a finger under my chin.

"Yes," I whisper. "I just… that was…"

"I know." Another kiss now, this one gentle, quick, lingering for only a promise-filled moment.

"What about Gemma?" I don't want to ask, but I have to, because if he's with her I can't do this.

"What about her?" he asks, taking a step back, a confused look on his face.

"Are you guys…?"

"Gemma and me? No. We're old friends and sometimes colleagues. I don't cheat, Tessa. Never have, never will."

"So you're not an asshole?" I ask, reaching out to play with the hem of his old T-shirt.

"Nope." He takes my hand and puts it on his chest, covering it with his own big hand.

"So what about the ringtone in the park?" I wince as I say it. But I'm dying to know.

"What about it?"

"You just let it ring and ring. And it was loud! And you sat there laughing. Kind of like a, well, asshole."

I shrug and he laughs.

"Yeah, I can see that," he says after a few moments. "OK. You remember that kid at my office? He's this really neat kid, and he's had a difficult time expressing his feelings. He's repetitive and closed off. Barely shows emotions. Really serious. I've been working with him on opening up, and one way he's starting doing that is through humor. So we've got this thing—it sounds stupid—but it's actually monumentally important. We play practical jokes on each other. I was letting him play a game on my phone during our session before the concert, and when my phone started ringing, I knew he'd changed the ring tone to the asshole calling one as a prank. So it seemed like I was being a dick, but I was so stunned and happy that I just wanted to listen to it until it stopped."

Shit. Now I feel like a jerk.

"Ben, I'm sorry…"

"I'm not. If you didn't think I was an asshole, we'd never have met." He pulls me close and kisses me once more. Regret fills his eyes as he breaks the kiss. "I have to get back to Joel." He rolls his eyes. "I'm sorry. I'd much rather do this again."

It's like we're teenagers, unable to keep our hands off each other. His hand grasps my ass, pulling me toward him, and I feel how hard he is. I strain my hips forward, feeling his length against my stomach. His other hand slides up my shirt, his hand warming the tender skin of my back.

I moan—it's unbidden, and I'm a little embarrassed to be so wonton. But he only kisses me harder.

When he stops, he puts his hands on my shoulders and grins, then runs one hand through his unruly hair. "Tessa," he says in a low voice. "What am I going to do with you?"

I shrug but smile in response. *Everything*, I want to say. *You're going to do everything with me.* But of course I could never say that out loud.

"Be safe," he whispers. "I'll see you this weekend."

"Yeah. You too." I watch as he jogs back to the studio. Then I get in my car and drive home.

My office is finally starting to look like a real office and not just a room with a desk and lots of cardboard boxes. A really, really small room. I seriously think the closet in my apartment is bigger. But at least it's mine, with a door I can shut if I need to speak privately with someone or just need time alone. I even have a tiny window, which is streaked and dirty, but I'll get to it soon.

Classes don't start for another week, but I'm busy making last minute changes to my syllabi and arranging my office and learning my way around campus.

I'm startled by a knock on the open door, and when I look up it's

Gemma. Ben's Gemma.

What the hell?

"Oh. Hi." I stand up from arranging volumes of poetry on a low shelf and cross my arms over my chest. *What is she doing here?*

"Hi," she says, looking around quickly. "What a cute little office!" I'm not sure if the condescending tone is real or a figment of my imagination.

"Thanks."

Her platinum blond pixied hair and elegant pants suit, paired with heels higher than I've ever worn, look out of place in this dusty book-riddled corridor of the English department, which somehow is at the bottom of the list for university renovations. It makes me feel at home, like the people who grace these halls care about the really important things, such as how to capture meaning in a handful of words or write a truly unique phrase that expresses what love feels like. But suddenly, instead of feeling proud of my job and position, I feel like a little, insignificant mouse.

"So listen. Tessa. I've got great news! The x-rays of my knee came back clear, and after a cortisone injection, I feel like new. So you don't have to take my place tomorrow in the competition."

My heart stops. "Oh. Um..."

"You don't mind, do you?"

Yes! I do! But I can't say it.

I want to. I try to. But when I open my mouth to speak, all I see is Gemma's cool confidence, and no words come out. Instead, I shake my head.

"Great. I'll let Ben know. And thanks for filling in so Ben could practice while I was out of commission."

"Yeah. Of course."

"Have a nice day," she says, glancing around my office one last time. I swear there's a tiny look of disdain on her face.

"You too," I mutter, but she's already gone. I can hear her heels clicking away down the hallway.

"What happened to *Tessa's Time*?" moans Jessica. "Why didn't you say you wanted to do it?"

"I don't know!" I wail. "She was so… professional and confident."

"You're professional too! You're a freaking professor, Tessa. And you're gorgeous. I don't know why you're so intimidated by her. You need to stick up for yourself."

"I know." She's right. "But the competition is tomorrow morning, and she's doing it. I was only the understudy." I stand still to allow the small white dog I'm walking to pee on a tree. Jessica and I are taking two of the shelter dogs from Happy Endings for a walk while I tell her my sad tale.

"You said he kissed you, right?" Jessica clicks her tongue at the German shepherd mix she's walking to distract him from the squirrel he's suddenly obsessed with.

"He did."

"So he likes you. You shouldn't just let him go."

"But how can I compete with a gorgeous neurologist who's already his best friend and, by the way, looks like a Victoria's Secret model?"

"What makes you think you have to?" she asks.

"Because it's obvious she likes him."

"But he likes you."

"I don't know, Jessica."

"You owe it to yourself to at least talk to him. Make sure he wants Gemma to be his partner and not you."

"All right," I say, as we turn to head back to the shelter. "I'll call him tonight."

But later, after I've given myself a pep talk and had a glass of wine for courage and called him, he doesn't answer his phone, and I don't leave a message. I think about texting him, but I already called, and I don't want to seem desperate. I go to bed and toss and turn all night, wishing I knew what he was thinking.

I wake up early and get dressed. I'm stunningly sad that instead of putting on bike shorts and a T-shirt I'm putting on a pair of jeans and a sweater. I know watching him carry Gemma through the course will be like rubbing salt in my wounds, but I need to go. Not showing up would be giving in completely, and I'm not about to do that.

I wish I could bring Jessica with me for moral support, but she took a red-eye out of town to some veterinary conference, so I'm on my own.

The parking lot is packed, and I have to park far away from the course. Smiles and laughter lighten the dark and cold day, and I huddle into my sweater as I make my way toward the course. Competitors, dressed in athletic wear, stretch and chit-chat.

I don't see Ben and Gemma, and though I know it's inevitable that I will, I savor the few minutes I have to ground myself before I have to face them.

"Tessa?"

I spin around and stare into Ben's eyes. "Hey," I say, trying to sound breezy.

"What are you doing here?"

"I came to, um, support you. And Gemma."

"Oh." His usual smile isn't there. In fact, I swear he's close to frowning at me.

"What's wrong?" I ask.

He shakes his head. "I really wanted to do the race with you, Tessa."

"I did too! But Gemma came to my office..."

"She said you seemed relieved that her knee was better," he interrupts. "And that you might have to go out of town? Something about a sick relative?"

I take a deep breath. I'm tired of hiding how I feel. I'm not going to do it any longer. "What? No. I don't have a sick anyone. And honestly? I was devastated when she said she was back in. I just... I couldn't say no to her, Ben. She was your original partner."

"I should have called you after I spoke with her. I was swamped..." His words trail off and he grabs me suddenly, his hand on my back, and looks into my eyes. "You're the one I want to be with." His words are savage, his eyes blazing. "I vaguely remember telling you once already that you shouldn't be afraid to say what you want."

I take a deep breath. "I want you, Ben. I mean, to race with you."

He chuckles. "Just to race with me?"

"Let's talk after the competition." Then reality hits me. "Wait! I'm not dressed for the race. I don't…"

"You're fine. I can carry you in jeans and a sweater."

"But I'll get soaked when we go through the water and be too heavy." I glance at the other teams stretching and getting ready, the women in bike shorts and sports bras despite the chilly morning.

Suddenly I don't want to play it safe anymore. Something opens inside me, like the sun breaking through gray clouds, triumphant and bursting with light. I pull my sweater off over my head.

Ben stands up straighter and raises an eyebrow at me, grinning as I toss my sweater at him. I shiver slightly in my black bra, then begin to unbutton my jeans.

"You're the best partner ever." Ben's grin is a full-fledged smile now.

"Oh yeah?" I shimmy my hips as I push the denim down my thighs, revealing a pair of black bikini underwear. I'm glad I match today, despite the fact that I had no idea I'd be stripping in front of a crowded field of people.

"Yup. Definitely the best partner." He laughs out loud as I toss my jeans at him.

"It's like wearing a bathing suit," I say with a shrug. "Like the beach volleyball players in the Olympics."

"It's, uh, better than a bathing suit. Here. Let me put your clothes and purse in my car. It's right over there."

"Great," I say. "Meet you at the start line." I try to ignore the stares of the people around me, but somehow, in the absurdity and fun of the entire event, I don't feel that out of place, and people aren't really paying me that much attention.

Ben runs back over to me. "Come on," he says. "It's almost time." He takes my hand and pulls me over to the starting line.

Gemma appears in front of us. She's wearing electric blue bike shorts that accentuate her gorgeous curves. She's got on a tight black tank top, the curves of her perfect boobs rising above the fabric. After looking at my bra and underwear, she pastes a fake smile on her face as she fights down the obvious surprise she feels at seeing me here.

"Tessa?" she asks.

I nod. "Hi, Gemma. Ben said he wasn't expecting me. Something about a sick relative? Must have gotten a mixed message, though, because I'm here." I shrug and give her a faux-confused smile.

"Great." She frowns and looks down.

I can tell she's embarrassed, and I feel a momentary flush of sympathy for her. It must be awful, caught in a lie in front of both people involved.

But there's no time to feel sorry for her because Ben's pulling me to the starting line. "We're in the first heat," he says. "Two teams compete. Winner advances."

He kneels down and I approach him in my underwear and bra and can't help noticing that he bites his lip as I approach. He makes a low growling sound as I straddle his shoulders and he stands.

Immediately the blood rushes to my head, and I tighten my grip with my knees around his neck and wrap my arms around his stomach.

"Oh, hey!" he yells over his shoulder. "My parents are right there!"

"Great," I yell back. "They get to see their son carry a strange girl in her underwear."

"Eh, you're not that strange," he teases. "And you'll be wearing clothes next time you meet them."

Next time. My heart flutters.

A gun shot signals the start of the race, and I shut my eyes and cling to Ben as he begins to jog up the incline that marks the beginning of the course.

His beard scratches the bare insides of my thighs, just like that first time in practice, and all I can think about is how it would feel if he was there with intent. If he was there kissing my thighs, biting my skin, moving closer and closer…

Ben's climbing over a giant log, and my body's jostled as he does. "Hang on!" he yells, but he doesn't have to tell me to. I'm clinging hard to him, both to keep from falling off and because I can. I mean, who wouldn't hold on tight to a guy like this if given the chance?

Cold spray splashes up and I shriek as he enters the water section of the course, a trench about thirty feet long filled with what feels like ice-cold dirty mud. I can hear Ben's laugh, and then suddenly he nips the inside of my right thigh with his teeth.

Electricity shoots through me, and I don't even care when I see the other couple pass us. Because Ben likes me! He kissed me. And he just bit my thigh.

We finish second, and when Ben sets me down on the ground and we're both standing upright, he grasps me around the waist and swings me around. "That was amazing!" he says.

"We lost," I counter, but I'm grinning ear to ear.

He shrugs and grins. "No. We didn't." He leans down to kiss me, but just before our lips meet we're swarmed by his parents and a bunch of guys whom he briefly introduces as his med school friends. Gemma's there, too, and I'm overwhelmed by so many people all at once.

"I'm going to get my phone for photos," he whispers to me and runs off to his car, while I stand there and awkwardly listen to everyone being familiar with each other.

He seems to take forever, but finally he lopes back, curls bouncing, holding his phone. He hands it to one of his buddies, then poses with me, his arm over my shoulder, for a photo by the finish line.

His friends surround him, slapping him on the back and talking over each other, and I introduce myself to his parents, who are really sweet and funny. They explain that it was always an annual tradition for Ben's friends to come out to watch them race. And now that Ben's taken over, they're here to see him.

"Benson! Carla!" Gemma insinuates herself between me and Ben's parents, hugging them and talking like she's known them forever, and I take a few steps away from the big group of Ben's people.

I glance over at Ben, and he's busy chatting up his med school friends and doesn't even notice me. I don't like crowds. I never have. I always end up feeling awkward, like if I left, nobody would notice.

Sighing, I head to his car to get my stuff that he stashed there. I keep hoping he'll stop me, but nobody notices that I'm leaving. At my own car, I pull my sweater and jeans on, then get inside and sit in the driver's seat, bummed and sad.

I consider calling Jessica to update her, but I'm too depressed. I like Ben. And I know he likes me. But maybe we're just too different. Maybe our worlds are too separate and not meant to collide.

I buckle up, ready to head home.

"Asshole calling. Asshole calling. There's an asshole on the other end of the line."

What the heck?

The voice is coming from my purse, which I pull onto my lap before rummaging around to find my phone. When I do, the screen is lit up, and a photo of Ben smiles at me as the stupid ring tone continues.

I burst out laughing. He must have taken the opportunity when he got his phone from the car to program his photo—and the ring tone—into my phone.

"Hello?" I answer somewhat breathlessly.

"Where are you?" he asks. "We're supposed to collect our money and drink your weight in beer!"

"Except we didn't win!" I object.

"Depends on how you define win."

His tone is heavy, heavier than I'm used to with him, and I don't know how to respond. My heart pounds.

"I want to take you out," he continues. "We keep getting interrupted, but now that the race is over, we're going to go somewhere and be alone. Like I've wanted to do with you since I met you at that concert in the park."

"OK," I murmur. "When?"

"Now."

A knock on the passenger side window startles me, and when I look up, he's peering in the window. He grins, and I press the unlock button so he can get in.

"Why'd you leave?" he asks, sitting down and shutting the passenger door.

"You seemed so busy…"

He interrupts me with a kiss, light at first. He's leaning over the center console, and he puts one hand around the back of my head as his lips open, teasing mine.

"I wish I'd caught you before you put your clothes on again," he whispers.

I laugh, but it's slightly strangled by my desire and his lips, which kiss me harder this time. He puts a hand on my knee, the warmth traveling straight through the denim and making my skin so, so hot. When his fingers move slightly up my leg, I remember the way his beard felt there, and a shudder of desire takes over my body.

He breaks off the kiss and laughs. "I feel like we're in high school, making out in a car and hoping nobody sees."

"And your parents are here!"

"Yeah. But I don't care if they see. I want everyone to know I'm with you."

"Really?" I ask.

"Yeah. Really. In fact, my mom will probably literally kill me if I don't bring you over for a late lunch today. She insisted."

"Well, I don't want you to literally die…"

Ben chuckles. "So we have…" He glances at his watch. "…about an hour to kill before then."

"What do you want to do?" I ask.

"Go park somewhere?" He winks at me. "You know, continue the high school theme?"

I laugh out loud. I know he's joking, but part of me thinks that's the best idea I've heard. Ever.

"There's a really cool coffee shop not far from here," he suggests.

"Tell me where to go," I say, turning the car on.

He puts his hand on my thigh as I pull out of the parking lot. The day is crisp and bright—the sun finally broke through the clouds—and I can't get the grin off my face. As we drive down the gravel road, through the tall trees that open up to the paved road ahead, I'm not sure exactly where we're going. But I know I'm headed somewhere amazing, with this guy who's definitely not an asshole at all.

About Maria Monroe

Hi! I'm Maria Monroe, contemporary romance author. I'm honored to be part of this anthology, which benefits such an important cause.

I hope you enjoyed Tessa and Ben's adventure participating in the Wife Carrying Competition (which is actually a real thing)! Tessa's friend Jessica is the star of my book **The Rescue**, which takes place in the same fictional town of Deerfield, ME, as this story does. And my novel **Julian & Lia** is about an innocent freshman at Maine University at Deerfield (MUD), who meets sexy college senior Julian.

I love connecting with readers. Please feel free to contact me!

Email: mariamonroeauthor@gmail.com

Website: www.graffitifiction.com

Facebook: www.facebook.com/mariamonroeauthor

Twitter: www.twitter.com/authormaria

Talking to the Moon

BY JEANNINE COLETTE

THE DINNER PARTY

"Another Wharton graduate in the family. Your father must be so proud," Aunt Ina boasts, her hands clasped in front of her heart.

Before I get a chance to answer, Father steps up to my side, his arm firm on my shoulder. "We are very proud of our Jules. Top of her class and still soaring. Only the best for our girl."

I look up at my father, his face beaming with immense pride.

In seven generations, there hasn't been a failure or scandal to the family name. My graduation from the Wharton Business School was not only expected—it was written in dogma.

Aunt Ina's cheeks are pinched with a rosy glow. "We're all dying to know where you accepted a position. Leave it to Franklin Bradford to host a bon voyage party for his daughter without sharing where it is she's traveling off to."

I open my mouth to respond, but Father cuts me off. "Nice try," he says with a pointed finger to his elder Aunt. "You'll just have to wait for the champagne toast like everyone else."

"If you'll excuse me. I have to use the ladies," I say and bow out of Father's arm.

I'm not three feet away when another relative is congratulating me on my accomplishments. My father's colleagues hand out business cards, telling me to stay in touch. Mother's socialites compliment me on the chiffon, aubergine-colored dress I'm wearing. I don't believe they've ever spoken to me about anything other than the couture on my body.

It's twenty minutes before I make it to the French doors leading to the veranda overlooking the ocean, the Long Island sun setting into the Atlantic. Splaying my hands on the rail, I take a moment to collect my thoughts. I love my parents and my life here at The Manor, but part of me can't wait to board that plane tomorrow and get away. I shouldn't complain—being a Bradford has had its privileges. I attended the best prep schools and now the most prestigious business school in the country. Weekly trips to the salon, a closet full of designer clothes, and everything I want at my fingertips is just the top of the iceberg of the life my father has been able to provide.

I respect where I've come from. I do not take it for granted.

But I want more.

I want an adventure.

And tomorrow, my new life begins.

Taking a deep breath, I inhale the salty air and listen to the waves as they crash into the shoreline. Rolling my head to the side, I see the lights of the carriage house are on. Inside that building is my Mercedes convertible that I adore. Mother thinks it's foolish I park it myself when one of the staff will bring it to the garage for me. I tell her I enjoy doing things myself. But that's not the real reason.

Looking through the French doors, into the party room, I see guests are still arriving. Father and Mother are busy in conversation, and cocktails are just being served.

I walk down the back steps and turn right onto the path to the carriage house. The workers are at the front of The Manor, valeting cars. Ducking in through the back door, I enter the large room that smells of wax and motor oil. It's silly I'd be in here all by myself. Perhaps it's force of habit.

I suppose I just wanted to come in here one last time.

"You wouldn't be thinking about leaving your party early, would you?" His deep baritone makes my heart race. A chill runs up my spine; I have to close my eyes to compose myself.

My back is to him, so I take a moment before turning around. I brush my palms against the soft fabric of my dress, gripping it lightly. Slowly, I turn around. My breath hitches at the sight of him.

Jameson Brock.

Dark hair curling up lightly at the ends. Blue-green eyes and pouty lips accentuated by a full beard I'm dying to run my hands through. His tan skin is slightly worn and rough showing off the rugged character of the man who works outside, shirtless, bent over the hood of a car. He's not like the stuffed shirt boys I went to business school with—the ones with manicured fingers and smooth pale skin from never seeing the light of day.

No, Jameson is the epitome of blue collar. Sunshine and steel, salty from the sea with eyes that appear older than his twenty-seven years.

"I ... had to get something from my car." I awkwardly point to where my Benz is parked.

"You could have rang. It's your special night. One of the valet would have run it up to you." He's standing about ten feet away. The deep searching look in his eyes has me scrambling to think of something to say.

I take in his attire. He's wearing blue jeans and a flannel shirt paired with worker boots. It's his signature look, one father lets him adorn when he's spending the day in the garage.

"Why are you in civilian clothes? I thought Father said the staff had to wear uniforms today?" I internally punch myself for uttering the most pretentious lines in the world.

His eyes shift to the side slightly. He places his hands deep in his pockets, his shoulders rounded. "I requested the night off."

Jameson is The Manor's mechanic. He maintains all of Father's cars. All *twenty-five* of them. Yes, it's a bit excessive, but father is a collector of vintage cars. The carriage house is where we house our everyday vehicles. Next door is a hangar where father's collection lives.

"Oh, well, you deserve it." I bite my lip and look down at the shiny concrete floor. Clinging onto my dress, I try to think of something witty to say. Nothing comes to mind.

"Can I help you get whatever it is you need from your car?" he offers.

My head jolts up. "No, I just realized it's not in there." I start to move toward the back entrance where I came in from but am compelled to spin around and look at him once again. "I'm leaving tomorrow."

"I know," he says, nodding slightly.

God, I'm pathetic. Twenty-two years old, harboring a crush on a man who has never looked twice at me. At least, not in that way. I'm just the rich brat he works for. Well, not anymore. By tomorrow evening, I'll be thousands of miles away and don't plan to come back. Not for a very long time.

Jameson releases his hands from his pockets and runs his hands through his hair. "I heard there's a big announcement tonight."

"Yes, Father is telling everyone that tomorrow I'm off to—"

"Don't say it."

"Okay." I fidget for a moment shifting my toes from side to side. "I'll being going then."

"Stay," he says. A plea that makes my heart stop.

I look back toward the door and the walkway that would bring me back to my party. My farewell party filled with people I adore and some I have never met yet are very important to my family.

Still, the only person I want to be with is in this room.

And he wants me to stay.

With *him*.

A small smile tugs on my face, and my body beats again from head to toe. A current that's drawing me back toward the center of the room where Jameson is standing.

I raise my brow. "What did you have in mind?"

Those blue-green eyes crinkle, the lines of life appearing with the action. He radiates when he smiles and my soul is about to burst at the sight of it.

"Wait here," he says and then walks quickly toward his office. When he's gone, the room feels entirely too big and lonely. I stand and wait for an eternity until he appears through the doorway holding a box with a red satin ribbon in his hands.

Jameson walks toward me and stops just two feet away. I look up into his purposeful gaze and get lost in the sheer magnitude of his larger-than-life presence.

He holds out the box to me. "This is for you. A going away gift."

My eyes widen in surprise as I take the box from him. "I wasn't expecting something from you." I turn around to hide my blush and walk the gift to a nearby table.

My fingers are untying the ribbon as he says, "I didn't know if I should give it to you."

I halt my movements and spin around. "Why not?"

"I just ... Doesn't matter. Open it." He gestures with one hand while running his other down the strands of his beard.

I'm grateful my back is to him when I lift the lid on the box and see the most beautiful necklace of gears, like the kind you see inside a watch. There are seven in total, all made of white and yellow gold, interlocking to create the most intricate piece of jewelry I've ever seen. I lift the necklace from the box and try to tame my insides from not bursting thought my skin. My eyes burn with tears that I can't let fall.

He made this.

For *me*.

Jameson Brock created a piece of jewelry for me. If he only knew what this meant to me, he may not have made it in the first place.

"You hate it," he says from behind me.

I clutch the piece to my chest and close my eyes. "I love it."

"No, it's OK. I know it was stupid. You have diamonds and pearls. What would you want with a piece of junk like that?"

"Are you kidding me?" I turn on my heels so fast, I think I've startled him.

He steps forward, his eyes looking at me with curiosity as he tilts his head and says, "Why are you crying?"

Brushing my palm against my cheek to wipe the tears I didn't want him to see, I say, "It's beautiful. I will cherish it forever."

"Why would you do that?"

"Because now I have a piece of you to take with me." My words are a whisper. A whisper that is shouted into his soul causing his body to fall at ease and take a step toward me with open arms and then abruptly stop, as if he caught himself doing something wrong. I want him near me but know the boundaries of our relationship. The ones we should never cross. Still, I need him close. Just for a moment. "Will you put it on me?"

I unclasp the necklace I'm wearing and place it on the table.

"Jules, that's the necklace your father gave you for graduating prep school. Don't take off your emeralds. Not for me."

I hold up his necklace to him. "You made this for me, right?"

He nods his head. The blue-greens fixed on mine. "Only for you."

I smile brightly. "Then I want to wear it."

I turn around and lift my hair. Jameson steps closer, his chest flush against my back as he locks his arms around me and then weaves the necklace around my neck.

He fixes the clasp before tracing a finger along the edge of the chain against my neck and then lets that finger trail down my collarbone to my clavicle. My chest rises with the touch. Just the slightest brush of his finger sends a shock of pleasure through my body.

I drop my hair and turn to him, his hand still resting at the base of my neck. When we are face to face, he traces fingers along the gears of the necklace, looking proudly at his handy work, his vision on my skin.

"Why did you make this for me?" I ask, hoping my question doesn't cause him to drop his hand. I've been dying for Jameson to touch me since he walked into The Manor seven years ago. I was just a child then, but I'm a woman now. And if I'm leaving tomorrow, it's with the slightest hope that maybe—just maybe—he feels something, *anything* for me, too.

My eyes are trained on his, but he's only staring at the necklace as if he's too afraid to look at me and see what's written all over my face.

"One gear is lonely. It can't move on its own. It's just stagnant." He takes a moment and swallows, his Adam's apple thick in his neck. "It probably doesn't know how alone it is until it's locked with another gear. You can't move one without the other. It's like they're sole purpose in life is to help the other move forward." He looks up, and I swear the whole world stops.

For the look he is giving me is *that* look.

From the slightly glazed-over shine in his eyes, to the way his brow is creasing lightly and the intense dilation of his pupils, he's looking at me with a yearning and a want and a despair that I've been looking at him with for years.

"Jameson," I whisper and place a hand over his heart. It's racing, wildly beating out of his chest. I dip my fingers inside the top buttons of his shirt and feel the heated skin. His chest rises with the touch.

"Jules." My name sounds like prayer on his lips. He moves a step closer, taking away any distance between us. His head falls to my forehead and our eyes close on instinct.

"Seven. There are seven gears," I say.

"For each year you've been in my life."

My body shoots up and I kiss him.

Without thinking, without considering consequences. No boundaries, or fear of being rejected, I rise up on my toes and kiss Jameson Brock. My lips firm on his, I hold onto him as I press my mouth so deeply into his I fear I may never surface.

His lips are warm and soft. The edge of his beard tickling my face as I part my lips slightly and interlock them with his.

But that's all that's happening.

My heart drops at the thought that I'm kissing him, but he's not kissing me back.

I fall back to my heels and look down. His hands are now at his side, ridding themselves of touching me. I remove my hands from him and step back.

Feeling foolish, I look down at the floor, the tires of the cars, the lighting that illuminates the aisles. Looking anywhere but at Jameson and the look of pity he must have on his face.

"I'm sorry. I don't know what got into me," I say, wiping the skin around my lips. So much for a grand farewell. Now, when I leave tomorrow, I'll know that I am leaving nothing behind.

"You don't understand," he says, taking a step toward me, but I retreat.

I hold a hand up. "This is embarrassing enough. You don't have to explain anything."

"No, Jules, I have *everything* to explain," he shouts, causing me to jump a little. His eyes are red-rimmed, and he's running his hands through his hair, pulling at the ends. "You're leaving tomorrow. And not just for a vacation or to school, you're leaving for a future. One that will be filled with business acquisitions and meetings, with fancy parties and men who will wine and dine you. You'll be living the life of a Bradford. The life you deserve."

"I don't understand. What does that have to do with us? Would you prefer I wasn't who I am?"

"No." He moves closer yet still far enough away. "No, I love who you are." Jameson reaches his hands out in explanation. "Jules, when I walked in here seven years ago, you were a fifteen-year-old kid who had more life in her than anyone I ever met. You would come in here after school and sit on my bench and tell me about your day while I worked. I never told you that I waited until three thirty just to see the smile on your face. And for as rich as you are, I couldn't believe how funny and smart and generous you are. I watched you grow up into this beautiful woman. When you went off to Wharton, I missed our talks. But when you came home, it was like we picked up right where we left off. I never understood why you weren't traveling off to Ibiza or St. Bart's with your friends. You always hung around here. And I was happy. Happy because I got to see you. And now you're leaving. No more coming back for winter break or staying home for the summer. You're moving on and you should be. You deserve everything you've worked for. Everything your family has given you. And everything a man worthy of having you can give you.

"That's why you can't kiss me," he continues. "And I sure as hell can't kiss you back. I'll never be a man worthy enough. It's why I almost didn't give you that ridiculous necklace. Looking at it now makes me feel like such a fool. What the hell can a guy like me give a girl like you?"

"Everything," I say, practically running toward him. "Jameson, I stayed for you. I'd rather sit here and talk to you than sit on a beach being waited on hand and foot while I listen to my friends complain about how dull their lives are. Being with you is—" I raise a hand and grab his face, pulling his gaze into mine. With those blue-green eyes looking into mine, I tell him with everything I have, "It's the only place I've ever wanted to be."

His cheek falls into my palm. The soft bristles of his face rubbing against my skin. He closes his eyes and savors the feel of my thumb tracing slight circles on his skin. I just want him to open those eyes and tell me what he's feeling. No, I don't want him to speak, I want him to kiss me. Kiss me with everything in his being and claim me as his own because that's exactly what I am.

I raise my other hand and run my fingers through his hair. He lets out a slight moan, which causes him to open his eyes.

The look he's giving me is carnal, hot with want and need.

And just when I think he's about to lean forward and kiss me, he speaks. "You should leave."

This time, it's not just my heart that falls to the ground but every single fiber of my being.

Lowering my hand, I sink backward. How many times does a man need to reject a woman before she finally gets the hint?

Apparently, for me, it's twice in one night.

I head out the back door and run up the winding path toward the veranda. The sun has lowered; the moonlight is the only thing illuminating the stairs as I head back up to my party.

"There she is!" Father beams, a glass of champagne in his hand. His arm outstretched, ushering me over to him.

The crowd parts as I make my way to the front of the room where Father is standing next to Mother. I smooth out my dress and take a step beside them, taming the hurried breath in my lungs. Mother smoothens the side of my hair, putting every last piece in its perfect place.

A waiter hands me a glass of champagne as Father raises his

again and speaks to our guests. "We'd like to thank everyone for coming to Jules' sendoff. Third generation Wharton Grad, not to mention Summa Cum Laude just like her old man," Father jokes and our guests clap. "Jules has always been an exemplary child. Captain of the swim and lacrosse teams in academy and spent her free time working at the Bradford Corporations. During her time at Wharton, she studied under the tutelage of Waxman and Bain who have been so impressed with her abilities that they have offered her a position."

Aunt Ina lets out a small gasp, quite possibly because she's excited about the possibility of me being close to home. What she doesn't know is that I turned that job down. I thought being four hours away from home, in Pennsylvania, would give me the space I needed from my family. What I hadn't planned on was Father's comrades to be everywhere. They infiltrated my internship and even my extracurriculars. Their sons and daughters were at my school inviting me to every function their families were hosting meaning mine were often there as well. That's why I turned down the position for something further away. Much further.

"But our Jules had other plans," Father continues. He's still talking when the French doors leading to the veranda open and with it a man that takes my breath away.

Father is speaking but I don't hear a word he says. All I can focus on is the sight of Jameson in the back of the room in his plaid shirt and jeans, looking wildly out of place amongst the summer suits and crisp khakis of our party guests. His stature towering over every male in the room with dark hair glistening in the lighting of the room and those eyes as clear as the sky on a cloudless day as they look straight at me.

I don't know why he's here. He's never been in our home unless summoned, and he certainly would never come to a party dressed as he is. Yet, he's here. And with purpose.

Father doesn't seem to notice, or perhaps he doesn't care that Jameson has entered because he is uttering the words, "and that's why tomorrow Jules is leaving for Paris to work with the prestigious Debois International."

Our guests clap, many awkwardly, as they're holding glasses.

Father raises his glass and cheers to the crowd who in turn drink their champagne. There are cordial cheers and many people start talking at once. Father kisses the side of my head, and Mother squeezes my hand.

All I can do is look out at Jameson.

Those eyes that were looking at me with purpose are now painted with defeat. He opens his mouth and takes three collective breaths. He looks around the room, at the chandelier, the servers, the guests, the Picasso on the wall, the grand piano in the corner. He looks at my father and mother by my side and then at the young man that is standing beside my mother.

"Jules," Mother says, "I want you to meet Kip Freghkerden. He is in Paris often on business and has offered to be an escort for you while you're in town."

I don't even look to Kip because my eyes are trained on Jameson as he is backing out of the room and, with the blink of an eye, has dipped out the French doors onto the veranda.

My feet move forward.

"Jules, where are you going?" Mother asks, seeming concerned.

"I'll be right back," I say over my shoulder and head through the crowd. This time, I don't stop for congratulations or cards. I head straight for the back doors.

Rushing up to the balcony, I look toward the carriage house but the lights are off. The breeze from the ocean pushes the hair off my face as I look out onto the beach.

And there he is, walking down the stairwell toward the sand.

I have no choice but to follow.

Because tonight is my last night, and if there's one thing I learned as a Bradford, it's to never take no for an answer.

THE BEACH

"**W**HY DID YOU REQUEST THE NIGHT OFF?" I shout as soon as my heels hit the sand.

Jameson turns around, the look of surprise to see me standing on the sandy beach, wind whipping through my hair, chasing him out into the dark of night.

He blinks at me, registering my question. "What did you say?"

I start to walk to him but my heels dig in the sand. I take them off and throw them toward the steps. The chiffon of my dress dragging in the sand. "I asked why you took the night off."

"You don't want to know the answer to that question."

"Yes, I do. I'm leaving tomorrow and the one thing I want to know before I go is why you took the night off only to stick around inside the carriage house? You say you're my friend. You said my smile is the highlight of your day. If that's true, then I need to know why. Why would you choose to stay away from me on my last day here?"

"Because I couldn't stand to see you leave." His voice rises over the ocean waves. "I didn't plan on being here, but for some reason I couldn't stay away. I just thought I could sit in the garage and be close to you. Just close enough without seeing you. I never expected you to come in."

"But I did."

"Yes, Jules, God damn it you did. What do you want from me?"

"I want you to tell me why you took the night off. Why you couldn't be here. And why, even though you tried to stay away, you still walked into that room and looked me straight in the eyes as if I were the only thing in it."

"Because you are," he yells, and the words hit me like an arrow in the chest. "God damn it. Is that what you want to hear? If so, then yes, yes, Jules. Yes, I took the night off because I'm in love with you. I have been for longer than is right. I have been gnawing away from the inside out wanting someone I can never have. For the last four years, the only thing that kept me sane was coming out here and staring at the moon, knowing that you were on the other side of it. I resigned myself to knowing that that is how I will live for the rest of my life. I wanted to stay away tonight, but I couldn't because I need to be near you. And you have no idea what it took from me not to kiss you back. I have been dreaming about that kiss for years and there it was, right in front of me and I had to push you away." He takes three large steps forward—his tall, strong body standing over me, commanding, powerful and full of raw, unadulterated male with carnal lust in his eyes and a little bit of anger. "I couldn't kiss you before, but fuck it if I'm not going to kiss you now."

His mouth crashes into mine. Strong, sensual lips part and sweep into me. Our tongues collide, and I fall so hard into his kiss, my head begins to spin.

This is the kiss of a man taking what he wants.

A man taking what he's wanted for years.

Jameson wraps his arms around my waist and pulls me in tight against his body. My hands find his beard and I pull gently. He lets out a low growl. The kiss becomes fierce. His hands are all over my body, circling my waist, running up and down my sides and trailing up my arms and neck, taking claim of me, holding me like he never wants to let go.

I unbutton his shirt and lay my hands against the hard plains of his chest. He's so strong and thick. My fingers rub over his nipples and the moan he growls into my mouth lets me know he likes it.

The ocean breeze whips through my hair, my dress cascading in the wind. I should move this party of two indoors but I can't seem to do anything but kiss him. And feel him. And undress him.

Pushing away the fabric from his shoulders, I lean down and kiss his neck and chest, tasting every bit of Jameson Brock. When my tongue darts out just below his ear, he shivers, and it's not from the cold.

"Jules," he breathes, as I continue to run my tongue along the skin, my fingers still deftly playing with his pecs. "Baby, look at me."

Looking up, I take in his perfect face silhouetted in the moonlight.

He raises his arms and hugs my face in his hands, forcing me to look him in the eye and take in the severity of what he's about to say.

"I am going to make love to you tonight," he says, "but not here. Not where anyone can see us."

"Yes, here," I say, and he frowns, not understanding. "I want you to make love to me under the moon so every night when I look up, I can think of you and remember this night. Remember the way you feel and taste. I can stare at the stars and know that you're on the other side, looking at the same sky. If there's one place I want to be, it's right here, under the moon, with you."

I look up to the sky and take in the moon. The beautiful full crescent moon on a summer night in Long Island. Amid the darkness of the shore, it is the only light, the only witness to this moment between a man and woman coming together. Their souls crashing along the Eastern Seaboard.

Jameson leans forward and caresses my neck with soft kisses that make my toes curl. I lean my head back and allow him to devour me with his mouth; his beard is like a course cushion.

His hand finds the zipper of my dress. The chiffon falls to the ground. Jameson releases me for a moment to take the dress and smooth it against the sand like a blanket. When he's done, he takes my hand and lowers me onto the aubergine. My back is cool against the dress but I'm instantly heated when two-hundred pounds of male lowers on top of me and claims me again with his fiery kisses. Our bodies rock together, his hard erection rubbing fiercely against my core.

Reaching down, I stroke him through his pants.

"Jules," he groans into my mouth, his body pressing firmer into me. "I dream of this. At night, when I look at the moon, I imagine, what it would be like to have you, with me, on my side. And here you are."

He's throbbing, hard as the steel rods that line the wall of the carriage house. I wrap my leg around him and pull him further into me. "I'm here. I've always been here."

He removes my bra; the night chill hardens my nipples until his mouth leans down and warms them. Swirling, sucking, pulling every intense amount of erotic pleasure from my skin. I push his pants down, needing to feel him, all of him. Using my toes, I push the denim down his legs, not wanting him to release himself from me to do it himself. I grab his incredibly firm ass and hiss at the feel of it and round my hands around his hips and take his cock in my hands.

"Sweet Jesus," he mutters as my fingers pump along the shaft, my thumb tracing the throbbing head. "This won't last long if you keep doing that. And I have plans for you. For us." He rubs my clit and my body arches back at the touch.

"Fuck me, Jameson. Please."

"You were always impatient. Ever since you were a kid," he says as he removes my panties and throws them with his pile of clothes.

"I'm not a kid anymore," I say, splayed out on the sand, ready to taken by the most incredible man.

"Don't I know it," he growls. His head dips down to my body and takes a nipple. His mouth greedy as he sucks hard and bites the end. I scream out in pleasure, which only makes him do it again to the other one. He rubs a thumb against my clit and the feeling of pleasure and pain is so intense, I may come all over the couture beneath me.

Jameson moves his hips against me. Rubbing, pumping, as if he's fucking yet he's not even inside me. The heavy weight of his cock against me, his hand rubbing my clit to intense levels of pleasure combined with his teeth sinking into nipples is lighting me on fire. My hips buck off the ground. My core clenches. And my body builds to a climax so high that I scream. Scream so loud the waves stop to listen.

I come. And I come hard. My release so powerful I think I've died and gone to heaven.

Jameson continues to move, continues to touch and taste and keeps the orgasm going. Running my fingers through his hair, I yank hard and try to control the build of the second wave.

Seven years of want. Seven years of touching myself in my room. Seven years of lusting after a man only to have him do this to me is more than my mind can comprehend. My body, on the other hand, is releasing seven years of lust.

I push on his shoulders and force Jameson up. On my knees, I take his mouth in mine and climb onto his lap kissing him hard and deep. His arms wrap around me and pull me in. We kiss forever, or at least it seems that long. We can't let go. Can't stop. Won't stop. His hands caress my body. There is nowhere he is not touching. My legs, my hips, my spine, my breasts.

I push him back onto the sand and run my tongue up and down the shaft.

"Condom," he hisses as he reaches back to find his pants, all while I'm lapping and sucking, trying to get as much of him into my mouth as possible.

He tears open the condom, and I rise to let him sheath himself in it. When he's fully coated, I climb back onto him and lower myself down onto his cock.

I moan.

He moans.

We both moan on impact.

He's so heavy and thick, too much to comprehend inside of me. I put my hands on his chest and begin to rock against him. My insides ignite, a spot deep inside me coming to life with each grind of my hips. I do it over and over again bringing myself intense pleasure with the action.

I do it faster.

I ride him like I was born to fuck him.

Jameson grabs my hips and starts pumping up into me. I sit up and lean my hands on his thighs and allow him to take over. His coarse hands clenching onto my skin, pulling me into him as he pulses pleasure through my veins. My breasts are out in the open wind. The feeling exhilarating. I should be cold but my body is on fire. On fire because our bodies are rocking together, and when I look down, the carnal gaze he's giving me, watching me come undone above him, because of him, for him, is all I need to start coming again.

"Jameson," I exhale.

He rises up to a seated position. His hands snake around my back and head. He kisses me as our bodies continue to grind against one another. I'm slick with orgasm. My body sliding up and down.

He places his forehead against mine and looks me in the eye. His head is creased, his mouth is open and his face is filled with pleasure so fierce he looks like he's in pain. He's gripping tighter, pumping harder, his cock feels like it's about to burst.

"Jules," he cries as he comes, hard, inside of me. I continue my stride and pull every bit of pleasure from him.

And when he's done, he kisses me again. Rolling me over, our bodies intertwine as we kiss.

Kiss in the sand.

Kiss by the sea.

Kiss under the moonlight.

THE GOODBYE

I wake to the scruffiness of Jameson's beard kissing my back, tickling my skin, forcing me to roll over and face him.

"You have freckles on your back," he says. He's just as beautiful first thing in the morning as I've imagined.

"How many," I ask, teasingly.

"Fourteen."

I lean back in surprise. "You counted?"

His blue-green eyes fall a bit. "You're leaving for Paris today. I'm trying to take in every piece of you before you disappear from my life."

My head falls to the pillow. I forgot about Paris. About my adventure and starting my new life away from Father and The Manor. About the dream job I took in the most romantic city in the world. Though, that romance will always pale in comparison to last night.

After we made love on the beach, we dressed and ran back to The Manor. I didn't want to, but Jameson was right—my family would be looking for me in worry. I tidied myself up and went back to my party telling Father I was tired and wanted to prepare for my trip the next day. It took me longer to leave than I wanted but when I made it back to my room, Jameson was there. I locked the door and escorted him into the shower where we laughed and talked and washed the sand off of each other in places people shouldn't have sand.

We spent the evening in my bed where we devoured each other again. I'm glad my parents sleep in another wing of the house otherwise the slaps Jameson gave on my ass would have been heard. And I'm not ashamed to say I wouldn't have stopped no matter who knocked on the door.

There were also sweet times. Like when he held me and told me all the times over the years I made his heart stop. And I told him mine.

"I'll be back." I lean on my elbow, facing him. "I can come back for Christmas. I wasn't planning on it but I can make the flight. Paris to New York is easy. Non-stop, too."

Jameson gives me a half smile. "You're not supposed to come back. That was the plan. I can't keep you from experiencing life anymore. You deserve better."

I sit up, holding the sheet to my body. "Better than you?"

"Way better than me. I do OK, your father pays me well but I can't give you this." He motions to my room which is larger than some Manhattan apartments. "I can't give you the home you dream of or the lifestyle you're used to. I can't give you what you want."

He runs his hands through his beard and down his neck. I pull his chin toward me, forcing him to look at me.

"What if I'm looking at everything I've ever wanted?"

Jameson sits up, his gorgeously sculpted torso on display. "Why did you wait until last night to tell me how you feel?"

His question causes me to stop gawking at his physique. With a tilt of my head I ask, "What do you mean?"

"You've been an adult for a while now. All those days we spent talking; you could have let me know how you felt. Instead, you waited until the last moment."

I know what he is implying. "If you think this was a goodbye fuck then you're wrong. I never said anything because I was too afraid of being rejected. Scared you'd laugh and tell me I was a spoiled little girl who knew nothing about real life."

I rise from the bed, taking the sheet with me. Jameson is left naked on the white Egyptian cotton.

Jameson opens his mouth to speak, but I continue, "I knew in high school I was too young for you. I knew in college Father would have fired you on the spot. But I'm a woman now, Jameson. A woman madly in love with you. I've been with other men. I've tried to fight this feeling, but I can't. I keep coming back to you. Always you."

A lopsided smile rises on Jameson's face. "You love me?"

"Yes, you idiot."

Jameson falls back on the bed, his hands propped behind his head on the pillow as he looks up at the ceiling with the goofiest grin I've ever seen.

I climb onto the bed and straddle Jameson, my long blonde hair falling around his face.

"Come to Paris with me," I say and kiss him. I can already feel him hardening beneath me.

"I can't hold you back." He raises his hands and undoes the sheet around me so my breasts are flush against his chest.

"You wouldn't be holding me back. You'd be pushing me forward. I can't start my next adventure always wondering about the one I left behind. I need you by my side." I kiss his neck and his erection rises to full mast. It's taking everything in me not to start riding him bare.

"What would I do in Paris?" he asks with labored breaths.

I lean down and stroke him. "Do you really need to ask that question?" I can't help my laugh.

Jameson grabs my head and pulls my face to his. The fun and games are over for in his eyes is concern. Way too much concern for a man who is being stroked by a naked woman.

I curve my brows at him in worry.

"You know what I mean, Jules. There's a reason why I could never share my feeling with you in the past. We're from different worlds. What could I possibly do in Paris that would benefit us in any way?"

I stare back at his blue-greens and the worry he has for being able to provide for me. I could tell him that I'm wealthy enough to support us both but I won't. Jameson is a proud man.

"You do know they have cars in Paris," I say, causing Jameson to roll his eyes. I pull his attention back to me. "What I mean is you can do anything you want, anywhere you want. I've seen you work on European cars. There's so much you can do and be a success."

I lean down and kiss him, and thank the heavens, he is kissing me back. "I need you, Jameson. I need you to take care of me. For the rest of my life."

Jameson leans back, seemingly stunned by my words. He pushes my hair back around my ear. His eyes crinkle. This time, with so much love and hope, I think I'm imagining it.

"Now, that's something I can do," he says.

"So you're coming with me?" I ask, hopefully.

"I'll go anywhere as long as I'm on your side of the moon."

About Jeannine Colette

Jeannine Colette is the author of the Abandon Collection, a series of standalone novels featuring dynamic heroines who have to abandon their reality in order to discover themselves . . . and love along the way.

A graduate of Wagner College and the New York Film Academy, Jeannine went on to become a Segment Producer for television shows on CBS and NBC. She left the television industry to focus on her children and pursue a full-time writing career. She lives in New York with her husband, the three tiny people she adores more than life itself, and a rescue pup named Wrigley.

Website: www.JeannineColette.com

Facebook: www.facebook.com/JeannineColetteBooks

Thou Shalt Not Beard

by Leslie McAdam

I took one look at him and let out a piercing shriek that would surely cause the Channel Island feral pigs to stampede, even though they lived oh, *twenty miles across the freaking Pacific Ocean from us.*

After being away for more than two weeks, I'd just stepped foot into our beach house south of Santa Barbara laden with suitcases and bags of presents, excited and happy to return to Ryan but also feeling nostalgic about my trip.

I'd been traveling with Marie, my best friend, on an extended quasi-bachelorette party to New York. We saw Times Square, three Broadway shows, MOMA, the Guggenheim, and all the flagship stores. At night, we hit the town or stayed in, ordered room service, and talked or watched movies until we fell asleep. In sum, best girl trip ever. Since this trip was the last time we'd be together with both of us single, Ryan had splurged, buying Marie and me first class plane tickets and a suite at the Plaza hotel, our home base for some final shopping before the wedding.

Our wedding. The wedding we weren't going to have in five days because I couldn't stand the sight of him.

I took a deep breath and prayed for serenity. Gathering myself, I asked in a slightly calmer voice, *"What on Earth did you do to yourself?"*

By "slightly calmer," I mean my decibel level would make seagulls take flight, but it wouldn't scare the feral pigs. That deep breath hadn't really done anything to help me find my inner Dalai Lama.

I glared at him.

My surfer boy, shirtless as usual, with ladder-like abs and golden curls I loved to touch, had been lounging on a couch watching television. He'd heard me come in, so he stood up, loping over with a broad grin and arms wide. "Amelia," he said in his raspy voice, ready to give me a welcome-home hug.

His blue plaid board shorts hung down below the divots in his hips, and as usual, I got distracted by the happy trail headed down his lean torso.

But once I'd caught sight of his face, I didn't see the abs or curls. I just saw red, like stop sign red. Fighting mad red. Bullfighter red. Like *no, absolutely not, this is not happening* red.

My beloved fiancé had grown a fucking beard right before our wedding.

Goddamn him. If I didn't love him so much, I'd hate him. As it was, I was so pissed I couldn't form sentences, and instead, resorted to shrieking like that haunted shack in Harry Potter.

His response?

A smile. One that cracked his face wide open and revealed his even, white teeth and glorious full lips. But that smile was surrounded by patchy blond hair that wasn't there two weeks ago.

Stubble, I could handle and actively liked.

But this?

No.

I stared at him, violet eyes wide, finger pointing at the hair on his chin, not sure what to do next.

Ryan chuckled and rubbed his beard like all hairy men do, whether their beard was just-grown-in or antediluvian. Thoughtful stroking must be part of Beard Ownership 101. That and being utterly fascinated with how it grows in.

But because his blond hair was so light, Ryan's monstrosity grew in unevenly, like it had been mowed by a particularly bored goat who couldn't be bothered to actually eat all the grass available. I'd heard Joel McHale make fun of Spencer's "creepy flesh-colored beard" on *The Hills*. Pretty much Ryan's fate.

It was scruffy.

This. Was. Not. Okay.

Our wedding did not allow scruffy. Our wedding was going to be elegant. I hadn't hired a wedding planner because I loved party planning. I liked pretty things. Our wedding had table settings that I had spent at least three solid weeks designing. I was just waiting for the shipments of imported napkins and vases any day now. I'd even choreographed our wedding so that it took place on the beach at sunset, during the magic hour when the wind was down and the waves were smooth. Our wedding was going to be perfect.

No beards allowed!

"I take it you're not a fan of the facial growth," he said, again doing the beard-stroke thing. Apparently me standing mute, pointing, and gawking gave him the hint.

I shook my dark hair. "No. I'm not. It doesn't . . . how could you . . . Ryan! It's our wedding! Why did you do this?"

"I always wanted to grow a beard."

"Are you going to shave it off?"

"Nope." He grinned annoyingly. "I like it." He leaned in for a kiss, unrepentant, but I took a step back, not ready.

"But couldn't you wait to do it until after we take pictures that we are going to look at for the rest of our lives?"

He came up in front of me and wrapped his arms around my waist, pulling me close to him. Ordinarily, I loved this, loved the way he smelled, and loved the feel of his muscles.

But right now all I felt was revulsion. I mean, he looked ridiculous.

How could I even give him a kiss? I'd need a machete to find his lips.

He'd changed something, and it was not acceptable. There was no possible way the whole entire universe, whether in our solar system, or in some distant galaxy, that this was acceptable.

"Does it really look that bad?"

I nodded.

Instead of agreeing that yes, Amelia, he was going to march his tight ass down to the bathroom and shave, he stretched up his arms, popping his goddamn abs (those abs), looked at me, and said, "Let's see if you change your opinion when you feel this beard between your legs."

A shudder rippled through my body involuntarily. Damn body. *Traitor.*

I started to say something that sounded like, "Guh," when he reached down, took my hand, and said, "I missed you." And he leaned down and kissed me, my first ever beard-kiss.

As he met my lips, the hair on his face scraped my pale skin. But because this beard-kiss came from Ryan, I soon forgot about the scratchiness and lost myself in his taste and his feel and his tongue, the love I felt for him and the love I knew he felt for me.

In short, *swoon.*

When we broke apart, under that facial hair I caught a glimpse of the face that I loved more than anything on this Earth. A face that had healed me. One that I loved to wake up to and was my favorite thing to see before I fell asleep. One that never failed to give me a visceral reaction of how handsome he was.

Before I could get another word in, he reached under my knees and lifted me up, carrying me like a bride. But instead of going to our bedroom, he headed directly to the couch he'd just got up from, and deposited me gently, kneeling right next to me. Leaning over me, radiant, muscly, shirtless, he whispered, "Give the beard a chance."

I went to shake my head no, but I mean, come on. It was *Ryan*.

That beardy eyesore didn't hide his striking green eyes.

"Give the beard a chance," he'd said. But I didn't stand a chance.

Cocking his head to the side, he started to kiss down my neck, and yes, it scratched, but more, it was warm lips and soft tongue, and in the time it took to make the jump to hyperspeed, I was willing to see what it felt like when cunnilingus became beard-a-lingus, and I told him so.

He grinned, and I got fascinated by the way the facial hair moved on his cheeks and chin, in a scientific way only, of course. Now his face moved differently, the way long grass moves on a hill in the wind.

But then I remembered I didn't like a beard on him.

He didn't let me get worked up again about his hairy abnormality on his otherwise perfect self, since he went straight to getting *me* worked up. He pulled, and off went my sandals. With flicks of his long, clever fingers, my khaki shorts came off my long legs. Peach peasant blouse off. Bra off, letting the ample girls loose. And he hooked his thumbs in the elastic of my pale peach cheeky panties and pulled them down my curvy hips.

Apparently I could go from zero to naked in six seconds these days on Ryan's couch.

He held my feet firmly, spread them apart, and started licking and sucking his way up my legs while I squirmed on the couch.

God, I'd missed him while I'd been gone. I missed the way he took care of me, always. My needs first.

Except this beard thing.

Was this the first sign that once we got married things were going to be different?

I went to open my mouth to have a discussion with him, but his cheeks brushed against my inner thigh—yes, I could feel that bristly fur—and then his long, delicious tongue found my pussy and went to work. With two fingers, he spread me open and gently rolled his tongue around my clit, then widened it and pressed along the side.

Oh God.

Beard? What beard?

I only felt tongue on my sex. No beard. No scratchy. No different.

The part of my brain that worried about things and tried to make everything just so turned off, and instead my thoughts went into this vacant room filled with light and, *fuck, give me more now, please.*

"I missed you. I missed your arms. I missed your hair. I missed your curves. I missed the fucking sexy smell of your pussy," he muttered as he ran his nose up and down the entire length of me. He put a finger inside me, curled up, and started pressing on the sensitive part—the rougher part with all the nerve endings—as he continued to go down, giving all of his attention to the bundle of nerves that he knew only he could affect.

Brain wiped. Not pissed about beard any more. Only processing tingling between my legs and blood rushing to my toes—heating them up—my hands scratching at the couch to the side of my hips, my body wiggling as he held me still by one hand on my hipbone.

He looked up, his mouth on me still, finger curled inside, and smiled with his verdant eyes.

Rubbing an extra good place with his fingers, because it had been two weeks since I'd seen him, I launched into orgasm, my brain lost and found again, my body shaking involuntarily. All the tension and nonsense in my brain vaporized and I entered a Zen-like state of nothingness. He kept going through my pulsing, the waves of the climax hitting again and again, and it was all I could do to not scream out in pleasure. All I could do to just let my body surrender to what it naturally did.

I felt better.

After I came to, I looked at him. "My God, Ryan, the things you get me to do."

He smiled. While my legs were jelly and my brain, mush, he'd pushed his board shorts down to his knees and pushed himself over me, hovering. Positioning his cock—his hard, veiny, lovely cock—right at my entrance, he waited, his arms on either side of my head, gazing down at me.

I could smell myself on him and see the lust in his eyes. "What is it?"

"I missed you so goddamn much, Amelia. I don't like going two weeks without you."

"I missed you too." I wrapped my arms around his ass and pressed him into me, and with a slow movement, he edged in inch by inch, until he fit all the way.

Finally.

"This is where you belong," I murmured.

"Yeah." He kissed me, and again, it was a beardy-kiss and smelled like me, but as he had started to move, started to thrust into me—gently, methodically, with a little tick up—I'd lost the ability to give a fuck about beards or anything else. I just wanted him to fuck me, and I wanted it now. I wanted the connection. I wanted to feel whole, the way I always felt whole with him.

As I wrapped my legs around him, he increased the pace and changed the angle. He grabbed a couch pillow and shoved it under my ass so that my back was arched, my head down, and my pelvis concave. As he fucked me, a blond curl dropped over his forehead and his eyes locked on mine.

Thrust, thrust, thrust.

I found myself tightening around him, and he reached down and rubbed my clit to finish. I came again, gasping, moaning, eyes on him. He watched me, satisfied, and it was beautiful in the way that anything pure is beautiful, anything sincere, anything loving.

When I settled down, he thrust five more times. With the sexiest groan, he threw his head back and came. He collapsed down onto me, and I grabbed him low on his waist, holding him close, never letting him go.

After a moment, snuggling his nose into the curve of my neck, he said, "Welcome home."

And I was home. Breathing against his warm body in the afternoon sunlight, with the waves breaking outside, I was home. I nodded into him and held him tighter.

That night, curled onto his bare chest in our big bed clad with white linens, listening to the sound of the ocean, I played with his curly locks, while he kept an arm around me. He'd just taken a shower after surfing, and he smelled clean, but still like the salty ocean.

Trying to deal with what he'd done, I tentatively ran my fingers through his attempt at a beard. My first lesson in Beard Ownership 101: stroking.

It felt funny. I was used to his smooth, tanned skin, with just a little stubble in the mornings. I'd memorized his freckles and the curves of his face.

Now they were obscured, and I didn't know what I thought about it anymore. I still didn't think I liked it. I pressed my nose against his nipple. He scooted against the pillows and tucked me in against him, kissing the top of my head.

Tired, jetlagged, I fell asleep on his broad chest as he combed my dark hair with his fingers.

When I woke up the next morning, my Sun God was on his back, arm thrown back, making a quiet, whiffling snore. In the morning sunlight, I got a good look at his beard.

Yep. Beard. Check. Still there. On his pretty face.

I still didn't like it. I wanted his face to go back to the way it was. Glancing over at the bathroom, I was tempted to creep in, get his kit, and shave it myself. Just lather my boy up with shaving cream and start while he was sleeping, so he'd have to finish or look ridiculous.

But that wasn't right.

If I changed my hair, I wouldn't want him cutting it while I was asleep.

Harrumph.

I looked over him out the window to the Pacific Ocean and watched the blue-green water shine in the morning, still calm. Guess the time difference made me get up extra early.

I padded downstairs, made a cup of coffee—sacrilege since Ryan made the best coffee—and settled on an arm chair looking out at the beach. A group of surfers gathered nearby, sitting on their boards. Ryan had left a stack of mail for me to look at, and I opened cards congratulating us on our nuptials.

Then I realized that I hadn't seen the shipments of the vases and napkins for our table settings.

Climbing out of my comfy chair cocoon, I went to the garage, with coffee cup in hand. No boxes. I started walking through all the rooms of the house, looking to see where he might have put them.

Nothing. Nowhere. Didn't see them.

I went to my computer, logged on, and found the confirmation email with the tracking number. But when I clicked on the link, I found out that my beautiful linens and decorations were back ordered.

Delayed.

For three weeks.

No.

NO.

They wouldn't come in time for our wedding.

I burst into tears. Ugly, heaving, wet, sobbing tears, way before six in the morning.

My wedding was ruined. Not only did my fiancé grow a wonky beard, but also the only thing I cared about—table settings—were not going to come.

Massive guilt washed over me for feeling this way. Here I was in a beach house, with the man of my dreams, crying because I didn't get imported vases and napkins. Seriously first world problems.

And the shame of how badly I was acting made me feel even worse.

As I sobbed, I became aware of a presence watching me.

Ryan leaned in the doorway wearing black boxer briefs, holding two cups of coffee. He padded over, barefoot, set a cup down next to me, and crouched down next to my chair, concerned.

"Hey," he said gently. "What's going on?"

Wiping the snot away, I didn't even want to look at him because I was being ridiculous and he had that stupid beard.

"Nothing."

"Babe. You don't cry like that for nothing. What is it?"

Holding my hands over my face, I muttered into my palms, "It looks like we're not going to get the table settings in. Our wedding is ruined."

Silence.

When I moved my hands and looked up, his facial expression registered utter amusement—eyebrow raised, eyes disbelieving, and that damn beard obscuring a twitch in his mouth.

"The table settings? Our wedding is going to be ruined because we don't have table settings?"

I nodded and sniffled.

"I know you love them, but is this really about table settings, Movie Star?"

I nodded and then thought better of it, so I shook my head. My voice wasn't louder than a whisper. "My last marriage was an utter failure. I want to get it right this time."

He set his hands on my knees. "No matter what the tables look like, no matter what you or I wear, no matter who attends, no matter what, it's going to be alright because I'm marrying you."

I wanted to believe him, but he was wrong.

Women like weddings. We *do* weddings. We want them to be pretty and romantic. I wanted it to be pretty and romantic. It's a special day. And if we have our heart set on something, then goddammit we have our heart set on something, and we'd better get it. That's it.

It's not being a bridezilla. It's about making the day you dreamed about *the day you dreamed about.*

Ryan called me Movie Star because I looked like Elizabeth Taylor. But decorating was my release from being an attorney. I loved to come home and thumb through glossy magazines. My hobby was to arrange things just so. It soothed me to arrange flowers, find the right china, and use my grandmother's tablecloths for a lunch with friends.

I started to shake my head, to argue with him, but he kept talking. "We'll make something fun for the tables. We can go gather seashells and get candles."

"The shells around here are small and gray and dirty and ugly."

"They'll mean more than anything you can buy."

"But they're not pretty!" I looked at the beard on his face again and burst into tears. I just wanted to crawl back into bed.

He ran his finger down my nose. "What is this, Amelia? Does it really look that bad? Or is it something else?"

"Nothing is going right. Everything is ruined. I wish you'd shave."

He tilted his head to the side. "It's just hair, babe. No big deal."

I still didn't like it.

Later that evening, I called Marie and told her about The Wedding Crises.

Instead of agreeing that yes, I was absolutely right to be upset, she laughed. "Dude, beards are hot. I wish Will would grow one. I don't know what your problem is." Marie, a therapist, lived about an hour away on a ranch with a cowboy, and I could hear him whistling to call his dog in the background.

"Ryan changed. He changed without telling me. Secretly. While we were gone." My voice sounded like a whine.

"It's no big deal, Amelia."

"But it is."

"You're seriously telling me that your wedding is threatened by a beard?"

I kicked at the ground. "Well, if you put it that way, it sounds stupid."

She adopted her professional tone of voice. "You're not stupid. You're getting married and scared, so you're looking for a reason to freak out."

"I am?" I stared at my feet on the floor.

"You are."

"I don't think so. I think it's just that I don't like beards."

She sighed. "Hipster hater."

That got a little laugh out of me—the mirthless kind of laugh.

"And I want my goddamn table settings."

"I'll be down tomorrow. Hang in there until then."

The rest of the day, I moped around. I researched online. I avoided Ryan.

By the end of the day, I headed for the cabinet with the tequila. I poured a shot, downed it without lime or salt, and burst into tears.

Ryan came up behind me and wrapped his arms around my waist. "What on Earth is going on? You never cry like this."

"I don't know," I sobbed.

"Is this really about the beard?"

I nodded. "You changed it without asking me."

"I don't think this is about the beard. I think you're scared of getting married, and I think you're scared of change."

I turned to him, my jaw dropping.

"You're scared of commitment," he continued.

My stomach sank into my shoes. No. That wasn't it. I loved Ryan. I wanted him more than anything. I wasn't scared. This was the right decision. Why would he think that? "I'm not."

He tilted his head and looked at me. "Our relationship is gonna change, Movie Star. It's not always going to be like this. Right now it's all new and exciting. Like anything brand new, you want to keep it new forever. But it's not always gonna be like that. We *have* to grow up, and I want to do it together. I want to do it with you. I want to go through life with you, my beautiful, smart, kind-hearted Amelia."

I stared at him. And I thought.

I did want everything to be like it was, with me crossing off rules and him making me experience new things. But at some point, we crossed everything off the list. We'd been back to places together, instead of experiencing them together for the first time. Things were becoming routine.

I liked the routine. I didn't want the scary changes and rule breaking again. Too risky. What if I changed or he changed and we didn't like each other, let alone love each other? Could I admit those awful truths?

What were we going to do in the middle of our lives? This was the beginning, but I was worried about what came next.

"I'm scared about the wedding," I whispered.

"I know," he whispered back. "We're taking a risk. But I want to do it with you."

"I'm scared about the future."

He lifted up my chin. "We're going to change. It's okay."

"I'm going to commit to you forever and ever, and right before we do that, you change?"

"I did. But this is no big deal, Amelia."

I asked the scariest question of them all. "What if you change more? What if after we make a legal binding contract to care for each other, we want out of it later because it wasn't what we thought?"

"I'm definitely going to change. So are you. No getting around it."

"But we might change in different ways, and we might not get along."

He gave me a hug. "That's really what you're scared of."

I nodded. "We're taking a risk."

"I think that's what marriage is. Taking a chance on someone, knowing that they are going to change. You're a real human being. We're not going to stay the same forever."

"So you think me not liking the beard means that I don't want you to change?"

He shrugged and stroked his beard. Beard Ownership 102, now.

"Yeah, that's what I think. If it freaks you out that much, I'll shave it off. You matter more."

I looked at him, let out a breath, and took a deep one. I loved Ryan. I would take the plunge with him no matter what. Even with nasty facial hair. "No. Leave it."

He looked surprised. "Really?"

I nodded. "Really. It's kind of growing on me." I reached around to hug him, and he snuggled his nose into the top of my hair.

"It's growing on me," he said with a wink.

I leaned back and groaned. Still, as usual, my surfer calmed me.

While I was in his arms, however, something came to me. I had to ask, but I was scared to death of the answer. Neuroses don't go away in a day. "Do you still want to marry me?"

"More than anything." He smiled his Sun God smile, and I felt bathed in his warmth again.

"I feel so insecure sometimes."

"Babe. We're both scared. I know I've wanted you my whole life. Ever since I saw you in high school. But does that mean I'm not scared? No. What if something happens to you? This is a chance we are both taking together. But you have to take chances. You don't live otherwise."

I nodded. He was right.

With a grin on his face, hidden by that beard, he got down on one knee before me. Solemnly. In board shorts and a Walden surf t-shirt. Barefoot. "Amelia. Will you marry me? Be my wife. Love me forever."

I burst into tears again and nodded. "I will." He gave me that beard-kiss. I could deal with it better this time.

And that night the beard-kiss felt even better between my legs.

The next day, Marie arrived with suitcases of clothes and a whole lot of bossiness and attitude. She was moving in to get me ready for the wedding.

The three of us walked up and down the beach, picking up sand dollars, starfish, and sea shells, which we soaked in bleach and water to get the sand off, scrubbed, and let dry. I ordered plain white linens from a local party supply store, and got tons of candles and hurricane glass holders.

Simplicity.

With the tent coming and the caterers, we would have a pared-down, but still elegant wedding, with beard and without fancy table settings.

Speaking of beards, Marie made me go online to look at a Tumblr site of beautiful men with scruffy beards. We sat next to each other at the desk and looked at the laptop, sipping margaritas.

I begrudgingly admitted that they looked okay. (Some of them more than okay.)

"Honestly, Amelia. Ryan is so hot, what does it matter?"

I still felt the need to defend my position. I was right, right? "I just like him better without it."

Of course she wouldn't let me get away with that. As she licked the salt off the rim of the glass, she said rather forcefully, "And what does his physicality matter? He's your soulmate, and you know it."

I took a deep breath and nodded. "You're right."

Satisfied, she giggled and took a sip of her drink. "Are you willing to take his beard to be your lawfully wedded beard?"

Clinking glasses with her, it was now a no-brainer. "I am."

"Good." She stood up and kissed the top of my head.

Our wedding day arrived, and I woke up ready to marry my beard. I mean, my best friend.

A white tent arrived, with tables for our guests—just close friends and family—and we decorated with piles of sea treasures, candles in glasses to protect from the wind, and simple linens and dishes.

It worked for the beach.

And that evening, I took my first step on the sand, barefoot. Still warm from the day, but not too warm, it felt just right. My knee-length, strapless white lace dress looked straight out of the 1950s, but it fit my curves.

My dad offered me his arm and said, "You ready, Princess?"

I beamed at him. I was.

I walked slowly with my dad toward the ocean, following Marie to the rows of chairs set up near the water's edge. Besides my family and Ryan's sister, I saw my friends, Jake and Lucy. Jessica and Mikey.

Hugo and Neveah. Will. Everyone had gone barefoot, a pile of shoes in a basket at the edge of the sand.

I took a step toward the aisle, and everyone stood.

Ryan's back had been turned away from me while he talked to the judge quietly. I could see his broad shoulders in his classic black tuxedo. He too was barefoot, with his pant legs rolled up, his hair glinting in the early evening sun.

Then he turned around, caught my eyes, and smiled.

And I felt like I did when I first saw him in the coffee shop. Like time stood still and nothing else existed except me and him. No noise. No waves. No other people.

Just his Sun God smile. His golden glow. Those green eyes that did me in the first time I saw him.

And all of a sudden, I was completely certain that I was doing the right thing. Ryan Fielding was meant for me and no other.

I made it down the aisle, pulled to his presence inevitably, like there was no place else I could go. No place else I wanted to go.

When I got to him, my dad, with tears in his eyes, placed my hand in Ryan's, and we turned toward the judge. I looked up to Ryan and never felt more whole in my entire life.

We promised each other before the judge and everyone with us to love each other and care for each other as long as we both shall live.

And I knew that I loved him more than I'd ever loved another person and that I would continue to love him, regardless of change. Regardless of what he looked like or what happened to us. I knew that we were meant for each other, despite knowing that things would change. We'd change together or apart, but we would be witnesses to each other's lives, and we would honor and respect each other.

I couldn't wait to start the middle part of our journey together.

Once we'd exchanged rings and the judge pronounced us married, Ryan Fielding, my new husband, leaned in to kiss me, and I realized.

He'd shaved.

I'd married him without noticing his facial hair at all. *It didn't matter anymore.* I saw him like I always had seen him—his soul, his passion, his sensuality, his love. Not his facial hair.

But he'd shaved it off for me.

"God, I love you," I whispered.

He smiled. "I love you, too. Forever and ever."

About Leslie McAdam

Bestselling author Leslie McAdam writes about the men you fantasize about. Her first published novel, The Sun and the Moon, won a 2015 Watty, which is the world's largest online writing competition. She lives in a drafty old farmhouse on a small orange tree farm in Southern California with her husband and two children.

Join her active Facebook fan group, Southwinds Coffee, for near-constant mancandy and giveaways: https://www.facebook.com/groups/SouthwindsCoffee/

Follow her everywhere!

Website: www.lesliemcadamauthor.com

Facebook: www.facebook.com/lesliemcdamauthor

Twitter: www.twitter.com/lesliemcadam

Instagram: www.instagram.com/mcadam_leslie

Newsletter:lesliemcadamauthor.us12.list-manage.com/subscribe?u=44afa3febf912dd02d197a1cb&id=44645c014d

Background Noise

BY R.C. MARTIN

Corie

"Heads up, babe—The Beard is here."

Jill's words filter through my ear and I gasp. I follow her instructions immediately, my head shooting up as my eyes shift and focus on the man I see through the storefront windows, approaching the coffee shop in all of his glory. My hands stop moving. My heart starts pounding. My lungs struggle for breath, and the sight of him catapults me into a different space-time continuum, where everything moves in slow motion, allowing me to capture every single detail of that fine specimen of a man walking toward us.

Over the last few weeks, I've surmised that he stands at the height of about six-foot-three. I know this because when he stands on the other side of the counter to order his red-eye, I have to look *up* into his eyes. At five-foot-nine, with approximately three feet of counter space between any given customer and myself, I don't usually have to tip my head *up*. For him, I can and *would* look up until my neck ached.

It's the middle of December in the middle of the mountains, so I've only seen him in jeans, thermal, long-sleeved t-shirts, and the occasional sweater; but I can tell by the way the fabric hugs his body that he's got a body worth hugging. And—oh, my *god*—can that man wear a pair of jeans. His legs, *that ass*, they were sculpted to perfection. Never before has a man been able to make my stomach clench walking *toward* me and walking away from me.

The bell jingles as he opens the front door, and my stomach is instantly full of a million little fireflies, lighting me up from the inside out as he continues to close the distance between us. He shakes off the chill of the frigid morning air, and the snow that has fallen across the shoulders of his big flannel coat begins to melt—seeping into the fabric that keeps him warm.

Oh, how I wish I could be the coat that keeps him warm.

As per usual, he's wearing a baseball cap over his over-grown, deep brown hair. It gets a little longer every week. If he lets it grow much more, it'll soon touch his shoulders. I wouldn't mind. His hair is gorgeous. The thick strands are so dark, they're almost black—but not quite. This, of course, I know with certainty. It's the shift in the space-time continuum. I swear.

I watch as he nods politely to a table full of little old ladies before his eyes focus behind the counter. He spots Jill first, and I know I only have another second before I have to stop staring. I won't dare look away before I have to, but it's imperative to my barista reputation that he not know I'm one bold move away from being his stalker on the down-low. These stolen moments have begun to carry me through each day. It's ridiculous, but it's true.

I attempt a deep breath as I admire his handsome hazel eyes, hooded beneath the bill of his cap. They're a perfect mix of dark brown and vibrant green. Regretfully, I don't let my eyes linger on his for long, my gaze drifting down to his lips. Lips I'm sure were made for long, languorous kisses; lips that are surrounded by that generously full beard that makes me positively weak at the knees.

Before I'm ready, his eyes find mine. Sucking in a quiet breath, I look away in an attempt to mask my blatant stare. I brush my hands against each other, for practically no reason at all, and then I plaster on my most confident smile, abandoning the task I can hardly remember I was doing as I approach the register. He sets his tablet, his journal, and his worn Bible on the counter—the items he brings with him every day—and reaches for his wallet.

"Good morning. Twenty-four ounce red-eye?" I ask, even though we both know I don't have to.

"Mornin'" he drawls in his unbelievably sexy southern accent, his voice a rich and delicious baritone that makes me press my thighs together. Every. Damn. Time. "A red-eye would be great, darlin'. Thank you."

I suppress the whimpering sigh that's *dying* to be set free from my throat, knowing good and well that it would embarrass the crap out of me if I made a single sound. Not to mention the fact that he calls everyone *darlin'*—and by everyone, I just mean Jill and me—so I shouldn't read into it. It's a southern gentleman thing.

"Coming right up," I announce after I've finished ringing up his order.

I pull the double shot of espresso for his beverage in seconds before filling his cup to the brim with our signature dark roast. After sliding the sleeve on, I set his drink on the counter in front of him, silently cursing myself for being so freaking efficient at my job.

"Let us know if you need anything else."

"Will do," he assures me. He then offers me a wink as he gathers his things and heads for the table that has somehow become *his* over the last month.

A month. He's been coming into Uncle Cal's coffee shop for an entire *month*, and all I really know about him is that he spends half of the day in that journal, sipping strong coffee, ignoring his phone. Yet, deep down inside of me, I've convinced myself that he's something special—some*one* special. I don't know why or how, as we exchange the same four sentences every day, revealing absolutely nothing personal, but my heart just *knows*.

When he's out of ear shot, I finally free the sigh I've been holding back. I can't help it. *The Beard*—whose name I'm not brave enough to ask for—is the man dreams are made of, and that's not a short order.

Escaping this little mountain town in backwoods Colorado is just about all I've wanted for as long as I can remember. It's a dream that seems to elude me at every turn. And yet, *The Beard* ignites my hope. It's as if the way he makes my body come alive just by entering a room is a daily awakening to the reality that life can be more.

I can be more.

Ashley

I shrug my way out of my coat, draping it over the back of the chair before I sit. This table right here is the best spot in the house—a window with a spectacular view to my right, and the coffee bar with a view of that gorgeous girl to my left. After being cooped up for four weeks in self-inflicted isolation, she has been a sight for sore eyes. This intimate and homey coffee shop was my first stop when I finally decided to venture into town, and I haven't been able to stay away since.

I manage one swallow of my coffee before my phone starts vibrating. I pull it from my pocket and see that it's my agent calling. I hit *ignore*, toss the device on the table, and reach for my cup. It doesn't even make it to my lips before the vibrating starts again. I pick up the phone once more, clenching my jaw in frustration when I see my manager's name light up the screen. I hit ignore—sure that I don't want to talk to him either—and set it aside, shifting my gaze out the window.

It's snowing. I know that out there, the morning is still young, and the silence that comes with the sunrise still lingers. It's all I want—it's what I *need*—the quiet that accompanies seclusion; the peace that comes when I'm out of the spotlight—in the background, where I am *home*.

I stifle a groan when, not five minutes later, my phone is buzzing across the table. I don't pick it up, but cough out a humorless laugh when I see it's my best friend calling. I wish I could answer. I wish I could talk to him. I wish he would understand. But these days, he's just like everyone else. I know he's not calling to wish me well today.

No, in his eyes, today is no different than yesterday, or the day before that, or the day before that. He's sold out. He's on *their* side. All he cares about is protecting my image, as if it even makes a lick worth of sense for me to fight against the lies people have chosen to believe.

When I'm halfway through with my coffee, the vibrating starts to grate on my nerves. I pick it up to turn the damn thing off, but then I see *Mama* is calling. A small smile tugs at the corner of my mouth as I slide my finger across the screen, accepting the call.

"Hey, mama."

"Happy birthday, honey," she greets.

I can tell by the tone of her voice that there's a smile on her face. I miss her; I miss my dad, too, but I can't go home. Not now. Not yet. I won't dare bring the attention I'm avoiding to their doorstep. No doubt it would follow me. It's not a secret that Tennessee is home. I'd touch down on familiar soil and the media would flock, circle, and harass like the vultures they truly are.

"Talk to me, Ashley—I so miss the sound of my boy's voice."

"You'd like it out here, mama. It's quiet."

"Now you know good and well that I don't do *snow*."

I chuckle, shaking my head at her before I reply, "I'll have to bring you 'round here in the fall."

"Sounds nice, honey." She sighs and a beat of silence passes between us. Then she sucks in a breath—a subtle warning for the words that are sure to follow. "Ricky's been tryin' to reach you."

"Yeah," I mutter, my smile fading.

"Ashley, he's your best friend. Don't shut him out. Especially not today."

"He doesn't give two shits about my birthday."

"Ashley—"

"He's worried about his meal ticket; wonderin' when I'll come out of hidin'. He's a musician first, mama—and that's a proven fact."

"Well, I won't argue with you when you're bein' bull-headed. But I will ask—when are you comin' home? Christmas is just around the corner, Ashley."

I don't respond right away, sure that I don't know the answer. Instead, I surrender to the tug in my chest that I feel every time I think of leaving. There are plenty of reasons why I'm here and not there—but one reason in particular that has me *here*, in this coffee shop, at this table. *Here*, I get the perfect view of that gorgeous girl.

I allow my eyes to wander in her direction, and I watch as she talks to the other girl behind the counter. She's smiling and carrying on like she does when she's not acting all shy. I like it. There's something incredibly natural about her, and it's sexy as I don't know what.

She's tall and curvy—generous tits, small waist, rounded hips, and a pair of thighs I've imagined myself sinking my teeth into. I think about it even now, causing my dick to press against the zipper of my pants. In an attempt to avoid growing even more uncomfortable, I steer my thoughts in a different direction.

I'd bet my left nut that her hair is just as soft as it looks—those brown, shiny, wavy locks always pulled back into a little ponytail at the nape of her neck. She's got a few stubborn strands that fall in her face regularly, and watching her tuck them behind her ear is way hotter than it should be. And those eyes—I swear on my grandmama's grave, that girl has the prettiest brown eyes I've ever seen. They're warm and inviting, even when she's timid and nervous.

I'm used to women treating me in a variety of different ways. The bold ones can be flat out frightening, and the quiet ones are often downright frustrating. I'm just a man, not a god. I don't deserve to be placed on the pedestal they've planted me on. I didn't ask for it, and yet I'm paying for it.

Nevertheless, *she's* different. She doesn't know who I am. She's shy because she feels the spark that lights up the room whenever we're both in it. Watching her respond to it is the cutest damn thing.

"Ashley?"

"Sorry, mama," I mutter, shaking my head clear.

Well, almost.

"I can't come home, yet. Got a few things I need to see to."

"Make it quick, honey. So long as my boy is stateside, I want him home for Christmas."

I nod, even though she can't see me do it, knowing that she has a point. I've missed my fair share of holidays over the last few years, and there's no real sense in me missing this one. Unlike a moment ago when she mentioned Ricky, I heed her advice now. It's time to *make it quick*.

"I hear you. I'll call you in a couple days, all right?"

"I'll hold you to that. Love you."

"Love you too, mama."

We disconnect and I toss my phone aside before looking back behind the coffee bar. My eyes lock with the pretty brown ones that I've been dreaming of for weeks. When she blushes and looks away, trying to appear busy, I can't help the grin that spreads across my face.

Yeah. It's time to make it quick, all right. I've done enough pussy-footin' around.

Corie

"Crap! Jill—oh, no! *Jill*," I hiss, my hands busy wiping down the counter I wiped down just two minutes ago.

"What's up, babe?" she asks, clearly oblivious to my current state of panic.

"*The Beard*," I whisper-shout. "He caught me staring, and now he's coming over here. Oh, my god, kill me now."

Jill only laughs before she comes to stand right next to me. "Be brave, Corie Flynn—be *brave*." She hip-checks me and then starts to back away from my side. With wide eyes, I look at her from over my shoulder, wondering why in the world she's leaving. She just smiles at me wickedly before waggling her fingers and disappearing behind the swinging kitchen door.

I cough out a sigh, appalled that I'm about to find myself alone and face to face with *The Beard*. Then I shut my eyes closed tight and try my hardest to cling to Jill's words. The truth is, she's right. He's just a guy. A really, incredibly, unbelievably *hot* guy—but a guy, nonetheless. It's time I stopped hiding behind my apron and the same *four* sentences we exchange every day.

I draw in a deep breath and then open my eyes just as he approaches the counter. Without his coat on, he looks even more appealing than he did before—his long-sleeved, black t-shirt serving as his PSA announcement that *The Beard* knows his way around a set of weights.

"Hi," he says, his voice deep and rumbly.

I squeeze my thighs together, silently laughing at myself, causing a smile to pull at my lips.

"Hi. Did you need something? A refill, maybe?"

"No," he replies, easing his fingertips into the front pockets of his jeans. "I've got my caffeine fix for the day. Thanks, darlin.'"

"Oh. Okay," I murmur, my nerves strangling my lungs as I realize he's no longer talking to Corie—*the barista*. No, he's talking to Corie—*the woman*.

"How would you like to come over for dinner tonight?"

My jaw drops open before I can stop it, and I find myself pressing a hand against my belly. I'm pretty sure my stomach just went cliff diving.

"Um," I manage, regaining control of my jaw. "Dinner? At—at *your* place?"

He chuckles softly before he reaches up and runs his hand over his lips and down his thick beard. "I reckon that might sound forward, but I'd rather stay in than go out—and tonight, I'd like your company."

"*My company*," I repeat dumbly. He grins at me and my stomach clenches. "You don't even know my name. How do you know you want *my* company?" The question tumbles from my lips before I think better of it, and I regret it almost immediately.

Dinner with The Beard? Yes, yes, yes! Why am I questioning him?

Crap. What if he changes his mind after he realizes that I've made a completely valid point?

I suck in a breath when he plants his hands on the counter, leaning toward me before he says, "Know your name, sugar. I like it, too. Never met a girl named Corie before."

I open my mouth to question how he knows my name, and then I see his eyes flick to the corner of my apron. I seal my lips closed and hum an embarrassed laugh as I remember that I wear a nametag.

God, I'm an idiot.

"I don't know your name," I admit softly, taking a step closer to the counter.

"I'm Ashley."

For reasons that I don't even care to figure out, this new knowledge puts me at ease and makes me feel safe—almost like he's trusted me with something personal, and I shouldn't be afraid to follow my heart right now.

Ashley.

It's just a name, but it's *his* name.

Suddenly, there are so many other things I'm dying to know about him.

"I like that. Never met a guy named Ashley before."

"You got a pen, sugar?" he asks.

It doesn't escape me that this is the second time he's called me that.

Sugar.

"Yeah," I mutter, trying to stay in the moment instead of wandering around aimlessly in my thoughts. I reach behind the register and grab a pen, handing it to him without delay.

"Paper?"

I hurriedly grab a slip of receipt paper, tearing off a blank piece and setting it before him.

"Do you like steak?" he asks as he writes.

"Sometimes."

I watch as a smirk twitches at the side of his mouth while he continues to write.

"You'll like mine. I promise."

I bite my bottom lip, fighting a huge smile before I say, "I haven't said *yes* yet."

"It's my birthday," he tells me, his eyes finding mine as he slides the paper across the counter. "You're not goin' to let me eat alone, are you?"

"You're all alone for your birthday?" I gasp.

"If you say yes, I'm not."

"Yes," I insist, nodding my head emphatically.

"Seven?"

"Yes."

"Good," he replies with a wink.

He starts to walk away, and my eyes immediately fall to take in that fine ass as my insides overflow with giddiness. Then, suddenly, he turns around and marches back toward me.

"Forgot somethin'," he grumbles before he extends his arm over the counter and reaches for me.

His fingers curl around the back of my neck, and the space-time continuum shifts as he gently pulls me toward him. Then I feel the tip of his tongue against my lips before he closes his mouth around mine. Time *stops*. I plant my hands on the counter, leaning into him further, unable to help myself. I feel drawn to him like a magnet, and not one single part of me wishes to ever pull away.

When he severs our connection, I'm afraid to open my eyes—afraid that if I do, everything that just happened will turn out to be nothing more than a dream. Then he speaks.

"Been wantin' to do that for a while now. Figured you wouldn't mind."

I peek my eyes open just enough to make out his lips, still so close to mine, surrounded by a beard I now long to feel all over my body.

"You figured right," I whisper, my cheeks heating in a blush.

"I'll see you tonight, sugar."

He presses a light peck against my lips before he lets me go and heads back to his table to gather his things.

This time, when he looks back at me, I don't bother hiding the fact that I'm staring. As I watch him leave, I can't stop myself from reaching up and tracing my fingers across my lips.

I was right.

Those lips were made for kisses.

I almost pee my pants when I turn into the driveway of the address that Ashley gave me this morning. I should have known by the unfamiliar street name that the neighborhood would be a foreign one, even to *me*—the townie that I am—which could only mean one thing. *Money*. As I put my little coupe into park, I start to question if this is such a good idea. I'm fairly certain that I *don't* belong in that house.

Then I remember the cupcakes I baked this afternoon, now sitting in the backseat. Lemon poppy seed, with copious amounts of blueberry frosting, because *every* birthday should come with frosting. Knowing that I can hardly justify standing the man up on his *birthday*, I pull in a deep breath and climb out of my car, cupcakes in hand.

The Ashley Manor—which I have dubbed his *not* so humble abode—is beyond breathtaking. More like *soul* crushingly beautiful. It's a stone-faced structure with three peaked roofs and a chimney. As I was driving up, I noticed an amazing wrap around porch out back, and a balcony just outside the second story. There are windows *everywhere*, and I can tell he's got just about every light on in the place. It's lit up like a Christmas tree.

As I approach his front door, I reach out to ring the doorbell and notice that my hands are trembling. I pull back, deciding to give myself a moment. It's freezing out here, but I need to calm down.

I close my eyes, remembering the feel of his lips pressed against mine. It's an incredible memory I wish not to forget. Furthermore, I won't deny that I desperately long to experience the pleasure of his touch again. His wealth doesn't change the moment we shared earlier; it doesn't alter each exchange between us that we've shared over the last month, all of which have somehow brought me to his doorstep. In the same vein, I must also accept the fact that my *lack* of wealth is just as insignificant.

Yes, I'm twenty-four years old and stuck working at the only local coffee shop in my hometown, but this doesn't define me. It's not who I *wish* to be, and I have every intention of getting out of Dillon, Colorado as soon as I can. Just because I'm here *now* doesn't mean I always will be. I refuse to accept that. I *have* to. If I don't, I'll turn into the person I always promised myself I wouldn't be.

I open my eyes, resolved to the fact that tonight I will be the girl who goes after what she wants. Tonight, I want Ashley; so I gulp down a breath of cold air, and I ring the doorbell.

Be brave, Corie Flynn—be brave.

Ashley

At the sound of the doorbell, I look away from the skillet, my heartbeat speeding up a notch in anticipation. I flip both steaks, sure that they have at least another fifteen minutes before they're ready, and then make my way to the entrance of the house.

I smile to myself, realizing that I'm a little nervous, and tug up the sleeves of my dark green sweater. I then run my fingers through my hair, still a bit damp from my shower, before I take a breath and open the door.

My God, this woman is a vision to behold.

Corie is shivering out on the porch, a domed rectangular container in her glove covered hands. Her hair, now loose and brushing the tops of her shoulders, is spotted with snow, and I wonder how long she's been standing outside.

"Hey, there," I greet, anxious to get her inside and out of the cold. "Come on in."

"Thanks," she murmurs, stepping over the threshold.

I close the door behind her, immediately reaching for the handle of the container before taking it away from her. She looks up at me curiously, and then I wrap my arm around her back, pulling her against my chest. When she sucks in a sharp intake of air, I wonder if I've made her uncomfortable; but then she rests her hands against my chest, leaning into me as if in my arms is a familiar place to be.

"How long you been here, sugar? You're covered in snow."

She blushes, but doesn't pull her gaze from mine, allowing me to explore her pretty brown eyes.

"Your house is huge. I may have been a little intimidated," she confesses.

I smirk down at her, tightening my grip around her back. Her body feels good pressed against mine. Soft and warm.

"Not my house, sugar."

"Um—what? Are you, like, squatting in someone's vacation

home or something?" she asks, her eyes growing wide in worry. It makes me laugh, really laugh—something I haven't done in a while.

I don't answer her right away. Instead, I dip my head and press a kiss against her luscious lips. The taste I had this morning about knocked me on my ass, and I've been waiting all day for the chance to kiss her some more. Tonight, I have every intention of savoring the flavor of her mouth. Bet she's sweet as apple pie.

"I'm not squattin', I swear," I assure her, my nose touching the end of hers. I can feel the short bursts of air that mark each one of her exhalations, and her excitement makes my dick twitch. "A friend o'mine owns the house. She's lettin' me borrow it for a while. Needed a place to lay low."

"Oh. That's awfully nice." As she speaks, I can feel her melting into me further, and I know already that my gut instinct was right. No way could I leave this town without getting to know the gorgeous girl behind the coffee bar.

"What's this?" I ask, holding up the container.

I don't bother looking at it, and neither does she, both of us still content with our current view.

"Cupcakes. Every birthday should be celebrated with frosting."

"You made me cupcakes?" My eyebrows shoot up in surprise, and I hold her tighter still.

"Yeah," she whimpers. "Lemon poppy seed with blueberry frosting. I wasn't quite sure what kind you'd like, but they're my favorite."

I kiss her again, resting my forehead against hers as I pull away. "Thank you, sugar."

"Don't thank me until after you've tried one," she insists with a nervous giggle.

She's too damn cute for her own good.

Too damn cute for my own good.

"Let me take your coat. The steaks are still on, but dinner should be ready soon."

"Okay."

I hang up her coat as she steps out of her boots, and then I take her hand, leading her to the kitchen. I let her go, setting the cupcakes on the kitchen island before hurrying to the stove to flip our steaks. I then head to the fridge, grabbing the butter I need for this particular recipe.

"Can I help with anything?"

"No," I say with a smile and wink. "Have a seat. Keep me company."

"So, you're a man who likes to cook, huh?"

I chuckle, dropping the butter in the skillet. When it melts, I'll add a bit of garlic and some thyme, and these babies will be just about ready.

"I *like* to cook, but my repertoire isn't all that impressive. Steak, I can do."

As soon as I've added all the necessary ingredients, I turn from the stove, my attention drawn to Corie. She's fidgeting with the sleeves of her white sweater—her white sweater with a wide neck, offering me the perfect peek at the tops of her tempting tits. My mouth waters and my pants suddenly feel too tight, but I tamp down my lust for the moment, reminding myself that I'm a gentleman.

"Are you a preacher?" she asks, titling her head to the side.

I choke out a laugh as I furrow my brow in confusion. "No, sugar, I'm no preacher. Far from it."

"Just checking," she says bashfully. "You always have that with you when I see you." She points to the edge of the counter, where I've left my tablet, my journal, and Grandma Joan's Bible.

A sad smile plays at my lips before I nod in its direction and explain, "It belonged to my grandma. She passed a little while back. I like to have it on me, especially when life gets stormy. She always said: *all the answers you'll ever need can be found in the Good Book.* She wasn't wrong, either. Might not always find the answers you want, but that's life."

"That's beautiful," she whispers.

"So are you, sugar. I think she'd approve," I reply with a wink, hoping to lighten the mood.

"Thank you." She tucks her hair behind her ear as she speaks, looking *away* from me. That, right there, let's me know she has no idea how gorgeous she really is.

"Can I get you something to drink?" I offer in an attempt to change the subject and get her to bring her eyes back up. "I've got wine, beer, coke, tea…"

"Actually, a beer would be great."

A grin spreads wide across my face when her pretty brown eyes lift to meet mine. Sitting before me is a woman who thinks birthdays should be celebrated with cupcakes and beer. All of a sudden, I think the shit storm I've endured, which brought me here, may just have been totally worth it.

"One beer, comin' up."

Corie

Note to self, Ashley doesn't break his promises.

Dinner is *delicious*. Our salad may have come from a bag, and the dinner rolls from the grocery's bakery, but the steak is *amazing*. It isn't just the food that's left me full and happy, either.

Ashley and I sit side by side at the kitchen island, foregoing the formal dining room as we eat and drink and talk. And talk. And *talk*. I thought I loved the sound of his voice before. Now I'm quite certain that I'm addicted. Not to mention the sound of his dark, sexy, belly laugh; coupled with his handsome smile, it's enough to make a girl swoon.

"Can I get you another beer?" he asks as he stands, taking our long abandoned plates to the sink.

I note the time, surprised to see that it's already well past nine. The last thing I want to do is go home, but I don't want to overstay my welcome, either.

"You're not goin' anywhere, Corie," he states, his tone both gentle and authoritative. "It's snowin' pretty heavy."

He nods out the window, and I feel both relieved and nervous when I see that he's right. I've definitely seen my fair share of snow; driven through some dangerous storms, too—life of a Rocky Mountain girl—but I won't argue with him. I don't have work tomorrow, and I don't want to leave. If he says I'm staying, I'm staying.

"Okay," I agree, reaching up to tuck my hair behind my ears. "I'll take that beer."

He nods once more, turning to pull two beers out of the fridge. He pops the caps off before he returns to my side. Though, instead of sitting, he holds out his hand.

"C'mon, sugar. I can offer you a more comfortable seat than that one."

I don't hesitate to slide my palm against his, and my stomach fills with a bunch of frenzied fireflies as he wraps his fingers around mine and holds on tight. He feels good—*really* good—and as we fall deeper and deeper into the night, I find myself getting lost in all that is Ashley.

He's incredibly sweet, really funny, and thoughtful, too. There's something about him that encourages me to feel at ease, like I can tell him anything. I think it's his eyes. They're familiar, somehow. I can't explain why or how, it's just an inkling I have. Those gorgeous hazel eyes make me feel safe and *warm*. And yet, at the same time, he has me on the verge of coming unhinged. His personality makes him *that* much more attractive, setting my entire body abuzz with nerves and an undeniable desire the likes of which I've never known.

He leads me into an absolutely *fabulous* sitting room. There's a fireplace, an assortment of plush, cream colored couches—decorated with an array of warm-colored throw pillows—and a wall covered with *huge* windows overlooking the backyard. I'm sure the view is absolutely stunning when it's not pitch black outside.

Ashley hands me my beer as I sit, then he occupies the space right next to me, resting his arm across the back of the couch behind me. It takes every ounce of will power that I have to stop myself from curling up into his side. When I first arrived and he pulled me into his arms, it felt so right. Now, with the little bit of alcohol in my system, I'm not sure I can trust myself to behave while pressed up against him.

I'm not what my late Aunt Edith would call *loose*. I'm no virgin, but intimacy is usually something that's *earned*. Normally, it takes months. Yet, tonight, as unprecedented as it may be—given that our first *real* conversation transpired only a couple of hours ago—I feel as though Ashley has earned my trust and stolen my heart in one fell swoop. I feel slightly ridiculous for justifying my desire in this way, but it's the only thing that makes sense. I've been lusting over him for weeks; but tonight, it's more than that.

I want as much of him as he'll give me.

I want to *give* as much as he'll take.

I swallow a pull from my beer, needing to shift the direction of my thoughts before I crawl into his lap and embarrass the crap out of myself. Needing a moment to calm down, I avoid his gaze and look about the room. When I spot a guitar, discarded on the couch kitty-corner to ours, I smile, pointing at it with my bottle.

"Do you play?"

He chuckles and then reaches up to run his fingers through his thick hair as he says, "Yeah. I play."

"Okay," I say teasingly, nudging his leg with my knee. "Let's hear it."

He studies me for a moment, unmoving, and then he shrugs before setting his beer aside. "Sure, why not?" he mutters, standing to grab the guitar.

I set my beer aside too, shifting to angle my body so that I'm facing his as he returns to his spot.

"Been workin' on some new stuff. No judgin', you hear?"

I can't help but grin, positively giddy that he's about to share this part of himself with me. I then nod enthusiastically as I reply, "I promise."

Ashley

It only takes a second for me to decide which new song I want to play for her. I just laid down the track to it this morning, in Britton's basement studio. As I strum my guitar, my fingers moving along the fret with hardly any effort, I sing the ballad that's been on my heart for the past few weeks.

The tempo is slow, but the lyrics are far from gentle. I've had a rough go of it the last couple of months, and I needed an outlet. Writing songs has always been my go-to; but even after scribbling out an entire album worth of lyrics, it wasn't until I pulled out my acoustic that I started to find peace.

I watch Corie closely as I play, and I'm surprised when her eyes start to fill with tears. This sure as hell isn't a serenade, but maybe the words appeal to her in ways I don't understand. I know I'm not the only one who feels trapped by the circumstances of life every now and again.

When I'm done playing, a single tear rushes down her cheek. I don't hesitate to reach over and lightly run the back of my fingers down her face, drying her soft skin. Before I can pull away, she leans toward me, grabbing hold of my bearded cheeks as she presses a firm kiss against my lips. When I react, I don't think before I *do*.

I open my mouth, sliding my tongue out to part her lips while I blindly set my guitar behind me. She opens up for me, and I pull her so close that she's almost in my lap. I plunge my tongue into her mouth, unable to restrain myself, anxious to taste her, and she whimpers. The sound goes straight to my groin, and my dick hardens in an instant.

I kiss her long and hard, and she kisses me right back—wet and sweet. I pull her even closer, her tits pushing against my chest, and all I want is to have her under me. I want to be inside of her. I want *all* of her.

"Mmm," she groans as I drag my lips away from hers, kissing my way along her jaw and down her neck. With a gasp, she arches her back and sticks out her chest as I lick the swell of her breasts just beneath the collar of her sweater. "*Ashley*," she sighs.

She buries her fingers in my hair, and the feel of her nails against my scalp is my undoing.

"I want you, sugar," I mutter, trailing kisses up the opposite side of her neck. When I reach the space just behind her jaw, I lick her again before pressing my lips against her ear as I whisper, "I swear to you, I didn't demand you stay and then offer you enough booze to take away your choice. You want me to stop, there are plenty of guest rooms upstairs. But I won't lie to you either, Corie—tried to be a gentleman, but I want you in my bed. Been dreamin' of havin' you there for weeks."

She shivers in my arms, gripping my shoulders tightly as she moans in my ear.

I'll be damned if that's not the sexiest sound I've ever heard.

"I think I've had enough *gentleman* for tonight," she murmurs ever so softly.

My face breaks out into a grin and I scoop her up in my arms, holding her against my chest as I stand and make my way to the stairs. She squeals and giggles—*so stinkin' cute*—holding onto me around my neck as she protests, "Ashley, I'm too heavy. Put me down. I can walk; it's okay."

I offer her no more than a smirk and a quick kiss as I ignore her and carry her all the way to the master-suite on the second level, all the way at the end of the hall. It isn't until I've reached the side of the bed that I set her on her feet. Looking up at me with those pretty eyes, she bites her bottom lip, as if she's embarrassed. I reach up and cradle her cheek with my hand before easing her lip free with my thumb. I then dip my head down and seal my mouth around hers, unable to deny myself another taste.

"I'll be right back, sugar. Don't move."

I'm gone just long enough to grab my wallet. When I find a couple condoms inside, I take that as a sign. Corie's about to be mine.

Corie

He leaves me for just a moment, and I try to calm my racing heart. It's no use. I'm too anxious, excited, and turned on. After the way he sang to me—the words so hauntingly perfect, the music so beautiful and captivating, his voice so dark and rumbly—I was sure that I could find the bravery to take what I want and offer all that I could give. He's special; he makes *me* feel special, and I don't want him to be the one I let slip away.

When he returns, I barely notice as he tosses two condoms on the nightstand beside me. In the next breath, I'm in his arms and his tongue is in my mouth.

I moan because I can't help it.

The feel of his strong, hard body wrapped around me is too much, and yet I want more. I can think of nothing else as he kisses me hungrily. Engulfed in his taste, his touch, and his scent, I succumb to the reality that *this* will change everything. I can feel it in my heart, in my gut, in my *core*. I don't know what tomorrow will bring, but I'll never be the same. Not after Ashley. I'm sure of it.

When he starts to pull off my sweater, I suck in a breath, disengaging my mouth from his as I look at him before frantically searching about the room.

"What? What's wrong?" he gasps, his fingers now gripping my waist with delicious ferocity.

I shake my head, needing a second to clear my thoughts.

"Um, the lights," I manage.

"What about them, sugar?" he asks, resting his forehead against mine.

His breathing is ragged, and I can feel each warm exhalation against my face. I stifle a whimper as I grip the fabric of his sweater at his broad shoulders.

"Aren't you going to turn them off?"

He pulls away just enough for me to make out the scowl on his face as he shakes his head.

"Why in God's name would I do that?"

My stomach clenches as my cheeks heat in a blush. "Uh—I—I've never had sex with the lights on." His scowl grows deeper and words start tumbling from my mouth in an attempt to smooth out his features. "I just thought, you know, it was more about *touch* than *sight*. I mean, I think maybe you'd enjoy it more if—"

"Is that what you think?" he asks, moving one of his hands up to grip the back of my neck. He tilts my head a little more, so he can look straight down into my eyes. "Is that what some scumbag made you believe, that you weren't worth lookin' at?"

I open my mouth to respond, but no words come out. I never thought about it like that. Not really. The truth is, I know I'm not a particularly small girl. My curves are nothing to be ashamed of, and I know that, but I've never really considered myself *sexy*.

"Corie," he groans softly, his fingers squeezing my neck as he runs his nose along the length of mine. "When I say I want you, I mean it, sugar. I want all of you—and I want to *see* all of you. Trust me, this body—" He pauses, his hand around my waist gripping me tighter as he pulls me closer. "It's meant to be *seen* and *savored*."

His declaration makes me dizzy with desire, and as I reach for the hem of my sweater, I realize I'm trembling. He lets go of me as I pull the fabric over my head, and my heart skips a beat when I see the lust in his eyes burn even hotter than before. Feeling vulnerable and exposed, I hesitantly slide my hands underneath his sweater, flatting my hands against his abs before I slide them up his chest, bringing his garment with me.

As soon as my palms graze over his nipples, he reaches behind his head and rips the fabric off of his body before he presses his bare skin against mine. He ducks his head down, his lips grazing my neck as his beard scratches my skin. It makes me shiver and squeeze my thighs together. My panties are soaked, and we've hardly done anything.

Ashley eases me back onto the bed, exploring every inch of me with his hands and his lips as he rids me of the rest of my clothing. When I'm naked, he stands up at the foot of the bed to finish removing his clothes, his eyes glued to mine the entire time. I feel silly and embarrassed, completely bare underneath his gaze, but then I catch sight of his erection. I watch as he reaches down and strokes his cock—which is magnificently proportional to the rest of him—and I realize that I'm turning him on.

Me, here, naked—I'm enough.

"*Damn*," he groans as he gives his cock a squeeze.

"What?" I ask, suddenly worried something is wrong.

He grins at me as he takes a step forward, climbing over the footboard before kneeling at my feet. He hooks his hands underneath my knees, bending my legs as he spreads me open. I suck in a startled breath, watching as he shakes his head. Then he flattens himself on the bed until his face is *right* between my thighs.

"Those bastards were missin' out, sugar. You're gorgeous."

Before I can respond, his tongue is making its way up my slit. It feels amazing. Then, as he reaches my clit, wrapping his lips around it, I feel his beard against the sensitive flesh of my center, and I immediately forget what words are.

Ashley

I lick her lazily, savoring the flavor of her sweet pussy. She tastes unlike anything I could have ever imagined. As I thrust my tongue inside of her, I don't even bother silencing my groan. She gasps, bucking her hips, and I drag my tongue up, swirling it around her swollen nub before I suck it into my mouth again.

"Oh, *Ashley*!" She thrusts her hips up again, her fingers in my hair as she silently begs for me to stay close. "I think—I think—"

She sucks in a sharp breath and I shove two fingers inside of her, working her pussy as I flick my tongue across her clit. With an uninhibited cry, she comes, her core tightening around me. I can feel the pre-cum leaking from the head of my dick, my body well aware that the next time her pussy flutters, it'll be around my cock.

Corie looks down at me as I suck my fingers clean. Her pretty brown eyes are smoldering, her lips parted as she tries to catch her breath. Somehow I know—we're about to cross a line I've never crossed before.

If tonight has proven anything, it's that the gorgeous girl behind the coffee bar is a risk I would take over and over again. This moment is ours, her ignorance my bliss. I've held her in my arms, I've tasted her mouth, I've savored her sweet desire, and I'm sure that when tomorrow dawns—I won't be the same.

When tomorrow comes, I won't be able to let her go.

How can I? She's a ray of light shining through the dark cloud of my reality. All I want is to get lost in her warmth.

I kiss my way up her stomach and between her perfect tits, suckling her hardened nipples before I press my lips to hers. She wraps her arms around me, pulling me closer, and I fit my hips between her legs, coating my dick with her arousal as I gently glide back and forth over her clit. When she whimpers, thrusting up, seeking more, I break our kiss and reach for a condom. I'm sheathed without delay;

and with not a word spoken, I slowly sink into her core.

I pause when I'm fully seated. Her mouth falls open in an adorable O shape as she arches her back, her beautiful eyes pleading with mine. I stare at her in return, silently promising her the world as I reach up and run my fingers through her hair.

After a moment, she pulls her bottom lip between her teeth, mewling softly as she reaches up to cup her hand around my cheek. When she grips hold of my beard and gives me a tug, I chuckle, smiling down at her before I press my forehead against hers.

"I'll take care of you, sugar," I murmur, pulling out slowly. Thrusting back inside of her, I graze my mouth over hers and whisper, "Always."

I take my time, loving her slowly as I try and make the moment last. She feels so damn snug around me, it's like she was made just for me. Every curve on her body, every dip and every plane, they're simply irresistible. I slide my hand down the length of her side, grabbing her thick thigh and hoisting it up and around my hip. Without further instruction, she brings up the other, locking her ankles behind my back.

"That's a good girl," I grunt, palming one of her breasts, pounding into her a little harder.

"You feel *incredible*," she moans, the delicate touch of her fingers sending tingles up my spine.

"You too, sugar. Can't hold on much longer. Need you to come again."

"Again?" she squeaks, her legs squeezing around me.

I groan, my restraint slipping and slipping fast. "Damn straight—*again*."

I reach down between us, rubbing her clit as I plunge into her core faster and with more force. When she starts to tremble, I know she's close.

"Ashley!" She gasps just as her pussy strangles my dick, pulling forth my release.

I manage one more thrust, burying myself until I'm balls deep as I fill the condom with my seed. When I'm spent, I roll onto my back, bringing her with me, needing the feel of her soft, plush body pressed against mine.

"Thank you," she whispers, pulling me from my daze.

"For what, darlin'?"

She buries her face in my neck, and I barely hear her when she admits, "No one has ever made me come twice."

With one hand, I sink my fingers into her soft hair. Holding her close against me with my other arm, I kiss the top of her head. "Sugar?"

"Yeah?"

"I'm not even close to bein' done with you."

She shivers and I chuckle, holding her even tighter.

"Ashley?"

"Yeah?"

"How old are you today?"

"Thirty."

She lifts her head and presses a sweet kiss against my cheek.

"Happy birthday."

She's the best damn birthday gift I've ever had.

Corie

Ashley is still sound asleep when I wake. As quietly and gingerly as I can manage, I slip out from underneath his heavy arm and climb out of the gigantic bed. Tucking my hair behind my ears, I search the floor for my panties. When I've found them, I pull them up my legs and start to hunt for my bra. I find Ashley's discarded sweater first and decide to wear it instead. I'm tugging it on as I make my way to the bathroom.

I do my business and then head to the sink to wash my hands. I freeze when I catch a glimpse of myself in the mirror. My wavy locks are a mess, and the small amount of makeup I had on yesterday is almost completely faded. Ashley's sweater hangs off one of my shoulders, and I look like a woman who spent all night having sex with a man I barely know.

And yet I *feel* absolutely, positively *beautiful*.

I smile at my reflection as I dry my hands and then turn to head back to the bedroom. As I go, I lift the collar of Ashley's sweater to my nose and breathe in deeply. My smile lingers, the memories I now associate with his scent some of the best of my entire life.

I think about climbing back in bed, but I know I wouldn't fall asleep. I also know that I could spend hours watching him sleep, and *that* is a level of creepy I don't think I'm ready to reveal to him. Instead, I decide to wander back down to the kitchen and treat myself to a cupcake.

Because if birthdays should come with copious amounts of frosting, the morning after the best sex of your life should definitely come with copious amounts of frosting.

As I lean against the kitchen island, consuming my favorite cupcake, I look at the remaining seven cakes. My stomach tingles when I remember Ashley suggesting we refuel with a birthday treat between round two and round three. He brought up four cakes, two for me and two for him, and then he proceeded to eat three—even stealing a bite of mine. I pretended to be offended, but I was giddy knowing that he loved them so much. Besides, he more than made up for it afterward.

When I'm finished eating, I clean up my mess and then wander to the sitting room he took me into last night, wishing to check out the view in the light of day. I almost lose my footing at the sight that awaits me, the sun rising over the snowcapped peaks beyond the wooded yard, blanketed in white. I make my way closer to the window, now curious about his friend who has loaned him this house. It didn't feel polite to ask last night, but the acres of land that seem to belong to this property look expansive.

I take a closer look around the room, wondering if there are any clues hiding in plain sight—hints that could potentially explain what his friend does for a living. When I see a few framed photos propped up on a bookshelf built into the back wall of the room, I go over to check them out. At first, I frown at the picture of a young girl smiling wide with her arms squeezing the neck of a man I'm guessing is her father. They're dressed in their ski gear, posing in front of a sign that tells me they're at the Breckenridge resort, just a fifteen-minute drive from here.

It's not the picture itself that makes me question my sanity, though; it's the *girl* in the picture—the girl who looks *crazily* familiar. When my eyes shift to another framed photo, I gasp, snatching it from the shelf to bring it closer to my face.

Holy crap!

Just then, a pair of big, strong arms wrap around my waist, pulling me back against a hard chest. Five minutes ago, I would have melted into him, unable to stop myself from surrendering to his touch. Now, however, I'm too busy freaking out.

I whirl around in his arms, holding up the picture before I cry, "You're friends with *Britton Cortnie?* The country music star? No—not *just* a country music star—*America's Pop-Country Princess?* Oh, my god—is this her house?"

I push my freehand against his chest, suddenly needing space to breathe, and he lets me go without protest. It isn't until I haphazardly return the photo to its rightful place that I realize that Ashley hasn't spoken. When my eyes look up into his handsome hazel ones, I'm startled to find him looking at me with *no* expression at all.

"Ashley?"

Out of nowhere, realization hits me square in the chest, causing an instant ache to overwhelm my heart.

"Oh. My. God. This *is* Britton's house. And you know her because—because—because you're freaking *Ashley Hicks!*"

I clap my hands on top of my head as I begin to pace, my brain trying to wrap itself around the truth while simultaneously piecing together all the clues that were *right underneath my nose—no, right between my legs—*all night long.

"I just spent the night with Ashley Hicks. Ashley Hicks! Possibly the greatest guitar player of my generation. Ashley Hicks, the most successful, drop dead gorgeous rock-n-roll god on the music scene today. Ashley Hicks, who *doesn't* have a beard *or* hair long enough to fall into his eyes. And—"

I gasp, the inhalation so sharp and so sudden, it sounds like a shriek. I turn to face him, dropping my hands at my sides as I cry, "Am I your *rebound*? What the hell? How is this happening to me?"

I ball my hands into fists, willing myself not to stomp my foot as I continue my tantrum.

"The man of my dreams is *not* supposed to be on the rebound—especially not after the drama plastered about his latest break-up all over the tabloids. And—*freaking hell!*" I wrap my arms around my chest, suddenly feeling like I'm wearing nothing at all, even though I'm drowning in Ashley's sweater. "I let you see me naked! Your last girlfriend was a freaking size two *movie star*, and I let you see me naked. Somebody, please, just kill me now."

"Are you done?" he asks, his eyes still void of any emotion, his morning voice low and gravely.

I press my thighs together, my eyes filling with tears as I realize that this is it. *Reality.* All of yesterday really *was* a dream. Now, it's time to wake up.

I nod at him in response to his question, dipping my chin to hide my tears as I begin to return to the bedroom to collect my things. I don't make it very far before I feel Ashley's hand around the side of my neck, his thumb pushing on my chin, encouraging me to look up. I tilt my head back, but I avoid his eyes, no longer feeling beautiful. Instead, I'm utterly humiliated.

"Corie, look at me."

I shake my head as much as his grip will allow as I whisper, "I can't."

"Yes, you can. Corie, *look* at me."

I shift my eyes to meet his, and that small movement is enough to send tears streaming down my cheeks. He reaches up with his other hand, gently brushing the wetness away with his thumb before he speaks.

"Why are you cryin', sugar?"

"I wanted it to be real. I wanted *us* to be real. Now I know that it's not."

"Who says?"

"Come on, Ashley. I'm not naïve."

"No, but you're pretty dumb if you think I'm gonna let you walk out that door."

I scrunch my brow at him in confusion. "So, what, now you're *kidnapping* me?"

His face lights up with a huge smile as his laugh fills the room. My belly clenches and my heart sinks, loving the sound but wishing I didn't.

"I'm not kidnappin' you, darlin'."

"What are you saying, then?"

His smile fades as he holds both sides of my neck, his gaze fixed intently on me.

"I'm only goin' to say this once, you hear?" He pauses, so I nod in reply before he continues. "You're not a rebound, and I'm not a *god*. To you, I'm just Ashley. And I'm *gonna keep bein'* just Ashley for as long as you'll have me."

"What?" I murmur in shock, my tears returning.

He props his forehead against mine as he says, "The woman of my dreams celebrates birthdays with cupcakes and beer before she loves on her man until the sun comes up."

His words wash over me and my knees grow unsteady, causing me to practically fall against his chest. He slides a hand down my back before wrapping his arm around my waist, holding me securely against him.

"Me?" I whimper.

"Yeah, sugar. Last night, it was just you and me. Corie and Ashley. Want a lot more, darlin'. I know a good thing when I see her; know for sure after I've been inside of her. Nobody compares, Corie. *Nobody.*"

I don't get a chance to respond before his lips are on mine. He possesses me with a deep, slow, *long* kiss. With each stroke of his tongue against mine, my panic and doubt are chased away. Soon, my arms are wound around his neck, my body pressed flush against his chest.

I don't protest when he bends down and grabs hold of the back of my thighs, lifting me from my feet. I wrap my legs around him and he carries me to the couch, laying me down before stripping me of my panties. When he reaches into the pocket of his sweatpants and pulls out a condom, I say a prayer of thanks that he found a forgotten stash amongst his things last night. We've been through a few—and by the look in his eyes, I get the distinct impression that we're bound to go through a few more.

He sheaths himself before he settles on top of me. Then he reaches down and rubs the head of his cock along my slick seam, coating himself in my arousal. He then guides himself into the heat of my core. As my body takes him in, adjusting to his length and girth, I free a long, contented sigh. He looks into my eyes, and I reach up to brush his hair away from his face. I hook my legs around the back of his thighs, studying him as he glides in and out of me. My entire body feels as though it's on fire with his gaze locked with mine, and my heart speaks loud and clear.

This is real.
This is us.
Ashley and Corie.

Ashley

"Will you tell me about it?"

I look up, watching as Corie enters the room. Her hair is wet from a shower, and she's being swallowed up by a pair of my sweatpants and an old tour t-shirt. Her tits sway as she makes her way toward me, and I have to remind my dick that we're giving her pussy a much needed break. I set aside my guitar, closing my journal as I lean back against the couch, opening my arms for her.

"Tell you about what?" I ask as she settles against my side, curling her legs beneath her.

"The storm," she answers simply.

Pressing my lips against her forehead, I grunt my understanding. I then pause, not because I wish to hide the truth, but because her request reassures me that this woman *deserves* the truth. She's still here, still looking at me like she did last night, still genuinely authentic, downright adorable, and undeniably sexy. Despite her knowledge of who I am, she still wants *just* Ashley.

"Natalie and I had been growing apart for months. When we broke up, it was a decision we *both* made. There were no tears. There was no fighting. It was just time."

Corie twists her neck so she can look up at me. I look right back, noting the lack of judgment in her eyes. I rub my hand up and down her side as I continue.

"The shit she pulled a couple months ago? It was a publicity stunt. The lie that I left her broken hearted was meant to cast her in some favorable light. It worked. Her film took the box office by storm. That, right there, was proof that I'd dodged a bullet. Had my management left it alone, it would have all blown over."

"*Your* management?"

"Yeah. It was Mitch's brilliant idea to toss me into the lion's den, completely unaware. He told me he set up a private dinner between Natalie and me, a chance for us to clear the air and come up with some kind of statement that would leak, showin' we could play nice—as if it's anyone's business.

"Anyway—I showed up, and halfway through the meal, Natalie started actin' like some crazy person. Before I could get out of there, the paparazzi came swarmin'. The next day, my face was everywhere, the headlines nothin' but lies. Mitch got a shit ton of attention thrown my way, but it sure as hell wasn't the kind of attention I ever wanted."

"That's so unfair. I'm sorry that happened to you," Corie murmurs softly, snuggling against me closer.

I rest my cheek atop her head, content to let the silence settle between us.

"I like the beard," she whispers after a while. "I like you *here*, too; but you can't hide forever, right?"

"I don't know," I mutter, circling both my arms around her before I give her a squeeze. "I kind of like it here, too."

"Yeah, but you've got a life to get back to." She turns her head, brushing her lips against my neck as she whispers, "The media doesn't know who you are. Not really. Your fans, on the other hand, you mean something to them. They won't remember this scandal. It's your lyrics they cling to. You've got songs to sing—lives to change."

"I doubt I change *lives*, sugar. I'm just a musician. I play because it's in my blood. I can't escape it; but the spotlight, that was never the plan."

I think about the years I spent in the background, playing other people's songs. It wasn't until someone recorded me while I wasn't paying attention, in the wee hours of the morning, on a tour bus traveling across the country, that I got discovered. Didn't take long before I was catapulted onto center stage. Times like these, I wonder if it was worth it.

"That might not have been the plan, but I guarantee you're more influential than you know. The song you sang to me last night? It resonated so deep within me, it almost scares me."

I scowl down at her, remembering her tears, wondering what I can do to ensure she doesn't feel trapped in the cage of her circumstances ever again.

"Tell me about it."

She inhales deeply and exhales slowly, nodding her head as she begins.

"I've wanted out of this town all my life. Tourists love it, but they come here willingly, and they're only ever passing through. I feel like I've been stuck here forever."

"What's keepin' you?"

"I don't know anymore. Until I was eighteen, I didn't have much of a choice. But home life is a huge reason why I've always wanted to escape. My dad drinks a lot. My mom died giving birth to me, and he never recovered. I used to think that the clothes on my back and the food in the fridge meant that he loved me, but I've come to learn that's not love."

"No, sugar, it isn't."

Her lips twitch in a small, sad smile I wish I could kiss away, but she continues before I get the chance.

"We didn't have the money for university, so I stuck around here. I went to community college, earning a degree in business management, hoping it would get me out of here. Then my Aunt Edith got sick and passed. Uncle Calvin and my cousin Jill needed help with the shop. I've worked there ever since. It's been a couple years, business is good, and I'm sure they could manage without me—but I don't know what I want or where I should go."

I stare down at her, all this talk of *leaving* causing a tug in my chest that's unwelcome. I just got her, I've only just begun to know her, and there's no way I'm ready to let her go. I think about what it would be like to simply pack her up and take her with me; and then a crazy idea pops into my head. I cough out a humorless laugh, wondering if I'm a love sick loon, or a brilliant opportunist.

"What? What are you thinking?" she asks, pulling me from my thoughts.

"You really ready to get out of here?"

"Like you wouldn't believe."

"Come with me."

She opens her mouth to speak, but no words come out. I read the doubt in her eyes, and a sly grin tugs at the corner of my mouth.

Damn, she's somethin' else.

"You wouldn't just be my girlfriend, sugar. I got a vacancy in my staff I need to fill. At least, I will after I make a quick phone call."

When her eyes light up, I know I've read her correctly. She's not interested in coming along for the ride as no more than the girl on my arm.

That, right there, is just another sign. The storm led me to this gorgeous girl behind the coffee bar, and I'm not lettin' her go.

"Wait—you're offering me a job?"

"Yup," I reply with a nod.

"What kind of job?"

"Need a new manager, sugar."

Her jaw falls open as she pulls away from me. "*What?*"

"You just said you studied business management in school. I need a manager for Ashley Hicks, *the business*."

She chokes out a sigh, shaking her head at me. "You're crazy! The most experience I have is helping to run a local coffee shop, and you want *me* to manage Ashley Hicks? *Ashley Hicks* is a multi-*million*-dollar business."

"Got a team of people who could show you the ropes, myself included. Somethin' tells me you could handle Ashley Hicks just fine," I reply with a smirk.

She gapes at me, her pretty brown eyes wide in shock and wonder. It makes me want to kiss her, so I grab hold of the back of her neck and do just that, brushing my lips against hers in a gentle kiss.

I pull away only to rest my forehead against hers as I softly speak, "Know a good thing when I see her, Corie. Say you'll do it. Come with me, sugar."

Her hand reaches up to grip my wrist, her fingers squeezing me tightly as she seals her eyes closed and starts to shake her head. I'm on the verge of begging when I hear her whisper to herself, "*Be brave, Corie Flynn—be brave.*"

A small grin plays at my lips, morphing into a full-on smile when she opens her eyes and offers me an enthusiastic nod.

"Yeah. Okay. I'm in."

Corie
Two Months Later

I take a look in the hotel suite's mirror, studying my made-up face. I hope I look okay. Then again, *okay* in the presence of *outrageously stunning* means I should probably just stay behind and let Ashley go without me.

Pressing my palms flat against my bare stomach, I close my eyes and take a deep breath. I feel like I'm about to throw up. Right now, I need my body to decide whether it can keep my cookies or not. The last thing I need is to slip into my gown *before* my nerves get the best of me.

The anxiety in my stomach ebbs, making room for the warm sensation of *love* I feel for the man whose lips now trail kisses across the length of my shoulder. His newly shortened beard is still present enough to scratch against my delicate skin, making my whole body break out in goosebumps.

"You look *amazin'*, sugar," he murmurs, his tone deep and sexy.

Even after all the time we've been spending together, his voice still makes me ache in the most delicious way. Yet, his opinion is so completely biased, it doesn't make me feel more confident.

"Are you sure I should go?" I ask, my eyes still closed. I'm afraid that if I even so much as catch a glimpse of his handsome hazel eyes in our reflection, I'll cave before I can reason with him that maybe I *shouldn't* go.

He doesn't respond right away. Instead, I feel it as he straightens behind me; then he places something cool and heavy around my neck. My curiosity gets the best of me and I open my eyes, gaping at the stunning display of diamonds now resting across my collarbone.

"*Ashley*," I barely manage. My eyes flick back and forth between the shirtless man behind me and the sparkly necklace on my chest.

He slides his arms around my middle, pulling me back against him as he rests his chin on my shoulder. When our gazes lock in our reflection, he says, "I love you. It's time the world knew it, too."

I grab hold of his forearms, my equilibrium slightly off after his declaration. I've *felt* his love in more ways than I can count over the last couple of months, but this is my first time hearing him say the words. He's been so patient and generous as I've begun to navigate my new role as his manager. I want to earn the right to my job title. I've been working so hard, and he has been so supportive, never allowing my status as his girlfriend to completely interfere with work.

More than that, *my Ashley* has become *my heart*. I don't know when I fell in love with him, only that when I was ready to admit it to myself, it was all consuming. I haven't spoken the words because I was afraid it was too soon. Now, here—wrapped in his arms—it feels like the words aren't enough.

I turn around, wishing to look directly at him, and cup my hands around his cheeks as I tell him, "I love you, too, Ashley—with my whole heart."

He responds with a kiss, parting my lips open with his tongue before he *owns* my mouth. I circle my arms around his neck, pulling him closer, and he grunts, kissing me deeper. I feel his erection through his sweatpants, and a small voice in the back of my head reminds me that we both need to get dressed. The car will be here in an hour to pick us up.

"Sweets," I start to say when he severs our kiss. I'm interrupted when he yanks my panties down my legs before he lifts me up onto the counter. "What—?"

I lose my words as his fingers graze over my core before he begins to play with my clit.

"I know you're nervous, sugar, but you're goin'," he insists, his breath hot against my lips. "Now hush and let me calm my woman down."

As he speaks, he pushes two fingers inside of me, and all I can manage is a nod. Then he's no longer standing in front me, but kneeling between my legs. He uses his free hand to grip the back of my knee and spread me wide as he sucks on my clit. With a moan, I throw my head back, bracing myself with my hands while he brings me closer and closer to my release.

He touches me just right, his warm, wet tongue igniting a need that only he can fulfill. When I come, I don't hold back my cry—knowing how much he likes to hear me scream. Not that it would matter. I couldn't stay silent even if I tried.

Panting, I right my neck and seek out his gaze mere seconds before he takes me by surprise, driving into me with his bare cock. He feels sensational, as always, and I'm no longer worried about whether or not we'll be late tonight. He's taking care of me, as he promised me he would, and I adore him for doing so. With every thrust, he chases my anxiety further and further away, reminding me that no matter what—we're Corie and *just* Ashley.

Just Ashley.

My Ashley.

My love.

When he reaches up and pulls down the cups of my strapless bra, instinct causes me to arch my back, offering him easy access to what he wants. I've been told that some men are tits men, and some men are ass men, but my sweets is a tits and *thigh* man.

I sigh as he wraps his lips around one of my nipples, sucking me *hard* into his mouth. I bury my fingers in his hair—trimmed just this morning, but still long enough for me to grip onto—and I arch my back even more. He groans and holds tight to each of my thighs as he pounds into me harder.

He swirls his tongue around my hardened peak before he lets me go, only to latch on to my other breast. I'm so wet, and the friction he elicits is so warm and perfect, I know it won't be long before he brings me to my second orgasm. I can feel it building, the pressure so pleasurable I can think of almost nothing else.

With a grunt, Ashley frees my nipple and then crashes his lips against mine. I whimper in surprise, but hold him close anyway. His kiss turns me on even more, and I mewl when my climax sneaks up on me.

"Ashley!" I cry as my core tightens and my body trembles.

"*Goddamn,*" he mutters, burying his face in my neck. He thrusts into me hard and fast a few more times before he stills, filling me with his release.

Wrapped in each other's arms, we don't move for a few minutes. We're silent as we work to catch our breath, and a part of me wishes we could stay here all night. I know that's not a possibility, though. Tonight is too important. It'll be Ashley's first big appearance in months. He's even performing the debut of a collaborative piece he was asked to do with the band Mountains & Men. Sage McCoy wrote a song that he was sure only Ashley could pull off with his electric guitar skills. He was right. The song is incredible, and I can't wait for the world to hear it. Furthermore, it's the perfect set up for his comeback.

Ashley got his start in the background. Tonight, he'll get that feeling back. He'll certainly never be hiding in the shadows again—not on stage, anyway—but he'll get to do what he loves best, *rock out* on that guitar. Then, next month, he'll be releasing his acoustic album. Just like that, no one will even remember the storm.

"Feel better, sugar?" he asks, pulling me from my thoughts.

I giggle, tightening my legs around him as he shifts to look into my eyes.

"Yeah, sweets, I do. Thank you."

"Love you," he says softly.

I reach up and kiss his lips before I reply, "I love you, too."

Ashley

I look down into Corie's lap, where she's absentmindedly fidgeting with my fingers, and smile. We're moments away from stepping out onto the red carpet, and she's a mess.

The most beautiful mess I've ever seen.

Her long, red gown hugs each and every curve of her gorgeous body—a body I know as intimately as my guitar. She looks stunning, and while I've already been inside of her once this evening, I know that when the night ends, I'll need to take her again. I can't get enough of her. I'll *never* get enough of her.

She's still the ray of light shining down on me, warming me from the inside out. The last couple of months have proven that I was right that first night, when I was sure I wouldn't be the same after I'd claimed her as mine. Now, my life is better. It's full. The woman at my side has a way of keeping me grounded in just the way that I need, inspiring me to be exactly who I am every day. She's taught me so much without even knowing it, and that's just one reason of many why I love her so damn much.

With Corie, all the bullshit that comes with being in the spotlight fades away. She's so quick to show me the ways in which my gift, my talent, and my music *matter*. Everything else is just background noise.

"Sugar?" I ask as the car comes to a stop.

"Hmm?" she hums, her head snapping in my direction.

"You good?"

"I'm at the Grammys," she whispers, her eyes wide with panic. "I'm going to be on national television. I'm *nobody*, and I'm going to go out there on the arm of Ashley Hicks. What will people say?"

"Darlin'," I start to speak, reaching over to grip the back of her neck. "I'm only going to say this once, you hear?" I pause, waiting for her to respond. When she nods, I stare into her pretty brown eyes as I tell her, "You've never been *nobody*. To me, you're everythin'. We don't give a shit what they say, remember? It's just you and me. Corie and Ashley."

She exhales, her shoulders sagging in relief before she leans toward me, resting her forehead against mine.

"You're right. I'm sorry."

I tilt my head up so that my lips graze her forehead as I mutter, "I love you. Don't you dare forget it."

"I love you, too. So, so much."
"All right, sugar—then there's just one thing you got'da do."
"What's that?" she asks, looking into my eyes.
"Be brave, Corie Flynn—*be brave*."

About R.C. Martin

R.C. Martin is a dreamer of stories and a writer of words. Forever a Colorado girl at heart, the Rocky Mountains is where her characters come to life and their journeys begin. For more from R.C. Martin, be sure to visit her social media pages!

Website: www.rcmartinbooks.com

Facebook: www.facebook.com/rcmartinbooks

Twitter: www.twittcer.com/AuthorRCMartin

Instagram: www.instagram.com/author_r.c.martin

Goodreads: www.goodreads.com/AuthorRCMartin

Rough and Reckless
A NOTORIOUS DEVILS SHORT STORY

BY HAYLEY FAIMAN

PART ONE

WEST

GREASE STARES AT ME.

It isn't a stare so much as a *glare*. I don't look away. I don't shift my eyes or back down, even though the dude is one of the ugliest motherfuckers I have ever seen in my entire goddamn life.

"I need you to be protection for my sister," he announces.

"Protection from what?" I ask, arching a brow.

"Some fucker ex is harassing her. He's followed her to her car a few times, harassing her outside of her work. I need presence there," he shrugs.

"Okay," I mutter. Easy job. Way easier than some of the fucking shit jobs they usually make us do around here.

I'm a prospect for the motorcycle club, the Notorious Devils—the original chapter. It's a big fuckin' deal, and I'll do whatever this ugly bastard wants me to so that I can earn my patch.

At twenty-two, I'm one of the oldest prospects waiting for my shot to patch-in. I wandered for a while after high school, trying my hand at college, then working, and finally this. *This* is where I was meant to be, with an entire family of brothers at my back.

"Ivy is off fucking limits; do you understand me?" he growls.

I almost laugh in his fuckin' ugly as shit face, but I don't. No way in *fuck* is his sister going to be anything I'd want to sink my cock into, not if she looks anything like him.

"Understood," I grunt as I bite the inside of my cheek to keep from laughing.

"She works at Carlotta's, off at three in the morning. I expect you there at two, and I expect you to escort her home, following behind her car on your bike until she's inside of her place, starting tonight," he instructs.

I nod my agreement then stand and turn to leave.

"Off fucking limits, prospect," he growls before stomping away.

"You watching over Grease's baby sister?" MadDog, the charter's president, asks.

"Yeah," I grunt, lifting my hand to rub the back of my neck.

"She's feisty. Good luck with that one," he chuckles.

I lift my chin as I walk away from him.

My assignment doesn't start until two. I have a few hours, but I need to get out of this stuffy as shit clubhouse. I've been cooped up, cleaning up after these fuckin' pigs since a big ass party they had a few days ago. Grunt work is a pain in the ass, but I know that the reward will be sweet once I'm patched in as a member.

I straddle my bike and start the engine, feeling her purr between my thighs before I take off into the pitch black night. Our clubhouse is in the middle of nowhere, between two towns, and about an hour away from the city.

Northern California is a gorgeous sight to see, day or night. Tonight, it's fuckin' epic. The air is crisp and clean. It smells like the trees that surround us and the lake that isn't too far from here.

Country living at its finest in the most beautiful part of the state. I couldn't imagine living anywhere else.

My bike hugs each curve as I wind down through the mountains toward my destination.

Carlotta's is a little dessert place in the middle of the downtown area. It's a hoppin' little spot, especially during the summer and winter months when tourists come to our quaint area and pretend to be enamored by our little towns and villages.

There's parking right in front, and I don't hesitate to pull my bike into a vacant stall. I switch off the motor and stare into the shop's front window.

It's a cute little place, but nowhere I would go. They serve fancy ass desserts and coffees. My sisters and mom love it, and they've talked about it often; but seeing as I have a dick, I've never stepped foot in the place.

IVY

"Are you fucking kidding me right now?" I breathe as I glance up at the motorcycle that's just pulled up and parked right in front of the shop.

The man straddling it isn't my brother, so I guess I should be grateful for that much. I can't see his face, but he has a full beard, and he's much thinner than my brother is—like half his size. My brother has a taste for food and he doesn't shy away from it, *ever*.

My eyes drift to the stranger's thighs, and I swear my belly clenches. I love thick thighs on a man. For whatever reason, I attribute that to his strength, and this guy has thighs that make me weak in the knees.

"Who's that?" Carlotta of Carlotta's, my boss and the owner of the shop, asks from behind me.

"Someone my brother knows," I sigh, turning away from the rough biker that's darkening our front parking area.

"What's he doing here?" she asks, arching a brow.

Carlotta knows who my brother is. I love her for not judging me because of him, but I've also warned him to keep himself and his shit away from my place of business. I don't want anything to do with their illegal bullshit of a gang. Oh, he'd be all over my ass if he knew that's what I thought of his little group. In my head, I scream the word *gang* all day long in reference to their *club*.

"Adam has been bothering me, following me around. I think this is my brother's way of protecting me or something," I shrug.

"Could be worse. He could not give a shit," Carlotta shrugs before she turns to head to the back.

I think about her words. Yeah, it could be worse. Barry could not give one shit about me. I've given him plenty of lip to wash his hands of me, but he hasn't yet. Maybe it was some dying wish of my father's, to keep me safe or something?

I chuckle to myself. *Yeah, right.*

The only thing my dad probably wished for on his deathbed was another shot of whiskey and maybe some nasty slut to be at his side.

For the next two hours, I try to ignore the man on the bike. I can feel his eyes scanning the window. I know he can't really see anything but shapes through the tinted glass, but I can still feel his presence. Something calls me to him, and I try to shake the feeling. He's definitely not the kind of man I need to be around.

"Go ahead and go home, girl," Carlotta says from the back.

The shop is completely dead, and it's only fifteen minutes until closing.

"I'll help clean up," I shrug as I take a broom from the side of the counter and start to sweep.

"Seriously. Joey will be here any minute to get me; you can sweep up before we open tomorrow. Get out of here," she urges.

I thank her and walk over to the counter, grabbing my purse before I remove my apron and hang it up. I walk over to the door and take a deep breath, unsure of who is waiting for me on the other side.

I would hope that my brother would send someone he trusts to protect me, but it's Barry, so who knows. He's always been a wildcard.

WEST

I watch the door open, fully prepared to see one ugly as shit chick—but that's not who steps outside of the little dessert shop. The woman is tall, but her curves are plentiful. Fuck me, her tits alone make my mouth water. There's way too much for me to look at. Waist, full hips, and her thighs—fuck, I could bury my face between them for hours. Everything about her is tempting. She was made to be fucked.

"So you're who Barry sent, huh?" she asks. My eyes snap up to meet hers.

She's gorgeous, with a round face and long honey colored hair. It looks soft as shit too.

"West," I grunt, trying to keep my dick under control. It's two seconds from finding its way out of my pants and inside of her cunt.

I stand and swing my leg over my bike, dismounting before I make my way to her side. She's tall for a woman; but at six-foot-three, she still stands a head shorter than me.

"Where's your car, babe?" I ask.

"Babe?" she scrunches her nose.

"Yeah," I grunt.

"My name is *Ivy*," she huffs as she starts to walk away from me.

I let her, not for any reason except wanting to watch her sweet ass move beneath her tight skirt.

"I'll follow you home as well," I announce as she unlocks her car.

It's a little piece of shit *Ford Focus*, and I wonder what in the fuck Grease is doing. He's obviously not taking care of his sister. I cringe when it sounds like metal scraping together as the engine starts. She needs a new ride and fuckin' fast, winter is just around the corner and there's no way in fuck this junk heap is going to last the harsh snow season that is on its way.

"I don't live far," she says.

"Wait for me. I don't have your address," I grunt.

To my amazement, she nods and doesn't attempt to back out of the parking stall. I jog to my bike and snap my helmet on as I start the engine and then pull out and wait for her. She slowly backs up and then takes off away from downtown.

She pulls into a tiny little house on the edge of town and my eyes narrow. The street is black, not one streetlight in sight, and the house itself is also dark. *It isn't safe.* There are trees and shrubs all around. Someone could just lie in wait for her, and nobody would probably even hear her scream. She's pretty fuckin' isolated out here.

"Thank you," she calls out as she walks toward her front door.

I shake my head as I jog up to her. Ivy's sliding her key into the door just as I catch up to her, and I wrap my hand around hers before I gently squeeze.

"Wh—," she tries to speak, but I don't let her.

I turn the key and leave her on the porch as I clear her house, turning on every light and checking every single room and closet for a possible intruder.

"Why'd you do that?" she asks from the living room as I make my way back to her.

"You live out in the fucking boonies. Anybody could be waiting for you," I announce.

"Adam wouldn't just walk inside of my house," she balks.

"Adam?" I ask.

"My ex, Adam, the guy who's been bothering me," she explains.

"Grease didn't tell me who it was, just said it was some guy bothering you after work," I grumble as I rub the back of my neck.

"Barry doesn't really listen to me," she murmurs.

"Look, you want me to stick around for a while?" I ask, not wanting to leave her out here all alone.

"No, I'll be okay."

"All right, babe. You workin' tomorrow night?" I ask.

"Yeah, I'll be off at the same time," she sighs. She looks beat to shit.

"See ya then. Lock up behind me," I order before I turn and walk away from her.

I *have* to walk away. If I don't, I'll fuck the shit out of her right there on her living room floor. She's the most beautiful woman I have ever seen. A fuckin' hard-on in heels, and she's off-fucking-limits. To do anything would be reckless as shit.

IVY

I press my back against my front door and pinch my eyes closed. Holy shit, West is beautiful. Like full on gorgeous. His dark, little-too-long and messy helmet hair, his full dark beard, and his eyes black as night.

I don't even *want* to think about his body—about his height, or how wide his shoulders are, and how trim his waist is, or the way his jeans hug his thick thighs. I shake my head, trying to rid myself of his image as I make my way toward my bathroom to shower before bed.

I want him. I want the bad boy, and I'm not sure I give one fuck that he's everything I've ever steered clear from.

I throw the covers off of my sweaty body and let out a huff of air. It's not even hot, and yet here I am, covered in sweat. I'd like to say it's because I had some creepy nightmare, but no—I had a sex dream.

West was the star, and he was spectacular. Well, his mouth was. I could even feel his beard against my thighs. It felt so real; and just when I was about to come, my eyes popped open.

I try to sleep for a few more minutes, but I can't. Instead, I get up and dress for some yoga. Cardio isn't really my thing, but I like yoga. It destresses and calms me.

I hope that it can clear my mind of the sexy biker that's taken residence front and center since last night. I don't even *like* bikers. Yet, one look at West and I was panting like one of their little groupies.

After an hour of yoga, I'm panting for a different reason. I feel rejuvenated and revitalized, but I still have that feeling in my belly that makes me think of *him*. I spend the rest of the day cleaning my house. In reality, I'm trying to purge that sexy as shit man from my head.

It doesn't work.

By the time I am dressed and headed toward Carlotta's, I'm feeling nothing but ridiculous giddy excitement at the fact that I'll be seeing him again tonight.

I'm so *stupid*.

Well, my head is smart. My body is stupid as all hell. It still wants that man that I know is going to do nothing but fuck me and leave me. It's their *MO*. It's what they do, men like my brother. Men like my father. Men like West. *Notorious Devils.*

I watched my father go through women like he was changing underwear. It was always one right after the other. Between that and his whiskey habit, I knew the kind of man I *didn't* want. A man exactly like West.

"Your head's in the clouds," Carlotta clucks as she starts to fill the dessert cabinet with delicious treats.

"Want to go get a drink tomorrow night?" I blurt out.

Tomorrow is Sunday, and Carlotta's is closed.

"Yeah, I could use a night out," she agrees with a smile.

The rest of the night, we're slammed from open to close. There's not one minute that I'm even available to think about West and his sexiness. That is, until he walks in, about one minute before closing, as I'm walking over to the door to lock it.

I watch as his eyes scan my body, from feet to hair, and it sends a chill over me. *Shit.* His tongue comes out and he licks his bottom lip before his teeth sink into it. *Shit.* I remember how that tongue felt in my dream. My body remembers, too. I grow wet just standing across from him.

"Need me to lock the door, babe?" he asks, his voice deep and husky.

"Sure," I whisper as I hold out the key.

I don't know why I agree, why I don't just do it my damn self; but as his long fingers wrap around my hand to take the key, I know it's because I want him to touch me. I want to feel his warm, calloused fingers caress my skin in some way, even if it is just my hand.

I turn around and busy myself with the duties that I need to do in order to close up the shop. Sweeping, wiping down tables, and everything else is done all while West leans against the locked front door, tracking my every move.

"Ready?" Carlotta says.

I look up to her with wide eyes, but she's not looking at me. She's transfixed on the captivating man behind me, and her lips tip in a grin before she looks at me and winks.

"What time do you want to meet up tomorrow, Ivy?" she asks loudly.

"Nine?" I ask, narrowing my eyes on her.

"Nine, at the *Bullseye*," Carlotta calls out as I walk toward West.

He doesn't say anything. He simply unlocks the door and opens it for me as he steps aside. Then he turns and locks if from the outside, locking Carlotta in, keeping her safe. We don't speak to one another. I'm tempted to look up at him, but I'm too scared I'll throw myself at him, so I just walk to my waiting car.

I cringe when I reach the pile of crap I call a car. It's on its last leg, and I'm afraid it's not going to make it through another cold, snowy winter. I open the door and start the engine, just in time to see West walking away from me.

I shouldn't have looked.

I haven't seen his ass before, and now I'm doomed. It's so perfect, and in his jeans—*I shiver*. I can only image just how spectacular it is completely bare.

I have a feeling it's going to be another long night. I wonder when he'll be called off and when creepy Adam will disappear?

WEST

It's taking everything inside of me to keep my hands to myself. *Fuck.* This bitch is white hot. If she thought she was coming out to *Bullseye* without me at her back, she thought fuckin' wrong. It's not a typical bar I would find myself in, but for tonight, I'm here.

I show up at nine-thirty, my eyes instantly drawn to the sexiest piece of ass I've ever seen in my life. Long, honey hair worn down, a skin tight, short as fuck, light pink dress that pretty much covers her from tits to just below her delicious ass.

My cock presses against my zipper when I catch a glimpse of her thick, bare thighs. *Christ.* I need those wrapped around me—my head, my waist, my back—fuckin' anywhere. *That ass?* I close my eyes and let out a breath, trying and failing not to imagine it in front of me.

Ivy is off fucking limits; do you understand me?

Grease's words replay over and over in my head as I sit at a booth in the back of the bar. I watch as Ivy drinks glass after glass of some girlie ass yellow cocktail. Just past twenty-one years old, she's the youngest woman in the bar, and she has, by far, the most attention thrown her way. Yet, every man that walks up to her, she's shooed off.

Bartender announces *last call*, and I watch as she and her girlfriend walk toward me. Her eyes skirt over me, and I don't think she's seen me—until her hand wraps around mine. She squeezes before she bends down, and her lips touch the shell of my ear as her soft voice speaks.

"You taking me home to actually fuck me, or are you just going to eye fuck me all night?"

Ivy tries to back up, thinking she's slick as shit, but her movements are slow from her alcohol consumption. My hand reaches out and grabs a handful of her ass as I stand. I dip my chin and brush my lips across hers. Then, lifting my head, I taste her off of my lips.

Lemons.

Fuck me, she tastes like lemons and sugar.

"You don't know what you're askin' for, babe," I grunt, not taking my hand off of her ass.

"I'm a big girl. I think I know what I want," she whispers, looking up at me through lowered lids.

"You want a man that has no qualms about fucking you even though I've watched you suck back cocktail after cocktail all night? Because once we step inside of your place, I'm fucking you. Trashed or not, whether you regret it in the morning, or not."

"I won't regret it," she murmurs.

Seconds later, she's on the back of my bike. Her warm pussy is pressed against my back, and her arms are wrapped tightly around my middle, fisting the fabric of my t-shirt. I pull onto her dark as fuck street and into her even darker driveway. I'm going to have to have a talk with her about leaving her house without a light on.

Ivy wobbles but doesn't trip or fumble as she digs her keys out of her little bag. I take them from her hand as soon as they're out of her bag, and I unlock her house.

Wrapping my fingers around her wrist, I tug her inside before slamming the front door behind me. Then I grab her by the waist and press her back against the closed door.

"West," she whispers. The sound goes straight to my cock.

Smashing my lips against hers, I take her in a hard, brutal, unrelenting kiss. My tongue invades her mouth, and her sugary lemon taste invades mine.

Moaning, I wrap my hands around the outside of her luscious thighs and I lift her off the ground a bit. Ivy responds just the way I want, with a moan of her own as her legs wrap around my waist, pressing her hot pussy against my middle.

"Fuck, you taste like sweet lemonade," I grunt as my lips move down the column of her neck.

"Lemon drops," she rasps.

I hum, moving my hands to her plump ass, groaning when I find it bare. One of my hands stays planted, my fingertips digging into the flesh of her cheek, while the other runs toward the crack of her delectable ass.

"West," she squeals.

"Thong panties," I murmur as my finger runs the length of the slim string, down to where it widens and covers her pussy.

"Yeah," she sighs as her head thumps against the door.

I scrape my beard down her neck and enjoy the intake of her breath when it reaches her chest.

"I need these tits in my mouth," I murmur against the tops of her breasts.

"Yes," she hisses.

I keep my hands wrapped around her ass as I take a step away from the door. I need a bed. I'm not going to do a quick fuck against the wall with Ivy. If I'm potentially fucking up my prospect position, if I'm being reckless as shit, then I'm going to damn well enjoy every second of it.

Luckily, I remember exactly where her room is. My nightly check of her house isn't solely for the benefit of keeping her safe. I'm a selfish bastard, and I knew I'd be in that bed, inside of her, eventually.

IVY

West lies me down on the bed, my legs dangling off of the edge. Slowly, he peels my dress off of me, leaving me wearing nothing but my heels and my lacy thong panties. He curses before he gently removes my shoes, dropping them to the floor at the foot of my bed. I'm soaking wet, my senses on overload. I'm drunk, I rode on the back of his bike, and now he's touching me.

Holy shit, it's like my dreams are finally coming true—well, my dreams over the past few nights.

"West," I whisper.

He's just looking at me, and I have the urge to cover up my entire body so that he can't see my imperfections. I start by pulling my legs closed, but his hands reach out quickly and wrap around my inner thighs, pushing my legs apart further than they were before.

My buzz is wearing off, and I'm wondering how on earth I became so bold and brazen as to come on to him? What is *wrong* with me?

"Been dreaming about having my head between these thighs for days," he mutters.

"*What?*" I breathe.

"Your body is rockin', Ivy. Fuckin' hell, it's like you were carved from my fantasies," he rasps as he sinks to the floor beside the bed and drapes my legs over his shoulders.

I gasp when his mouth covers me over the center of my panties before he sucks. Then I feel his tongue flatten against it, and all I want is his tongue against my skin. I lift my hips closer to his mouth and he chuckles, his breath washing over my sensitive center.

"Greedy," he murmurs.

I don't even care. *Shit, yes, I'm greedy.* He just told me I looked like a fantasy, and he looks like every bad boy I've ever seen and run from. I want it all from him, all that dirty nasty, bad boy sex that oozes out of him.

Laying bare before him, it's like a vault has been blown wide open, and I'm forced to admit that this is my fantasy, too. My very own fantasy I've never allowed myself to voice. I was lying to myself, watching those men who came and went as I grew up; watching the bad boys that grew into bad men who hung around the house. I shiver at the truth. I've always wanted to take a walk on the wild side. With West, *his* wild seems a bit safer than any other *Devil* I've seen.

West's finger slips beneath my panties and his knuckle grazes my center, then my clit, causing me to hiss. Then, as if he's read my mind, he shifts my panties to the side and lowers his face to my center again. When his lips wrap around my clit, I can't help but tighten my thighs around his head.

He hums as his tongue flicks me in quick, rapid moves. I cry out and arch my back, trying to get closer to his face. My whole body shakes as his tongue leaves my clit and fills my pussy, giving me exactly what I crave.

"Holy shit," I curse as he fucks me.

I can feel his beard rubbing against my thighs and against my pussy with each move he makes. When his lips and tongue are playing my clit again, my eyes roll in the back of my head. I'm unable to control myself, my hips moving and searching of their own volition.

I'm on the verge of coming, my body wound so tightly that I feel as though I'm going to detonate into a million pieces at any given second.

Then. He. Stops.

I open my mouth to protest, but he's already pulling his clothes off. The sight of his bare chest makes my mouth hang open. He's the most built man I've ever seen up close and personal. When his pants fall to the floor, I snap my mouth closed and my eyes widen at the sheer size of his cock.

"See something you like, babe?" he asks. I look up to his face to find him smirking.

Unsure of what to say, I nod before I lick my bottom lip and sink my teeth into it. I like everything that I see. I have no clue where to start. He instructs me to ditch my panties and get into the middle of the bed. I do as he orders as quickly as I can.

"Show me that sweet pussy," he murmurs as he crawls up from the foot of my bed between my legs.

I spread my thighs, my bashfulness completely gone for the moment. All I can think about is having him inside of me. I don't want him there, I *need* him there, all of him—*every single fucking inch.*

West bends his neck and sucks one of my nipples into his mouth, his teeth sinking into the hardened bud and gently tugging. I move my hands to the back of his head, twisting my fingers into his hair and arching my back, trying to get closer to his mouth—to him.

He slips his cock between my folds and then, with one quick thrust, he's completely inside of me. Ripping his head away from my breast, he lets out the deepest, sexiest groan I have ever heard in my life.

"Fuck me, you're so goddamn tight," he grunts. His eyes connect with mine and his expression is no longer cocky and smug. It's serious.

One of his hands lifts and moves my hair from my face, his fingers sliding down to the side of my neck while he shifts his hips, pulling almost completely out of me before he slides back inside to the root.

"Ivy," he rasps.

I have no words to respond with. My eyes just stay glued to his as he slowly pulls out and slams back inside of me with his strength.

It's hard but slow, his rhythm never changing, never breaking. I lift my knees higher and whimper as my body climbs again toward my release. I can already feel that when it happens, it's going to be huge.

"Want this pussy to strangle the fuck outta me, babe. I need you to come," he murmurs.

His lips touch mine and then, as if it's the permission my body needs, I come, crying out into his mouth. My fingers, wrapped around his forearms, are surely scoring nail marks into his flesh. He thrusts his hips a few more times before he stills, rips his lips from mine, and then lets out the most beautiful moan while he fills me with his own climax.

I blink, suddenly realizing there was no condom used between us.

"West," I whisper.

"Shh," he murmurs as he continues to rock his hips, lazily sliding in and out of me.

"West, you didn't use a condom," I blurt out.

"You got birth control taken care of, right?" he mutters against my neck as his lips make a path from below my ear to the center of my throat.

"Against babies, yes; against incurable diseases, no," I grind out.

"I'm clean," he murmurs, still seated inside of me with his mouth on my neck.

"How many clubwhores have you fucked without protection?" I grind out.

It's then that he lifts his head and narrows his eyes slightly before he smirks.

"None. I don't have time to fuck those whores. I'm a prospect. And even if I did have the time, they're disgusting. My cock has never been bare inside anybody but you," he continues, grinning.

"Why me?" I ask quietly.

"I want you," he says. I look at him with apprehension, but he eases that as he speaks again. "*Only* you, Ivy."

"But you barely know me," I whisper.

"I like what I know," he says, as though that is explanation enough. He eases out of me, rolling to the opposite side of the bed and dragging me with him so that I'm tucked into his side. "You're fuckin' feisty, Ivy, and I like it a helluva lot."

We spend the rest of the night and morning in each other's arms, fucking hard, fast, slow, and gentle. After we're completely exhausted and totally spent, he wraps me in his arms. With my head against his chest, my arm around his middle—one of his buried in my hair, and the other resting on my hip—he sighs a contented sigh.

"Never letting you go, Ivy," he murmurs against my hair.

I suck in a breath. It's then that I realize, I only want *him* too. I wasn't supposed to, I never intended on it, and yet here I am, wrapped in his strong arms.

PART TWO

WEST

PATCHED MEMBER.

I grin at my brothers. I can call them that now, because they are—my *brothers*.

There are whores dancing and putting on a show, drinks are coming at me from all different directions, and yet, the only person I want to celebrate with isn't here. Even if she was, I couldn't let on that she's my girl.

Ivy.

"Hey, man, I just want to say thanks for keeping an eye on Ivy. She said that shitbag hasn't been around once looking for her since you been watching out," Grease says, slapping my shoulder.

"Yeah," I nod, trying not to give anything away.

That *shitbag* hasn't made an appearance because I've been staying at her place every single night for the past two months, escorting her to and from *Carlotta's* every night she works.

Grease leaves shortly after his thanks with a whore on his arm.

"You aren't enjoying your party?" MadDog asks.

"I am," I nod.

"Ivy is a good girl. Would hate to see her get hurt," MadDog mutters.

My head swings over to him in surprise, and he just grins.

"She just for fun or more?" he asks.

"More," I murmur.

"You're young. You sure about that?"

"She's *mine*," I grunt.

"Better man up and tell her brother that, then," he chuckles.

"What'll he *do* to me?" I ask, taking a shot of whatever is in front of me, not tasting the liquor.

"Probably beat the shit out of you. He won't kill you, you're patched in now, but he might shoot you," MadDog chuckles as he walks away.

I think about his words. I *should* man up. I want to show my woman off to my brothers, and I want to show her that we aren't as bad as the image she's painted in her head. I look over at Grease and cringe. Tonight is not that night. He's got a whore bent over the pool table, and he's fucking her so hard, I swear I see that big ass table jump.

I quietly slip away from my own party and make my way out the back door.

"You aren't getting your party on. This is your night, Camo," Smoke mutters.

Camo, my new road name—because they say I blend in like camouflage. No longer am I only known as *prospect*. It feels damn good, too.

I shrug as my answer.

"Go to your girl," he chuckles. I turn and look at him in surprise. "Written all over your face, brother. Don't know who she is, but if she's keeping you from a fuckfest with easy pussy, then she's where you need to be," he grins as he stands and walks inside.

I take his advice.

I walk over to my bike and leave. Ivy has tonight off. She knows where I am. She said she was just going to hang around her place and she'd see me in the morning. No drama, no tantrum, no fuckin' bullshit. Another reason why I love her.

Yeah, I do.

I love her.

She's my woman, and I want her to be my Old Lady, too. After I talk to her brother, of course, and accept my punishment for blatantly disrespecting him and ignoring his orders—the orders of my VP. Then I'm going to brand her and make her mine for the world to see.

IVY

Patch-in party.

It's tonight, and I've never felt so uneasy in all of my life.

I wish I were working to take my mind off of what West is or isn't doing.

I don't know much about the MC lifestyle, or all that happens behind clubhouse doors. I've always stayed far away; but I do know that drugs, booze, and sex flow freely. I can imagine that it's doubled at a big party. And tonight is West's night, which means all those things will flow freely toward *him*.

I throw myself down on the sofa in a huff, and then I hear a noise on my back patio. It makes me pause. West always uses my back entrance.

He parks his bike behind my fence. I know we're supposed to be a secret, but it's starting to annoy me. I don't want to feel like a dirty secret anymore. I want to go out in public with him; I want all the other women around to know he's mine, that he's taken and definitely not available.

I hear another unidentifiable noise. I stand up and walk around the sofa, on my way to where I hear the sound yet a-freaking-again.

"You're finally alone," a deep voice says from my dining room. I freeze.

"Adam," I whisper as I retreat a step, bumping into the back of my sofa.

"Did you think I would give up? I didn't give up when I wanted you; I'm not giving up now," he laughs.

"I don't want you anymore. I've moved on, and you need to as well," I announce.

Adam was a mistake.

I thought he was cute when he would come into Carlotta's. He would flirt with me, and eventually he asked me out. We dated for a few months and I was constantly fending him off, until one night I finally gave in and we had sex. It was awful. He didn't care if I even liked it, let alone if I got off.

I broke up with him shortly after, and then he started harassing me. At first, it was phone calls; then he would randomly show up outside my work, my house, the grocery store. That was when I called my brother and asked for help. I don't ask Barry for much, so he knew it was important when I asked him for help with Adam.

"Well, too bad, because I'm not through with you yet. Though, when I am, I won't want *you* anymore, and neither will that piece of shit you've been fucking," he says, smirking.

I open my mouth to speak but he's on me, and his hand covers my mouth before I can get a word out. Then he spins me around, and I can feel his body against my back, pushing me against the sofa, trying to bend me over.

"He ain't here to protect you anymore, and when he sees what I've done to you, he won't want you. Nobody will," he whispers against my ear.

I try to scream, knowing it will be fruitless; knowing that my neighbors are all too far away to hear me; knowing that in no way whatsoever will West get to me in time. He won't be by until tomorrow evening when he takes me to work.

I'm going to be brutalized, and there's nothing I can do about it. Fighting will only make it worse, and unless there's a way for me to get out of Adam's tight grasp, I'm done for.

I feel his hand wrap around my breast and squeeze so tight that I know there are going to be bruises. Then I hear a loud blast and Adam's weight falls against me, pushing me even further down against the sofa before it's lifted from me almost immediately.

Spinning around, I gasp at the sight of the man standing in my kitchen. The man who has a piece of my heart. *West.* He's got a gun dangling from his hand and his eyes are focused on the body that's at my feet.

"West," I whisper.

His eyes lift before something flashes through them, and then I'm off. I run into his arms and wrap myself around him.

"He hurt you, baby?" he rasps as his free hand tangles in the back of my hair, pulling me even closer to his chest. It's almost as if he's trying to pull me into his body.

"No, no you came just in time," I whisper against his shirt.

He smells like booze, leather, and sweat. My favorite combination of scents. I tip my head back and look into his eyes. They're darker than normal but focused on me.

"You're mine, Ivy. I'm tellin' your brother and I'm claiming you," he grunts. "You're my Old Lady and nobody fuckin' touches you. Never again."

"Claiming me?" I ask.

"Yeah, fuckin' yeah, Ivy. Nobody touches you again. Never."

"I love you, West," I murmur.

We haven't been together very long, but I do. I love him. He's everything in a man I convinced myself I never wanted, but he's also everything I need.

"Gonna need to get him outta your place and get it cleaned up," he murmurs as his eyes drift from mine to Adam's dead body.

I feel a pang of sadness that he hasn't told me he loves me as well. But maybe his vow of love is claiming me, making me his Old Lady to his club. Maybe that's what love is to him? *Protection.*

What seems like minutes later, my house is filled with bikers. Men I never thought I would want traipsing through my place are here, and they're a welcome sight.

Then Barry shows up.

West's arm is wrapped around my hip, his hand just on the outside of my ass, and he's talking to the president of their club, *MadDog*. He hasn't seen my brother yet, but my brother's seen him. I'm guessing by the fire in his eyes, he isn't happy that West is touching me.

"Get your hands off my sister," Barry grunts. I open my mouth, but West squeezes my hip and shushes me. "What in the fuck are you doin' at her place right now?"

"Wanted to talk to you tomorrow about that," West mutters.

"'Bout what?" Barry growls.

"I want Ivy to be my Old Lady," West announces. The men that were helping to clean up all freeze.

"She's off fucking limits," Barry yells.

"Now, Grease," MadDog warns. Barry narrows his eyes on him.

"Told you months ago she was off limits. You been fuckin' my baby sister for months?" Barry asks.

"*Barry,*" I hiss.

"Shut the fuck up," he says, pointing at me. West gently slides me behind his body—his tightly held body.

"Don't talk to my woman like that," West growls.

"She's not your fuckin' woman. She's off-limits, and you fucked her anyway."

"He's doin' right by her, Grease," MadDog mutters.

"Shouldn't be doin' *shit* with her," Barry grunts.

"His punishment will come tomorrow. We'll hold church and decide. But for now, let's focus on what's happened here. He saved her before shit could have really gone down with that asswipe ex of hers," MadDog rationally explains.

"You okay, Ivy?" Barry asks, his tone softer and all big brothery.

"Yeah," I murmur.

I disengage from West and make my way over to my big brother, wrapping my arms around his neck and hugging him close.

"You wanna be this jackhole's Old Lady? If not, I'll kill him right here and right now," Barry whispers in my ear.

I pull back a bit and grin.

"Yeah, I really do," I admit.

"I thought you hated the club and all bikers?" he asks, narrowing his eyes.

"I love you, and I love him, so you can't be all bad," I shrug.

"You love him?"

"I do," I admit.

"Fuck me. I'll kill him if he hurts you, you know that right?" Barry asks.

"Of course I do," I smile.

WEST

I hear the shower start and I take a deep breath. My patch in party—what a *clusterfuck*. I'm not mad I decided to skip it and come home to my woman. She needed me, and my gut instinct was right. What kind of Notorious Devil would I be if I didn't listen to my gut?

I don't know what tomorrow will bring with church and whatever verdict I get thrown at me for deliberately disobeying orders, but whatever it is, it'll be worth it. Ivy is now my Old Lady. *She's mine*, and

I don't have to hide her or hide us for a second longer.

The water turns off and the door opens. I look up, and there she is.

The woman who stole my fuckin' heart.

Ivy.

My Ivy.

She's wrapped in a towel, her wet hair dripping, and she's never looked more beautiful.

"C'mere," I grunt.

I watch as she takes a few steps toward me. Spreading my thighs, I wrap my hands around her waist and pull her between my legs. I cup her cheeks with my hands and tilt my head slightly to look up at her. Most beautiful fuckin' woman in the entire goddamn world.

"I love you too, Ivy," I murmur. I watch as she sucks in a breath and then smiles wide.

"Will you make love to me?" she asks.

"You sure you want that tonight, after everything?" I ask, running the pad of my thumb across her bottom lip.

"I want you inside of me. I love the way you make me feel, the way you make me forget the rest of the world even exists. And he's gone, West. He's gone and he's never coming back to scare me again," she whispers.

"Yeah, baby, I'll make love to you," I murmur.

Keeping my hands on her cheeks, I stand before I press my lips to hers. She tastes like mint and Ivy with a hint of lemon.

"You been drinkin' those lemon cocktails you like?" I ask as I lift my lips from hers.

"I had a couple shots of lemon flavored vodka, to calm my nerves after Barry left," she admits with a shy smile.

"Taste's good," I grunt before I pick her up and turn her around, lying her down on the bed.

Slowly, I unknot the towel at her breasts and let it fall open, displaying all of her gorgeous, milky white skin. It's all mine, every single inch of her, from now until the end of time. All the easy pussy in the world couldn't make me feel the way this one woman does.

"West," she whispers.

"I'm just lookin' at my woman, baby. Takin' in all this beauty that's just for me."

"West," she chokes.

I quickly peel off my own clothes and spread her thighs apart. I want to taste her, but my cock needs to claim her more. I crawl up her body and sink inside of her wet cunt as my forehead rests on hers. She's so fuckin' tight, every single time. Every inch of her was made for me.

"I love you, West," she murmurs, repeating her words from earlier.

Words that I know she wanted me to say back right then and there. I've loved her for a while now, but didn't know how to say the words. She needed to hear them, so between us, *alone*, I gave them to her. I couldn't say them with a dead man on her living room floor, or with the house full of my brothers. I needed to share them when we were completely alone.

Just us.

"I love you too, Ivy," I murmur as I pick up my pace.

I growl when her fingernails scrape my beard. Fuck, it feels so good when she does that. I thrust a little harder, hitting her a little deeper, forgetting that she asked me to make love to her, not fuck her. I'm on the verge of coming and I need her to get there before I do.

Slipping my hand between us, I begin to stroke her clit. She moans and throws her head back, exposing her neck to me. I suck on the sweet skin of her neck, and her pussy starts to flutter around my dick, urging me on. My thrusts become more erratic with every moan that escapes her lips.

"Oh, shit," she cries. That's when she squeezes me like a fucking vice.

I release her neck and rear back on my knees before I fuck her with earnest, drawing her orgasm out and chasing mine simultaneously. I plant myself deep inside of her before I let out a long moan as I come—hard. Then I collapse on top of her, ignoring the fact that I'm probably crushing her soft body with my heavy one.

"I feel too young to be labeled an Old Lady. Can't I be like... a Young Lady or something?" she asks a few minutes later. I lift my head and laugh, looking into her dancing eyes.

"How about when we're here, you're just my Ivy?" I ask. "At the club, you're Camo's Old Lady; but when it's just us, you're my Ivy?"

"Camo?" she asks, furrowing her brows.

"My road name. Got it tonight," I shrug as I slip out of her and roll onto my back. Ivy rolls with me and plasters her front to my side.

"I like it," she admits with a grin. "You are sneaky, and you blend in."

"Glad you like it, baby, because it's gonna be tattooed on your sexy as fuck body," I smile.

"Tattooed?" she blinks in surprise.

"Yeah. You're an Old Lady, so you have your man's brand on you. You know this shit, don't you?" I question in confusion.

"Well, yeah, I mean, but I thought that was after you were married or whatever," she mutters.

"Being my Old Lady is just as good as being married, babe," I say, starting to get irritated.

"I'm afraid of needles," she admits.

I wrap my hand around the back of her head and pull her into my chest chuckling.

"Fuck, baby, I thought you were reconsidering," I say, continuing to laugh.

"No, never. I just, I really hate needles," she confesses.

"I have to get my ink next week. You'll come with me, feel it out."

"Okay," she nods.

"Get some sleep," I murmur against the top of her head.

IVY

Hours later, I feel the bed dip and then West's lips graze my cheek. I ask him where he's going without even opening my eyes. They're too heavy. I'm too exhausted from our love making, which lasted the rest of the evening and into the morning, well after the sun rose.

"Got that meeting this afternoon, baby. Get some sleep," he grunts into the quiet room.

"I have to work tonight," I remind.

"If I'm not back before you need to get to the shop, I'll be there before it closes."

His voice is sounding further away, and I know that he's walking out of the bedroom. Seconds later, the room is bathed in quiet again, and I fall asleep.

I know that this meeting has something to do with us being publically together, but I don't really see what the issue is. Barry likes him well enough to consider him a brother, so wouldn't he want us to be happy?

The hours tick by, and I find myself ready for work and walking out of the door without a word from West. No phone call and no text. I can't shake off that feeling of worry as I drive toward downtown.

The shop is busy, so busy that I shouldn't even have the time to worry about West, but I do. I'm distracted, and my eyes keep drifting toward the front door every time it opens with a new customer. None of them are West, and my stomach is in complete knots by the time we close the shop's door.

"You okay?" Carlotta asks me as we start cleaning up for the night.

"I'm just worried. West had a meeting, and I haven't heard from him all day." I shrug as I gather my bag and throw it over my shoulder.

"He's a pretty big boy, I'm sure he's fine," she chuckles.

I leave the shop not feeling any better, since he didn't show. He's been there every single night I've worked for the past two months. It feels just plain weird without either hopping on the back of his bike, or having it rumble behind my car as I drive home.

My house is dark as I pull up the drive, but I see West's bike in its normal spot. I furrow my brow at the sight of it and hurry toward the front porch. I throw open the door and gasp at what greets me.

West is lying on my sofa, looking half dead. His face is swollen, along with both of his eyes. There is blood dripping from his mouth, and scrapes are all over the rest of his face. His clothes are dirty and ripped, and I stand frozen to my spot, afraid to take one more step forward; afraid that he is, indeed, dead.

"Ivy?" he moans.

His voice breaks my frozen state, and I run next to his side and sink down on the floor beside him.

"What on earth happened, West?" I ask, trying to keep the horrified sound out of my voice.

"That bad, eh?" He coughs and then moans.

"Did Barry do this to you?" I whisper.

"Yeah," he rasps.

"Because of me?"

"No, because I defied his orders," he explains.

"Which were to stay away from *me*?" I ask.

West grunts as his response. I close my eyes and inhale deeply, disgusted with what's happened. I can't believe my brother beat him so badly that he can't even open his eyes. He's struggling to breathe, and it's all because Barry told West I was off limits and we fell in love with each other anyway.

"It's cool now, baby. It's done and over, and we're good to be together," he mutters.

"It's not cool, not even a little. I'm so upset and angry right now," I growl.

"Grease dropped me off here 'cause he knew you'd take good care of me. I had to be tried and punished for my disobedience. It could have been worse, baby," he says. He's so nonchalant about the whole thing that it's making me even more irritated.

"I don't see how it could have been any worse, West."

"I could be dead right now," he says. I wait for him to laugh, but he doesn't. He's completely serious, and I feel my stomach drop.

"Dead?" I say, sucking in a breath.

"Yeah, baby, disobedience isn't tolerated. Trust is really fuckin' important, and I fucked up. I should have gone to Grease before we ever began, instead of hiding it from him."

"Do you regret me?" I whisper.

"Never. I'd do this all over again every day of my life if it meant coming home to you," he murmurs.

"You're full of shit."

"Get over here and take care of your man," he grumbles.

It takes me a few hours to get him cleaned up and into bed. I'm furious at Barry, and the club, and at West, too. They're all assholes, every single one of them. I don't slide into bed next to West, but instead go out to the couch and turn a movie on the television. I don't even know what it is; I'm just staring at the characters as they go through their motions.

"Ivy," a voice grunts next to me. I feel my body being shaken a bit.

"What?"

I sit up bleary eyed, looking around the room, and then my eyes meet West's bruised and battered face.

"Baby, what are you doing out here?" he rasps with concern.

"I couldn't sleep," I shrug.

"I'm fine. We're fine. It's all good, baby," he murmurs as he sits down next to me with a groan.

"You're not good, and it's partly my fault, and your own club did this to you. How can you be okay with all of this?" I ask as tears well in my eyes.

"This life has its own set of rules, Ivy. I broke one, a big fuckin' one. I should have done things differently, but I didn't. I don't regret not doing them differently, either. Had I, then I would have missed out on the past two months. So, yeah, being banged up like this fuckin' sucks. But it ain't the end of the world, and now there's no more hiding for us," he shrugs.

"I hate how optimistic that whole speech was," I grumble.

"Come to bed, babe, make your man feel better," he chuckles.

"How? You're a disaster," I point out.

"You can give me a mouth hug," he murmurs.

I can't help it, I burst out laughing. Together, we walk toward the bedroom and I do give him that mouth hug. He comes with his hands wrapped in the back of my hair and his cock down my throat.

"Love you, Ivy," he murmurs into my ear when I curl into his side, careful not to touch him too much.

"I love you, West—but I'm still pissed."

"Yeah, baby, I know," he sighs.

WEST

A week passes, and though my bruises are turning the color of bananas and my swelling is down, Ivy is still pissed. She tries to hide it from me, but I know she's not talking to her brother. Grease has eyed me warily a few times but hasn't come outright and asked me anything. I hope that tonight will clear the air a bit. Tonight is party night, and I'm taking my Old Lady to show her off to my brothers.

"Is this okay?" Ivy asks from the bedroom.

I make my way over to the room and my mouth drops when I take in the sight of her. She's standing in the middle of the bedroom in a tiny, little black skirt that barely covers her ass, and a skin tight, low cut tank that her tits are practically hanging out of.

Then my eyes scan down to her shoes. I have never fought not to get hard—not as much as I'm fighting it now—in my entire life. Her shoes are the tallest heels I've ever seen her wear.

I don't speak. Instead, I walk up to her and wrap my hand in the back of her hair, wrenching her neck back and smashing my lips to hers as I lift her skirt with my other hand. I take the string on the side of her panties and rip it to shreds.

Ivy gasps in my mouth, but I could give a fuck. I need her, right here and right now. I slide my hand from her hip, down to her thigh, and then her knee, hitching her leg around my waist before I plunge my tongue into her mouth and consume her.

I walk toward the dresser, until her ass is pressed against it, then I move my hand from her hair and lift her until she's on the edge of the piece of furniture. Ivy fumbles with my pants and pulls my cock out. Her small hand wraps around it and gently strokes me as I fuck her mouth with my tongue.

"West," she moans.

"Need this pussy, hard and fast, baby," I whisper against her lips.

"Take it," she urges before she squeezes my dick.

I growl and then I move her hand and plunge deep inside her to the hilt. She throws back her head with a long groan. I don't give her time to adjust to my size before I pull almost completely out of her and then sink back inside. I don't stop, I don't slow, I just fuck her with all of my strength as I watch her accept me, take me, and find her pleasure in what I'm giving her.

Sliding a hand between us, I start rubbing firm circles against her clit as my other hand drifts up her spine, twisting into the back of her hair. I can't look at her face a second longer, or I'll come too soon. Instead, I bury my face in her neck and inhale her sweet scent.

"West," she whispers as her legs shake on either side of me.

"Come, baby," I grunt, sweat dripping from my forehead.

"Oh, shit," she curses. Then she yells out my name as her body goes taunt beneath me.

I don't slow my movements or even reduce my power as I thrust into her tight body. I'm chasing my own release; and when I find it, I can't stop my head from falling back or silence the loud groan that fills the air around us.

"So you like my outfit?" Ivy asks on a chuckle once we've both caught our breath.

"Fuck, it's going to be difficult not to bend you over every single piece of furniture in the clubhouse and fuck you senseless," I murmur, brushing my lips over hers and pulling out of her warm, tight heat.

"I don't think Barry would like that," she mutters as she rights her skirt and starts walking to the bathroom to clean up.

"He can't say dick about it, even if he hated it. You're my Old Lady," I say as I tuck my dick in my pants and walk into the bathroom as she's fixing her hair.

"What?" she asks with wide eyes.

"You're mine now. He can't say anything. Doesn't mean I'd ever do anything to disrespect him like that or make you feel uncomfortable in any way," I shrug.

Ivy walks up to me and wraps her arms around my neck before she presses her lips to mine.

"I love you, West," she whispers.

"Let's get the fuck outta here," I grunt before I grab her ass and squeeze.

IVY

I'm thankful that nobody is outside of the clubhouse when we pull up. I hadn't thought out my outfit all that well. There's no modest way to get off of West's bike in the miniskirt I'm wearing. Luckily, I changed my panties, so at least I have those on underneath to cover myself a little.

"Ready?" West asks after I've righted my skirt and fluffed up my helmet head hair.

"Not really," I deadpan.

"You'll be fine, babe. I won't leave your side," he promises, kissing the side of my head.

Together, we walk into the clubhouse. I'm surprised by all of the smoke that lingers in the air. I haven't ever been to a party here, and I'm in knots in anticipation of what's going to happen.

When my eyes finally adjust, I see some scantily clad women walking around; but then there are also women dressed in jeans and tanks, just hanging on the arm of who I assume are their men. West walks us right over to them and, suddenly, I feel like I stick out like a sore thumb in my teeny, tiny skirt and low-cut tank.

My eyes travel over to the girl standing next to MadDog, the president. She has long, dark hair and she looks to be around my age. MadDog wraps his hand around her waist and I blink in surprise. He's old enough to be my dad, but now that I look at him—not completely stressed out with a dead guy on my living room floor—I notice that he's hot. For a guy old enough to be my dad, he doesn't look it. His blond hair is just a little grey at the temples, and he's got a few wrinkles from being in the sun, but his body is tall and solid and he's a total silver fox.

"Hey, everyone. This is Ivy," West announces, shaking me out of my pervy thoughts about MadDog.

Everybody greets me with their names or road names, then MadDog smiles and introduces the girl at his side as Mary-Anne. He doesn't say that she's his Old Lady or anything, and it has me curious as to who exactly she is to him.

I look over to the bar and see my brother bellied up to it. I excuse myself and make my way over to him, West's eyes never leaving me. I can feel them on my back, burning into me with his intense gaze.

"I'm still fucking angry," I announce as I reach Barry's side.

"Yeah?" he grunts, tipping his head slightly to look at me.

"Fuck yeah, you beat the shit out of my boyfriend," I practically shriek.

"Don't fuck with the bull; you'll get the horns," he grumbles, sounding exactly like our dad. I wrinkle my nose at the phrase and he chuckles, taking a pull from his beer.

"One day you're going to come at me with some chick, and I'm going to beat the shit out of her just for the hell of it," I announce.

I watch as Barry throws his head back in laughter, his booming voice filling the room around us.

"You do that, baby sister, I'll fuckin' sell tickets to the public," he chuckles. I roll my eyes but give my big brother a hug, because I love the dumb bastard.

"Do it again and I'll make your life hell," I whisper against his ear.

"How?" he rumbles.

"I have all the baby albums," I explain before I turn and walk away from him.

As the night progresses, I look around and find that the scantily clad women from earlier are now naked women, and they're having sex, and everything else, with the rest of the men. Nobody seems to mind. Then my eyes find my brother's, and I gasp when I notice he's getting a blow job from one of the women.

My *brother*.

I honestly didn't know how tonight was going to go, but obviously he's in his element. He's perfectly content and disgusting all at the same time.

"Just don't look," Mary-Anne murmurs next to me, interrupting my thoughts.

"That's my brother," I groan, taking a drink of beer.

"Yeah, my brother is a Devil, but in Idaho," she grimaces. "The more you come, the more shit you'll see. Just think of it kinda like Vegas—what happens at the clubhouse stays at the clubhouse," she shrugs.

"So are you...?" I ask, moving my eyes to MadDog, whose hand has fallen down to her ass now.

"We're *something*," she smiles.

"Let's get the fuck to bed, baby," West whispers in my ear.

"We're too drunk to drive," I point out.

"Got a room here, babe. Come upstairs and fuck your man," he grunts, making me giggle.

"You better go take care of him, girl," Mary-Anne giggles.

"He ain't the only one needs some attention, sweetness," MadDog points out with a grin.

I wave to Mary-Anne and say goodbye as West drags me toward his room. Once we're inside and the door is locked, I turn around to face him and my belly clenches. His eyes are like liquid fire, and they're aimed right at me.

"Fucked you hard and fast earlier, baby. Now, I need you to ride me nice and slow," he murmurs.

"Yeah?" I breathe.

"Yeah. Then I'm gonna fuck you from behind. I've been thinking about that sweet ass all night, and I want to stare at it while my dick sinks into your tight pussy."

I can't stop my legs from quivering at his words. My pussy clenches and my nipples tighten. I want all of that, every single thing he's describing. West walks over to me and wraps his hands around my waist, yanking me into his chest. His lips brush mine.

"I love you, Ivy," he whispers against my lips.

"I love you too, West," I reply.

"Come ride my face, babe," he grins.

I don't respond. I don't need to. What woman is going to turn such an enticing offer down after a night of drinking beside her man?

I spend the night making love to him, then being fucked by him; and although there's a difference in the way he takes me, it's always consistently with love. He fills me with it from the inside out.

I know that this man, no matter how reckless he was by breaking the rules to be with me, he would never be reckless with me or my heart. He loves me with all that he is. I'm his, and he's mine, and together—we're going to make a beautiful life together.

One beautifully reckless moment at a time.

About Hayley Faiman

Hayley Faiman is an only child, born in California. She currently resides in Texas with her husband, of twelve years, their two boys, and a chocolate lab named Optimus Prime.

Website: hayleyfaiman.com/

Facebook: www.facebook.com/authorhayleyfaiman

Twitter: twitter.com/AuthorHayleyF

First Class Distraction

by Ruthie Henrick

One: LAYOVER

Blake

From my table along the outside railing of the airport bar, I could keep tabs on the other travelers as they made their way to or from their flight. It wasn't exciting, but it was a good way to kill some time until my plane departed. Mostly I kept tabs on the sexy as fuck woman seated halfway across the room nursing a girly drink with an umbrella. She was a contradiction.

I liked contradictions.

Hispanic with long, loose curls falling down her back, a little on the petite side, yet curvy in all the places a guy needed a handhold. She wore a halter dress in some lightweight stretchy fabric and a fun, bright crimson, yet she perched on the edge of her chair with her skirt draped over her knees and her handbag piled in her lap.

Her deep-set eyes darted around the area as if searching out terrorists who'd happened to elude TSA. She caught me watching her and froze, then relaxed into her seat, her dark gaze laughing. Her lips tugged up in a brilliant half smile. Definitely a contradiction.

My phone rang. Again. I let it go. My buddy Deke had been trying to reach me since before I left Honolulu this afternoon. My two-week hiatus was up and I was on my way home. I had paid a shitload of non-refundable cash for a tropical honeymoon it turned out I had no use for. Deke badgered me until I agreed a beach bungalow away from the wagging tongues of the Moreover gossipmongers would be a welcome reprieve. I let my ex hang around town and explain to everyone how she figured her dentist could give her a better life.

I should return Deke's call, but before I did, I let my phone rest in my palm while the woman across the room took a sip and slid her tongue over her glossy lips. Rosy, full, lush. Fuck. I did not need that shit in my life. I opened Deke's contact and typed in a text.

Me: Layover in LA. Red-eye home boards soon. I'll meet you at Baggage Claim. You still have the arrival time?

The woman across the room lifted her drink and met my gaze … Then sucked through her straw. Her cheeks hollowed and my dick twitched. Fuck. Me. Did she really just do that? Did she mean it for me? I glanced around. The tables on either side of me were vacant.

My phone dinged as Deke finally responded.

Deke: I have it. You could have called me back this morning.

Fucker. He was only pissed because I bailed on two weeks of basketball practice and the season opener was fast approaching. It was difficult enough for both of us to keep the boys focused on the court rather than the cheerleaders. I reached for my beer and drained it. Then flagged down my waitress. A few moments later she bounced over to my side. "Need a refill, hon?"

I slid my empty to the edge of the table. "Kim, right?" Her eyes lit, and she moved half a step closer till her tits were shoved into my arm. She gave me a smile she might imagine would earn her a bigger tip. It probably would have a month ago.

"I've got whatever you need, hon."

Twelve ounces, Kim. I tapped the rim of the empty Corona. "Um, yeah, another bottle."

Kim hung around for an expectant moment until she realized all I wanted from her was a little more beer. She noted my order on her pad and sulked off toward the end of the bar, bringing my lady back into view.

She was watching me. My heartrate picked up. What the fuck! I picked up my phone again.

Me: Dude, I'm waiting in a bar and this chick's eye-fucking me. I've been off the market too long. What do I do?

What was I thinking? Deke only had a clue when it came to Dixie. How would he know?

Deke: Ignore her! You're never touching another woman ever!

Point made.

Deke: Fuck, man! Dixie was looking over my shoulder. Are you sure about the girl? Because if you're sure, hit it!

Me: How do you know? What have you been reading?

Deke: Cosmo. Don't tell Dixie.

I laughed and dropped my phone to the table. Was I sure? Well, yeah. I knew the signals. I was rusty, but I'd been brushing up for the past two weeks. I had time before they called my flight. Enough to finish my beer and . . . practice.

My drink arrived and I dropped some money on Kim's tray, then ignored her as I focused on plump, shiny red lips wrapped around a thin plastic straw. And how they would feel stretched around my thick, pulsing cock. I considered walking over and introducing myself. We could finish our drinks, bore each other with small talk, then go our separate ways and never see each other again. I cast my glance in her direction again. She leaned forward, her shoulders pressed together, her cleavage gaping as she wrapped those lips I was obsessed with around her straw and slid it in and out. If she was trying to get my attention, she had it all. I relaxed back in my chair and lifted my bottle to her in a toast. If she wanted to put on a show for me, I'd sit right here and enjoy it. I wasn't fucking going anywhere.

A tall dude in a yuppie leather jacket and metro-styled hair stepped into view and scanned the open room as he oh-so-casually slid his ring off his left hand and slipped it into his pocket. He took off toward the bar like his hall pass expired any moment, and I let him go. I was just getting over the train wreck that was my own life. I had no desire to witness his.

I returned my attention to the table across the room to find the waitress clearing away the empty; my woman was gone. I'd only been distracted a minute; she couldn't have gone far. I craned my neck for a quick search and located her in a gate area across the concourse— *my* gate area, according to the lighted sign—joined by a pair of men. She held a Styrofoam cup of coffee with both hands and sipped from the slotted lid. The younger of the two men sat beside her, attempting to capture her hand between his. She batted him away. The jerk appeared to be in his early thirties, several years older than her, tall and wiry. The man pacing the floor before her, jacking his jaw and alternating between waving his arms and jabbing his sausage finger in her face, was stocky and gray.

The woman kept her eyes lowered and mouth pressed into a firm line while the older man blustered, but when grab-hands stood over her and planted his fists on his hips as garbage spewed from his thin lips, she surged to her feet. The next instant, her coffee flew at him and soaked his starched dress shirt. I was on my feet before the command to rise hit my brain. *What the everlovin' fuck, Blake?* I didn't even know this chick.

Her chin jerked up and her gaze met mine over the several yards that separated us, but she wasn't laughing this time. Oh, no. Girl was pissed. Her lips were flatlined, and she gave me a short shake of her head so I lowered myself back into my chair. Was she in trouble?

Within moments my woman had the situation under control, though, as she threw her handbag over her shoulder, then grabbed dickwad's soaked sleeve in one fist and Don Julio's shirt in the other and dragged them both down the walkway, jabbering in non-stop Spanish till they disappeared in the crowd. My grin stretched across my face. *Slam dunk!*

The attendant at my gate caught my attention when she announced boarding for First Class over the loudspeaker. My phone dinged again and I opened the text to read while I walked.

Deke: Shane will also be coming to the airport. The new principal is flying in from Los Angeles tomorrow, too. Isabel Fernandez. Maybe you'll see her.

I gulped my drink, then collected my backpack and made my way in line with my eyes on my phone. Deke must be bored. And have Dixie peeking over his shoulder again. His messages were beginning to sound like a girl.

Deke: Dixie wants to know what you thought of Hawaii. Have a good time? She's thinking honeymoon.

Jesus.

Me: Lot of sun. Lot of trees. Fucking lot of water.

Deke: Still an ass, I see. Still have the beard, too?

The result of my no-shave summer, and apparently, the straw that broke Donna's back. *Oh, yeah.* I stroked what was left of it after trimming it this morning, and out of the blue imagined rubbing the short scruff against the naked tawny skin of a fuckin' hot stranger.

Me: Best decision ever.

Two: SEAT ASSIGNMENT

Sophie

As quickly as I could in these ridiculous heels, I hurried back to my departure gate. The blood still pounded through my veins at the thought of Antonio's foolishness. If I had any lingering doubt that taking a new job on the other side of the country was the right move, it was just shot down. And what was that *idiota* thinking, dragging *mi papa* along to help change my mind? As if that would ever happen! It had been months since I broke up with him. My mind was set. And if I did not want to date him any longer, I sure as hell did not want to marry the overbearing ass.

It took every bit of patience and civility in me to help him refund the tickets he bought to pass through security. The only reason I did not let him eat the cost was I was afraid he would return to harass me even more. If I never saw him again in my lifetime, it would be a week too soon.

A crowd was gathered around a bank of monitors announcing arrivals and departures. I changed course and skirted the throng. I had just checked the status of my red-eye when I was at the ticket counter selling back the moron's tickets. Right on time, although I was so wound up I would not sleep for hours. *Damn those men!*

Ugh, mi papa! I would deal with him later. Or maybe I would give *mi mama* a call. She would take care of the problem with the notorious sharp edge of her tongue. The idea made me grin, but then I jerked out of my vindictive fantasy and halted mid-stride when I realized I was about to pass my gate.

The line to board snaked through the waiting area, and I took my place at the end behind a family with a young girl and a teenage son—who managed to give hormonal fourteen-year-old males the world over a bad rap by gluing his eyes to my chest. Where was Pokémon Go when I needed it? I tugged the edges of my denim jacket together and glared at him until his mom happened to notice and bopped him on his head. Was it bad I wanted to fist bump her?

Toward the head of the line, I spotted the guy from earlier in the bar—hot surfer type with a beard and tribal ink. The one I was flirting with only minutes before. The one who witnessed the showdown with my father and my ex. The dude was glued to his phone. Probably still saying good-bye to his girlfriend; he did not look *settled* enough to be a married man. He had played along, but then, an airport bar offered a great deal of anonymity. I was also someone I normally was not, brave and daring . . . and a little bit slutty. But he had every nerve ending in my body on high alert. Which was really too bad. I had lived in LA my entire life, where the guys were all the same. They might be pretty to look at, but they wore their brains somewhere south of their waistbands.

Thank God, the line started moving. Somewhere behind me a baby fussed. I knew the feeling. Overnight transcontinental flights were never fun. The best you could hope for was you fell asleep fast and the passenger beside you didn't snore. Or drool.

I craned my neck to look for the surfer dude once I got through the jetway and reached the door to the plane. I had heard grumblings about our flight being overbooked since I got in line, and once I saw how packed the coach section already was—and how many people were still behind me—the rumors seemed to have merit. It was disappointing, but not as much as realizing I had not caught sight of a dark beard on a casually dressed beach bum.

"Ticket, please." The flight attendant interrupted my musings and I opened the app on my phone to show her my seat assignment. "Twenty-Five-A," she directed, and pointed to my right. I was still behind the gawky teenager, but I had learned to deal with hormonal adolescents years ago. My immediate concern was to locate the seat number that matched my boarding pass. I remained a half step back to keep from kicking the wheeled carry-on ahead of me, and a moment later arrived at my destination. What I did not find was an empty seat.

As passengers bumped around me, I lifted my voice to reach the man dozing in the window seat. *My* window seat. "Sir. Sir! I believe you are in the wrong place. I have been assigned this seat." I held out my phone with the boarding pass app loaded. He stirred and glared at me through unfocused eyes.

"I'm sitting here. This is my seat. I have a boarding pass here somewhere." He patted his shirt pocket, then reached under the seat in front of him and produced a printout that matched the information on my phone app. *Exactly*. How could this be?

I let my eyes wander Coach to search for a flight attendant, but they were all occupied with seating the other passengers. I would have to return to the attendant who already helped me. Like a salmon swimming upstream, I fought my way back down the aisle as passengers found seats and loaded belongings in overhead compartments on either side of me. I was nearly breathless by the time I arrived at her side.

I pulled out my cell phone again and waited the few seconds it took for the boarding pass app to load. The man asleep in my seat was only one more frustration in a day—and night—full of them, but I was finally escaping the cage I had lived in my entire life. The hour was late and we were all tired, but I could manage this situation with grace. Make *mi mama* proud. I offered the attendant a smile when she gave me her attention.

"I am sorry to interrupt you, but it seems they double booked my seat." I offered her my phone, and again she peered at my electronic boarding pass. Then she glanced down the aisle way and at the clipboard in her hand. "Not a problem. Wait here and I'll be right back." She waded through the line of final people trying to find their seats until she came to my window seat over the wing. She woke the snoozing man again, and he snarled as he presented his boarding document. Her brow furrowed and she checked it again, then made her way back to me. With a determined set to her features, she grabbed the sleeve of another attendant who happened to pass by. "John, can you take over here for a moment, please? I need to seat this passenger." John simply nodded and took the clipboard from her, then resumed her duties.

I felt much like the child left standing in a game of musical chairs. I let my gaze sweep over the passengers one more time. Where was my sexy surfer? Would it not be something if he noticed me and stood... and announced the seat beside him was free?

The attendant led me out of Coach, swept the privacy curtain aside as we approached First Class, and I reluctantly abandoned my fantasy. She spoke over her shoulder as I stepped through to enter. "Don't worry. Follow me in here. Dan will have just the seat for you."

Three: TAKEOFF

Blake

I HADN'T BEEN SEATED LONG ENOUGH TO FINISH MY FIRST FREE beer when a commotion in the aisle alerted me that the window seat beside me wouldn't remain vacant after all. I raised my tray, and the swish of my girl's skirt brushed my bare legs as she passed in front of me. My heart gave a healthy kick. My cock gave a playful lurch as well, but I put an end to that shit immediately. I didn't even know her name.

The attendant helped her find overhead storage for her carry-on. Dan, his nametag said. Dude already looked tired, as if he couldn't wait for everyone to nod off so he could grab a nap, too. "We're almost ready to take off. Can I get you something to drink?"

We both turned to my new seatmate expectantly. She offered him a sweet smile. "Do you have lemonade?" *Innocent.* The cock tease from earlier realized maybe she'd gone overboard. *Dammit!*

Dan nodded. "Sure. A can okay?"

"A can is fine." And before he could turn to me she added, "And one of those little bottles of vodka." She showed me her laughing eyes. *Well, okay, then.*

I picked up my bottle to check the level. Dan raised a brow, guy code for *you gonna let the chick outdrink you? Fuck you, Dan.* I set the bottle back on my lowered tray. "Sure, bring me another." *Why the hell not?*

She'd added a short jacket over her dress since the bar, and covered a good amount of skin. *Too bad.* Our seats were wide and we had plenty of leg room. My seatmate possessed the beauty that inspired poets to write sonnets. But once she stowed her oversized handbag she turned to peer out the window. Into the black night. Where the only thing to see was pinpoints of light in the distance and our reflections in the open porthole.

I could let that go. Be a gentleman and allow her to pretend she hadn't been blowing a straw less than an hour ago to wind me up. But who was I kidding? There was no fun in that. I bristled my hand over the short whiskers on my cheek and made a show of checking my watch. "So, forty minutes ago your lips made my dick hard. Now we're strangers?"

She slammed the cover down over the glass and whipped her head my way; her hair flew to settle over her shoulders and curl over the curve of her breasts. Nice. Her cheeks had gone pink under the tan of her natural skin tone. "I . . . I . . ."

I let her off the hook and extended my hand. I even added a grin so she knew I was teasing. "I'm Blake." The cabin lights had been dimmed and individual spotlights were blinking off throughout our area. The older gentleman across the aisle from me was already snoring softly.

She put her much smaller hand in mine. It was soft and smooth. "Blake. I am . . . Sophie." She added a short nod at the end of her introduction, as though she needed to convince herself as much as me. "I should apologize." Her cheeks flushed to a deep shade. "My behavior—"

"Oh, please, don't apologize on my behalf." I laughed. "I enjoyed the hell out of it. Any time you feel the need to continue—"

"*Dios mio*," she groaned. "I was bored, and I tend to be . . . reckless . . . when I have too much time on my hands." She spread her hands helplessly. "I've never done anything like that before. My friend Melissa, she encourages me to be more outgoing since I broke up with my boyfriend, but I think maybe that is not what she has in mind, no?"

I chuckled. "Well, Sophie, unless your friend Melissa is a hooker, I think maybe no."

Sophie's mouth dropped open and her eyes rounded, then she dissolved into laughter. "Melissa?" Her voice rose in a squeak and got her laughing again. "Oh, no! Kindergarten. She is an angel with the little ones." There was a mixture of pride and mirth in her tone to go along with the amusement in her features. "As a matter of fact, she was also my kindergarten teacher so many years ago." One of Sophie's finely arched eyebrows rose. "She will retire soon, but she will enjoy knowing I listened to her advice. I do not think I will give her the details, though." Sophie giggled, but the laughter died in her throat and her hands flew to clutch the armrests when the plane's engines fired up and vibrated throughout the cabin. Her gaze darted from point to point.

"Relax. They're just starting the plane. You don't fly often, huh?" Muted instructions for the attendants came over the speakers from the cockpit. Someone closed the door to the jetway.

She shook her head. "Not often. But *mi papa*, he did not want me to drive all the way across the country alone."

I reached up and flicked off my reading light, leaving only Sophie's and one other some distance away. Dan arrived with our drinks and Sophie lowered her tray.

"Here, let me get that for you." I took her can and bottle from him so he wouldn't have to reach over me and set them on her tray. He handed me my new beer and grabbed my now-empty bottle. "Thanks, man."

Sophie opened her drinks and measured a portion of the liquor into the plastic cup Dan had also provided, then filled it with lemonade. It seemed an odd combination. I waved my finger to indicate her concoction. "That's really a thing, huh? Or did you just make it up?" She lifted her cup and took a sip, then considered me over the rim as the tip of her tongue swept her lips. My eyes followed the motion. She cocked her head, her face framed by a fall of thick, dark curls. Her glistening lips tipped up at the corners.

"You have never had a dirty Mexican?" *Fuck me.* Suddenly, my cock was jumping up and down and waving and volunteering as tribute. *Dirty Mexican? Yes, please!*

Hit it. I took a tropical vacation and came up empty. But I had a feeling my two-week dry spell might end in the last place I would have imagined.

Four: CRUISING ALTITUDE

Sophie

Oh, Sophie, when will you learn to be more careful *what you wish for?* The man was delicious to look at with his combination of dark hair and brilliant blue eyes. His T-shirt strained over his muscular biceps and fell smoothly over what appeared to be a rock-solid torso. Little tremors kicked up in my belly, and my breasts seemed fuller and heavier in the halter top of my dress. The engine grew suddenly louder, and my tremoring heart now felt as though it would beat out of my chest. My hands gripped the armrests so tightly I could not feel my fingertips.

"Sophie."

I closed my eyes. The plane started moving down the runway faster and faster . . .

"Sophie!"

We lifted into the air with a jolt, and my thundering heart fell to my stomach. Warm, calloused hands covered mine, and my eyes flew open. Blake was there, his nose on mine, the smell of beer in my face, his soothing southern accent that had come as a sweet surprise calming me.

"It's only a lot of noise. Everything is fine. We're right here buckled in our seats and safe. I'm right here with you. It will be over soon." He crooned as my nana would to a fussing child. I nodded as though I understood, but I did not understand.

I loosened my grip but did not pull my hands out from under his. Truthfully, the heat and weight of them was pleasant. I lowered my voice to a murmur as the only sound in our section of the plane seemed to come from our seats. The one other light had been flicked off moments ago, turning my reading lamp into a spotlight. "Thank you. I am being ridiculous. Look around us; none of the other passengers are freaking out."

Blake's eyes did not stray from my face. "I don't want to look anywhere else." He turned my palms over in his and linked our fingers. It was an oddly intimate thing to do. I hardly knew him. Yet, I played sexy games with him in the bar because I was attracted to him. We were becoming more and more alone in our corner of the airplane, with passengers surrendering to sleep all around us.

Eyes dark and cloudy, Blake released my hands to turn off my light and throw us into shadows. As he lowered his arm, he lifted the divider between us and his face was close enough for me to cup his cheek and feel the soft bristles of his beard on my palm. He lifted both of his hands to my jaw and ran one thumb along my chin. And then my lower lip. The vodka had done its job. I kept my eyes locked on his and parted my lips, then touched the tip of my tongue to his thumb. His chest expanded in his snug T-shirt as he inhaled a deep, choppy breath.

He drew me closer until our cheeks rubbed together, the soft hairs of his beard prickly against my sensitive skin. Warm air caressed my earlobe when he whispered in my ear, "There's about to be another really loud noise. Just go with it." And then his mouth was on mine.

Heat and wet and tongues sliding together. My hands found his shoulders, and then his chest, and I may have pawed at him through his shirt. In the background, behind the thrashing of my blood and the pounding of my heartbeat, I registered the loud, grinding noise Blake warned me of. I broke away to look up at him with the question in my eyes. Then I realized he could not see me in the dark, but I was not afraid. Not now. "What is that?"

His hands framed my face, holding me as he whispered in the dark. "Landing gear." His thumb traced my lip again, and I drew it into my mouth. His lips turned up around it, and his smile gleamed. "You like playing games, do you?" All around us, our fellow passengers were sleeping. The flight attendant who brought our drinks had pulled the curtain to separate their darkened area.

I grinned back at Blake. Until he dragged his thumb from my mouth, letting the collected moisture chase it and trickle down my chin. My heart skipped a beat as my eyes found his and our gazes locked. In a swift, sure movement he spread his hand along my jaw and thrust his thick middle finger between my lips. The length of it slipped deeper and deeper into the hot, wet, dark space and slid over the smooth surface of my tongue.

¡Dios mio! My sex clenched as my tongue circled his digit the same way I teased him with the straw. But this time, I was my own victim. I clutched his forearms to keep from mauling him. Or something. The background hum of the engine, the slight jostling of the plane in the air, the fullness of Blake's thick finger bumping the back of my throat as it pulsed in and out of my mouth were more effective than any sex toy I'd ever played with.

The plunging neckline of my dress was not designed for wearing a bra, and my ragged breaths dragged my bare breasts against the fabric until my nipples were stiff and achy. I needed . . . I needed . . . "Blake . . ." My whisper was a shadow in the darkened cabin, but he was so focused on me that he was already aware. He drew his finger from between my parted lips and trailed it down my chin, and then my throat. Then his lips swooped down to cover my mouth and his tongue glided in to replace it, flicking against mine with a never-ending series of licks and swipes.

¡Ay, Dios! His lips were firm but surprisingly soft against mine. My hands slid down his arms to land on his T-shirt—and the firm muscles of his torso beneath the soft fabric I wanted to bury my hands in. Was his skin smooth or did he have a crisp matting of hair on his chest?

"Blake!" I threw my head back and nearly forgot my surroundings when his roaming hand slid in the low cut front of my dress to cover my sensitive breast. When he rolled my nipple between his fingers, I cast my face forward to bite his shoulder. If I screamed, we would wake the entire plane. My center pulsed and throbbed, my desire so acute it was painful. I lowered one hand to cup it. If I rubbed just a little . . .

Blake's chuckle vibrated through my chest that seemed suddenly fuller. "I think I can help you with that, baby." He turned so he sat with his back to the aisle, and as if I were a rag doll, turned me on the seat so my back leaned against his upright chest, my feet planted on the wide leather cushion. A thin airline blanket appeared from nowhere to cover my lower half as he spread my knees and lifted my skirt. But his hand... His fingers dove into my panties to spread my sensitive, swollen lips, then unerringly found that bundle of nerves that begged for attention. He alternated slow circles followed by rapid pulses and I pitched and bucked into his hand, biting my lip to remain silent. I tilted my head back to watch his face as he pleasured me. Eyes dark, lips parted, chest heaving with his shifting breaths. My breath stuttered as his hand claiming my breast pinched my nipple and then rolled it to soothe it. On and on, slow, quick, pinch, roll until I was sure I would lose my mind.

His erection was a steel rod that poked against my back. The friction of it when I moved my hips only added to my frustration. Panting, I yanked his hand out of my panties. "I want you, Blake." My voice was shaky with pent up need. *How horny could one woman possibly get?* I had a feeling my First Class distraction was a bad boy, and I wanted his naked body in my hands. His fascinating tats exposed to me. His solid muscles under my fingers. His rigid cock in my mouth. This flight would end soon, and I would go back to my ordinary life. But for these few hours I was in a bubble, insulated from the outside world. Nobody knew who I was; nobody knew how boring my life had become. I could be Sophie from LA, who was fun. And a little bit slutty. I allowed my lips to form a self-satisfied grin. Even the thought of it would bring mi papa after me with a shotgun.

Five: TURBULENCE

Blake

"Goddamn, Sophie, I smell you, and it's so fucking hot." I inhaled and let the aroma of her desire fill my senses. "I can taste you, and I haven't put my mouth on anything except your lips. That ends now." She swallowed a gasp when I grazed her earlobe between my teeth, then trailed my way down her throat. My hands covered her breasts over the flimsy material of her dress. I wanted to yank her jacket down to trap her arms, rip her clothes away until she was naked and spread out before me. But that was a fantasy for another lifetime. When I wanted my own woman again. When I cared to be caught. Tonight was . . . what?

Tits jiggling in my face begging to be sucked. Hips, soft and fleshy, for my palms to grasp. After our flirtation at the bar, Sophie and I were both after the same prize tonight. A harmless distraction. She wanted to get off with no strings attached. My dick was cool with that.

She reclined against the window, the unused blanket wadded behind her back as a pillow. Her legs were spread wide, one foot propped on the seat cushion, the other slid to the floor. I inched forward to nuzzle the cleavage between her breasts and caught the light musky scent of her arousal. My cock throbbed in my shorts. Her nipple poked my cheek. I towered over her on my knees, grinning at her through the dark. The safety lights in the ceiling gave the area an otherworldly feel, and the soft snores from all around us assured us we were still quite alone.

I unfastened her dress at the nape and her heavy breasts fell free. She was perfection, and I took a moment to appreciate the gift. This girl was sin wrapped in feisty confidence. It was almost too bad I'd never see her again. Almost.

Her areolas were dark and puckered, her nipples engorged. *So pretty.* I lifted the weighted mounds in my palms and flicked my thumb across one. She arched her back with a sharp inhale. The dusky target shot straight to my mouth. *Two points.*

Her hands groped in the dim light until they found a place to land. One found a home on my bicep and gripped as my arm flexed beneath her fingertips. Her other hand landed midway up my thigh and even now was burrowing through the leg of my shorts. I had a better idea...

I released her breast and covered her hand, then slid back so I rested on my feet. I reclined a little further and brought her with me. "Baby, what about..." I removed her hand from under the wide hem and lifted it over the tent that was about to cause permanent damage to a favorite part of my anatomy. My hips jerked when her fingers wrapped around my cock through the thin fabric of my basketball shorts. Dude was straining to get out. Weeping for it. I was on board.

Sophie faced me on both knees, breasts barely concealed by the short denim jacket she wore over her dress. The dress that now hung from her waist. This girl. Whoever she was, she was the last thing I expected to find tonight. After two weeks of tropical boredom, I was ready to return to my students, to the team, and hit it hard. I was good. And the ex had better be happy with the dentist she traded me in on because I had no more use for the ball and chain. Donna who? Fuck her.

Sophie's rounded breasts swung free when she leaned forward to kiss me. Her lips were soft and sweet, her tongue testing now that she was the one initiating a kiss. Fuck that. I grabbed the back of her neck, pulled her close, and showed her I didn't mind if she sucked my face on her way to sucking me off. With her tongue working the interior of my mouth and her hand working my dick like a porn star, the only thing that could make it better was a little skin on skin...

Fingers splayed, her free hand traveled up my torso, bunching up my shirt as it moved upward. I sucked in a breath as her fingers grazed over each of my abs. She spread her hands over the width of my pecs, and without warning, pinched a nipple. I about came in my pants. "Fuck, Sophie!" I yanked her hands away and trapped them behind her back. Her back arched and forced the jacket to fall away. Her tits grazed my chest. *Oh, that was nice.*

"Blake." Her lips left my mouth to travel down the rasp of my chin and took my earlobe between her teeth. She murmured soft words into my ear. Melodic, foreign. I didn't understand a goddamn thing she said.

Her lips lowered to lick at the flat disc, then suck my nipple into her mouth. Jesus Christ, that was hot! She moved lower over my abs, her head bobbing as she retraced the path her hands had taken only minutes ago. I had a fucking puddle on the front of my shorts, and my dick was about to poke through the nylon fabric of my shorts.

Someone grunted and snuffled in the aisle seat two rows up and I froze. Dear God, no! Not with Sophie's mouth and her tits and her hands all promising magic. *For the love of God, go back to sleep!*

Sophie continued to kiss her way down my stomach. She lapped at the trail of short hairs that led into my waistband. Her tits bumped my dick through a fucking thin barrier that I wanted gone like now. The curtain to the attendant's quarters scraped open. *Fuck, no!* Sophie's breasts grazed against my cock with every one of her movements. God, what I still imagined doing with those tits. When she grabbed my elastic waistband, it took every bit of my willpower to stop her hands.

Six: FINAL APPROACH

Sophie

BLAKE STILLED MY HANDS FROM UNCOVERING HIS COCK, AND I was ready to scream all the obscenities my three brothers taught me over the course of my lifetime. In both my languages. My blood pounded hot through my veins, and pulsed and throbbed between my thighs. I was amped and lethargic at once, and frantic for relief. If I had known I would need my vibrator, I would not have packed it away in the luggage compartment. "Damn it, Blake, this flight will be over soon. I want..."

His cock was still stretching out his silky shorts, clearly outlined, and I longed to explore his buried treasure. I reached for his waistband again. I needed him in me—some part of him in some part of me—but he clamped his fingers around my wrists. "Baby, *shh*. Listen."

Listen? What? My eyes darted over his shoulder to search the darkened compartment. Then I heard it. The low mumble of conversation and a quiet racket coming from the attendants' area. *¡Madre de Dios, no!* Desperation flooded me. Not now. Not yet. My gaze flew back to meet Blake's. "Perhaps someone only wished for a Coke, and they will soon buckle back in their seat?" Everything else seemed normal, although who could hear over the rumble of the elderly gentleman snoring across the aisle?

Blake bracketed my face in his hands and pressed his lips to mine. Smooth and gentle, dry lips pressed together, a first date peck. Not the frenzied, erotic kiss he gave me five minutes ago. And not the connection I had wanted in the seconds before I fed his cock into my mouth to see how far down my throat it would go.

I reached up to pull his hands to my breasts. The mass of them overfilled his large palms, and when he massaged his thumbs over the uber sensitive nipples, I had to swallow a moan. Blake's hips bucked beneath my own. "Soph." He straightened one of his legs and I moved to straddle his thigh. "There you go, baby." He lifted the fabric of my skirt so I no longer sat on it, then reached beneath it to slide my panties to the side. "Ride me, baby."

When I leaned forward, I could slide my breasts close enough for him to latch on with his mouth. He stroked me with his tongue and then sucked me in. The dart of impatient desire shot directly to my clit. Blake urged me toward a climax with determined purpose. He slid one finger, then two inside me as he flicked his thumb on my clit. I humped his leg to the steady, frustrated rhythm of his hips jerking up to bump his cock against my core.

With Blake's hand occupied, my breasts swung free to graze against the line of crisp hair on his abdomen where his shirt had been lifted. The rasp of my overly sensitive skin against the coarse trail was nearly punishing, and it sent a volley of needy sensation throughout my limbs.

Blake's first two fingers thrust in and out of my core, his thumb circled and flicked, his hips jerked against me as he desperately sought his own release. The pitch of the plane's engine changed. Lowered. "We have only minutes, *papi*." We were about to lose our seclusion. "I can wait no longer. Please . . ." This time, he did not argue when I lowered his shorts and exposed his erection. Long. Thick. Angry red, a drip of thick fluid clinging to the tip.

I pushed myself up his body, letting the solid length of him glide down the center of my torso until I thrust my tongue into his mouth in a kiss that was impatient and demanding. His cock was not the only thing angry. His erection rested against his belly, and I released his mouth with regret to slide back down to where it waited.

When I arrived, I let it slide between the fullness of my breasts, cupping it, trapping it, even as my nipples rubbed furiously over the cleanly trimmed area of his groin. I rocked back and forth over the hard length of him, letting him pull nearly out before I hid him again within my flesh. "Blake, please tell me you enjoy this." I imagined this was close to heaven. I closed my eyes to savor the feeling and was surprised at the explosion of pleasure that attacked me. It was fireworks and shooting stars—

"Sophie!" Blake's hands disappeared. His hips stilled.

Not yet! "Tell me this feels good to you, too." I nipped at his ab and stroked his pre-cum slickened erection between my swollen breasts. I rubbed my thighs together to create the friction I now missed. *I was so close!*

"Sophie!" Contact vanished between my breasts and Blake's erection. I opened my eyes to find Blake's beautiful blue unwavering gaze, dark with desire as he slid my halter between us and fastened it to cover my exposed skin. The first dim overhead lights flashed on to reveal a cabin full of sleepy passengers in various stages of wakefulness.

Blake lifted his shorts from his rapidly deflating erection, and I scrambled off his legs and to my seat by the window. We had mere seconds to right our clothing, our hair, our attitudes before we were discovered. Blake was already situated in his wide leather seat, wrestling with his restraint as if nothing was amiss. I pulled a brush from the bag I had stashed. My clothing and hair I could manage. But the fevered blood still buzzing through my veins told me I clearly needed to get myself together before our plane reached the airport and I had to make a good first impression. My new life depended on it.

Seven: ROUGH LANDING

Blake

Sitting beside Sophie as we awaited our landing was both the same as and different from preparing for takeoff. Her window was uncovered again, and intermittent streaks of lightning flashed in the rain-streaked glass as we bounced through the turbulent sky. She kept her gaze determinedly focused out the window, but this time there was plenty to command her attention.

"Hey, Sophie." The first time she startled at the flash of light in the distance, I reached for her hands bundled together in her lap.

"No. No." She slipped her palms out of mine and wrapped them together again. But not before I caught sight of her luscious breasts heaving with her heavy breaths. A hint of her profile and the high color that had stolen over her cheeks. The tears that glossed her chocolate brown eyes. Was she afraid? Angry? I was growing hard in my shorts again and it fucking pissed me off. Why did this woman leave me with no more control than the horny high schoolers I dealt with back home? I wasn't looking for love—wasn't looking for a committed relationship. But we were both headed somewhere near the same place, and this woman knew how to use her body to rock my world. Might be nice to have her on speed dial.

I reached for a single hand and entwined our fingers. My skin was tanned from days basking in the tropical sunshine. Hers was genetics.

Again she pulled away. "I am fine. Thank you."

She pulled her legs up onto the seat and tugged her dress down over her knees. I didn't hear another word from her, so I let her be. *Well, fuck.*

With a few hours' sleep behind them, the passengers in our section of the plane were stirring, stretching, standing in line for a turn at the restroom. Reading lights popped on one by one. Dan made his way down our aisle with a cart of breakfast.

I lowered my tray, which finally drew Sophie's attention from the gray clouds and flashes of light. Now that my cock was tucked away, it seemed she didn't find me any more interesting than the weather, but bring on eggs and OJ, and she was all in.

I took a quick inventory of Dan's offering when he stopped beside me. "Bagel and orange juice, thanks." Dan handed me my food. Sophie hadn't spoken up yet so I raised a brow. "Don't think he's serving lemonade this morning."

Her eyes widened and her brow creased just long enough for me to feel like a prick before she smoothed out her features and offered Dan an apologetic smile. "The cranberry juice sounds nice, please."

We ate and drank in silence and had just finished when Dan reappeared with his clattering cart to collect our empties. I stretched my neck to peer out the porthole as he reached for Sophie's trash, then relaxed back in my seat. "How much longer until we reach our destination?"

Dan opened his mouth to answer, and at that same moment, the grinding gnash of gears signaled the landing gear being deployed. Dan nodded. "Not much longer now. Y'all will want to lift your trays and keep your seatbelts fastened."

It had been an endless day of travel for me, and very little sleep the night before. For Sophie, too, I imagined, and then it was compounded by the emotional upheaval brought on by our mind-blowing—if unfulfilled—sexcapades. I turned my head to study her profile, which finally seemed more relaxed. A couple of times during the night we were frantic about our lack of privacy, our vanishing window of time, but it was all a part of the game.

Game? Our clock was running down, and the buzzer was about to go off. I had to score soon because there would be no chance at extra periods.

"So, this new job you're moving to Tennessee for. What will you be doing?"

She leveled a perfectly sensible gaze on me. "No, Blake. We will not start the small talk now. I'm very glad I had a chance to meet you. We had a mostly enjoyable flight." The corners of her lips kicked up.

"I think we will both go home and finish what we started, no?" Fuck! This woman with the fabulous tits, the body of a goddess, the lips I'd jack off to the moment I got home...

The plane dove in a wide arc as it made its final approach and I waited for her to cry out. To clutch at the armrests—or me. When she didn't, I leaned forward to catch her eye. "You're only afraid to go up, not afraid of going down?"

She shrugged. That bare shoulder under my lips was smooth and scented. Entirely feminine. "Perhaps I only have the fear when it is dark."

My heartbeat increased. She was slipping away. "What if I need you to hold my hand so I'm not afraid?" I added a teasing grin—hoped it was playful and not desperate. Would she give me a smile in return? I'd seen her smile. Knew her lighthearted side. *Dammit, Sophie. What if it wasn't the storm I was afraid of?*

The plane's wheels hit the tarmac and in fraught silence we rolled to the jetway and jerked to a stop.

Eight: BAGGAGE CLAIM

Sophie

As soon as the seat belt light dinged off, it was chaos in the plane as everyone stood to reach for their stored belongings. They were eager to leave the confined space, but then, so was I. Without much effort I could be coerced into continuing this relationship with Blake. But, no! I was only now beginning my own life. Without a father deciding where I worked. Where I lived. Without a brother deciding who I dated.

Blake rose with the backpack he had stored at his feet. At a break in the stream of traffic, he stepped into the aisle, then waited while I stepped before him. His hand on my arm made me look back and glance at my abandoned seat. "Did I leave something—"

He paused before answering, his touch heavy on my sleeve. "No. I want your number."

I rolled my eyes. "You are a stubborn man. Wherever you are from, it cannot be near where I am moving. It is a small town. The people all know each other." I continued to walk until I was off the plane and amid the crowd hurrying down the jetway. Blake came up beside me.

"How do you know I'm not nearby? What's the name of your town?"

Was the man obtuse? I halted in the midst of the sea of moving bodies to gape at him, then continued to move with the flow. "Blake, what we had was nice. Pleasant." He raised an eyebrow. I shrugged. "I am not your hookup. I have a life and a serious career. I must protect those things."

I followed the directional sign to Baggage Claim, Blake's possessive hand at the small of my back and my heels clacking on the floor tiles. I had two large suitcases to collect, both brand new. Red, which I determined was my new signature color. *Bold.* I had given everything in my apartment—*everything except my clothes*—to my sister who was moving into her first apartment. In a sense, we were both starting over.

At the baggage terminals, I lost sight of Blake. Perhaps he had no luggage to collect and left without saying good-bye. My heartbeat tripped over that thought until I reminded it that was probably for the best. *New job. New life. No time for a new love also.*

I spotted one of my suitcases on the conveyor belt and shouldered my way through the crowd. It was tempting to put my uncomfortable high heels to use, but I was a newcomer to this area where I hoped the people would warm to me; so instead, I used care not to step on toes. By the time I arrived, a tall—*very tall, impossibly handsome*—man with his dark hair up in a man bun had already wrestled my bag to the floor and was reaching for the second. He hefted it to stand beside the first. Blake accepted a large postcard from a third man, folded it and stashed it in his backpack. They did that handshake, shoulder grab, chest bump guy thing; then my hero approached Blake and they executed an elaborate handshake fist bump performance that only longtime friends cared about remembering.

As they apparently knew each other, I left them to catch up and let my eyes slide over the periphery of the crowd. From time to time one or more of them peered over at me as though he was solving a puzzle.

I was to be picked up by a member of the school board. A man I had spoken to on the telephone, but had never met in person. I had tried to stalk him on Facebook and LinkedIn to find a photograph but had no luck. *Who did not have a social media profile?*

"Sophie, come on over here. I'd like you to meet a couple of my friends." Blake waved me over to his little reunion. I moved to stand beside my luggage, stepping from one foot to the other in the uncertainty of my present situation.

He jabbed the tall guy in the arm. "This is Deke McAllister. We work together."

Deke stuck out his hand. "How was your trip?"

I let the corners of my lips climb and met Blake's gaze as I answered Deke. "Memorable." Blake snorted.

Then Blake's introduction registered and my heart thumped in my chest. McAllister. *McAllister?* But Deke. That was not the correct name. Blake indicated the third man, maybe in his early thirties. "This is Deke's brother, Shane. He's the local vet in our town. Volunteers on the school board. Great guy."

Por Dios, of all the guys I could meet in all the bars . . . I lifted my eyes to meet Deke's gaze, and he was laughing. Amused as though he already had this figured out. Had *me* figured out. I had no words, but I managed to meet Shane McAllister's outstretched palm in a handshake. "It is very nice to meet you, Mr. McAllister. And I appreciate the opportunity to work in your school."

He laughed. "Not my school personally, and your resume speaks for itself. You come highly recommended, and I'm sure you'll do an excellent job for our students and our community. We welcome you to Moreover. Now, let's get you there, shall we?" He released the handle to one of the suitcases and tipped it on its wheels. I took the pull-out handle of the companion luggage and followed him toward the exit.

Blake and his friend Deke followed close behind. I kept my hearing tuned to their conversation—it seemed everything Blake did was zeroed in on my radar. I was nearly to the automatic glass door—nearly to freedom—when Blake called to me from behind. Shane and I both stopped walking. Blake jogged to meet me and took the suitcase from my hand. "We're not done, Sophie. Not by a goddamn longshot."

He cupped my jaw in both hands, much as he had the night before in the quiet and the dark. When we were alone, not surrounded by a building full of strangers.

He lowered his face until his forehead pressed against mine. Our noses bumped. Our lips brushed.

Then fused.

Blake's tongue traced the seam of my lips and parted them, then swept the inside of my mouth while the warmth of his hands bracketed my face. I found my hands whispering up the front of his T-shirt. The same soft fabric I shoved up over his abs so I could explore his sun-kissed-skin with soft nibbles. My palms reached his shoulders, and I hung on as our kiss grew fevered, desperate, punishing. Did he understand how badly I hated to say good-bye? I wrapped my forearms around his neck and clung as our kiss pushed all our limits. When Blake's hands stroked the sides of my torso, and his thumbs grazed my breasts, the sensation awoke me to the realization of our surroundings. Shane and Deke stood side by side, both breathless with laughter.

Shane McAllister recovered himself and once again moved toward the exit doors. I pulled my arms away from Blake's neck, stepped back with a final brush of his whiskers against my palm, reclaimed my suitcase. What a terrible first impression I must be making!

Blake's friend Deke wheezed and nearly choked on his words. "What the fuck was that?"

His exclamation sent Shane into another round of chuckles.

Blake's gaze—as blue as the Pacific we left behind us, more full of self-assured promise than the kiss we just shared—locked on mine. "The start of overtime."

I lowered my brow. *This man.* "What does that . . . What do you—"

"Miss Fernandez, you coming?" I glanced at Shane, waiting near the door, then back at Blake, who wore a smug grin on his face. I must leave. Get away from here. My heart would only be safe if our paths never crossed again.

¡Ay, Dios mio! Overtime?

About Ruthie Henrick

Ruthie's an Arizona girl, married to her high school sweetheart and mama to three grown sons. She writes contemporary romance with heroes who make you swoon, yet might live right next door. She's a true romance junkie and a lifetime avid reader who spent far too much time shushing the voices in her head—until the day she sat down at her keyboard to see what all those voices had to say.

She's a big fan of coffee and easy to cook meals, and she loves country music. It's generally the soundtrack to whatever she has going on. At work, doing housework, in the car—the music is always on. Except when she writes—that she does in silence.
Ruthie loves chatting with other readers, sharing her favorite books and authors, and discovering those new to her. Go by and hang out with her on any of her social media!

Facebook: bit.ly/RuthieHenrick

Instagram: instagram.com/ruthiehenrick

Pinterest: www.pinterest.com/ruthiehenrick

Twitter: twitter.com/RuthieHenrick

Goodreads: bit.ly/1fah8dG

Opening Hearts

By Jerica MacMillan

Hannah watched the blond surf instructor while he taught his little group of students. There weren't many other people on the beach, so their activity naturally drew her attention. And the instructor's tall form encased in black neoprene that molded to his athletic body was droolworthy enough to draw attention. He'd led his students right past her and Elena where they played in the water, his blue eyes locking with hers, spray from the water catching in the scruffy stubble on his face. She'd been stunned into immobility by the electricity that ran through her when their gazes met, unable to look away, even though it embarrassed her to have been caught checking him out.

She tried to ignore them the rest of the time, but was largely unsuccessful. Elena kept giving her shit about it. "I think you might have some drool there," she said at one point, wiping at her own chin.

Hannah narrowed her eyes at her best friend. "Haha. Shut up." Elena cackled and went back to the book she'd brought with her. Hannah tried to focus on her book—she was rereading *Harry Potter* for the millionth time. It seemed like appropriate vacation reading. And while Harry, Ron, and Hermione could usually keep her attention, today they were usurped by the surf god carelessly straddling his surfboard, bobbing on the waves, watching his students take turns trying to surf. He made it look effortless when he caught a wave while his students watched. She wished she could be in his class. Maybe she could convince Elena to take a surf lesson with her. If they dragged Elena's fifteen-year-old brother along, maybe they'd have enough for a group lesson.

"What's that face?"

Hannah turned to look at Elena, consciously relaxing the wrinkle in her nose. "Nothing."

"You looked like you smelled something bad. What are you thinking?"

Hannah shrugged. "It's nothing, really. I was just thinking." On second thought, having Elena's little brother along for a surf lesson didn't sound like such a great idea after all. In fact, she didn't even really want Elena along. Maybe the surf god gave private lessons. Should she ask him?

"You should talk to him when he's done."

Hannah whipped around to stare at Elena again. "What?"

Elena laughed again. "The surf instructor. You keep staring at him. Just talk to him. Give him your number or ask for his. *For God's sake, do something.*"

"You really think I should?"

"Yes. Totally. What's the worst that could happen?"

"He could laugh in my face."

Elena shrugged, her eyes going back to her book. "So? It's not like you'll ever see him again. And if you do, it'll only be around here. We'll go home in a few weeks and then you'll definitely never see him again. But the way he was looking at you when he walked past, I doubt he'll laugh at you."

Hannah nodded, thinking about it some more. Yeah, she'd wait until his students left, and then she'd ask about surf lessons. That could work.

Decision made, she tried to go back to her book, but she kept reading the same page over and over. Eventually she just gave up and closed the book, setting it aside and watching the end of the surf lesson. Her heart rate kicked up when she realized they were all heading back toward shore. It must be over. Soon, she'd have to stand up and walk over to him. She hoped she didn't stutter or sound like a complete idiot.

She kept her eyes on him the whole time, blushing when he walked back up the beach and caught her staring. But she couldn't help it. Especially after his students left and he pulled down the top of his wetsuit, the sun pouring over his bare torso. He faced mostly away from her, and his muscles rippled along his back as he bent to pull a water bottle out of a backpack, his head tipping back as he guzzled the water, his longish hair slicked back away from his face.

"You better get over there before he leaves or something."

Elena's voice startled her out of her examination of the newly revealed parts of his body. "Right. Good point." She pulled her feet under her, kicking hot sand on the edge of their beach blanket. Her stomach twisted with nerves, and her heart rate sped higher as she approached him.

He faced away from her so she cleared her throat, but he didn't turn, the sound lost in the surf and wind before it reached him. Gathering up her courage, she pitched her voice to be heard clearly above the ambient noise. "Do you ever teach private surf lessons?"

The water bottle came down and he turned, his eyes wandering over her body before they met hers. "Yeah, I take on private students."

The words in his deep voice sent a thrill through Hannah. She shifted her feet, trying to seem cool and unaffected. "Oh, um. So, how do I sign up? Do you work for a surf shop or something? Or can I just give you my number?" Oh God. Really? Did she just offer to give him her number? Obvious much?

A slow smile spread across his face. "Sure. I'd love to get your number. You sure you just want surf lessons?"

Heat spread down her chest, and she could see his eyes tracking the flush taking over her body that she couldn't possibly blame on the sun. "Well, uh, yeah. Surf lessons sound like fun." She flapped a hand at the water. "You seem like a good teacher."

He shifted closer, his blue eyes twinkling. "Oh, I am."

She tried to keep her eyes on his face, which wouldn't normally be a challenge with his strong cheekbones, bright blue eyes, straight nose, wide mouth with full, slightly chapped lips that curved at the corners, and the dusting of scruff she noticed earlier, like he hadn't bothered shaving in a few days. Except that his ripped torso was on display in front of her, and good Lord, he didn't look like he had a spare ounce of fat anywhere. He was tall and lean, his pecs and biceps bulging as he flexed his hands around his water bottle, his abs rippling when he bent to retrieve his phone from his backpack.

When he stood back up, her eyes traveled slowly back to his face, taking in the V at his hips, the golden happy trail that caught the sunlight, and his flat, brown nipples that tipped the bulges of his pecs. He winked at her when her eyes met his again, and she blushed even more. She must look about the same color as a lobster. And in only a bikini, the blush that covered almost her entire torso was on full display. Fan-freaking-tastic.

He raised an eyebrow, his smile growing wider at her body's response, and held out his phone. "Here, why don't you put in your number. I'll check my schedule at the surf shop, and we can coordinate a time for you to get lessons. My name's Matt, by the way."

She took the phone, her fingers brushing his, and she had to stop herself from swaying toward him and making an even bigger fool of herself. But she smiled wide, unable to contain her giddiness at getting his name and programming her phone number into his phone. "I'm Hannah."

"Nice to meet you, Hannah." He crossed his arms over his chest, his pecs and biceps bulging once more and distracting her. He chuckled, a low sound that she almost couldn't hear over the crash of the waves and the wind whipping past them. "Are you going to just hold my phone, or are you going to give me your number?"

She ripped her eyes away from his chest, prickly heat washing over her once more. Good God, she needed to get a handle on her blushing around this guy. What the hell was wrong with her? She typed her full name—Hannah Glover—and handed his phone back to him.

He typed something into it, then smiled at her before tucking it back into his backpack. "I just sent you a text, so now you have my number too. I was going to surf for a while longer today. I'd offer to give you a lesson now, but you don't have any equipment, so I'll check in with the surf shop later this afternoon. Then we can touch base tonight. Sound good?"

She nodded, trying not to seem overeager, but probably failing. "That sounds great!" The huge grin on her face still wouldn't calm down to a normal, polite smile. But Matt just grinned back at her, obviously not put off by her enthusiasm.

"If you want, we could meet up later to discuss the schedule. There's a group of us getting together at the Jetties at eight. Wanna come?" He lifted his chin over her shoulder, indicating where Elena sat. "You can bring your friend, if you want."

Hannah stopped breathing for a second. This super hot surf god was inviting her to hang out with his friends? "Yes, please!" she blurted out before she could stop herself, probably louder than necessary, too.

He laughed, but not in a mean way. "Great. I'll see you there, then."

"Yeah. Good. Okay. See you then." She turned away and walked back to Elena before he could see her blush yet again. Good Lord, she was blushing way too much today. Hopefully tonight she could keep a handle on it.

Matt sat in the sand, his long sleeve t-shirt pulled down to protect his arms from the chill in the air this late in the evening. He glanced at his phone again, checking the time. Eight twelve. He'd said eight o'clock, and he'd been so antsy that he'd gotten here early, helping Ben, his friend from high school, get the fire started. The others sat closer to the fire, talking and laughing, a few people already dancing to the music playing on a speaker dock for an old school iPod that someone had brought. And Hannah was late. He swigged his beer, his eyes scanning the bluff hiding the parking lot. Should he text her? See if she was still coming? Or—

Someone bumped his shoulder and he turned to see Ben standing next to him, his hairy legs sticking out of a pair of tan cargo shorts next to Matt's shoulder. "Dude, what are you doing? You were here early. I figured you'd be eager to hook up with someone or at least hang out and have a good time."

Matt shrugged. "I'm waiting for someone. She's not from around here, so I want to make sure she knows she's in the right place."

Ben laughed. "You're bringing a date, but you didn't even offer to pick her up?"

"I never said it was a date."

Ben shook his head, laughing some more. "Whatever, man. How are you planning on scoring if she came separately? That's amateur hour right there. You know better than that."

"I never said I was meeting a girl." Matt glanced up at his old friend with his eyebrows raised.

Ben just chuckled and nudged Matt's shoulder with his knee again. "With the way you're over here checking your phone every three seconds and staring at the parking lot, I know it's not a dude. Unless there's something you'd like to share?"

Matt punched Ben in the thigh. "Shut up, dude. I'm not gay."

Ben backed up, laughing harder. "Alright, alright. I know. And you did say she and her. But it'd be cool with me if you were gay. I'm enlightened like that." He swigged his beer, holding in a laugh and backed away, kicking up sand as he moved to escape Matt's second punch. "I don't need a dead leg, dude. I plan on dancing tonight."

Matt stood up, brushing sand from his shorts, his eyebrows raised. "Oh, yeah? Anyone special?"

Ben rubbed a hand over his close-cropped brown hair, calming down. "Mindy's here."

Matt's eyebrows climbed further up his forehead. "You guys still a thing?" Mindy and Ben had dated for their entire senior year.

Ben tilted his head. "Not really, but we hook up sometimes when we're both in town. She went to school in California, though, and I'm at UW, so it's not like we could really be together anyway. You know how long distance stuff is."

"Not really. But I can't imagine it would be easy. Did you guys even try?"

Ben shook his head, "Nah. We both decided it wouldn't be worth it. But it's not like we broke up because we hate each other. And neither of us have anything serious going on with anyone else, so why not fuck and be friends while we're in the same place?"

Matt nodded, taking another pull out of the beer bottle in his hand. "Yeah, sure." He didn't know if he could be that casual about sex with a former girlfriend, but if that's what Ben and Mindy wanted, who was he to judge?

Ben said something else, but Matt didn't catch it, because Hannah appeared on top of the dunes blocking the parking lot from the beach. The wind off the water caught strands from her ponytail and pulled them free, whipping them around her face, the evening light making her hair more golden.

He nodded. "Uh-huh. Cool, man. My date's here. I'll catch up with you later." He was vaguely aware of Ben's laughter behind him, but he couldn't give a shit right now. She came. He strode toward the dunes to meet her, a smile stretching his lips wide, relief that she showed up settling over him, calming his nervous energy.

Her dark-haired friend walked beside her, both of them wearing short shorts and tank tops, and the friend had a bag slung over one shoulder. Matt's brow creased when he saw a guy with dark hair trailing behind them, about the same height as the girls. Why would she bring along a guy?

Matt stopped at the base of the dune. None of them had seen him yet, their attention focused on their feet as they took large steps down the steep dune.

Finally, Hannah looked up, her face lighting up in a big smile. "Hey."

"Hey." His smile matched hers. Maybe the guy was with her friend.

She came to a stop in front of him, and he barely noticed the other two stopping beside her, all his attention on Hannah. She motioned to her friend. "This is Elena. I don't think you guys introduced yourselves earlier today."

He shook his head, turning his attention briefly to the friend. "Hey. I'm Matt."

She huffed a laugh, her lips tilted in a private smile. "Yeah, I know. Nice to meet you." She was pretty, too, curvy and stacked, long dark hair and a deep tan. He'd noticed her this morning, too, thinking either girl was a nice possibility. But it had been Hannah who'd ultimately captured his attention. When her green eyes had locked with his on his way into the water something had passed between them, and he found himself drawn to her. Given that she'd approached him on the beach, the feeling seemed to be mutual.

Elena hooked a thumb over her shoulder. "This is my little brother, Tomás. He's the reason we're late."

Matt turned a quizzical look on Hannah. She nodded. "He begged to come. I'm here with Elena's family for the summer. Her parents weren't going to let us come if we didn't bring him along."

"Okay. No big deal. We have pop and beer in the coolers by the fire. Everyone's cool, though. It's fine." He gestured toward the growing group of people surrounding the fire. There were probably twenty or thirty people there now, all their old friends from high school that were home for the summer gathering by the Jetties like they always had growing up. As long as they didn't get too loud or rowdy, no one bothered them down on the beach.

He led the way, wanting to reach for Hannah's hand, but stopping himself. He'd get her to dance with him, then he'd have an excuse to touch her. The orangey quality of the light made it harder to tell, but she still seemed to be blushing half the time he talked to her. He didn't want to scare her off by being too forward too soon.

Hannah walked a few steps behind Matt, Elena and Tomás behind her, trying to keep up with his long strides in the sand. She'd worn cute strappy sandals, and regretted the choice now that sand kept getting under her feet. At the first chance, she'd take them off. And then get her sweatshirt from Elena's bag. The wind made it colder than she'd expected down here by the water. The condo buildings shielded the parking lot from the wind most of the time, so it hadn't felt that cool when they'd gotten in the car to drive into town.

Matt stopped by the coolers and cast a look at her over his shoulder. The way his eyes raked over her body, bolder and more appreciative than anyone ever before, had goosebumps rippling up her arms and over her chest. She shivered.

He turned to face her. "Cold? It gets chilly here at night. Here, let's get you closer to the fire so you can get warm." He pressed his hand to her lower back, guiding her toward the fire, and then wrapped an arm around her, his hand rubbing up and down her arm. Leaning down, he pitched his voice so just she could hear. "I'll keep you warm."

Oh. Maybe she'd let Elena hang onto her sweatshirt after all. Matt keeping her warm? Yes, please. She sent a wide-eyed look at Elena, who smirked and gave a little wave of her fingers before fishing drinks out of the cooler for her and her brother.

Hannah held herself stiffly, unused to people she barely knew wrapping themselves around her, even for the ostensible purpose of keeping her warm, but as his heat enveloped her from behind, she couldn't help but relax against him, enjoying the feel of his firm torso against her side, and the way his muscles moved as he continued to rub her arm. A rush of heat spread from her chest to her face. She'd blame that on the fire this time. She wasn't blushing again, dammit.

"Better?"

She turned her face up to see him smiling down at her. She nodded. "Much." And she tried to keep herself from blushing again while she cast about for something else to talk about. Matt didn't seem too worried about their silence, his hand slowing, but still stroking up and down her bare arm, the movement turning more sensual and less the business-like chafing intended to warm her up. She couldn't suppress another shiver and the goosebumps that popped out on her arm and chest, even though she felt hot all over.

"I thought you said you were better?" He chuckled and moved behind her. "Here. Maybe this'll help." He pressed his chest against her back and wrapped his arms around her, holding her tight against him. Now she felt positively hot, but no way was she going to move away, even if nerves fluttered in her belly, and another wave of heat washed over her front, which was definitely not from the fire.

After a moment she felt his chin come to rest on top of her head. "This okay?"

She nodded. "Yeah."

"You know," his voice rumbled in his chest, and she could feel it where she pressed against him. "We're not going to be able to dance or anything if we have to stay here like this in front of the fire all night."

"Oh." Should she tell him that she had a sweatshirt? This was so great, but dancing with him sounded like fun, too. Screw it. Hopefully he wouldn't immediately let her go when she told him she did have a sweatshirt after all. "Well, Elena—my friend—she has sweatshirts for all of us in her bag. I can get it whenever."

"Okay. Good." She could hear the smile in his voice, but he made no move to release her. She smiled and snuggled further into his arms, and he tightened them around her. "So you said you were here for the summer. When do you go back home?"

"Early August. We got here about a week ago." Elena's mom was a teacher, and her dad ran some kind of online company. Hannah wasn't clear on the details but it meant that they could go away for like two months every summer. This year, Hannah got invited along, and her parents had said yes.

"Wow. That's some vacation."

"I know. My parents could never do that, but Elena's dad can work from anywhere, and her mom has the summers off from school, so they always pick somewhere different and get a vacation rental for a couple months."

"You must be good friends with Elena, huh?"

She smiled again. "Yeah. We've been friends since elementary school. She knows all my deep, dark secrets."

He laughed—a full, throaty laugh—his chin lifting off her head for a moment. The sound warmed her as much as the fire and his body. She liked hearing him laugh.

"All your deep, dark secrets, huh? I'm not sure I believe you have many of those. You seem far too sweet and innocent for that."

His words had her twisting her head around to look at him. "You think so, huh?" He was right, but she'd never admit it to him. She was tired of being the sweet, innocent good girl, always doing what she was told, never having any fun. That was part of why Elena had egged her on today when Hannah had drooled over Matt at the beach, and why Elena had agreed to basically babysit her younger brother at a party full of strangers. Hannah loved her parents, but they were ridiculously overprotective, not letting her date until last summer, and even then mostly with groups. Elena's parents were more relaxed, and this summer was her chance to do things her restrictive parents would never allow. Like go to a party to meet a guy she barely knew and snuggle in his arms to stay warm. Who knew what else could happen?

A bemused smile met the challenge in her words, but he just shrugged. "Babe, I've seen you blush more times than I can count today. Yeah, you're definitely a sweet and innocent little thing."

Another blush flamed over her face at his words. Shit, she wished she could get that under control. But she couldn't, and she had no comeback to his statement, so she turned back around, staring into the fire again.

His mouth came down near her ear, his breath fanning over her skin, raising more goosebumps down her neck. "You wanna know one of my secrets?" He paused, waited for her to nod, and then went on. "I like your blushes. And the goosebumps that you get when I touch you or whisper in your ear. I like that you're all sweet and innocent." She shivered in his arms. "And I like that you shiver against me like that, especially since I know you can't be cold now."

Mortification that she was so transparent washed through her, followed by pleasure at his words. He liked her reactions. He liked her.

He nuzzled her ear for a second, sending another wave of goosebumps and heat washing down her neck, then rested his chin on top of her head again.

"What about you?"

"Hmm?" Matt had no idea what the girl in his arms was asking about, distracted by the feel of her body against his, the fruity smell of her shampoo and the lingering scent of sunscreen from her day at the beach.

She turned her head to look back at him over her shoulder again. Maybe he should let her get her sweatshirt so they could sit and face each other while they talked. But he was enjoying holding her too much to let go just yet. And he hoped he'd get to hold her some more later. She really was so innocent with her blushes that stained her skin the prettiest pink. Would she know how to dance? How to kiss? More? She wasn't that young, probably only a year or so younger than him, so he doubted she'd never been kissed. But had she gone any further? He made sure to keep space between his hips and her ass, no matter how much he wanted to grind himself against her. She blushed when he whispered in her ear. She'd freak if he let her feel his hard-on right now.

"I said, 'what about you?' How long are you here for?"

Oh, right. "I leave the first week of August. Football practice starts a few weeks before classes."

"Oh. Where do you go to school?" There was something strange in her voice.

He gave her a quizzical look. "Marycliff University over in Spokane."

"Oh. Cool. Yeah, I've heard of it." That strange quality was still there, and she seemed stiffer in his arms.

"What about you? Where do you go to school?"

She turned her face away from him and mumbled something that he couldn't catch.

"What? I couldn't hear you."

Her chest swelled under his arms as she took a deep breath before turning her face toward him once more, but she wouldn't look at him. "I said Hanford High School."

He froze. High school? She started to squirm in his arms, but he didn't let her go. "Wha—" He cleared his throat. "What year are you?"

She stopped moving, but held herself stiffly against him, the only reason she touched him at all was because he still held her back pressed against his chest. "I'll be a senior in the fall."

"So you're seventeen?"

She gave a short nod. "I'll be eighteen next week."

He relaxed, his arms draping around her again rather than clamping in frozen dread. She was eighteen, or would be soon enough. That wasn't so bad. "Cool. I'll be a sophomore at Marycliff next year."

She relaxed against him again. "Oh. So that makes you …?"

"Nineteen."

She relaxed some more, the tension leaving her body, resuming the comfortable way they'd been standing before. "Cool. You like Marycliff?"

"Yeah. It's a good school. I got a football scholarship that covers most of my tuition, so it's been a good deal."

"Wow." Her voice was full of admiration. "No wonder you're ripped." She stiffened in his arms again, like maybe she was embarrassed that she'd said that.

He laughed. "Yeah. Between surfing and football I work out a lot. What about you? Do you have college plans for next year?"

She nodded, relaxing once more. "Yeah. My parents really want me to go to WSU since it's close to home, but I'd rather go to UW."

"So you'd spend your school year over in my part of the state."

She chuckled. "Yup. But you'll be in Spokane, so it's not like we'd see each other."

He opened his mouth to say something about maybe meeting in the middle on breaks, but stopped himself. Where the hell had that come from anyway? He barely even knew this chick. "True."

They fell silent, and Matt wasn't sure what to say after his almost blurted out desire to see her again after tonight, after they both left for the summer, going back to their real lives. Even though he'd grown up in Westport, it no longer felt like his real life after just one year of school. The only thing he really missed in Spokane was being able to surf more than just the few weeks he was home in the summer. He'd come home a few times in the spring before the surf got really gentle, but his dad had been annoyed with him, telling him he needed to stay at school, focus on classes, and give up his stupid dreams of surfing. The only reason his dad was okay with him surfing as much as he did during the summer was because he got paid decently to teach lessons. Even then, his dad almost constantly told him how much more money he'd make working on a fishing charter. But he couldn't stomach doing that. Yeah, he'd get to spend all day on the water, but not like he wanted.

When his dad went off about that stuff he mostly just nodded and kept his head down. Arguing didn't ever do anything except start a yelling match, and he hated those, hated the confrontation, and hated that even when he was right, he'd lose. Sometimes he'd mention how he'd given his word to Trip, the owner of the surf shop that he taught for, and his dad had raised him to be a man of his word. His dad would grumble a bit, usually something about Trip being a hippie stoner—which wasn't entirely untrue—but then drop the subject. For a while. Usually until he saw Matt getting ready to go surfing or coming home after being on the beach. He'd learned to avoid his dad for the most part, which wasn't too hard since the man worked long hours as the harbor master, so this summer he'd escaped most of the lectures.

Hannah shifted in his arms, bringing him back to the present. For now he had this girl who he wanted to get to know better, in every meaning of the word. He unclasped his arms from around her, rubbing her arms a few times. "Let's get your sweatshirt from Elena, then we'll get a drink and dance."

Hannah sipped her Dr. Pepper, wrapped in the warm cotton of her favorite hoody. Matt had fished a bottle of beer out of the cooler first, twisted off the top and handed it to her. She'd never had beer before, but didn't want to tell him that. He could already tell that she wasn't used to having a guy pay this much attention to her, touching her as much as he did. He didn't need to know that she'd never had any alcohol before now, especially since he obviously assumed she had with the casual way he passed her the beer, expecting her to want that over a can of pop.

She'd taken a sip and wrinkled her nose at the bitter, fermented taste of the beer. Ugh. Why did people drink this stuff? It was awful.

Matt had laughed and taken the bottle out of her hand, setting the other bottle in his hand back in the cooler. "Not a fan of beer, huh?"

She shook her head. "No. That's gross. How do you drink it?"

He took a swig, his eyes dancing in the sunset. "Acquired taste, I guess. Sorry. Would you rather have a pop? It looks like there're a couple bottles of water, too."

She could make out different colored cans floating in the icy water of the cooler. "Yeah. A pop would be great."

He fished out a Dr. Pepper, offering it to her with a raised eyebrow. Now they stood chatting with some of his friends, Matt standing on her left, occasionally brushing against her, guiding her to the different groups with his hand on her back, making sure to include her in conversation. She stayed mostly quiet, only chiming in when someone asked her a question, but laughing along with everyone, enjoying the easy way Matt had with his friends. He was like a chameleon, fitting in with each group, moving easily between his former football teammates and his surfing buddies, changing his tone and demeanor slightly with each one. It was impressive watching him slide so smoothly between groups, and she could see that he was well liked by everyone.

Finally, he tangled his fingers with hers, tugging her behind him closer to where the music was playing. "Let's dance for a bit."

She smiled and nodded, draining the last of her Dr. Pepper. He took her can and stuck it in a big black garbage bag by one of the coolers. It made her happy that they had those, because she was not okay with littering, especially on a beach like this.

He caught her wide smile when he straightened up from getting rid of their trash. "What?"

She shook her head. "Nothing. I'm just having a good time. And I'm glad you guys don't litter."

"Oh?" He took her hands, pulling her into the mix of swaying bodies, wrapping her hands behind his neck before reaching for her hips. "You an environmentalist?"

She cocked her head. "Sort of. I mean, I guess so. I feel like we should take care of the environment. It's not right for animals to get caught in plastic rings or choke on trash because people are too lazy or stupid to clean up after themselves. I mean, that's something you learn before kindergarten, right? Cleaning up your own mess? I guess some people's mamas didn't do such a good job with that."

He chuckled. "I guess so. So our mamas must've done an okay job, huh?"

"Must've. You guys are cleaning up after yourselves."

"Well, most of us are surfers. We don't like surfing surrounded by trash, so we do what we can to keep our beaches clean. Plus, like you said, it's not fair to the wildlife. Tell me more about your environmental streak."

"Really? Are you sure? Most people get bored when I talk about this kind of stuff."

He shook his head, his eyes on her lips. "I don't think I could get bored with anything you decide to talk about."

She blushed. Again. The sun was so low now, that she hoped he couldn't tell. But with the way a smile tugged at the corners of his mouth, she thought he probably could. "Okay. Well, I'm in an environmental club at school. We organize roadside cleanups and stuff. We spend a lot of time picking up litter, it seems like. We go out once a month or so, and I try to get us down by the river every other time we go out. The pollution of the waterways seems more awful to me than some roadside trash. I mean, I know it's all bad, but the roadways are already kind of polluting everything. There's more animal life at risk in the river."

Matt's eyes were intent on her face, and he nodded. "I get that. I care more about the litter on the beach than even in the parking lot, much less on the highway."

"Yeah." She nodded, licking her lips. His eyes zeroed in on the movement. "Um, so, anyway. We also do fund raisers when there's a major natural or environmental disaster. Like, with the tsunami in Japan, we raised money for victims and to help with the Fukushima cleanup." She shook her head, her enthusiasm for the subject taking over. "I don't get why people don't care more about the environment, you know? I mean, it affects everyone. If the ocean is polluted with toxic waste, it affects the food supply and where do people think we get our water from? I mean, I know it goes through a cleaning process in the city, but it comes from rivers and lakes and underground aquifers. If we pollute the groundwater, what do people think we're going to drink? We can't exactly live without clean water."

One corner of Matt's mouth pulled up like he was suppressing a smile, and she stopped, realizing she'd been talking fast and loud about it. "Yeah. Sorry, I'm getting carried away. I'll stop now."

He chuckled again and shook his head. "No, I like it. I like how passionate you are about it. It's good. People should be passionate about things they care about, and it's great that you care so much about the environment. Someone needs to care about it."

"What about you? Do you care about it?" She held her breath waiting for his answer while their bodies swayed to the slow music. She was glad it was slow so they could still talk while they danced. She liked talking to him.

He shrugged one shoulder, the movement lifting her hand slightly. "As much as a normal person, I guess. I agree with you that people should clean up after themselves and that polluting the water supply is stupid." A smile split his face. "I'm not nearly as passionate as you are, but that's okay."

She nodded. She was used to people not caring about things as much as she did. At least he didn't think she was stupid and respected it, even if he didn't fully share her passion for the environment. "Yeah. Okay. Good." She paused, and his fingers flexed on her hips, pulling her against him more, so his hips pressed into her belly. "What about you? What are you passionate about?"

His smile fell off his face, and his jaw clenched, the easygoing expression on his face replaced by an unreadable mask. He shook his head. "It doesn't matter. Let's talk more about you."

She opened her mouth to protest, but then the music changed to something with a faster, driving beat, and Matt pulled her tightly against him, moving them to the music, and neither of them spoke anymore for a while.

Matt held Hannah close, enjoying the feel of her body against his, the way the sweet scent of her shampoo mingled with the smoky smell of the fire and the salty tang from the ocean. He had a feeling that any one of those scents would now trigger this memory. Acting more on instinct than thought, he dipped his head toward hers, one hand traveling from her hips up to cup the base of her skull, tipping her head back. He pressed his lips to hers.

She didn't respond at first, her mouth unmoving under his. He was about to back away and let her go, thinking he'd completely misread the situation, when she pressed herself closer to him, her lips pushing back against his. With a swipe of his tongue along her lower lip, she opened for him. He explored her mouth, seeking out her tongue. She was tentative at first, only briefly touching his tongue with hers. His other hand came up to her face, cupping her cheek, angling her head so he could devour her, her response unleashing something inside him. Something that couldn't get enough of her. He wouldn't let her hide, showing her what he wanted from her, seeking out her tongue with his and sliding them together. Again she responded quickly, giving as good as she got, her initial hesitation disappearing.

This was more like the confident girl who'd approached him on the beach. But that initial hesitation niggled at the back of his mind. She blushed like a virgin. And she was still in high school, even if she was almost eighteen. Could she be?

He pushed the thought away to consider later, more concerned with this, right here, right now. His hips moved against her, and he gripped her hips with one hand again, pulling her tight against him, letting her feel what she did to him, what he wanted, dancing long forgotten.

Until someone bumped into him. "Dude! Get a room!"

Hannah stiffened, pulling back, her face flaming. Matt glared at Ben, partly for interrupting him, partly for embarrassing Hannah. Yeah, he liked seeing her blush, but when he was the reason for it, not from his friend being a dickhead. "Fuck off, Ben."

Ben laughed, moving away. Matt turned his attention back to Hannah, who'd now put as much space between them as she could with people dancing all around them, her hands pressed to her cheeks. He reached for her, pulling one hand down and threading his fingers through hers. "Come on." He tugged her after him, pulling her away from the crowd of his friends who loved nothing more than to give him shit. He didn't mind, but Hannah didn't know them, didn't realize it was all harmless teasing, and he didn't want her to feel embarrassed or self conscious.

"Where are we going?"

He glanced back at her, the sand kicking up behind her as she tried to keep up with him. He slowed his pace so she could walk beside him and grinned down at her. "Just over here a little ways, away from my obnoxious friends."

She looked back at the group, her brows creased with concern and upper lip caught between her teeth.

"Hey." He stopped and waited for her to look at him. "You're not from the coast, right? Have you seen the green flash when the sun sets into the ocean?"

She shook her head, concern still written on her face.

He pulled her in close and wrapped an arm around her. "Relax. We won't do anything you don't want to do, okay? We'll just hang out over here for a bit until you're ready to go back."

She glanced back one more time before she faced him again and nodded. "Okay. I just don't want to leave Elena."

"We won't. And if she's ready to leave before you are, I'll give you a ride home, okay?"

She shook her head. "No, we'll all get in trouble if we don't come home together. That was one of the conditions for getting to come tonight."

He nodded. "Alright. Either way, I just want to spend some more time with you, without Ben being a dick, okay?"

She nodded, still chewing on her lip. "Okay."

Unable to help himself, he cupped her cheek and dipped his head for another kiss, savoring the feel of her soft lips against his.

He wanted to stay there, just like that, losing himself in the feel of her, the scent of her in his nostrils, her soft skin under his hands. He really wanted to lay her down in the sand, still warm from the day's sunshine, strip her clothes off her and cover her with his body, using his own warmth to block the chill from the evening air. But that obviously couldn't happen tonight. The only privacy on this beach was to get away from the crowd, nowhere near enough for what he really wanted to do. And she had to go home with her friend, so there was no chance of taking their private party elsewhere. And truthfully, he wasn't sure if she'd be up for moving that fast anyway. Maybe it was for the best that he knew how things stood tonight anyway. But God, he was going to be hurting later from how keyed up she had him already.

He broke away, leading her a little further down from the shore, far enough away that the sound of the waves overpowered the noise from the party around the fire further up the beach. Settling himself in the sand, he pulled Hannah down between his legs, leaning her back against his chest, his arms going around her, both of them facing the sun, now little more than an orange-gold sliver above the water.

He leaned down so he could whisper in her ear. "Watch. It'll only take a few more minutes. Don't blink or you'll miss it."

He felt as much as saw her sharp intake of breath, and he couldn't hold back the smile that spread across his face at the goosebumps racing down her neck when he whispered against her skin. That expanse of skin peeking out of her sweatshirt was too tempting. He dropped his head further, brushing his lips below her ear, then trailing kisses down her neck, tracing the path of her goosebumps with his mouth.

She gasped, her head pressing back against him, and he smiled against her skin before scraping his teeth over the tendon where her neck met her shoulder.

"I'm going to miss what you want me to see if you keep that up." Her voice came out breathy and tortured sounding.

Matt kissed her once more on the neck before sitting up, snuggling her back into him. They didn't have to wait much longer, the sun sinking lower and lower into the ocean, until it disappeared with a green flash.

Hannah let out a soft gasp, and he shifted, trying to make more room for his rock hard dick in his shorts. That was the same sound as when he'd started kissing down her neck.

She turned her head up to look at him. "That's amazing. I'd heard about that, but didn't know if it was really real or not."

He grinned at her. "It doesn't happen every night, but it's not uncommon. I'm glad you got to see it."

"I'm glad you made me watch it, even if you did try to distract me before I could see it."

"You like that kind of distraction, though?"

He could just make out the pink tinge on her cheeks in the deepening twilight. She nodded.

His grin grew wider, and he lowered his face to hers. "I'd be happy to keep up the distractions then." And with that he kissed her, turning her so she could straddle him, and he could give her a taste of everything he wanted to do to her.

They stayed there, making out as the twilight deepened around them, the sky fading to navy. Matt thought he could kiss her all night long. And he would've happily done so, but far too soon a voice in the distance called, "Hannah!"

When her name was called again, Hannah pulled back, her face turning in the direction of the party still over by the fire. The music had stopped, and it looked like some people had started leaving, though he knew from experience that a few would stay there until midnight or later, hanging out, laughing and drinking until the fire burned down to embers and they could kick sand over it and go home. Apparently Hannah and her friend would not be part of that group.

He saw a shadow detach itself from the rest of the group, and that voice called Hannah's name again.

Hannah sighed. "That's Elena. I know she saw us coming over here. It must be getting close to ten. That's when we have to be home."

Matt couldn't help chuckling. "Really? Ten? It's not exactly a school night or anything."

He felt more than saw her shrug. "Yeah, well, it was agree to that or not come at all."

She detached herself from his grip and climbed off his lap. He sighed from the loss of contact, then stood and adjusted himself, resigning himself to walking her back to her car. At least he had her number already. He was sure she'd agree to see him again. He laced his fingers through hers and led her back to the group.

Elena and her brother stood on the edge closest to the parking lot, the bag now slung over Elena's shoulder. "Come on, Han. We're going to be late if you don't get a move on." She turned and started for the parking lot, not even acknowledging that Matt was there.

He and Hannah trailed after the other two. On the edge of the parking lot he stopped, turning Hannah to face him. He kissed her once more, briefly, not the kind of kiss he really wanted, but there wasn't time for that. "We still have to figure out our surf lesson. I get off work tomorrow at four. I'll come pick you up after, okay?"

She nodded, the light from the parking lot washing over her pale skin, her teeth sunk into her lower lip. "Okay."

One more kiss, and he let her go, watching her climb into the car with her friend and drive away. He hadn't been all that excited about being home for the summer, except for getting to surf most days. But after meeting Hannah, it was looking like this might end up being a great summer after all. The kind you didn't want to end. He couldn't wait.

Want to read the rest of Matt and Hannah's story? Check out *Managed Hearts* now!

About Jerica MacMillan

Jerica MacMillan is a lifelong reader and lover of romance. Nothing beats escaping into a book and watching people fall in love, overcome obstacles, and find their happily ever after. She is the author of six books in two series: Players of Marycliff University and The Rebound Series. She was named a semifinalist in Harlequin's So You Think You Can Write 2015 contest.

Jerica is living her happily ever after in North Idaho with her husband and two children. She spends her days building with blocks, admiring preschooler artwork, and writing while her baby naps in the sling. Sign up to join her Book Club at www.JericaMacMillan.com and get a free book! You can hang out with her in her closed reader group on Facebook—Jerica MacMillan's Book Junkies.

Facebook: www.facebook.com/jericamacmillan

Twitter: www.twitter.com/jericamacmillan

Pinterest: www.pinterest.com/jericamacmillan

Goodreads: www.goodreads.com/jericamacmillan

Hometown Prince

BY EVIE LAUREN

A BEAD OF SWEAT SLOWLY DRIPS DOWN THE SMALL OF MY BACK, following the trail of the one before.

That's how you know it's hot.

I don't sweat, but it's the middle of August in Arizona, so even I'm not immune to the heat. Standing on the black asphalt of this parking lot is like standing on the surface of the sun. I unconsciously shuffle my feet to keep my cheap flip flops from sticking to the ground.

I don't even know what I'm staring at. Wafts of steam rise from under the popped up hood of the old beat-up car that I've had since high school. I'm not a mechanic, so who knows what's actually causing it not to start. Truthfully, even if I did know, it wouldn't matter. It's not as if I'd know how to fix it, and I definitely don't have the money to take it to a shop. Actually, I don't even have the money to have it towed to a shop. I feel awful, but I'll have to call my Dad tomorrow to have him come take a look at it. Our relationship is mostly non-existent, but he knows his way around a car, so he's my only hope.

Staring at the hoses and wires for a few more seconds, I pray that the answer to all my problems will magically appear, and the engine will roar to life if I stand here in the searing heat and glare. Maybe it's shear desperation that keeps me held in place, or the fact that I don't want to walk back to my apartment and have to ask my downstairs neighbor, Ms. Honey, to borrow her car.

She'd lend it to me, but there's not much I hate more than needing someone's help. If this wasn't an emergency, I'd never consider it. But, unfortunately, it is.

I trudge up the sidewalk, defeated and beaten down. I'm one of the most positive people you'll ever meet, but I've had a string of bad luck lately that is unreal. At some point, I'm only human, and I've got to admit that this just plain sucks.

No matter how I feel though, I plaster a smile on my face for the one person who needs me to be strong. My son, Finn. He's my whole world. He's every happy moment I could have ever asked for wrapped in one small, energetic little man. And, as I come in to view of Ms. Honey's apartment, I find him staring out her window watching for me. His small cheek is pressed against the glass, smushing his face. My smile transforms from being tight and fake, to real and warm. The sight of him puts everything in to perspective. We'll be all right, as long as we have each other.

He waves, his little hand moving so fast it's a blur. I blow him a kiss before I realize that in my haste to get back to him, I forgot my purse on the front seat of the car. The last thing I need right now is to have that stolen, too.

I put up my finger to him to let him know I will be back in one minute and he nods his head in understanding. His dark brown locks bob with the movement. Winking in his direction, I head back in a hurry to the parking lot.

Finn has a plane to catch that leaves in three hours, and we should have been on the road ten minutes ago. I'm a nervous wreck about him leaving—and flying without me—but my sister lives in California and spent the entire year begging for him to come and stay with her for two weeks. She's an amazing aunt, and I know he'll be safe, and loved. Not to mention, he'll have the time of his life.

My sister graciously offered to fly here, only to turn around and fly right back to California with him. She knew there was no way I could afford to take off work to go with him, though I desperately wish I could. We always need the money, and my vacation days are like gold, typically only used when Finn is sick.

I finally relented and told my sister he could go, and besides being a basket case this entire last week over his leaving, now I'm afraid he may just miss his flight if I don't pull myself together and solve our latest problem.

A small throng of college boys pass me on the sidewalk, backpacks strewn over their shoulders. College students flock to this complex because we are only a few blocks from the school. The men stare as I pass, definitely interested, but I don't meet their eyes. Purposefully, I twist my head away, and shield myself from their glare with my long, blonde locks. I know I'm not bad looking. That's not one of my problems. I'm always able to attract men just fine—it's attracting *good* men that I seem to have a problem with.

I break into a slow jog the last few feet to my car, grateful that Ms. Honey lives in the apartment below ours. There is no way Finn could have stood out in this heat while I tried to figure out what's wrong with our car. She's been our neighbor for the last four years, since Finn was only a year old. I know I can trust her, and that she loves him. Even so, I don't want to take advantage of her kindness.

I don't like to accept help from people, no matter how big or how small. It's a problem of mine. Maybe a flaw? But after having Finn when I was only twenty years old, it felt as if everyone doubted my ability to raise a child on my own when I was barely more than one myself—and I have always wanted to prove them wrong. Make them eat their words. I think somewhere deep down it feels as though accepting help means I'm failing.

Finally within view of my car, I breathe a sigh of relief that my purse is still on the front seat. If the ground wasn't thermo-nuclear hot right now, I would get down on my hands and knees and thank God it's where I left it. Instead, I raise my face to the sky and murmur a quiet "thank you," before opening the door to lean down and retrieve it. I nearly burn my hand on the door handle, and then again on the seatbelt in my small endeavor. One day I'll get a new car, one with a warranty and roadside assistance, and these stupid problems will be a thing of the past. At least I have a car. Well, it doesn't work, but I have one. That counts for something, I'm pretty sure.

"Hannah!" A deep husky voice, coming from a few rows behind me, commandeers my thoughts.

I jump so much that I nail my head on the door frame of the car. Dropping my purse, I rush both hands up to the spot that throbs on the back of my head. I'm pretty sure I'm in danger of passing out from the pain. With my eyes squeezed shut, I release one of my hands and robotically reach for where I can feel the purse strap on my foot, grabbing it before it melts to the pavement. I'm not in a hurry to open my eyes because I'd recognize the timbre of that voice anywhere, and it sounds much angrier than when he normally speaks to me. *Much angrier.*

Frustrated, I ease them open and focus through the pain on the six and a half foot wall of muscle that is sauntering toward me. *Rhett Prince.* He's got his practice uniform on, covered in dirt. I'd love to peruse him from his head straight down to his toes, because I could get lost in him, and forget all of my troubles, but I don't. His deep brown eyes lock on mine, and the questioning in them sends my body throwing up caution flags in my brain. I'm about to get in trouble, and not the kind of trouble I enjoy.

His chiseled jawline is tense with worry and anger. I've been victim to that same expression on his face since we were kids, so you'd think by now I'd be immune to it, but I'm not. It affects me each and every time he directs it my way.

Rhett and I grew up next door to each other, both born and raised in those homes. Best friends from the beginning. Nothing could come between us when we were younger. That is, until high school, when the hormones started raging. And then a lot came between us. Namely every girl in our school and all of the surrounding areas. It's not like we were dating. We never dated. Don't get me wrong, he showed interest, but I was scared. I couldn't lose him. He meant everything to me. And getting in to a relationship would only make the possibility of something going wrong between us very, very real. And then where would I be?

I never had much of a connection to my parents, or any of my family other than my sister. She's older than I am, and after she moved out to start her life, there were many times where it felt as though I was living with strangers. Rhett was my salvation. I needed him to be in my life. He was much too important a part of it to mess up over a stupid attraction. Something I knew even when I was young.

But there was plenty to be attracted to. Models in magazines had nothing on him. There wasn't a single part of Rhett that wasn't perfect. It'd always been that way. He was the object of every girl's affections since forever. And as the years passed, and he went from cute boy, to gorgeous teenager, to this beautiful man prowling my way, I could do nothing but watch as every other girl got parts of him that I would never have.

Rhett flirted with me in the beginning. When we finally got old enough to realize that he was a boy and I was a girl, and that meant something. But the terror I felt over replacing the relationship we had with one that would be more physical, and able to fall apart, kept me from acting on it. Until eventually he gave in, and stopped pushing the subject. He never asked me why. He never pressed me to respond to any of his advances, he just seemed to understand that this is how I wanted things.

Regardless, through all of my ups and downs, he's always been there for me. Through the high school years when his popularity far outshone my own. Through his college years, when he was the star player on his baseball team being scouted by the major leagues, and I was simply the old friend juggling a job and some online classes—definitely not living the college dream the way he was. And most importantly, through a pregnancy with a man that I came to realize much too late that I couldn't count on. I'd turn around and there he'd be, in some quiet way, but there nonetheless. No questions, no judgements, just love and support. No matter what, Rhett's stood by me.

Right now though, it looks as though he'd like to throttle me. Not a usual look, nor one I am accustomed to.

Rhett stops directly in front of me, and stands wordless, staring. The silence is worse than anything he could actually say, because I think I see disappointment. He reaches up to run his hands through the scruff of his beard. I wasn't sure at first how I felt about the added facial hair. He started growing it out right about the time I had Finn. It was a time when I was looking for familiarity, so any small change to my world freaked me out. He was such a big part of my world that this change to his appearance made me unsure. Crazy, I know, but true. Now I can't imagine him without it. I have to admit it's incredibly sexy. Just a little longer than a five o'clock shadow, and framing his jawline in a way that makes him appear haunting, serious, and all man. No trace of that little boy that I knew once upon a time.

"Hey, Rhett—" The words barely leave my lips before he starts in on me.

"Hannah! Seriously! I have to hear from Ms. Honey that you're in trouble? I told you five years ago when you had Finn that you needed a reliable car. I offered to buy you one a million times! Why do you have to be so stubborn?" His eyes flash to a darker shade the more upset he gets. I'm reminded of burning coal when he stares from the heavens back to me. He motions toward my old coupe with disgust on his normally composed face. Whether the look is directed toward my car, or me, I'm not sure. Probably both.

His jaw ticks and his chest moves in one long exhale, a tell-tale sign that he's chewing over things he'd like to say before he settles on, "I can afford to buy you a car, Hannah. This is crazy!" Rhett's deep voice rises at the end of his rant, his hands thrown in the air.

"Yeah, I know you can." My hand instinctually flings to my hip, to match his stance, upset not only with him giving me grief, but because of my pounding head, my broken car, and the fact that I'm about to leave my baby at the airport. Don't even get me started on the blazing heat now beating down on me, making it hard to think and react to everything he's spouting at me. I'm a good foot shorter than him, so it's hard to look intimidating, but I'm doing my best to win this staredown.

He could afford a car and so much more. Rookie of the Year straight out of college, with a huge contract for the Diamondbacks. Our very own hometown hero. Money is not one of his worries. But that's not the point. That's his money not mine, and I don't need anyone's help.

"Why didn't you just call?" His irritation winds down to an acceptable level, finally.

"Because I'll figure it out, Rhett. The way I do everything else. I'll either call a cab or ask to borrow Ms. Honey's car. No big deal." I try to convince him, but he knows asking her for help is a very big deal to me, and he sees right through my calm façade.

"Well, lucky for you, you won't need to do that now, because I'm here. Just load him into my truck and take him to the airport. I'll wait at your apartment until you get back."

"Rhett, you really don't need to do that. I can just ask her. Go about your day. We're fine, really."

"Are you serious?" His face falls at the same time his temper heats back up. Rhett's forehead creases as his eyes scorch me. He's taking complete offense to my attitude. His muscular chest heaves a sigh so huge I'm surprised it doesn't blow down the mesquite tree we are standing next to. "Yeah, I can tell you are." Shadows cast disappointment across his face, as he studies mine. "How long will it take before you realize I'm here for you? That I want to be here for you both?"

I stand stock still. Afraid to move, afraid to answer. Because I don't know what the answer is. I know he's here for me, always has been. And that fact, makes me feel things that I just can't feel when it comes to him. Rhett is my safe haven, my proverbial light in the storm. But our chance for something more came and went a long time ago, and I passed it up because I was afraid of losing him.

And while I hate it when he has to drop whatever he's doing to come and rescue me, my biggest fear is the day that he no longer does.

But one day it will happen. One day, Rhett will meet someone he can get serious with, instead of all of these girls who pass through. She'll be put together, successful, and perfect in every way, no doubt. And that's what he deserves—nothing less. Definitely not a girl like me who had to stop my college education in order to raise my son, and who is slowly creeping toward my degree one class at a time. Someone who has to work her fingers to the bone to get by. No, he deserves someone who can focus her energy on showing him nothing but the love he deserves. In time, he'll move on with her and forget about me. I want for him to be happy, but the thought of my world without him is so bleak that I don't like to think about it.

While my brain scrutinizes all of the possibilities of what his life will eventually be, he moves on answering his own question, his handsome face sullen. "You know what, just forget it." His expression is dreary. I'm so lost in my own world of hurt over my imaginary someday that I don't stop to consider the reason he looks that way. "Look, you'll be doing me a favor." His voice turns smooth and comforting while he tries to convince to me accept his help. "I need to get cleaned up, and your apartment is closer than my house. Just take my keys and get Finn to the airport. I'll grab a shower while you're gone."

"Okay," the word whooshes reluctantly from my mouth. My voice, now weak from my defeat, quietly utters, "Whatever you say, Mr. Prince." Hesitantly, I reach for his palm. My fingers slide over his skin as I timidly grab the keys. Every time I touch him it feels intimate, and the small brush of my skin against his own right now is no different. I'm not the only one who feels the fire each time we make contact. I can see it in his eyes, where they are stuck on his palm, and the area that my fingers just vacated. Much less slowly, I thrust my keychain out to him. When his obsidian eyes meet my own, he gives me a tense perusal that leaves me with goosebumps.

Rhett's muscled body leans my direction, and it takes everything in me not to meet him halfway, but I stand still. He nuzzles the hair away from my temple, and leaves a kiss there in its wake. Breathing me in, he apologizes, his breath caressing my ear. "I'm sorry I raised my voice." I want to wrap myself in his words, and then in his arms, like always, but I don't give in to need.

Tears, unwanted, form at the corners of my eyes, but I blink them back. I hate to get all weepy, but he's caught me on an off day. Needing to say goodbye to Finn later has left my normally steadfast nerves in a fray, and Rhett being Rhett has left my emotions in a tailspin.

He notices the tears anyways, and looks me long and hard in the eyes. I want nothing more than for him to look away, but he doesn't, so I break contact first. "You okay?" Concern instantly clouds his voice, as he smoothes his tan palm over my cheek, tucking my hair behind my ear. When I don't look at him, he takes one strong finger and gently directs my chin his way.

"I'm good." The promise leaves my lips with more conviction than I feel. "I just want this day to be over with. Once Finn gets to California and is having fun, I'll feel much better."

Another prominent sigh escapes Rhett's full lips causing me to stare at them, my focus absolute. How I've dreamed about them over the years. I know first hand how soft they can be. I also know how strong they can be.

Once, years ago, when we were barely out of high school, we both gave in to the tension that flows between us, erupting in a kiss that if I lived a thousand years, I would never be able to forget. I didn't stop him. I didn't want to.

If my parents hadn't returned home, who knows where that kiss might have led? In that moment, I was giving in to the pull Rhett always had over me, and I would have followed him anywhere.

Not many days pass that I don't think about that day that feels like a lifetime ago. One that, for better or for worse, could have been a turning point for us. Instead of winding up together on that fateful afternoon, we pulled away from each other, breathing hard, neither of us wanting it to come to an end.

Each and every time Rhett tried to bring it up in the weeks that followed, I changed the subject. After he left that afternoon, I had time to realize that the possibility of what could go wrong with a relationship between us, far outweighed what I felt could go right if we followed that path. Eventually, Rhett resigned himself with the fact that I didn't want to talk about it, and it was never brought up again.

Back in my present day mess, my preoccupation with his lips and the memory is absolute, until he shifts, pulling me from my daze, and my eyes spring up to his own waiting pair. I'm sure Rhett notices that I was looking at his mouth as though it was my next meal, but he doesn't say a word. Instead, his powerful forearms brush my shoulders as he reaches to grasp the sides of my face, leaning in to press his lips to the top of my head. "Come on, let's get you out of this heat and up to get Finn. I'll help you get him in the truck."

"You don't need to—" I begin, but he quiets me with a domineering glance. His glare keeps my mouth sealed for the remainder of our walk. I'd never admit it, but that look is smoldering, and I find it far too hot to be scared of it.

Finn squeals and jumps up and down the second his eyes lock on Rhett. He rushes his tiny body out of the window and to the door in a flash. Finn knows better than to open it without Ms. Honey, but I can hear the excited patter of his feet on the other side.

Ms. Honey swings the door open with the most innocent of smiles. Innocent she is not, but dang it if she doesn't pull it off. "Well, hello, dear!" Her pearly whites are aimed directly up at Rhett's breathtaking face, putting on a show for him. Women, no matter their age, can never resist him. "You sure did make it here in no time!" Ms. Honey applauds him.

Not able to wait any longer, Finn wrenches his little body forward and wraps himself completely around one of Rhett's long, muscular legs. He greets him with his typical baseball in one hand and glove on the other. Rhett keeps him in a steady supply of both. Finn looks up to him. He's his hero, plain and simple.

Rhett immediately pries Finn from his leg, picking him up and hugging him tightly to his body. The sight does things to my chest that I don't have words for. These two men have my heart. One knows it, the other doesn't.

Once dislodged from Rhett's chest, Finn runs his fingers across Rhett's beard. "It tickles," he grins at him. Rhett knows this is his cue to lean forward and rake his beard across Finn's soft little cheeks. Giggling ensues, and Finn is still laughing when Rhett lowers him to the floor. He skips away happily, looking for his shoes.

With Finn gone, Rhett redirects back to Ms. Honey. "I left as soon as I got your call."

"I can see that." She eyes his practice uniform up and down from behind her glasses, and the appreciation there is not to be missed. It makes me laugh, but I'm able to cover it by looking away toward where Finn has disappeared. The inappropriateness of her action does not stop the flirty smirk that immediately forms on the older lady's lips.

Ms. Honey is nothing short of a walking piece of history. A sweet and sassy blast from the nineteen sixties. Her pants are largely polyester and her glasses definitely lend themselves toward the cat-eye phenomenon of that decade. The bouffant bun that her hair is never without could probably withstand hurricane force winds. She's nosy, and talks more than she listens, but I'm grateful for her presence each and every day. It's nice to have someone who I know sincerely cares about Finn and I who lives so close by. She always keeps tabs on the two of us, even though she acts as if she doesn't.

I clear my throat pointedly, my hand flying back to my hip. "And just when did the two of you exchange numbers?" My eyes shoot from Ms. Honey back to Rhett, not sure who I should focus on.

Rhett looks shyly away, knowing that I don't like for anyone to intrude on my behalf, he knows what he's going to say won't be well received by me. Staring a little too intently at a leaf on a potted plant by the door, he fiddles with it between his thumb and forefinger. "I left my number for her a long time ago. You know, in case you ever needed something."

My mouth is poised to argue, when Rhett stops his inspection of the leaf. "What if there was an emergency? She needed someone that she could get ahold of. It helps me worry less about the two of you when I can't be here." Innocent eyes sweep first to Ms. Honey, and then back to mine. The sexy vulnerability on his face is something I can't resist. Honestly, after that last part of his argument, how can I be mad?

In lieu of saying anything at all, I roll my hazel eyes. If nothing else, I need to be polite to Ms. Honey for taking time to watch Finn, and even for calling Rhett, no matter how misguided that may have been. She did it with the best of intentions—I think.

"Thank you for calling Rhett." I politely hug her. "And for watching the little one." My hand finds Finn's shoulder as he scampers back my way, ready to go.

Ms. Honey gives me a wink, reaching towards Finn, her arms spread wide. "Give Honey a hug! And tell me you'll miss me!"

Finn launches in to her arms, wrapping himself tightly around her neck. I worry that he'll hurt her, but she seems to enjoy every second of it. "I'll miss you!" he nearly shouts.

"Promise to wave to me from the sky!" Ms. Honey shoos him out the door toward Rhett and I.

"I promise!" His bellow is only eclipsed by the massive wave he gives her. Pulling on my hand, Finn forces me into a slow jog toward the parking lot.

Rhett follows in an easy stride, his legs carrying him much quicker than my shorter ones.

Finn's pace speeds up, causing me to reach desperately behind me to grab Rhett's hand, before we leave him in our dust. His hand is already outstretched, anticipating this very thing. Our fingers glide together to form a strong grip, one that sends warmth running up my arm and into my chest.

Finn's giggles are infectious when he catches a glimpse of the human chain that Rhett and I have formed behind him. His little legs come to an abrupt stop when he gets close to Rhett's truck, nearly causing me to collide with him. My feet skid before I stumble and almost lose my balance.

From behind, Rhett wraps his powerful arm around my waist; his hand fanning out on my lower stomach. His grip is strong, and with my back pressed tightly to his front, I can feel every hard inch of him. Those practice pants leave nothing to the imagination. Suddenly, I'm breathing harder than I want, and it has nothing to do with the short jog. Rhett notices. The pressure of his hand increases and pulls me further in to him. His breath closes in on my neck, sending chills through me, even though with the sun beating down on us, I should have been burning up. Being close to Rhett is hard enough, but having this much contact with him sends my mind reeling until I don't even know who I am. Because even with this simple touch, I'm not Hannah, I'm his. Always his.

I swear I feel the lightest touch of Rhett's lips to my neck just as Finn's excited chatter lulls me from the obscene pull Rhett always has over my senses. "I'm ready," he announces, jumping up and down next to the door of the mammoth truck, breaking my concentration.

Rhett's hand loosens from its protective grip allowing me to step away. Always stepping away. Always trying to do what's right. It's exhausting. I can't look Rhett in the eyes, so I focus on Finn.

Luckily, Finn's love of Rhett's truck has kept him preoccupied and oblivious to what's happening. The massive vehicle is intimidating, just like the man who drives it. From its blacked out paint to the lift that makes it look like a 4x4 on steroids, the quad cab behemoth suits Rhett perfectly.

He opens the back passenger door, lifting Finn into the booster seat he keeps in there. He pulls the seatbelt out and around him, letting Finn buckle it himself. Rhett eases his body in the door, very close to Finn, and murmurs a few quiet words to him. After a small nod from his tiny face, Rhett backs up. "Love you, buddy. Be good for your aunt. Okay?"

"I will," Finn promises. "Love you, too."

Rhett closes the door before turning on me. I already started the truck and have the a/c cranked on high. He brushes his thumb across my cheek. There's nothing he can say to make this hard moment better. "I'll be here when you get back."

I nod. It's all I can do.

Climbing in the truck, I melt into the leather seats while I watch him walk away. Rhett exudes power in every action. Even in the sweeter moments he and I have shared through the years, he's always in control. It frustrates him that I fight that control. He wants nothing more than to save me, but I know I need to save myself. I think he realizes that too, but dang it if it doesn't wear on him. I can see it now, in the way his normally broad shoulders slump ever so slightly as he makes his way off the hot parking lot and onto the sidewalk.

His frame, his persona, his shine, it's all larger than life, and much too big for this apartment complex. But here he is anyway, looking decidedly out of place. For me.

Pushing all of the problems of the last few hours aside, I take in his retreating form, from his long powerful legs to the way that baseball uniform clings to his perfect backside. It's little wonder all of the sports and fitness magazines have been beating down his door for the last few years since he hit the big time. They'd be crazy not to. His agent persuaded him to take part in more than Rhett really wants to. He's one who usually shuns the limelight, but it's smart business to get as much endorsement and spotlight as he can, for as long as he can, and he understands that.

He doesn't live an extravagant lifestyle, though he certainly can afford to. He does have a beautiful home in Scottsdale, near a gorgeous golf course, with more rooms than he really needs. He's offered for Finn and I to come live there so many times I've lost count. As nice of an offer as it is, I don't think I could stand to watch girls coming and going, nor would I want to explain that to Finn. I can't help but wonder if he really wants us there, or if he simply feels obligated to offer. It's been easier to stay put and not delve in to any of it. So that's what I've done.

Wanting to stay lost in this mirage of perfectly toned man instead of my actual reality and sad moment of taking my son to the airport, I slowly close my eyes, and let his form burn in to my brain for a moment longer. I remind myself that I can get through this goodbye, and then while Finn is off having fun, I can get our current mess straightened out before he returns home. I'm not sure where I'll find the energy because I'm burning both ends of the candle these days, but I always find a way. And I'm not going to stop now.

Dragging myself back up to my apartment after leaving half of my heart at the airport, exhaustion and gloom engulf me. I've never spent time away from Finn before, and while I have piles of stuff to keep me busy, I'm so used to going non-stop and having his perfect little face peeking in and out of every aspect of my life, I honestly don't know what I'll do for the next few weeks. My sister swears I'll be fine, and that I need some time alone to just be me. Usually she's right, but this time, I'm not sure. I'm still struggling with the notion that maybe I've made a mistake in letting him go, when I open my apartment door.

The silence that meets me is odd. Rhett's a busy guy. Always moving, always planning, constantly in motion. I wonder if he's left?

"Rhett?" I call out, ducking my head around the wall that separates the living room from the kitchen, checking to see if he's in there. I'm seconds away from texting him when I wander in to my room.

His strong form lays motionless in my bed, fast asleep. The deep rise and fall of his chest means he'll be out for a few hours more, at least. He doesn't settle down to sleep very often, but when he does, you can set a bomb off next to him and he won't wake up. "The Prince sleeps," I mutter to myself, amused.

My eyes roam from his prominent jawline dusted with soft bristles to his chiseled golden brown abs, and land on the small towel wrapped around his waist. A quiet laugh escapes my lips. Those towels envelope Finn's small body, and work for me, but barely cover him. The opening slit of the towel faces the front, running the length of his tanned and toned thigh, and up towards his waist. If he shifts just slightly, he'll be exposed to the world. Knowing a girl can only deny herself so much temptation, I pull my quilt up and over him to his chest.

Rhett settles further into the sheets, relaxing into the softness. His large frame makes my bed look miniature. Before I even register what I'm doing, I'm sitting on the edge of it, staring like a creeper. I can't help it. He's generally so busy, and there are very few times that he remains still. And even fewer times where I let myself take him in completely like this. I discovered years ago I can only take so much of it. He's perfect, truly, and not only on the outside. He's perfect on the inside, too. Well, at least for me. I'm sure there'd be a line of girls who would tell you differently. Ones who undoubtedly feel scorned by him. Several are bitter, because Rhett's the kind of guy who makes every girl want more. But he never wants more with any of them. It doesn't win him any fans. They all think they'll be the girl to make him want a commitment. And each and every one of them is crushed when he doesn't. I never want to be one of those girls.

Easing off the side of the bed, I dance my fingers through his short dark beard, and up into the hair above his ear. After the long day, I'd like to crawl into the bed with him, but I know I shouldn't. Besides he doesn't have any spare clothes here, so I need to wash his practice uniform so he'll have something clean to wear home.

Hours pass while I troll around my apartment trying to keep myself busy. I don't exactly work quietly, and our old washer is noisy, but he sleeps through it all.

On my final pass through my bedroom to stack clean towels in the linen closet, Rhett's sleeping form springs up like a jack-in-the-box. He loops his large palm around my wrist and yanks me toward him before wrapping his other arm around my waist. I'm pulled over him and into the empty space next to him, all in one swift move. Rhett's lying atop of me before I can even fight back.

I scream. And not a normal scream, either. This one is high pitched and full of fright. Which, of course, only adds to his amusement. My much smaller hand lands a smack to his bare chest. He loves that I'm so much more petite than him. It makes holding me against my will that much easier. I'd like to say it doesn't happen often, but it does. Reaching for my palm, he brings it to his lips, kissing it.

"You scared me," I chide.

He only laughs harder.

"Seriously!" Feigning more anger than I feel, I push at his chest. He's not budging, and he's really enjoying himself, so there's no way I'm putting an end to this until he's good and ready. He's always in control.

"Really? I couldn't tell." He winks down at me with his stupid, smug, perfect smile plastered on his stupid, smug, perfect face. He mocks me by impersonating my scream, high pitched squeal and all.

My eyes roll out of habit because it's all I have at the moment, and now I'm trying not to laugh.

He shifts his hips, a small move, but it's then that realization hits me. He's still in a towel, mostly naked, on top of me. Without a doubt, my face registers my sudden awareness, and Rhett, ever vigilant of my expressions, immediately catches on.

I watch his own awareness rush through him, and though I fight hard to keep the thoughts from entering my head, I can't help it. It feels so good to lay here, with his weight on me, in my bed, laughing. All of it. It feels right.

Before I can stop myself, I dance the very tips of my fingers through the beard that covers his cheek, up the side of his face and in to his hair, just as I had earlier.

"Hannah," he breaths through an exhale, reverently, his full lips capturing my attention.

His eyes smolder, and he shifts his hips again, this time intentionally, as though he can't stop himself.

My body takes over, my eyes shutting of their own accord in pleasure. A light gasp escapes my lips when his movement hits me where I need him the most. My back arches in the slightest, wanting to feel him more than I care to admit, or have him know.

Like a fast moving storm, his lips are on my neck, layering kisses that fall in a steady line leading directly to my own. I do nothing to stop it. Tilting my head to the other side, I give him room to work. The brush of his beard and the wetness of his tongue overload my senses. I only tip my head back in his direction when I know his lips are nearly to my own, and I need to feel them more than I need anything else right now.

The kiss doesn't start out gently like the one we shared years before, but hard and absolutely weighed down with rampant desire and yearning. Longing that's built up over years of denying myself. He may have been the one who started this kiss, but I want it just as much, and there's no denying it.

I press my chest up, needing every inch of our bodies to connect. My legs wrap around his waist in an instant, and by then it's too late.

Rhett's rough hands push my shirt up, his tongue running a line from my belly button all the way to my breasts. I'm shivering when my shirt vanishes. I don't even register that action because after years of dreaming about the kiss we shared, all I know is I need his mouth on mine again, and I need it now.

Placing my hands on either side of his face, I pull him urgently to me, straining to connect my face with his. He obliges all too willingly, falling back in to me, his weight hitting me in all the right spots. I moan, rolling my head on the pillow, before Rhett's lips find my own.

I latch on to them, my need for him almost embarrassing, but I just don't care. I'm too far gone. After years of thinking I'd never feel them again, I can't get enough.

Rhett makes an effort to slow down this erratic frenzy we're both in. He knows all I want are his lips on mine, so instead he pulls his away infinitesimally, teasing me. I have no shame, so I search his out.

His willpower must be as nonexistent as my own because it doesn't take much for him to give me what I want. His lips graze mine tauntingly before they disappear and are replaced with his tongue. The very tip of it sweeps across my mouth, before he pulls his face just out of my reach again. I whine, needing him. His body trembles where it touches my own—a sign that the restraint he's showing right now isn't coming easy. However, true to Rhett, he's found control and he's holding on to it. Easing his mouth back to mine, he flicks his tongue across my top lip, never fully giving me his. It's the sweetest torture I've ever known.

I break, so crazy with need I can't think straight. My voice is unrecognizable when I cry out to him. "Rhett, please!"

Never able to deny me, the heat of his mouth is against my own almost immediately. He's in control, as always, and now I know it.

Both of his palms slide smoothly up my sides, one resting behind my back pulling me to him, the other coming to rest behind my neck, holding me possessively. The kiss deepens, all the while we grind our bodies together until I feel like I could fall apart, but never once does he take his lips off of mine again.

The way his body moves against my own is skilled and fluid. Every motion a masterpiece I want to savor. Rhett never does anything small, he's all in, and the master of every domain he endeavors to conquer. And this, what we are doing in my bed, is no different. He has me exactly where he wants me and is filling every one of my senses so full that I don't think I'll ever find my way out again. Suddenly, nothing feels like enough. His body isn't close *enough*, the kiss isn't deep *enough*, his hands aren't holding me tight *enough*.

My mind starts to crash all around me, and my euphoria at being the only place I've ever wanted to be is replaced with my fears from years past that I've been using to deny myself this type of relationship with Rhett.

My once frantic lips still, and our intertwined bodies start to slow.

"Hannah?" Rhett whispers against my swollen mouth. "Baby, what's wrong?" He pulls his head back enough to really give my face a once over.

He knows me too well and I can't hide my panic from him even if I want to.

Rhett's massive frame rolls off of me in one quick movement, and even through my fear, I still miss the warmth of him instantly, pulling the blanket up to cover myself.

"I'm sorry, Hannah. I never meant—" Rhett pauses in the middle of sitting up, his beautiful lips struggling noticeably with the words. He rubs the back of his neck, worked up, and clearly having a hard time rectifying what just happened. "That's not true." He finally finishes his thought, staring away from me and at my bedroom door. "I did mean to, it's just—" He stops talking again, sending my heart racing, scared for what he will say next. His face is tormented.

Anxiety takes over, and I can't stop myself from wondering if he's already realized what a mistake he was about to make. That thought spurs me to start babbling out of nervousness. "Look, I know you probably don't want me like this. You don't have to make any excuses. We got caught up in the moment. It's been a long day. I get it, I do." I'm not even sure what I'm saying, only that I want this moment—which was just short of heaven a few seconds ago, and that I had wanted to last forever—to now end as soon as possible.

At my words, Rhett turns to me so swiftly I worry he may get whiplash. Under his intense gaze, I pull the blanket up tighter over my chest, wishing I had even the slightest idea where my shirt is.

"Probably don't want you like this?" he repeats, his anger undeniable. The burning coal has returned behind his stormy eyes.

I don't even know how to respond. In all of the years we've known each other, and everything that we've been through, I've never seen this look that he's giving me. It stuns me to silence, and makes me want to take back everything I just said, so he'll stop staring directly into the depths of my soul.

Rhett's mouth opens, poised to say something, before he closes it, shuts his eyes sadly, and hangs his head. I know defeat when I see it, and that's exactly what this is. Why though? I don't know. I'm so lost in my own head over everything that's transpired over the last few minutes I don't even know where to start with questions.

Tongue tied and reeling, I can only watch as he picks his face back up to meet mine. "After everything, that's what you think?" He shakes his head just once and wraps the towel tighter around his waist, before heaving his body out of my bed. I get the distinct feeling he wants to be alone. Having already eyed his clean uniform that sits folded in a chair next to my bed, he unceremoniously drops his towel, his back to me.

Modest he is not, but he has zero reason to be. I stare in awe of this entire situation as he pulls his pants on over his naked backside, the one that my legs had just been wrapped around. After sitting in the chair to slip his shoes on, Rhett stands before my bed, not even so much as looking at me. His stare is fixated on the hat in his hands.

Rhett's voice rings out over the hurtful silence, frustrated. "Come to my game tonight," he implores me. His face is blank, looking lost, as he continues to stare away from me, and in a second I would have agreed to just about anything to make that look disappear.

"If that's what you want." My voice breaks with barely contained emotion.

"It's what I want." His response is definitive, leaving no room for argument. "I'll send a car for you." His hand shoots up to stop my protests at the same time I begin to eek one out. "The driver will have your ticket."

"Okay," the word is nothing more than a puff of air as it leaves my mouth. I pull myself up to sit, running my hand through my hair, and tightening the sheet across my chest. I hate being so naked.

As though he can read my thoughts, Rhett picks my shirt up off the floor where it lays next to his feet. Leaning across my bed, he places it in my lap before running his lips across my cheek. They hover over my skin longer than normal and I don't really know what that means, but with everything that has happened, their feather light touch emphasizes the big gaping hole that I now have in my chest from what we've just done.

"Thanks," I stare shyly away, feeling defenseless to his pull. I know that I'll replay these last few moments with him in my mind every day for the rest of my life. For a few short seconds, everything in my world felt right. This memory no doubt blows the one of our kiss from years ago, right out of the water.

He nods wordlessly, his emotions so prominent it feels as if they are electrifying the air around us. I hold my breath until he walks out of my bedroom and through my apartment door, locking it on his way out.

I want to sit, stare and wallow, but I can't. Finn's plane landed a while ago, and my sister promised to have him call as soon as she got him to her house and he was settled. That call should be coming any minute. Plus, I have to get ready for the game. I told Rhett I would go, so I need to be there.

An hour later, I've resigned myself with the fact I can't take back what Rhett and I have done, so I need to move on and focus on other things. I pull the cutest pair of jeans I own out of my closet. They're fitted and even I can admit they look good on me. I have several jerseys with Rhett's last name, Prince, emblazoned on them and I always wear one when I go to his games. Always. I may not be his girl, but I am his best friend, and so proud of him that I usually can't even talk about his accomplishments without tearing up.

Tonight I pick a red one and partner it with some splashy red polish on my nails. I'm a little down in the dumps, and a lot confused, so this simple act helps me to refocus on something else. Not one to typically wear much makeup, I spend more time on that than usual, too. By the time I'm done with my hair and put on some earrings, the car service calls to say they're downstairs. I feel good, having taken the time to primp, which is rare for me given my limited time these days. And I look good, too, even if I do say so myself.

The car service takes me to the players' entrance so I don't have to fight the crowds. Rhett always puts me with the players' wives. Most of them are sweet, and I don't mind. My jean clad legs have an extra sashay as I approach my seat next to Andre Garcia's wife, Sheila. Andre's the pitcher for the team, and he and Sheila were high school sweethearts. If I was playing favorites, Sheila would be it. She's sincere, and funny. She loves the sport of baseball almost as much as her husband, and is always there early for the games. A hardcore fan.

Sheila's overjoyed to see me here, I can tell. "Hey, you!" She wraps her arms around me, and my face gets swamped by her long blond curls. Her taller frame dwarfs me, but the hug feels good. "How've you been, sweetheart?" Grabbing my purse from my shoulder, she guides me to my seat.

"Good," I return her infectious smile. And I am. The troubles of the day have melted away, and I'm finally able to take my first full deep breath since I woke up this morning. Something about the smell of the stadium and the buzz of excitement that surrounds it ropes me in every time, relaxing me. I love it here just as much as Sheila does.

She and I spend the remainder of the time before the game catching up, and the minutes fall away. As a few of the players begin to mill about, Sheila rises from her seat to look for Andre. I follow her gaze, and find that Rhett has appeared. I wonder if he made his way out to the field just to check on me. His eyes immediately go to the seat he knows I'll be in.

The smile that lights his face does things to me. Our whole lives a feeling like no other always encompasses me when he looks at me that way. It's like a jolt right to my emotions. The happy ones. I blow him a kiss, feeling much lighter than I did when he left my apartment earlier. The haze of not knowing what we did, and what to do about it, has lifted. I need to get our friendship back on track and stop this craziness.

Rhett stares at me too long. I can't deny it. I can't explain it away. His eyes trail from my own and down to the jersey I'm wearing. His jersey. His eyes heat at seeing his name on me so I stand, turn around and give him a show of pointing to the "Prince" emblazoned across my back. Glancing over my shoulder, I sweep my long blonde hair out of the way, giving him my best mega-watt smile. The intensity and hunger I see in his stare makes my breath stutter. Before I collapse under it, he kisses two of his fingers and holds them out toward me, disappearing back in to the dugout.

I love that man. There's no way around it.

My bottom isn't back in my seat before three curvy, vivacious young women, wearing homemade shirts with Rhett's name all over them make their way to the railing near the dugout, screaming his name. With a last name like "Prince," it's easy to come up with catchy sayings. Some fans get super creative, but clearly these girls did not. One of the women has the old, used up, "Be my Prince?" emblazoned right across her huge chest. From their bubble gum pink lips to their shorts that show the whole bottom quarter of their butts, these three are in this thing to land themselves a baseball player. It always irritates me, but today especially so. I can't take my eyes off of them and their pursuits. Rhett's the best looking guy on the team, or any team, in my opinion. And that's saying a lot because baseball does not lack hot men. He's also extremely talented, and exceedingly smart. A triple threat.

Not able to ignore their chants, a few of Rhett's teammates wander out to the screaming trio, trying to placate them. No matter their efforts, when they leave, the screams for Rhett always start back up. After an unsuccessful attempt by his teammate, Rousing, to appease them, I watch as he clearly prods Rhett to join them. Timidly, Rhett's head clears the dugout, heading their way.

The women jump up and down at Rhett's approach, giggling with excitement. The way their chests bounce is nothing short of pornographic, and Rousing's eyes bug out of his head. Rhett, on the other hand, is cool as a cucumber. Not fazed at all by their display.

It's funny that I forget how determined girls can be when it comes to Rhett. It never helps to see it in real life, and I can feel Sheila watching my reaction. Besides all the complications a relationship with Rhett would bring to our friendship, this is another downside, the girls. Day after day, night after night, literally throwing themselves at him. I'm not sure I could handle it.

"You know it means nothing, right?" Sheila nudges me. "Don't let it bother you." Her hand wraps around my own. Her voice sounds far away even though she's sitting right next to me. My focus is absolute.

Sheila's words begin to sink in and I momentarily drop my eyes from the scene of Rhett with the bimbos. "What?" I feign innocence.

Sheila gives me a tight look. "Cut the crap, Hannah."

"Seriously." I try to convince her. "It totally doesn't even matter to me. It's not like we're dating. Rhett's free to do whatever." I wave my hand in the direction that I know he's still talking to them, and turn my attention to the opposite side of the field.

"Okay, well, I'll just let you sit in your own denial then." Sheila shrugs, laughing at me under her breath. "But a word of advice?"

Reluctantly, I turn back to her, swallowing hard. I'm not sure I want to hear her advice.

"Rhett is a good man. A good man who cares about you. Deeply," she emphasizes the last word. "Don't let someone else's intentions cloud you from seeing what his intentions are."

My eyes tear involuntarily for the millionth time that day. It's been an eternity since I've had such little control over my emotions, but it's been a long day. "Honestly, Sheila," I breathe, feeling the fight leave my body as I say the words. They come out weaker than I mean for them to. "It's not like that between us. We're just friends, and he's free to do what he wants."

"That's what you want?" She dishes out some tough love.

"I—"My voice stutters, my eyes cutting back to Rhett. The woman with the cheesy slogan plastered across her chest is hanging over the railing holding out a piece of paper. As I watch, he takes it from her outstretched fingertips. It has to be a phone number. One tear escapes as I look on. Rhett takes a step away from the girls, and unfortunately his deep brown eyes kick my direction as I wipe it from my cheek. Alarm colors his face before he comes to a stop at the entrance to the dugout. I pull my gaze from his and back to Sheila, who watched the whole scene along with me. "It doesn't matter what I want," I whisper, wishing now that I'd just stayed home.

Sheila's smart enough to let the subject drop, strengthening her grip on my hand, though I'm sure she has more she wants to say.

No more than a few minutes pass before Rhett is back out of the dugout, beckoning for me to meet him at the railing. I already know he's worried about me. I really wish he hadn't seen me cry. I only have about two seconds before he's swarmed by fans, so I jump from my seat and rush to him.

"You okay?" He stealthily peers around us for prying ears. Rhett takes his cap off, smoothing out his hair and pulling it back on lower over his brow this time. He's delectable, and it makes my heart wrench with need.

"Yeah, I'm fine," I lie unconvincingly. He doesn't have time to discuss this, and even if he did this is not the time or place.

"Just tell me," he orders in a huff. He isn't trying to be unkind, he just can't stand it when I keep things from him. All semblance of the high and mighty, star baseball player fade, and all that remains is my Rhett. The one who used to sit against the old tree in my backyard with me for hours on end while my parents screamed at each other just a few feet away in our tiny house—so I didn't have to be alone.

"Honestly, I was just talking with Sheila, and it's not something you need to worry about." I try again to ease his fear. "I'm fine."

Precious seconds that we don't have are wasted while he stares at me, waiting on an honest answer—which is fine by me because I don't especially want to have this conversation. Where are the fans when you need them?

"Hannah, if it was the girls..." He cuts to the chase.

I look away guiltily. I don't mean to. Sometimes you can't help your gut reaction to things.

"You know I don't go for that kind of thing." Rhett begins to plead his case, but I don't want to hear it.

"You don't?" I purposefully act surprised and not a little rude. Definitely out of line. I have no right to make him feel bad.

Rhett's head jerks backward, as shocked by my attitude as I am. We never fight. Ever.

I continue, apparently set on making a fool of myself. "Look, I saw her give you her number, and that's fine by me. You owe me no explanations. Okay? If that's the kind of girl you want, then so be it."

One chuckle escapes his lips, but not out of humor. "Well, you're really full of zingers today aren't you?" His eyes flash to a pair of fans hovering at the top of the stands, looking very much as if they are deciding whether to interrupt us. I find myself for the first time hoping for the disruption.

"Hannah!" Rhett commands my attention when I don't turn back to him. That doesn't help my mood. "Look at me!" His voice turns deep. It's not often that I act this insolent, but I'm two seconds away from leaving so he's trying to get the situation back on track.

My eyes beat down into his, showing my resentment at this

whole conversation.

"You actually believe that's the kind of girl I want?" His face holds mine captive.

"Yeah," I state simply, and I really don't believe it, but I'm angry and saying whatever I can to cause him the hurt that I feel.

"Yeah?" He half questions, half mimics me. The anger that he's trying to keep below the surface springs free.

"Why are you repeating everything I say?" I strike back.

"Because I can't actually believe that you are saying it! I feel like I need clarification that I'm hearing you correctly!"

Rhett's outburst catches a few sideways glances. He braces both hands on the wall that separates us and drops his head to steady his nerves.

"You know what, don't worry about it. Just go play your game," I urge him. Anger drips from my voice, as present as it is in his, coupled with a sadness I know he can hear.

"Don't worry about it. Sure. No problem." Rhett shakes his head, the words spilling from his mouth lifeless.

His tone causes me enough alarm to be concerned, but that is diminished by the fact that he's repeating me again, making my temper flare back up.

Taking control, because that's what he does, his angry stare lessens, and his voice turns as soothing as possible given the situation. "Hannah, just do me a favor and wait for me after the game. Please? I can't do this here, you know that, but we'll talk this through. Okay? I'll give you a ride home. Take you out for dinner?"

He's so painfully handsome that I don't know where I find the strength to tell him no, but I'm hurting too much, and I think I've had a day where I can officially say, enough is enough.

My eyes slide from his, unable to look at him. "I can't Rhett. I've got to leave here early. I promised my department manager I'd get some work to her by tomorrow morning and I haven't even started it." It's a lie. And I'm pretty certain he knows.

I wait a heartbreaking second, then return my attention to him, seeing the hurt plastered all over his face. Not anger, only hurt. Here he is holding out an olive branch, once again, and I'm breaking it, once again. And that makes me feel like the worst kind of person. Because someone like Rhett who has bent over backwards for me my whole life, should never look hurt like that, and definitely not because of something I did. I almost give in and tell him I'll go, before he half-heartedly answers, "Fine."

He pushes off of the wall, done with this conversation, and maybe with me. I can't tell. Without so much as a glance in my direction, he calls over his shoulder, "I'll have the car waiting for you. It'll be there whenever you're ready."

I know part of the reason he walked away before saying that is because it's harder for me to refuse his help if he doesn't give me the chance. But the other part is because he can't bear to look at me right now, and that hurts worse than any rejection I've ever had. And that's saying a lot, seeing as though I've been rejected by a man I actually birthed a child for. But this is Rhett. My Rhett.

The slow shuffle that I make on the way back to my seat is pathetic. To most people, what just happened between Rhett and I would be no big deal. However, since we never fight, this is monumental.

Sheila, short on words, weaves her arm around my shoulders. It's a comforting weight, until it's time to start clapping for our boys. I'm worried that my argument with Rhett before the game will affect his playing, and I think it did. But luckily, it's working in his favor. He's always formidable and strong, but the brutal force he's using to swing the bat during the opening innings is something superhuman. I imagine he's probably seeing my face on every one of those balls he's crushing.

When it comes time, I don't want to leave, but I lied to him and set the ball in motion so I need to make good on my pathetic excuse. Riveted by the game, and even more riveted by Rhett himself, I reluctantly peel myself from my seat close to the top of the ninth inning, giving Sheila a huge hug. She tries to make me promise to be back the next night, but I evade her as best I can. I'm worried Rhett won't offer me the ticket after our little episode, and I don't want to admit that to her.

I sulk the entire ride home, disappointed in myself not just for tonight, but for more things than I can count. All of the pieces of my life are held together by the thinnest thread, and the weight on my shoulders of what would happen if even one of those threads break is overwhelming.

Pulling up to my apartment complex I turn an evil eye towards my broken down car like it has personally affronted me, taking out my anger on an inanimate object. I don't know where to start with trying to fix it. I hope and pray it'll be cheap, and my sad excuse for a vehicle will back on the road soon because I don't know what I'll do if it isn't.

Ms. Honey's TV flickers in her living room when I walk past her front window and up the steps to my apartment door. It feels good to know I'm not the only one still awake. Somehow it makes me feel a fraction less lonely.

I go through my nightly routine, minus the smiling little face of Finn, washing off the make-up that seemed like a great idea a few hours ago, and showering all of the product out of my hair. Once I'm in my comfy sweatpants and an old Diamondbacks T-shirt with Rhett's face on it—What can I say, I'm a glutton for punishment—I decide sleep is my only option. And who knows, maybe tomorrow will bring some clarity? I could always hope.

I never hear his footsteps on the stairs outside, or the latch on the door opening, but I do hear Rhett's voice softly call, "Hannah?" from the direction of my living room, not long after my head hits the pillow.

"Rhett?" I'm surprised, and wonder if I imagined it. Feeling confused, I slowly pull myself up. Maybe I've finally lost it and am hearing voices? At this point it wouldn't shock me.

I'm two seconds from laying back down, convinced I'm going whacko, when the light flicks on in my room, flooding it with a soft glow. The sudden brightness startles me so much, I jump.

"Sorry," Rhett immediately apologizes when he sees my fright, coming my way with deliberate strides to comfort me. "I didn't mean to scare you." He takes up residence on the end of my bed, laying his warm palm on my calf. Trying to calm me. He's showered from his game, and smells divine.

"Working hard?" His eyebrow pops up, irritated that I lied to him. I'm very obviously not working.

I divert my eyes to my lap. There's one thing we don't do to each other, and that's lie. Big or small, they all count. "I'm sorry, Rhett," I start to explain, but never finish. I'm out of excuses.

Mercifully, he lets me off the hook. "Hannah, just don't." His gentle tone beckons me to meet his gaze. "Be honest with me, okay? What happened here today," he nods towards my bed, "did that upset you?"

My eyes dart away from his again, fiddling with my fingers.

"Hannah?" Rhett's doing his best to get me to talk.

"There's no easy answer to that, Rhett." My brain is spinning a million miles a minute. "I mean, yeah, it upset me because things aren't like that between you and I, and look, the one time they are, we're fighting. This is why we should never do this. This is why we just need to be friends." My arms flare out, encompassing the both of us and this bed, as though somehow that drives home the point.

"You're scared?" A strange expression crosses his eyes, as if a piece of a puzzle finally locked in place for him. They squint in concentration, taking in more than just my words. He can read me like a book.

"Of course, I'm scared. You're my whole world, Rhett. I can't lose you." I finally admit in a true moment of honesty. More honesty than I've ever given him before.

Scooting closer to me, he braces his hands on either side of my thighs. His massive chest is very close to my own. "That's why you always turn me down? That's why you pull away? Each and every time." He breathes the last few words, almost to himself, his thoughts far away though he's still staring at me, as if he's reliving all of those moments.

"Rhett, you know my family is all but non-existent, and it's always been you and I. You're the one constant in my life. I know my mistakes are my fault. And I've learned from them, and dealt with them the best way I can. But you? You can't be one of those mistakes. I've spent every day of my life protecting that one thing. I know I'm not the perfect girl. I know I'm not the girl for you, but I can't lose you. I just can't." My confession leaves me feeling panicked.

Something in Rhett shifts. I can't physically see it, but I feel it all the way to my core. His voice is a caress when he speaks again. "How can you think I'd ever leave you? You think that you could push me away? Hannah, I stood by you when the bullies in school tried to knock you down. I stood proudly by your side, in all of the times that you were confused, scared, and wrong, just as much as I did when you were happy, and life was going your way. I stood by you while you were pregnant with another man's baby. I stood by you while he left. And I'll be standing by you until the day I die, Hannah." Rhett's hand gently sweeps up the side of my face and through my hair, cradling the side of my head. "What's going on up here in this beautiful head of yours that you think for one minute I'd ever leave you? Why would you ever think I don't want you? What have I ever done to make you feel that way?"

I shake my head, feeling myself tremble. Rhett's never done anything to make me feel that way, and yet, I've never been brave enough to tell him how I feel. And while he knows me inside and out, and knows every other fear I've ever had, he never knew my fear over him vanishing from my life. I start to worry that letting him in on it is a mistake.

"Do you want me, Hannah?" The absolute look of sincerity and love that he is giving me would bring me to my knees if I wasn't already sitting. "Answer that, and be honest with me about us, for once, please." His voice is pleading, giving way to an undercurrent of pain. I've always avoided the topic of him and I, and it's obvious he's afraid that I'm going to do it again.

I'm trapped. No matter what I say, there's no denying he'll see through it. Even though admitting it terrifies me, I have to tell him. There'll be no turning back after I do.

"Always." The simple word leaves my mouth in a rush before I lose my nerve. "I've always wanted you, Rhett. Long before you became our hometown hero, and Finn's personal hero, you were mine. I fell in love with you when I was so young I didn't even know what love was and what my feelings for you meant. I don't know anything else but loving you, and wanting you." My head hangs at the end of my confession, terrified that now that he knows, he'll start to pull away. Maybe I've just scared him off for good.

A second doesn't pass before he has my face pulled back up to his, and his grip, while still gentle, turns more forceful. "You want me?" The words fall from his mouth as though he can't believe them and needs one more verification. "All this time?" He stares at me in disbelief, as the truth sinks in.

Shock is written all over his face, but I'm not sure he needs an answer at this point. I nod my head anyway. His thumb pushes away from my cheek to stroke my lower lip in the lightest wisp.

"It's always been you, too, Hannah, but I didn't think you felt the same. You and Finn are the first thing I think about every morning, and the last thing I think about every night. You have to know that? No more being stubborn and trying to do this on your own. No more being scared," he orders softly. "We've wasted too much time as it is. You're mine now, both of you. And you'll be mine forever."

His solid chest closes the small distance to mine, lowering me in a torturous pace to my back. Rhett hovers over me with the most possessive look in his eyes I've ever seen him don, and his beautiful lips zero in on my own. I love that look. It's my new favorite.

"Just like that," I whisper, not believing that the only thing I ever wanted could possibly be coming true, after fighting it for so long.

Rhett's lips lower the rest of the way to mine until we are sharing the same breath, and every word he speaks causes them to brush against my own.

"Just like that?" The tiniest of laughs spills from his mouth. "Hannah, I've been chasing after you for the better part of twenty years. I wouldn't say, 'just like that.' I'd say, 'it's about time.'"

Before I can reciprocate his smile or utter another word, his lips take my own. Rhett possesses them, and makes them his. The kiss lets me know they always will be. My hand searches out his face, running my fingers through the soft stubble on his cheek, as I fall into every dream I've ever had, with my Prince.

About Evie Lauren

Evie Lauren resides near the beautiful mountains of Arizona, but was born and raised in Florida and is a beach girl at heart. She writes young adult fiction under the pen name R.S. Reed. While her passion has always been her young adult series, L.I.A., romance at any age is a story that she loves to tell, and the characters from her short story Hometown Prince have quickly become two of her favorites. Thank you for the support and the love, and for taking time to spend a few minutes in Hannah and Rhett's little corner of the world. To keep up to date on all of her new projects, check out her website, and follow the links on that page for her social media.

Website: www.rsreedbooks.com

Facebook: www.facebook.com/evielaurenauthor

Twitter: www.twitter.com/elaurenauthor

Instagram: www.instagram.com/evielaurenauthor

Goodreads: www.goodreads.com/author/show/15722910.Evie_Lauren

All or Nothing

by M. Andrews

Chapter One

Zoe

Looking up at the clock hanging above the dishwashing station, I anxiously wait for the minute hand to click over the three. Everything around me seems to be moving in slow motion. Each second that goes by feels like a lifetime. I hold my breath as the minute hand moves. My heart beats excitedly out of my chest when I hear the door to the café creak open, and the strand of bells hanging from the handle jingle, signaling he's here. My sweet SWAT officer is here. Technically he's not mine…at least not yet.

I wipe my floury hands on my apron then check my hair in the tiny mirror hanging on the door. Smoothing back the fly-away strands of hair, I push open the door and step out into the café where the sexy officer, Dylan Edwards, is standing, waiting for his coffee and his two passion fruit donuts.

Dylan has been coming into the shop every morning at six-fifteen for the past three months. He never misses a day. At least, not since I started working the morning shift. I've been working at Sprinkles Donut shop for the past year. I started out working the late shift, due to my rehearsal schedule with the Pacific Northwest Ballet School. Now that I am a principle with the company, rehearsals are later in the day and go well into the evening. The Delarosa's were kind enough to change my shift so I could continue working. It's not easy having to be up at four a.m., five days a week, but seeing Dylan's sexy smile makes it all worth it.

"Good morning, Officer Edwards," I say, giving him a warm smile. While my eyes drink in the view of Dylan in his dark navy blue uniform, I catch a glimpse of silver hidden away on his gun belt; it's his handcuffs...instantly, wild images of being cuffed to his bed run rampant in my mind. That, mixed with his neatly trimmed beard and chocolate brown eyes, has my panties completely soaked.

"How is my favorite honeybee this morning?" He returns my smile as he takes the closest seat at the counter near me.

My heart flutters every time he calls me his honeybee. A nickname I'd earned one morning when he spotted the gold bumble bee necklace my sister, Nora, gave me when I found out I was going to be a principle dancer. Now I wear it every single day.

"I am doing much better now." I wink over at him as I reach into the donut case and grab out two of his favorite donuts. The still wet icing drips down my fingers. I slide the plate over to him and, before I can move my hand away, Dylan grabs it in his strong fingers. He holds me in his intense gaze as he brings my hand up to his mouth.

"I'm done waiting," he whispers under his breath.

A soft moan escapes my lips as he licks the icing from each of my fingers. His warm tongue and dark hungry stare makes all logical brain function fly out the window. Is this really happening? This is so damn erotic. All I wanted this morning was for Dylan to finally ask me out to dinner. Now all I want is his tongue lavishing every inch of my body.

"I've been playing my hand cautiously for the past three months.

Waiting for the right time to make my move and make you mine. I've wanted you, Zoe, since the moment I laid eyes on you. I had to make sure you were ready for me, but my patience has run dry. I know you don't have rehearsals tonight, so there is no excuse why you can't have dinner with me. I will pick you up at seven."

It's not a question, it's a demand. Not that I would even say no. I've been waiting for this since the morning he first stepped foot into the shop. I want to pinch myself to see if I'm dreaming. God, I hope this isn't a dream.

Still holding my hand, Dylan stands up from his stool and leans over me. His other hand cups my chin and tilts my lips up to his. "I'll see you tonight my sweet little honeybee," he murmurs before capturing my lips in a warm soft kiss, his tongue sweeping in my mouth. He tastes better than I imagined.

In my daze, I manage to give him my number and my address. I can't believe this is all happening. I watch as he confidently strides out of the shop, tucking the slip of paper in his breast pocket. He steps outside, stops in front of the window, and gives me a wave before he makes the short walk down the street to the police station.

"Oh fuck that was hot." I fan myself with the coffee menus. My heart is still racing and my clit is throbbing. There is no way I am going to be able to function with all the blood currently rushing down between my legs. I drop the menus on the counter and turn for the kitchen doors. Once in the kitchen, I head straight for the bathroom. I lock the door behind me and lean back against the cold wood. Slipping my hand inside my jeans, rubbing my clit in rough fast circles, I close my eyes and imagine Dylan is fucking me against this door.

His face is buried in my neck, lips and tongue caressing my delicate skin. The image of his cock thrusting in and out of my cunt has me dripping down my hand. I push three fingers inside my tight channel, pumping them in and out while strumming my clit with my thumb. "Make you mine," plays over and over in my head until I'm coming all over my hand. My legs shake as my orgasm surges through me. Dylan is not even here, and he's already made me come better than any of the losers I've dated in the past. If this is the effect he has on me from just a kiss, then I can't wait to see what he can do with the rest of him.

I step over to the sink and wash my hands. My cheeks are still flushed, and I can't wipe the smile Dylan has given me off my face. By the end of tonight, officer Dylan Edwards will finally be mine.

Chapter Two

Dylan

I knock on Zoe's door right at seven. I was so anxious and excited about tonight I pulled up to her building at six-forty-five. I've been planning this entire night for the past week. To be honest, I've been planning this since the day we met. I walked into that donut shop three months ago and saw the most beautiful woman I'd ever seen. With eyes as blue as the ocean, hair as golden as the sun, and a smile that could melt the coldest of hearts. Zoe looked like a fucking angel, and she turned my whole world upside down. She has consumed my every thought, making it even harder for me to concentrate at work. I keep imagining her long lean legs wrapped around my waist while I fuck her tight little cunt. My name spilling from her perfect sweet lips.

It took everything I had not to grab her by her hair and drag her back into the kitchen like a fucking caveman after that kiss. I've only had a small taste, and I'm already addicted to my sweet honeybee. She has awakened this primal need in me to make her mine. I want her by my side and in my bed. More than anything, I want her heart. I want her mine.

A man like me doesn't deserve a real woman like Zoe. I'm no saint when it comes to my past. My dad and my brothers all used drugs to cope with their bullshit, and I used women. Used them to fill the emptiness I was feeling. Zoe is making that pit smaller and smaller. Every morning I look forward to waking up. I get so excited to see her face and hear her voice that I get to the donut shop early and watch her from outside. She likes to dance while she makes the donuts. It's pretty damn cute. I want to see her dance around my house every day. I want her face to be the first thing I see when I wake up, and I want to watch her come every night before she falls asleep in my arms.

The door slowly opens and it's agony waiting to see her face. I've been waiting all day to see her smile and feel her in my arms. When she finally appears, she is wearing a red flannel robe, her eyes are red, and her cheeks are stained with tears. Seeing her in tears is ripping my heart out.

"I'm sorry Dylan, but I had an accident with my dress. It ripped when the zipper got stuck, and I can't go on our date tonight."

"Don't you have another one you can change into? I don't mind waiting."

"Thing is, I bought this dress today because I don't have any other dresses and, looking at you in your nice blue suit and tie, my t-shirts and jeans won't go with wherever it is you are taking me for dinner." Her voice trembles as she fights back more tears. No way am I letting her get out of this date. I've waited three long months for this fucking night, and no way am I letting a ripped dress stand in the way of getting what's mine.

I reach up and pull off my tie and stuff it into my jacket pocket. "Okay, so here is what we are going to do." I reach into my breast pocket and pull out a handkerchief and wipe Zoe's tear soaked cheeks. "We will stay in tonight and I will cook us dinner."

"Do you like boiled chicken and steamed kale, because that is all I have." She winces. I share in her wince, that sounds awful and not the romantic meal I had planned.

"That sounds terrible. Let's walk down to Whole Foods and pick up dinner, and we can have our own little house party. Why don't you go get dressed before you have another clothing malfunction on your hands. Because right now, I would really rather tear you out of that robe and fuck you on the floor of this hallway, and I am pretty sure your neighbors wouldn't appreciate that."

A shy smile graces her face, and her cheeks turn an adorable shade of pink. She thinks I'm kidding but I'm not. My hands are itching to pull open the sash on her robe and see the beauty hiding beneath it. My dick is already growing hard at the thought of touching and tasting every inch of her creamy skin.

"You are terrible Officer Edwards." She giggles. I love the way she calls me Officer Edwards. She will be calling me that in bed later tonight.

"You have no idea my little honeybee. Now go get dressed," I demand, feeling the blood rushing from my head down to my pants. It's only a matter of time before my dick wins this fight. Zoe is the kind of girl that deserves romance and candle light. She deserves to be treated like a queen before I fuck her like a dirty little slut.

Chapter Three

Zoe

I'm standing in front of the buffet at Whole Foods staring at the trays full of mac and cheese, fried rice, breaded fish, and chicken. None of which have ever entered my mouth, never. I hold my little brown box feeling completely flustered. When I was five, my mom decided I needed a hobby to help get me out of my shell. I was a shy kid who used to hide behind my mother's hip whenever anyone would try to talk to me. After the art classes and swimming lessons were a bust, she put me in ballet classes at the community center, and it was just what I needed. Dancing up on that stage made me feel like a different person, one who wasn't actually afraid of her own shadow. I could lose myself in the music and the choreography, letting the weight of my insecurities float away. Turns out I was really good. So good, in fact, that I got a scholarship to the Pacific Northwest Ballet Academy. A part of being a dancer with the PNWB is you are expected to stay a certain weight, which means missing out on pizza, ice cream, basically all things carb, sugar, and good tasting.

I can feel Dylan watching me, he's probably wondering why it's taking me so long to pick something to eat. "I don't normally eat food like this." My cheeks burn red. If he didn't think I was weird before, he does now.

"What did you like to eat before you became a dancer?" he asks.

"I've never actually eaten any junk food," I reply shyly.

"So wait, you've never had pizza or burgers? What about French fries? You've had to of had cake and ice cream when you were a kid."

I hide my face behind my empty food box. "Nope, I didn't have any of it. I was very disciplined, even as a child. You must think I'm a freak." You can't even imagine how difficult it was as a nine-year-old at birthday parties to be eating carrots and celery while the other kids were stuffing their faces with cake and candy.

"No, not at all. All I'm thinking is how I want to stuff you with cheeseburgers and desserts." He taps his index finger against his chin. "How about for tonight, calories don't count, and you can eat whatever your heart desires." He closes the space between us and bends down to my ear. "Besides, we will be working off all those calories later." His lustful words make my pussy clench. "What do you want to eat?"

Besides his cock? I want every fattening thing in this fucking store. I drop the container on the silver buffet. My first instinct is to go for the steamed vegetables, instead, I guide my hand over to the spoon resting in the tray of five cheese and bacon macaroni and cheese. I scoop up a huge spoonful and drop it in my box.

"That's my girl." Dylan flashes me an approving smile.

Next, I go for the pork samosas and spring rolls. If its deep fried and breaded it goes right into my box. Once my box is full, I bring it up to my nose and breathe in all the delicious smells. I place my box into the basket Dylan is holding, and then we walk over to the bakery. I figure if calories don't count tonight then ordering one of every little fruit and pudding tart won't hurt. Dylan just watches in proud amazement while I order a big slice of chocolate cake on top of all the other mouthwatering desserts I ordered. I plan on eating every last crumb of this cake off Dylan's naked body when we get back to my apartment.

"Oh my God, this is the best thing I've ever eaten," I moan, licking the bacon grease and cheese off my lips. After our stop at Whole Foods, Dylan took me to get bacon cheeseburgers from Red Mill Burger, and pizza from Hot Mama's. I've been stuffing my face with all of it. I'm probably going to get sick from eating all this, but it will be so worth it.

This is not how I saw our night going after the fiasco with my dress. I spent the afternoon with Nora trying on every dress at Nordstrom's. I found a gorgeous teal lace dress that hit me just above my knee and hugged what little curves I do have perfectly. Most of my wardrobe consists of black tights, jeans, t-shirts, and converse. Not exactly date attire. Then that damn zipper got stuck and, when I tried to pull it loose, the lace ripped. It was a blessing in disguise because now I have Dylan in my apartment all to myself and have had some of the best food I have ever eaten.

"Just wait until you try the pizza." Dylan smiles, sliding the pizza box across the counter.

I gaze longingly at the cheese and pepperoni goodness. My mouth already watering. "It smells and looks amazing," I say, picking up a slice. The gooey mozzarella cheese strings dangle down from the crust. I take a small bite and let out an almost orgasmic moan. I officially love pizza.

"Dylan, can I ask you something?"

"You can ask me anything," he replies.

"What made you want to be a cop?" I ask. Working around cops for the past year, I've heard a lot of interesting stories of how they became cops. Most were following in the footsteps of their fathers, others just wanted to keep the streets safe and serve their community. I'm fascinated to hear Dylan's reasoning. My sister told me Dylan comes from money, his step father owns the biggest lumber yards in all of Washington. He could have easily taken over the family business and had a cushy desk job. Instead, he puts his life on the line every day to be a SWAT officer.

"My dad and my brothers were my biggest motivation," he replies.

"Are they cops too?" I ask, taking another bite of my pizza.

Dylan lets out a hardy laugh. "No, my dad and my brothers lived and died on the wrong side of the law. Back in Boston my life was completely different. I grew up in one of the roughest neighborhoods in Boston, Charlestown. I was surrounded by armored truck robbers, drug dealers, and gun runners. All three shared a roof with me. Our house was raided by the FBI at least three times a year, and my dad and brothers were constantly in and out of jail. By the time I was fifteen, my mom had had enough of the lies and abuse my father offered up, so one morning, while my dad and brothers were out pulling a job, she packed me up in her car, and we headed for Seattle where my aunt and uncle lived at the time. My mom lost three sons and her husband to the streets, she didn't want to lose me too. I never really fit in with my family in Boston. I always knew what they were doing was wrong and especially hated how they treated my mom. I made a promise to myself when I was eight years old that I was going to be a cop when I grew up. I wanted to keep people like my dad off the streets."

I'm completely blown away by how forthcoming Dylan is about his past. My ex, Elliot, had never talked about his life before meeting me. He didn't even tell me if he still had parents living.

"Thank you for telling me." I feel even closer to him having heard this. Anyone in his shoes could have easily fallen victim to the streets, but Dylan used his father's mistakes as ammunition to make his life better. He became a better man for it.

"I want you to know everything about me, Zoe, even the dark parts." He grabs my hand and pulls me off of my stool and into his lap. "There are no secrets with me, Zoe. I'm an open book. I've done things I'm not proud of, but it's a part of who I am. Loving me means loving all…the good, and the ugly. Do you think you can do that?" His tone deepens. One hand slides around the back of my neck, while his other hand trails up my inner thigh, making the heat pool between my legs. All I can do is nod yes. I will take any piece of him I can get as long as he is mine.

"You're my girl, Zoe. I will never let you go," he says, sealing our lips in a kiss, his tongue tracing along my lips, pleading for entrance. I part my lips letting him in. Our tongues dance in my mouth. He wants me and only me, and that has my whole body on fire. I need him now more than I need air.

"Dylan, I need you," I murmur. My hands glide up his crisp white shirt, feeling every firm sculpted muscle on his chest. One by one, I open each little white button, exposing more and more of his golden tanned skin. My lips move along his strong chiseled jaw and down his neck. A low moan escapes from deep in Dylan's chest when my hands make contact with his bare skin. Sliding his shirt off, I dip my head down and place a gentle kiss on his chest just above his heart.

"Take me to bed, Dylan."

He envelops me in his strong arms and stands to his feet, carrying me to my bedroom. Gently, he places me back on my feet at the foot of the bed. His hands grip the hem of my shirt, pulling it up over my head, letting it drop to the floor next to my feet. A hand reaches behind my back and, with a quick flick of his wrist, the clasp is open, and the straps are sliding down my arms. He licks his lips hungrily at the sight of my bare breasts. My nipples are hard and ready for his mouth.

"Touch me, please." My voice is deep and pleading.

His fingers ghost down between my breasts. "So perfect." He mouths in a hushed tone.

"You're even more beautiful than I imagined." His thumb grazes over my left nipple, sending a surge of electricity through my body. Our lips come together in a deep seductive kiss, hands exploring each other's bodies.

Trailing my fingers down to his belt, I work open the smooth leather and pop the button open. I slip a hand inside his pants, running it along his thick hard length. He groans into our kiss, pressing himself harder against my palm. I pull away from his lips and start to sink down to my knees, but Dylan stops me.

"There will be plenty of time for you to suck my cock later. Tonight is all about you. Lay back on the bed," he orders.

I work my jeans down off my hips, leaving my panties on. I'm giving Dylan the gift of me, and it only seems fitting that he unwraps it. I crawl over to the center of the bed, lie back against my elbows, and watch while Dylan removes the rest of his clothes. When his cock springs free from his boxers, my pussy clenches, and the breath in my lungs is sucked out of my body.

"I see the nickname is true," I absentmindedly say. The rumors of the snake in Dylan's pants run rampant amongst the badge bunnies. I try not to think about how many of them have actually seen him like this. I must focus on the fact that he and that big fucking dick of his are all mine.

"What nickname might that be?" He cocks a curious eyebrow up at me.

"The girls around the bar call you Big Dick Dylan." I blush at my own words and fall back against the pillows.

He lets out a chuckle as he climbs up on the bed. "I've been called a lot of things, but that one is a first." He grips his cock in his hand, gently stroking it as he looks down at me. "All ten inches of this dick are yours my little honeybee."

Chapter Four

Dylan

Zoe reaches down and releases my hand from my cock, replacing it with hers. "Mine," she softly moans, making my dick twitch against her palm. I rock my hips in rhythm with her strokes. A deep primal growl escapes from my chest. My cock is hungry for a taste of my little honeybee, but I need her coming on my mouth first. Once my dick enters her cunt, he won't be leaving it for the rest of the night.

I release her hand from me, my body already missing her touch. Slipping my fingers under the white cotton of her panties, I slide them off and bring them to my nose. A drop of cum drips out of my cock when I feel the wet spot against my lips. I take in a deep breath, letting her sweet honey scent fill my senses. I want her intoxicating scent all over me. I toss the panties over my shoulder.

"I'm going to take you bare, Zoe. I want to feel every pulse of this pretty..." My fingers dance up along her the soft creamy skin of her thighs. "...little." Her head rolls back against the pillows as I spread her lips open with my fingers, exposing her swollen clit. It's pink and plump and throbbing between my fingers. All it would take is one good suck and I'd have her coming in an instant. "... pussy." Her greedy hips buck up. Her pussy is so hungry for me.

"You want my cock, huh honeybee? Don't worry, I'll give him to you. Only after I get a taste." I grip her hips and bring her up to my mouth. Her sweet juices are dripping down to her ass. My tongue glides across her right cheek then to her left, lapping up every drop of her sweet nectar. Oh fuck she tastes so damn good. My tongue plunges deep inside her tight channel, eating her like a man who has been stranded in the Sahara getting his first drink of water.

"Oh God, Dylan," Zoe screams, hands gripping the metal bars of her headboard. Maybe I will tie her to it later. I reach a hand up to her flawless creamy little tits, they are small, but they fit perfectly in my hand. Her rosy pink nipples are standing at full attention. I pinch one between my fingers, making her clench around my tongue.

My mouth latches onto her sweet little bud, and she almost launches off the bed as the pleasure hits her like a tidal wave. Wiggling my head back and forth, I let my beard graze her flesh, leaving her thighs pink and tender. I want her to remember who owns her, with every step she takes, tomorrow and for the next week.

Her body begins to quiver, she's close. As much as I wanted her coming in my mouth, my need to feel her coming on my cock is stronger. Releasing her from my mouth, I lean back on my knees and pull her into my lap, straddling me. She is trembling in my arms. "Dylan, please..." Her voice is just a faint whisper. She's aching to come. I have her right where I want her.

Positioning my tip at her entrance, I slowly push her down on my length. We both cry out in unison. She is so warm and wet and she's gripping me tighter than a fist. It's the most exquisite feeling in the world. The sounds she is making have me about to come already. I haven't laid hands on another woman since I met Zoe, and no other woman will ever feel my touch again. Zoe is it for me.

I grip her golden locks in my hand and, with a quick flick of my wrist, her head is back, and my mouth is on her neck, tongue licking at her pulse point. Her nails dig into my back as she rides me. I wrap my free hand around her tiny waist and hold her tight against my chest while I leave my mark on her neck. Everyone will know she is mine. She is so tight and warm; I don't know how much longer I can hold on.

Her pussy pulses around every inch of my length. "That's it baby, choke my cock with this tight fucking pussy. Come with me, Zoe." Each pulse pulls us closer to the edge.

Zoe holds me tighter as her orgasm takes her over. My name spills from her lips over and over, and it sets me off like a fucking gun. I come hard and fast, filling her with every last drop I have.

Her body goes limp against mine. I hold her steady in my arms as the last of the waves wash over her body. Gently stroking her sweat laced back, I kiss her softly. I knew we would be good together, but

I never thought it could be this damn good. We were made for each other and nothing will ever take that away.

Chapter Five

Zoe

"You are amazing." I giggle, as we fall back against the bed. Dylan is still deeply rooted inside me and hard as a rock, ready for more. He lazily thrusts in and out of my channel while his fingers dance along my curves.

"Oh no, you're the one that is amazing. If my cock wasn't so cozy in your pussy, I would bury my face in that sweet honey pot of yours." His warm lips trail down my neck, his beard tickling my skin. I'm going to have beard burn over every inch of me by the time the sun comes up. I fucking love it.

"We're amazing together." I roll Dylan on his back. Straddling his waist, I kiss a trail over his honed muscular chest. Every inch of him is sculpted perfection. I sit up, slowly rocking my hips. He feels so good inside me, I never want this feeling to end. "I could get use to this."

"Use to what?" he groans, hands settling on my hips, working me harder along his length.

"To you, in my bed, fucking me, holding me, loving me." My head falls back and our moans fill the small space. I want him in my bed every night. I want his arms around me when I fall asleep, and I want him between my legs when I wake up in the morning. Just as I plunge over the edge of ecstasy, I find myself falling even harder for him. In this beautiful moment, I realize I'm in love with Dylan Edwards.

"I love you, Zoe." His words set me off. I chant, "I love you too," over and over until I collapse on top of him.

The loud grumbling of my stomach wakes me from a dead sleep.

Dylan was right, we did work off all of the calories from dinner. It's two in the morning, and I am ravenous for something to eat. I carefully slip out of bed as to not wake up Dylan. After the marathon of love making we just had, he needs his rest because, the moment he wakes up, we are going for the world record of how many orgasms two people can have in twenty-four hours. The rumors about Dylan's talents between the sheets are true, he's a fucking sex god. In just a few hours with him I'm completely addicted.

I walk out to the living room and pick up his shirt from the floor and slip it on, buttoning up two of the tiny buttons. Bringing the collar up to my nose, I breathe in his scent. He smells like a pine forest after a spring rain. I step into the kitchen and head straight for the fridge. Pulling the door open, I pull out the box of tarts and the massive slice of chocolate cake. I set both boxes down on the counter then grab a fork from the drawer.

I pop open the lid on the cake and look down longingly at the rich chocolate frosting and the moist dark chocolate cake. This simple dessert reminds me a little of our relationship, sweet and decadent and oh so bad for you. It makes it all the sweeter now that he said he loves me. It's crazy fast, but who fucking cares. We've spent the past three months getting to know each other, that's long enough for me to know that the feelings I have for him are genuine.

Just as stab my fork into the cake, I feel a pair of arms slide around my waist and a warm set of lips on my neck.

"Can I get a bite of that?" Dylan asks.

I scoop up a bite of cake and feed it to him. He lets out a satisfied hum when the chocolate touches his tongue.

"What are you doing awake?" I ask.

"I rolled over and you were gone, had to find out where my girl went." He takes the fork from my hand and cuts another bite from the cake and offers it to me. I let the fork slide into my mouth. The sweet chocolate explodes around my taste buds.

"I had to get something to eat. You successfully worked off my dinner." I slyly grin, turning in his arms. I give him a once over and see that he is naked, and that ten-inch monster of his is already hard. I bet his cock would taste pretty damn good covered in chocolate.

"Told you we'd work off all those extra calories." With a cocky grin sliding across his face, he reaches behind me and pushes the cake box out of the way then lifts me up on the counter. He opens the two buttons and slides my shirt off, tossing it to the floor. "When we are alone you will be naked. I don't want anything coming between me and what's mine." His dark possessive words send a chill through my whole body. He pulls me closer to the edge of the marble counter, lining up his fat tip at my entrance then slowly pushes inside me.

He scoops up another bite of cake and feeds it to me while he slowly fucks me in my kitchen. I dip my finger into the luscious frosting and smear the cold concoction over each of my nipples. He's feeding me a snack; he might as well get one too. Resting my hands back on the counter, I offer up my chocolate covered nipples to him. Like a magnet his head dips down, and his tongue lavishes my tits.

Dylan reaches his hand into the box and grabs a handful of cake. He brings it up to my mouth and I take a big bite. The frosting and bits of cake cover my lips. His mouth comes crashing down on mine, sucking and licking me clean. Dylan smears the rest of the cake down my chest and over my breasts.

"Hey, I'm supposed to be eating that off of you," I pout. Dylan reaches back into the box and scoops up more cake then wipes it down his chest.

"There, now we can eat it off each other." We both laugh. I wrap my hands around the back of his neck and pull him to my lips.

"I love you so damn much."

"I love you too, honeybee."

There is no guarantee as to what life will throw at us, but I know whatever it is, Dylan and I will be ready to take it head on. Our love may be new, but it is strong, and nothing will ever tear us apart.

About M. Andrews

M. Andrews resides in the suburbs of Seattle with her husband and two daughters. She is a self-proclaimed cupcake hound and coffee addict who loves to write sticky sweet erotic romance. M is the author of the Gambling on Love Series and the Sticky Sweet Series.

Website: mandrewsauthor.com

Facebook: www.facebook.com/Author-M-Andrews-851376491601312/

Twitter: twitter.com/Whiskeysoaked

Instagram: www.instagram.com/authormandrews/

Pinterest: www.pinterest.com/AuthorMAndrews/

Goodreads: www.goodreads.com/author/show/14035728.M_Andrews

Confessions of a Beard Lover

by Adrienne Perry

Internally, Chase Adams was cursing up a shit storm. Externally, he remained calm, even pleasant as he repeatedly told the waitress who was ineffectually mopping up maple syrup from his thigh and moving in a direction that was getting dangerously close to his crotch, that really, he was fine. To please, just let it go. He'd clean it up himself.

The waitress didn't seem to want to let it go. Whether it was because she genuinely felt guilty about being responsible for the sticky goo that covered most of his front side, or whether she just was looking for a cheap thrill, Chase wasn't quite sure. Her smile told him she knew just how to show a man a good time, and probably had more than a time or two.

But she'd have to save that smile for another man, another day. The only thing on Chase's mind at the moment was getting out of this impossibly small Tennessee town, and doing so, hopefully, in clean clothes. But at 6:30 am on a Sunday morning, Chase recognized the chances he'd find an open clothing store were slim to none.

Chase finally managed to push the waitress away, but not before shooting her an apologetic smile that was also a definite "no" to what she had unofficially offered.

He threw some money down on the diner table and strode out into the humid morning air, his right hand rubbing absently at his beard. The Ben Franklin down the street didn't open until noon. Chase needed a change of clothes now, and according to the waitress, the nearest town that might offer stores that opened before lunchtime was at least an hour's drive away. Still, Chase found himself walking down Main Street.

The place was like a ghost-town. Aside from in the diner, he had yet to see another car or person.

Chase sighed, and turned to head back to his truck, when a blast of hot air hit him. Turning his head to follow the heat, he saw the door of a dry-cleaners swinging open slightly. Strange, since there wasn't a breeze, but a moving door meant an unlocked door, and maybe the dry cleaner would be able to help Chase out. How, he wasn't quite sure, but he figured it was worth a chance.

Saturday "Daisy" Fontaine had never been a religious person. She'd often give a shout out to the big guy/girl upstairs, but she found the rules and restrictions of formalized religion far too constricting. However, Daisy also loved her Nana, which was why, with less than six hours until her deadline to submit her next travel blog on the awesomeness of the Great Smoky Mountains and the micro-towns nestled within their rolling peaks and valleys, Daisy had been kicking up dust along a deserted Appalachian highway in desperate need of a Catholic priest.

Her precious Nana had called Daisy to tell her that "it was her time," and she had "gotten the call from the man in charge," and her only wish at that moment was for Daisy to go to confession and be absolved of her sins. The connection had been spotty, and it had been hard to hear everything her Nana was saying, but Daisy caught the gist of the message before her cell coverage had cut out, and hadn't come back. Daisy had considered telling her Nana she'd gone to confession without actually following through, but some amount of Catholic guilt was ingrained in her head, and she felt like she owed it to her Nana to really do it.

Frantic with worry for her Nana, and driven by the need to fulfill her wishes, Daisy had punched in "Catholic Church" into her GPS. She'd complied when the robotic yet soothing female voice urged her to exit the already questionable main highway. Which was why, when her tire had blown and Daisy discovered there was no spare, she remained stranded on the side of a dirt road with no rescue in sight. She knew her Nana would scold her for not checking the rental's trunk before driving it off the lot. "Always make sure you have a spare," was one of the life lessons her sweet grandmother had reiterated over the years.

But she'd ignored her Nana's advice to check the spare, and with few other options available to her, Daisy did the only other thing she could think of: she looked both ways down the road, and started walking.

"Hello?"

Chase's greeting as he walked into the dry cleaner's was met with silence.

"Hello? Anyone here?" he called again.

Nothing.

Looking around, and even peeking in the back revealed an empty store. Bummed that he'd struck out, Chase moved to walk back out, when he noticed the bag swaying gently on the clothes rack.

The thought that popped into Chase's mind was wrong. He knew it was wrong, but his maple syrup pants were too damn uncomfortable. Instead of walking out, taking his sticky pants with him, he found himself striding across the cracked linoleum floor towards the plastic garment bag. He ripped the top corner open. Chase glanced at the clothes ever so quickly, and noted a pair of black pants in his size. He registered there was also a black shirt. He didn't look any closer, just grabbed the bag off the rack before he thought too closely about what he was doing and changed his mind. It might be the right thing to do to walk away empty-handed, but he was going to start chafing down there, and that would be a frigging nightmare.

Chase wasn't completely beyond redemption, though. Before leaving he threw a hundred dollar bill down on the counter and made a promise to himself that he'd send the clothes back as soon as he could.

As soon as Chase was on the sidewalk, he ripped open the bag all the way to see his haul.

"God dammit all to hell!" he exclaimed as the plastic fell away to reveal the outfit inside.

The door clicked shut behind him.

"You've got to be fucking kidding me!"

Chase stared at the black clerical shirt and pants dangling from the wire hanger. The white collar tab flashed mockingly at Chase as the sun glanced off its shiny brightness.

A priest's outfit? A goddamn priest's outfit? Chase ran his hand over his chin, letting the rough scruff raze his palm. *Was this some kind of a cosmic joke?*

Chase thought about all the bad things he'd done in his life. The beds he'd snuck out of in the pre-dawn hours, the promises he'd made and failed to keep, the lies he'd told to protect himself. He wondered if someone, something, was trying to send him a message.

He tried the door again, but this time it was locked tight. Stuck with two undesirable options, Chase's natural go-with-the-flow approach to life bubbled to the surface and he let out a bellowing laugh at the sheer hilarity of the situation. Shaking his head, he shucked off his soiled clothes, right there on the sidewalk. *Let 'em look*, he thought to himself, *if there's even anyone alive in this town. They'll get a good show.*

No one was watching, at the moment, but if they had been, they definitely would have gotten a good show. It wasn't bragging for Chase to think women would line up for the chance to glimpse his shirtless torso. Tall and muscular, Chase looked good, really good, both clothed and not. He kicked the dirty jeans and T-shirt into a pile on the ground, and stepped into the polyester blend pants and shirt. Even though he refrained from putting the white tab into the shirt, there was no denying he was dressed like a priest. He looked up at the sky for a moment, wondering if lightening was going to strike him down. When nothing happened, he gathered up his dirty pile and tossed it in the back seat of his truck.

Chase didn't notice the white collar sticking to the syrup on his pants. Nor did he notice it detach itself and flutter down onto the floor of the front seat.

Chase started the engine and rolled out of town. *It's been real,* he said silently, watching the town shrink out of sight in his rearview mirror.

While she walked, Daisy worried. She worried about her Nana, she worried about her blog, she worried about werewolves roaming the woods, she worried she'd find herself in the middle of the movie *Deliverance*.

While she walked, Daisy also checked her phone for a signal. Nothing.

Between walking and worrying and checking her phone, Daisy also let her mind wander, traveling to places that made her uncomfortable. She considered the fact that she'd been driving a while without passing any towns or houses, and that maybe walking wasn't the best plan to follow. She also thought about *Deliverance* again, and *Texas Chainsaw Massacre*, and The *Hills Have Eyes*, and every other horror movie in which bad things happen to people who are stranded and alone in the middle of nowhere. Daisy concluded she should find a weapon. She might not have a spare tire in the truck, but surely there'd be one of those tire-iron things that you always saw people holding in movies—the ones with the sharp poky bit on one end?

Daisy returned to her car. After poking about in the trunk for a bit revealed nothing of real use for protection, Daisy did something completely out of character. She lifted her head up to the sky and prayed for help.

A moment later, she heard the faint rumble of a car engine in the distance.

<hr />

Chase was surprised when he noticed the car stopped ahead in the breakdown lane of the narrow two-lane road. Tough luck. His first instinct was to keep on driving, let the unfortunate SOB fend for himself.

But then Chase noticed the legs. Unquestionably female, they were long and lean and stretched for miles before ending in faded denim shorts. They were attached to an equally impressive top half, with a narrow waist and tight, pert breasts highlighted in the black tank top she was wearing. Chase probably would have pulled over regardless of his instinct to keep going, even if the stranded traveler had been a fat, balding guy. But he'd be lying if he said he didn't appreciate that his potential passenger was a woman with a smoking hot body. He eased his foot off the accelerator and prepared to slow down.

As he got closer, he was able to see more details. Her light brown hair was pulled back in a messy ponytail. Stray bits fell in soft curls around her face. Blurry facial features resolved themselves into the visage of an undeniably gorgeous woman with high cheekbones, luminous eyes, and a wide, generous mouth.

The only drawback was that currently the mouth was turned down in a scowl. Chase saw her squinting at the truck. He guessed she was trying to see who was driving and if he was safe or not, so he tried to mold his expression into one that looked harmless and kind. He ran his hand over his jaw, and reflected that his scruffy beard probably made him look like a backwoods derelict. Nothing he could do about that now, though. He'd just have to do or say whatever he could to ease any concerns she'd have about his intentions.

He hadn't seen a single other car while he'd been driving, and he'd been on the road for almost thirty minutes already. He'd bet his was the first car that had come by, and he knew she couldn't turn down his offer of help. Besides, with the scowl and squinty eyes, she looked positively fearsome. Maybe he should be worried about his own safety instead of worrying about hers.

Daisy felt equal parts relieved and scared when she heard the engine noise approaching. *Please, please don't be a murderer.* She gripped her cell phone tightly in one hand, and impulsively grabbed a medium sized rock off the ground in the other. She kept this hand behind her back. She figured if it was someone dangerous, she'd tell him she had the police on the line to scare him off, and if that didn't work, she'd bash him in the head with the rock. She made a mental note to sign up for a self-defense class when she made if back to civilization.

A dust cloud preceded the vehicle, and she felt a pang of dismay at the hulking pick-up truck that finally rumbled into view. This was no benign Prius or safe-looking sedan that would be driven by a woman, or possibly a family with 2.5 kids and a dog in the back. This was a truck that screamed masculinity and testosterone. Daisy felt another tingle of anxiety. But then again, she tried to reassure herself, hadn't she read somewhere that 98% of the people in the world are basically good, and with good intentions, and only a small minority have bad plans?

The truck was approaching and it was slowing as it got closer to her. Daisy squinted at the driver's seat, trying to see who was behind the wheel, but the sun glared harshly off the windshield and she couldn't make out any details. Just as the truck reached within about a hundred feet of her, Daisy heard her phone ding, letting her know she had a new text message. Which meant she also had a signal! A huge grin of relief spread across her face, and she looked down at her phone to see who was trying to reach her. It was Nana. The message read *The Good Lord provides*, followed by praying hands and a smiley emoji.

At that moment, the truck stopped next to Daisy and the driver rolled down the window.

When Chase saw the woman smile, she literally took his breath away. The air actually caught in his lungs and hovered there, paralyzed. It felt like his heart stilled and his blood stopped flowing as her face transformed into something fucking dazzling. She was pretty before, but her smile lit up her face, made her eyes shine, and she radiated happiness and goodness with her expression. She made the world a brighter, kinder place. Just with a smile.

Chase felt a growing unease that this woman might have the power to bewitch him like no one ever had before. They hadn't even spoken, and already he wanted nothing more than to do something, anything, to be the one who brought a smile like that back to her face, to the world. Just one look, one hit, and already he was addicted, already hooked on the high he got when he saw it.

His heart began to beat again, but faster now, pounding in his chest. His blood rushed in a frenzy through his veins. His breath took a moment longer to return, and when it did, it came in rapid, rasping gulps. He struggled to pull in enough oxygen, his head growing dizzy. But it was already too late. Chase was drowning. He was sunk.

When the truck stopped and the driver rolled down the window, Daisy gasped.

It took her less than a second to take in the man (HOT!), the outfit, and the white priest's collar on the floor of the truck. *Seriously? She was being rescued by a priest? Thanks Nana! She thought to herself. And thanks whoever else is up there who sent him to me. And you made him fucking hot, too?*

Wait…wasn't that like, against the rules or something. Weren't priests supposed to be old and grandfatherly? And what's with the facial hair? Priests are allowed to have five day old scruff now? Didn't they have personal grooming rules? And how wrong was it that Daisy was feeling a ping of attraction to this guy?

"Hey, you having some car trouble?" he asked. "Need some help?"

His voice was deep and smooth, like melted caramel on a scoop of ice cream, coating her insides with warmth and satisfaction. Daisy didn't give herself a chance to acknowledge the tremble she felt in her stomach, and her knees, when she heard his voice. Instead, she focused on the fact that she'd been searching for a priest, and now here one was, practically dropped into her lap. Daisy also ignored the burst of arousal she felt when she thought about him in her lap.

"Wow, thanks! Yeah, I got a flat and the spare is missing. It's a rental. And even though Nana told me to always check the spare before I leave, I forgot. I've been stuck here, and I have no phone reception, and I cannot believe how crazy, and how perfect, it is that you… you! are the one who pulled up. I totally need you right now, and this is like a miracle!"

The words exploded out of Daisy's mouth before she could think or filter. She needed a priest, she needed to go to confession, and she'd gotten one. Bonus because he was so good looking. Or maybe that wasn't a bonus, because instead of thinking about repentance, all she could focus on was how sexy he was. And once that thought was in her head, she couldn't keep her eyes from roaming over his body and noticing how hard his thighs looked straining against the fabric of the pants. And it was really impossible to ignore the ropy muscles in his forearms, or the way they led up to sculpted biceps that Daisy suddenly, inexplicably, wanted to lick. *Jesus, where had that come from?*

Stop. Stop looking at his muscles. Look somewhere else instead. Unfortunately for Daisy, her eyes rested on his face, and sweet baby Jesus, it was like looking at someone who could be a cover model for GQ. He had dark, longish hair that looked like his only nod to grooming was to run a hand through it. It was mussed and wild, dangerously inviting someone to smooth it down into tameness. A stray lock flopped onto his forehead, and Daisy's hand actually itched to brush it back.

His dark eyes were framed with long lashes that would have made a less masculine man look pretty rather than handsome. On him, though, it just drew attention to those eyes. Deep, dark brown, like a cup of hot chocolate on a cold winter's day. Straight nose, strong, with character. And then his lips. Full and wide, tasty.

The look was capped off with the scruff. Definitely more than 5 o'clock shadow. More, even, than two day's growth, but not yet a full blown beard. It was the facial hair of a man who'd spend days in bed with his woman, not wanting to leave her even long enough to shave. He radiated a laid-back, bit of a devil-may-care attitude, though that must just be in her imagination, because he was a priest after all. Daisy wondered if the scruff would be scratchy or soft, or some wonderful combination of the two. And if it would feel different on her face as compared to between her legs.

Stop! Daisy ordered herself. *He's a priest. He's not available for dating…or more.*

Daisy realized he was saying something, and she had no idea what it was. She stared at him blankly until he repeated the question.

"Do you need a ride somewhere? I haven't had signal on my phone either, but I'm heading to Bellington. It should be about 45 minutes from here."

The gears in Daisy's brain were grinding so slowly that she had to dissect each word to figure out what he was saying. Her mind fought with itself, one part wanting to think about his hands exploring her curves, his long fingers dipping into forbidden places, another part warning her to stop. Fuck!

He held up his hands, palms open, and smiled at her. "I swear I'm safe. Scout's honor!"

Daisy forced her mind to clear again. No more sexy thoughts. But he should be safe. Daisy found she instinctively trusted him, and not, she thought, just because he was a priest. It just seemed as though there was something inherently honest about him. And anyway, she didn't really have much choice. His was the first car she'd seen since her tire had blown, and who knew how long it would be before someone else drove by?

Also, the memory of Nana's request still echoed in her head, and the message she'd sent resonated. The appearance of this man made too many things fall into place. She could ride with him to the town, get her car fixed or towed or whatever, and confess to satisfy Nana.

His good looks had no power over her. She could talk to him without fantasizing about stripping him naked and sampling every inch of his body with her fingers, with her tongue.

And then he smiled at her. And Daisy was lost.

Chase hadn't been paying much attention to what the woman was saying. He'd been distracted by how alluring she was and how he longed to wind his fingers in her hair so he could tug her head back before kissing her neck.

She had a flat tire; that part he got. Then there was something about her grandma, nana? But the part that had come through loud and clear was when she said he was perfect, and that she needed him. Everything else was unimportant. Chase caught the important part: she wanted him!

God knew, he wanted her, too. He felt a tightening in his groin even thinking about it, and he shifted slightly to accommodate. He'd always been a man who appreciated the beauty of women, and enjoyed their pleasures when he could. But he couldn't remember ever having had such an instant and intense attraction to someone before.

He thought she might still be a little wary; she had hesitated when he offered her a ride. So he'd thrown his hands up in mock surrender, declaring himself safe. Of course, he figured any decent serial killer would proclaim himself safe, so maybe that didn't help make him appear more trustworthy to her. Absently, he ran his hand over his chin again, a habit that was becoming increasing comforting to him, and then pulled at the gold chain around his neck. It was a memento from his grandmother, a strong and fierce matriarch of their family, who had pressed the chain, which held a gold cross into his palm the last time he'd visited her, an occurrence that happened far too seldom for both of them. Before he'd grown the facial hair, and taken to rubbing that when he needed to think or distract himself, he'd often pulled at the cross and fingered it instead. He did so now, and watched as the woman's eyes widened in…shock?…before she stuck her hand in the window.

"I'm Daisy, and yes, I could really use your help."

Chase took her hand in his. Her skin was soft, like silk, and her hand was tiny in his giant paw. But her grip was surprisingly strong and confident.

"Daisy, nice, like the flower. I'm Chase. Nice to meet you."

"I'm actually named 'Saturday', but when I was three I insisted everyone start calling me Daisy. My parents really challenged me with their choice for my name. It's good to meet you too. And should I really just call you Chase? It seems a little informal, but whatever. Can we do it now, or do you have to be on duty, or something? Oh! And do we need to be anywhere special for this, or is in the car ok? It's been a while. Years, really. I and was never really into it before. I don't even really remember how to get started."

Chase was pretty sure she couldn't possibly be talking about what it sounded like she was talking about. Because it sure sounded like she was propositioning him for sex. Not that he'd be opposed. His dick was in full agreement with her idea. But was she offering him sex in exchange for the ride? He guessed people did that sometimes, but she seemed too wholesome for that. She didn't seem innocent, exactly, but she didn't look like the type of person who made it a habit to trade sex for favors.

Maybe he was wrong, though. Maybe that was what she was offering. And if she was, did he dare take her up on it? He wanted it. Lord knows he wanted it. She did something to his insides that was unexpected and unfamiliar. He wanted to drink her in. But he also felt protective of her, and he didn't want her feeling beholden to him and giving her body to him out of a sense of obligation. He actually could think of little worse than pushing himself inside of her and seeing a grimace of duty cross her features before she turned her face away.

Yes, he wanted her, and with a fierceness that challenged the reality that he'd only just met her, but he wanted her panting under him with the same arousal that he felt. He wanted her begging for his touch, his mouth. He wanted her to want him, and not just be there. He yearned to strip her control and wariness away as much as he wanted to strip her clothes off. Anything less would be disappointing.

"I think first names are appropriate, don't you? We're not so deep in the south that we ought to go by Mr. and Mrs. until we're formally introduced, are we? And all I'm doing is offering a ride. Nothing else is required or asked for. I really do just want to give you a lift. So please don't feel like anything more is needed. At most, I'll ask for some pleasant, banal conversation to pass the time before we get to town. Okay?"

"Conversation? Is that what it's called now? Last time I did it, which was probably when I was in seventh or eighth grade, it was still called confession."

Confession? Was that a euphemism for sex he'd never heard before? Chase thought he'd heard, and used, them all, but this would be a new one.

And then it clicked. His outfit. The collar. She thought we was a goddamn priest! He should have figured it out sooner, but he'd been distracted by her long legs and honeyed skin.

Here he'd been thinking she was asking him for sex, and she thought he was a priest. He should clear this up right away. By now Daisy had opened the door and settled herself into the passenger seat. But even though the words of explanation formed in his brain, when he opened his mouth, instead of the truth, he asked, "Confession, huh? What would a good girl like you have to confess?"

He knew he shouldn't, but he couldn't quite resist having a little fun with her.

Daisy sighed and crossed her arms over her chest. Chase pretended not to notice her breasts as she did that. "I don't know. My Nana is really into it, you know? She wants me to do this, so I'm really just doing it for her."

"Sounds to me," and Chase was no expert, but he was sure about this part, "That if you give a confession, it's supposed be because it's something you really want to do."

"Yeah." She nodded. "It is. But still. I'm kinda hoping it'll be good Karma to do it for her."

"Okay, then." He tried not to let his smile escape into a laugh. "If you were going to confess. What it is you'd want to say, do you think?"

"Forgive me Father…Chase…for I have sinned. It's been, well, a long time since my last confession."

Then Daisy began.

He didn't expect what came next.

Daisy hadn't thought she'd be so nervous. She also hadn't thought she'd be confessing to a hot priest, especially one that had sounded like he was flirting with her. That shouldn't be allowed. How was she supposed to tell him about all the sins she'd committed when she was thinking about how sexy his lips were? Wait! Did she have to confess that? Oh god, she probably did. And now she'd said 'god', in vain, even if only in her head. So she had more to confess. Shit. And she didn't even think she needed to confess, and that was probably a sin, too

"Ok, so I've lied, like, a lot of times. But never anything too big. I mean, a couple times I called in sick to work when really I felt fine. But it was more of a mental health day for me. I just needed to recharge, and mental health is really a big part of overall health, so those don't even count as lies. It's kind of a travesty that mental health isn't considered a part of overall health, and that there isn't more compensation for people trying to manage their issues.

"But that's off topic. I also lied to my friend recently when I told her I was busy when she invited me to a Pampered Chef party, and then stayed home watching The Bachelor instead. It was already recorded so I was actually free to go to the party. I felt really bad about that later, because she only had two other people show up, so it was kind of embarrassing for her, but mostly just felt relieved that I hadn't had to be there. And, well, I'm sure there are more. I don't remember them all, so maybe I can just lump them all into one big sin, and leave it at that?"

Daisy snuck a sideways glance at Chase. His eyes were on the road, and he seemed to be listening intently, though he had a hint of a smile at the corner of his mouth. When she hesitated, he cast a quick glance her way and nodded encouragement for her to continue. She was sure she'd seen amusement in his grin.

"I swear. Also a lot. And I say 'god' all the time. I don't mean anything by it, though. It's just an expression. But, I'm sorry.

"Ummm…I envy things? Like the new Tory Burch purse my editor just got. I didn't even really like it, I just wanted it because of the name. Though, oh my god, that leather felt good. I wanted to take a nap on it, it was so soft. Oh, and I've done the 'name in vain' one again. Sorry. Wait…actually, I kind of lied again. I'm not really sorry about that. I don't truly think that's a really big deal. I mean, I don't think God is really sitting up in heaven keeping a tally of all the times someone says 'Oh god!' But I will try to be better about that, and the swearing. Does that count?

"And, what else? I don't really know. I think I'm basically a good person. I haven't murdered anyone, and I like to think that I'm mostly nice. I don't go to church, though. Is that a sin? If yes, then sorry. But I probably won't start going more often. So I apologize in advance for that."

Daisy paused. She felt simultaneously that she'd said too much and hadn't said enough. She thought about the story her Nana had told her once about her grandfather. Her grandparents had immigrated to the US from Italy, and spoke no English when they arrived. But her grandfather had wanted to go to confession, so he'd written a list of sins in Italian and asked a neighbor's child to translate them into English, which he then memorized. His confession went flawlessly as he recited his sins until the priest demanded one more sin before his penance would be delivered. But her grandfather didn't know the words to come up with one more.

Daisy sympathized with her grandfather and his need to pull one more sin out when he'd thought he was done. Right now, she felt like she needed to come up with something that had a bit more meat.

Chase, glanced over at her again.

"I should…" he said at the same time that Daisy began to speak again.

"Please," she said, not wanting to stop in case she lost her nerve. She was feeling increasingly nervous around him partly because she couldn't ignore her growing attraction to him. "Can I keep going?"

Chase looked like he wanted to say something, but after a moment of hesitation, he simply nodded and said, "Go on."

"Thanks. So, I, uh, don't think birth control is wrong. I mean, there are too many people in this world anyway, and I think it's just irresponsible not to use condoms. So I guess that means I don't think premarital sex is wrong. And," Daisy felt her face turn a bright red as she blushed, "I've you, know, had it a few times. The sex that is, and the birth control."

Daisy picked nervously at the hem of her shorts, pulling at the frayed denim. She could pretend that she was just confessing sins to please her Nana, but if she was being honest, she'd have to admit that she was really bringing up sex specifically to see what his reaction would be. She wasn't flirting, exactly, but she was trying to push the boundaries, trying to see if she could get a rise (haha) out of him. It was out of character for her to be this forward, and she was uncertain about it, but at the same time, something about being around him made her feel both bold and safe.

She snuck another sideways glance at Chase. He was just as good-looking in profile as he was from the front. Damn, there should seriously be a rule against good-looking priests. It was kind of a waste to have such a good looking guy off the market for no good reason. Not that being a priest wasn't a good reason, a noble job. Spiritual, and all. But still, it was a little unfortunate.

Or, maybe he was there as a plant. Someone deliberately gorgeous so that women would lust after him…that was one of the big sins, wasn't it? Lust. So he was like a trap, God trying to rack up as many deadly sins as he could so he'd get more repentance. Maybe God fed off of repentance. Maybe it was like heroin to him.

Daisy mentally slapped herself. Had she really just called God a drug addict? What was wrong with her? But despite the conflicting emotions about blaspheming God filling her head, Daisy didn't stop her next words from coming.

"I've also had impure thoughts." Daisy paused, then sighed before continuing. "And, I just lied again. When I said I'd *had* impure thoughts. I made it seem like it was something in the past. But it's not. I still have them. I'm having them right now."

"Daisy, I really need to tell you…" Chase interrupted, but Daisy couldn't let him cut in.

"No, just wait until I finish. If I don't keep going I'll lose my nerve. The lustful thoughts I'm having, actually, are about, um, you. And I know that's wrong, and it's so embarrassing, but I sort of have to tell you because this is confession after all. I'm supposed to be feeling sorry for all the things I've done that are bad, and all I can think about is the bad things I want to do to you. Right now."

Daisy's voice had lowered to almost a whisper. That, along with the words she was saying, had created a bubble of intimacy in the cab of the truck. It felt like the air had thickened and stilled, that time had slowed. Outside, everything was speeding by, but in the cab of the truck, it was just the two of them in a moment that stretched every second into a thousand ticks. She felt reckless. Her pulse was racing.

"I have an almost overwhelming desire to put my hand on your thigh, just to see what happens. I want to feel the muscles in your leg tense, and I want to see your jaw clench when I run my hand up your thigh towards your cock. I want to run my hands over the zipper of your pants to see if you're hard. I want you to be hard. I want to feel you straining against the fabric even though you're not supposed to. I want to feel that especially because you're not supposed to. I want to turn you on because you're not supposed to get turned on. I want to tempt you, and I want to make you break your vows."

Chase felt like he'd been hit in the chest with a sledgehammer. It was suddenly a struggle to breathe. He pulled at the tight, polyester collar of his shirt, wishing the neckline wasn't sticking up and itching his neck. He also wished the smoking hot woman sitting next to him didn't think he was a priest.

He knew, of course he knew, that he needed to stop her. He'd encouraged her in the beginning because it was fun, and silly. He'd loved hearing her talk, was intrigued by the game. He figured she'd come up with some easy sins, and then they'd have a good laugh about the situation. But suddenly her confession had morphed into something dirty, and sexy and he wanted to listen to her voice forever. He needed to tell her the truth. But God help him, he wasn't strong enough to stop her from talking.

So Chase didn't explain, didn't stop her from going on.

When Daisy had started confessing, she'd really been sincere in trying to tell the priest everything, as truthfully and openly as possible. But not too long after she'd started, her confession had become something else. And when she'd seen Chase swallow when she'd mentioned his cock, when his hands tightened on the steering wheel and the bead of sweat appeared on his temple when she said she imagined pulling his pants zipper down with her teeth, she forgot all about the fact that she was supposed to be unburdening her soul of its sins and she just wanted Chase. She wanted his hands and his mouth and his fucking beard scratching at the skin between her thighs while his tongue dived into the core of her.

"Tell me more," Chase said, his voice rough.

"Maybe," Daisy responded, her voice low and sultry, "It would be better if I show you. Just so you know exactly what I mean."

A breath of air whooshed from Chase's lungs. Daisy could see his pulse thumping in his neck, and she felt powerful and sexy that her words were having such an effect on him. She glanced down at his lap, pleased to see his erection pressing against his pants.

"Maybe," Daisy repeated, "you should pull over so you can… concentrate…better."

Chase didn't need a second request. In a blur of gravel and dust, he slid onto the shoulder and threw the truck in park. Seconds later both his and Daisy's seatbelts were off. He half lifted her, and she half shifted herself over the center console until she was facing him, her legs straddling his lap. He thrust his hips up into her pelvis, his erection pushing into her. He rotated under her, grinding into Daisy and pulling from her a deep moan.

This was like a fucking fantasy coming to life. How was it possible that this was actually happening?

Chase pulled Daisy's face to his, and their lips met with heat and desire. This was no slow, building kiss. This was all fire. Chase thrust his tongue deep into her mouth, demanding that she open for him. He scraped his teeth along her lips while his beard scratched her cheeks. Daisy responded by pulling Chase's bottom lip into her mouth and nipping at it with her teeth. Chase drew her tongue into his mouth and sucked on it hard. At the same time, his hands ran up and down her body, slowing as they passed the sides of her breasts and ending up cupping her ass, pulling her harder onto him.

She was perfect. The sensation of her, the taste of her, it was almost unbearable she felt so good.

He wanted this. He wanted it so damn bad. But the voice in his head screaming at him that he was taking advantage became too loud to ignore. And Chase did the unthinkable. He stilled his hands on her waist and held her steady on his lap. It took more effort than he had imagined to pull away from her, but he couldn't let this happen without first telling her the truth.

Before he could do that, though, he felt Daisy freeze in his embrace. Her expression morphed from pleasure into regret and she scrambled back over to her side of the cab.

"Oh my god," Daisy spoke in a horrified voice. "I can't even believe I just did that. I'm going to hell. I just made out with a priest! How is this okay for you? Do you have to quit the priesthood now?"

"No, listen, slow down." Chase struggled to find the words to explain. "What just happened wasn't bad. It's not what you think. I'm not what you think."

Chase rubbed at his chin again, watching Daisy's eyes narrow in confusion and suspicion.

"What do you mean you're not what I think? What I think is you're a priest, and that we just kissed. And there is something so, so wrong about that."

She was fucking gorgeous, and Chase wished he'd been truthful sooner. He feared he'd blown it by holding back, for letting her go on with her confession for as long as he had. He hated himself for being the one that had encouraged her to do something that made her feel badly. He'd taken advantage of her, and he could never expect her to forgive him for that. Forget that she'd started it, that she'd been the one to suggest it. He should have been stronger for her. He should have told her the truth, no matter that he'd been more turned on by her words than he'd been by anything or anyone before, and he had a raging case of blue balls to prove it.

He sighed. It was already too late. The proper time had already passed, but he still needed to tell her the truth.

"So, uh, I actually have my own confession."

Daisy's head popped up, her eyes still filled with guilt.

"I'm not actually a priest."

Her mouth opened in the sexiest little "oh" he'd ever seen. And he'd seen a lot. He'd watched women try for the wide-eyed, open-mouthed surprised look, pouting their lips into a perfect circle to accept the hard tip of a dick, and they hadn't even come close to looking as fuck-able as Daisy looked right now. And she was doing it completely unintentionally.

"Yeah, so, it's a funny story, actually. I was in this little town, having break—"

Chase broke off as he watched Daisy's face transform from surprise, to disbelief, to full-on fury. Chase had seen his share of angry women before, but no one had ever looked as lethal as Daisy did. He would have sworn that her amber eyes actually turned red.

"Whoa. Let me explain. I swear, this is not as crazy as you think. Well, maybe it is that crazy, but I don't make it a habit to lure innocent women stuck on the side of the road to confession."

As he took a breath to launch into the story, prepared to do anything to convince her to forgive him, even though he knew that chances of that were slim, Daisy flung open the door and leaped from the seat. On the dusty side of the highway, she leaned over, hands on her knees. Chase couldn't tell if she was hyperventilating or trying not to vomit. He got out of his side of the car and began walking cautiously towards her.

She held up one hand, and without looking at him, spoke in a clipped voice. "Do not come near me," she ordered. "You are the biggest fucking asshole ever, and I need you to leave. Now." Then she mumbled to herself, "Oh my god, oh my god, what did I do? What do I do?"

Chase had never been good with emotions. Not his own, and especially not women's. It had never bothered him before, but suddenly, at that moment, he wished he knew what to say, what to do. It actually hurt him that she was so upset. It hurt him even more knowing he was the cause.

Everything had just happened so quickly, and he didn't know of a man who would have turned down what Daisy had offered

Chase's normal MO would be to drive off and leave her there, per her wishes. He couldn't deny that he'd adopted a love 'em and leave 'em philosophy a time or two in the past. He could call for a tow truck or highway patrol to rescue her once he was far enough away. They'd only known each other for a heartbeat of time.

But already he was changed. He wanted to become the kind of man who deserved a woman like her. He didn't want her to be angry at him, and more than that, he didn't want their relationship, if you could even call it that, over before they'd even started. He didn't want this to be it. She was undeniably gorgeous, but more than the way she looked, what attracted him to her was the way she talked, and the silly way she had of explaining her actions, her outlook on what was right and wrong and how she struggled with knowing the difference, her conviction that good intentions might outweigh your actions, and the love she had for her grandmother. He wanted more of that.

"Please, Daisy, I really am sorry, but the story is actually kind of funny. If you just let me explain…"

"Funny?!? You think this is funny?" Daisy had never felt fury like this before. And now this guy, this liar and cheat, and who knew what else, was trying to tell her this was funny? She'd told him about everything she'd done wrong, and he let her, without trying to stop her. And then she'd talked dirty to him, had kissed him. Daisy felt her cheeks flush again with embarrassment. Oh god, she was going to hell.

"I just confessed to you, and you let me? You knew I thought you were a priest! Why didn't you say something? And then you kissed me! How could you do that?"

She wondered if anyone had ever actually died of shame, because if so, she was sure to follow. She just needed him gone, and she needed to do her best to forget this ever happened. Even though already a secret part of her brain was telling her she'd remember this forever, that she'd compare every man from now on to Chase and wish they didn't fall short. Shut up, she ordered herself, her breath coming in raspy, irregular gasps.

She sensed Chase was still standing there, could feel the uncertainty and wariness radiating off him. She snuck a quick glance at him and noted that he really did look sincerely sorry.

"Just go."

She needed him to leave.

She hoped he wouldn't go.

Daisy remained facing away from him, her hands still on her knees. She stayed there for what felt like years, before she finally heard the crunch of gravel under his feet as he walked back to the truck.

"I'll send help for you," he said. The sound of the door slamming, closing him in, echoed with finality in the humid air.

Daisy felt her eyes well with tears as the engine roared and the truck pulled back onto the highway. She'd never felt more alone.

When Chase walked away from Daisy, his heart actually hurt. He didn't know that could happen, but there it was, the ache in his chest.

When he started to drive, he had every intention of leaving her behind. She was just a blip in his life, something he'd forget before he could even form a solid memory of it, or of her. And then something tripped in his soul.

Dammit, he didn't want to leave. He couldn't explain why, but he didn't want this to be it. He wanted the chance to explain, to prove to her that he wasn't the asshole she thought he was. And he wanted to know her better, for however long he could. He didn't know where it would lead. He didn't know if they'd have a chance at a future, but if he drove away now, he knew for sure they wouldn't. And he wasn't quite ready to accept that.

Skidding the truck to a stop, he launched himself out of the door and strode toward her. He saw her turn and look at him with surprise. Confusion. He thought he even saw some interest in her eyes, and he hoped it wasn't just his in his mind.

Her mouth fell open as he stepped toward her. He knew she was getting ready to lay into him again, that she was going to tell him to leave, to go to hell. He deserved it. Of course he did, and he'd take it. He'd take everything, but not yet. He had something more important to get to first.

And so, when Chase reached Daisy, and before she had a chance to yell at him, he pulled her into his arms and crushed his lips to hers, silencing whatever it was she intended to say. He knew they both had more to get out, but he was taking this first.

He wanted her with a ferocity that was heavy and hard, but her needs superseded his own, and he deliberately softened his touch. He lightly ran his tongue along her lip, asking, not demanding, her to open for him. For a moment she stayed stiff in his arms, but she didn't push him away. Encouraged, he pulled her bottom lip into his mouth, sucking gently. His hold on her changed, and he went from gripping her to caressing her, embracing her. She could back away if she wanted. She stayed. She didn't kiss him back, but she stayed.

Lifting his head from hers, Chase spoke before Daisy could.

"Daisy, sweetheart, I did not intend to trick you. When I pulled over, I forgot I was even wearing this damn outfit. And the story really is kind of funny how it all happened. I'm not a very good person. I lie," he gestured down at his outfit. "I steal. Sort of. And so many other things, and I will tell them all to you if it helps. I have definitely had impure thoughts, and never so strongly or as intense as just now, thinking about you.

"But one thing I can't admit to is trying to make a fool of you. I never meant to trick you, and the reason I didn't stop you right away way was because I loved listening to you talk. And when other things started to happen, I didn't stop you because I thought I'd die if I did.

I have never, ever, felt as good as I did when you were kissing me. Touching me. And goddammit, I may have ruined it all by not telling you the truth, but I didn't want it to end. I still don't want it to end. I want this to be the beginning. If you still want me to leave, I will, but I really hope you don't. I don't want to go."

If life was a romance novel, Daisy would have swooned at his declaration. He was pretty smooth, Daisy mused, though he also seemed sincere about it. Daisy could read the regret and remorse in his eyes.

He was still holding her waist, but gently, and she could step out of his embrace if she wanted. It had taken everything in her to resist kissing him back, but she still felt betrayed and embarrassed. And even now she had the nagging thought in the back of her head that her Nana wanted her to confess.

Nana, who never asked for much…although she did drop some pretty heavy hints about how the buttons on her old phone had been so small, she didn't know if she'd be able to see the numbers well enough to call Daisy anymore. Or the doctor for help if she ever fell and couldn't get up. And she hadn't said no when Daisy showed up a week later with a brand new, larger phone for her. And she had then said she'd need to start using one of her old canvas grocery bags as a purse, since the new phone would take up too much space in her current purse…if only she could afford the Coach bag she'd seen online…that would be the perfect size (and it was at the outlet and on sale). So Daisy had surprised Nana with the purse. Maybe Nana did, actually, ask for a lot. But those were mostly little things, and Daisy adored her, and loved the look of happiness on Nana's face when Daisy could deliver something Nana wanted. This was something bigger, more important, than a purse or a phone. This was eternal life.

At that moment, Daisy heard a faint chiming sound. It took her a second to recognize that it was her phone ringing! She stepped out of Chase's grasp to dig through her purse, yanking out her phone triumphantly. She held it up to the sky as if it were a victory trophy and then swiped to answer. It was Nana!

"Daisy? Are you there honey? It's happening." Nana sounded faint and frail.

"I'm here Nana, I'm going to go to confession. I just tried, but, well, it didn't really work out. But I'm going. Right now. Just...please hold on a little longer."

"Hold on longer? Why would I do that? I'm ready now."

"No Nana, just...I'm coming to see you."

"Well, honey, you can come if you want, but I won't be here anymore."

"Nana, please, don't say that. Just stay a little longer. For me?"

"But Daisy, why would I want to stay here? I've been on the waiting list for that apartment for nearly an entire year, and it's finally opened up! Poolside, brand new kitchen, not that I cook much anymore, but it's always nice to have those fancy appliances, and the best part is that handsome Mr. Pritchard lives just two doors down from my new place. He moved just two months ago, after his wife passed. He's Catholic! And it's just blocks from the beach. I know how much you young ladies like to sun yourselves on these Florida beaches. And even I can go in the ocean here it's so warm! I can even get a little golf cart to drive down to the beach whenever I want. I'd love to see you, Daisy, but it'd be better if you wait a few weeks while I settle in. In fact, that's why I'm calling you now. I'm having a little moving-in party in a couple weeks, and I'd love for you to come."

"Wait, what? You're moving?"

"Well, of course, just like I told you. It was almost my time... and now it's here. I cannot wait to move. You know I've been wanting this."

"Yes, but, I thought when you said it was your time, you meant you were dying. You're not?"

"Well, Daisy, I suppose we all are, but I'm not planning on making that move anytime soon. The Good Lord will call to me, but I don't think it's imminent. I just saw Dr. Clark, and he said I am healthier than most of his patients half my age."

"But why did you want me to go to confession just so you could get into a new apartment? You know I don't go to church, and isn't it kind of wrong to make me go and confess just so you can get a new place to live? I don't know much about all that, but it doesn't seem completely appropriate."

"Confession? I never said you should go to confession? Where would you get that idea? Of course, you know I pray for you and for God to forgive you, and I am always happy to take you to church with me, anytime. You just let me know. But I also know you and your stubbornness well enough not to put a guilt trip on you like that."

"But you said, and I quote you here, *you need to make a confession.*"

"I did no such thing! Oh wait...do you mean when I told you need to make *concessions* if you want to meet a nice gentleman. I just meant you might need to be a little more open to men you might not initially think are right for you—you do have a pattern of finding something wrong in every man you meet, and dear, you're not getting any younger. You really do need to open up your mind to some different types. And I have a very nice young man in mind for you. Mr. Pritchard's grandson is quite nice, and if you wear flats, the height difference won't be so noticeable. His personality is...lovely."

"Oh, my god, Nana. I thought you wanted me to make my confession before it was too late. I thought you were going to die!"

Daisy looked up from the ground, where she had been digging patterns in the pebbles with the toe of her shoe, and straight into Chase's eyes. She wanted to drown in those eyes.

Her Nana continued to talk, but Daisy wasn't listening anymore. She focused on Chase, and thought about her crazy behavior since meeting him. It was possible, not probable, but she was willing to admit *possible* that Chase wasn't completely at fault for deceiving her. He'd never actually *said* he was a priest. Of course she assumed he was, he had the outfit on for god's sake, but she hadn't given him much of a chance to correct her assumption.

And she had, after all, been the one who'd started the dirty talk, who'd been deliberately provocative, knowing that it was wrong.

And he'd been the one to stop her from going further than the kiss, when he must have sensed he'd been willing to continue, do more. It was, in a way, admirable. She'd felt how hard he was, so it must have been uncomfortable for him to stop.

So maybe he deserved another chance. Maybe.

Daisy said something, she couldn't remember what, to end the call with her Nana.

"Okay," she said. "Maybe you're not completely at fault. Maybe I jumped to conclusions just a little bit and didn't give you much of a chance to explain." She held up a hand. "You're not totally excused. You could have tried harder to stop me. You could have let me know sooner. But anyway, I guess I'm willing to hear your story now, and it had better be good." She waved the phone vaguely in the air. "Anyway, that was my Nana, and she is *not* dying, and she did not want me to go to *confession*. So, you can just forget everything I just told you."

Daisy shrugged. She didn't quite know where she and Chase would go from here. She watched him rub his chin. She'd known him only a few hours, and already she knew that gesture meant he was thinking something over. After such a short amount of time, she already felt like she *got* him. She loved the way he listened to her, and the easy way he offered that sexy half smile of his when he was amused, which seemed like most of the time. And the way he kissed. Damn! If he did other things as well as he kissed, she'd be a satisfied woman. Her Nana was wrong. If she ended up with Chase, she wouldn't have to make any concessions. If anything, she'd be reaching higher.

Chase didn't quite know how it had happened, but it seemed that he was no longer on Daisy's shit list. She was smiling at him. He couldn't remember a time he'd felt happier about something. This was a woman he wanted to spend his days making happy. That smile. God, that smile.

"First of all, I'm glad to hear your Nana's not dying. And second, I truly am sorry for deceiving you. But there is no way in hell that I'm am going to forget *anything* you just said. There was some pretty good content in there. Parts of me, in fact, still have a pretty vivid memory of your confessions."

Daisy quirked an eyebrow at him.

"Oh yeah? Which parts would those be?"

"My, uh, mind, of course. Gee, what were you thinking?"

"Your mind, huh? Yeah, I'm sure that's what's remembering what I said about wanting to hold your cock in my hand. In my mouth."

She was right, it definitely wasn't his mind that was thinking about that.

She paused, then continued.

"And is it your mind that's interested in knowing that I'm imagining your fingers unbuttoning my shorts and slipping under the fabric of my panties?"

Damn, she was hot. And he was hot for her.

"You know that dirty talk is going to get you in trouble. Aren't you supposed to be some proper Catholic girl or something?"

"I never was a very good Catholic. But there are other things I'm excellent at." She wiggled her eyebrows at him, partly in jest, but also with a hint of promise.

"Since you're starting up with the sex talk again, maybe instead of forgetting, we just start fresh." He held out a hand to her. "Hi, I'm Chase, ersatz priest who has been known to withhold the truth unwisely, who has a really interesting story about a jar of maple syrup and a haunted dry cleaners, and is amazingly attracted to you."

Daisy held her hand out to him.

"I'm down with starting new. I'm Daisy. I'm a little bit crazy, a little impetuous, and sometimes I don't allow other people the chance to talk. I'm a hugely lapsed Catholic, and a prolific sinner. I'm a travel blogger with a deadline that I'm going to miss, and I'm in need of a ride to Florida to attend a house-warming party for my Nana. She said I can bring a guest."

Her eyebrow quirked up at him again. "So Chase, you up for it? Road trip to Florida? I think you'd like my Nana. And you do still owe me that explanation."

Yep he was up for it. That and a whole lot more. Smiling in return, he clasped her hand in his. "I'm in." He opened the passenger door for Daisy and gestured her in.

"Let's get started."

About Adrienne Perry

Adrienne Perry writes contemporary erotic romance with plenty of heat and humor. When she's not writing fiction, she is a professional science writer and in her spare time she likes to warp young minds (but only those of her own children and sometimes her nieces and nephew).

For more information about Adrienne and her two real-life sisters, who also write romance novels visit graffitifiction.com.

Facebook: www.facebook.com/AdriennePerryAuthor/

Twitter: www.www.twitter.com/authoradrienne

Eternal Embrace

BY THOMAS SWEENEY

Why is death described as black? When I died, all the colors became crystal clear to my mind's eye. I could see everything. I could see the entire universe all in one blink. The colors shot out at me almost violently, engulfing me completely like a white hot bath of love and joy. It was so bright and so refreshing. I felt free. I felt happiness. I felt ecstasy. I felt incredible energy. I had been encased in a physical body for so many years that I thought was me, only to discover that I was far more. I was a light being, an energetic entity. It was beauty beyond my wildest dreams: perfection in balance.

In the throws of my reintroduction to eternal bliss, there was a tiny silver cord of thought pulling me toward something. A presence that guided my heart. The love and desire that pulled at me were palpable, like the soft warmth of an evening fire that hypnotizes the eye. I couldn't deny the gravity of this thought and felt my essence being drawn more and more rapidly toward it. I wanted it, longed for it, needed it, and it needed me. We were compelled to meet and be together, forever.

    The first time I saw her was my tenth birthday. Father had agreed that it was time I got to see the big city. She appeared to glow through the glass of her father's general store counters. Initially, I was mesmerized by the candy the glass display held captive just out of my reach. When she peeked through the first time from behind the display, I caught my breath. Somehow she seemed familiar. The candy no longer held any interest to me. Her eyes caught mine and she darted out of sight again, only to return a moment later wide-eyed and curious. We stared at each other for what felt like an eternity, only to be startled back to reality by my father's deep baritone voice booming directions for me to take the supplies outside to our vehicle. When I looked back through the glass again, she was gone.

    The next few weeks in the high country held me prisoner, hundreds of miles away from my new obsession. She was in my dreams and thoughts daily. Her emerald green eyes burned into my skull like brands on a beast of burden. The young girl through the glass had permanently marked herself inside me, yet I had no idea what her name was. My fascination was downright distracting. There was no comparison for the aching need that pulled at my psyche to learn more about her. My age allowed only the limited experience that my parents would indulge. However, my imagination was untethered. By the next time I was able to make a trip with my family into the city for supplies again, this mystery girl had become an enigma beyond reproach. She was perfect in every way to me.

    When my family entered the city limits, my heart started beating so fast that I broke out in a light sweat. My mother touched my forehead, checking for fever and suggested I wait in our lift. My outburst may have been unnecessary, but seemed to serve its purpose. Permission was granted to visit the store. Once inside, I immediately began to scour the entire shop for my maiden. Her name was my goal. The only challenge was that my father kept demanding my focus to gather the essentials for the next period of time in the high country. The ore we mined was extremely valuable, but our territory wasn't completely settled yet and squatters were ever threatening. Father kept trying to hire new workers, but they never seemed to stay and the automated systems required constant monitoring. Even I had been trained to manage them at eight years old, so the work wasn't difficult—just tedious. Finally, everything had been gathered and packed. Just as we were about to leave, she came in through the main entrance to her father's store carrying a bag in each hand. When she saw me, I saw the blood drain from her face until she looked porcelain. Only my mother caught the exchange as we walked toward my angel and her mother entering after. Ever the doting parent, my mother slowed and greeted the young girl and her parent. This gave me precious few moments to say something, but my mouth wouldn't move and I began to fidget uncontrollably. I could see the young girl's eyes pasted to the floor while our mothers exchanged pleasantries until my father insisted our time for safe passage home was growing short. I'll never forget the feeling of defeat as I crossed the threshold of the entrance and glanced back as my goal faded into the shadows of the isles filled with products and supplies. The entire flight home, I wept silently in my seat, pretending I was asleep. The agony was unbearable, and it felt as if there were no hope or joy in the entire universe.

This was the way of it for several years. Every few months we would head into the city for supplies, and every few months I would be scared silent when my angel would appear—if she would appear. There were a few times she wasn't present at all. If ever life held needles of stinging pain, not seeing my dream in the flesh even briefly brought on suffering like I never imagined possible. Doubt and fear would creep into my thoughts that she was avoiding me or was disgusted by the simple, mute boy that occasionally frequented her father's shop. The list of reasons for her absence grew infinite and without restraint as my mind raced to explain all the reasons she would have to not want to see me. Until I did catch a glimpse of her, it would weigh relentlessly on my conscious and unconscious thoughts, distracting me from the beauty of life around me in our high mountain sanctuary.

By my fifteenth year of life, I was able to run the entire mine by myself. My father and I worked side by side with the occasional seasonal worker. It was a good time in my childhood because I got to know my father well. He was a hard working man that enjoyed a challenge as much as he enjoyed the full beard he sported year-round. His facial hair was a point of pride for him, but served a very practical purpose during the sub-zero winters we weathered in the high country. I looked forward to emulating my father and growing my own beard one day. Perhaps a strong, masculine beard would win my angel's heart as it had my mother. My parents were so in love. It was inspiring to see the devotion they shared for each other, despite the hard work of running a family business in the unsettled territory.

In the spring of that year, my father died in the mine repairing one of the roadheaders. The giant machine had become jammed, requiring direct assistance to clear the debris. While directing the droids, the tunnel had collapsed. The hydraulic wall supports had done their job and saved the roof from crumbling completely, but a stray piece of rock managed to strike my father's temple, killing him instantly. My mother took it hard and almost lost herself in her despair. I began running the business alone until my mother could gather herself again. In the process of learning to keep everything going, a powerful discovery revealed itself to me. My parents were incredibly rich. The ore we'd been mining was extremely rare and difficult to acquire and my parents had saved and invested everything they made into several profitable financial ventures. Thanks to the success of owning the mine, our family's future had been secured. I had no idea my father was so close to never needing to enter a mine again. It almost broke my heart knowing he'd come so close to reaching his dream. For his memory, and my mother's emotional health, I decided to find a management company to run our mine and move to the city. Secretly, I longed to be closer to my angel. With my mother's guidance and assistance, I secured a reputable firm to run the family business and made arrangements to move. The move actually seemed to improve my mother's depression. She dove in head first to completing the interviews and documents required by the management firm and instructed me about the nuances and details of each piece as my formal business education. I think she wanted to escape the memory of the high country as much as I longed to be close to my obsession.

Once in the city comfortably, a new challenge arose. I had no need for buying supplies from my favorite store anymore. Our new home was part of a purchased housing facility that we now owned. It included office staff, maintenance, maids, and various other assistants to procure our every desire. My hands had been my tools for so long that allowing others to serve me became a real challenge. In my eighteenth year, I realized that I hadn't seen my dream girl for almost three years. The distractions of burying my father, moving, hiring the management firm, studying the documents and laws at my mother's direction, and finally adjusting to living in a city teeming with people and activity had made time rocket by without much notice. Suddenly, I had to go to her, but the fear of seeing her engulfed me like a powerful morning tide raging against the rocks of the shore. Several times I tried to go to her father's store, even made it to the door of the shop, only to flee in desperate disgust at my own inadequacy. My mother called me a man now and reveled in the beard I'd begun growing in memory of my father, but the thought of my angel would instantly drag me back to that frightened and embarrassed ten-year-old peering through the cloudy display glass. I was hopeless.

I discovered quickly that the city was abundant in a great many things, including young, eligible women. Being rich, young, and eligible myself made the buffet even more enticing. Girls would swoon over me regularly: often to my own embarrassment in public. My mother would tease me, insisting that I choose one as a future mate. This idea from her seemed completely contrary to the devotion and passion she and my father had expressed during their relationship. They had loved each other madly. While logical, settling for a suitable mate was the furthest thing from my mind, though some of the beautiful, young girls did provide some pleasant distraction occasionally. My heart still longed for my missing angel, yet I had no courage to seek her out seriously. The thought alone would make my knees weak.

One weekend while out on a sunny Summer afternoon with friends, I found myself in the neighborhood of the old supply shop that held my prize. It was a moment of joyous abandoned inspired by my company that caused my brazen entrance into the small storefront. My friends followed closely on my heels with wide-eyed curiosity at what had caught my attention in such a bland, boring, and otherwise unentertaining venue. The building looked so much smaller than I remembered from my childhood. At first, it appeared that no one was working the store. Then suddenly, a young woman stood up from behind the candy counter. She didn't look up at first and began to open her mouth to speak. Before words could escape her ruby red lips, her eyes caught mine and my heart stopped. I felt as if I might pass out. The tugging on my arms from my friends snapped me out of the panic that had soaked me to my marrow. They were insisting we leave due to the lack of stimulation the establishment provided. I refused to move, but failed to speak too. Finally, the young woman behind the counter offered assistance with finding our needs, but my friends filed out the front door impatiently. My feet unconsciously guided me closer to the counter. Drawing near, it was easy to see that the young girl I'd worshiped had become a stunning young woman. Stammering, I introduced myself. It was amazing that I was able to form words at all, but my angel's response surprised me. She recognized me despite my full beard. She explained that my similarity in appearance to my father was uncanny. Her brilliant green eyes sparkled in the dim light of the shop. I was mesmerized. We spoke at length, leaving my friends to their own devices. It came to my awareness that she'd lost both her parents to a terrible accident in the bustling flight paths of the large city. She maintained the shop out of nostalgia for them, but secretly longed for more. I promised that I would come to visit frequently if she would allow it. Her smile at my request made my heart leap.

From that day forward, I would find any reason possible to stop in the small shop and visit with my angel—even purchasing small presents for my mother to justify the trip. Mother noticed the change in behavior immediately and began encouraging me to invite the girl to dinner. When I gathered enough courage and offered the invite, my angel accepted more quickly than I expected. I felt emboldened by her reaction. That first evening with her was magical and perfect. It was that night that I decided to arrange to ask for her hand in marriage and a refusal would not be tolerated. Spending more time with her only served to increase my desire for her. I became a tall, flaming beacon fire in the dark of night, burning a message of love across the sky. Nothing had ever meant more to me.

The day I married my angel was one of the single most joyful days of my life. My mother wouldn't stop crying. She repeatedly told me how proud my father would have been of me. My new wife shed a few tears too. During our honeymoon, she explained that she never stopped thinking of me from the first time we met at her father's candy counter. Her suffering had paralleled my own for all these years of separation. My words flowed easily now and I shared my heart's longing for her and vowed to never leave her side. She was my universe: my heart's reason for beating. I'd never been happier than I was with my love by my side.

The first few years of our relationship were like living in a dream that you read about or see in screenings. We traveled the entire planet together and experienced everything that caught our preferences. Life has so much to offer and we both wanted to see it all. Sharing all those wonderful days with my angel gave me satisfaction deep within my soul. When we entered our fourth year of marriage, we began preparing for a family of our own only to discover that she was incapable of bearing children. With all the technologies our civilizations had discovered and mastered, this was one challenge yet to be overcome. We were both devastated, but my angel took it the hardest. She felt inadequate and useless. In her mind, her value came from the ability to bear and rear offspring. Adoption was suggested and quickly rejected. It was our bloodline that was vital to her psyche. Anything less was fraudulent. It took a few more years for her to recover from this mind-trap, but eventually she did. She began to volunteer her time more and more with troubled or abused children and foster homes. At times, it felt as if she was running away from me. Constantly, I would remind her of my love and devotion, but it still felt different. She didn't love herself anymore.

Our marriage settled into a comfortable routine of busy work and avoidance for many years with occasional blips of happiness, but never the untethered joy and bliss we had in the beginning. As the decades flew by, we barely noticed the changes occurring in our bodies until my mother passed peacefully in her sleep. That moment jarred me out of the hypnosis of comfortable sameness I'd entered. I decided that moment to win my soulmate back and engaged a campaign of relentless, unconditional love immediately. I showered her with affection and attention, performed extraordinary tasks of devotion, and made passionate love to her at every opportunity. The secret I discovered was that if we acted like we were in love, we found ourselves in love…meaningfully. It worked. She slowly began to brighten the rooms of our homes again with her smile and laughter. Plans for trips and excursions became commonplace. She even mentioned adoption again without pain. The heat in our embrace had returned and it warmed my soul completely. She was my everything and I hers.

We never actually adopted, but the long list of children we helped and grew to be successful, productive members of their community gave us both reason to be proud. Letters and awards were bestowed upon us by our communities and the families we'd helped. It was all very flattering, but unnecessary. Much more time passed and my beard followed my hair's lead by turning a bright silver tone that made my beautiful wife's green eyes glow with delight when she kissed me. I began to look more and more like my father, but my beautiful wife remained timeless. She made me smile every morning when we woke together in the gathering daylight of our twin suns. Occasionally, we would remain in bed, lazily sharing the day together until prior agreements demanded our attentions again. Every time I would hug her, I could feel the tension from a busy day instantly melt away. The sensation of waking in the middle of the night and curling up to her back close enough to breathe in her scent from the exposed skin of her beautiful neck was enough to inspire prayers of thanks to our creators.

If someone had told me that falling in love could continue in perpetuity, I would have thought them mad, until I first met my angel and finally won her heart in marriage. Each day that passed, a new discovery of the depth of her complexity and subtlety would surface and surprise me. How could I have lived so closely with this gorgeous woman and still feel that I only know a small part of her? While we were adventuring through life together, I often found myself wondering at the personal adventure of discovery I had embarked on by becoming her partner, lover, and best friend. The world was our playground and our hearts were priceless jewels.

Our companies and charities grew and prospered each year with exciting challenges and experiences abounding: some more preferable than others, but all appreciated with my love by my side. Together, there was nothing we couldn't do. For several years, we traveled and met great leaders of many of the different continents that made up our vast planet. The homelands of so many different cultures and civilizations gave us unlimited inspiration. We loved every second we were together. Never having children of our own ironically gave us the freedom to travel at a moments notice, which we did habitually—indulging our wandering whims freely. The amassed fortune from my parents and sizable rivers of revenue from our own various business ventures afforded us generosity that was difficult to rival in any culture we'd ever visited. We actually became something of a legend for some peoples. Legends are always exaggerated, of course, but our constant movement and acts of public generosity garnered regular notoriety.

As we grew older and began to extend our stays at certain preferred properties, it became customary for me to celebrate our wedding anniversary in some unusual manner with friends and loved ones. The events grew every year in size and extravagance until an annual fair developed around the date of our union. Our largest estate in the city where we met would be opened to the public for thirty-six hours: the equivalent of one day. We would make a brief appearance as per tradition for the celebration, but quickly excuse ourselves to allow our guests the freedom to enjoy the evening. It was nice to be remembered each year and flattering for the size of the event, but it became a small burden at times that felt as if it might take the fun out of the initial intention of the act of devotion. That inspired us to begin taking private retreats back to my homeland in the high country. My angel and I would spend weeks rediscovering the beauty of the endless mountain ranges of my father's property. Our rationale to the public for the excursions was always to check in and monitor our mining concerns in the region, but privately we both craved the time alone. Each trip seemed to center us around the love we still held deeply with our hearts for the other. Nature had a magical way of reminding us of what's really important. We would sit on the massive porch of our mountain estate and watch the sunset, only to wake the next morning in each other's embrace. In the high country, the days would blur together until our staff would remind us of the date and impending agreements that required our attentions. Begrudgingly, we would always make our way back to the racing speed of life on our planet, but each year the trips to the mountains became our most desired appointment.

I can still remember my angel's hair changing from her youthful light brown to a shimmering silver like my beard. She never liked the idea of genetic manipulation for vanity. She considered her body's decision to change a sacred event that connected directly with her subconscious that should be respected. The new color made her even more beautiful to me. I always loved the idea of matching clothes and colors that she would sport—much to her own chagrin. However, now we could match and she couldn't accuse me of doing it purposefully. Nature herself dictated that we should be in harmony emotionally and physically, so who was I to argue. This didn't always amuse my lovely wife, but made me chuckle every time it came up.

We lived this way for so long that I could barely remember my life without her. The years I'd grown up longing for my glowing girl behind the counter felt as a brief moment in comparison to the extremely satisfying decades that had followed. We worked hard together. We played hard together. We dreamed big dreams together. We made passionate love together. We grew old together. Life was perfect in all its imperfections with her. Every challenge we faced, we faced together—and there were many. However, our passion and love for each other made each moment worthwhile. Doubt didn't exist in our world thanks to our union. She had been made from the fires of the universe's first breath of life and sent to guide me through eternity. She was my angel.

It would have been our tenth trip to our properties in the high country if our flight had made it to the landing port. We were scheduled to review the mines and stay at our private retreat in the mountains for the summer. It was a pleasant reprieve from the bustle of the giant city that had grown so large over the decades. The quiet seclusion of the mountains gave us time to be together uninterrupted and focus on our love for each other. This was a hard earned habit that we'd developed over the years, especially when so many distractions can be entertaining and tempting. My angel was always my primary focus and me hers, so the decision for the repeat trip was easy to agree on. Unfortunately, the malfunctioning engines had other ideas for our trip and drove us headlong into the side of one the famous peaks of the region. I'll never forget the look on my angel's face as the plane plummeted to the ground. She looked serene: almost peaceful. Holding her hand, I leaned in to kiss her face once more in those final seconds and we stared into each other's eyes for as long as we had left.

There was a huge cracking sound and a force that knocked the wind out of me, then suddenly I was blinded by a bright white light that burned through the core of my being. Colors slowly began to dance around me in vibrant streams of flashes that raced by. I was moving, but couldn't see to where. It was just a feeling, a sense of knowing, that convinced me of my motion. Everything I'd ever known before felt like entertainment I'd been viewing and not experiencing in person. It was my life, but it wasn't really me. I had participated, but was only one actor in a vast play that included countless other souls who all helped make it possible. Appreciation for the complexity of life and wonder at the idea of it actually occurring in perfect orchestration overtook me. There was much more to the inner-workings of the universe than I'd ever imagined before. So much I'd taken for granted became revealed as small miracles.

A burst of energy pulsed through me suddenly and the wonder of creation filled my awareness: everything, people, civilizations, planets, stars, singularities, galaxies, the entire universe, and beyond. Time became a construct I could manipulate with just my thoughts. I could see the past. I could see the future. All answers rushed to me uninhibited. I was in bliss. That's when I felt it—the pull. It was calling to me like a whisper in the rain. The dancing lights around me sped up and grew brighter, blurring together as I flew through infinity. My heart knew what was pulling me, and I knew it was good, so no restraint was offered. The joy of approaching the calling was building inside the center of who I was. There was no doubt that love was at the source of this message. Compelled to answer, I moved faster.

It was my angel calling. When I reached her, the familiar feeling of her surrounded me. Pulling her into me, I encased her in a protective cocoon of love and swirled through space and time, satisfying my unquenchable need for her presence. Over an undefinable amount of time, things became more focused. There were lines now instead of blurred colors, and blotches of darkness separating them. It was these lines that we both decided to explore, just as we had explored our previous lives together. With my angel again by my side, I could go anywhere and do anything. Swirling in and out of each other in ecstasy, we rushed forward on a joyous journey of discovery—just as we always had. Holding onto each other through each new cycle, we searched the universe for its undiscovered secrets. The lines became visions of beauty and wonder that we marveled at for eons: never boring of the infinite possibilities that unfolded before us. We had become joyous wanderers and explorers of the infinite. Then came the moment my angel consciously decided to take shape. There was a pull inside me again and I felt her desire. Always the doting lover, I joined her in her adventure. If we're together, I'm willing to follow her anywhere.

It took a considerable amount of focus for us both, but there was no rush since time had no sway on us anymore. We swam through space spinning close to each other, basking in the warm glow of a nearby star. The newcomer offered its warm yellow rays of love to us as we spiraled through the void. I could see my lover's colors begin to take the shape of a new world. The beautiful glow of her green rushed into my view, accompanied by a deep blue that took my breath away. She twirled for me to share her new experience as I orbited her with a familiar silver glow beaming down and my heart full of love. Not long after, she shared a feeling of life with me from inside her. Miraculously, something had joined our journey and taken hold of her presence. My angel finally had children of her own growing on her surface. The impossible had come true and we both shouted with joy from our hearts. My lovely bride was a mother, and I was a father pushing and pulling lovingly on her as she continuously gave birth to more and more souls. Each and every child that joined our journey added to our happiness as we raced through time and space circling each other in our eternal embrace. She is mine, and I am hers—forever.

About Thomas Sweeney

Thomas Sweeney is a first-time novelist. Having found success through music with a number one hit on MP3.com, beating Alanis Morissette and Blink 182 in 2000, Thomas has been a singer, songwriter and musician for over 25 years. His music has appeared on major radio stations nationally and internationally and Thomas has performed with several internationally acclaimed artists.

Wanting to expand his creativity and storytelling skills beyond music, Thomas has now added being an indie author to his repertoire. He's already working on two new stories, one of which is a continuation of his first novel, "The Harem."

Thomas has read a lot of great and inspiring books over the years. From training and experience in this wonderful thing we call life, he was inspired to become an author.

Facebook: www.facebook.com/TheHaremBook

Twitter: www.twitter.com/theharembook

Instagram: www.instagram.com/theharembook

Pinterest: www.pinterest.com/theharembook

Goodreads: www.goodreads.com/ThomasSweney

Google+: google.com/+TheHaremBook

Website: www.theharembook.com

Highland Pursuits

by Emmanuelle de Maupassant

It had been in the back of a taxi, in the summer of 1928, that Lady Ophelia Finchingfield had first realized her views on the wedded state. Perhaps it was his awkward, overly lubricated kiss, or the inept grope upon her breast that brought the revelation. Perhaps it was the conviction that her suitor lacked the brooding depth of a Heathcliff, or a Rochester. Whatever the substance behind her discovery, she accordingly turned down an offer of marriage from the Honourable Percival Huntley-Withington who, at the tender age of twenty-two, had recently succeeded his father as Earl of Woldershire.

Some months earlier, just after Easter, Ophelia had begun her debutante season. She had since attended twelve balls, nineteen cocktail parties, and eleven dinners. Most mornings had seen her riding in Hyde Park, along Rotten Row and Ladies' Mile, returning to a formal breakfast of kippers, scrambled eggs and sausages.

She had attended polo and cricket matches, had played croquet and lawn tennis, and had tried her hand at archery and at bowls. Her attendance had been sought at intimate concerts, garden parties and picnics.

There had been nights at the opera (where no one listened), and nights at the ballet (where no one watched). It was all too apparent that the real purpose was to be seen. Ophelia had fallen into bed, exhausted, often no earlier than two in the morning.

Not yet halfway through the marathon of endurance, at the end of May, she'd wondered how she would maintain the pace. Her own debutante ball had been scheduled for the first week in August, and she'd begun to feel that her feet would be worn to stumps before it arrived. Moreover, it being her own dance, she'd have no choice but to endure the clutches of every decrepit old wart and every young toad wishing to shuffle her about. She would have a moldy time of it.

There had been little need for her mother, Lady Daphne, to court favor on her behalf, since the family's wealth alone inspired others to solicit her presence. The Honourable Sir Peter Finchingfield, MP for King's Lyppe, was heir to a successful turkey farming business. Moreover, he was a rising star in the Conservative party, tipped for a cabinet position, having recently led a vital debate in the House on subsidization of root vegetable growing, with particular reference to swedes and turnips.

What Sir Peter lacked in charm was provisioned by Lady Daphne, herself the daughter of a duke, though one of constrained means. She believed in her own infallible taste: in clothes, literature, art, music, and interior décor. It was of no regard that her acquaintance with them resembled that of a bee flitting from flower to flower without collecting a grain of pollen.

Those confident in the marvel of their own brilliance are never shaken by the criticisms of lesser creatures. In her eyes, all things connected with herself were highly sought after. Since social standing and money happily met in the Finchingfield household, the world at large was disposed to agree.

At the birth of her baby daughter, Lady Daphne was confronted with the uninspiring option of naming her after Sir Peter's mother, Edna, or his grandmother, Elsie. Pretending a great love of Shakespeare, she landed upon Ophelia, a name that she hoped would bestow her (as it turned out) only daughter with a love of literature.

For all her espousal of the arts, she'd never read a word of the Bard, though she had once attended a performance of *Hamlet*. In the dark, none had noticed that she'd dozed from Act Two through to the final bloody end. Naturally, she was much congratulated on her originality and, since neither of the grand matriarchs were alive to see injustice done, the matter was settled.

Lady Daphne had been preparing for at least twelve months for this momentous occasion in her daughter's life. The preceding summer and autumn months had been spent in Paris, attending the Louvre, the Philharmonie de Paris, the Musée d'Orsay and the Palais Garnier, so that Ophelia might improve her knowledge of music and the fine arts.

To Ophelia's delight, her mother had at last conceded that they should both visit Antoine in the Galleries Lafayette to have their hair styled in the boyish manner. In matters of fashion, Lady Daphne could not bear to lag behind, and emerged with a sleek bob. Ophelia, who, in all things, was more unruly, found that her curls refused to sit quietly, even under the expert hands of Monsieur Antoine. She emerged with hair springing wildly about her dainty face, heightening her wide set eyes. Her mother was unable to hide her dismay, but the cut gave Ophelia great satisfaction. Not only would it be easier to wash, but it well-matched her mischievous attitude. The overall effect was impish.

They had been outfitted lavishly, as regular visitors at Maison Worth, and other ateliers. How many hours had she stood, in one pose and then another, as satins, tulles and velvets were draped and pinned, and silks held to her face. Her mother had insisted on several suitably virginal evening gowns in white, embroidered in diamante and silver thread, georgette crêpe day dresses in cornflower blue, apricot and apple green, new riding attire, head-dresses of ostrich feathers, and shoes dainty of heel, destined to be danced to their graves upon the polished floors of London residences. Ophelia had embraced the novelty, having been previously confined to sensible wool for winter and summer cottons.

For Lady Daphne, as chaperone, the season would be almost as onerous. In gold brocade and lamé, diamonds glittering against pale skin, she had every intention of rising to the occasion. Even had she worn the rough serge of a nun, her elegance would have marked her as superior among her sex. Her dark-haired beauty had been admired in her youth, and was admired still.

"A smiling visage and demure bearing Ophelia," she had advised, on the evening before it all began. "All else, you may leave to me."

It could not be said that Ophelia hadn't tried with Percival, although she had vowed never to lose her senses over a man. She had no intention of her life imitating that of her Shakespearean namesake.

Early on in the season, she had taken her place among thirty strangers for dinner, all but a second cousin on her father's side perfectly unknown to her. Percival had been seated to her left, at the express direction of her mother. Well-mannered and agreeable, though sporting the pimples of youth and an over-fondness for hair oil, Percival was perfectly pleasant. Sadly, he lacked intellect: the result of interbreeding by certain old families, which had largely resulted in brains being replaced by the fluffiest of meringues.

They had next met at Grosvenor House, Percival rescuing her from a retired major whose toupée, in vivid tangerine, would have looked quite at home in the jungles of Borneo. Percival had swooped in, taken her hand, and led her into the throng for a foxtrot. She'd been more than willing to overlook a few crushed toes.

At their third meeting, she had begun to view him as a good egg, despite his poor conversation. He had escorted her into supper, had eaten without spilling anything over her or himself, and had given her a chaste kiss upon the forehead on departure, uttered with a cheery 'toodle-pip'.

The following evening, they had taken lemon ices on a balcony at the Connaught Hotel, and she had allowed Percival's aristocratic hand to creep about her waist. She'd prepared herself for a 'lunge', and had been all too ready to engage him on equal ground, but he had merely given her a playful pinch and licked, somewhat provocatively, the cherry from the top of her sorbet.

It had been on the fifth evening of their acquaintance, as Percival had escorted her from pre-dinner drinks at the Savoy to Devonshire House (her mother intentionally removing herself to a cab directly behind) that he'd seized the opportunity to make known his ardor. He'd clamped his wet lips to hers, tongue probing at her upper molars and, despite her utmost readiness to surrender to the moment, to allow Percival to prove himself masterful, she'd been struck by a sense of absurdity.

She knew that wives were obliged to put up with things they found distasteful, and that a woman's passions were secondary to those of her husband, if they existed at all. Moreover, Ophelia was not averse to wedlock as a means to further her social position, to secure her financial future, and to access a lifestyle that would include regular trips to the Continent, and attendance at soirees hosted by the elite of her class. Marriage, she had long ago decided, was a contract and, in signing it, she was determined to acquire the very best terms. As Lady Daphne would say, "You were born, and you will die. What you make of the middle is your own affair."

Her reluctance to commit to the wedded state might have been attributed to her age. In no more than the twinkling of an eye, Ophelia, like the rest of her cohort, had been transported from gawky childhood to the realms of eligible womanhood. "Ah!" we might say. "What could be more fitting then, that Lady Ophelia Finchingfield, a radiant example of the innocent feminine, would cast down her eyes, and resist the eagerness of her suitor."

Were we to reach inside the mind of our young heroine, we'd discover that far from being averse to physical intimacy, it was a subject she'd examined most thoroughly, and with regular indulgence, often while daydreaming in a long, hot bath. Rather than being coy, she looked forward keenly to her place at the lovers" table, in anticipation of sampling all its dishes.

As Percival had withdrawn his tongue, dabbing saliva from the edges of his mouth, he'd extracted from his pocket a ring, and alarmed repugnance had welled within her.

It was at that moment that the placement of her head within a noose became apparent. If she failed to wriggle free, she'd find herself being kissed by Percival Huntley-Withington for the rest of her miserable life.

Ophelia's rejection of marriage to the Earl of Woldershire so incensed Lady Daphne (the opinion of Sir Peter was of no matter) that Ophelia had been placed on the next overnight sleeper to Scotland, to stay with her grandmother until she saw sense. If Lady Finchingfield could overlook Percival's mother expelling cigarette smoke from her nostrils in the manner of a horse snorting steam on a chilly morning, then Ophelia could put up with marriage to a man lacking sex appeal. In fact, thought Lady Daphne, the less pizzazz on that front the better; in her experience, less appealing husbands were rather easier to manage.

Unceremoniously banished from the social whirl of London, Ophelia lay on her bunk, rocked by the rhythm of the Scotch Express to Inverness. She had never met Lady Morag MacKintoch but she feared her grandmother feeding her nothing but bread and water (physically and sexually) until she relented and threw herself back upon her mother's mercy.

Yet, despite these forebodings, Ophelia could not deny a certain excitement. Scotland, she decided, would be the place to run into an artist, the sort who would be expertly experienced: a marvelous kisser, and much besides. In fact, she mused, *wild Bohemians are probably thicker on the ground in the Highlands than they are in Bloomsbury. They'll be everywhere, painting grand views and sighing for want of a woman upon which to pour their passion...*

And then another thought crossed her mind.

What if I woke up in the morning and found that I wasn't female anymore but a man. I'd still be me, but I'd be able to do as I liked. I'd be the apple pie instead of the whipped cream. I'd be valued for what I say, and what I do, rather than for how I look, or who I was married to.

She closed her eyes, and wriggled under the covers.

The last hour of the train journey, following her change onto a rackety branch line, had taken her truly into the depths of the towering Highlands, past fast-running streams and looming granite crags. A deep violet sky overhung hillsides of russet and mustard, draped in a mist of drizzle.

When she emerged from her carriage, she found that the platform of her station comprised no more than some raised wooden boards placed at the side of the track. She looked about, but there was no one to collect her, so Ophelia waited forlornly under a tree, water dripping down her collar. It was a clear half hour before she heard the sound of a car engine.

The driver, rather than coming out to help her, honked the horn and motioned for her to climb in. *Bloody rude*, thought Ophelia, wrenching open the door, and breaking a nail in the process. She was obliged to bundle her cases onto the back seat.

"Thank you ever so much," she snapped, unpinning her sodden hat.

"No trouble," came the reply, in an accent broadly Scottish, but clear enough for Ophelia to understand. "I'm supposed to be felling trees today, but the rain made it difficult. Not so bad having to stop for a while to come and get you."

The man behind the wheel was a rough looking character in shabby clothing, unkempt, and with a beard full of hedgerow. He'd been undertaking manual labour, as was apparent not just from his appearance, spattered in woodchips and sawdust, but from the aroma filling the car: a cocktail of male sweat and damp tweed.

"Whisky?" he offered, passing a hipflask.

"Certainly not. It's eleven in the morning!"

"Please yourself," he replied and stepped on the accelerator.

Horribly uncouth! Ophelia fumed, her resentment growing. *And woefully undertrained.*

"I say, please slow down," she directed, as the car took a bend at speed, jolting her sideways.

"Too much to do to take it any slower. I don't have all day London-Miss. Don't worry, I know these roads like the back of my hand."

"I shall jolly well complain about you when we arrive. You're making me feel unwell with this awful handling of the car. You're not fit to drive!" declared Ophelia.

"Do as you like."

She felt too nauseous to argue.

The dense forest through which they motored soon opened out into a glen, hemmed in by steep-rising peaks, snow-topped despite the summer month. For some miles they passed only modest dwellings, few and far between. Turning towards the crags, they entered a tunnel through the rock and the car plunged into cool, silent darkness. It emerged upon the view of a great loch, amid pinnacles black and barren. At the water's edge stood the solid, grey stonework of a castle. Beautiful yet mournful, the scene could have been one from an old Celtic tale. Nestled within its mountain embrace, Castle Kintochlochie looked ancient.

The car descended the hillside at speed, sweeping to a halt before the stately home of generations of MacKintochs. Ophelia staggered out of the vehicle, and managed three steps before ejecting the contents of her stomach. She was watched with interest by the crowd gathered to welcome her: a party comprising her grandmother, Morag's companion Lady Devonly, and the entire staff of Castle Kintochlochie.

"Don't worry a bit," said Lady Morag. "The dogs'll eat it in a jiffy. Let's get you inside."

"Darling, you look so much like your mother," Morag exclaimed, once Ophelia had joined her and Lady Devonly in the drawing room. The driver had absented himself but she made a mental note to relate her treatment at the first opportunity. Tea poured and fruitcake eaten, Ophelia was feeling already rather better.

"I must agree that you've been rather naughty. An earldom is not to be sniffed at," began her grandmother. "Wedlock lends respectability."

Ophelia made to interject but Morag was clearly in the mood for speeches. "Even though you'll come into your own fortune in a few years' time, you must consider your social position." Morag helped herself to a buttered muffin. "Naturally, I can quite guess the truth of it. No doubt, you have a secret, vastly unsuitable lover." She held up one finger sternly, forbidding interruption. "Now my dear, I'm all for a little harmless 'sin' but a woman must, at last, select the right horse for her carriage."

Ophelia decided to let her grandmother believe whatever appealed to her.

Morag nodded to her companion. "Perhaps you have heard of my dear friend Constance? She is a keen amateur naturalist, and the author of several acclaimed editions. We met while I was travelling in West Africa, with my dear Hugo, God rest his soul, making our study of the tribes of Dahomey."

Looking about, Ophelia could see that the drawing room boasted ample evidence of those travels: a set of most alarming masks being placed upon the far wall, sporting what appeared to be real hair and teeth.

"Lady Devonly, though married at the time to the British Ambassador, accompanied us on trips into the interior several times, compiling her own fascinating catalogue of native parrot species. Take us as your example Ophelia; choose wisely, and marriage need not be too much of a bore."

Constance smiled benignly and patted Ophelia's hand.

Morag lowered her voice. "My own marriage was a blissful joining of the sexes, founded on equality of intellect and passion. Not so my brother Hector, whose bride ran away with the gamekeeper. He has never been the same. His own estate he gambled away and has spent most of his life in abject resentment against the world and all in it. My darling husband, having the empathy of the angels, insisted that Hector should live out his days with us, but I fear the arrangement is not always inclined to make us merry."

"Of course, there's Hamish, Constance's nephew. Darling boy has been with us about five years now, managing the estate. He's a wonderful help, so practical! It's his way of coping. So much tragedy; a man needs to keep busy…"

"You'll meet Hector this evening. Poor thing has been suffering with the flu. He's been creeping towards the grave so long that the Reaper has grown tired of waiting for him to shamble within arm's reach."

Ophelia, pouring everyone another cup of tea, wondered if she might help herself to a third slice of cake.

"You must tell us about Paris dear," Constance prompted. "It's so long since I've been. Are the women still as chic? I recall their corsets being laced so tightly that they daren't even laugh. I could never wait until the end of the day, to whisk mine off. You're lucky to have avoided those fearful contraptions. Today's fashions are much less constricting."

"It was wonderful," Ophelia began, relating some of her excursions and adventures. Even under the watchful eye of her mother, between clothes fittings and endless trips to galleries, she had tasted a little of the bohemian lifestyle: artists lounging in cafés, discussing all manner of philosophical topics. They spoke of sex as they might of the weather. She'd strained to listen, employing her schoolgirl French to eavesdrop on those conversations. Breathing the Parisian air had surpassed all expectations. The place positively buzzed with possibilities.

"Ah yes," sighed Constance, recalling her own youthful days in that enchanting city.

Morag admitted, "We're generally quiet here, but we'll have twenty to dinner on the occasion of my birthday. Among them will be the Comte de Montefiore, whom you may find amusing, and his sister. Their mother was a dear friend of Lady Devonly many years ago. We have hopes that, perhaps, there may yet be wedding bells in a certain quarter." She clapped her hands excitedly. "They spent some days here last spring. We're very fond of them."

Ghastly, thought Ophelia. *I expect the Comte will be a cad: all moustache and teeth. He'll want me to laugh at his awful jokes and there will be constant pouncing. No doubt his sister will be frightful too, full of simpering. It'll be like London all over again.*

"Ah, it's past midday," beamed Lady Morag, beckoning the butler forward. "Haddock, it's time for a cocktail. Three gin fizzes if you please."

Meanwhile, down in the servants" quarters, a parallel conversation was afoot. "It's been a goodly time coming," said the cook. "Mr. Hamish has been too long without a wife. No man should be left lonely in his bed of a night." Neither the footman nor the gardener could disagree. As for little Hettie, the scullery maid, she sighed forlornly and continued scrubbing the potatoes. She'd keep Mr. Hamish's bed warm anytime he liked, with or without a wedding band on her finger.

"My angel, what jolly company we are," declared Morag, as Ophelia joined her grandmother, heading down the stairs to dinner that evening.

"Tripe!" proclaimed Sir Hector, blowing his nose noisily into a handkerchief.

Ophelia felt inclined to agree, looking at the fearsome visage of her great uncle and at the army of atrocious ancestors glaring at her from the walls, the eyes of some disdainful, others demented, like nocturnal creatures disturbed by the sudden lighting of the dining candles.

"So difficult to find suitable guests," Morag continued. "Just us, I'm afraid. Most of our neighbors are half-wits, and the rest have criminal tendencies. There's barely a teaspoon to be found after they've visited."

"Ah, here's Hamish. You've met, of course, dear. Our chauffeur, Brodie, is laid up with lumbago, otherwise he'd have met you from the station. Hamish kindly stepped in, despite being so busy. What would we do without you Hamish?" said Morag, turning a smile of affection on the gentleman newly entered.

Here was the uncouth individual from earlier in the day, except that he had taken a bath, and removed the leaves and debris from his person. Standing tall, the broadness of his chest was all too apparent, straining against the formality of his dinner suit. His hair curled at his neck, luxuriantly auburn, as was his beard.

Hamish, eyes a-glitter, looked at her with ill-concealed

amusement and greeted her with a wry smile. "Our delightful London guest, here to teach us true refinement."

She glared, answering, "I'm sure that the ladies of this house have refinement in abundance."

Though she turned away to engage Constance in conversation, she remained aware of his physique, so alarmingly athletic. A vision came to her of him in loincloth and helmet, striding forth to do battle before the walls of Troy. He would put the most noble and virile of the demi-gods to shame. She'd be damned if she'd give him the satisfaction of seeing her squirm.

Still, she was glad to be wearing her crimson velvet. Open across the shoulders, and upper back, it made her a trifle chill, but bestowed undeniable sex-appeal.

It took much self-control for Ophelia to avoid looking down the table at the infuriating Hamish. Yet, how badly she wished to do so. To her dismay, and excitement, it was apparent that he was not only attractive but a wit. Of course, the more she commanded herself not to give him the slightest thought, the more he became all she could think of.

Wishing to offer her hostess praise, Ophelia commented, "The smoked trout pâté was divine, and the salmon en croute. Wonderfully fresh; quite the best I've eaten anywhere."

"All from our own estate. I caught the trout and salmon myself this morning," Hamish called down to her, fixing her with a steely gaze.

"It's true," added her grandmother. "We are fortunate in our cook, Mrs. Beesby, but we must thank darling Hamish for providing us with our supper tonight."

"Perhaps he might take me out and show me how to catch them too," Ophelia found herself saying, then cursing herself. *Fiddlesticks! He'll think I'm in a spin for him and his head is undoubtedly big enough as it is.*

"Groping for trout!" interjected Sir Hector. "A filthy euphemism! Keep a look-out Morag or they'll be rutting in the open air with the livestock!"

"Really Hector! Not all young people are debauched, despite the

Bright Things and jazz and flappers and what-not. Behave yourself!" commanded Lady MacKintoch.

Ophelia dared not look at Hamish, feeling that he would certainly be laughing at her now. The shame! She felt flushed from head to toe. Rutting indeed!

"How is your season going my dear?" asked Constance. "Have you made new friends?"

Ophelia smiled at Lady Devonly, thankful for the change of subject.

"I did meet two lovely sisters, Baba and Nancy Beaton, whose brother, Cecil, takes the most delightful photographs. He's promised to take mine one day, wearing nothing but feathers. I know it sounds naughty, but he's not like that at all. It's simply artistic."

"As for the Bright Young Things, my mother vetoed any invitations that appeared unsuitable. I heard about midnight car chases and other escapades, of course. I'd have loved to attend Elizabeth Ponsonby's 'bath and bottle' party. Daddy knows her father; they say he'll become labor leader of the House of Lords. Well, they had the most spiffing time at St. George's Swimming Baths. The dowagers sat like plump hens roosting, watching all the 'improper' behavior through their lorgnettes."

Ophelia continued excitedly. "There was a top-notch Negro band from New York, playing the latest jazz. They danced until dawn and then spilled out to catch buses, still wearing their bathing costumes. Can you imagine!"

Haddock placed a dish of raspberry mousse before her, into which Ophelia plunged her spoon. "The newspapers called it depraved. Baba tells me there was a lot more going on in the pool besides swimming."

"Nancy boys and mental defectives!" barked Hector, his moustache twitching.

"Well dear, perhaps no more about that!" Morag laughed, shaking her head. How she would have enjoyed being there, taking her place among the dowager hens.

"However, I'm all for young people's frivolity. We who sent our men to fight in that dreadful war can be so dour, always looking over our shoulder for the 'black dog.'"

Her gaze fell on the family crest on her dessert spoon. "My dear Hugo and my son, your uncle Teddy, Ophelia — both fell at the Somme."

She raised her eyes and gave a small smile. "Let the young have their fun. Let them live. There's been enough darkness."

After dinner, as they gathered at the fire, Morag asked if Constance might recite some poetry. "Something clever... some Edith Sitwell?"

"Driveling idiotism," grumbled Sir Hector.

Lady Devonly began, with an emotional air; clearly, Miss Sitwell was a favorite.

"What's the trollop saying?" grunted Hector. "Speak up. All this mumbling!"

"Hector, you are too dreadful! What will Ophelia think? Perhaps you might play us something on the piano dear," prompted Morag.

Ophelia began with some pastoral pieces. Sir Hector could be heard muttering, "That instrument needs tuning again. Bloody awful racket!"

On a whim, she broke into the Gershwins' *Someone to Watch Over Me*, and then *S'Wonderful*. This delighted everyone; even Hector stopped grumbling and began tapping his foot.

She had continued to avoid Hamish's eye but now found him at her elbow, the warmth of his body beside her on the piano stool. He invited her to join him in a duet of *Lady Be Good*.

"Delightful, my darlings," cooed Morag, "The Gershwins are such a wonderful team, just as husband and wife should be: lyrics and music in perfect complement."

Ophelia, caught between feelings of pleasure and embarrassment, fought to control her blushes. Hamish's thigh was undeniably pressed against hers.

They played *Tea For Two*, which had Constance and Morag singing along, then Hamish broke into *Sweet Georgia Brown*, and Ophelia let him take over. His mastery of the piano far surpassed her own.

"Can't beat some decent jazz. We just need Louis Armstrong on his trumpet," said Hamish, his eyes alight with the music.

"I've most of the Creole Jazz Band's records," Ophelia admitted. "My mother hates all this, even though the BBC has been playing it on the radio. She says it's immoral, that it encourages riotous behavior, but Daddy bought a gramophone and keeps bringing home new songs. He's a fan too."

"Do you remember, Constance," began Morag, "When we stayed with the Batammariba tribe for the Eho festival? The drumming went straight through your bones. We kicked off our shoes and joined in barefoot. This song makes me want to get up and do a jig."

Hamish finished with a flourish, to much applause.

"Bloody good I say. Makes a man feel half his age," declared Hector, looking remarkably chirpy.

"Hamish, it's been so long since I've heard you play. What a tonic!" beamed Constance. "We must have this jolly music more often."

Morag agreed. "Thank you Ophelia. You've inspired us. Now, we ladies should repair to bed. Hamish, you'll stay up and play dominoes with Hector won't you. Haddock, some cocoa to my room as usual, please."

As Ophelia made to retire, she saw Hamish tug his forelock, and smirk in her direction. She scurried to bed.

In the days that followed, Ophelia explored the house, and the tranquil beauty of the grounds. She strolled the loch, and the lower slopes of the purple-heathered hills, gazing up at the more brutal peaks surrounding the castle. She hoped always, though without admitting it, to run into Hamish.

His work roused him early in the morning, so that he did not take breakfast with them, and then took him out in the forest through the long day. He failed even to appear at dinner, Lady Devonly explaining that he was spending his time largely in a hillside cabin while he undertook some clearing of the woodlands.

Ophelia roamed the castle's long and draughty corridors, musing on the forty-three generations who had done so before her. The dungeons, she heard, dated from the twelfth century. It seemed that living in a state of permanent chill was the surest recipe for a long life, since innumerable aged Scots scrutinized her from their portraits. She imagined them rendered irritable by the scratchiness of their tartans and their icy beds.

While some parts of the castle were Spartan in appearance, cold seeping from the very stonework, most of the living areas had been decorated luxuriously, warmed by dark oak panelling and tapestries. Frolicking satyrs appeared to be a favorite theme. There were heavy brocades at the windows, deep sofas and plump cushions. Her room was no exception, boasting purple velvet drapes, a small bookcase of French novels, Russian poetry, and the plays of Oscar Wilde, and an inviting wing-backed chair, placed directly before the fire. The sensual air of her bedchamber could not have been more in contrast with her lace-frilled room in London; decorated in shades of peach, it was her mother's idea of a fitting place for a young virgin to sleep.

Ophelia found herself often in the kitchen, since Mrs. Beesby enjoyed a natter, particularly if her helper were prepared to beat a bowl of egg white into submission. It was not long before Ophelia was able to turn the conversation to the mysterious Hamish.

"Dearie me, so very sad. No man should have to suffer such torment: ah, the perils of childbirth. It's the Lord's way and we kinna argue," lamented Mrs. Beesby. "Nigh on five year ago, he lost his wife, and his wee bairn, within a few short hours one from t'other. 'Twas a night as black as the Earl of Hell's waistcoat, and the mist thick all aboot the place, so the doctor couldnae reach the castle. Mr. Hamish'd only arrived a month, bein' in Edinburgh wi' his wife's folk afore that. Oh the tragedy!" she wailed, indulging in the pathos of the sorry tale.

"How devastating…" choked Ophelia. She felt most dreadful for his poor wife and baby, and for him. No wonder he so often disappeared into the forest. She'd certainly been rude on first meeting. And he'd been such a brick, improvising on the piano; it had been a lovely surprise. She felt ashamed of herself. Beastly snobbery!

It was not long after this that the weather turned muggy. Even the biting midges seemed too oppressed to bother in their labors. Without a single Bohemian artist yet to distract her, Ophelia's thoughts turned with regularity to the figure of Hamish. As she sat in the lightest of her muslin dresses, fanning herself and reading the novels of Miss Braddon and Mrs. Gaskell, her imagination transformed the heroes into dashing figures, sporting beards of auburn.

Noticing her dreamy expression and general listlessness, Morag suggested that Ophelia take out one of the horses, and she agreed readily. She was inspecting them, to see which might best suit her, when she heard footsteps in the tack room and turned to see Hamish, looking as handsome as she remembered. A flush bloomed through her body.

"Heard you were riding. Don't mind if I join you? Here, take Esmeralda. She's quietest," he offered.

"That's very kind," Ophelia conceded, as Hamish saddled up the mare, fingers working swiftly. He whispered into the horse's ear as he worked, stroking her neck. Esmeralda was, evidently, under his spell. She reached to nibble his sleeve as he placed the bit in her mouth.

Hamish could not help but notice that Ophelia was in good looks. Still, her London ways were rather irritating: fancy wearing a plumed hat and formal riding coat for a hack in the Highlands, especially in this heat.

"Remember," warned Hamish, leading the horse out for her, "Take it easy. Esmeralda's a good filly but she'll take her head if you give her the chance."

Ophelia felt a twinge of annoyance. She'd had enough of being told what to do under her mother's eye. Moreover, standing in close proximity to Hamish was sending her knees a-quiver. It was a pathetic state of affairs. It was below her dignity to let him see the effect he was having on her. If, at that moment, he'd lunged at her in the same way that Percival had in the taxi, she knew for certain that she would not have struggled to get away.

I must take myself in hand, she thought and, rather out of the blue, found herself saying, "You needn't be so patronizing. I've been riding since I was four! I know how to handle a horse."

Red-cheeked, and wishing to hide her trembling lip, she set off at a gallop, heading towards the dense forest west of the loch. Hamish, barely having had time to saddle his own ride, leapt on. Standing high in the stirrups, he called out to her. "Slow down you fool!"

Ophelia, however, heard not a word, the wind having picked up. It came blowing down from the mountains, whisking away all good sense. She disappeared from view, spurring on Esmeralda to enter the trees.

As she rounded the second bend in the path, they came upon a stag, antlers lowered. Esmeralda, panicked, made an ill-timed leap to the side, to avoid being pierced by the deer's horns. Ophelia clung on desperately as the horse twisted in mid-air, but found herself unseated, and thrown.

Hamish appeared moments behind her, as the stag darted away through the pines. Ophelia, dazed, reclined in a puddle of mud. It had taken some of the impact of her fall but she was sodden, and the stuffing had been knocked from her.

"Well, I don't suppose you'll do that again in a hurry," Hamish said, his temper calming.

Ophelia could see, and feel, that she lay in filth. Slime oozed between her fingers, and her legs. She rather felt that she should sit up, but somehow lacked the will, or the inclination. Her mind felt disordered and she wondered if she might cry. Her ankle was throbbing.

"There, there," she heard Hamish say. "We'll get you up and sort you out. You've had a shock."

He lifted her, one arm under her knees and the other across her back. She hadn't been carried since she was a child, taken up the stairs by her father. Even in her muddled state, she thought how nice it was.

As he approached his horse, wondering the best way to place Ophelia on the saddle, Hamish realized that it had grown dark, menacing clouds having emerged over the crags. Fat raindrops began to fall, rustling the leaves above them.

The first flash of brilliance split the sky, and Hamish's stallion let out a snort of fear. Esmeralda, who had been watching, also gave a fearful whinny. As a deep, monstrous rumble travelled across the canyon of the glen, the two horses decided that enough was enough, and bolted clear.

"Damn!"

"What's the matter, Hamish," mumbled Ophelia. "Do you want to kiss me? You can if you like. I expect you're a very good kisser..." Her eyes closed and her body went limp in his arms.

He wasn't bothered for the horses. They'd find their way back. He couldn't carry Ophelia far though and she was beyond walking.

Another lightning tongue lashed the peaks, followed closely by thunder. The storm was coming closer.

She awoke upon a cottage sofa, to the sweet smell of burning wood. Hamish was crouched before the stove, feeding it logs from a basket.

Her velvet coat had been draped over a chair to dry. Rain beat heavily upon the window.

"I'm cold," she said, making him look up.

"You're awake then. That's good. Your ankle is swelling. Try to keep it raised."

"It's because I'm wet through," she went on, and she was, every bit of her. The storm had finished what the puddle had begun. "Do you have a blanket?"

She began to lift off layers, casting each in a damp heap on the floor. There wasn't much in the room but, from a cupboard, he brought her an old shirt, and two rugs.

"Don't look." She pulled her chemise over her head, and wriggled out of the last of her under things. She put on the shirt. It had been sitting a while and smelt of mildew. It was too rough to button closely, so she left the upper fasteners loose.

"This is your cabin isn't it?" she said, rather obviously. Leaning against the wall were variously sized axes and other tools.

"Good that you're talking again." Hamish lifted down a bottle and poured some of the liquid into a tin cup. "Drink this. It'll warm you."

He took his handkerchief and dabbed a corner in the whisky, using it to wipe a streak of mud from her cheek.

A bright flash lit the gloom, followed by a low growl, as of a subterranean monster waking in its lair. The door shook.

"Who's out there?" she whimpered.

"No one. It's just the wind."

"They're shaking the door. Don't let them in," she sobbed, drawing a blanket close to her chin.

He sat beside her on the little sofa, and moved her legs across his lap, so that her foot was elevated. He held the cup and she took a sip. The fiery whisky numbed her lips, making them tingle.

She smiled. "It's turning me warm inside; it's the same feeling I have when I look at you."

"You may not remember any of this in the morning," he laughed.

The wind chose that moment to rattle the door again, in savage spite, and she jumped.

"Do you miss her?" she asked abruptly. It was a subject which, in her usual state, she would not have dared broach.

Hamish didn't answer. The wind blew down the chimney, making the woodstove flare. At last, responding to her candour, he said, "I do think of her, often, yes."

They sat in silence, she listening to his breathing, and looking at his profile as he gazed at the fire.

"Many have it a great deal worse than me but, sometimes, it's as if I'm on a bridge and can't see the other side. Not sure where I'm going. Can't go back and too afraid to move forward."

He paused.

"They all think I should marry again. There's a woman, the daughter of an old friend of my aunt. It would be an easy choice: become a husband again, have children."

He smiled wanly.

The storm and failing daylight had made the room darker. Lit only by the stove, the shadows were palpably thick. Tremors continued to shake the roof and windows of the cabin.

How beautiful he is, she thought. There were golden threads in his beard and in his hair, like the copper brightness of the flames.

She fumbled with the buttons on the front of her shirt, opening them one by one. The glow from the stove lit the curve of her breasts.

Taking his hand, she placed it on her skin. His palm was more calloused than she'd expected.

He sat very still, as if to touch her further would break the enchantment.

He looked long at her, all but naked, light and dark dancing across her body. She felt him eating the sight of her. His eyes then moved upwards, found hers, and stared hard.

I should be blushing, she thought. *I should turn away.* But she didn't.

He leaned forward, lips parted, and there was nothing in her but the melting desire to return the force of his mouth, to be wrapped tight in his arms, to feel the strength of him. Drinking deeply from her, his kiss was an ocean of torment and need.

He caught her face between his hands, looking again into her eyes, holding her still, suspended between past and present. Then, longing overcame him, and he became a creature of hunger, his mouth at her breast, consuming her, his beard rough at her nipple.

He grazed her belly, travelling an inevitable path. His hands were under her hips, raising her sex to meet his mouth, and the shock of his tongue made her gasp: a wonderful, terrible rapture. She forgot almost to breathe, choking with the pleasure of it.

His hands gripped harder, under her buttocks now, his face forcing her thighs wider, his tongue stroking her, plunging, curling to the nub of her sex, teasing her, making her twist in agonized joy. He devoured the openness of her.

She writhed, wanting more, knowing that there was more.

She took a handful of his hair in her fist, whimpering with the dreadful delight of it. He raised his head, eyes darkly dilated.

She watched as Hamish unbuttoned his shirt, and then his trousers, discarding them. It was the first time she had seen a naked man. His length, veined, and glistening, stood proudly from a shock of hair, golden red.

"I'm not afraid," she said. There was nothing brutish here, she thought, nothing clumsy or awkward.

Calmer now, yet moving as if in the daze of waking sleep, of night-dreaming lust, he lowered his body to hers, pushing into the soft swell of her. She met each thrust as if she had known all her life for what her tender flesh was intended. Wordless, beyond language, she allowed herself to be enfolded in pleasure.

A last crack of electricity split the sky.

She woke to grey early light and chill, the fire having gone out. The brutal howling had passed and it was quiet, as if all nature had ceased breathing.

Ophelia was thirsty and muddle-headed, her limbs languorously limp, as if heavy with memories. Sitting up, looking expectantly for Hamish, her ankle throbbed. Tentatively, as if afraid of whom she might summon, she called out for him. There was no reply.

From outside, she heard the crack of splitting wood. She eased herself up, wincing, and hobbled into the morning air.

Hamish raised the axe again, letting it swing a full arc into the waiting log, tossing kindling to one side. She stood, without speaking, propped against the door, watching the strength of his shoulders.

How much can change in a single day, she thought. Never before had she felt such fluttering from her heart. Breathing now required concentration. It was happiness, she realized: an overwhelming joy.

He stooped to pick up the wood and turned, seeing her.

"You're up then." He smiled wanly but without the warmth she had been expecting, and without meeting her eye. "Go in and sit down. You need to keep that foot up."

Searching his face, she felt the blood drain from her. A chasm opened in her chest, dark and cold.

"Hamish?" she prompted, feeling her voice quiver.

"I'll chop more wood, and then head up to the house to collect the horses. Clearly, you can't walk on that ankle."

"Last night…" she began, but words failed her. There was too much she wanted to say.

He looked over his shoulder, and she saw that his expression was closed. He gave no reply.

Her tears welled, and died, curbed by anger. What had happened between them had been wondrous. She refused to believe that he couldn't feel the same way.

She sat watching the flames after he had left, her heart numb.

It was some time before she heard footsteps running up the track and, shuffling out, saw that Hamish had brought Murray, the stable lad, with him.

"Oh Miss Ophelia," he puffed. "Mr. Hamish says you've turned your ankle an' spent the night 'ere in the cabin. Must've been right awful. Come on m'lady, put your arm over me shoulder an' I'll help ye onto Rosie. She's slow but sure. You won't come to no 'arm."

She felt Hamish's avoidance of touching her, letting Murray take most of her weight, helping more to steady the horse than to support her as she pushed her good foot into the stirrup. He'd fitted a side-saddle, so that she might sit more comfortably, but the awkwardness of it still had her wincing. She bit her lip.

Murray led her horse, while Hamish went on slightly ahead. They made their way slowly, tree branches having come down, making the going difficult. It was little more than two miles to return, but the uneven path jolted her repeatedly.

It was impossible for her to speak to Hamish with Murray there. No doubt, that was why he'd brought him.

To compose herself, she focused on the stream filled to brimming, rippling over stones and roots, and then the loch, running high upon its banks. Her eyes, however, kept straying to Hamish's back, turned adamantly against her. The air, cool and clean, was like breathing cold water, rushing in, raw and ragged.

At last, arriving at the castle, Murray helped her down. Indecorously, Ophelia was obliged to slide off the saddle into his arms; he was stronger than she expected.

"I'll take over from here," Hamish told him curtly, leaving Murray to lead the horses away. He offered her his arm stiffly.

"My dear! Oh! How worried we were!" exclaimed Morag, appearing on the steps, rushing forward to hug Ophelia. "That terrible storm!"

She took Ophelia's other arm. "Murray said he saw you both ride out yesterday, only minutes before the storm started gathering. Constance assured me that Hamish would look after you both, and she guessed of course that he'd take you to the cabin if there was any trouble."

Ophelia smiled wanly. Morag's warmth brought a lump to her throat. How lovely it was to have someone saying kind things to her, although she feared it would make her cry.

Constance appeared then, full of solicitous concern. "Your poor ankle! And you must be ravenous my dear, not having eaten since yesterday luncheon. Hamish, would you tell cook to bring up some venison stew to Ophelia's room, with plenty of thickly buttered bread, and a pot of tea."

Hamish nodded his assent and departed, leaving her in the care of the two dowagers.

"Let's get you upstairs and into the bath first," said Morag, "Then, we'll tuck you into bed."

They took her, step by step, most carefully, and then undressed her as the water ran, making Ophelia feel quite four years old again.

"We'll be back in a few minutes dear," Constance said, once they'd helped her into the tub. "Just call if you need us."

Feeling most dreadfully tired, Ophelia eased her shoulders under the water.

Hamish had brought alive some new part of her. With no thought for decency, she'd surrendered to him, and he had surrendered to her. A light had flared brightly within her, and had been just as abruptly extinguished.

She closed her eyes, against the welling tears.

Ophelia spent the next few days in bed, visited regularly by the two elderly ladies, bringing her treats to tempt her appetite, and news on the plans for Morag's coming birthday dinner.

Listless, she reclined, gazing vaguely out of the window, knowing that the visitor she most wanted would be unlikely to appear, yet longing to see him. She picked up books repeatedly, but without the will to read them. She endured the days as best as she could, cursing and crying, then retreating into silence.

The doctor came and pronounced the ankle merely sprained rather than fractured. He bandaged it and said she'd be fine within the week, and to try her weight on it as soon as she felt able.

By the time Morag's birthday arrived, she was able to hobble down to the drawing room, giving heartfelt kisses and her birthday gift (the improvised wrapping of some of her own Penhaligon's soap), but retired back upstairs afterwards, wishing to avoid the flurry of activity as their guests arrived through the day. Hamish was nowhere to be seen.

"Do come down tonight my darling," Morag had entreated her. "We'd so love to have you join us."

From her bedroom window, she watched cars arriving, and greetings being given. Towards early evening, a very smart Daimler pulled up, its occupants already in dinner attire. For them, Hamish appeared, coming down the steps to welcome them: a tall, slim man, with dark hair and a moustache, and an elegant woman, her hair white-blonde, wearing a silver coat. Ophelia watched as Hamish took her kisses not only on each cheek but on the lips. She placed her arm through his and they disappeared inside, laughing.

So that's it! Ophelia realized, her anger returning.

She pushed a brush roughly through her hair, slicked rouge to her cheeks, and gave herself a boldly painted lip. Her appearance was improved but her eyes bore evidence of anguish, looking more huge than ever in her pale face.

She chose a comfortable favorite from her wardrobe, a dark dress speckled in emerald green beads. It had a stain on the back of the hem, which wouldn't shift, but she doubted anyone would see. She slipped it over her head, and rang for Constance's maid to help her limp downstairs. Mary brought with her a garish orange and brown checked sash: the tartan worn for centuries by the MacKintochs.

"It's for you to wear m'lady," explained Mary. "Lady Morag sent it for you."

Among those at dinner were spinster cousins of the family, Evelyn and Alice, the reverend of the local kirk, a sprinkling of the few respectable neighbors, and Colonel Faversham, who'd served with Morag's husband years ago. She'd known his type as soon as she'd laid eyes on him: a member of the bottom-pinching brigade. Even Lady Devonly's posterior wouldn't be safe.

Glamor was provided by the owners of the Daimler: the Comte de Montefiore, and his sister, Felicité. The latter was a vision, her tall, lithe frame clothed in a diaphanous gown of rose-petal pink.

Ophelia felt disheveled in contrast, as if her vitality had been sucked away, much like the mulligatawny soup, slurped into the quivering mouths of this seeming sea of ancients at her end of the table.

Further down, she could see quite clearly that the Comte's sister, all elegance, was flirting with Hamish. A throb of shame suffused her cheeks, almost as vivid as the aching pulse in her ankle.

"No better than dogs," she heard Sir Hector mutter, to her right, seeing Hamish place a kiss upon Felicité's hand.

The tartan sash felt suddenly as if it were suffocating her. She pulled it over her head, casting it behind her.

On her left, the Comte de Montefiore, without speaking, perused her décolleté. *Despicable man, I shall ignore him!* He had a particular Mediterranean air, darkly dangerous, with features in unusual proportion, his nose and eyebrows being too large for his face.

The Comte nodded at the unassuming personage of Lady Mildred Faucett-Plumbly, and her rotund spouse, enjoying his lamb chop with gusto. "There is a place for physical allure. If a woman cultivates the sexual appeal of a parsnip, she will find herself bedding a cabbage."

"I'm sure they're both perfectly lovely, and deliriously happy," she snapped, adding, "In their own way." Of course, she didn't believe so for a moment, but felt that to agree with the Comte would be disloyal to the more vulnerable members of her sex.

Colonel Faversham caught her eye. "Now young lady," he began. "Nice looking gel like you oughtn't to be single; too much temptation to fall into wicked ways. Don't deny it! I know the urges of the young. Best put a husband in your bed!"

"Lascivious swine!" grumbled Sir Hector.

Ophelia felt a surge of warmth towards him.

"Don't you agree, vicar?" barked the Colonel, jabbing a conspiratorial elbow at his dining companion. Reverend McAdam looked most alarmed. Of the Presbyterian faith, the abundant charms of Mrs. McAdam had warmed his marital bed for nigh on forty years. He felt the Colonel's remark impertinent.

Ophelia's gaze was upon Hamish, willing that he look at her, that he show some sign as to what had passed between them, some acknowledgment.

Misses Evelyn and Alice Craigmore, meanwhile, were admiring the figure of the Colonel, falling upon his lamb with energetic mastication. They had lived their whole lives in respectable spinsterhood, at 17 Durness Walk, in the grand city of Aberdeen.

"Not bad for his age Evelyn," remarked Alice. "Solidity of frame, a decent moustache, and good teeth."

"Yes, he might do. Powerful stamina I'd imagine," replied her sister.

It was a game of theirs, to weigh up the merits of gentlemen as prospective husbands. They liked to be thorough in their examination. Most men, sadly, failed to meet their exacting standards. Sixty-two years of spinsterhood quite spoils a woman, since she is permitted indulgence of every fancy, and finds herself much freer, in mind and body, than her married counterparts. The sisters had never found a man (it had not occurred to them that, in fact, they might require two) worthy of their surrender. However, the Colonel was scoring highly.

"One can sense some men's enthusiasm," Alice mused. "He'd be like a terrier down a rabbit hole."

"Dreadful you!" exclaimed Evelyn.

Ophelia wondered if the spinsters realized their supposedly private conversation was perfectly audible to others around them.

It was Lord Faucett-Plumbly who turned the conversation to politics, remarking to Ophelia his surprise at her father's recent support of the women's cause.

Ophelia, in no mood to be challenged, flew to his defence. "Daddy is more forward-thinking than most people realize. He's always been in favour of women's suffrage."

"With all women over the age of twenty-one now voting, we've added five million to the electoral roll. We may outnumber the men at the next election," declared one of the Ms. Craigmores.

"Poppycock!" spluttered Hector, "Women are physically, mentally and morally inferior to men. Can't be trusted to vote! They should be at home, raising their children. Leave politics to the men, eh Hamish?"

Before Hamish had a chance to reply, Morag intervened. "Really Hector, we are not utterly incapable of understanding the issues of the day, despite our late Queen Victoria's thoughts on the matter. I too was a Suffragist, in my younger days."

"Hear, hear," declared Ophelia, "Look at Lady Astor, taking her place in the House, and Margaret Bonfield. Who knows what they, and other women, might achieve. We could soon have women serving on the cabinet, or even as Prime Minister! I wouldn't mind standing myself, perhaps, one day…"

She heard Hector snort and mutter, but found herself suddenly animated. She'd had no idea that her grandmother had been active in promoting votes for women. Her mother's support for the movement had been more in thought than in deed; Ophelia couldn't imagine Lady Daphne chaining herself to railings.

She urged, "Women do need to be heard. My father voted for the Women's Employment Act too; it's a travesty that marrying precludes so many women from working. Can our lives have purpose in simply looking after a husband? It's abominable that it didn't pass the House."

Looking the length of the table, she saw then that Hamish's eyes were upon her, gazing intently, as if seeing something for the first time. He held her in that look, and her heart, which she had been trying so hard to steel against him, trembled in her breast.

Several conversations erupted, everyone now having an opinion to contribute; all but Félicité, who was whispering to Hamish, allowing her hair to brush his face. Ophelia saw him turn and smile in return.

Hussy! thought Ophelia. Never had she been thrown into such a paroxysm of jealousy. It was too sick-making. She took her glass and emptied it in three gulps. None of the dry sticks surrounding her seemed to notice. Haddock, however, appeared over her shoulder, to refill.

Resentment gnawed at her, making her feel the ache in her ankle all the more.

"I see who you are watching. The ring is almost upon the finger, I believe." The Comte's voice was cool.

She felt a pang of fear but retorted, "I've no ambition in that direction; to marry is to become an exhibit."

"You wish to flutter free." He nodded. "But beware of scorching your wings. The deadliest flames are the most enticing, and to you especially, I think."

Ophelia glared at him and took another swig of Pouilly-Fumé.

Fortified by alcohol, Ophelia declared most loudly, "I've been reading Radclyffe Hall's *Well of Loneliness*. They're saying that she'll be tried for obscenity, just for writing about women falling in love with other women. Where's the freedom if we can't even write what we like!"

Lady Faucett-Plumbly looked most uncomfortable, but Morag came to Ophelia's aid.

"Sounds marvelous my dear. Please do lend me your copy."

Constance remarked, with seeming innocence, "Hamish has lent me his copy of *Lady Chatterley's Lover*. Would you believe, Mr. Lawrence's heroine bears my name. And he's quite right; woman cannot live for the mind alone. Love only ripens when body and mind are content."

The Comte leaned close to Ophelia, his fingers creeping to her thigh. "I know what women want, and I would vouch that you are no different."

Ophelia slapped his hand away.

"Perhaps you have less idea than you imagine." Recalling some gossip exchanged between her grandmother and Constance the day before, she added, "If I'm not mistaken, your wife spends most of the year between Monaco and Milan, having found attractions elsewhere."

At the other end of the table, Hamish, apparently unafraid of ruffling feathers, returned to the subject of Mr. Lawrence's scandalous book.

"He makes some interesting observations on the classes. Men are working in dangerous conditions, given less thought than we might to a dog. It's a travesty that the miners have been cut off from striking again. Every man deserves a fair wage and fair hours."

This brought Lord Faucett-Plumbly's fist upon the table. "No one in their right mind can have approved of the general strike. It brought the country to a standstill, all those men refusing to do their jobs."

The Colonel nodded, "I heard the Prime Minister on the radio, calling it an attack on Britain's democracy. We all have our duty. Must knuckle down, however hard the conditions, like we did in the war. More to living than personal comfort."

The sentiment was somewhat spoilt by his helping himself to another portion of potatoes.

"Servants of Beelzebub!" grumbled Sir Hector, though at no one in particular, and without raising his head from the last scrapings of his mashed celeriac.

"Now, now," said Morag quickly, wishing to turn the conversation to lighter matters. "Felicité, you were telling me about the cinema and these new talking films."

"J'adore Mademoiselle Clara Bow," mused Felicité. "Our Ophelia looks like her does she not, with her head of curls, and her passionate ways. All her emotion is in the present moment, and she does not conform. There is something noble in this, is there not?"

Ophelia felt the compliment and turned away, only to catch the eye of the Comte, filled with a certain malicious, erotic glitter. His fingers lifted her skirt beneath the table, warm on her knee, then climbing to the top of her stocking. He hooked them under the garter.

"I do believe, my little rose, that, given half the chance, you'd have every man line up to kiss your bloomers." The Comte's hand crept higher still, reaching the soft inner flesh of her thigh.

"Your whispered indecencies are nothing but hot air," Ophelia hissed, endeavoring to remove the offending hand without causing a stir.

Felicité continued to babble on. "I have seen *The Jazz Singer*, with Monsieur Al Jolson, six times. And this Louise Brooks, they say she posed for a photograph without her clothes, and that she has kissed the belle Garbo. My secret wish is to be like the great Greta. Like me, she speaks little English, but she says all with her eyes, commanding the men to fall at her feet. She is mysterious and alluring, is she not?"

Her lashes fluttered wildly at Hamish. Ophelia didn't for a minute believe they were real.

Hamish then rose from his seat and proposed a toast. "We are gathered here to celebrate the eightieth birthday of our beloved Lady MacKintoch. Let us raise our glasses to a life well-lived, a life of love and adventure. May we all be so fortunate."

Having touched his glass to Morag's, he looked down fondly at the fair head of Felicité. As glasses were raised in response, she leapt up, gasping, "Mon cœur! Mon ange!" and took a kiss from him, full on the lips.

Ophelia felt a wave of heat pass over her, and became fearful that she might faint. Bile rising, she stumbled from the table, caring not for the searing pain in her ankle, out through the library, into the conservatory, where the windows were left ajar in the summer months. She leaned out and breathed deeply, endeavoring to calm her pulse, battling the pricking of her tears.

The room smelt over-sweet, of jasmine and honeysuckle, begonias and orchids, but the cool air revived her a little.

At last, she heard a footstep. She turned, thinking that perhaps Hamish had come to find her. He must, surely! He needed to tell her that it had all been acting; that it was her he loved.

However, it was the Comte, removing his tie and dinner jacket, throwing them carelessly over a table of geraniums. He was holding a glass of brandy.

Her heart plummeted. She could see now that it was better to have no heart.

She turned to leave, but he grasped her wrist firmly. "I think there is something you have all but promised me my charming maiden."

He brought his face close to hers, his breath sour with cigar smoke. A wave of nausea swept over her again but she held still as he kissed her, teeth raking her lips.

Voices drifted out from the library, that of Felicité laughing and of Hamish. She heard a heavily accented voice, laced with coquetry.

"Really! This Colonel is telling me that my beautiful Paris is rempli with pots of flesh!"

"Fleshpots, Felicité," corrected Hamish, "No doubt the old bugger is well familiar with them."

Ophelia was brought back to the moment by the Comte giving her a savage nip, then growling in her ear. "Don't lie to yourself. I know what it is that you want."

Why not lose myself in this, and forget Hamish, thought Ophelia. *Falling in love is nothing but poison.*

"You wish me to tear you, little rose, to pluck off your petals and crush them. Women have many secrets, but yours are not so difficult to read."

It would serve Hamish right to come in and catch us, thought Ophelia. "If you've something to show me, jolly well get on with it. My ankle is throbbing."

There is only the thinnest of divides between what we want and what we fear, and the two often intersect. All that happened next, she thought later, occurred as if she were watching herself from a distance.

Ophelia, disgusted and yet strangely thrilled, allowed the Comte to bend her over a chaise and lift her skirts. He drew down her knickers (peach silk, at twenty shillings) leaving them at her ankles. He gave her bare bottom a vicious squeeze, and then stabbed his thumb into her slit, nestling it there, within her dark fur. He drew it back and forth, with measured relish.

"What sort of girl invites a man she has only just met to behave in this manner?" mused the Comte. "A very wicked one I think. A girl who deserves to be punished."

The first smack of his open palm was well aimed, catching her on the underside of her right cheek. He followed it immediately with another, on the same spot, and then a third, leaving a sharp sting upon her skin.

Bastard! thought Ophelia, but whatever snake resided in her womb unfurled and shivered.

Another three blows were delivered, each sharper than the last. She went to cry out, but the shriek died in her throat. Two of his fingers found their way back to her wet lips, and slipped easily inside. Her lust, though reluctant, was molten.

"You are impatient," whispered the Comte.

She felt then the warmth of the Comte's manhood, his hand stroking the thickening column of his cock, rubbing it against her. He cupped her buttocks, parting them, directing his erection to her cleft. Nudging the slick tip forward, he teased her, entering little by little.

Her burning cunt grasped at him, urging him to proceed. He laughed then, knowing that he had conquered her, young and ripe and glorious. So the hunter greedily consumes its prey; too late for the bird to flutter.

She was no more than flesh receiving flesh, swept on waves of shame and excitement. The wolf in his groin rose to howl, letting her feel its full savagery, and he erupted hard, each hot spurt drenching her in delightful depravity. The carnal pleasure was not only his, as the conquering male, but hers too.

In the shadows, someone had been watching, unseen to our young heroine, although perhaps not to the Comte, whose gratification went beyond the easy seduction of silly girls. He had no compunction about consuming them, as he did the finest wines; afterwards, he cared not what happened to the empty bottles.

Steps crossed the library. Had Ophelia's ears not been filled with her own ragged breath, and the thud of her heart, she would have heard the click of the door.

Ophelia had lain awake for hours, wracked with a terrible headache, and tumultuous feelings of shame and intoxication. She was less discomfited by her liaison with the Comte than by her naivety, of having allowed herself to be duped by Hamish. She had thrown her heart out into the ring and he had stepped upon it.

Her ankle continued to ache but the pain of it was nothing compared to the anger, and anguish, she directed at herself.

She was also aware that she had moved from her virgin state to that of having taken two lovers in no more than the blink of an eye.

Some match, of incredible intensity, had been struck, and she could not imagine how the resulting fire would be quenched.

If the world at large were to offer its moral judgement, it would surely have something to say.

Ophelia scrutinized herself in the mirror. I'm corrupted and unable to be what I was before, she thought, but her reflection looked just the same, if rather weary.

I'm trying on versions of myself, she concluded, *that's all, to see how they fit. Aren't I doing just as I planned, exploring what it means to be a woman, without becoming a dreary wife?* She supposed she was but, somehow, she did not feel satisfied.

The breakfast room was quiet, most revellers from the night before having chosen to lie late abed, taking their toast and marmalade, bacon and eggs on trays. Morag was already down however, and the Comte, accompanied by his sister and Hamish, discussing plans for a trip to Edinburgh.

"Délicieux," Felicité declared, clapping her hands girlishly. "I would so adore to see the upper apartments at Holyrood Palace. Perhaps we shall encounter the ghost of poor Rizzio, and see that mysterious blood stain which refuses to be scrubbed clean? Fifty-six stabbings! Mon Dieu! C'est horrible! Dépravé!"

"Bonne idée chéri," declared the Comte. "And perhaps petite Ophelia will come too. There is room in the car, is there not Hamish? We might book rooms at The Caledonian."

By the glint in his villainous eye, the Comte's intentions were clear. In the cold light of day, they did not appeal to her.

Meanwhile, the thought of watching Hamish flirt with Felicité was more than she could bear. Let him place his hand on her knee, or wherever else he liked; she wouldn't be there to see it.

Hamish did not give her the opportunity to answer. "I think not Comte. Ophelia is here to spend time with Lady MacKintoch. It would be unfair of us to deprive our hostess. From what I have seen, Ophelia is most accommodating to others. Even her ankle is no impediment to her efforts in this regard. You would agree, no doubt, having last night received a tour of the conservatory in her capable hands."

He looked pointedly at the Comte and Ophelia felt her face burn.

"Our Ophelia is most passionate in all matters," leered the Frenchman and, caddish to the last, slipped a hand between the cheeks of her bottom. Really! It was the assumption of consent she minded more than anything.

The three then took their leave, Hamish refusing to speak directly to Ophelia or to meet her eye, and Felicité in a flurry of extravagant cheek kissing.

Detestable creature! She's pure varnish; nothing of substance… Ophelia seethed. *And Hamish is simply foul. Has he no decent feeling?*

The remaining guests stayed only another day before departing, allowing Ophelia to return to her former pastimes: reading a great deal; playing cards with Constance and Morag, or backgammon with Hector; learning how to knit, thanks to Lady Devonly; playing the piano; and chatting with Mrs. Beesby, helping her often (she could now make a tolerable scone).

When her ankle felt steadier, Ophelia began taking out Esmeralda again, stopping often at the cabin. Morag expected Hamish not to stay away more than a few weeks. There was so much to attend to on the estate.

She also helped in the stables and, within a short while, became quite friendly with Murray, who showed her things she'd never known about horses: how to brush them down properly and bathe them, how to clean and polish the tack, what to feed them (and not), even how to draw pus from a boil inside the hoof. It gave Ophelia satisfaction to think how horrified her mother would be.

She considered kissing Murray, even though he was barely her own age, with a face as smooth as a baby's, but she soon realized that this would be folly. He was cordial company, nothing more. Soon afterwards, she heard from Mrs. Beesby that Hettie and Murray were courting, and felt glad that she hadn't interfered.

Afternoon tea became a highlight. Ophelia grew accustomed to Morag's declaration that 'few situations cannot be transformed by a strong cup of Earl Grey'. After her third, she would evoke her other belief, that 'a buttered crumpet cheers even the most miserable'. *How we do unite over simple comforts*, thought Ophelia.

Lady Devonly would agree, and there would begin tales not only of living on beetles and bananas, but of utmost violence and degeneracy, set in the snake-swarmed jungles of Dahomey. A favorite anecdote involved cannibals offering marriage to the highly respectable married persons of Morag, or Constance, or to both together. The details seemed to grow more outrageous with each telling.

Ophelia would play for them, her fingers always seeming to choose Gershwin's *Man I Love or If I Had You*. Even her mother had approved of that one, since it was said to be a favorite of the Prince of Wales. She thought back to her first evening, when Hamish had sat beside her on the stool, thumping out their duets and laughing.

She much appreciated the easy chatter of Lady Devonly and her grandmother, and that of Mrs. Beesby, in the warm kitchen. Also, she came to hold dearer the murmuring streams, and the rugged mountains, towering on all sides, watching over the castle.

The solemn beauty of the estate, increasingly, gave her fortitude and a sense of contentment: the loch reflecting the ethereal depth of the sky and the grass shivering in the wind. When the rolling clouds parted, golden beams would dart across the hillside, surprising russet deer, invisible to her until they leapt away, over splintered crags. With each passing day, her eyes, though wistful, became brighter and her cheeks rosier. She would walk for hours without becoming tired, the landscape invigorating her.

In the still, dark hours, Ophelia would often rise, put on her robe, and stare out into the ink blue of the night, following the moon's glimmer on the loch. If she gazed long enough, she thought, some mystery might be revealed. There was so much yet for her to understand, but the ancient earth and rock kept their silent council.

One day, Ophelia saw an eagle, sweeping overhead, circling and scanning for rabbits in the heather; so majestic and self-contained, neck outstretched, powerful in its independence. Wouldn't it be wonderful if she might be the same?

She had often dreamt of learning to fly, like Amelia Earhart. Not across the Atlantic (she doubted she'd be brave enough), but to soar with a feeling of freedom.

It seemed so long ago that she'd fantasized of taking a host of lovers. She knew her soul a little better now, including a few of its secret caves.

In London, it had felt as if the many doors in the long corridor of her life had all been shut, but for two: one marked 'marriage' and the other 'spinsterhood'. Neither had appealed to her under Lady Daphne's terms. Strangely, her time in Scotland had opened up the doors; some led to places she was unsure she wished to venture, but she appreciated having the choice. Morag and Constance, she felt certain, would encourage her in whatever she chose to do next.

She didn't care what her mother thought. Her father, though a largely absent figure, was indulgent. He'd ensured a modest income for her since turning eighteen, and this would become more substantial when she reached twenty-one. She might do something interesting with it, if she had a mind to.

I might achieve anything really; do anything, she mused. *Perhaps even, like Morag, I'll head off on an expedition into the unknown. Well, perhaps not the unknown, but further abroad. The world has so many treasures.*

It was in this contented, if not yet truly happy, state of mind that she set out for a walk around the loch, on one of the last warm afternoons of the summer. There is always a faintly melancholy air about those last days of warmth, when birds are already contemplating their flight to more temperate climes. She felt the stirrings of change; that this season was ending, and another was to begin.

Having passed through the trees on the eastern bank of the loch, she emerged into the sun and, there, what awaited her...? A view more wondrous than sun-dappled water or the solemn glitter of the stars. She saw the muscular shoulders and curve of a man's naked back, his thighs, and firm buttocks: a man entirely stripped, ready to take a swim. A feast for any woman's eyes but for hers especially, for who should that man be but Hamish, returned at last.

She watched him wade in, until his lower half was decently submerged, and then, hardly knowing what to say, she settled upon shouting, "I see you're back."

The look upon his face, startled, his head twisting to see who had called out, brought a smile to hers. In turning, he showed her the width of his chest, the smoothness of his lower abdomen, and the depth of his pelvic muscles. Ophelia took in the contours of that glorious body and he stood, silent, allowing her to do so.

He said nothing but, after some moments, began to move, slowly, and purposefully, back towards the bank, into shallower water. He revealed, inch by tantalizing inch, the last portion of his lower torso, leading into thick, auburn hair, and the solidity of his meat, well-girthed. He planted his legs boldly and folded his arms upon his chest. Ophelia could have sworn that he'd angled his pelvis forward, as if defying her not to look, as if saying: "Here it is; admire all you like!"

He gave her a smile that could have been any man's smile, given to any woman: a smile that went back into the forest and its shaded dells, into the granite almost. It was the same smile men have been giving to women for centuries. The smile of an ordinary man's amour, the sort that goes unwritten in the annals of history, but runs just as deep. His smile was one of complicity, of intimacies shared, and of remembrance of touch.

A flood of heat threatened to overwhelm her. Her body, an archive of desire, remembered everything.

At last, she gathered herself to speak.

"Felicité must be delighted," she said softly, letting him see where her eyes lingered.

His tone was of resignation, acceptance of what had failed to yield fruit. "I thought she might consider staying in Scotland, but it appears I'm not a good judge of women."

He hesitated.

"What I'm offering isn't enough to tempt her, although she did sample at her leisure," said Hamish wryly. "She's currently on a grand tour of the European capitals. She's in no haste to be wed, or so I believe."

"In some ways that's very sensible of her," admitted Ophelia, with a sudden rush of happiness. "The 'not-marrying' part and planning to enjoy herself; of that, I must confess I approve."

"You'll soon be off then I take it? The Comte has gone to his villa on the Riviera; he tells me you're always welcome," Hamish added archly.

"That's tempting," she answered, unable to resist the mischief of it. "However, I've become rather devoted to the glen, and the loch, and to the mountains. Nature has its charms. Also, I've grown very fond of everyone here… even Hector."

Hamish's eyes held her fast, filled not only with the heat of desire but with tenderness. In the long silence between them she felt his uncertainty. At last, he spoke.

"Could you be fond of me?"

In answer, she kicked off her shoes, rolled down her stockings and tucked up her muslin dress, leaving her legs bare, feeling Hamish look upon their length. She paddled out, through the reeds, almost losing her balance in the slippery mud. She put down her hands to steady herself then pushed a lock of hair from her face, leaving a streak of pondweed slime. She advanced, carefully, through the water, until she almost faced him.

She cast down her eyes, fearful suddenly of meeting his, willing her heart to calm itself. When she raised them, she found that Hamish had moved considerably closer and had lowered his face to hers. He licked his thumb to wipe away the smear on her cheek.

"Why is it that you only want to kiss me when I'm covered in filth?" she asked.

He took that as an invitation.

About Emmanuelle de Maupassant

Emmanuelle de Maupassant lives with her husband (maker of tea and fruit cake) and her hairy pudding terrier (connoisseur of squeaky toys and bacon treats).

She is best known for her 'Noire' series: named by Stylist Magazine as among the sexiest reads of 2015. Her latest work, a feast of the unsettling and the erotic, is Cautionary Tales, inspired by Russian folklore and superstitions.

Website: www.emmanuelledemaupassant.com

Facebook: www.facebook.com/EMaupassant

Twitter: twitter.com/EmmanuelledeM

Goodreads: www.goodreads.com/author/show/8528528.Emmanuelle_de_Maupassant

Pinterest: uk.pinterest.com/emmanuelledeM/

Printed in Great Britain
by Amazon